Chatham River Press
Readers Bookshelf

AGATHA CHRISTIE

FIVE COMPLETE HERCULE POIROT NOVELS

DEATH ON THE NILE

MURDER ON THE ORIENT EXPRESS

THE ABC MURDERS

CARDS ON THE TABLE

THIRTEEN AT DINNER

CHATHAM RIVER PRESS • NEW YORK

This omnibus edition contains the complete and unabridged texts of the original editions. It has been completely reset for this volume.

This book was originally published as five separate volumes.

This 1984 edition is published by Chatham River Press, a division of Arlington House, Inc., distributed by Crown Publishers, Inc., by arrangement with Dodd, Mead & Company.

Manufactured in the United States of America.

Library of Congress Cataloging in Publication Data

Christie, Agatha, 1890-1976.
Five complete Hercule Poirot novels.

Contents: Thirteen at dinner—Murder on the Orient Express—The ABC murders—[etc.]
1. Detective and mystery stories, English. I. Title.
PR6005.H66A6 1984 823'.912 83-26251
ISBN: 0-517-439999

r q p o n m l k

CONTENTS

THIRTEEN AT DINNER

To
Dr. and Mrs. Campbell Thompson

CONTENTS

Chapter

CHAPTER 1
A Theatrical Party

The memory of the public is short. Already the intense interest and excitement aroused by the murder of George Alfred St. Vincent Marsh, fourth Baron Edgware, is a thing past and forgotten. Newer sensations have taken its place.

My friend, Hercule Poirot, was never openly mentioned in connection with the case. This, I may say, was entirely in accordance with his own wishes. He did not choose to appear in it. The credit went elsewhere—and that is how he wished it to be. Moreover, from Poirot's own peculiar private point of view, the case was one of his failures. He always swears that it was the chance remark of a stranger in the street that put him on the right track.

However that may be, it was his genius that discovered the truth of the affair. But for Hercule Poirot I doubt if the crime would have been brought home to its perpetrator.

I feel therefore that the time has come for me to set down all I know of the affair in black and white. I know the ins and outs of the case thoroughly and I may also mention that I shall be fulfilling the wishes of a very fascinating lady in so doing.

I have often recalled that day in Poirot's prim neat little sitting-room when, striding up and down a particular strip of carpet, my little friend gave us his masterly and astounding resumé of the case. I am going to begin my narrative where he did on that occasion—at a London theatre in June of last year.

Carlotta Adams was quite the rage in London at that moment. The year before she had given a couple of matinées which had been a wild success. This year she had a three weeks' season of which this was the last night but one.

Carlotta Adams was an American girl with the most amazing talent for single-handed sketches unhampered by make-up or scenery. She seemed to speak every language with ease. Her sketch of an evening in a foreign hotel was really wonderful. In turn, American tourists, German tourists, middle-class English families, questionable ladies, impoverished Russian aristocrats and weary discreet waiters all flitted across the scene.

Her sketches went from grave to gay and back again. Her dying Czecho-Slovakian woman in hospital brought a lump to the throat. A minute later we were rocking with laughter as a dentist plied his trade and chatted amiably with his victims.

Her programme closed with what she announced as "Some Imitations."

Here again, she was amazingly clever. Without make-up of any kind, her features seemed to dissolve suddenly and re-form themselves into those of a famous politician, or a well-known actress, or a society beauty. In each character she gave a short typical speech. These speeches, by the way, were remarkably clever. They seemed to hit off every weakness of the subject selected.

One of her last impersonations was Jane Wilkinson—a talented young American actress well known in London. It was really very clever. Inanities slipped off her tongue charged with some powerful emotional appeal so that in spite of yourself you felt that each word was uttered with some potent and fundamental meaning. Her voice, exquisitely toned, with a deep husky note in it, was intoxicating. The restrained gestures, each strangely significant, the slightly swaying body, the impression even, of strong physical beauty—how she did it, I cannot think!

I had always been an admirer of the beautiful Jane Wilkinson. She had thrilled me in her emotional parts, and I had always maintained in face of those who admitted her beauty but declared she was no actress, that she had considerable histrionic powers.

It was a little uncanny to hear that well-known, slightly husky voice with the fatalistic drop in it that had stirred me so often, and to watch that seemingly poignant gesture of the slowly closing and unclosing hand, and the sudden throw back of the head with the hair shaken back from the face that I realised she always gave at the close of a dramatic scene.

Jane Wilkinson was one of those actresses who had left the stage on her marriage only to return to it a couple of years later.

Three years ago she had married the wealthy but slightly eccentric Lord Edgware. Rumour went that she left him shortly afterwards. At any rate eighteen months after the marriage, she was acting for the films in America, and had this season appeared in a successful play in London.

Watching Carlotta Adams' clever but perhaps slightly malicious imitation, it occurred to me to wonder how such imitations were regarded by the subject selected. Were they pleased at the notoriety—at the advertisement it afforded? Or were they annoyed at what was, after all, a deliberate exposing of the tricks of their trade? Was not Carlotta Adams in the position of the rival conjurer who says: "Oh! this is an old trick! Very simple. I'll show you how this one's done!"

I decided that if *I* were the subject in question, I should be very much annoyed. I should, of course, conceal my vexation, but decidedly I should not like it. One would need great broad-mindedness and a distinct sense of humour to appreciate such a merciless exposé.

I had just arrived at these conclusions when the delightful husky laugh from the stage was echoed from behind me.

I turned my head sharply. In the seat immediately behind mine, leaning forward with her lips slightly parted, was the subject of the present imitation—Lady Edgware, better known as Jane Wilkinson.

I realised immediately that my deductions had been all wrong. She was leaning forward, her lips parted, with an expression of delight and excitement in her eyes.

As the "imitation" finished, she applauded loudly, laughing and turning to her companion, a tall extremely good-looking man, of the Greed god type, whose face I recognised as one better known on the screen than on the stage. It was Bryan Martin, the hero of the screen most popular at the moment. He and Jane Wilkinson had been starred together in several screen productions.

"Marvellous, isn't she?" Lady Edgware was saying.

He laughed.

"Jane—you look all excited."

"Well, she really is too wonderful! Heaps better than I thought she'd be."

I did not catch Bryan Martin's amused rejoinder. Carlotta Adams had started on a fresh improvisation.

What happened later is, I shall always think, a very curious coincidence.

After the theatre, Poirot and I went on to supper at the Savoy.

At the very next table to ours were Lady Edgware, Bryan Martin and two other people whom I did not know. I pointed them out to Poirot and, as I was doing so, another couple came and took their places at the table beyond that again. The woman's face was familiar and yet strangely enough, for the moment I could not place it.

Then suddenly I realised that it was Carlotta Adams at whom I was staring! The man I did not know. He was well-groomed, with a cheerful, somewhat vacuous face. Not a type that I admire.

Carlotta Adams was dressed very inconspicuously in black. Hers was not a face to command instant attention or recognition. It was one of those mobile sensitive faces that pre-eminently lend themselves to the art of mimicry. It could take on an alien character easily, but it had no very recognisable character of its own.

I imparted these reflections of mine to Poirot. He listened attentively, his egg-shaped head cocked slightly to one side whilst he darted a sharp glance at the two tables in question.

"So that is Lady Edgware? Yes, I remember—I have seen her act. She is *belle femme*."

"And a fine actress too."

"Possibly."

"You don't seem convinced."

"I think it would depend on the setting, my friend. If she is the centre of the play, if all revolves round her—yes, then she could play her part. I doubt if she could play a small part adequately or even what is called a character part. The play must be written *about* her and *for* her. She appears to me of the type of women who are interested only in themselves." He paused and then added rather unexpectedly: "Such people go through life in great danger."

"Danger?" I said, surprised.

"I have used a word that surprises you, I see, *mon ami*. Yes, danger. Because, you see, a woman like that sees only one thing—herself. Such women see nothing of the dangers and hazards that surround them—the million conflicting interests and relationships of life. No, they see only their own forward path. And so—sooner or later—disaster."

I was interested. I confessed to myself that such a point of view would not have struck me.

"And the other?" I asked.

"Miss Adams?"

His gaze swept to her table.

"Well?" he said, smiling. "What do you want me to say about her?"

"Only how she strikes you."

"*Mon cher*, am I to-night the fortune-teller who reads the palm and tells the character?"

"You could do it better than most," I rejoined.

"It is a very pretty faith that you have in me, Hastings. It touches me. Do you not know, my friend, that each one of us is a dark mystery, a maze of conflicting passions and desires and aptitudes? *Mais oui, c'est vrai*. One makes one's little judgments—but nine times out of ten one is wrong."

"Not Hercule Poirot," I said smiling.

"Even Hercule Poirot! Oh! I know very well that you have always a little idea that I am conceited, but, indeed, I assure you, I am really a very humble person."

I laughed.

"You—humble!"

"It is so. Except—I confess it—that I am a little proud of my moustaches. Nowhere in London have I observed anything to compare with them."

"You're quite safe," I said dryly. "You won't. So you are not going to risk judgment on Carlotta Adams?"

"*Elle est artiste!*" said Poirot simply. "That covers nearly all, does it not?"

"Anyway, you don't consider that she walks through life in peril?"

"We all do that, my friend," said Poirot gravely. "Misfortune may always be waiting to rush out upon us. But as to your question, Miss Adams, I think, will succeed. She is shrewd and she is something more. You observed without doubt that she is a Jewess?"

I had not, But now that he mentioned it, I saw the faint traces of Semitic ancestry. Poirot nodded.

"It makes for success—that. Though there is still one avenue of danger—since it is of danger we are talking."

"You mean?"

"Love of money. Love of money might lead such a one from the prudent and cautious path."

"It might do that to all of us," I said.

"That is true, but at any rate you or I would see the danger involved. We could weigh the pros and cons. If you care for money too much, it is only the money you see, everything else is in shadow."

I laughed at his serious manner.

"Esmeralda, the gypsy queen, is in good form," I remarked teasingly.

"The psychology of character is interesting," returned Poirot, unmoved. "One cannot be interested in crime without being interested in psychology. It is not the mere act of killing, it is what lies *behind* it that appeals to the expert. You follow me, Hastings?"

I said that I followed him perfectly.

"I have noticed that when we work on a case together, you are always urging me on to physical action, Hastings. You wish me to measure footprints, to analyse cigarette-ash, to prostrate myself on my stomach for the examination of detail. You never realise that by lying back in an armchair with the eyes closed one can come nearer to the solution of any problem. One sees then with the eyes of the mind."

"I don't," I said. "When I lie back in an armchair with my eyes closed one thing happens to me and one thing only!"

"I have noticed it!" said Poirot. "It is strange. At such moments the brain should be working feverishly, not sinking into sluggish repose. The mental activity, it is so interesting, so stimulating! The employment of the little grey cells is a mental pleasure. They and they only can be trusted to lead one through fog to the truth . . ."

I am afraid that I have got into the habit of averting my attention whenever Poirot mentions his little grey cells. I have heard it all so often before.

In this instance my attention wandered to the four people sitting at the next table. When Poirot's monologue drew to a close I remarked with a chuckle:

"You have made a hit, Poirot. The fair Lady Edgware can hardly take her eyes off you."

"Doubtless she has been informed of my identity," said Poirot, trying to look modest and failing.

"I think it is the famous moustaches," I said. "She is carried away by their beauty."

Poirot caressed them surreptitiously.

"It is true that they are unique," he admitted. "Oh, my friend, the 'toothbrush' as you call it, that you wear—it is a horror—an atrocity—a wilful stunting of the bounties of nature. Abandon it, my friend, I pray of you."

"By Jove," I said, disregarding Poirot's appeal. "The lady's getting up. I believe she's coming to speak to us. Bryan Martin is protesting, but she won't listen to him."

Sure enough, Jane Wilkinson swept impetuously from her seat and came over to our table. Poirot rose to his feet, bowing, and I rose also.

"M. Hercule Poirot, isn't it?" said the soft husky voice.

"At your service."

"M. Poirot, I want to talk to you. I must talk to you."

"But certainly, Madame, will you not sit down?"

"No, no, not here. I want to talk to you privately. We'll go right upstairs to my suite."

Bryan Martin had joined her. He spoke now with a deprecating laugh.

"You must wait a little, Jane. We're in the middle of supper. So is M. Poirot."

But Jane Wilkinson was not so easily turned from her purpose.

"Why, Bryan, what does that matter? We'll have supper sent up to the suite. Speak to them about it, will you? And, Bryan—"

She went after him as he was turning away and appeared to urge some course upon him. He stood out about it, I gathered, shaking his head and frowning. But she spoke even more emphatically and finally with a shrug of the shoulders he gave way.

Once or twice during her speech to him she had glanced at the table where Carlotta Adams sat, and I wondered if what she were suggesting had anything to do with the American girl.

Her point gained, Jane came back, radiant.

"We'll go right up now," she said, and included me in a dazzling smile.

The question of our agreeing or not agreeing to her plan did not seem to occur to her mind. She swept us off without a shade of apology.

"It's the greatest luck just seeing you here this evening, M. Poirot," she said as she led the way to the lift. "It's wonderful how everything seems to turn out right for me. I'd just been thinking and wondering what on earth I was going to do and I looked up and there you were at the next table, and I said to myself: 'M. Poirot will tell me what to do.'"

She broke off to say "Second Floor" to the lift-boy.

"If I can be of aid to you—" began Poirot.

"I'm sure you can. I've heard you're just the most marvellous man that ever existed. Somebody's got to get me out of the tangle I'm in and I feel you're just the man to do it."

We got out at the second floor and she led the way along the corridor, paused at a door and entered one of the most opulent of the Savoy suites.

Casting her white fur wrap on one chair, and her small jewelled bag on the table, the actress sank on to a chair and exclaimed:

"M. Poirot, somehow or other I've just *got* to get rid of my husband!"

CHAPTER 2
A Supper Party

After a moment's astonishment Poirot recovered himself!

"But Madame," he said, his eyes twinkling. "Getting rid of husbands is not my specialty."

"Well, of course, I know that."

"It is a lawyer you require."

"That's just where you're wrong. I'm just about sick and tired of lawyers. I've had straight lawyers and crooked lawyers, and not one of them's done me any good. Lawyers just know the law, they don't seem to have any kind of natural sense."

"And you think I have?"

She laughed.

"I've heard that you're the cat's whiskers, M. Poirot."

"*Comment?* The cat's whiskers? I do not understand."

"Well—that you're *It*."

"Madame, I may or may not have brains—as a matter of fact I have—why pretend? But your little affair, it is not my *genre*."

"I don't see why not. It's a problem."

"Oh! a problem!"

"And it's difficult," went on Jane Wilkinson. "I should say you weren't the man to shy at difficulties."

"Let me compliment you on your insight, Madame. But all the same, me, I do not make the investigations for divorce. It is not pretty—*ce métier là*."

"My dear man, I'm not asking you to do spying work. It wouldn't be any good. But I've just got to get rid of the man, and I'm sure you could tell me how to do it."

Poirot paused awhile before replying. When he did, there was a new note in his voice.

"First tell me, Madame, why you are so anxious to 'get rid' of Lord Edgware?"

There was no delay or hesitation about her answer. It came swift and pat.

"Why, of course. I want to get married again. What other reason could there be?"

Her great blue eyes opened ingenuously.

"But surely a divorce should be easy to obtain?"

"You don't know my husband, M. Poirot. He's—he's—" she shivered. "I don't know how to explain it. He's a queer man—he's not like other people."

She paused and then went on.

"He should never have married—anyone. I know what I'm talking about. I just can't describe him, but he's—queer. His first wife, you know, ran away from him. Left a baby of three months behind. He never divorced her and she died miserably abroad somewhere. Then he married me. Well—I couldn't stick it. I was frightened. I left him and went to the States. I've no grounds for a divorce, and if I've given him grounds for one he won't take any notice of them. He's—he's a kind of fanatic."

"In certain American states you could obtain a divorce, Madame."

"That's no good to me—not if I'm going to live in England."

"You want to live in England?"

"Yes."

"Who is the man you want to marry?"

"That's just it. The Duke of Merton."

I drew in my breath sharply. The Duke of Merton had so far been the despair of matchmaking mammas. A young man of monkish tendencies, a violent Anglo-Catholic, he was reported to be completely under the thumb of his mother, the redoubtable dowager duchess. His life was austere in the extreme. He collected Chinese porcelain and was reputed to be of aesthetic tastes. He was supposed to care nothing for women.

"I'm just crazy about him," said Jane sentimentally. "He's unlike anyone I ever met, and Merton Castle is too wonderful. The whole thing is the most romantic business that ever happened. He's so good-looking too—like a dreamy kind of monk."

She paused.

"I'm going to give up the stage when I marry. I just don't seem to care about it any more."

"In the meantime," said Poirot dryly, "Lord Edgware stands in the way of these romantic dreams."

"Yes—and it's driving me to distraction." She leaned back thoughtfully. "Of course if we were only in Chicago I could get him bumped off quite easily, but you don't seem to run to gunmen over here."

"Over here," said Poirot, smiling, "we consider that every human being has the right to live."

"Well, I don't know about that. I guess you'd be better off without some of your politicians, and knowing what I do of Edgware I think he'd be no loss—rather the contrary."

There was a knock at the door, and a waiter entered with supper dishes. Jane Wilkinson continued to discuss her problems with no appreciation of his presence.

"But I don't want you to kill him for me, M. Poirot."

"Merci, Madame."

"I thought perhaps you might argue with him in some clever way. Get him to give in to the idea of divorce. I'm sure you could."

"I think you overrate my persuasive powers, Madame."

"Oh! but you can surely think of *something*, M. Poirot." She leaned forward. Her blue eyes opened wide again. "You'd like me to be happy, wouldn't you?"

Her voice was soft, low and deliciously seductive.

"I should like everybody to be happy," said Poirot cautiously.

"Yes, but I wasn't thinking of everybody. I was thinking of just me."

"I should say you always do that, Madame."

He smiled.

"You think I'm selfish?"

"Oh! I did not say so, Madame."

"I dare say I am. But, you see, I do so hate being unhappy. It affects my acting, even. And I'm going to be ever so unhappy unless he agrees to a divorce—or dies.

"On the whole," she continued thoughtfully. "It would be much better if he died. I mean, I'd feel more finally quit of him."

She looked at Poirot for sympathy.

"You *will* help me, won't you, M. Poirot?" She rose, picking up the white wrap, and stood looking appealingly into his face. I heard the noise of voices outside in the corridor. The door was ajar. "If you don't—" she went on.

"If I don't, Madame?"

She laughed.

"I'll have to call a taxi and go round and bump him off myself."

Laughing, she disappeared through a door to an adjoining room just as Bryan Martin came in with the American girl, Carlotta Adams, and her escort, and the two people who had been supping with him and Jane Wilkinson. They were introduced to me as Mr. and Mrs. Widburn.

"Hello!" said Bryan. "Where's Jane? I want to tell her I've succeeded in the commission she gave me."

Jane appeared in the doorway of the bedroom. She held a lipstick in one hand.

"Have you got her? How marvellous. Miss Adams, I do admire your performance so. I felt I just had to know you. Come in here and talk to me while I fix my face. It's looking too perfectly frightful."

Carlotta Adams accepted the invitation. Bryan Martin flung himself down in a chair.

"Well, M. Poirot," he said. "You were duly captured. Has our Jane persuaded you to fight her battles? You might as well give in sooner as later. She doesn't understand the word 'no.'"

"She has not come across it, perhaps."

"A very interesting character, Jane," said Bryan Martin. He lay back in his chair and puffed cigarette smoke idly towards the ceiling. "Taboos have no meaning for her. No morals whatever. I don't mean she's exactly immoral—she isn't. Amoral is the word, I believe. Just sees one thing only in life—what Jane wants."

He laughed.

"I believe she'd kill somebody quite cheerfully—and feel injured if they caught her and wanted to hang her for it. The trouble is that she *would* be caught. She hasn't any brains. Her idea of a murder would be to drive up in a taxi, sail in under her own name and shoot."

"Now, I wonder what makes you say that?" murmured Poirot.

"Eh?"

"You know her well, Monsieur?"

"I should say I did."

He laughed again, and it struck me that his laugh was unusually bitter.

"You agree, don't you?" he flung out to the others.

"Oh! Jane's an egoist," agreed Mrs. Widburn. "An actress has got to be, though. That is, if she wants to express her personality."

Poirot did not speak. His eyes were resting on Bryan Martin's face, dwelling there with a curious speculative expression that I could not quite understand.

At that moment Jane sailed in from the next room, Carlotta Adams behind her. I presume that Jane had now "fixed her face," whatever that term denoted, to her own satisfaction. It looked to me exactly the same as before and quite incapable of improvement.

The supper party that followed was quite a merry one, yet I sometimes had the feeling that there were undercurrents which I was incapable of appreciating.

Jane Wilkinson I acquitted of any subtleties. She was obviously a young woman who saw only one thing at a time. She had desired an interview with Poirot, and had carried her point and obtained her desire without delay. Now she was obviously in high good humour. Her desire to include Carlotta Adams in the party had been, I decided, a mere whim. She had been highly amused, as a child might be amused, by the clever counterfeit of herself.

No, the undercurrents that I sensed were nothing to do with Jane Wilkinson. In what direction did they lie?

I studied the guests in turn. Bryan Martin? He was certainly not behaving quite naturally. But that, I told myself, might be merely characteristic of a film star. The exaggerated self-consciousness of a vain man too accustomed to playing a part to lay it aside easily.

Carlotta Adams, at any rate, was behaving naturally enough. She was a quiet girl with a pleasant low voice. I studied her with some attention now that I had a chance to do so at close quarters. She had, I thought, distinct charm, but charm of a somewhat negative order. It consisted in an absence of any jarring or strident note. She was a kind of personified soft agreement. Her very appearance was negative. Soft dark hair, eyes a rather colourless pale blue, pale face and a mobile sensitive mouth. A face that you liked but that you would find it hard to know again if you were to meet her, say, in different clothes.

She seemed pleased at Jane's graciousness and complimentary sayings. Any girl would be, I thought—and then—just at that moment—something occurred that caused me to revise that rather too hasty opinion.

Carlotta Adams looked across the table at her hostess who was at that moment turning her head to talk to Poirot. There was a curious scrutinising quality in the girl's gaze—it seemed a deliberate summing up, and at the same time it struck me that there was a very definite hostility in those pale blue eyes.

Fancy, perhaps. Or possibly professional jealousy. Jane was a successful actress who had definitely arrived. Carlotta was merely climbing the ladder.

I looked at the three other members of the party. Mr. and Mrs. Widburn, what about them? He was a tall cadaverous man, she a plump, fair, gushing soul. They appeared to be wealthy people with a passion for everything connected with the stage. They were, in fact, unwilling to talk on any other subject. Owing to my recent absence from England they found me sadly ill-informed, and finally Mrs. Widburn turned a plump shoulder on me and remembered my existence no more.

The last member of the party was the dark young man with the round cheerful face who was Carlotta Adams' escort. I had had my suspicions from the first that the young man was not quite so sober as he might have been. As he drank more champagne this became even more clearly apparent.

He appeared to be suffering from a profound sense of injury. For the first half of the meal he sat in gloomy silence. Towards the latter half he unbosomed himself to me apparently under the impression that I was one of his oldest friends.

"What I mean to say," he said. "It isn't. No, dear old chap, it isn't—"

I omit the slight slurring together of the words.

"I mean to say," he went on, "I ask you? I mean if you take a girl—well, I mean—butting in. Going round upsetting things. Not as though I'd ever said a word to her I shouldn't have done. She's not the sort. You know—Puritan fathers—the Mayflower—all that. Dash it—the girl's straight. What I mean is—what was I saying?"

"That it was hard lines," I said soothingly.

"Well, dash it all, it is. Dash it, I had to borrow the money for this beano from my tailor. Very obliging chap, my tailor. I've owed him money for years. Makes a sort of bond between us. Nothing like a bond, is there, dear old fellow. You and I. You and I. Who the devil are you, by the way?"

"My name is Hastings."

"You don't say so. Now I could have sworn you were a chap called Spencer Jones. Dear old Spencer Jones. Met him at the Eton and Harrow and borrowed a fiver from him. What I say is one face is very like another face—that's what I say. If we were a lot of Chinks we wouldn't know each other apart."

He shook his head sadly, then cheered up suddenly and drank off some more champagne.

"Anyway," he said, "I'm not a damned nigger."

This reflection seemed to cause him such elation that he presently made several remarks of a hopeful character.

"Look on the bright side, my boy," he adjured me. "What I say is, look on the bright side. One of these days—when I'm seventy-five or so, I'm going to be a rich man. When my uncle dies. Then I can pay my tailor."

He sat smiling happily at the thought.

There was something strangely likeable about the young man. He had a round face and an absurdly small black moustache that gave one the impression of being marooned in the middle of a desert.

Carlotta Adams, I noticed, had an eye on him, and it was after a glance in his direction that she rose and broke up the party.

"It was just sweet of you to come up here," said Jane. "I do so love doing things on the spur of the moment, don't you?"

"No," said Miss Adams. "I'm afraid I always plan a thing out very carefully before I do it. It saves—worry."

There was something faintly disagreeable in her manner.

"Well, at any rate the results justify you," laughed Jane. "I don't know when I enjoyed anything so much as I did your show to-night."

The American girl's face relaxed.

"Well, that's very sweet of you," she said warmly. "And I guess I appreciate your telling me so. I need encouragement. We all do."

"Carlotta," said the young man with the black moustache. "Shake hands and say thank you for the party to Aunt Jane and come along."

The way he walked straight through the door was a miracle of concentration. Carlotta followed him quickly.

"Well," said Jane, "what was that that blew in and called me Aunt Jane? I hadn't noticed him before."

"My dear," said Mrs. Widburn. "You mustn't take any notice of him. Most brilliant as a boy in the O.U.D.S. You'd hardly think so now, would you? I hate to see early promise come to nothing. But Charles and I positively must toddle."

The Widburns duly toddled and Bryan Martin went with them.

"Well, M. Poirot?"

He smiled at her.

"*Eh bien*, Lady Edgware?"

"For goodness' sake, don't call me that. Let me forget it! If you aren't the hardest-hearted little man in Europe!"

"But no, but no, I am not hard-hearted."

Poirot, I thought, had had quite enough champagne, possibly a glass too much.

"Then you'll go and see my husband? And make him do what I want?"

"I will go and see him," Poirot promised cautiously.

"And if he turns you down—as he will—you'll think of a clever plan. They say you're the cleverest man in England, M. Poirot."

"Madame, when I am hard-hearted, it is Europe you mention. But for cleverness you say only England."

"If you put this through I'll say the universe."

Poirot raised a deprecating hand.

"Madame, I promise nothing. In the interests of the psychology I will endeavour to arrange a meeting with your husband."

"Psycho-analyse him as much as you like. Maybe it would do him good. But you've got to pull it off—for my sake. I've got to have my romance, Mr. Poirot."

She added dreamily: "Just think of the sensation it will make."

CHAPTER 3
The Man with the Gold Tooth

It was a few days later, when we were sitting at breakfast, that Poirot flung across to me a letter that he had just opened.

"Well, *mon ami,*" he said. "What do you think of that?"

The note was from Lord Edgware and in stiff formal language it made an appointment for the following day at eleven.

I must say that I was very much surprised. I had taken Poirot's words as uttered lightly in a convivial moment, and I had had no idea that he had actually taken steps to carry out his promise.

Poirot, who was very quick-witted, read my mind and his eyes twinkled a little.

"But yes, *mon ami,* it was not solely the champagne."

"I didn't mean that."

"But yes—but yes—you thought to yourself, the poor old one, he has the spirit of the party, he promises things that he will not perform—that he has no intention of performing. But, my friend, the promises of Hercule Poirot are sacred."

He drew himself up in a stately manner as he said the last words. "Of course. Of course. I knew that," I said hastily. "But I thought that perhaps your judgment was slightly—what shall I say—influenced."

"I am not in the habit of letting my judgment be 'influenced' as you call it, Hastings. The best and driest of champagne, the most golden-haired and seductive of women—nothing influences the judgment of Hercule Poirot. No, *mon ami,* I am interested—that is all."

"In Jane Wilkinson's love affair?"

"Not exactly that. Her love affair, as you call it, is a very commonplace business. It is a step in the successful career of a very beautiful woman. If the Duke of Merton had neither a title nor wealth his romantic likeness to a dreamy monk would no longer interest the lady. No, Hastings, what intrigues me is the psychology of the matter. The interplay of character. I welcome the chance of studying Lord Edgware at close quarters."

"You do not expect to be successful in your mission?"

"*Pourquoi pas?* Every man has his weak spot. Do not imagine, Hastings, that because I am studying the case from a psychological standpoint, I shall not try my best to succeed in the commission entrusted to me. I always enjoy exercising my ingenuity."

I had feared an allusion to the little grey cells and was thankful to be spared it.

"So we go to Regent Gate at eleven to-morrow?" I said.

"We?" Poirot raised his eyebrows quizzically.

"Poirot!" I cried. "You are not going to leave me behind. I always go with you."

"If it were a crime, a mysterious poisoning case, an assassination—ah! these are the things your soul delights in. But a mere matter of social adjustment?"

"Not another word," I said determinedly. "I'm coming."

Poirot laughed gently, and at that moment we were told that a gentleman had called.

To our great surprise our visitor proved to be Bryan Martin.

The actor looked older by daylight. He was still handsome, but it was a kind of ravaged handsomeness. It flashed across my mind that he might conceivably take drugs. There was a kind of nervous tension about him that suggested the possibility.

"Good-morning, M. Poirot," he said in a cheerful manner. "You and Captain Hastings breakfast at a reasonable hour, I am glad to see. By the way, I suppose you are very busy just now?"

Poirot smiled at him amiably.

"No," he said. "At the moment I have practically no business of importance on hand."

"Come now," laughed Bryan. "Not called in by Scotland Yard? No delicate matters to investigate for Royalty? I can hardly believe it."

"You confound fiction with reality, my friend," said Poirot, smiling. "I am, I assure you, at the moment completely out of work, though not yet on the dole. *Dieu merci*."

"Well, that's luck for me," said Bryan with another laugh. "Perhaps you'll take on something for me."

Poirot considered the young man thoughtfully.

"You have a problem for me—yes?" he said in a minute or two.

"Well—it's like this. I have and I haven't."

This time his laugh was rather nervous. Still considering him thoughtfully, Poirot indicated a chair. The young man took it. He sat facing us, for I had taken a seat by Poirot's side.

"And now," said Poirot, "let us hear all about it."

Bryan Martin still seemed to have a little difficulty in getting under way.

"The trouble is that I can't tell you quite as much as I'd like to." He hesitated. "It's difficult. You see, the whole business started in America."

"In America? Yes?"

"A mere incident first drew my attention to it. As a matter of fact, I was travelling by train and I noticed a certain fellow. Ugly little chap, clean-shaven, glasses, and a gold tooth."

"Ah! a gold tooth."

"Exactly. That's really the crux of the matter."

Poirot nodded his head several times.

"I begin to comprehend. Go on."

"Well, as I say. I just noticed the fellow. I was travelling, by the way, to New

York. Six months later I was in Los Angeles, and I noticed the fellow again. Don't know why I should have—but I did. Still, nothing in that."

"Continue."

"A month afterwards I had occasion to go to Seattle, and shortly after I got there who should I see but my friend again, *only this time he wore a beard*."

"Distinctly curious."

"Wasn't it? Of course I didn't fancy it had anything to do with me at that time, but when I saw the man again in Los Angeles, beardless, in Chicago with a moustache and different eyebrows and in a mountain village disguised as a hobo—well, I began to wonder."

"Naturally."

"And at last—well, it seemed odd—but not a doubt about it. I was being what you call shadowed."

"Most remarkable."

"Wasn't it? After that I made sure of it. Wherever I was, there, somewhere near at hand, was my shadow made up in different disguises. Fortunately, owing to the gold tooth, I could always spot him."

"Ah! that gold tooth it was a very fortunate occurrence."

"It was."

"Pardon me, M. Martin, but did you never speak to the man? Question him as to the reason of his persistent shadowing?"

"No, I didn't." The actor hesitated. "I thought of doing so once or twice, but I always decided against it. It seemed to me that I should merely put the fellow on his guard and learn nothing. Possibly once they had discovered that I had spotted him, they would have put someone else on my track—someone whom I might not recognise."

"*En effet*—someone without that useful gold tooth."

"Exactly. I may have been wrong—but that's how I figured it out."

"Now, M. Martin, you referred to 'they' just now. Whom did you mean by 'they'?"

"It was a mere figure of speech used for convenience. I assumed—I don't know why—a nebulous 'they' in the background."

"Have you any reason for that belief?"

"None."

"You mean you have no conception of who could want you shadowed or for what purpose?"

"Not the slightest. At least—"

"*Continuez*," said Poirot encouragingly.

"I *have* an idea," said Bryan Martin slowly. "It's a mere guess on my part, mind."

"A guess may be very successful sometimes, Monsieur."

"It concerns a certain incident that took place in London about two years ago. It was a slight incident, but an inexplicable and an unforgettable one. I've often wondered and puzzled over it. Just because I could find no explanation of it at the time, I am inclined to wonder if this shadowing business might not be connected in some way with it—but for the life of me I can't see why or how."

"Perhaps I can."

"Yes, but you see—" Bryan Martin's embarrassment returned. "The awkward thing is that I can't tell you about it—not now, that is. In a day or so I might be able to."

Stung into further speech by Poirot's inquiring glance he continued desperately.

"You see—a girl was concerned in it."

"Ah! parfaitement! An English girl?"

"Yes. At least—why?"

"Very simple. You cannot tell me now, but you hope to do so in a day or two. That means that you want to obtain the consent of the young lady. Therefore she is in England. Also, she must have been in England during the time you were shadowed, for if she had been in America you would have sought her out then and there. Therefore, since she has been in England for the last eighteen months she is probably, though not certainly, English. It is good reasoning that, eh?"

"Rather. Now tell me, M. Poirot, if I get her permission, will you look into the matter for me?"

There was a pause. Poirot seemed to be debating the matter in his mind. Finally he said:

"Why have you come to me before going to her?"

"Well, I thought—" he hesitated. "I wanted to persuade her to—to clear things up—I mean to let things be cleared up by you. What I mean is, if *you* investigate the affair, nothing need be made public, need it?"

"That depends," said Poirot calmly.

"What do you mean?"

"If there is any question of crime—"

"Oh! there's no crime concerned."

"You do not know. There may be."

"But you would do your best for her—for us?"

"That, naturally."

He was silent for a moment and then said:

"Tell me, this follower of yours—this shadow—of what age was he?"

"Oh! quite youngish. About thirty."

"Ah!" said Poirot. "That is indeed remarkable. Yes, that makes the whole thing very much more interesting."

I stared at him. So did Bryan Martin. This remark of his was, I am sure, equally inexplicable to us both. Bryan questioned me with a lift of his eyebrows. I shook my head.

"Yes," murmured Poirot. "It makes the whole story very interesting."

"He *may* have been older," said Bryan doubtfully, "but I don't think so."

"No, no, I am sure your observation is quite accurate, M. Martin. Very interesting—extraordinarily interesting."

Rather taken aback by Poirot's enigmatical words, Bryan Martin seemed at a loss what to say or do next. He started making desultory conversation.

"An amusing party the other night," he said. "Jane Wilkinson is the most high-handed woman that ever existed."

"She has the single vision," said Poirot, smiling. "One thing at a time."

"She gets away with it, too," said Martin. "How people stand it, I don't know!"

"One will stand a good deal from a beautiful woman, my friend," said Poirot with a twinkle. "If she had the pug nose, the sallow skin, the greasy hair, then—ah! then she would not 'get away with it' as you put it."

"I suppose not," conceded Bryan. "But it makes me mad sometimes. All the same, I'm devoted to Jane, though in some ways, mind you, I don't think she's quite all there."

"On the contrary, I should say she was very much on the spot."

"I don't mean that, exactly. She can look after her interests all right. She's got plenty of business shrewdness. No, I meant morally."

"Ah! morally."

"She's what they call amoral. Right and wrong don't exist for her."

"Ah! I remember you said something of the kind the other evening."

"We were talking of crime just now—"

"Yes, my friend?"

"Well, it would never surprise me if Jane committed a crime."

"And you should know her well," murmured Poirot thoughtfully. "You have acted much with her, have you not?"

"Yes. I suppose I know her through and through, and up and down. I can see her killing anybody quite easily."

"Ah! she has the hot temper, yes?"

"No, no, not at all. Cool as a cucumber. I mean if anyone were in her way she'd just remove them—without a thought. And one couldn't really blame her—morally, I mean. She'd just think that anyone who interfered with Jane Wilkinson had got to go."

There was a bitterness in his last words that had been lacking heretofore. I wondered what memory he was recalling.

"You think she would do—murder?"

Poirot watched him intently.

Bryan drew a deep breath.

"Upon my soul, I do. Perhaps, one of these days, you'll remember my words . . . I *know* her, you see. She'd kill as easily as she'd drink her morning tea. *I mean it, M. Poirot.*"

He had risen to his feet.

"Yes," said Poirot quietly. "I can see you mean it."

"I know her," said Bryan Martin again, "through and through."

He stood frowning for a minute, then with a change of tone, he said:

"As to this business we've been talking about, I'll let you know, M. Poirot, in a few days. You will undertake it, won't you?"

Poirot looked at him for a moment or two without replying.

"Yes," he said at last. "I will undertake it. I find it—interesting."

There was something queer in the way he said the last word.

I went downstairs with Bryan Martin. At the door he said to me:

"Did you get the hang of what he meant about that fellow's age? I mean, why was it interesting that he should be about thirty. I didn't get the hang of that at all."

"No more did I," I admitted.

"It doesn't seem to make sense. Perhaps he was just having a game with me."

"No," I said. "Poirot is not like that. Depend upon it, the point has significance since he says so."

"Well, blessed if I can see it. Glad you can't either. I'd hate to feel I was a complete mutt."

He strode away. I rejoined my friend.

"Poirot," I said. "What was the point about the age of the shadower?"

"You do not see? My poor Hastings!" He smiled and shook his head. Then he asked: "What did you think of our interview on the whole?"

"There's so little to go upon. It seems difficult to say. If we knew more—"

"Even without knowing more, do not certain ideas suggest themselves to you, *mon ami?*"

The telephone ringing at that moment saved me from the ignominy of admitting that no ideas whatever suggested themselves to me. I took up the receiver.

A woman's voice spoke, a crisp, clear efficient voice.

"This is Lord Edgware's secretary speaking. Lord Edgware regrets that he must cancel the appointment with M. Poirot for to-morrow morning. He has to go over to Paris to-morrow unexpectedly. He could see M. Poirot for a few minutes at a quarter-past twelve this morning if that would be convenient."

I consulted Poirot.

"Certainly, my friend, we will go there this morning."

I repeated this into the mouthpiece.

"Very good," said the crisp business-like voice. "A quarter-past twelve this morning."

She rang off.

CHAPTER 4
An Interview

I arrived with Poirot at Lord Edgware's house in Regent Gate in a very pleasant state of anticipation. Though I had not Poirot's devotion to "the psychology," yet the few words in which Lady Edgware had referred to her husband had aroused my curiosity. I was anxious to see what my own judgment would be.

The house was an imposing one—well-built, handsome and slightly gloomy. There were no window-boxes or such frivolities.

The door was opened to us promptly, and by no aged white-haired butler such as would have been in keeping with the exterior of the house. On the contrary, it was opened by one of the handsomest young men I have ever seen. Tall, fair, he might have posed to a sculptor for Hermes or Apollo. Despite his good looks there was something vaguely effeminate that I disliked about the softness of his voice. Also, in a curious way, he reminded me of someone—someone, too, whom I had met quite lately—but who it was I could not for the life of me remember.

We asked for Lord Edgware.

"This way, sir."

He led us along the hall, past the staircase, to a door at the rear of the hall.

Opening it, he announced us in that same soft voice which I instinctively distrusted.

The room into which we were shown was a kind of library. The walls were lined with books, the furnishings were dark and sombre but handsome, the chairs were formal and not too comfortable.

Lord Edgware, who rose to receive us, was a tall man of about fifty. He had dark hair streaked with grey, a thin face and a sneering mouth. He looked bad-tempered and bitter. His eyes had a queer secretive look about them. There was something, I thought, distinctly odd about those eyes.

His manner was stiff and formal.

"M. Hercule Poirot? Captain Hastings? Please be seated."

We sat down. The room felt chilly. There was little light coming in from the one window and the dimness contributed to the cold atmosphere.

Lord Edgware had taken up a letter which I saw to be in my friend's handwriting.

"I am familiar, of course, with your name, M. Poirot. Who is not?" Poirot bowed at the compliment. "But I cannot quite understand your position in this matter. You say that you wish to see me on behalf of"—he paused—"my wife."

He said the last two words in a peculiar way—as though it were an effort to get them out.

"That is so," said my friend.

"I understood that you were an investigator of—crime, M. Poirot?"

"Of problems, Lord Edgware. There are problems of crime, certainly. There are other problems."

"Indeed. And what may this one be?"

The sneer in his words was palpable by now. Poirot took no notice of it.

"I have the honour to approach you on behalf of Lady Edgware," he said. "Lady Edgware, as you may know, desires—a divorce."

"I am quite aware of that," said Lord Edgware coldly.

"Her suggestion was that you and I should discuss the matter."

"There is nothing to discuss."

"You refuse, then?"

"Refuse? Certainly not."

Whatever else Poirot had expected, he had not expected this. It is seldom that I have seen my friend utterly taken aback, but I did on this occasion. His appearance was ludicrous. His mouth fell open, his hands flew out, his eyebrows rose. He looked like a cartoon in a comic paper.

"*Comment?*" he cried. "What is this? You do not refuse?"

"I am at a loss to understand your astonishment, M. Poirot."

"*Ecoutez*, you are willing to divorce your wife?"

"Certainly I am willing. She knows that perfectly well, I wrote and told her so."

"You wrote and told her so?"

"Yes. Six months ago."

"But I do not understand. I do not understand at all."

Lord Edgware said nothing.

"I understood that you were opposed to the principle of divorce."

"I do not see that my principles are your business, M. Poirot. It is true that I did not divorce my first wife. My conscience would not allow me to do so. My second marriage, I will admit frankly, was a mistake. When my wife suggested a divorce, I refused point blank. Six months ago she wrote to me again urging the point. I have an idea she wanted to marry again—some film actor or fellow of that kind. My views had, by this time, undergone modification. I wrote to her at Hollywood telling her so. Why she has sent you to me I cannot imagine. I suppose it is a question of money."

His lips sneered as he said the last words.

"Extremely curious," murmured Poirot. "Extremely curious. There is something here I do not understand at all."

"As regards money," went on Lord Edgware. "I have no intention of making any financial arrangement. My wife deserted me of her own accord. If she wishes to marry another man, I can set her free to do so, but there is no reason why she should receive a penny from me and she will not do so."

"There is no question of any financial arrangement."

Lord Edgware raised his eyebrows.

"Jane must be marrying a rich man," he murmured cynically.

"There is something here that I do not understand," said Poirot. His face was perplexed and wrinkled with the effort of thought. "I understand from Lady Edgware that she had approached you repeatedly through lawyers?"

"She did," replied Lord Edgware dryly. "English lawyers, American lawyers, every kind of lawyer, down to the lowest kind of scallywag. Finally, as I say, she wrote to me herself."

"You having previously refused?"

"That is so."

"But on receiving her letter, you changed your mind. Why did you change your mind, Lord Edgware?"

"Not on account of anything in that letter," he said sharply. "My views happened to have changed, that is all."

"The change was somewhat sudden."

Lord Edgware did not reply.

"What special circumstances brought about your change of mind, Lord Edgware?"

"That, really, is my own business, M. Poirot. I cannot enter into that subject. Shall we say that gradually I had perceived the advantages of severing what—you will forgive my plain speaking—I considered a degrading association. My second marriage was a mistake."

"Your wife says the same," said Poirot softly.

"Does she?"

There was a queer flicker for a moment in his eyes, but it was gone almost at once.

He rose with an air of finality and as we said good-bye his manner became less unbending.

"You must forgive my altering the appointment. I have to go over to Paris to-morrow."

"Perfectly—perfectly."

"A sale of works of art as a matter of fact. I have my eye on a little statuette—a perfect thing in its way—a *macabre* way, perhaps. But I enjoy the *macabre*. I always have. My taste is peculiar."

Again that queer smile. I had been looking at the books in the shelves near. There were the Memoirs of Casanova. also a volume on the Comte de Sade, another on medieval tortures.

I remembered Jane Wilkinson's little shudder as she spoke of her husband. That had not been acting. That had been real enough. I wondered exactly what kind of a man George Alfred St. Vincent Marsh, fourth Baron Edgware, was.

Very suavely he bid us farewell, touching the bell as he did so. We went out of the door. The Greek god of a butler was waiting in the hall. As I closed the library door behind me, I glanced back into the room. I almost uttered an exclamation as I did so.

That suave smiling face was transformed. The lips were drawn back from the teeth in a snarl, the eyes were alive with fury and an almost insane rage.

I wondered no longer that two wives had left Lord Edgware. What I did marvel at was the iron self-control of the man. To have gone through that interview with such frozen self-control, such aloof politeness!

Just as we reached the front door, a door on the right opened. A girl stood at the doorway of the room, shrinking back a little as she saw us.

She was a tall slender girl, with dark and hair and a white face. Her eyes, dark and startled, looked for a moment into mine. Then, like a shadow, she shrank back into the room again, closing the door.

A moment later we were out in the street. Poirot hailed a taxi. We got in and he told the man to drive to the Savoy.

"Well, Hastings," he said with a twinkle, "that interview did not go at all as I figured to myself it would."

"No, indeed. What an extraordinary man Lord Edgware is."

I related to him how I had looked back before closing the door of the study and what I had seen. He nodded his head slowly and thoughtfully.

"I fancy that he is very near the border line of madness, Hastings. I should imagine he practises many curious vices, and that beneath his frigid exterior he hides a deep-rooted instinct of cruelty."

"It is no wonder both his wives left him."

"As you say."

"Poirot, did you notice a girl as we were coming out? A dark girl with a white face."

"Yes, I noticed her, *mon ami*. A young lady who was frightened and not happy."

His voice was grave.

"Who do you think she was?"

"Probably his daughter. He has one."

"She did look frightened," I said slowly. "That house must be a gloomy place for a young girl."

"Yes, indeed. Ah! here we are, *mon ami*. Now to acquaint her ladyship with the good news."

Jane was in, and after telephoning, the clerk informed us that we were to go up. A page boy took us to the door.

It was opened by a neat middle-aged woman with glasses and primly arranged grey hair. From the bedroom Jane's voice, with its husky note, called to her.

"Is that M. Poirot, Ellis? Make him sit right down. I'll find a rag to put on and be there in a moment."

Jane Wilkinson's idea of a rag was a gossamer negligée which revealed more than it hid. She came in eagerly, saying: "Well?"

Poirot rose and bowed over her hand.

"Exactly the words, Madame, it *is* well."

"Why—how do you mean?"

"Lord Edgware is perfectly willing to agree to a divorce."

"What?"

Either the stupefaction on her face was genuine, or else she was indeed a most marvellous actress.

"M. Poirot! You've managed it! At once! Like that! Why, you're a genius. How in mercy's name did you set about it?"

"Madame, I cannot take compliments where they are not earned. Six months ago your husband wrote to you withdrawing his opposition."

"What's that you say? *Wrote to me?* Where?"

"It was when you were at Hollywood, I understand."

"I never got it. Must have gone astray, I suppose. And to think I've been thinking and planning and fretting and going nearly crazy all these months."

"Lord Edgware seemed to be under the impression that you wished to marry an actor."

"Naturally. That's what I told him." She gave a pleased child's smile. Suddenly it changed to a look of alarm. "Why, M. Poirot, you didn't go and tell him about me and the duke?"

"No, no, reassure yourself. I am discreet. That would not have done, eh?"

"Well, you see, he's got a queer mean nature. Marrying Merton, he'd feel, was perhaps a kind of leg up for me—so then naturally he'd queer the pitch. But a film actor's different. Though, all the same, I'm surprised. Yes, I am. Aren't you surprised, Ellis?"

I had noticed that the maid had come to and fro from the bedroom tidying away various outdoor garments which were lying flung over the backs of chairs. It had been my opinion that she had been listening to the conversation. Now it seemed that she was completely in Jane's confidence.

"Yes, indeed, m'lady. His lordship must have changed a good deal since we knew him," said the maid spitefully.

"Yes, he must."

"You cannot understand his attitude. It puzzles you?" suggested Poirot.

"Oh, it does. But anyway, we needn't worry about that. What does it matter what made him change his mind so long as he has changed it?"

"It may not interest you, but it interests me, Madame."

Jane paid no attention to him.

"The thing is that I'm free—at last."

"Not yet, Madame."

She looked at him impatiently.

"Well, going to be free. It's the same thing."

Poirot looked as though he did not think it was.

"The duke is in Paris," said Jane. "I must cable him right away. My—won't his old mother be wild!"

Poirot rose.

"I am glad, Madame, that all is turning out as you wish."

"Good-bye, M. Poirot, and thanks awfully."

"I did nothing."

"You brought me the good news, anyway, M. Poirot, and I'm ever so grateful. I *really* am."

"And that is that," said Poirot to me, as we left the suite. "The single idea—herself! She has no speculation, no curiosity as to why that letter never reached her. You observe, Hastings, she is shrewd beyond belief in the business sense, but she has absolutely no intellect. Well, well, the good God cannot give everything."

"Except to Hercule Poirot," I said slyly.

"You mock yourself at me, my friend," he replied serenely. "But come, let us walk along the Embankment. I wish to arrange my ideas with order and method."

I maintained a discreet silence until such time as the oracle should speak.

"That letter," he resumed when we were pacing along by the river. "It intrigues me. There are four solutions of that problem, my friend."

"Four?"

"Yes. First, it was lost in the post. That *does* happen, you know. But not very often. No, not very often. Incorrectly addressed, it would have been returned to Lord Edgware long before this. No, I am inclined to rule out that solution—though, of course, it may be the true one.

"Solution two, our beautiful lady is lying when she says she never received it. That, of course, is quite possible. That charming lady is capable of telling any lie to her advantage with the most childlike candour. But I cannot see, Hastings, how it could be to her advantage. If she knows that he will divorce her, why send me to ask him to do so? It does not make sense.

"Solution three. Lord Edgware is lying. And if anyone is lying it seems more likely that it is he than his wife. But I do not see much point in such a lie. Why invent a fictitious letter sent six months ago? Why not simply agree to my proposition? No, I am inclined to think that he *did* send that letter—though what the motive was for his sudden change of attitude I cannot guess.

"So we come to the fourth solution—that someone suppressed that letter. And there, Hastings, we enter on a very interesting field of speculation, because that letter could have been suppressed at either end—in America or England.

"Whoever suppressed it was someone who did not want that marriage dissolved. Hastings, I would give a great deal to know what is behind this affair. There is *something*—I swear there is something."

He paused and then added slowly:

"Something of which as yet I have only been able to get a glimpse."

CHAPTER 5
Murder

The following day was the 30th of June.

It was just half-past nine when we were told that Inspector Japp was below and anxious to see us.

It was some years since we had seen anything of the Scotland Yard inspector.

"*Ah! ce bon Japp*," said Poirot. "What does he want, I wonder?"

"Help," I snapped. "He's out of his depth over some case and he's come to you."

I had not the indulgence for Japp that Poirot had. It was not so much that I minded his picking Poirot's brains—after all, Poirot enjoyed the process, it was delicate flattery. What did annoy me was Japp's hypocritical pretence that he was doing nothing of the kind. I liked people to be straightforward. I said so, and Poirot laughed.

"You are the dog of the bulldog breed, eh, Hastings? But you must remember that the poor Japp he has to save his face. So he makes his little pretence. It is very natural."

I thought it merely foolish and said so. Poirot did not agree.

"The outward form—it is a *bagatelle*—but it matters to people. It enables them to keep the *amour propre*."

Personally I thought a dash of inferiority complex would do Japp no harm, but there was no point in arguing the matter. Besides, I was anxious to learn what Japp had come about.

He greeted us both heartily.

"Just going to have breakfast, I see. Not got the hens to lay square eggs for you yet, M. Poirot?"

This was an allusion to a complaint from Poirot as to the varying sizes of eggs which had offended his sense of symmetry.

"As yet, no," said Poirot, smiling. "And what brings you to see us so early, my good Japp?"

"It's not early—not for me. I've been up and at work for a good two hours. As to what brings me to see you—well, it's murder."

"Murder?"

Japp nodded.

"Lord Edgware was killed at his house in Regent Gate last night. Stabbed in the neck by his wife."

"By his wife?" I cried.

In a flash I remembered Bryan Martin's words on the previous morning. Had he had a prophetic knowledge of what was going to happen? I remembered, too, Jane's easy reference to "bumping him off." Amoral, Bryan Martin had called her. She was the type, yes. Callous, egoistical and stupid. How right he had been in his judgment.

All this passed through my mind while Japp went on:

"Yes. Actress, you know. Well known. Jane Wilkinson. Married him three years ago. They didn't get on. She left him."

Poirot was looking puzzled and serious.

"What makes you believe that it was she who killed him?"

"No belief about it. She was recognised. Not much concealment about it, either. She drove up in a taxi—"

"A taxi—" I echoed involuntarily, her words at the Savoy that night coming back to me.

"—rang the bell, asked for Lord Edgware. It was ten o'clock. Butler said he'd see. 'Oh!' she says, cool as a cucumber. 'You needn't. I am Lady Edgware. I suppose he's in the library.' And with that she walks along and opens the door and goes in and shuts it behind her.

"Well, the butler thought it was queer, but all right. He went downstairs again. About ten minutes later he heard the front door shut. So, anyway, she hadn't stayed long. He locked up for the night about eleven. He opened the library door, but it was dark, so he thought his master had gone to bed. This morning the body was discovered by a housemaid. Stabbed in the back of the neck just at the roots of the hair."

"Was there no cry? Nothing heard?"

"They say not. That library's got pretty well sound-proof doors, you know. And there's traffic passing, too. Stabbed in that way, death results amazing quick. Straight through the cistern into the medulla, that's what the doctor said—or something very like it. If you hit on exactly the right spot it kills a man instantaneously."

"That implies a knowledge of exactly where to strike. It almost implies medical knowledge."

"Yes—that's true. A point in her favor as far as it goes. But ten to one it was a chance. She just struck lucky. Some people do have amazing luck, you know."

"Not so lucky if it results in her being hanged, *mon ami,*" observed Poirot.

"No. Of course she was a fool—sailing in like that and giving her name and all."

"Indeed, very curious."

"Possibly she didn't intend mischief. They quarrelled and she whipped out a penknife and jabbed him one."

"Was it a penknife?"

"Something of that kind, the doctor says. Whatever it was, she took it away with her. It wasn't left in the wound."

Poirot shook his head in a dissatisfied manner.

"No, no, my friend, it was not like that. I know the lady. She would be quite incapable of such a hot-blooded impulsive action. Besides, she would be most unlikely to have a penknife with her. Few women have—and assuredly not Jane Wilkinson."

"You know her, you say, M. Poirot?"

"Yes. I know her."

He said no more for the moment. Japp was looking at him inquisitively.

"Got something up your sleeve, M. Poirot?" he ventured at last.

"Ah!" said Poirot. "That reminds me. What has brought you to me? Eh? It is not merely to pass the time of day with an old comrade? Assuredly not. You have here a nice straightforward murder. You have the criminal. You have the motive—what exactly is the motive, by the way?"

"Wanted to marry another man. She was heard to say so not a week ago. Also heard to make threats. Said she meant to call round in a taxi and bump him off."

"Ah!" said Poirot. "You are very well informed—very well informed. Someone has been very obliging."

I thought his eyes looked a question, but if so, Japp did not respond.

"We get to hear things, M. Poirot," he said stolidly.

Poirot nodded. He had reached out for the daily paper. It had been opened by Japp, doubtless while he was waiting, and had been cast impatiently aside on our entry. In a mechanical manner, Poirot folded it back at the middle page, smoothed and arranged it. Though his eyes were on the paper, his mind was deep in some kind of puzzle.

"You have not answered," he said presently. "Since all goes in the swimming fashion, why come to me?"

"Because I heard you were at Regent Gate yesterday morning."

"I see."

"Now, as soon as I heard that, I said to myself, 'Something here.' His lordship sent for M. Poirot. Why? What did he suspect? What did he fear? Before doing anything definite, I'd better go round and have a word with him."

"What do you mean by 'anything definite?' Arresting the lady, I suppose?"

"Exactly."

"You have not seen her yet?"

"Oh! yes, I have. Went round to the Savoy first thing. Wasn't going to risk her giving us the slip."

"Ah!" said Poirot. "So you—"

He stopped. His eyes, which had been fixed thoughtfully and up to now unseeingly on the paper in front of him, now took on a different expression. He lifted his head and spoke in a changed tone of voice.

"And what did she say? Eh! my friend. What did she say?"

"I gave her the usual stuff, of course, about wanting a statement and cautioning her—you can't say the English police aren't fair."

"In my opinion foolishly so. But proceed. What did milady say?"

"Took hysterics—that's what she did. Rolled herself about, threw up her arms and finally flopped down on the ground. Oh! she did it well—I'll say that for her. A pretty bit of acting."

"Ah!" said Poirot blandly. "You formed, then, the impression that the hysterics were not genuine?"

Japp winked vulgarly.

"What do you think? I'm not to be taken in with those tricks. *She* hadn't fainted—not she! Just trying it on, she was. I'll swear she was enjoying it."

"Yes," said Poirot thoughtfully. "I should say that was perfectly possible. What next?"

"Oh! well, she came to—pretended to, I mean. And moaned—*and* groaned and carried on and that sour-faced maid of hers doped her with smelling salts and at last she recovered enough to ask for her solicitor. Wasn't going to say anything without her solicitor. Hysterics one moment, solicitor the next, now I ask you, is that natural behaviour, sir?"

"In this case quite natural, I should say," said Poirot calmly.

"You mean because she's guilty and knows it."

"Not at all, I mean because of her temperament. First she gives you her conception of how the part of a wife suddenly learning of her husband's death should be played. Then, having satisfied her histrionic instinct, her native shrewdness makes her send for a solicitor. That she creates an artificial scene and enjoys it is no proof of her guilt. It merely indicates that she is a born actress."

"Well, she can't be innocent. That's sure."

"You are very positive," said Poirot. "I suppose that it must be so. She made no statement, you say? No statement at all?"

Japp grinned.

"Wouldn't say a word without her solicitor. The maid telephoned for him. I left two of my men there and came along to you. I thought it just as well to get put wise to whatever there was going on before I went on with things."

"And yet you are sure?"

"Of course I'm sure. But I like as many facts as possible. You see, there's going to be a big splash made about this. No hole and corner business. All the papers will be full of it. And you know what papers are."

"Talking of papers," said Poirot. "How do you account for this, my dear friend. You have not read your morning paper very carefully."

He leant across the table, his finger on a paragraph in the society news. Japp read the item aloud.

> Sir Montagu Corner gave a very successful dinner-party last night at his house on the river at Chiswick. Among those present were Sir George and Lady du Fisse, Mr. James Blunt, the well-known dramatic critic, Sir Oscar Hammerfelt of the Overton Film Studios, Miss Jane Wilkinson (Lady Edgware) and others.

For a moment Japp looked taken aback. Then he rallied.

"What's that got to do with it? This thing was sent to the Press beforehand. You'll see. You'll find that our lady wasn't there, or that she came in late—eleven o'clock or so. Bless you, sir, you mustn't believe everything you see in the Press to be gospel. You of all people ought to know better than that."

"Oh! I do, I do. It only struck me as curious, that was all."

"These coincidences do happen. Now, M. Poirot, close as an oyster I know you to be by bitter experience. But you'll come across with things, won't you? You'll tell me why Lord Edgware sent for you?"

Poirot shook his head.

"Lord Edgware did not send for me. It was I who requested him to give me an appointment."

"Really? And for what reason?"

Poirot hesitated a minute.

"I will answer your question," he said slowly. "But I should like to answer it in my own way."

Japp groaned. I felt a sneaking sympathy with him. Poirot can be intensely irritating at times.

"I will request," went on Poirot, "that you permit me to ring up a certain person and ask him to come here."

"What person?"

"Mr. Bryan Martin."

"The film star? What's he got to do with it?"

"I think," said Poirot, "that you may find what he has got to say interesting—and possibly helpful. Hastings, will you be so good?"

I took up the telephone-book. The actor had a flat in a big block of buildings near St. James's Park.

"Victoria 49499."

The somewhat sleepy voice of Bryan Martin spoke after a few minutes.

"Hello—who's speaking?"

"What am I to say?" I whispered, covering the mouthpiece with my hand.

"Tell him," said Poirot, "that Lord Edgware has been murdered, and that I should esteem it a favour if he would come round here and see me immediately."

I repeated this meticulously. There was a startled exclamation at the other end.

"My God," said Martin. "*So she's done it then!* I'll come at once."

"What did he say?" asked Poirot. I told him.

"Ah!" said Poirot. He seemed pleased. "*So she's done it then*. That is what he said? Then it is as I thought, it is as I thought."

Japp looked at him curiously.

"I can't make you out, M. Poirot. First you sound as though you thought the woman might not have done it after all. And now you make out that you knew it all along."

Poirot only smiled.

CHAPTER 6
The Widow

Bryan Martin was as good as his word. In less than ten minutes he had joined us. During the time that we awaited his arrival, Poirot would only talk of extraneous subjects and refused to satisfy Japp's curiosity in the smallest degree.

Evidently our news had upset the young actor terribly. His face was white and drawn.

"Good heavens, M. Poirot," he said as he shook hands. "This is a terrible business. I'm shocked to the core—and yet I can't say I'm surprised. I've always half-suspected that something of this kind might happen. You may remember I was saying so yesterday."

"*Mais oui, mais oui,*" said Poirot. "I remember perfectly what you said to me yesterday. Let me introduce you to Inspector Japp who is in charge of the case."

Bryan Martin shot a glance of reproach at Poirot.

"I had no idea," he murmured. "You should have warned me."

He nodded coldly to the inspector.

He sat down, his lips pressed tightly together.

"I don't see," he objected, "why you asked me to come round. All this has nothing to do with me."

"I think it has," said Poirot gently. "In a case of murder one must put one's private repugnances behind one."

"No, no. I've acted with Jane. I know her well. Dash it all, she's a friend of mine."

"And yet the moment that you hear Lord Edgware is murdered, you jump to the conclusion that it is she who has murdered him," remarked Poirot dryly.

The actor started.

"Do you mean to say—?" His eyes seemed starting out of his head. "Do you mean to say that I'm wrong?That she had nothing to do with it?"

Japp broke in.

"No, no, Mr. Martin. She did it right enough."

The young man sank back again in his chair.

"For a moment," he murmured. "I thought I'd made the most ghastly mistake."

"In a matter of this kind friendship must not be allowed to influence you," said Poirot decisively.

"That's all very well, but—"

"My friend, do you seriously wish to range yourself on the side of a woman who has murdered? Murder—the most repugnant of human crimes."

Bryan Martin sighed.

"You don't understand. Jane is not an ordinary murderess. She—she has no sense of right or wrong. Honestly she's not responsible."

"That'll be a question for the jury," said Japp.

"Come, come," said Poirot kindly. "It is not as though you were accusing her. She is already accused. You cannot refuse to tell us what you know. You have a duty to society, young man."

Bryan Martin sighed.

"I suppose you're right," he said. "What do you want me to tell you?"

Poirot looked at Japp.

"Have you ever heard Lady Edgware—or perhaps I'd better call her Miss Wilkinson—utter threats against her husband?" asked Japp.

"Yes, several times."

"What did she say?"

"She said that if he didn't give her her freedom she'd have to 'bump him off.'"

"And that was not a joke, eh?"

"No. I think she meant it seriously. Once she said she'd take a taxi and go round and kill him—*you* heard that, M. Poirot?"

He appealed pathetically to my friend.

Poirot nodded.

Japp went on with his questions.

"Now, Mr. Martin, we've been informed that she wanted her freedom in order to marry another man. Do you know who that man was?"

Bryan nodded.

"Who?"

"It was—the Duke of Merton."

"The Duke of Merton! Whew!" The detective whistled. "Flying at high game, eh? Why, he's said to be one of the richest men in England."

Bryan nodded more dejectedly than ever.

I could not quite understand Poirot's attitude. He was lying back in his chair, his fingers pressed together and the rhythmic motion of his head suggested the complete approval of a man who has put a chosen record on the gramophone and is enjoying the result.

"Wouldn't her husband divorce her?"

"No, he refused absolutely."

"You know that for a fact?"

"Yes."

"And now," said Poirot, suddenly taking part once more in the proceedings. "You see where I come in, my good Japp. I was asked by Lady Edgware to see her husband and try and get him to agree to a divorce. I had an appointment for this morning."

Bryan Martin shook his head.

"It would have been of no use," he declared confidently. "Edgware would never have agreed."

"You think not?" said Poirot, turning an amiable glance on him.

"Sure of it. Jane knew that in her heart of hearts. She'd no real confidence that you'd succeed. She'd given up hope. The man was a monomaniac on the subject of divorce."

Poirot smiled. His eyes grew suddenly very green.

"You are wrong, my dear young man," he said gently. "I saw Lord Edgware yesterday, *and he agreed to a divorce*."

There was no doubt that Bryan Martin was completely dumbfounded by this piece of news. He stared at Poirot with his eyes almost starting out of his head.

"You—you saw him yesterday?" he spluttered.

"At a quarter-past twelve," said Poirot in his methodical manner.

"And he agreed to a divorce?"

"He agreed to a divorce."

"You should have told Jane at once," cried the young man reproachfully.

"I did, M. Martin."

"You did?" cried Martin and Japp together.

Poirot smiled.

"It impairs the motive a little, does it not?" he murmured. "And now, M. Martin, let me call your attention to this."

He showed him the newspaper paragraph.

Bryan read it, but without much interest.

"You mean this makes an alibi?" he said. "I suppose Edgware was shot some time yesterday evening?"

"He was stabbed, not shot," said Poirot.

Martin laid the paper down slowly.

"I'm afraid this does no good," he said regretfully. "Jane didn't go to that dinner."

"How do you know?"

"I forget. Somebody told me."

"That is a pity," said Poirot thoughtfully.

Japp looked at him curiously.

"I can't make you out, Monsieur. Seems now as though you don't want the young woman to be guilty."

"No, no, my good Japp. I am not the partisan you think. But frankly, the case as you present it, revolts the intelligence."

"What do you mean, revolts the intelligence? It doesn't revolt mine."

I could see words trembling on Poirot's lips. He restrained them.

"Here is a young woman who wishes, you say, to get rid of her husband. That point I do not dispute. She told me so frankly. *Eh bien*, how does she set about it? She repeats several times in the loud clear voice before witnesses that she is thinking of killing him. She then goes out one evening, calls at his house, has herself announced, stabs him and goes away. What do you call that, my good friend? Has it even the commonsense?"

"It was a bit foolish, of course."

"Foolish? It is the imbecility!"

"Well," said Japp, rising. "It's all to the advantage of the police when criminals lose their heads. I must go back to the Savoy now."

"You permit that I accompany you?"

Japp made no demur and we set out. Bryan Martin took a reluctant leave of us. He seemed to be in a great state of nervous excitement. He begged earnestly that any further development might be reported to him.

"Nervy sort of chap," was Japp's comment on him.

Poirot agreed.

At the Savoy we found an extremely legal-looking gentleman who had just arrived, and we proceeded all together to Jane's suite. Japp spoke to one of his men.

"Anything?" he inquired laconically.

"She wanted to use the telephone!"

"Who did she telephone to?" inquired Japp eagerly.

"Jay's. For mourning."

Japp swore under his breath. We entered the suite.

The widowed Lady Edgware was trying on hats in front of the glass. She was dressed in a filmy creation of black and white. She greeted us with a dazzling smile.

"Why, M. Poirot, how good of you to come along. Mr. Moxon" (this was to the solicitor) "I'm so glad you've come. Just sit right by me and tell me what questions I ought to answer. This man here seems to think that I went out and killed George this morning."

"Last night, madam," said Japp.

"You said this morning. Ten o'clock."

"I said ten p.m."

"Well, I can never tell which is which—a.m.'s and p.m.'s."

"It's only just about ten o'clock now," added the inspector severely.

Jane's eyes opened very wide.

"Mercy," she murmured. "It's years since I've been awake as early as this. Why, it must have been Early Dawn when you came along."

"One moment, Inspector," said Mr. Moxon in his ponderous legal voice. "When am I to understand that this—er—regrettable—most shocking—occurrence took place?"

"Round about ten o'clock last night, sir."

"Why, that's all right," said Jane shortly. "I was at a party—Oh!" She covered her mouth up suddenly. "Perhaps I oughtn't to have said that."

Her eyes sought the solicitor's in timid appeal.

"If, at ten o'clock last night, you were—er—at a party, Lady Edgware, I—er—I can see no objection to your informing the inspector of the fact—no objection whatever."

"That's right," said Japp. "I only asked you for a statement of your movements yesterday evening."

"You didn't. You said ten something m. And anyway you gave me the most terrible shock. I fainted dead away, Mr. Moxon."

"About this party, Lady Edgware?"

"It was at Sir Montagu Corner's—at Chiswick."

"What time did you go there?"

"The dinner was for eight-thirty."

"You left here—when?"

"I started about eight o'clock. I dropped in at the Piccadilly Palace for a moment to say good-bye to an American friend who was leaving for the States—Mrs. Van Dusen. I got to Chiswick at a quarter to nine."

"What time did you leave?"

"About half-past eleven."

"You came straight back here?"

"Yes."

"In a taxi?"

"No. In my own car. I hire it from the Daimler people."

"And whilst you were at the dinner party you didn't leave it."

"Well—I—"

"So you did leave it?"

It was like a terrier pouncing on a rat.

"I don't know what you mean. I was called to the telephone when we were at dinner."

"Who called you?"

"I guess it was some kind of hoax. A voice said 'Is that Lady Edgware?' And I said 'Yes, that's right,' and then they just laughed and rang off."

"Did you go outside the house to telephone?"

Jane's eyes opened wide in amazement.

"Of course not."

"How long were you away from the dinner table?"

"About a minute and a half."

Japp collapsed after that. I was fully convinced that he did not believe a word she was saying, but having heard her story he could do no more until he had confirmed or disproved it.

Having thanked her coldly, he withdrew.

We also took our leave but she called Poirot back.

"M. Poirot. Will you do something for me?"

"Certainly, Madame."

"Send a cable for me to the Duke in Paris. He's at the Crillon. He ought to know about this. I don't like to send it myself. I guess I've got to look the bereaved widow for a week or two."

"It is quite unnecessary to cable, Madame," said Poirot gently. "It will be in the papers over there."

"Why, what a headpiece you've got! Of course it will. Much better not to cable. I feel it's up to me to keep up my position now everything's gone right. I want to act the way a widow should. Sort of dignified, you know. I thought of sending a wreath of orchids. They're about the most expensive things going. I suppose I shall have to go to the funeral. What do you think?"

"You will have to go to the inquest first, Madame."

"Why, I suppose that's true." She considered for a moment or two. "I don't like that Scotland Yard inspector at all. He just scared me to death. M. Poirot?"

"Yes?"

"Seems it's kind of lucky I changed my mind and went to that party after all."

Poirot had been going towards the door. Suddenly, at these words, he wheeled round.

"What is that you say, Madame? You changed your mind?"

"Yes. I meant to give it a miss. I had a frightful headache yesterday afternoon."

Poirot swallowed once or twice. He seemed to have a difficulty in speaking.

"Did you—say so to anyone?" he asked at last.

"Certainly I did. There was quite a crowd of us having tea and they wanted me to go on to a cocktail party and I said 'No.' I said my head was aching fit to split and that I was going right home and that I was going to cut the dinner too."

"And what made you change your mind, Madame?"

"Ellis went on at me. Said I couldn't afford to turn it down. Old Sir Montagu pulls a lot of strings, you know, and he's a crochetty creature—takes offence easily. Well, I didn't care. Once I marry Merton I'm through with all this. But Ellis is always on the cautious side. She said there's many a slip, etc., and after all I guess she's right. Anyway, off I went."

"You owe Ellis a debt of gratitude, Madame," said Poirot seriously.

"I suppose I do. That inspector had got it all taped out, hadn't he?"

She laughed. Poirot did not. He said in a low voice:

"All the same—this gives one furiously to think. Yes, furiously to think."

"Ellis," called Jane.

The maid came in from the next room.

"M. Poirot says it's very lucky you made me go to that party last night."

Ellis barely cast a glance at Poirot. She was looking grim and disapproving.

"It doesn't do to break engagements, m'lady. You're much too fond of doing it. People don't always forgive it. They turn nasty."

Jane picked up the hat she had been trying on when we came in. She tried it again.

"I hate black," she said disconsolately. "I never wear it. But, I suppose, as a correct widow I've just got to. All those hats are too frightful. Ring up the other hat place, Ellis. I've got to be fit to be seen."

Poirot and I slipped quietly from the room.

CHAPTER 7
The Secretary

We had not seen the last of Japp. He reappeared about an hour later, flung down his hat on the table and said he was eternally blasted.

"You have made the inquiries?" asked Poirot sympathetically.

Japp nodded gloomily.

"And unless fourteen people are lying, she didn't do it," he growled.

He went on:

"I don't mind telling you, M. Poirot, that I expected to find a put-up job. On the face of it, it didn't seem likely that anyone else could have killed Lord Edgware. She's the only person who's got the ghost of a motive."

"I would not say that. *Mais continuez.*"

"Well, as I say, I expected to find a put-up job. You know what these theatrical crowds are—they'd all hang together to screen a pal. But this is rather a different proposition. The people there last night were all big guns, they were none of them close friends of hers and some of them didn't know each other. Their testimony is independent and reliable. I hoped then to find that she'd slipped away for half an hour or so. She could easily have done that—powdering her nose or some excuse.

But no, she did leave the dinner table as she told us to answer a telephone call, but the butler was with her—and, by the way, it was just as she told us. He heard what she said. 'Yes, quite right. This is Lady Edgware.' And then the other side rang off. It's curious, that, you know. Not that it's got anything to do with it."

"Perhaps not—but it is interesting. Was it a man or a woman who rang up?"

"A woman, I think she said."

"Curious," said Poirot thoughtfully.

"Never mind that," said Japp impatiently. "Let's get back to the important part. The whole evening went exactly as she said. She got there at a quarter to nine, left at half-past eleven and got back here at a quarter to twelve. I've seen the chauffeur who drove her—he's one of Daimler's regular people. And the people at the Savoy saw her come in and confirm the time."

"*Eh bien*, that seems very conclusive."

"Then what about those two in Regent Gate? It isn't only the butler. Lord Edgware's secretary saw her too. They both swear by all that's holy that it was Lady Edgware who came there at ten o'clock."

"How long has the butler been there?"

"Six months. Handsome chap, by the way."

"Yes, indeed. *Eh bien*, my friend, if he has only been there six months he cannot have recognised Lady Edgware since he had not seen her before."

"Well, he knew her from her pictures in the papers. And anyway the secretary knew her. She's been with Lord Edgware five or six years, and she's the only one who's absolutely positive."

"Ah!" said Poirot. "I should like to see the secretary."

"Well, why not come along with me now?"

"Thank you, *mon ami*, I should be delighted to do so. You include Hastings in your invitation, I hope?"

Japp grinned.

"What do you think? Where the master goes, there the dog follows," he added in what I could not think was the best of taste.

"Reminds me of the Elizabeth Canning Case," said Japp. "You remember? How at least a score of witnesses on either side swore they had seen the gipsy, Mary Squires, in two different parts of England. Good reputable witnesses, too. And she with such a hideous face there couldn't be two like it. That mystery was never cleared up. It's very much the same here. Here's a separate lot of people prepared to swear a woman was in two different places at the same time. Which of 'em is speaking the truth?"

"That ought not to be difficult to find out?"

"So you say—but this woman—Miss Carroll, really *knew* Lady Edgware. I mean she'd lived in the house with her day after day. She wouldn't be likely to make a mistake."

"We shall soon see."

"Who comes into the title?" I asked.

"A nephew, Captain Ronald Marsh. Bit of a waster, I understand."

"What does the doctor say as to the time of death?" asked Poirot.

"We'll have to wait for the autopsy to be exact, you know. See where the dinner had got to." Japp's way of putting things was, I'm sorry to say, far from refined. "But ten o'clock fits in well enough. He was last seen alive at a few minutes past nine when he left the dinner table and the butler took whiskey and soda into the library. At eleven o'clock when the butler went up to bed the light was out—so he must have been dead then. He wouldn't have been sitting in the dark."

Poirot nodded thoughtfully. A moment or two later we drew up to the house, the blinds of which were now down.

The door was opened to us by the handsome butler.

Japp took the lead and went in first. Poirot and I followed. The door opened to the left, so that the butler stood against the wall on that side. Poirot was on my right and, being smaller than I was, it was only just as we stepped into the hall that the butler saw him. Being close to him, I heard the sudden intake of his breath and looked sharply at the man to find him staring at Poirot with a kind of startled fear visible on his face. I put the fact away in my mind for what it might be worth.

Japp marched into the dining-room, which lay on our right, and called the butler in after him.

"Now then, Alton, I want to go into this again very carefully. It was ten o'clock when this lady came?"

"Her ladyship? Yes, sir."

"How did you recognise her?" asked Poirot.

"She told her name, sir, and besides I've seen her portrait in the papers. I've seen her act, too."

Poirot nodded.

"How was she dressed?"

"In black sir. Black walking dress, and a small black hat. A string of pearls and grey gloves."

Poirot looked a question at Japp.

"White taffeta evening dress and ermine wrap," said the latter succinctly.

The butler proceeded. His tale tallied exactly with that which Japp had already passed on to us.

"Did anybody else come to see your master that evening?" asked Poirot.

"No, sir."

"How was the front door fastened?"

"It has a Yale lock, sir. I usually draw the bolts when I go to bed, sir. At eleven, that is. But last night Miss Geraldine was at the Opera so it was left unbolted."

"How was it fastened this morning?"

"It was bolted, sir. Miss Geraldine had bolted it when she came in."

"When did she come in? Do you know?"

"I think it was about a quarter to twelve, sir."

"Then during the evening until a quarter to twelve, the door could not be opened from the outside without a key? From the inside it could be opened by simply drawing back the handle."

"Yes, sir."

"How many latchkeys were there?"

"His lordship had his, sir, and there was another key in the hall drawer which Miss Geraldine took last night. I don't know if there were any others."

"Does nobody else in the house have a key?"

"No, sir. Miss Carroll always rings."

Poirot intimated that that was all he wished to ask, and we went in search of the secretary.

We found her busily writing at a large desk.

Miss Carroll was a pleasant efficient-looking woman of about forty-five. Her fair hair was turning grey and she wore pince-nez through which a pair of shrewd blue eyes gleamed out on us. When she spoke I recognised the clear business-like voice that had spoken to me through the telephone.

"Ah! M. Poirot," she said as she acknowledged Japp's introduction. "Yes. It was with you I made that appointment for yesterday morning."

"Precisely, Mademoiselle."

I thought that Poirot was favourably impressed by her. Certainly she was neatness and precision personified.

"Well, Inspector Japp?" said Miss Carroll. "What more can I do for you?"

"Just this. Are you absolutely certain that it was Lady Edgware who came here last night?"

"That's the third time you've asked me. Of course I'm sure. I saw her."

"Where did you see her, Mademoiselle?"

"In the hall. She spoke to the butler for a minute, then she went along the hall and in at the library door."

"And where were you?"

"On the first floor—looking down."

"And you were positive you were not mistaken?"

"Absolutely. I saw her face distinctly."

"You could not have been misled by a resemblance?"

"Certainly not. Jane Wilkinson's features are quite unique. It was her."

Japp threw a glance at Poirot as much as to say: "You see."

"Had Lord Edgware any enemies?" asked Poirot suddenly.

"Nonsense," said Miss Carroll.

"How do you mean—nonsense, Mademoiselle?"

"Enemies! People in these days don't have *enemies*. Not English people!"

"Yet Lord Edgware was murdered."

"That was his wife," said Miss Carroll.

"A wife is not an enemy—no?"

"I'm sure it was a most extraordinary thing to happen. I've never heard of such a thing happening—I mean to anyone in our class of life."

It was clearly Miss Carroll's idea that murders were only committed by drunken members of the lower classes.

"How many keys are there to the front door?"

"Two," replied Miss Carroll promptly. "Lord Edgware always carried one. The other was kept in the drawer in the hall, so that anybody who was going to be late in could take it. There was a third one, but Captain Marsh lost it. Very careless."

"Did Captain Marsh come much to the house?"

"He used to live here until three years ago."

"Why did he leave?" asked Japp.

"I don't know. He couldn't get on with his uncle, I suppose."

"I think you know a little more than that, Mademoiselle," said Poirot gently.

She darted a quick glance at him.

"I am not one to gossip, M. Poirot."

"But you can tell us the truth concerning the rumours of a serious disagreement between Lord Edgware and his nephew."

"It wasn't so serious as all that. Lord Edgware was a difficult man to get on with."

"Even you found that?"

"I'm not speaking of myself. I never had any disagreements with Lord Edgware. He always found me perfectly reliable."

"But as regards Captain Marsh—"

Poirot stuck to it, gently continuing to goad her into further revelations.

Miss Carroll shrugged her shoulders.

"He was extravagant. Got into debt. There was some other trouble—I don't know exactly what. They quarrelled. Lord Edgware forbade him the house. That's all."

Her mouth closed firmly. Evidently she intended to say no more.

The room we had interviewed her in was on the first floor. As we left it, Poirot took me by the arm.

"A little minute. Remain here if you will, Hastings. I am going down with Japp. Watch till we have gone into the library, then join us there."

I have long ago given up asking Poirot questions beginning "Why?" Like the Light Brigade "Mine not to reason why, mine but to do or die," though fortunately it has not yet come to dying! I thought that possibly he suspected the butler of spying on him and wanted to know if such were really the case.

I took up my stand looking over the banister. Poirot and Japp went first to the front door—out of my sight. Then they reappeared walking slowly along the hall. I followed their backs with my eye until they had gone into the library. I waited a minute or two in case the butler appeared, but there was no sign of anyone, so I ran down the stairs and joined them.

The body had, of course, been removed. The curtains were drawn and the electric light was on. Poirot and Japp were standing in the middle of the room looking round them.

"Nothing here," Japp was saying.

And Poirot replied with a smile:

"Alas! not the cigarette ash—nor the footprint—nor a lady's glove—nor even a lingering perfume! Nothing that the detective of fiction so conveniently finds."

"The police are always made out to be as blind as bats in detective stories," said Japp with a grin.

"I found a clue once," said Poirot dreamily. "But since it was four feet long instead of four centimetres no one would believe in it."

I remembered the circumstances and laughed. Then I remembered my mission.

"It's all right, Poirot," I said. "I watched, but no one was spying upon you as far as I could see."

"The eyes of my friend Hastings," said Poirot in a kind of gentle mockery. "Tell me, my friend, did you notice the rose between my lips?"

"The rose between your lips?" I asked in astonishment. Japp turned aside spluttering with laughter.

"You'll be the death of me, M. Poirot," he said. "The death of me. A rose. What next?"

"I had the fancy to pretend I was Carmen," said Poirot quite undisturbed.

I wondered if they were going mad or if I was.

"You did not observe it, Hastings?" There was reproach in Poirot's voice.

"No," I said, staring. "But then I couldn't see your face."

"No matter." He shook his head gently.

Were they making fun of me?

"Well," said Japp. "No more to do here, I fancy. I'd like to see the daughter again if I could. She was too upset before for me to get anything out of her."

He rang the bell for the butler.

"Ask Miss Marsh if I can see her for a few moment."

The man departed. It was not he, however, but Miss Carroll who entered the room a few minutes later.

"Geraldine is asleep," she said. "She's had a terrible shock, poor child. After you left I gave her something to make her sleep and she's fast asleep now. In an hour or two, perhaps."

Japp agreed.

"In any case, there's nothing she can tell you that I can't," said Miss Carroll firmly.

"What is your opinion of the butler?" asked Poirot.

"I don't like him much and that's a fact," replied Miss Carroll. "But I can't tell you why."

We had reached the front door.

"It was up there that you stood, was it not, last night, Mademoiselle?" said Poirot suddenly, pointing with his hand up the stairs.

"Yes. Why?"

"And you saw Lady Edgware go along the hall into the study?"

"Yes."

"And you saw her face distinctly?"

"Certainly."

"But you could not have seen her face, Mademoiselle. You can only have seen the back of her head from where you were standing."

Miss Carroll flushed angrily. She seemed taken aback.

"Back of her head, her voice, her walk! It's all the same thing. Absolutely unmistakable! I tell you I *know* it was Jane Wilkinson—a thoroughly bad woman if there ever was one."

And turning away she flounced upstairs.

CHAPTER 8
Possibilities

Japp had to leave us. Poirot and I turned into Regent's Park and found a quiet seat.

"I see the point of your rose between the lips now," I said laughing. "At the moment I thought you had gone mad."

He nodded without smiling.

"You observe, Hastings, that the secretary is a dangerous witness. Dangerous because inaccurate. You notice that she stated positively that she saw the visitor's *face?* At the time I thought that impossible. Coming *from* the study—yes, but not going *to* the study. So I made my little experiment which resulted as *I* thought, and then sprung my trap upon her. She immediately changed her ground."

"Her belief was quite unaltered, though," I argued. "And after all, a voice and a walk are just as unmistakable."

"No, no."

"Why, Poirot, I think a voice and the general gait are about the most characteristic things about a person."

"I agree. And therefore they are the most easily counterfeited."

"You think—"

"Cast your mind back a few days. Do you remember one evening as we sat in the stalls of a theatre—"

"Carlotta Adams? Ah! but then she is a genius."

"A well-known person is not so difficult to mimic. But I agree she has unusual gifts. I believe she could carry a thing through without the aid of footlights and distance—"

A sudden thought flashed into my mind.

"Poirot," I cried. "You don't think that possibly—no, that would be too much of a coincidence."

"It depends how you look at it, Hastings. Regarded from one angle it would be no coincidence at all."

"But why should Carlotta Adams wish to kill Lord Poirot? She did not even know him."

"How do you know she did not know him? Do not assume things, Hastings. There may have been some link between them of which we know nothing. Not that that is precisely my theory."

"Then you have a theory?"

"Yes. The possibility of Carlotta Adams being involved struck me from the beginning."

"But, Poirot—"

"Wait, Hastings. Let me put together few facts for you. Lady Edgware, with a complete lack of reticence, discusses the relations between her and her husband, and even goes so far as to talk of killing him. Not only you and I hear this. A waiter hears it, her maid probably has heard it many times, Bryan Martin hears it, and I imagine Carlotta Adams herself hears it. And there are the people to whom these people repeat it. Then, on that same evening, the excellence of Carlotta Adams' imitation of Jane is commented upon. Who had a motive for killing Lord Edgware? His wife.

"Now supposing that someone else wishes to do away with Lord Edgware. Here is a scapegoat ready to his hand. On the day when Jane Wilkinson announces that she has a headache and is going to have a quiet evening—*the plan is put into operation*.

"Lady Edgware must be seen to enter the house in Regent Gate. Well, she is seen. She even goes so far as to announce her identity. *Ah! c'est un peu trop, ca!* It would awaken suspicion in an oyster .

"And another point—a small point, I admit. The woman who came to the house last night wore black. *Jane Wilkinson never wears black*. We heard her say so. Let us assume, then, that the woman who came to the house last night was *not* Jane Wilkinson—that it was a woman impersonating Jane Wilkinson. Did that woman kill Lord Edgware?

"Did a third person enter that house and kill Lord Edgware? If so, did the person enter before or after the supposed visit of Lady Edgware? If after, what did the woman say to Lord Edgware? How did she explain her presence? She might deceive the butler who did not know her, and the secretary who did not see her at close quarters, but she could not hope to deceive a husband. Or was there only a dead body in the room? Was Lord Edgware killed *before* she entered the house—sometime between nine and ten?"

"Stop, Poirot!" I cried. "You are making my head spin."

"No, no, my friend. We are only considering possibilities. It is like trying on the clothes. Does this fit? No, it wrinkles on the shoulder? This one? Yes, that is better—but not quite large enough. This other one is too small. So on and so on—until we reach the perfect fit—the truth."

"Who do you suspect of such a fiendish plot?" I asked.

"Ah! that is too early to say. One must go into the question of who has a motive for wishing Lord Edgware dead. There is, of couse, the nephew who inherits. A little obvious that, perhaps. And then, in spite of Miss Carroll's dogmatic pronouncement, there is the qustion of enemies. Lord Edgware struck me as a man who very easily might make enemies."

"Yes," I agreed. "That is so."

"Whoever it was must have fancied himself pretty safe. Remember, Hastings, but for her change of mind at the last minute, Jane Wilkinson would have had no alibi. She might have been in her room at the Savoy, and it would have been difficult to prove it. She would have been arrested, tried—probably hanged."

I shivered.

"But there is one thing puzzles me," went on Poirot. "The desire to incriminate her is clear—but what then of the telephone call? Why did someone ring her up at Chiswick and, once satisfied of her presence there, immediately ring off? It looks, does it not, as if someone wanted to be sure of her presence there before proceeding to—what? That was at nine-thirty, almost certainly before the murder. The intention then seems—there is no other word for it—*beneficent*. It *cannot* be the murderer who rings up—the murderer has laid all his plans to incriminate Jane. Who, then, was it? It looks as though we have here two entirely different sets of circumstances."

I shook my head, utterly fogged.

"It might be just a coincidence," I suggested.

"No, no, everything cannot be a coincidence. Six months ago, a letter was suppressed. Why? There are too many things here unexplained. There must be some reason linking them together."

He sighed. Presently he went on:

"That story that Bryan Martin came to tell us—"

"Surely, Poirot, that has got no connection with this business."

"You are blind, Hastings, blind and willfully obtuse. Do you not see that the whole thing makes a pattern? A pattern confused at present but which will gradually become clear . . ."

I felt Poirot was being over-optimistic. I did not feel that anything would ever become clear. My brain was frankly reeling.

"It's no good," I said suddenly. "I can't believe it of Carlotta Adams. She seemed such a—well, such a thoroughly nice girl."

Yet, even as I spoke, I remembered Poirot's words about love of money. Love of money—was that at the root of the seemingly incomprehensible? I felt that Poirot had been inspired that night. He had seen Jane in danger—the result of her strange egoistical temperament. He had seen Carlotta led astray by avarice.

"I do not think she committed the murder, Hastings. She is too cool and level-headed for that. Possibly she was not even told that murder would be done. She may have been used innocently. But then—"

He broke off, frowning.

"Even so, she's an accessory after the fact now. I mean, she will see the news to-day. She will realise—"

A hoarse sound broke from Poirot.

"Quick, Hastings. Quick! I have been blind—imbecile. A taxi. At once."

I stared at him.

He waved his arms.

"A taxi—at once."

One was passing. He hailed it and we jumped in.

"Do you know her address?"

"Carlotta Adams, do you mean?"

"*Mais oui, mais oui*. Quickly, Hastings, quickly. Every minute is of value. Do you not see?"

"No," I said. "I don't."

Poirot swore under his breath.

"The telephone book? No, she would not be in it. The theatre."

At the theatre they were not disposed to give Carlotta's address, but Poirot managed it. It was a flat in a block of mansions near Sloane Square. We drove there, Poirot in a fever of impatience.

"If I am not too late, Hastings. If I am not too late."

"What is all this haste? I don't understand. What does it mean?"

"It means that I have been slow. Terribly slow to realise the obvious. Ah! *mon Dieu*, if only we may be in time."

CHAPTER 9
The Second Death

Though I did not understand the reason for Poirot's agitation, I knew him well enough to be sure that he had a reason for it.

We arrived at Rosedew Mansions, Poirot sprang out, paid the driver and hurried into the building. Miss Adams' flat was on the first floor, as a visiting-card stuck on a board informed us.

Poirot hurried up the stairs, not waiting to summon the lift which was at one of the upper floors.

He knocked and rang. There was a short delay, then the door was opened by a neat middle-aged woman with hair drawn tightly back from her face. Her eyelids were reddened as though with weeping.

"Miss Adams?" demanded Poirot eagerly.

The woman looked at him.

"Haven't you heard?"

"Heard? Heard what?"

His face had gone deadly pale, and I realised that this, whatever it was, was what he had feared.

The woman continued slowly to shake her head.

"She's dead. Passed away in her sleep. It's terrible."

Poirot leaned against the doorpost.

"Too late," he murmured.

His agitation was so apparent that the woman looked at him with more attention.

"Excuse me, sir, but are you a friend of hers? I do not remember seeing you come here before."

Poirot did not reply to this directly. Instead he said:

"You have had a doctor? What did he say?"

"Took an overdose of a sleeping draught. Oh! the pity of it! Such a nice young lady. Nasty dangerous things—these drugs. Veronal, he said it was."

Poirot suddenly stood upright. His manner took on a new authority.

"I must come in," he said.

The woman was clearly doubtful and suspicious.

"I don't think—" she began.

But Poirot meant to have his way. He took probably the only course that would have obtained the desired result.

"You must let me in," he said. "I am a detective and I have got to inquire into the circumstances of your mistress's death."

The woman gasped. She stood aside and we passed into the flat.

From there on Poirot took command of the situation.

"What I have told you," he said authoritatively, "is strictly confidential. It must not be repeated. Everyone must continue to think that Miss Adams' death was accidental. Please give me the name and address of the doctor you summoned."

"Dr. Heath, 17 Carlisle Street."

"And your own name?"

"Bennett—Alice Bennett."

"You were attached to Miss Adams, I can see, Miss Bennett."

"Oh! yes, sir. She were a nice young lady. I worked for her last year when she were over here. It wasn't as though she were one of those actresses. She were a real young lady. Dainty ways she had and liked everything just so."

Poirot listened with attention and sympathy. He had now no signs of impatience. I realised that to proceed gently was the best way of extracting the information he wanted.

"It must have been a great shock to you," he observed gently.

"Oh! it was, sir. I took her in her tea—at half-past nine as usual and there she was lying—asleep I thought. And I put the tray down. And I pulled the curtains—one of the rings caught, sir, and I had to jerk it hard. Such a noise it made. I was surprised when I looked round to see she hadn't woken. And then all of a sudden something seemed to take hold of me. Something not quite natural about the way she lay. And I went to the side of the bed, and I touched her hand. Icy cold it was, sir, and I cried out."

She stopped, tears coming into her eyes.

"Yes, yes," said Poirot sympathetically. "It must have been terrible for you. Did Miss Adams often take stuff to make her sleep?"

"She'd taken something for a headache now and again, sir. Some little tablets in a bottle, but it was some other stuff she took last night, or so the doctor said."

"Did anyone come to see her last night? A visitor?"

"No, sir. She was out yesterday evening, sir."

"Did she tell you where she was going?"

"No, sir. She went out about seven o'clock."

"Ah! How was she dressed?"

"She had on a black dress, sir. A black dress and a black hat."

Poirot looked at me.

"Did she wear any jewellery?"

"Just the string of pearls she always wore, sir."

"And gloves—grey gloves?"

"Yes, sir. Her gloves were grey."

"Ah! Now describe to me, if you will, what her manner was. Was she gay? Excited? Sad? Nervous?"

"It seemed to me she was pleased about something, sir. She kept smiling to herself. As though there were some kind of joke on."

"What time did she return?"

"A little after twelve o'clock, sir."

"And what was her manner then? The same?"

"She was terribly tired, sir."

"But not upset? Or distressed?"

"Oh! no, sir. I think she was pleased about something, but just done up, if you know what I mean. She started to ring someone up on the telephone, and then she said she couldn't bother. She'd do it to-morrow morning."

"Ah!" Poirot's eyes gleamed with excitement. He leaned forward and spoke in a would-be indifferent voice.

"Did you hear the name of the person she rang up?"

"No, sir. She just asked for the number and waited and then the Exchange must have said: 'I'm trying to get them' as they do, sir, and she said 'All right,' and then suddenly she yawned and said 'Oh! I can't bother. I'm too tired.' and she put the receiver back and started undressing."

"And the number she called? Do you recollect that? Think. It may be important."

"I'm sorry I can't say, sir. It was a Victoria number and that's all I can remember. I wasn't paying special heed, you see."

"Did she have anything to eat or drink before she went to bed?"

"A glass of hot milk, sir, like she always did."

"Who prepared it?"

"I did, sir."

"And nobody came to the flat that evening?"

"Nobody, sir."

"And earlier in the day?"

"Nobody came that I can remember, sir. Miss Adams was out to lunch and tea. She came in at six o'clock."

"When did the milk come? The milk she drank last night?"

"It was the new milk she had, sir. The afternoon delivery. The boy leaves it outside the door at four o'clock. But, oh! sir, I'm sure there wasn't nothing wrong with the milk. I had it myself for tea this morning. And the doctor he said positive as she'd taken the nasty stuff herself."

"It is possible that I am wrong," said Poirot. "Yes, it is possible that I am entirely wrong. I will see the doctor. But, you see, Miss Adams had enemies. Things are very different in America—"

He hesitated, but the good Alice leapt at the bait.

"Oh! I know, sir. I've read about Chicago and them gunmen and all that. It must be a wicked country and what the police can be about, I can't think. Not like our policemen."

Poirot left it thankfully at that, realising that Alice Bennett's insular proclivities would save him the trouble of explanations.

His eye fell on a small suitcase—more of an attaché case, that was lying on a chair.

"Did Miss Adams take that with her when she went out last night?"

"In the morning she took it, sir. She didn't have it when she came back at teatime, but she brought it back last thing."

"Ah! You permit that I open it?"

Alice Bennett would have permitted anything. Like most canny and suspicious women, once she had overcome her distrust she was child's play to manipulate. She would have assented to anything Poirot suggested.

The case was not locked. Poirot opened it. I came forward and looked over his shoulder.

"You see, Hastings, you see?" he murmured excitedly.

The contents were certainly suggestive.

There was a box of make-up materials, two objects which I recognised as elevators to place in shoes and raise the height an inch or so, there was a pair of grey gloves and, folded in tissue paper, an exquisitely-made wig of golden hair, the exact shade of gold of Jane Wilkinson's and dressed like hers with a centre parting and curls in the back of the neck.

"Do you doubt now, Hastings?" asked Poirot.

I believe I had up to that moment. But now I doubted no longer.

Poirot closed the case again and turned to the maid.

"You do not know with whom Miss Adams dined yesterday evening?"

"No, sir."

"Do you know with whom she had lunch or tea?"

"I know nothing about tea, sir. I believe she lunched with Miss Driver."

"Miss Driver?"

"Yes, her great friend. She has a hat-shop in Moffatt Street, just off Bond Street. Genevieve, it's called."

Poirot noted the address in his notebook just below that of the doctor.

"One thing more, Madame. Can you remember anything—*anything at all*—that Mademoiselle Adams said or did after she came in at six o'clock that strikes you as at all unusual or significant?"

The maid thought for a moment or two.

"I really can't say that I do, sir," she said at last. "I asked her if she would have tea and she said she'd had some."

"Oh! she said she had had it," interrupted Poirot. "*Pardon*. Continue."

"And after that she was writing letters till just on the time she went out."

"Letters, eh? You do not know to whom?"

"Yes, sir. It was just one letter—to her sister in Washington. She wrote her sister twice a week regular. She took the letter out with her to post because of catching the mail. But she forgot it."

"Then it is here still?"

"No, sir. I posted it. She remembered last night just as she was getting into bed. And I said I'd run out with it. By putting an extra stamp on it and putting it in the late fee box it would go all right."

"Ah!—and is that far?"

"No, sir, the post office is just round the corner."

"Did you shut the door of the flat behind you?"

Bennett stared.

"No, sir. I just left it to—as I always do when I go out to post."

Poirot seemed about to speak—then checked himself.

"Would you like to look at her, sir?" asked the maid tearfully. "Looks beautiful she does."

We followed her into the bedroom.

Carlotta Adams looked strangely peaceful and much younger than she had appeared that night at the Savoy. She looked like a tired child asleep.

There was a strange expression on Poirot's face as he stood looking down on her. I saw him make the sign of the Cross.

"*J'ai fait un serment,* Hastings," he said as we went down the stairs.

I did not ask him what his vow was. I could guess.

A minute or two later he said:

"There is one thing off my mind at least. I could not have saved her. By the time I heard of Lord Edgware's death she was already dead. That comforts me. Yes, that comforts me very much."

CHAPTER 10
Jenny Driver

Our next proceeding was to call upon the doctor whose address the maid had given us.

He turned out to be a fussy elderly man somewhat vague in manner. He knew Poirot by repute and expressed a lively pleasure at meeting him in the flesh.

"And what can I do for you, M. Poirot?" he asked after this opening preamble.

"You were called this morning, M. le docteur, to the bedside of a Miss Carlotta Adams."

"Ah! yes, poor girl. Clever actress too. I've been twice to her show. A thousand pities it's ended this way. Why these girls must have drugs I can't think."

"You think she was addicted to drugs, then?"

"Well, professionally, I should hardly have said so. At all events she didn't take them hypodermically. No marks of the needle. Evidently always took it by the mouth. Maid said she slept well naturally, but then maids never know. I don't suppose she took veronal every night, but she'd evidently taken it for some time."

"What makes you think so?"

"This. Dash it—where did I put the thing?"

He was peering into a small case.

"Ah! here it is."

He drew out a small black morocco handbag.

"There's got to be an inquest, of course. I brought this away so that the maid shouldn't meddle with it."

Opening the pochette he took out a small gold box. On it were the initials C.A. in rubies. It was a valuable and expensive trinket. The doctor opened it. It was nearly full of a white powder.

"Veronal," he explained briefly. "Now look what's written inside."

On the inside of the lid of the box was engraved:

C.A. from D. Paris, Nov. 10th.
Sweet Dreams

"November 10th," said Poirot thoughtfully.

"Exactly, and we're now in June. That seems to show that she's been in the habit of taking the stuff for at least six months, and as the year isn't given, it might be eighteen months or two years and a half—or any time."

"Paris. D," said Poirot, frowning.

"Yes. Convey anything to you? By the way, I haven't asked you what your interest is in the case. I'm assuming you've got good grounds. I suppose you want to know if it's suicide? Well, I can't tell you. Nobody can. According to the maid's account she was perfectly cheerful yesterday. That looks like accident, and in my opinion accident it is. Veronal's very uncertain stuff. You can take a devil of a lot and it won't kill you, and you can take very little and off you go. It's a dangerous drug for that reason.

"I've no doubt they'll bring it in Accidental Death at the inquest. I'm afraid I can't be of any more help to you."

"May I examine the little bag of Mademoiselle?"

"Certainly. Certainly."

Poirot turned out the contents of the pochette. There was a fine handkerchief with C.M.A. in the corner, a powder puff, a lipstick, a pound note and a little change, and a pair of pince-nez.

These last Poirot examined with interest. They were gold-rimmed and rather severe and academic in type.

"Curious," said Poirot. "I did not know that Miss Adams wore glasses. But perhaps they are for reading?"

The doctor picked them up.

"No, these are outdoor glasses," he affirmed. "Pretty powerful too. The person who wore these must have been very short-sighted."

"You do not know if Miss Adams—"

"I never attended her before. I was called in once to see a poisoned finger of the maid's. Otherwise I have never been in the flat. Miss Adams, whom I saw for a moment on that occasion, was certainly not wearing glasses then."

Poirot thanked the doctor and we took our leave.

Poirot wore a puzzled expression.

"It can be that I am mistaken," he admitted.

"About the impersonation?"

"No, no. That seems to me proved. No, I mean as to her death. Obviously she had veronal in her possession. It is possible that she was tired and strung up last night and determined to ensure herself a good night's rest."

Then he suddenly stopped dead—to the great surprise of the passers-by and beat one hand emphatically on the other.

"No, no, no, no!" he declared emphatically. "Why should that accident happen so conveniently? It was no accident. It was not suicide. No, she played her part and in doing so she signed her death warrant. Veronal may have been chosen simply because it was known that she occasionally took it and that she had that box in her possession. But, if so, the murderer must have been someone who knew her well. Who is D? Hastings? I would give a good deal to know who D. was."

"Poirot," I said, as he remained wrapt in thought. "Hadn't we better go on. Everyone is staring at us."

"Eh? Well, perhaps you are right. Though it does not incommode me that people should stare. It does not interfere in the least with my train of thought."

"People were beginning to laugh," I murmured.

"That has no importance."

I did not quite agree. I have a horror of doing anything conspicuous. The only thing that affects Poirot is the possibility of the damp or the heat affecting the set of his famous moustache.

"We will take a taxi," said Poirot, waving his stick.

One drew up by us, and Poirot directed it to go to Genevieve in Moffatt Street.

Genevieve turned out to be one of those establishments where one nondescript hat and a scarf display themselves in a glass box downstairs and where the real centre of operations is one floor up a flight of musty-smelling stairs.

Having climbed the stairs we came to a door with "Genevieve. Please Walk In" on it, and having obeyed this command we found ourselves in a small room full of hats while an imposing blonde creature came forward with a suspicious glance at Poirot.

"Miss Driver?" asked Poirot.

"I do not know if Modom can see you. What is your business, please?"

"Please tell Miss Driver that a friend of Miss Adams would like to see her."

The blonde beauty had no need to go on this errand. A black velvet curtain was violently agitated and a small vivacious creature with flaming red hair emerged.

"What's that?" she demanded.

"Are you Miss Driver?"

"Yes. What's that about Carlotta?"

"You have heard the sad news?"

"What sad news?"

"Miss Adams died in her sleep last night. An overdose of veronal."

The girl's eyes opened wide.

"How awful!" she exclaimed. "Poor Carlotta. I can hardly believe it. Why, she was full of life yesterday."

"Nevertheless it is true. Mademoiselle," said Poirot. "Now see—it is just on one o'clock. I want you to do me the honour of coming out to lunch with me and my friend. I want to ask you several questions."

The girl looked him up and down. She was a pugilistic little creature. She reminded me in some ways of a fox terrier.

"Who are you?" she demanded bluntly.

"My name is Hercule Poirot. This is my friend Captain Hastings."

I bowed.

Her glance travelled from one to the other of us.

"I've heard of you," she said abruptly. "I'll come."

She called to the blonde:

"Dorothy?"

"Yes, Jenny."

"Mrs. Lester's coming in about that Rose Descartes model we're making for her. Try the different feathers. By-by, shan't be long, I expect."

She picked up a small black hat, affixed it to one ear, powdered her nose furiously, and then looked at Poirot.

"Ready," she said abruptly.

Five minutes afterwards we were sitting in a small restarant in Dover Street. Poirot had given an order to the waiter and cocktails were in front of us.

"Now," said Jenny Driver. "I want to know the meaning of all this. What has Carlotta been getting herself mixed up in?"

"She had been getting herself mixed up in something, then, Mademoiselle?"

"Now then, who is going to ask the questions, you or me?"

"My idea was that I should," said Poirot, smiling. "I have been given to understand that you and Miss Adams were great friends."

"Right."

"*Eh bien*, then I ask you, Mademoiselle, to accept my solemn assurance that what I do, I am doing in the interests of your dead friend. I assure you that that is so."

There was a moment's silence while Jenny Driver considered this question. Finally she gave a quick assenting nod of the head.

"I believe you. Carry on. What do you want to know?"

"I understand, Mademoiselle, that your friend lunched with you yesterday."

"She did."

"Did she tell you what her plans were for last night?"

"She didn't exactly mention last night."

"But she said something?"

"Well, she mentioned something that maybe is what you're driving at. Mind you, she spoke in confidence."

"That is understood."

"Well, let me see now. I think I'd better explain things in my own words."

"If you please, Mademoiselle."

"Well, then. Carlotta was excited. She isn't often excited. She's not that kind. She wouldn't tell me anything definite, said she'd promised not to, but she'd got something on. Something, I gathered, in the nature of a gigantic hoax."

"A hoax?"

"That's what she said. She didn't say how or when or where. Only—" She paused, frowning. "Well—you see—Carlotta's not the kind of person who enjoys practical jokes or hoaxes or things of that kind. She's one of those serious, nice-minded, hard-working girls. What I mean is, somebody had obviously put her up to this stunt. And I think—she didn't say so, mind—"

"No, no, I quite understand. What was it that you thought?"

"I thought—I was sure—that in some way money was concerned. Nothing really ever excited Carlotta except money. She was made that way. She'd got one of the best heads for business I've ever met. She wouldn't have been so excited and so pleased unless money—quite a lot of money—had been concerned. My impression was that she'd taken on something for a bet—and that she was pretty sure of winning. And yet that isn't quite true. I mean, Carlotta didn't bet. I've never known her to make a bet. But anyway, somehow or other, I'm sure money was concerned."

"She did not actually say so?"

"N-n-o. Just said that she'd be able to do this, that and the other in the near future. She was going to get her sister over from America to meet her in Paris. She was crazy about her little sister. Very delicate, I believe, and musical. Well, that's all I know. Is that what you want?"

Poirot nodded his head.

"Yes. It confirms my theory. I had hoped, I admit, for more. I had anticipated that Miss Adams would have been bound to secrecy. But I hoped that, being a woman, she would not have counted revealing the secret to her best friend."

"I tried to make her tell me," admitted Jenny. "But she only laughed and said she'd tell me all about it some day."

Poirot was silent for a moment. Then he said:

"You know the name of Lord Edgware?"

"What? The man who was murdered? On a poster half an hour ago."

"Yes. Do you know if Miss Adams was acquainted with him?"

"I don't think so. I'm sure she wasn't. Oh! wait a minute."

"Yes, Mademoiselle?" said Poirot eagerly.

"What was it now?" she frowned, knitting her brow as she tried to remember. "Yes, I've got it now. She mentioned him once. Very bitterly."

"Bitterly?"

"Yes. She said—what was it?—that men like that shouldn't be allowed to ruin other people's lives by their cruelty and lack of understanding. She said—why, so she did—that he was the kind of man whose death would probably be a good thing for everybody."

"When was it she said this, Mademoiselle?"

"Oh! about a month ago, I think it was."

"How did the subject come up?"

Jenny Driver racked her brains for some minutes and finally shook her head.

"I can't remember," she confessed. "His name cropped up or something. It might have been in the newspaper. Anyway, I remember thinking it odd that Carlotta should be so vehement all of a sudden when she didn't even know the man."

"Certainly it is odd," agreed Poirot thoughtfully. Then he asked:

"Do you know if Miss Adams was in the habit of taking veronal?"

"Not that I knew. I never saw her take it or mention taking it."

"Did you ever see in her bag a small gold box with the initials C.A. on it in rubies?"

"A small gold box—no, I am sure I didn't."

"Do you happen to know where Miss Adams was last November?"

"Let me see. She went back to the States in November, I think—towards the end of the month. Before that she was in Paris."

"Alone?"

"Alone, of course! Sorry—perhaps you didn't mean that! I don't know why any mention of Paris always suggests the worst. And it's such a nice respectable place really. But Carlotta wasn't the week-ending sort, if that's what you're driving at."

"Now, Mademoiselle, I am going to ask you a very important question. Was there any man Miss Adams was specially interested in?"

"The answer to that is 'No,'" said Jenny slowly. "Carlotta, since I've known her, has been wrapped up in her work and in her delicate sister. She's had the 'head of the family all depends on me' attitude very strongly. So the answer's NO—strictly speaking."

"Ah! and not speaking so strictly?"

"I shouldn't wonder if—lately—Carlotta hadn't been getting interested in some man."

"Ah!"

"Mind you, that's entirely guesswork on my part. I've gone simply by her manner. She's been—different—not exactly dreamy, but abstracted. And she's looked different, somehow. Oh! I can't explain. It's the sort of thing that another woman just feels—and, of course, may be quite wrong about."

Poirot nodded.

"Thank you, Mademoiselle. One thing more. Is there any friend of Miss Adams whose initial is D?"

"D," said Jenny Driver thoughtfully. "D? No, I'm sorry. I can't think of anyone."

CHAPTER 11
The Egoist

I do not think Poirot had expected any other answer to his question. All the same, he shook his head sadly. He remained lost in thought. Jenny Driver leant forward, her elbows on the table.

"And now," she said, "am I going to be told anything?"

"Mademoiselle," said Poirot. "First of all let me compliment you. Your answers to my questions have been singularly intelligent. Clearly you have brains, Mademoiselle. You ask whether I am going to tell you anything. I answer—not very much. I will tell you just a few bare facts, Mademoiselle."

He paused, and then said quietly:

"Last night Lord Edgware was murdered in his library. At ten o'clock yesterday evening a lady whom I believe to have been your friend Miss Adams came to the house, asked to see Lord Edgware, and announced herself as Lady Edgware. She wore a golden wig and was made up to resemble the real Lady Edgware who, as you probably know, is Miss Jane Wilkinson, the actress. Miss Adams (if it were she) only remained a few moments. She left the house at five minutes past ten but she did not return home till after midnight. She went to bed, having taken an overdose of veronal. Now, Mademoiselle, you see the point, perhaps, of some of the questions I have been asking you."

Jenny drew a deep breath.

"Yes," she said. "I see now. I believe you're right, M. Poirot. Right about its having been Carlotta, I mean. For one thing, she bought a new hat off me yesterday."

"A new hat?"

"Yes. She said she wanted one to shade the left side of her face."

Here I must insert a few words of explanation as I do not know when these words will be read. I have seen many fashions of hats in my time—the cloche that shaded the face so completely that one gave up in despair the task of recognising one's friends. The tilted forward hat, the hat attached airily to the back of the head, the beret, and many other styles. In this particular June the hat of the moment was shaped like an inverted soup plate and was worn attached (as if by suction) over one ear, leaving the other side of the face and hair open to inspection.

"These hats are usually worn on the right side of the head?" asked Poirot.

The little modiste nodded.

"But we keep a few to be worn on the opposite side," she explained. "Because there are people who much prefer their profile to the left or who have a habit of parting hair on one side only. Now, would there be any special reason for Carlotta's wanting that side of her face to be in shadow?"

I remembered that the door of the house in Regent Gate opened to the left, so that anyone entering would be in full view of the butler that side. I remember also that Jane Wilkinson (so I had noticed the other night) had a tiny mole at the corner of the left eye.

I said as much excitedly. Poirot agreed, nodding his head vigorously.

"It is so. It is so. *Vous avez parfaitement raison*, Hastings. Yes, that explains the purchase of the hat."

"M. Poirot?" Jenny sat suddenly bolt upright. "You don't think—you don't for one moment think—that Carlotta did it? Killed him, I mean. You can't think that? Not just because she spoke so bitterly about him."

"I do not think so. But it is curious, all the same—that she should have spoken so, I mean. I would like to know the reason for it. What had he done—what did she know of him to make her speak in such a fashion?"

"I don't know—but she didn't kill him. She's—oh! she was—well—too refined."

Poirot nodded approvingly.

"Yes, yes. You put that very well. It is a point psychological. I agree. This was a scientific crime—but not a refined one."

"Scientific?"

"The murderer knew exactly where to strike so as to reach the vital nerve centres at the base of the skull where it joins the cord."

"Looks like a doctor," said Jenny thoughtfully.

"Did Miss Adams know any doctors? I mean, was any particular doctor a friend of hers?"

Jenny shook her head.

"Never heard of one. Not over here, anyway."

"Another question. Did Miss Adams wear pince-nez?"

"Glasses? Never."

"Ah!" Poirot frowned.

A vision rose in my mind. A doctor, smelling of carbolic, short-sighted eyes magnified by powerful lenses. Absurd!

"By the way, did Miss Adams know Bryan Martin, the film actor?"

"Why, yes. She used to know him as a child, she told me. I don't think she saw much of him, though. Just once in a while. She told me she thought he'd got very swollen-headed."

She looked at her watch and uttered an exclamation.

"Goodness, I must fly. Have I helped you at all, M. Poirot?"

"You have. I shall ask you for further help by and by."

"It's yours. Someone staged this devilry. We've got to find out who it is."

She gave us a quick shake of the hand, flashed her white teeth in a sudden smile and left us with characteristic abruptness.

"An interesting personality," said Poirot as he paid the bill.

"I like her," I said.

"It is always a pleasure to meet a quick mind."

"A little hard, perhaps," I reflected. "The shock of her friend's death did not upset her as much as I should have thought it would have done."

"She is not the sort that weeps, certainly," agreed Poirot dryly.

"Did you get what you hoped from the interview?"

He shook his head.

"No—I hoped—very much I hoped—to get a clue to the personality of D, the person who gave her the little gold box. There I have failed. Unfortunately Carlotta Adams was a reserved girl. She was not one to gossip about her friends or her possible love affairs. One the other hand, the person who suggested the hoax may not have been a friend at all. It may have been a mere acquaintance who proposed it—doubtless for some 'sporting' reason—on a money basis. This person may have seen the gold box she carried about with her and made some opportunity to discover what it contained."

"But how on earth did they get her to take it? And when?"

"Well, there was the time during which the flat door was open—when the maid was out posting a letter. Not that that satisfies me. It leaves too much to chance. But now—to work. We have still two possible clues."

"Which are?"

"The first is the telephone call to a Victoria number. It seems to me quite a probability that Carlotta Adams would ring up on her return to announce her success. On the other hand, where was she between five minutes past ten and midnight? She may have had an appointment with the instigator of the hoax. In that case the telephone call may have been merely one to a friend."

"What is the second clue?"

"Ah! that I do have hopes for. The letter, Hastings. The letter to the sister. It is possible—I only say possible—that in that she may have described the whole business. She would not regard it as a breach of faith, since the letter would not be read till a week later and in another country at that."

"Amazing, if that is so!"

"We must not build too much upon it, Hastings. It is a chance, that is all. No, we must work now from the other end."

"What do you call the other end?"

"A careful study of those who profit in any degree by Lord Edgware's death."

I shrugged my shoulders.

"Apart from his nephew and his wife—"

"And the man the wife wanted to marry," added Poirot.

"The Duke? He is in Paris."

"Quite so. But you cannot deny that he is an interested party. Then there are the people in the house—the butler—the servants. Who knows what grudges they may have had? But I think myself our first point of attack should be a further interview with Mademoiselle Jane Wilkinson. She is shrewd. She may be able to suggest something."

Once more we made our way to the Savoy. We found the lady surrounded by boxes and tissue paper, whilst exquisite black draperies were strewn over the back of every chair. Jane had a rapt and serious expression and was just trying on yet another small black hat before the glass.

"Why, M. Poirot. Sit down. That is, if there's anything to sit on. Ellis, clear something, will you?"

"Madame, you look charming."

Jane looked serious.

"I don't want exactly to play the hypocrite, M. Poirot. But one must observe appearances, don't you think? I mean, I think I ought to be careful. Oh! by the way, I've had the sweetest telegram from the Duke."

"From Paris?"

"Yes, from Paris. Guarded, of course, and supposed to be condolences, but put so that I can read between the lines."

"My felicitations, Madame."

"M. Poirot." She clasped her hands, her husky voice dropped. She looked like an angel about to give vent to thoughts of exquisite holiness. "I've been thinking. It all seems so *miraculous*, if you know what I mean. Here I am—all my troubles over. No tiresome business of divorce. No bothers. Just my path cleared and all plain sailing. It makes me feel almost religious—if you know what I mean."

I held my breath. Poirot looked at her, his head a little on one side. She was quite serious.

"That is how it strikes you, Madame, eh?"

"Things happen right for me," said Jane in a sort of awed whisper. "I've thought and I've thought lately—If Edgware was to die. And there—he's dead! It's—it's almost like an answer to prayer."

Poirot cleared his throat.

"I cannot say I look at it quite like that, Madame. Somebody killed your husband."

She nodded.

"Why, of course."

"Has it not occurred to you to wonder who that someone was?"

She stared at him. "Does it matter? I mean—what's that to do with it? The Duke and I can be married in about four or five months . . ."

With difficulty Poirot controlled himself.

"Yes, Madame, I know that. But apart from that has it not occurred to you to ask yourself *who killed your husband*?"

"No." She seemed quite surprised by the idea. We could see her thinking about it.

"Does it not interest you to know?" asked Poirot.

"Not very much, I'm afraid," she admitted. "I suppose the police will find out. They're very clever, aren't they?"

"So it is said. I, too, am going to make it my business to find out."

"Are you? How funny."

"Why funny?"

"Well, I don't know." Her eyes strayed back to the clothes. She slipped on a satin coat and studied herself in the glass.

"You do not object, eh?" said Poirot, his eyes twinkling.

"Why, of course not, M. Poirot. I should just love you to be clever about it all. I wish you every success."

"Madame—I want more than your wishes. I want your opinion."

"Opinion?" said Jane absently, as she twisted her head over her shoulder. "What on?"

"Who do you think likely to have killed Lord Edgware?"

Jane shook her head. "I haven't any idea!"

She wriggled her shoulders experimentally and took up the hand-glass.

"Madame!" said Poirot in a loud, emphatic voice. "WHO DO *you* THINK KILLED YOUR HUSBAND?"

This time it got through. Jane threw him a startled glance. "Geraldine, I expect," she said.

"Who is Geraldine?"

But Jane's attention was gone again.

"Ellis, take this up a little on the right shoulder. So. What, M. Poirot? Geraldine's his daughter. No, Ellis, the *right* shoulder. That's better. Oh! must you go, M. Poirot? I'm terribly grateful for everything. I mean, for the divorce, even though it isn't necessary after all. I shall always think you were wonderful."

I only saw Jane Wilkinson twice again. Once on the stage, once when I sat opposite her at a luncheon party. I always think of her as I saw her then, absorbed heart and soul in clothes, her lips carelessly throwing out the words that were to influence Poirot's further actions, her mind concentrated firmly and beatifically on herself.

"*Épatant*," said Poirot with reverence as we emerged into the Strand.

CHAPTER 12
The Daughter

There was a letter sent by hand lying on the table when we got back to our rooms. Poirot picked it up, slit it open with his usual neatness, and then laughed.

"What is it you say—'Talk of the devil'? See here, Hastings."

I took the note from him.

The paper was stamped 17 Regent Gate and was written in very upright characteristic handwriting which looked easy to read and, curiously enough, was not.

> "DEAR SIR, (it ran)
>
> I hear you were at the house this morning with the inspector. I am sorry not to have had the opportunity of speaking to you. If convenient to yourself I should be much obliged if you could spare me a few minutes any time this afternoon.
>
> Yours truly,
> GERALDINE MARSH."

"Curious," I said. "I wonder why she wants to see you?"

"Is it curious that she should want to see me? You are not polite, my friend."

Poirot has the most irritating habit of joking at the wrong moment.

"We will go round at once, my friend," he said, and lovingly brushing an imagined speck of dust from his hat, he put it on his head.

Jane Wilkinson's careless suggestion that Geraldine might have killed her father seemed to me particularly absurd. Only a particularly brainless person could have suggested it. I said as much to Poirot.

"Brains. Brains. What do we really mean by the term? In your idiom you would say that Jane Wilkinson has the brains of a rabbit. That is a term of disparagement. But consider the rabbit for a moment. He exists and multiplies, does he not? That, in Nature, is a sign of mental superiority. The lovely Lady Edgware she does not know history, or geography, nor the classics *sans doute*. The name of Lao Tse would suggest to her a prize Pekingese dog, the name of Molière a *maison de couture*. But when it comes to choosing clothes, to making rich and advantageous marriages, and to getting her own way—her success is phenomenal. The opinion of a philosopher as to who murdered Lord Edgware would be no good to me—the motive for murder from a philosopher's point of view would be the greatest good of the greatest number, and as that is difficult to decide, few philosophers are murderers. But a careless opinion from Lady Edgware *might* be useful to me because her point of view would be materialistic and based on a knowledge of the worst side of human nature."

"Perhaps there's something in that," I conceded.

"Nous voici," said Poirot. "I am curious to know why the young lady wishes so urgently to see me."

"It is a natural desire," I said, getting my own back. "You said so a quarter of an hour ago. The natural desire to see something unique at close quarters."

"Perhaps it is you, my friend, who made an impression on her heart the other day," replied Poirot as he rang the bell.

I recalled the startled face of the girl who had stood in the doorway. I could still see those burning dark eyes in the white face. That momentary glimpse had made a great impression on me.

We were shown upstairs to a big drawing-room and in a minute or two Geraldine Marsh came to us there.

The impression of intensity which I had noticed before was heightened on this occasion. This tall, thin, white-faced girl with her big haunting black eyes was a striking figure.

She was extremely composed—in view of her youth, remarkably so.

"It is very good of you to come so promptly, M. Poirot," she said. "I am sorry to have missed you this morning."

"You were lying down?"

"Yes, Miss Carroll—my father's secretary, you know—insisted. She has been very kind."

There was a queer grudging note in the girl's voice that puzzled me.

"In what way can I be of service to you, Mademoiselle?" asked Poirot.

She hesitated a minute and then said:

"On the day before my father was killed you came to see him?"

"Yes, Mademoiselle."

"Why? Did he—send for you?"

Poirot did not reply for a moment. He seemed to be deliberating. I believe, now, that it was a cleverly calculated move on his part. He wanted to goad her into further speech. She was, he realised, of the impatient type. She wanted things in a hurry.

"Was he afraid of something? Tell me. Tell me. I must know. Who was he afraid of? Why? What did he say to you? Oh! why can't you speak?"

I had thought that that forced composure was not natural. It had soon broken down. She was leaning forward now, her hands twisting themselves nervously on her lap.

"What passed between Lord Edgware and myself was in confidence," said Poirot slowly.

His eyes never left her face.

"Then it was about—I mean, it must have been something to do with—the family. Oh! you sit there and torture me. Why won't you tell me? It's necessary for me to know. It's necessary, I tell you."

Again, very slowly, Poirot shook his head, apparently a prey to deep perplexity.

"M. Poirot." She drew herself up. "I'm his daughter. It is my right to know—what my father dreaded on the last day but one of his life. It isn't fair to leave me in the dark. It isn't fair to him—not to tell me."

"Were you so devoted to your father, then, Mademoiselle?" asked Poirot gently.

She drew back as though stung.

"Fond of him?" she whispered. "Fond of him. I—I—"

And suddenly her self-control snapped. Peals of laughter broke from her. She lay back in her chair and laughed and laughed.

"It's so funny," she gasped. "It's so funny—to be asked that."

That hysterical laughter had not passed unheard. The door opened and Miss Carroll came in. She was firm and efficient.

"Now, now, Geraldine, my dear, that won't do. No, no. Hush, now. I insist. No. Stop it. I mean it. Stop it at once."

Her determined manner had its effect. Geraldine's laughter grew fainter. She wiped her eyes and sat up.

"I'm sorry," she said in a low voice. "I've never done that before."

Miss Carroll was still looking at her anxiously.

"I'm all right now, Miss Carroll. It was idiotic."

She smiled suddenly. A queer bitter smile that twisted her lips. She sat up very straight in her chair and looked at no one.

"He asked me," she said in a cold clear voice, "if I had been very fond of my father."

Miss Carroll made a sort of indeterminate cluck. It denoted irresolution on her part. Geraldine went on, her voice high and scornful.

"I wonder if it is better to tell lies or the truth? The truth, I think. I wasn't fond of my father. I hated him!"

"Geraldine dear."

"Why pretend? You didn't hate him because he couldn't touch you! You were one of the few people in the world that he couldn't get at. You saw him as the employer who paid you so much a year. His rages and his queernesses didn't interest you—you ignored them. I know what you'd say. 'Everyone has got to put up with something.' You were cheerful and uninterested. You're a very strong woman. You're not really human. But then you could have walked out of the house any minute. I couldn't. I belonged."

"Really, Geraldine, I don't think it's necessary going into all this. Fathers and daughters often don't get on. But the less said in life the better, I've found."

Geraldine turned her back on her. She addressed herself to Poirot.

"M. Poirot, I *hated* my father! I am glad he is dead! It means freedom for me—freedom and independence. I am not in the least anxious to find his murderer. For all we know the person who killed him may have had reasons—ample reasons—justifying that action."

Poirot looked at her thoughtfully.

"That is a dangerous principle to adopt, Mademoiselle."

"Will hanging someone else bring Father back to life?"

"No," said Poirot dryly. "But it may save other innocent people from being murdered."

"I don't understand."

"A person who has once killed, Mademoiselle, nearly always kills again—sometimes again and again."

"I don't believe it. Not—not a real person."

"You mean—not a homicidal maniac? But yes, it is true. One life is removed—perhaps after a terrific struggle with the murderer's conscience. Then—danger threatens—the second murder is morally easier. At the slightest threatening of suspicion a third follows. And little by little an artistic pride arises—it is a *métier*—to kill. It is done at last almost for pleasure."

The girl had hidden her face in her hands.

"Horrible. Horrible. It isn't true."

"And supposing I told you that it *had* already happened? That already—to save himself—*the murderer has killed a second time*?"

"What's that, M. Poirot?" cried Miss Carroll. "Another murder? Where? Who?"

Poirot gently shook his head.

"It was an illustration only. I ask pardon."

"Oh! I see. For a moment I really thought—Now, Geraldine, if you've finished talking arrant nonsense."

"You are on my side, I see," said Poirot with a little bow.

"I don't believe in capital punishment," said Miss Carroll briskly. "Otherwise I am certainly on your side. Society must be protected."

Geraldine got up. She smoothed back her hair.

"I am sorry," she said. "I am afraid I have been making rather a fool of myself. You still refuse to tell me why my father called you in?"

"Called him in?" said Miss Carroll in lively astonishment.

"You misunderstand, Miss Marsh. I have not refused to tell you."

Poirot was forced to come out into the open.

"I was only considering how far that interview might have been said to be confidential. Your father did not call me in. *I* sought an interview with *him* on behalf of a client. That client was Lady Edgware."

"Oh! I see."

An extraordinary expression came over the girl's face. I thought at first it was disappointment. Then I saw it was relief.

"I have been very foolish," she said slowly. "I thought my father had perhaps thought himself menaced by some danger. It was stupid."

"You know, M. Poirot, you gave me quite a turn just now," said Miss Carroll. "When you suggested that woman had done a second murder."

Poirot did not answer her. He spoke to the girl.

"Do you believe Lady Edgware committed the murder, Mademoiselle?"

She shook her head.

"No, I don't. I can't see her doing a thing like that. She's much too—well, artificial."

"I don't see who else can have done it," said Miss Carroll. "And I don't think women of that kind have got any moral sense."

"It needn't have been her," argued Geraldine. "She may have come here and just had an interview with him and gone away, and the real murderer may have been some lunatic who got in afterwards."

"All murderers are mentally deficient—of that I am assured," said Miss Carroll. "Internal gland secretion."

At that moment the door opened and a man came in—then stopped awkwardly.

"Sorry," he said. "I didn't know anyone was in here."

Geraldine made a mechanical introduction.

"My cousin, Lord Edgware. M. Poirot. It's all right, Ronald. You're not interrupting."

"Sure, Dina? How do you do, M. Poirot? Are your grey cells functioning over our particular family mystery?"

I cast my mind back trying to remember. That round, pleasant, vacuous face, the eyes with slight pouches underneath them, the little moustache marooned like an island in the middle of the expanse of face.

Of course! It was Carlotta Adams' escort on the night of the supper party in Jane Wilkinson's suite.

Captain Ronald Marsh. Now Lord Edgware.

CHAPTER 13
The Nephew

The new Lord Edgware's eye was a quick one. He noticed the slight start I gave.

"Ah! you've got it," he said amiably. "Aunt Jane's little supper party. Just a shade bottled, wasn't I? But I fancied it passed quite unperceived."

Poirot was saying good-bye to Geraldine Marsh and Miss Carroll.

"I'll come down with you," said Ronald genially.

He led the way down the stairs talking as he went.

"Rum thing—life. Kicked out one day, lord of the manor the next. My late unlamented uncle kicked me out, you know, three years ago. But I expect you know all about that, M. Poirot?"

"I had heard the fact mentioned—yes," replied Poirot composedly.

"Naturally. A thing of that kind is sure to be dug up. The earnest sleuth can't afford to miss it."

He grinned.

Then he threw open the dining-room door.

"Have a spot before you go."

Poirot refused. So did I. But the young man mixed himself a drink and continued to talk.

"Here's to murder," he said cheerfully. "In the space of one short night I am converted from the creditor's despair to the tradesman's hope. Yesterday ruin stared me in the face, to-day all is affluence. God bless Aunt Jane."

He drained his glass. Then, with a slight change of manner, he spoke to Poirot.

"Seriously, though, M. Poirot, what *are* you doing here? Four days ago Aunt Jane was dramatically declaiming. 'Who will rid me of this insolent tyrant?' and lo and behold she is ridded! Not by your agency, I hope? The perfect crime, by Hercule Poirot, ex-sleuth-hound."

Poirot smiled.

"I am here this afternoon in answer to a note from Miss Geraldine Marsh."

"A discreet answer, eh? No, M. Poirot, what are you really doing here? For some reason or other you are interesting yourself in my uncle's death."

"I am always interested in murder, Lord Edgware."

"But you don't commit it. Very cautious. You should teach Aunt Jane caution. Caution and a shade more camouflage. You'll excuse me calling her Aunt Jane. It amuses me. Did you see her blank face when I did it the other night? Hadn't the foggiest notion who I was."

"En verité?"

"No. I was kicked out of here three months before she came along."

The fatuous expression of good-nature on his face failed for a moment. Then he went on lightly.

"Beautiful woman. But no subtlety. Methods are rather crude, eh?"

Poirot shrugged his shoulders.

"It is possible."

Ronald looked at him curiously.

"I believe you think she didn't do it. So she's got round you too, has she?"

"I have a great admiration for beauty," said Poirot evenly. "But also for—evidence."

He brought the last word out very quietly.

"Evidence?" said the other sharply.

"Perhaps you do not know, Lord Edgware, that Lady Edgware was at a party at Chiswick last night at the time she was supposed to have been seen here."

Ronald swore.

"So she went after all! How like a woman! At six o'clock she was throwing her weight about, declaring that nothing on earth would make her go, and I suppose about ten minutes after she'd changed her mind! When planning a murder never depend upon a woman doing what she says she'll do. That's how the best laid plans of murder gang agley. No, M. Poirot, I'm not incriminating myself. Oh, yes, don't think I can't read what's passing through your mind. Who is the Natural Suspect? The well-known Wicked Ne'er-do-Well Nephew."

He leaned back in his chair chuckling.

"I'm saving your little grey cells for you, M. Poirot. No need for you to hunt round for someone who saw me in the offing when Aunt Jane was declaring she never, never, never would go out that night, etc. I was there. So you ask yourself did the wicked nephew in very truth come here last night disguised in a fair wig and a Paris hat?"

Seemingly enjoying the situation, he surveyed us both. Poirot, his head a little on one side, was regarding him with close attention. I felt rather uncomfortable.

"I had a motive—oh! yes, motive admitted. And I'm going to give you a present of a very valuable and significant piece of information. I called to see my uncle yesterday morning. Why? To ask for money. Yes, lick your lips over that. To ASK FOR MONEY. And I went away without getting any. And that same evening—that very same evening—Lord Edgware dies. Good title that, by the way. Lord Edgware Dies. Look well on a bookstall."

He paused. Still Poirot said nothing.

"I'm really flattered by your attention, M. Poirot. Captain Hastings looks as though he had seen a ghost—or were going to see one any minute. Don't get so strung up, my dear fellow. Wait for the anti-climax. Well, where were we? Oh! yes, case against the Wicked Nephew. Guilt is to be thrown on the hated Aunt by Marriage. Nephew, celebrated at one time for acting female parts, does his supreme histrionic effort. In a girlish voice he announces himself as Lady Edgware and sidles past the butler with mincing steps. No suspicions are aroused. 'Jane,' cries my fond uncle. 'George,' I squeak. I fling my arms about his neck and neatly insert the penknife. The next details are purely medical and can be omitted. Exit the spurious lady. And so to bed at the end of a good day's work."

He laughed and rising, poured himself out another whisky and soda. He returned slowly to his chair.

"Works out well, doesn't it? But you see, here comes the crux of the matter. The disappointment! The annoying sensation of having been led up the garden. For now, M. Poirot, we come to the alibi!"

He finished off his glass.

"I always find alibis very enjoyable," he remarked. "Whenever I happen to be reading a detective story I sit up and take notice when the alibi comes along. This is a remarkably good alibi. Three strong, and Jewish at that. In plainer language, Mr. Mrs. and Miss Dortheimer. Extremely rich and extremely musical. They have a box at Covent Garden. Into that box they invite young men with prospects—as good a one, shall we say, as they can hope to get. Do I like the opera? Frankly, no. But I enjoy the excellent dinner in Grosvenor Square first, and I also enjoy an excellent supper somewhere else afterwards, even if I do have to dance with Rachel Dortheimer and have a stiff arm for two days afterwards. So you see, M. Poirot, there you are. When uncle's lifeblood is flowing, I am whispering cheerful nothings into the diamond encrusted ears of the fair (I beg your pardon, dark) Rachel in a box at Covent Garden. Her long Jewish nose is quivering with emotion. And so you see, M. Poirot, why I can afford to be so frank."

He leaned back in his chair.

"I hope I have not bored you. Any questions to ask?"

"I can assure you that I have not been bored," said Poirot. "Since you are so kind, there is one little question that I would like to ask."

"Delighted."

"How long, Lord Edgware, have you known Miss Carlotta Adams?"

Whatever the young man had expected, it certainly had not been this. He sat up sharply with an entirely new expression on his face.

"Why on earth do you want to know that? What's that got to do with what we've been talking about?"

"I was curious, that was all. For the other, you have explained so fully everything there is to explain that there is no need for me to ask questions."

Ronald shot a quick glance at him. It was almost as though he did not care for Poirot's amiable acquiescence. He would, I thought, have preferred him to be more suspicious.

"Carlotta Adams? Let me see. About a year. A little more. I got to know her last year when she gave her first show."

"You knew her well?"

"Pretty well. She's not the sort of girl you ever got to know frightfully well. Reserved and all that."

"But you liked her?"

Ronald stared at him.

"I wish I knew why you were so interested in the lady. Was it because I was with her the other night? Yes, I like her very much. She's sympathetic—listens to a chap and makes him feel he's something of a fellow after all."

Poirot nodded.

"I comprehend. Then you will be sorry."

"Sorry? What about?"

"That she is dead!"

"What?" Ronald sprang up in astonishment. "Carlotta dead?"

He looked absolutely dumbfounded by the news.

"You're pulling my leg, M. Poirot. Carlotta was perfectly well the last time I saw her."

"When was that?" asked Poirot quickly.

"Day before yesterday, I think. I can't remember."

"*Tout de même*, she is dead."

"It must have been frightfully sudden. What was it? A street accident?"

Poirot looked at the ceiling.

"No. She took an overdose of veronal."

"Oh! I say. Poor kid. How frightfully sad."

"N'est-ce pas?"

"I *am* sorry. And she was getting on so well. She was going to get her kid sister over and had all sorts of plans. Dash it, I'm more sorry than I can say."

"Yes," said Poirot. "It is sad to die when you are young—when you do not want to die—when all life is open before you and you have everything to live for."

Ronald looked at him curiously.

"I don't think I quite get you, M. Poirot?"

"No?"

Poirot rose and held out his hand.

"I express my thoughts—a little strongly perhaps. For I do not like to see youth deprived of its right to live, Lord Edgware. I feel—very strongly about it. I wish you good-day."

"Oh—er—good-bye."

As I opened the door I almost collided with Miss Carroll.

"Ah! M. Poirot, they told me you hadn't gone yet. I'd like a word with you if I may. Perhaps you wouldn't mind coming up to my room.

"It's about that child, Geraldine," she said when we had entered her sanctum and she had closed the door.

"Yes, Mademoiselle?"

"She talked a lot of nonsense this afternoon. Now don't protest. Nonsense! That's what I call it and that's what it was. She broods."

"I could see that she was suffering from over-strain," said Poirot gently.

"Well—to tell the truth—she hasn't had a very happy life. No, one can't pretend she has. Frankly, M. Poirot, Lord Edgware was a peculiar man—not the sort of man who ought to have had anything to do with the upbringing of children. Quite frankly, he terrorised Geraldine."

Poirot nodded.

"Yes, I should imagine something of the kind."

"He was a peculiar man. He—I don't quite know how to put it—but he enjoyed seeing anyone afraid of him. It seemed to give him a morbid kind of pleasure."

"Quite so."

"He was an extremely well-read man, and a man of considerable intellect. But in some ways—well, I didn't come across that side of him myself, but it was there. I'm not really surprised his wife left him. This wife, I mean. I didn't approve of her, mind. I've no opinion of that young woman at all. But in marrying Lord Edgware she got all and more than she deserved. Well, she left him—and no bones broken, as they say. But Geraldine couldn't leave him. For a long time he'd forget all about her, and then, suddenly, he'd remember. I sometimes think—though perhaps I shouldn't say it—"

"Yes, yes, Mademoiselle, say it."

"Well, I sometimes thought he revenged himself on the mother—his first wife—that way. She was a gentle creature, I believe, with a very sweet disposition. I've always been sorry for her. I shouldn't have mentioned all this, M. Poirot, if it hadn't been for that very foolish outburst of Geraldine's just now. Things she said—about hating her father—they might sound peculiar to anyone who didn't know."

"Thank you very much, Mademoiselle. Lord Edgware, I fancy, was a man who would have done much better not to marry."

"Much better."

"He never thought of marrying for a third time?"

"How could he? His wife was alive."

"By giving her her freedom, he would have been free himself."

"I should think he had had enough trouble with two wives as it was," said Miss Carroll grimly.

"So you think there would have been no question of a third marriage. There was no one? Think, Mademoiselle. No one?"

Miss Carroll's colour rose.

"I cannot understand the way you keep harping on the point. Of course there was no one."

CHAPTER 14
Five Questions

"Why did you ask Miss Carroll about the possibility of Lord Edgware's wanting to marry again?" I asked with some curiosity as we were driving home.

"It just occurred to me that there was the possibility of such a thing, *mon ami*."

"Why?"

"I have been searching in my mind for something to explain Lord Edgware's sudden *volte face* regarding the matter of divorce. There is something curious there, my friend."

"Yes," I said thoughtfully. "It is rather odd."

"You see, Hastings, Lord Edgware confirmed what Madame had told us. She had employed the lawyers of all kinds, but he refused to budge the inch. No, he would not agree to the divorce. And then, all of a sudden, he yields!"

"Or so he says," I reminded him.

"Very true, Hastings. It is very just, the observation you make there. *So he says*. We have no proof, whatever, that that letter was written. *Eh bien*, on one part, ce Monsieur is lying. For some reason he tells us the fabrication, the embroidery. Is it not so? Why, we do not know. But, on the hypothesis that he *did* write that letter, there must have been a *reason* for so doing. Now the reason that presents itself most naturally to the imagination is that he has suddenly met someone whom he desires to marry. That explains perfectly his sudden change of face. And so, naturally, I make the inquiries."

"Miss Carroll turned the idea down very decisively," I said.

"Yes. Miss Carroll . . ." said Poirot in a meditative voice.

"Now what are you driving at?" I asked in exasperation.

Poirot is an adept at suggesting doubts by the tone of his voice.

"What reason should she have for lying about it?" I asked.

"*Aucune—aucune*.

"But, you see, Hastings, it is difficult to trust her evidence."

"You think she's lying? But why? She looks a most upright person."

"That is just it. Between the deliberate falsehood and the disinterested inaccuracy it is very hard to distinguish something."

"What *do* you mean?"

"To deceive deliberately—that is one thing. But to be so sure of your facts, of your ideas and of their essential truth that the details do not matter—that, my friend, is a special characteristic of particularly honest persons. Already, mark you, she has told us one lie. She said she saw Jane Wilkinson's face when she could not possibly have done so. Now how did that come about? Look at it this way. She looks down and sees Jane Wilkinson in the hall. No doubt enters her head that it *is* Jane Wilkinson. She *knows* it is. She says she saw her face distinctly because—being so sure of her facts—exact details do not matter! It is pointed out to her that she could not have seen her face. Is that so? Well, what does it matter if she saw her face or not—it *was* Jane Wilkinson. And so with any other question. She *knows*. And so she answers questions in the light of her knowledge, not by reason of remembered facts. The positive witness should always be treated with suspicion, my friend. The uncertain witness who doesn't remember, isn't sure, will think a minute—ah! yes, that's how it was—is infinitely more to be depended upon!"

"Dear me, Poirot," I said. "You upset all my preconceived ideas about witnesses."

"In reply to my question as to Lord Poirot's marrying again she ridicules the idea—simply because it has never occurred to her. She will not take the trouble to remember whether any infinitesimal signs may have pointed that way. Therefore we are exactly where we were before."

"She certainly did not seem at all taken aback when you pointed out she could not have seen Jane Wilkinson's face," I remarked thoughtfully.

"No. That is why I decided that she was one of those honestly inaccurate persons, rather than a deliberate liar. I can see no motive for deliberate lying unless—true, that is an idea!"

"What is?" I asked eagerly.

But Poirot shook his head.

"An idea suggested itself to me. But it is too impossible—yes, much too impossible."

And he refused to say more.

"She seems very fond of the girl," I said.

"Yes. She certainly was determined to assist at our interview. What was your impression of the Honourable Geraldine Marsh, Hastings?"

"I was sorry for her—deeply sorry for her."

"You have always the tender heart, Hastings. Beauty in distress upsets you every time."

"Didn't you feel the same?"

He nodded gravely.

"Yes—she has not had a happy life. That is written very clearly on her face."

"At any rate," I said warmly, "you realise how preposterous Jane Wilkinson's suggestion was—that she should have had anything to do with the crime, I mean."

"Doubtless her alibi is satisfactory, but Japp has not communicated it to me as yet."

"My dear Poirot—do you mean to say that even after seeing her and talking to her, you are still not satisfied and want an alibi?"

"*Eh bien*, my friend, what is the result of seeing and talking to her? We perceive that she has passed through great unhappiness, she admits that she hated her father and is glad that he is dead, and she is deeply uneasy about what he may have said to us yesterday morning. And after that you say—no alibi is necessary!"

"Her mere frankness proves her innocence," I said warmly.

"Frankness is a characteristic of the family. The new Lord Edgware—with what a gesture he laid his cards on the table."

"He did indeed," I said, smiling at the remembrance. "Rather an original method."

Poirot nodded.

"He—what do you say?—cuts the ground before our feet."

"From under," I corrected. "Yes—it made us look rather foolish."

"What a curious idea. You may have looked foolish. I did not feel foolish in the least and I do not think I looked it. On the contrary, my friend, I put him out of countenance."

"Did you?" I said doubtfully, not remembering having seen signs of anything of the kind.

"*Si, si*. I listen—and listen. And at last I ask a question about something quite different, and that, you may have noticed, disconcerts our brave Monsieur very much. You do not observe, Hastings."

"I thought his horror and astonishment at hearing of Carlotta Adams' death was genuine," I said. "I suppose you will say it was a piece of clever acting."

"Impossible to tell. I agree it *seemed* genuine."

"Why do you think he flung all those facts at our head in that cynical way? Just for amusement?"

"That is always possible. You English, you have the most extraordinary notions of humour. But it may have been policy. Facts that are concealed acquire a suspicious importance. Facts that are frankly revealed tend to be regarded as less important than they really are."

"The quarrel with his uncle that morning, for instance?"

"Exactly. He knows that the fact is bound to leak out. *Eh bien*, he will parade it."

"He is not so foolish as he looks."

"Oh! he is not foolish at all. He has plenty of brains when he cares to use them. He sees exactly where he stands and, as I said, he lays his cards on the table. You play the bridge, Hastings. Tell me, when does one do that?"

"You play bridge yourself," I said, laughing. "You know well enough—when all the rest of the tricks are yours and you want to save time and get on to a new hand."

"Yes, *mon ami*, that is all very true. But occasionally there is another reason. I have remarked it once or twice when playing with *les dames*. There is perhaps a little doubt. *Eh bien, la dame*, she throws down the cards, says 'and all the rest are mine,' and gathers up the cards and cuts the new pack. And possibly the other players agree—especially if they are a little inexperienced. The thing is not obvious, mark you. It requires to be followed out. Half-way through dealing the next hand, one of the players thinks: 'Yes, but she would have to have taken over that fourth diamond in dummy whether she wanted to or not, and then she would have had to lead a little club and my nine would have made.'"

"So you think?"

"I think, Hastings, that too much bravado is a very interesting thing. And I also think that it is time we dined. *Une petite omelette, n'est ce pas?* And after that, about nine o'clock, I have one more visit I wish to make."

"Where is that?"

"We will dine first, Hastings. And until we drink our coffee, we will not discuss the case further. When engaged in eating, the brain should be the servant of the stomach."

Poirot was as good as his word. We went to a little restaurant in Soho where he was well known, and there we had a delicious omelette, a sole, a chicken and a Baba au Rhum of which Poirot was inordinately fond.

Then, as we sipped our coffee, Poirot smiled affectionately across the table at me.

"My good friend," he said. "I depend upon you more than you know."

I was confused and delighted by these unexpected words. He had never said anything of the kind to me before. Sometimes, secretly, I had felt slightly hurt. He seemed almost to go out of his way to disparage my mental powers.

Although I did not think his own powers were flagging, I did realise suddenly that perhaps he had come to depend on my aid more than he knew.

"Yes," he said dreamily. "You may not always comprehend just how it is so—but you do often and often point the way."

I could hardly believe my ears.

"Really, Poirot," I stammered. "I'm awfully glad. I suppose I've learnt a good deal from you one way or another—"

He shook his head.

"*Mais non, ce n'est pas ça*. You have learnt nothing."

"Oh!" I said, rather taken aback.

"That is as it should be. No human being should learn from another. Each individual should develop his own powers to the uttermost, not try to imitate those of someone else. I do not wish you to be a second and inferior Poirot. I wish you to be the supreme Hastings. And you are the supreme Hastings. In you, Hastings, I find the normal mind almost perfectly illustrated."

"I'm not abnormal, I hope," I said.

"No, no. You are beautifully and perfectly balanced. In you sanity is personified. Do you realise what that means to me? When the criminal sets out to do a crime his first effort is to deceive. Who does he seek to deceive? The image in his mind is that of the normal man. There is probably no such thing actually—it is a mathematical abstraction. But you come as near to realising it as is possible. There are moments when you have flashes of brilliance when you rise above average, moments (I hope you will pardon me) when you descend to curious depths of obtuseness, but take it all for all, you are amazingly normal. *Eh bien,* how does this profit me? Simply in this way. As in a mirror I see reflected in your mind exactly what the criminal wishes me to believe. That is terrifically helpful and suggestive."

I did not quite understand. It seemed to me that what Poirot was saying was hardly complimentary. However, he quickly disabused me of that impression.

"I have expressed myself badly," he said quickly. "You have an insight into the criminal mind, which I myself lack. You show me what the criminal wishes me to believe. It is a great gift."

"Insight," I said thoughtfully. "Yes, perhaps I have got insight."

I looked across the table at him. He was smoking his tiny cigarettes and regarding me with great kindliness.

"*Ce cher* Hastings," he murmured. "I have indeed much affection for you."

I was pleased but embarrassed and hastened to change the subject.

"Come," I said in a business-like manner. "Let us discuss the case."

"*Eh bien*." Poirot threw his head back, his eyes narrowed. He slowly puffed out smoke.

"*Je me pose des questions,*" he said.

"Yes?" I said eagerly.

"You, too, doubtless?"

"Certainly," I said. And also leaning back and narrowing my own eyes I threw out:

"Who killed Lord Edgware?"

Poirot immediately sat up and shook his head vigorously.

"No, no. Not at all. Is it a question, that? You are like someone who reads the detective story and who starts guessing each of the characters in turn without rhyme or reason. Once, I agree, I had to do that myself. It was a very exceptional case. I will tell you about it one of these days. It was a feather in my cap. But of what were we speaking?"

"Of the questions you were 'posing' to yourself," I replied dryly. It was on the tip of my tongue to suggest that my real use to Poirot was to provide him with a companion to whom he could boast, but I controlled myself. If he wished to instruct then let him.

"Come on," I said. "Let's hear them."

That was all that the vanity of the man wanted. He leaned back again and resumed his former attitude.

"The first question we have already discussed. *Why did Lord Edgware change his mind on the subject of divorce?* One or two ideas suggest themselves to me on that subject. One of them you know.

"The second question I ask myself is *What happened to that letter?* To whose interest was it that Lord Edgware and his wife should continue to be tied together?

"Three. *What was the meaning of the expression on his face that you saw when you looked back yesterday morning on leaving the library?* Have you any answer to that, Hastings?"

I shook my head.

"I can't understand it."

"You are sure that you didn't imagine it? Sometimes, Hastings, you have the imagination *un peu vif*."

"No, no." I shook my head vigorously. "I'm quite sure I wasn't mistaken."

"*Bien*. Then it is a fact to be explained. My fourth question concerns those pince-nez. Neither Jane Wilkinson nor Carlotta Adams wore glasses. What, then, are the glasses doing in Carlotta Adams' bag?

"And for my fifth question. *Why did someone telephone to find out if Jane Wilkinson were at Chiswick and who was it?*

"Those, my friend, are the questions with which I am tormenting myself. If I could answer those, I should feel happier in my mind. If I could even evolve a theory that explained them satisfactorily my *amour propre* would not suffer so much."

"There are several other questions," I said.

"Such as?"

"Who incited Carlotta Adams to this hoax? Where was she that evening before and after ten o'clock? Who is D who gave her the golden box?"

"Those questions are self-evident," said Poirot. "There is no subtlety about them. They are simply things we do not know. They are questions of *fact*. We may get to know them any minute. My questions, *mon ami*, are psychological. The little grey cells of the brain—"

"Poirot," I said desperately. I felt that I must stop him at all costs. I could not bear to hear it all over again.

"You spoke of making a visit to-night?"

Poirot looked at his watch.

"True," he said. "I will telephone and find out if it is convenient."

He went away and returned a few minutes later.

"Come," he said. "All is well."

"Where are we going?" I asked.

"To the house of Sir Montagu Corner at Chiswick. I would like to know a little more about that telephone call."

CHAPTER 15
Sir Montagu Corner

It was about ten o'clock when we reached Sir Montagu Corner's house on the river at Chiswick. It was a big house standing back in its own grounds. We were admitted into a beautifully-panelled hall. On our right, through an open door, we saw the dining-room with its long polished table lit with candles.

"Will you come this way, please?"

The butler led the way up a broad staircase and into a long room on the first floor overlooking the river.

"M. Hercule Poirot," announced the butler.

It was a beautifully-proportioned room, and had an old-world air with its carefully-shaded dim lamps. In one corner of the room was a bridge table, set near the open window, and round it sat four people. As we entered the room one of the four rose and came towards us.

"It is a great pleasure to make your acquaintance, M. Poirot."

I looked with some interest at Sir Montagu Corner. He had a distinctly Jewish cast of countenance, very small intelligent black eyes and a carefully-arranged toupée. He was a short man—five foot eight at most, I should say. His manner was affected to the last degree.

"Let me introduce you. Mr. and Mrs. Widburn."

"We've met before," said Mrs. Widburn brightly.

"And Mr. Ross."

Ross was a young fellow of about twenty-two with a pleasant face and fair hair.

"I disturb your game. A million apologies," said Poirot.

"Not at all. We have not started. We were commencing to deal the cards only. Some coffee, M. Poirot?"

Poirot declined but accepted an offer of old brandy. It was brought us in immense goblets.

As we sipped it, Sir Montagu discoursed.

He spoke of Japanese prints, of Chinese lacquer, of Persian carpets, of the French impressionists, of modern music and of the theories of Einstein.

Then he sat back and smiled at us beneficently. He had evidently thoroughly enjoyed his performance. In the dim light he looked like some genie of the mediaeval age. All round the room were exquisite examples of art and culture.

"And now, Sir Montagu," said Poirot. "I will trespass on your kindness no longer but will come to the object of my visit."

Sir Montagu waved a curious claw-like hand.

"There is no hurry. Time is infinite."

"One always feels that in this house," sighed Mrs. Widburn. "So wonderful."

"I would not live in London for a million pounds," said Sir Montagu. "Here one is in the old-world atmosphere of peace that—alas!—we have put behind us in these jarring days."

A sudden impish fancy flashed over me that if someone were really to offer Sir Montagu a million pounds, old-world peace might go to the wall, but I trod down such heretical sentiments.

"What is money, after all?" murmured Mrs. Widburn.

"Ah!" said Mr. Widburn thoughtfully, and rattled some coins absent-mindedly in his trousers pocket.

"Archie," said Mrs. Widburn reproachfully.

"Sorry," said Mr. Widburn and stopped.

"To speak of crime in such an atmosphere is, I feel, unpardonable," began Poirot apologetically.

"Not at all." Sir Montagu waved a gracious hand. "A crime can be a work of art. A detective can be an artist. I do not refer, of course, to the police. An inspector has been here to-day. A curious person. He had never heard of Benvenuto Cellini, for instance."

"He came about Jane Wilkinson, I suppose," said Mrs. Widburn with instant curiosity.

"So it seems," said Sir Montagu. "I asked her here knowing that she was beautiful and talented and hoping that I might be able to be of use to her. She was thinking of going into management. But it seems that I was fated to be of use to her in a very different way."

"Jane's got luck," said Mrs. Widburn. "She's been dying to get rid of Edgware and here's somebody gone and saved her the trouble. She'll marry the young Duke of Merton now. Everyone says so. His mother's wild about it."

"I was favourably impressed by her," said Sir Montagu graciously. "She made several most intelligent remarks about Greek art."

I smiled to myself picturing Jane saying "Yes" and "No," "Really how wonderful," in her magical husky voice. Sir Montagu was the type of man to whom intelligence consisted of the faculty of listening to his own remarks with suitable attention.

"Edgware was a queer fish, by all accounts," said Widburn. "I daresay he's got a good few enemies."

"Is it true, M. Poirot," asked Mrs. Widburn, "that somebody ran a penknife into the back of his brain?"

"Perfectly true, Madame. It was very neatly and efficiently done—scientific, in fact."

"I note your artistic pleasure, M. Poirot," said Sir Montagu.

"And now," said Poirot, "let me come to the object of my visit. Lady Edgware was called to the telephone when she was here at dinner. It is about that telephone call that I seek information. Perhaps you will allow me to question your domestics on the subject?"

"Certainly. Certainly. Just press that bell, will you, Ross?"

The butler answered the bell. He was a tall middle-aged man of ecclesiastical apparance.

Sir Montagu explained what was wanted. The butler turned to Poirot with polite attention.

"Who answered the telephone when it rang?" began Poirot.

"I answered it myself, sir. The telephone is in a recess leading out of the hall."

"Did the person ask to speak to Lady Edgware or to Miss Jane Wilkinson?"

"To Lady Edgware, sir."

"What did they say exactly?"

The butler reflected for a moment.

"As far as I remember, sir, I said 'Hello.' A voice then asked if I was Chiswick 43434. I replied that that was so. It then asked me to hold the line. Another voice then asked if that was Chiswick 43434 and on my replying 'yes' it said 'Is Lady Edgware dining there?' I said her ladyship *was* dining here. The voice said, 'I would like to speak to her, please.' I went and informed her ladyship who was at the dinner table. Her ladyship rose, and I showed her where the 'phone was."

"And then?"

"Her ladyship picked up the receiver and said: 'Hello—who's speaking?' Then she said: 'Yes—that's all right. Lady Edgware speaking.' I was just about to leave her ladyship when she called to me and said they had cut her off. She said someone had laughed and evidently hung up the receiver. She asked me if the person ringing up had given any name. They had not done so. That was all that occurred, sir."

Poirot frowned to himself.

"Do you really think the telephone call has something to do with the murder, M. Poirot?" asked Mrs. Widburn.

"Impossible to say, Madame. It is just a curious circumstance."

"People do ring up for a joke sometimes. It's been done to me."

"*C'est toujours possible, Madame.*"

He spoke to the butler again.

"Was it a man's voice or a woman's who rang up?"

"A lady's, I think, sir."

"What kind of a voice, high or low?"

"Low, sir. Careful and rather distinct." He paused. "It may be my fancy, sir, but it sounded like a *foreign* voice. The R's were very noticeable."

"As far as that goes it might have been a Scotch voice, Donald," said Mrs. Widburn, smiling at Ross.

Ross laughed.

"Not guilty," he said. "I was at the dinner table."

Poirot spoke once again to the butler.

"Do you think," he asked, "that you would recognise that voice if you were to hear it any time?"

The butler hesitated.

"I couldn't quite say, sir. I might do so. I think it is possible that I should do so."

"I thank you, my friend."

"Thank you, sir."

The butler inclined his head and withdrew, pontifical to the last.

Sir Montagu Carter continued to be very friendly and to play his rôle of old-world charm. He persuaded us to remain and play bridge. I excused myself—the stakes were bigger than I cared about. Young Ross seemed relieved also at the prospect of someone taking his hand. He and I sat looking on while the other four played. The evening ended in a heavy financial gain to Poirot and Sir Montagu.

Then we thanked our host and took our departure. Ross came with us.

"A strange little man," said Poirot as we stepped out into the night.

The night was fine and we had decided to walk until we picked up a taxi instead of having one telephoned for.

"Yes, a strange little man," said Poirot again.

"A very rich little man," said Ross with feeling.

"I suppose so."

"He seems to have taken a fancy to me," said Ross. "Hope it will last. A man like that behind you means a lot."

"You are an actor, Mr. Ross?"

Ross said that he was. He seemed sad that his name had not brought instant recognition. Apparently he had recently won marvellous notices in some gloomy play translated from the Russian.

When Poirot and I between us had soothed him down again, Poirot asked casually:

"You knew Carlotta Adams, did you not?"

"No. I saw her death announced in the paper to-night. Overdose of some drug or other. Idiotic the way all these girls dope."

"It is sad, yes. She was clever, too."

"I suppose so."

He displayed a characteristic lack of interest in anyone else's performance but his own.

"Did you see her show at all?" I asked.

"No. That sort of thing's not much in my line. Kind of craze for it at present, but I don't think it will last."

"Ah!" said Poirot. "Here is a taxi."

He waved a stick.

"Think I'll walk," said Ross. "I get a tube straight home from Hammersmith."

Suddenly he gave a nervous laugh.

"Odd thing," he said. "That dinner last night."

"Yes?"

"We were thirteen. Some fellow failed at the last minute. We never noticed it till just the end of dinner."

"And who got up first?" I asked.

He gave a queer little nervous cackle of laughter.

"I did," he said.

CHAPTER 16
Mainly Discussion

When we got home we found Japp waiting for us.

"Thought I'd just call round and have a chat with you before turning in, M. Poirot," he said cheerfully.

"*Eh bien*, my good friend, how goes it?"

"Well, it doesn't go any too well. And that's a fact."

He looked depressed.

"Got any help for me, M. Poirot?"

"I have one or two little ideas that I should like to present to you," said Poirot.

"You and your ideas! In some ways, you know, you're a caution. Not that I don't want to hear them. I do. There's some good stuff in that funny-shaped head of yours."

Poirot acknowledged the compliment somewhat coldly.

"Have you any idea about the double lady problem—that's what I want to know? Eh, M. Poirot? What about it? Who was she?"

"That is exactly what I wish to talk to you about."

He asked Japp if he had ever heard of Carlotta Adams.

"I've heard the name. For the moment I can't just place it."

Poirot explained.

"Her! Does imitations, does she? Now what made you fix on her? What have you got to go on?"

Poirot related the steps we had taken and the conclusion we had drawn.

"By the Lord, it looks as though you were right. Clothes, hat, gloves, etc., and the fair wig. Yes, it must be. I will say—you're the goods, M. Poirot. Smart work, that! Not that I think there's anything to show she was put out of the way. That seems a bit far fetched. I don't quite see eye to eye with you there. Your theory is a bit fantastical for me. I've more experience than you have. I don't believe in this villain-behind-the-scenes motif. Carlotta Adams was the woman all right, but I should put it one of two ways. She went there for purposes of her own—blackmail, maybe, since she hinted she was going to get money. They had a bit of a dispute. He turned nasty, she turned nasty, and she finished him off. And I should say that when she got home she went all to pieces. She hadn't meant murder. It's my belief she took an overdose on purpose as the easiest way out."

"You think that covers all the facts?"

"Well, naturally there are a lot of things we don't know yet. It's a good working hypothesis to go on with. The other explanation is that the hoax and the murder had nothing to do with each other. It's just a damned queer coincidence."

Poirot did not agree, I knew. But he merely said non-committally:

"*Mais oui, c'est possible*."

"Or, look here, how's this? The hoax is innocent enough. Someone gets to hear of it and thinks it will suit their purpose jolly well. That's not a bad idea?" He paused, and went on: "But personally I prefer idea No. 1. What the link was between his lordship and the girl we'll find out somehow or other."

Poirot told him of the letter to America posted by the maid, and Japp agreed that that might possibly be of great assistance.

"I'll get on to that at once," he said, making a note of it in his little book.

"I'm the more in favour of the lady being the killer because I can't find anyone else," he said, as he put the book away. "Captain Marsh now, his lordship as now is. He's got a motive sticking out a yard. A bad record too. Hard up and none too scrupulous over money. What's more he had a row with his uncle yesterday morning. He told me that himself as a matter of fact—which rather takes the taste out of it. Yes, he'd be a likely customer. But he's got an alibi for yesterday evening. He was at the opera with the Dortheimers. Rich Jews. Grosvenor Square. I've looked into that and it's all right. He dined with them, went to the opera and they went on to supper at Sobranis. So that's that."

"And Mademoiselle?"

"The daughter, you mean? She was out of the house too. Dined with some people called Carthew West. They took her to the opera and saw her home afterwards. Quarter to twelve she got in. That disposes of *her*. The secretary woman seems all right—very efficient decent woman. Then there's the butler. I can't say I take to him much. It isn't natural for a man to have good looks like that. There's something fishy about him—and something odd about the way he came to enter Lord Edgware's service. Yes, I'm checking up on him all right. I can't see any motive for murder, though."

"No fresh facts have come to light?"

"Yes, one or two. It's hard to say whether they mean anything or not. For one thing, Lord Edgware's key's missing."

"The key to the front door?"

"Yes."

"That is interesting, certainly."

"As I say, it may mean a good deal or nothing at all. Depends. What *is* a bit more significant to my mind is this. Lord Edgware cashed a cheque yesterday—not a particularly large one—a hundred pounds as a matter of fact. He took the money in French notes—that's why he cashed the cheque, because of his journey to Paris to-day. Well, that money has disappeared."

"Who told you of this?"

"Miss Carroll. She cashed the cheque and obtained the money. She mentioned it to me, and then I found that it had gone."

"Where was it yesterday evening?"

"Miss Carroll doesn't know. She gave it to Lord Edgware about half-past three. It was in a Bank envelope. He was in the library at the time. He took it and laid it down beside him on a table."

"That certainly gives one to think. It is a complication."

"Or a simplification. By the way—the wound."

"Yes?"

"The doctor says it wasn't made by an ordinary penknife. Something of that kind but a different shaped blade. And it was amazingly sharp."

"Not a razor?"

"No, no. Much smaller."

Poirot frowned thoughtfully.

"The new Lord Edgware seems to be fond of his joke," remarked Japp. "He seems to think it amusing to be suspected of murder. He made sure we did suspect him of murder, too. Looks a bit queer, that."

"It might be merely intelligence."

"More likely guilty conscience. His uncle's death came very pat for him. He's moved into the house, by the way."

"Where was he living before?"

"Martin Street, St. George's Road. Not a very swell neighbourhood."

"You might make a note of that, Hastings."

I did so, though I wondered a little. If Ronald had moved to Regent Gate, his former address was hardly likely to be needed.

"*I* think the Adams girl did it," said Japp, rising. "A fine bit of work on your part, M. Poirot, to tumble to that. But there, of course, you go about to theatres and amusing yourself. Things strike you that don't get the chance of striking me. Pity there's no apparent motive, but a little spade work will soon bring it to light, I expect."

"There is one person with a motive to whom you have given no attention," remarked Poirot.

"Who's that sir?"

"The gentleman who is reputed to have wanted to marry Lord Edgware's wife. I mean the Duke of Merton."

"Yes, I suppose there is a *motive*." Japp laughed. "But a gentleman in his position isn't likely to murder. And anyway, he's over in Paris."

"You do not regard him as a serious suspect, then?"

"Well, M. Poirot, do you?"

And laughing at the absurdity of the idea, Japp left us.

CHAPTER 17
The Butler

The following day was one of inactivity for us, and activity for Japp. He came round to see us about tea-time.

He was red and wrathful.

"I've made a bloomer."

"Impossible, my friend," said Poirot soothingly.

"Yes, I have. I've let that (here he gave way to profanity)——of a butler slip through my fingers."

"He has disappeared?"

"Yes. Hooked it. What makes me kick myself for a double-dyed idiot is that I didn't particularly suspect him."

"Calm yourself—but calm yourself then."

"All very well to talk. *You* wouldn't be calm if you'd been hauled over the coals at headquarters. Oh! he's a slippery customer. It isn't the first time he's given anyone the slip. He's an old hand."

Japp wiped his forehead and looked the picture of misery. Poirot made sympathetic noises—somewhat suggestive of a hen laying an egg. With more insight into the English charcter, I poured out a stiff whisky and soda and placed it in front of the gloomy inspector. He brightened a little.

"Well," he said. "I don't mind if I do."

Presently he began to talk more cheerfully.

"I'm not so sure even now that he's the murderer! Of course it looks bad his bolting this way, but there might be other reasons for that. I'd begun to get on to him, you see. Seems he's mixed up with a couple of rather disreputable night clubs. Not the usual thing. Something a great deal more recherché and nasty. In fact, he's a real bad hat."

"*Tout de même,* that does not necessarily mean that he is a murderer."

"Exactly! He may have been up to some funny business or other, but not necessarily murder. No, I'm more than ever convinced it was the Adams girl. I've got nothing to prove it as yet, though. I've had men going all through her flat to-day, but we've found nothing that's helpful. She was a canny one. Kept no letters except a few business ones about financial contracts. They're all neatly docketed and labelled. Couple of letters from her sister in Washington. Quite straight and aboveboard. One or two pieces of good old-fashioned jewellery—nothing new or expensive. She didn't keep a diary. Her pass-book and cheque-book don't show anything helpful. Dash it all, the girl doesn't seem to have had any private life at all!"

"She was of a reserved character," said Poirot thoughtfully. "From our point of view that is a pity."

"I've talked to the woman who did for her. Nothing there. I've been and seen that girl who keeps a hat shop and who, it seems, was a friend of hers."

"Ah! and what do you think of Miss Driver?"

"She was a smart wide-awake bit of goods. She couldn't help me, though. Not that that surprised me. The amount of missing girls I've had to trace and their family and their friends always say the same things. 'She was a bright and affectionate disposition and had no men friends.' That's never true. It's unnatural. Girls ought to have men friends. If not there's something wrong about them. It's the muddle-headed loyalty of friends and relations that makes a detective's life so difficult."

He paused for want of breath, and I replenished his glass.

"Thank you, Captain Hastings, I don't mind if I do. Well, there you are. You've got to hunt and hunt about. There's about a dozen young men she went out to supper and danced with, but nothing to show that one of them meant more than another. There's the present Lord Edgware, there's Mr. Bryan Martin, the film star, there's half a dozen others—but nothing special and particular. Your man behind idea is all wrong. I think you'll find that she played a lone hand, M. Poirot. I'm looking now for the connection between her and the murdered man. That must exist. I think I'll have to go over to Paris. There was Paris written in that little gold box, and the late Lord Edgware ran over to Paris several times last Autumn, so Miss Carroll tells me, attending sales and buying curios. Yes, I think I must go over to Paris. Inquest's to-morrow. It'll be adjourned, of course. After that I'll take the afternoon boat."

"You have a furious energy, Japp. It amazes me."

"Yes, you're getting lazy. You just sit here and *think!* What you call employing the little grey cells. No good, you've got to go out to things. They won't come to you."

The little maidservant opened the door.

"Mr. Bryan Martin, sir. Are you busy or will you see him?"

"I'm off, M. Poirot." Japp hoisted himself up. "All the stars of the theatrical world seem to consult you."

Poirot shrugged a modest shoulder, and Japp laughed.

"You must be a millionaire by now, M. Poirot. What do you do with the money? Save it?"

"Assuredly I practise the thrift. And talking of the disposal of money, how did Lord Edgware dispose of his?"

"Such property as wasn't entailed he left to his daughter. Five hundred to Miss Carroll. No other bequests. Very simple will."

"And it was made—when?"

"After his wife left him—just over two years ago. He expressly excludes her from participation, by the way."

"A vindictive man," murmured Poirot to himself.

With a cheerful "So long," Japp departed.

Bryan Martin entered. He was faultlessly attired and looked extremely handsome. Yet I thought that he looked haggard and not too happy.

"I am afraid I have been a long time coming, M. Poirot," he said apologetically. "And, after all, I have been guilty of taking up your time for nothing."

"*En verité?*"

"Yes. I have seen the lady in question. I've argued with her, pleaded with her, but all to no purpose. She won't hear of my interesting you in the matter. So I'm afraid we'll have to let the thing drop. I'm very sorry—very sorry to have bothered you—"

"*Du tout—du tout,*" said Poirot genially. "I expected this."

"Eh?" The young man seemed taken aback.

"You expected this?" he asked in a puzzled way.

"*Mais oui*. When you spoke of consulting your friend—I could have predicted that all would have arrived as it has done."

"You have a theory, then?"

"A detective, M. Martin, always has a theory. It is expected of him. I do not call it a theory myself. I say that I have a little idea. That is the first stage."

"And the second stage?"

"If the little idea turns out to be right—then I *know!* It is quite simple, you see."

"I wish you'd tell me what your theory—or your little idea—is?"

Poirot shook his head gently.

"That is another rule. The detective never tells."

"Can't you suggest it even?"

"No. I will only say that I formed my theory as soon as you mentioned a gold tooth."

Bryan Martin stared at him.

"I'm absolutely bewildered," he declared. "I can't make out what you are driving at. If you'd just give me a hint."

Poirot smiled and shook his head.

"Let us change the subject."

"Yes, but first—your fee—you must let me."

Poirot waved an imperious hand.

"*Pas un sou!* I have done nothing to aid you."

"I took up your time—"

"When a case interests me, I do not touch money. Your case interested me very much."

"I'm glad," said the actor uneasily.

He looked supremely unhappy.

"Come," said Poirot kindly. "Let us talk of something else."

"Wasn't that the Scotland Yard man whom I met on the stairs?"

"Yes, Inspector Japp."

"The light was so dim, I wasn't sure. By the way, he came round and asked me some questions about that poor girl, Carlotta Adams, who died of an overdose of veronal."

"You knew her well—Miss Adams?"

"Not very well. I knew her as a child in America. I came across her here once or twice but I never saw very much of her. I was very sorry to hear of her death."

"You liked her?"

"Yes. She was extraordinarily easy to talk to."

"A personality very sympathetic—yes, I found the same."

"I suppose they think it might be suicide? I knew nothing that could help the inspector. Carlotta was always very reserved about herself."

"I do not think it was suicide," said Poirot.

"Far more likely to be an accident, I agree."

There was a pause.

Then Poirot said with a smile:

"The affair of Lord Edgware's death becomes intriguing, does it not?"

"Absolutely amazing. Do you know—have they any idea—who did it—now that Jane is definitely out of it?"

"*Mais oui*—they have a very strong suspicion."

Bryan Martin looked excited.

"Really? Who?"

"The butler has disappeared. You comprehend—flight is as good as a confession."

"The butler! Really, you surprise me."

"A singularly good-looking man. *Il vous ressemble un peu,*" he bowed in a complimentary fashion.

Of course! I realised now why the butler's face had struck me as being faintly familiar when I first saw it.

"You flatter me," said Bryan Martin with a laugh.

"No, no, no. Do not all the young girls, the servant girls, the flappers, the typists, the girls of society, do they not all adore M. Bryan Martin? Is there one who can resist you?"

"A lot, I should think," said Martin. He got up abruptly.

"Well, thank you very much, M. Poirot. Let me apologise again for having troubled you."

He shook hands with us both. Suddenly, I noticed, he looked much older. The haggard look was more apparent.

I was devoured with curiosity, and as soon as the door closed behind him, I burst out with what I wanted to know.

"Poirot, did you really expect him to come back and relinquish all idea of investigating those queer things that happened to him in America?"

"You heard me say so, Hastings."

"But then—" I followed the thing out logically.

"Then you must know who this mysterious girl is that he had to consult?"

He smiled.

"I have a little idea, my friend. As I told you, it started from the mention of the gold tooth, and if my little idea is correct, I know who the girl is, I know why she will not let M. Martin consult me, I know the truth of the whole affair. And so could you know it if you would only use the brains the good God has given you. Sometimes I really am tempted to believe that by inadvertence He passed you by."

CHAPTER 18
The Other Man

I do not propose to describe either the inquest on Lord Edgware or that on Carlotta Adams. In Carlotta's case the verdict was Death by Misadventure. In the case of Lord Edgware the inquest was adjourned, after evidence of identification and the medical evidence had been given. As a result of the analysis of the stomach, the time of death was fixed as having occurred not less than an hour after the completion of dinner, with possible extension to an hour after that. This put it as between ten and eleven o'clock, with the probability in favour of the earlier time.

None of the facts concerning Carlotta's impersonation of Jane Wilkinson were allowed to leak out. A description of the wanted butler was published in the Press, and the general impression seemed to be that the butler was the man wanted. His story of Jane Wilkinson's visit was looked upon as an impudent fabrication. Nothing was said of the secretary's corroborating testimony. There were columns concerning the murder in all the papers, but little real information.

Meanwhile Japp was actively at work, I knew. It vexed me a little that Poirot adopted such an inert attitude. The suspicion that approaching old age had something to do with it flashed across me—not for the first time. He made excuses to me which did not ring very convincingly.

"At my time of life one saves oneself the trouble," he explained.

"But, Poirot, my dear fellow, you mustn't think of yourself as old," I protested.

I felt that he needed bracing. Treatment by suggestion—that, I know, is the modern idea.

"You are as full of vigour as ever you were," I said earnestly. "You're in the prime of life, Poirot. At the height of your powers. You could go out and solve this case magnificently if you only would."

Poirot replied that he preferred to solve it sitting at home.

"But you can't do that, Poirot."

"Not entirely, it is true."

"What I mean is, we are doing nothing! Japp is doing everything."

"Which suits me admirably."

"It doesn't suit me at all. I want you to be doing things."

"So I am."

"What are you doing?"

"Waiting."

"Waiting for what?"

"*Pour que mon chien de chasse me rapporte le gibier,*" replied Poirot with a twinkle.

"What *do* you mean?"

"I mean the good Japp. Why keep a dog and bark yourself? Japp brings us here the result of the physical energy you admire so much. He has various means at his disposal which I have not. He will have news for us very soon, I do not doubt."

By dint of persistent inquiry, it was true that Japp was slowly getting together material. He had drawn a blank in Paris, but a couple of days later he came in looking pleased with himself.

"It's slow work," he said. "But we're getting somewhere at last."

"I congratulate you, my friend. What has happened?"

"I've discovered that a fair-haired lady deposited an attaché-case in the cloakroom at Euston at nine o'clock that night. They've been shown Miss Adams' case and identify it positively. It's of American make and so just a little different."

"Ah! Euston. Yes, the nearest of the big stations to Regent Gate. She went there doubtless, made herself up in the lavatory, and then left the case. When was it taken out again?"

"At half-past ten. The clerk says by the same lady."

Poirot nodded.

"And I've come on something else too. I've reason to believe that Carlotta Adams was in Lyons Corner House in the Strand at eleven o'clock."

"*Ah! c'est très bien ça!* How did you come across that?"

"Well, really more or less by chance. You see, there's been a mention in the papers of the little gold box with the ruby initials. Some reporter wrote it up—he was doing an article on the prevalence of dope-taking among young actresses. Sunday paper romantic stuff. The fatal little gold box with its deadly contents—

pathetic figure of a young girl with all the world before her! And just a wonder expressed as to where she passed her last evening and how she felt and so on and so on.

"Well, it seems a waitress at the Corner House read this and she remembered that a lady she had served that evening had had such a box in her hand. She remembered the C.A. on it. And she got excited and began talking to all her friends—perhaps a paper would give her something?

"A young newspaper man soon got on to it and there's going to be a good sobstuff article in to-night's *Evening Shriek*. The last hours of the talented actress. Waiting—for the man who never came—and a good bit about the waitress's sympathetic intuition that something was not well with her sister woman. You know the kind of bilge, M. Poirot?"

"And how has it come to your ears so quickly?"

"Oh! well, we're on very good terms with the *Evening Shriek*. It got passed on to me while their particular bright young man tried to get some news out of me about something else. So I rushed along to the Corner House straight away—"

Yes, that was the way things ought to be done. I felt a pang of pity for Poirot. Here was Japp getting all this news at first hand—quite possibly missing valuable details, and here was Poirot placidly content with stale news.

"I saw the girl—and I don't think there's much doubt about it. She couldn't pick out Carlotta Adams' photograph, but then she said she didn't notice the lady's face particularly. She was young and dark and slim, and very well dressed, the girl said. Had got on one of the new hats. I wish women looked at faces a bit more and hats a bit less."

"The face of Miss Adams is not an easy one to observe," said Poirot. "It had the mobility, the sensitiveness—the fluid quality."

"I daresay you're right. I don't go in for analysing these things. Dressed in black the lady was, so the girl said, and she had an attaché-case with her. The girl noticed that particularly, because it struck her as odd that a lady so well dressed should be carrying a case about. She ordered some scrambled eggs and some coffee, but the girl thinks she was putting in time and waiting for someone. It was when the girl came to give her the bill that she noticed the box. The lady took it out of her handbag and had it on the table looking at it. She opened the lid and shut it down again. She was smiling in a pleased dreamy sort of way. The girl noticed the box particular because it was such a lovely thing. 'I'd like to have a gold box with my initials in rubies on it!'" she said.

"Apparently Miss Adams sat there some time after paying her bill. Then, finally, she looked at her watch once more, seemed to give it up and went out."

Poirot was frowning.

"It was a *rendez-vous*," he murmured. "A *rendez-vous* with someone who did not turn up. Did Carlotta Adams meet that person afterwards? Or did she fail to meet him and go home and try to ring him up? I wish I knew—oh! how I wish I knew."

"That's *your* theory, M. Poirot. Mysterious Man-in-the-Background. That Man-in-the-Background's a myth. I don't say she mayn't have been waiting for someone—that's possible. She may have made an appointment to meet someone there after her business with his lordship was settled satisfactorily. Well, we know what happened. She lost her head and stabbed him. But she's not one to lose her head for long. She changes her appearance at the station, gets out her case, goes to the rendezvous, and then what they call the 'reaction' gets her. Horror of what she's done. And when her friend doesn't turn up, that finishes her. He may be someone who knew she was going to Regent Gate that evening. She feels the game's up. So she takes out her little box of dope. An overdose of that and it'll be all over. At anyrate she won't be hanged. Why, it's as plain as the nose on your face."

Poirot's hand strayed doubtfully to his nose, then his fingers dropped to his moustaches. He caressed them tenderly with a proud expression.

"There was no evidence at all of a mysterious Man-in-the-Background," said Japp, pursuing his advantage doggedly. "I haven't got evidence yet of a connection between her and his lordship, but I shall do—it's only a question of time. I must say I'm disappointed about Paris, but nine months ago is a long time. I've still got someone making inquiries over there. Something may come to light yet. I know you don't think so. You're a pig-headed old boy, you know."

"You insult first my nose and then my head!"

"Figure of speech, that's all," said Japp soothingly. "No offence meant."

"The answer to that," I said, "is 'Nor taken.'"

Poirot looked from one to the other of us completely puzzled.

"Any orders?" inquired Japp facetiously from the door.

Poirot smiled forgivingly at him.

"An order, no. A suggestion—yes."

"Well, what is it? Out with it."

"A suggestion that you circularise the taxi-cabs. Find one that took a fare—or more probably two fares—yes, two fares—from the neighbourhood of Covent Garden to Regent Gate on the night of the murder. As to time it would probably be about twenty minutes to eleven."

Japp cocked an eye alertly. He had the look of a smart terrier dog.

"So that's the idea, is it?" he said. "Well, I'll do it. Can't do any harm—and you sometimes know what you're talking about."

No sooner had he left than Poirot arose and with great energy began to brush his hat.

"Ask me no questions, my friend. Instead bring me the benzine. A morsel of omelette this morning descended on my waistcoat."

I brought it to him.

"For once," I said. "I do not think I need to ask questions. It seems fairly obvious. But do you think it really is so?"

"*Mon ami*, at the moment I concern myself solely with the toilet. If you will pardon me saying so, your tie does not please me."

"It's a jolly good tie," I said.

"Possibly—once. It feels the old age as you have been kind enough to say I do. Change it, I beseech you, and also brush the right sleeve."

"Are we proposing to call on King George?" I inquired sarcastically.

"No. But I saw in the newspaper this morning that the Duke of Merton had returned to Merton House. I understand he is a premier member of the English aristocracy. I wish to do him all honour."

There is nothing of the Socialist about Poirot.

"Why are we going to call on the Duke of Merton?"

"I wish to see him."

That was all I could get out of him. When my attire was at last handsome enough to please Poirot's critical eye, we started out.

At Merton House, Poirot was asked by a footman if he had an appointment. Poirot replied in the negative. The footman bore away the card and returned shortly to say that His Grace was very sorry but he was extremely busy this morning. Poirot immediately sat down in a chair.

"Très bien," he said. "I wait. I will wait several hours if need be."

This, however, was not necessary. Probably as the shortest way of getting rid of the importunate caller, Poirot was bidden to the presence of the gentleman he desired to see.

The Duke was about twenty-seven years of age. He was hardly prepossessing in appearance, being thin and weakly. He had nondescript thin hair going bald at the temples, a small bitter mouth and vague dreamy eyes. There were several crucifixes in the room and various religious works of art. A wide shelf of books seemed to contain nothing but theological works. He looked far more like a weedy young haberdasher than like a duke. He had, I knew, been educated at home, having been a terribly delicate child. This was the man who had fallen an immediate prey to Jane Wilkinson! It was really ludicrous in the extreme. His manner was priggish and his reception of us just short of courteous.

"You may, perhaps, know my name," began Poirot.

"I have no acquaintance with it."

"I study the psychology of crime."

The Duke was silent. He was sitting at a writing-table, an unfinished letter before him. He tapped impatiently on the desk with his pen.

"For what reason did you wish to see me?" he inquired coldly.

Poirot was sitting opposite him. His back was to the window. The Duke was facing it.

"I am at present engaged on investigating the circumstances connected with Lord Edgware's death."

Not a muscle of the weak yet obstinate face moved.

"Indeed? I was not acquainted with him."

"But you are, I think, acquainted with his wife—with Miss Jane Wilkinson?"

"That is so."

"You are aware that she is supposed to have had a strong motive for desiring the death of her husband?"

"I am really not aware of anything of the kind."

"I should like to ask you outright, your Grace, Are you shortly going to marry Miss Jane Wilkinson?"

"When I am engaged to marry anyone the fact will be announced in the newspapers. I consider your question an impertinence." He stood up. "Good-morning."

Poirot stood up also. He looked awkward. He hung his head. He stammered.

"I did not mean . . . I . . . *Je vous demande pardon . . .*"

"Good-morning," repeated the Duke, a little louder.

This time Poirot gave it up. He made a characteristic gesture of hopelessness, and we left. It was an ignominious dismissal.

I felt rather sorry for Poirot. His usual bombast had not gone well. To the Duke of Merton a great detective was evidently lower than a blackbeetle.

"That didn't go too well," I said sympathetically. "What a stiff-necked tartar the man is. What did you really want to see him for?"

"I wanted to know whether he and Jane Wilkinson are really going to marry."

"She said so."

"Ah! she said so. But, you realise, she is of those who say anything that suits their purpose. She might have decided to marry him and he—poor man—might not yet be aware of the fact."

"Well, he certainly sent you away with a flea in the ear."

"He gave me the reply he would give to a reporter—yes." Poirot chuckled. "But I know! I know exactly how the case stands."

"How do you know? By his manner?"

"Not at all. You saw he was writing a letter?"

"Yes."

"*Eh bien,* in my early days in the police force in Belgium I learned that it was very useful to read handwriting upside down. Shall I tell you what he was saying in that letter? '*My dearest, I can hardly bear to wait through the long months. Jane, my adored, my beautiful angel, how can I tell you what you are to me? You who have suffered so much! Your beautiful nature—*'"

"Poirot!" I cried, scandalised, stopping him.

"This was as far as he had got. '*Your beautiful nature—only I know it.*'"

I felt very upset. He was so naïvely pleased with his performance.

"Poirot," I cried. "You can't do a thing like that. Overlook a private letter."

"You say the imbecilities, Hastings. Absurd to say I 'cannot do' a thing which I have just done!"

"It's not—not playing the game."

"I do not play games. You know that. Murder is not a game. It is serious. And anyway, Hastings, you should not use that phrase—playing the game. It is not said any more. I have discovered that. It is dead. Young people laugh when they hear it. *Mais oui,* young beautiful girls will laugh at you if you say 'playing the game' and 'not cricket.'"

I was silent. I could not bear this thing that Poirot had done so light-heartedly.

"It was so unnecessary," I said. "If you had only told him that you had gone to Lord Edgware at Jane Wilkinson's request, then he would have treated you very differently."

"Ah! but I could not do that. Jane Wilkinson was my client. I cannot speak of my client's affairs to another. I undertake a mission in confidence. To speak of it would not be honourable."

"Honourable!"

"Precisely."

"But she's going to marry him?"

"That does not mean that she has no secrets from him. Your ideas about marriage are very old-fashioned. No, what you suggest, I couldn't possibly have done. I have my honour as a detective to think of. The honour, it is a very serious thing."

"Well, I suppose it takes all kinds of honour to make a world."

CHAPTER 19
A Great Lady

The visit that we received on the following morning was to my mind one of the most surprising things about the whole affair.

I was in my room when Poirot slipped in with his eyes shining.

"*Mon ami,* we have a visitor."

"Who is it?"

"The Dowager Duchess of Merton."

"How extraordinary! What does she want?"

ou accompany me downstairs, *mon ami*, you will know.”

tened to comply. We entered the room together.

Duchess was a small woman with a high-bridged nose and autocratic eyes. n she was short one would not have dared to call her dumpy. Dressed she was in unfashionable black, she was yet every inch a *grande dame*. She npressed me as having an almost ruthless personality. Where her son was tive, she was positive. Her will-power was terrific. I could almost feel waves of force emanating from her. No wonder this woman had always dominated all those with whom she came in contact!

She put up a lorgnette and studied first me and then my companion. Then she spoke to him. Her voice was clear and compelling, a voice accustomed to command and to be obeyed.

“You are M. Hercule Poirot?”

My friend bowed.

“At your service, Madame la Duchesse.”

She looked at me.

“This is my friend, Captain Hastings. He assists me in my cases.”

Her eyes looked momentarily doubtful. Then she bent her head in acquiescence.

She took the chair that Poirot offered.

“I have come to consult you on a very delicate matter, M. Poirot, and I must ask that what I tell you shall be understood to be entirely confidential.”

“That without saying, Madame.”

“It was Lady Yardly who told me about you. From the way in which she spoke of you and the gratitude she expressed, I felt that you were the only person likely to help me.”

“Rest assured, I will do my best, Madame.”

Still she hesitated. Then, at last, with an effort, she came to the point, came to it with a simplicity that reminded me in an odd way of Jane Wilkinson on that memorable night at the Savoy.

“M. Poirot, I want to ensure that my son does not marry the actress, Jane Wilkinson.”

If Poirot felt astonishment, he refrained from showing it. He regarded her thoughtfully and took his time about replying.

“Can you be a little more definite, Madame, as to what you want me to do?”

“That is not easy. I feel that such a marriage would be a great disaster. It would ruin my son’s life.”

“Do you think so, Madame?”

“I am sure of it. My son has very high ideals. He knows really very little of the world. He has never cared for the young girls of his own class. They have struck him as empty-headed and frivolous. But as regards this woman—well, she is very beautiful, I admit that. And she has the power of enslaving men. She has bewitched my son. I have hoped that the infatuation would run its course. Mercifully she was not free. But now that her husband is dead—”

She broke off.

“They intend to be married in a few months’ time. The whole happiness of my son’s life is at stake.” She spoke more peremptorily. “It must be stopped, M. Poirot.”

Poirot shrugged his shoulders.

“I do not say that you are not right, Madame. I agree that the marriage is not a suitable one. But what can one do?”

"It is for you to do something."

Poirot slowly shook his head.

"Yes, yes, you must help me."

"I doubt if anything would avail, Madame. Your son, I should say refuse to listen to anything against the lady! And also, I do not think there much against her to say! I doubt if there are any discreditable incidents to be up in her past. She has been—shall we say—careful?"

"I know," said the Duchess grimly.

"Ah! So you have already made the inquiries in that direction."

She flushed a little under his keen glance.

"There is nothing I would not do, M. Poirot, to save my son from this marriage." She reiterated that word emphatically, *"Nothing!"*

She paused, then went on:

"Money is nothing in this matter. Name any fee you like. But the marriage must be stopped. You are the man to do it."

Poirot slowly shook his head.

"It is not a question of money. I can do nothing—for a reason which I will explain to you presently. But also, I may say, I do not see there is anything to be done. I cannot give you help, Madame la Duchesse. Will you think me impertinent if I give you advice?"

"What advice?"

"Do not antagonise your son! He is of an age to choose for himself. Because his choice is not your choice, do not assume that you must be right. If it is a misfortune—then accept misfortune. Be at hand to aid him when he needs aid. But do not turn him against you."

"You hardly understand."

She rose to her feet. Her lips were trembling.

"But yes, Madame la Duchesse, I understand very well. I comprehend the mother's heart. No one comprehends it better than I, Hercule Poirot. And I say to you with authority—be patient. Be patient and calm, and disguise your feelings. There is yet a chance that the matter may break itself. Opposition will merely increase your son's obstinacy."

"Good-bye, M. Poirot," she said coldly. "I am disappointed."

"I regret infinitely, Madame, that I cannot be of service to you. I am in a difficult position. Lady Edgware, you see, has already done me the honour to consult me herself."

"Oh! I see." Her voice cut like a knife. "You are in the opposite camp. That explains, no doubt, why Lady Edgware has not yet been arrested for her husband's murder."

"Comment, Madame la Duchesse?"

"I think you heard what I said. Why is she not arrested? She was there that evening. She was seen to enter the house—to enter his study. No one else went near him and he was found dead? And yet she is not arrested! Our police force must be corrupt through and through."

With shaking hands she arranged the scarf round her neck, then with the slightest of bows, she swept out of the room.

"Whew!" I said. "What a tartar! I admire her, though, don't you?"

"Because she wishes to arrange the universe to her manner of thinking?"

"Well, she's only got her son's welfare at heart."

Poirot nodded his head.

"That is true enough, and yet, Hastings, will it really be such a bad thing for M. le Duc to marry Jane Wilkinson?"

"Why, you don't think she is really in love with him?"

"Probably not. Almost certainly not. But she is very much in love with his position. She will play her part carefully. She is an extremely beautiful woman and very ambitious. It is not such a catastrophe. The Duke might very easily have married a young girl of his own class who would have accepted him from the same reasons—but no one would have made the song and the dance about that."

"That is quite true, but—"

"And suppose he marries a girl who loves him passionately, is there such a great advantage in that? Often I have observed that it is a great misfortune for a man to have a wife who loves him. She creates the scenes of jealousy, she makes him look ridiculous, she insists on having all his time and attention. Ah! *non*, it is not the bed of roses."

"Poirot," I said. "You're an incurable old cynic."

"*Mais non, mais non*, I only make the reflections. See you, really, I am on the side of the good mamma."

I could not refrain from laughing at hearing the haughty Duchess described in this way.

Poirot remained quite serious.

"You should not laugh. It is of great importance—all this. I must reflect. I must reflect a great deal."

"I don't see what you can do in the matter," I said.

Poirot paid no attention.

"You observed, Hastings, how well-informed the Duchess was? And how vindictive. She knew all the evidence there was against Jane Wilkinson."

"The case for the prosecution, but not the case for the defence," I said, smiling.

"How did she come to know of it?"

"Jane told the Duke. The Duke told her," I suggested.

"Yes, that is possible. Yet I have—"

My telephone rang sharply. I answered it.

My part consisted of saying Yes at varying intervals. Finally I put down the receiver and turned excitedly to Poirot.

"That was Japp. Firstly, you're 'the goods' as usual. Secondly, he's had a cable from America. Thirdly, he's got the taxi-driver. Fourthly, would you like to come round and hear what the taxi-driver says. Fifthly, you're 'the goods' again, and all along he's been convinced that you'd hit the nail on the head when you suggested that there was some man behind all this! I omitted to tell him that we'd just had a visitor who says the police force is corrupt."

"So Japp is convinced at last," murmured Poirot. "Curious that the Man-in-the-Background theory should be proved just at the moment when I was inclined to another possible theory."

"What theory?"

"The theory that the motive for the murder might have nothing to do with Lord Edgware himself. Imagine someone who hated Jane Wilkinson, hated her so much that they would have even had her hanged for murder. *C'est une idee, ça!*"

He sighed—then rousing himself:

"Come, Hastings, let us hear what Japp has to say."

CHAPTER 20
The Taxi-Driver

We found Japp interrogating an old man with a ragged moustache and spectacles. He had a hoarse self-pitying voice.

"Ah! there you are," said Japp. "Well, things are all plain sailing, I think. This man—his name's Jobson—picked up two people in Long Acre on the night of June 29th."

"That's right," assented Jobson hoarsely. "Lovely night it were. Moon and all. The young lady and gentleman were by the tube station and hailed me."

"They were in evening dress?"

"Yes, gent in white waistcoat and the young lady all in white with birds embroidered on it. Come out of the Royal Opera, I guess."

"What time was this?"

"Some time afore eleven."

"Well, what next?"

"Told me to go to Regent Gate—they'd tell me which house when they got there. And told me to be quick, too. People always say that. As though you wanted to loiter. Sooner you get there and get another fare the better for you. They never think of that. And, mind you, if there's an accident you'll get the blame for dangerous driving!"

"Cut it out," said Japp impatiently. "There wasn't an accident this time, was there?"

"N-no," agreed the man as though unwilling to abandon his claim to such an occurrence. "No, as a matter of fact, there weren't. Well, I got to Regent Gate—not above seven minutes it didn't take me, and there the gentleman rapped on the glass, and I stopped. About number 8 that were. Well, the gentleman and lady got out. The gentleman stopped where he was and told me to do the same. The lady crossed the road, and began walking back along the houses the other side. The gentleman stayed by the cab—standing on the sidewalk with his back to me, looking after her. Had his hands in his pockets. It was about five minutes when I heard him say something—kind of exclamation under his breath and then off he goes too. I looks after him because I wasn't going to be bilked. It'd been done afore to me, so I kept my eye on him. He went up the steps of one of the houses on the other side and went in."

"Did he push the door open?"

"No, he had a latchkey."

"What number was the house?"

"It would be 17 or 19, I fancy. Well, it seemed odd to me my being told to stay where I was. So I kept watching. About five minutes later him and the young lady came out together. They got back into the cab and told me to drive back to Covent Garden Opera House. They stopped me just before I got there and paid me. Paid me handsome, I will say. Though I expect I've got into trouble over it—seems there's nothing but trouble."

"You're all right," said Japp. "Just run your eye over these, will you, and tell me if the young lady is among them."

There were half a dozen photographs all fairly alike as to type. I looked with some interest over his shoulder.

"That were her," said Jobson. He pointed a decisive finger at one of Geraldine Marsh in evening dress.

"Sure?"

"Quite sure. Pale she was and dark."

"Now the man."

Another sheaf of photographs was handed to him.

He looked at them attentively and then shook his head.

"Well, I couldn't say—not for sure. Either of these two might be him."

The photographs included one of Ronald Marsh, but Jobson had not selected it. Instead he indicated two other men not unlike Marsh in type.

Jobson then departed and Japp flung the photographs on the table.

"Good enough. Wish I could have got a clearer identification of his lordship. Of course it's an old photograph, taken seven or eight years ago. The only one I could get hold of. Yes, I'd like a clearer identification, although the case is clear enough. Bang go a couple of alibis. Clever of you to think of it, M. Poirot."

Poirot looked modest.

"When I found that she and her cousin were both at the opera it seemed to me possible that they might have been together during one of the intervals. Naturally the parties they were with would assume that they had not left the Opera House. But a half-hour interval gives plenty of time to get to Regent Gate and back. The moment the new Lord Edgware laid such stress upon his alibi, I was sure something was wrong with it."

"You're a nice suspicious sort of fellow, aren't you?" said Japp affectionately. "Well, you're about right. Can't be too suspicious in a world like this. His lordship is our man all right. Look at this."

He produced a paper.

"Cable from New York. They got into touch with Miss Lucie Adams. The letter was in the mail delivered to her this morning. She was not willing to give up the original unless absolutely necessary, but she willingly allowed the officer to take a copy of it and cable it to us. Here it is, and it's as damning as you could hope for."

Poirot took the cable with great interest. I read it over his shoulder.

> Following is text letter to Lucie Adams, dated June 29th, 8 Rosedew Mansions, London, S.W.3. Begins, Dearest little Sister, I'm sorry I wrote such a scrappy bit last week but things were rather busy and there was a lot to see to. Well, darling, it's been ever such a success! Notices splendid, box office good, and everybody most kind. I've got some real good friends over here and next year I'm thinking of taking a theatre for two months. The Russian dancer sketch went very well and the American woman in Paris, too, but the Scenes at a Foreign Hotel are still the favourites, I think. I'm so excited that I hardly know what I'm writing, and you'll see why in a minute, but first I must tell you what people have said. Mr. Hergsheimer was ever so kind and he's going to ask me to lunch to meet Sir Montagu Corner, who might do great things for me. The other night I met Jane Wilkinson and she was

ever so sweet about my show and my take off of her, which brings me round to what I am going to tell you. I don't really like her very much because I've been hearing a lot about her lately from someone I know and she's behaved cruelly, I think, and in a very underhand way—but I won't go into that now. You know that she really is Lady Edgware? I've heard a lot about him too lately, and he's no beauty, I can tell you. He treated his nephew, the Captain Marsh I have mentioned to you, in the most shameful way—literally turned him out of the house and discontinued his allowance. He told me all about it and I felt awfully sorry for him. He enjoyed my show very much, he said 'I believe it would take in Lord Edgware himself. Look here, will you take something on for a bet?' I laughed and said 'How much?' Lucie darling, the answer fairly took my breath away. Ten thousand dollars. Ten thousand dollars, think of it—just to help someone win a silly bet. 'Why,' I said, 'I'd play a joke on the King in Buckingham Palace and risk lèse majesté for that.' Well then, we laid our heads together and got down to details.

"I'll tell you all about it next week—whether I'm spotted or not. But anyway, Lucie darling, whether I succeed or fail, I'm to have the ten thousand dollars. Oh! Lucie, little sister, what that's going to mean to us. No time for more—just going off to do my 'hoax.' Lots and lots and lots of love, little sister mine.

"Yours,

"Carlotta."

Poirot laid down the letter. It had touched him, I could see.

Japp, however, reacted in quite a different way.

"We've got him," said Japp exultantly.

"Yes," said Poirot.

His voice sounded strangely flat.

Japp looked at him curiously.

"What is it, M. Poirot?"

"Nothing," said Poirot. "It is not, somehow, just as I thought. That is all."

He looked acutely unhappy.

"But still it must be so," he said as though to himself. "Yes, it must be so."

"Of course it is so. Why, you've said so all along!"

"No, no. You misunderstand me."

"Didn't you say there was someone back of all this who got the girl into doing it innocently?"

"Yes, yes."

"Well, what more do you want?"

Poirot sighed and said nothing.

"You are an odd sort of cove. Nothing ever satisfies you. I say, it was a piece of luck the girl wrote this letter."

Poirot agreed with more vigour than he had yet shown.

"*Mais oui,* that is what the murderer did not expect. When Miss Adams accepted that ten thousand dollars she signed her death warrant. The murderer thought he had taken all precautions—and yet in sheer innocence she outwitted him. The dead speak. Yes, sometimes the dead speak."

"I never thought she'd done it off her own bat," said Japp unblushingly.

"No, no," said Poirot absently.

"Well, I must get on with things."

"You are going to arrest Captain Marsh—Lord Edgware, I mean?"

"Why not? The case against him seems proved up to the hilt."

"True."

"You seem very despondent about it, M. Poirot. The truth is, you like things to be difficult. Here's your own theory proved and even that does not satisfy you. Can you see any flaw in the evidence we've got?"

Poirot shook his head.

"Whether Miss Marsh was accessory or not, I don't know," said Japp. "Seems as though she must have known about it, going there with him from the opera. If she wasn't, why did he take her? Well, we'll hear what they've both got to say."

"May I be present?"

Poirot spoke almost humbly.

"Certainly you can. I owe the idea to you!"

He picked up the telegram on the table.

I drew Poirot aside.

"What is the matter, Poirot?"

"I am very unhappy, Hastings. This seems the plain sailing and the aboveboard. But *there is something wrong*. Somewhere or other, Hastings, there is a fact that escapes us. It all fits together, it is as I imagined it, and yet, my friend, there is something wrong."

He looked at me piteously.

I was at a loss what to say.

CHAPTER 21
Ronald's Story

I found it hard to understand Poirot's attitude. Surely this was what he had predicted all along?

All the way to Regent Gate, he sat perplexed and frowning, paying no attention to Japp's self-congratulations.

He came out of his reveries at last with a sigh.

"At all events," he murmured, "we can see what he has to say."

"Next to nothing if he's wise," said Japp. "There's any amount of men that have hanged themselves by being too eager to make a statement. Well, no one can say as we don't warn them! It's all fair and aboveboard. And the more guilty they are, the more anxious they are to pipe up and tell you the lies they've thought out to meet the case. They don't know that you should always submit your lies to a solicitor first."

He laughed and said:

"Solicitors and coroners are the worst enemies of the police. Again and again I've had a perfectly clear case messed up by the Coroner fooling about and letting the guilty party get away with it. Lawyers you can't object to so much, I suppose. They're paid for their artfulness and twisting things this way and that."

On arrival at Regent Gate we found that our quarry was at home. The family were still at the luncheon table. Japp proferred a request to speak to Lord Edgware privately. We were shown into the library.

In a minute or two the young man came to us. There was an easy smile on his face which changed a little as he cast a quick glance over us. His lips tightened.

"Hello, Inspector," he said. "What's all this about?"

Japp said his little piece in the classic fashion.

"So that's it, is it?" said Ronald.

He drew a chair towards him and sat down. He pulled out a cigarette case.

"I think, Inspector, I'd like to make a statement."

"That's as you please, my lord."

"Meaning that it's damned foolish on my part. All the same, I think I will. 'Having no reason to fear the truth,' as the heroes in books always say."

Japp said nothing. His face remained expressionless.

"There's a nice handy table and chair," went on the young man. "Your minion can sit down and take it all down in shorthand."

I don't think that Japp was used to having his arrangements made for him so thoughtfully. Lord Edgware's suggestion was adopted.

"To begin with," said the young man. "Having some grains of intelligence, I strongly suspect that my beautiful alibi has bust. Gone up in smoke. Exit the useful Dortheimers. Taxi-driver, I suppose?"

"We know all about your movements on that night," said Japp woodenly.

"I have the greatest admiration for Scotland Yard. All the same, you know, if I had really been planning a deed of violence I shouldn't have hired a taxi and driven straight to the place and kept the fellow waiting. Have you thought of that? Ah! I see M. Poirot has."

"It had occurred to me, yes," said Poirot.

"Such is not the manner of premeditated crime," said Ronald. "Put on a red moustache and horn-rimmed glasses and drive to the next street and pay the man off. Take the tube—well—well, I won't go into it all. My Counsel, at a fee of several thousand guineas, will do it better than I can. Of course, I see the answer. Crime was a sudden impulse. There was I, waiting in the cab, etc., etc. It occurs to me, 'Now, my boy, up and doing.'

"Well, I'm going to tell you the truth. I was in a hole for money. That's been pretty clear, I think. It was rather a desperate business. I had to get it by the next day or drop out of things. I tried my uncle. He'd no love for me, but I thought he might care for the honour of his name. Middle-aged men sometimes do. My uncle proved to be lamentably modern in his cynical indifference.

"Well—it looked like just having to grin and bear it. I was going to try and have a shot at borrowing from Dortheimer, but I knew there wasn't a hope. And marry his daughter I couldn't. She's much too sensible a girl to take me, anyway. Then, by chance, I met my cousin at the opera. I don't often come across her, but she was always a decent kid when I lived in the house. I found myself telling her all about it. She'd heard something from her father anyway. Then she showed her mettle. She suggested I should take her pearls. They'd belonged to her mother."

He paused. There was something like real emotion, I think, in his voice. Or else he suggested it better than I could have believed possible.

"Well—I accepted the blessed child's offer. I could raise the money I wanted on them, and I swore I'd turn to and redeem them even if it meant working to manage it. But the pearls were at home in Regent Gate. We decided that the best thing to do would be to go and fetch them at once. We jumped in a taxi and off we went.

"We made the fellow stop on the opposite side of the street in case anyone should hear the taxi draw up at the door. Geraldine got out and went across the road. She had her latchkey with her. She would go in quietly, get the pearls and bring them out to me. She didn't expect to meet anyone except, possibly, a servant. Miss Carroll, my uncle's secretary, usually went to bed at half-past nine. He, himself, would probably be in the library.

"So off Dina went. I stood on the pavement smoking a cigarette. Every now and then I looked over towards the house to see if she was coming. And now I come to the part of the story that you may believe or not as you like. A man passed me on the sidewalk. I turned to look after him. To my surprise he went up the steps and let himself in to No. 17. At least I thought it was No. 17, but, of course, I was some distance away. That surprised me very much for two reasons. One was that the man had let himself in with a key, and the second was that I thought I recognised in him a certain well-known actor.

"I was so surprised that I determined to look into matters. I happened to have my own key of No. 17 in my pocket. I'd lost it or thought I'd lost it three years ago, had come across it unexpectedly a day or two ago and had been meaning to give it back to my uncle this morning. However, in the heat of our discussion, it had slipped my memory. I had transferred it with the other contents of my pockets when I changed.

"Telling the taxi man to wait, I strode hurriedly along the pavement, crossed the road, went up the steps of No. 17, and opened the door with my key. The hall was empty. There was no sign of any visitor having just entered. I stood for a minute looking about me. Then I went towards the library door. Perhaps the man was in with my uncle. If so, I should hear the murmur of voices. I stood outside the library door, but I heard nothing.

"I suddenly felt I had made the most abject fool of myself. Of course the man must have gone into some other house—the house beyond, probably. Regent Gate is rather dimly lighted at night. I felt an absolute idiot. What on earth had possessed me to follow the fellow, I could not think. It had landed me here, and a pretty fool I should look if my uncle were to come suddenly out of the library and find me. I should get Geraldine into trouble and altogether the fat would be in the fire. All because something in the man's manner had made me imagine that he was doing something that he didn't want known. Luckily no one caught me. I must get out of it as soon as I could.

"I tiptoed back towards the front door and at the same moment Geraldine came down the stairs with the pearls in her hand.

"She was very startled at seeing me, of course. I got her out of the house, and then explained."

He paused.

"We hurried back to the opera. Got there just as the curtain was going up. No one suspected that we'd left it. It was a hot night and several people went outside to get a breath of air."

He paused.

"I know what you'll say: Why didn't I tell you this right away? And now I put it to you: Would you, with a motive for murder sticking out a yard, admit light-heartedly that you'd actually been at the place the murder was committed on the night in question?

"Frankly, I funked it! Even if we were believed, it was going to be a lot of worry for me and for Geraldine. We'd had nothing to do with the murder, we'd seen nothing, we'd heard nothing. Obviously, I thought, Aunt Jane had done it.

Well, why bring myself in? I told you about the quarrel and my lack of money because I knew you'd ferret it out, and if I'd tried to conceal all that you'd be much more suspicious and you'd probably examine that alibi much more closely. As it was, I thought that if I bucked enough about it it would almost hypnotise you into thinking it all right. The Dortheimers were, I know, honestly convinced that I'd been at Covent Garden all the time. That I spent one interval with my cousin wouldn't strike them as suspicious. And she could always say she'd been with me there and that we hadn't left the place."

"Miss Marsh agreed to this—concealment?"

"Yes. Soon as I got the news, I got on to her and cautioned her for her life not to say anything about her excursion here that night. She'd been with me and I'd been with her during the last interval at Covent Garden. We'd walked in the street a little, that was all. She understood and she quite agreed."

He paused.

"I know it looks bad—coming out with this afterwards. But the story's true enough. I can give you the name and address of the man who let me have the cash on Geraldine's pearls next morning. And if you ask her, she'll confirm every word I've told you."

He sat back in his chair and looked at Japp.

Japp continued to look expressionless.

"You say you thought Jane Wilkinson had committed the murder, Lord Edgware?" he said.

"Well, wouldn't you have thought so? After the butler's story?"

"What about your wager with Miss Adams?"

"Wager with Miss Adams? With Carlotta Adams, do you mean? What has she got to do with it?"

"Do you deny that you offered her the sum of ten thousand dollars to impersonate Miss Jane Wilkinson at the house that night?"

Ronald stared.

"Offered her ten thousand dollars? Nonsense. Someone's been pulling your leg. I haven't got ten thousand dollars to offer. You've got hold of a mare's nest. Does *she* say so? Oh! dash it all—I forgot, she's dead, isn't she?"

"Yes," said Poirot quietly. "She is dead."

Ronald turned his eyes from one to the other of us. He had been debonair before. Now his face had whitened. His eyes looked frightened.

"I don't understand all this," he said. "It's true what I told you. I suppose you don't believe me—any of you."

And then, to my amazement, Poirot stepped forward.

"Yes," he said, "I believe you."

CHAPTER 22
Strange Behaviour of Hercule Poirot

We were in our rooms.

"What on earth—" I began.

Poirot stopped me with a gesture more extravagant than any gesture I had ever seen him make. Both arms whirled in the air.

"I implore of you, Hastings! Not now. Not now."

And upon that he seized his hat, clapped it on his head as though he had never heard of order and method, and rushed headlong from the room. He had not returned when, about an hour later, Japp appeared.

"Little man gone out?" he inquired.

I nodded.

Japp sank into a seat. He dabbed his forehead with a handkerchief. The day was warm.

"What the devil took him?" he inquired. "I can tell you, Captain Hastings, you could have knocked me down with a feather when he stepped up to the man and said: 'I believe you.' For all the world as though he were acting in a romantic melodrama. It beats me."

It beat me also, and I said so.

"And then he marches out of the house," said Japp. "What did he say about it to you?"

"Nothing," I replied.

"Nothing at all?"

"Absolutely nothing. When I was going to speak to him he waved me aside. I thought it best to leave him alone. When we got back here I started to question him. He waved his arms, seized his hat and rushed out again."

We looked at each other. Japp tapped his forehead significantly.

"Must be," he said.

For once I was disposed to agree. Japp had often suggested before that Poirot was what he called "touched." In those cases he had simply not understood what Poirot was driving at. Here, I was forced to confess, I could not understand Poirot's attitude. If not touched, he was, at any rate, suspiciously changeable. Here was his own private theory triumphantly confirmed and straight away he went back on it.

It was enough to dismay and distress his warmest supporters. I shook my head in a discouraged fashion.

"He's always been what I call peculiar," said Japp. "Got his own particular angle of looking at things—and a very queer one it is. He's a kind of genius, I admit that. But they always say that geniuses are very near the border line and liable to slip over any minute. He's always been fond of having things difficult. A straightforward case is never good enough for him. No, it's got to be tortuous. He's got away from real life. He plays a game of his own. It's like an old lady playing at patience. If it doesn't come out, she cheats. Well, it's the other way round with him. If it's coming out too easily, he cheats to make it more difficult! That's the way I look at it."

I found it difficult to answer him. I was too perturbed and distressed to be able to think clearly. I, also, found Poirot's behaviour unaccountable. And since I was very attached to my strange little friend, it worried me more than I cared to express.

In the middle of a gloomy silence, Poirot walked into the room.

He was, I was thankful to see, quite calm now.

Very carefully he removed his hat, placed it with his stick on the table, and sat down in his accustomed chair.

"So you are here, my good Japp. I am glad. It was on my mind that I must see you as soon as possible."

Japp looked at him without replying. He saw that this was only the beginning. He waited for Poirot to explain himself.

This my friend did, speaking slowly and carefully.

"*Ecoutez,* Japp. We are wrong. We are all wrong. It is grievous to admit it, but we have made a mistake."

"That's all right," said Japp confidently.

"But it is not all right. It is deplorable. It grieves me to the heart."

"You needn't be grieved about that young man. He richly deserves all he gets."

"It is not he I am grieving about—it is you."

"Me? You needn't worry about me."

"But I do. See you, who was it set you on this course? It was Hercule Poirot. *Mais oui,* I set you on the trail. I direct your attention to Carlotta Adams, I mention to you the matter of the letter to America. Every step of the way it is I who point it!"

"I was bound to get there anyway," said Japp coldly. "You got a bit ahead of me, that's all."

"*Cela ce peut*. But it does not console me. If harm—if loss of prestige comes to you through listening to my little ideas—I shall blame myself bitterly."

Japp merely looked amused. I think he credited Poirot with motives that were none too pure. He fancied that Poirot grudged him the credit resulting from the successful elucidation of the affair.

"That's all right," he said. "I shan't forget to let it be known that I owe something to you over this business."

He winked at me.

"Oh! it is not that at all." Poirot clicked his tongue with impatience. "I want no credit. And what is more, I tell you there will be no credit. It is a fiasco that you prepare for yourself, and I, Hercule Poirot, am the cause."

Suddenly, at Poirot's expression of extreme melancholy, Japp shouted with laughter. Poirot looked affronted.

"Sorry, M. Poirot." He wiped his eyes. "But you did look for all the world like a dying duck in a thunderstorm. Now look here, let's forget all this. I'm willing to shoulder the credit or the blame of this affair. It will make a big noise—you're right there. Well, I'm going all out to get a conviction. It may be that a clever Counsel will get his lordship off—you never know with a jury. But even so, it won't do me any harm. It will be known that we caught the right man even if we couldn't get a conviction. And if, by any chance, the third housemaid has hysterics and owns up she did it—well, I'll take my medicine and I won't complain you led me up the garden. That's fair enough."

Poirot gazed at him mildly and sadly.

"You have the confidence—always the confidence! You never stop and say to yourself—Can it be so? You never doubt—or wonder. You never think: This is too easy!"

"You bet your life I don't. And that's just where, if you'll excuse me saying so, you go off the rails every time. Why shouldn't a thing be easy? What's the harm in a thing being easy?"

Poirot looked at him, sighed, half threw up his arms, then shook his head.

"*C'est fini!* I will say no more."

"Splendid," said Japp heartily. "Now let's get down to brass tacks. You'd like to hear what I've been doing?"

"Assuredly."

"Well, I saw the Honourable Geraldine, and her story tallied exactly with his lordship's. They may both be in it together, but I think not. It's my opinion he bluffed her—she's three parts sweet on him anyway. Took on terribly when she found he was arrested."

"Did she now? And the secretary—Miss Carroll?"

"Wasn't too surprised, I fancy. However, that's only my idea."

"What about the pearls?" I asked. "Was that part of the story true?"

"Absolutely. He raised the money on them early the following morning. But I don't think that touches the main argument. As I see it, the plan came into his head when he came across his cousin at the opera. It came to him in a flash. He was desperate—here was a way out. I fancy he'd been meditating something of the kind—that's why he had the key with him. I don't believe that story of suddenly coming across it. Well, as he talks to his cousin, he sees that by involving her he gains additional security for himself. He plays on her feelings, hints at the pearls, she plays up, and off they go. As soon as she's in the house he follows her in and goes along to the library. Maybe his lordship had dozed off in his chair. Anyway, in two seconds he's done the trick and he's out again. I don't fancy he meant the girl to catch him in the house. He counted on being found pacing up and down near the taxi. And I don't think the taxi-man was meant to see him go in. The impression was to be that he was walking up and down smoking whilst he waited for the girl. The taxi was facing the opposite direction, remember.

"Of course, the next morning, he has to pledge the pearls. He must still seem to be in need of the money. Then, when he hears of the crime, he frightens the girl into concealing their visit to the house. They will say that they spent that interval together at the Opera House."

"Then why did they not do so?" asked Poirot sharply.

Japp shrugged his shoulders.

"Changed his mind. Or judged that she wouldn't be able to go through with it. She's a nervous type."

"Yes," said Poirot meditatively. "She is a nervous type."

After a minute or two, he said:

"It does not strike you that it would have been easier and simpler for Captain Marsh to have left the opera during the interval by himself. To have gone in quietly with his key, killed his uncle, and returned to the opera—instead of having a taxi outside and a nervous girl coming down the stairs any minute who might lose her head and give him away."

Japp grinned.

"That's what you and I would have done. But then we're a shade brighter than Captain Ronald Marsh."

"I am not so sure. He strikes me as intelligent."

"But not so intelligent as M. Hercule Poirot! Come, now, I'm sure of that!" Japp laughed.

Poirot looked at him coldly.

"If he isn't guilty why did he persuade the Adams girl to take on that stunt?" went on Japp. "There can be only one reason for that stunt—to protect the real criminal."

"There I am of accord with you absolutely."

"Well, I'm glad we agree about something."

"It might be he who actually spoke to Miss Adams," mused Poirot. "Whilst really—no, that is an imbecility."

Then, looking suddenly at Japp, he rapped out a quick question.

"What is your theory as to her death?"

Japp cleared his throat.

"I'm inclined to believe—accident. A convenient accident, I admit. I can't see that he could have had anything to do with it. His alibi is straight enough after the opera. He was at Sobranis with the Dortheimers till after one o'clock. Long before that she was in bed and asleep. No, I think that was an instance of the infernal luck criminals sometimes have. Otherwise, if that accident hadn't happened, I think he had his plans for dealing with her. First, he'd put the fear of the Lord into her—tell her she'd be arrested for murder if she confessed the truth. And then he'd square her with a fresh lot of money."

"Does it strike you—" Poirot stared straight in front of him. "Does it strike you that Miss Adams would let another woman be hanged when she herself held evidence that would acquit her?"

"Jane Wilkinson wouldn't have been hanged. The Montagu Corner party evidence was too strong for that."

"*But the murderer did not know that*. He would have had to count on Jane Wilkinson being hanged and Carlotta Adams keeping silence."

"You love talking, don't you, M. Poirot? And you're positively convinced now that Ronald Marsh is a white-headed boy who can do no wrong. Do you believe that story of his about seeing a man sneak surreptitiously into the house?"

Poirot shrugged his shoulders.

"Do you know who he says he thought it was?"

"I could guess, perhaps."

"He says he thought it was the film star, Bryan Martin. What do you think of that? A man who'd never even met Lord Edgware."

"Then it would certainly be curious if one saw such a man entering that house with a key."

"Chah!" said Japp. A rich noise expressive of contempt. "And now I suppose it will surprise you to hear that Mr. Bryan Martin wasn't in London that night. He took a young lady to dine down at Molesey. They didn't get back to London till midnight."

"Ah!" said Poirot mildly. "No, I am not surprised. Was the young lady also a member of the profession?"

"No. Girl who keeps a hat shop. As a matter of fact, it was Miss Adams' friend, Miss Driver. I think you'll agree her testimony is past suspicion."

"I am not disputing it, my friend."

"In fact, you're done down and you know it, old boy," said Japp, laughing. "Cock and bull story trumped up on the moment, that's what it was. Nobody entered No. 17—and nobody entered either of the houses either side—so what does that show? That his lordship's a liar."

Poirot shook his head sadly.

Japp rose to his feet—his spirits restored.

"Come, now, we're right, you know."

"Who was D, Paris, November?"

Japp shrugged his shoulders.

"Ancient history, I imagine. Can't a girl have a souvenir six months ago without its having something to do with this crime? We must have a sense of proportion."

"Six months ago," murmured Poirot, a sudden light in his eyes. "*Dieu, que je suis bête!*"

"What's he saying?" inquired Japp of me.

"Listen." Poirot rose and tapped Japp on the chest. "Why does Miss Adams' maid not recognise that box? Why does Miss Driver not recognise it?"

"What do you mean?"

"Because the box was *new!* It had only just been given to her. Paris, November—that is all very well—doubtless that is the date of which the box is to be a *souvenir*. But it was given to her *now*, not *then*. It has just been bought! Only just been bought! Investigate that, I implore you, my good Japp. It is a chance, decidedly a chance. It was bought not here, but abroad. Probably Paris. If it had been bought here, some jeweller would have come forward. It has been photographed and described in the papers. Yes, yes, Paris. Possibly some other foreign town, but I think Paris. Find out, I implore you. Make the inquiries. I want—I so badly want—to know who is this mysterious D."

"It will do no harm," said Japp good-naturedly. "Can't say I'm very excited about it myself. But I'll do what I can. The more we know the better."

Nodding cheerfully to us he departed.

CHAPTER 23
The Letter

"And now," said Poirot, "we will go out to lunch."

He put his hand through my arm. He was smiling at me.

"I have hope," he explained.

I was glad to see him restored to his old self, though I was none the less convinced myself of young Ronald's guilt. I fancied that Poirot himself had perhaps come round to this view, convinced by Japp's arguments. The search for the purchaser of the box was, perhaps, a last sally to save his face.

We went amicably to lunch together.

Somewhat to my amusement at a table at the other side of the room, I saw Bryan Martin and Jenny Driver lunching together. Remembering what Japp had said, I suspected a possible romance.

They saw us and Jenny waved a hand.

When we were sipping coffee, Jenny left her escort and came over to our table. She looked as vivid and dynamic as ever.

"May I sit here and talk to you a minute, M. Poirot?"

"Assuredly, Mademoiselle. I am charmed to see you. Will not M. Martin join us also?"

"I told him not to. You see, I wanted to talk to you about Carlotta."

"Yes, Mademoiselle?"

"You wanted to get a line on to some man friend of hers. Isn't that so?"

"Yes, yes."

"Well, I've been thinking and thinking. Sometimes you can't get at things straight away. To get them clear you've got to think back—remember a lot of little words and phrases that perhaps you didn't pay much attention to at the time. Well, that's what I've been doing. Thinking and thinking—and remembering just what she said. And I've come to a certain conclusion."

"Yes, Mademoiselle?"

"I think the man that she cared about—or was beginning to care about—was Ronald Marsh—you know, the one who has just succeeded to the title."

"What makes you think it was he, Mademoiselle?"

"Well, for one thing, Carlotta was speaking in a general sort of way one day. About a man having hard luck, and how it might affect character. That a man might be a decent sort really and yet go down the hill. More sinned against than sinning—you know the idea. The first thing a woman kids herself with when she's getting soft about a man. I've heard the old wheeze so often! Carlotta had plenty of sense, yet here she was coming out with this stuff just like a complete ass who knew nothing of life. 'Hello,' I said to myself. 'Something's up.' She didn't mention a name—it was all general. But almost immediately after that she began to speak of Ronald Marsh and that she thought he'd been badly treated. She was very impersonal and offhand about it. I didn't connect the two things at the time. But now—I wonder. It seems to me that it was Ronald she meant. What do you think, M. Poirot?"

Her face looked earnestly up into his.

"I think, Mademoiselle, that you have perhaps given me some very valuable information."

"Good." Jenny clapped her hands.

Poirot looked kindly at her.

"Perhaps you have not heard—the gentleman of whom you speak, Ronald Marsh—Lord Edgware—has just been arrested."

"Oh!" Her mouth flew open in surprise. "Then my bit of thinking comes rather late in the day."

"It is never too late," said Poirot. "Not with me, you understand. Thank you, Mademoiselle."

She left us to return to Bryan Martin.

"There, Poirot," I said. "Surely that shakes your belief."

"No, Hastings. On the contrary—it strengthens it."

Despite that valiant assertion I believed myself that secretly he had weakened.

During the days that followed he never once mentioned the Edgware case. If I spoke of it, he answered monosyllabically and without interest. In other words, he had washed his hands of it. Whatever idea he had had lingering in his fantastic brain, he had now been forced to admit himself that it had not materialised—that his first conception of the case had been the true one and that Ronald Marsh was only too truly accused of the crime. Only, being Poirot, he could not admit openly that such was the case! Therefore he pretended to have lost interest.

Such, I say, was my interpretation of his attitude. It seemed borne out by the facts. He took no faintest interest in the police court proceedings, which in any case were purely formal. He busied himself with the other cases and, as I say, he displayed no interest when the subject was mentioned.

It was nearly a fortnight later than the events mentioned in my last chapter when I came to realise that my interpretation of his attitude was entirely wrong.

It was breakfast time. The usual heavy pile of letters lay by Poirot's plate. He sorted through them with nimble fingers. Then he uttered a quick exclamation of pleasure and picked up a letter with an American stamp on it.

He opened it with his little letter-opener. I looked on with interest since he seemed so moved to pleasure about it. There was a letter and a fairly thick enclosure.

Poirot read the former through twice, then he looked up.

"Would you like to see this, Hastings?"

I took it from him. It ran as follows:

> "Dear M. Poirot,—I was much touched by your kind—your very kind letter. Apart from my terrible grief, I have been so affronted

by the things that seem to have been hinted about Carlotta—the dearest, sweetest sister that a girl ever had. No, M. Poirot, she did *not* take drugs. I'm sure of it. She had a horror of that kind of thing. I've often heard her say so. If she played a part in that poor man's death, it was an entirely innocent one—but of course her letter to me proves that. I am sending you the actual letter itself since you ask me to do so. I hate parting with the last letter she ever wrote, but I know you will take care of it and let me have it back, and if it helps you to clear up some of the mystery about her death, as you say it may do—why, then, of course it must go to you.

You ask whether Carlotta mentioned any friend specially in her letters. She mentioned a great many people, of course, but nobody in a very outstanding way. Bryan Martin, whom we used to know years ago, a girl called Jenny Driver, and a Captain Ronald Marsh were, I think, the ones she saw most of.

I wish I could think of something to help you. You write so kindly and with such understanding, and you seem to realise what Carlotta and I were to each other.

Gratefully yours,

LUCIE ADAMS.

P.S.—An officer has just been here for the letter. I told him that I had already mailed it to you. This, of course, was not true, but I felt somehow or other that it was important you should see it first. It seems Scotland Yard need it as evidence against the murderer. You will take it to them. But, oh! please be sure they let you have it back again some day. You see, it is Carlotta's last words to me."

"So you wrote yourself to her," I remarked as I laid the letter down. "Why did you do that, Poirot? And why did you ask for the original of Carlotta Adams' letter?"

He was bending over the enclosed sheets of the letter I mentioned.

"In verity I could not say, Hastings—unless it is that I hoped against hope that the original letter might in some way explain the inexplicable."

"I don't see how you can get away from the text of that letter. Carlotta Adams gave it herself to the maid to post. There was no hocus pocus about it. And certainly it reads as a perfectly genuine ordinary epistle."

Poirot sighed.

"I know. I know. And that is what makes it so difficult. Because, Hastings, as it stands, that letter is *impossible*."

"Nonsense."

"*Si, si*, it is so. See you, as I have reasoned it out, certain things *must* be—they follow each other with method and order in an understandable fashion. But then comes this letter. It does not accord. Who, then, is wrong? Hercule Poirot or the letter?"

"You don't think it possible that it could be Hercule Poirot?" I suggested as delicately as I was able.

Poirot threw me a glance of reproof.

"There are times when I have been in error—but this is not one of them.

Clearly then, since the letter seems impossible, it *is* impossible. There is some fact about the letter which escapes us. I seek to discover what that fact is."

And thereupon he resumed his study of the letter in question, using a small pocket microscope.

As he finished perusing each page, he passed it across to me. I, certainly, could find nothing amiss. It was written in a firm fairly legible handwriting and it was word for word as it had been telegraphed across.

Poirot sighed deeply.

"There is no forgery of any kind here—no, it is all written in the same hand. And yet, since, as I say, it is impossible—"

He broke off. With an impatient gesture he demanded the sheets from me. I passed them over, and once again he went slowly through them.

Suddenly he uttered a cry.

I had left the breakfast table and was standing looking out of the window. At this sound, however, I turned sharply.

Poirot was literally quivering with excitement. His eyes were green like a cat's. His pointing finger trembled.

"See you, Hastings? Look here—quickly—come and look."

I ran to his side. Spread out before him was one of the middle sheets of the letter. I could see nothing unusual about it.

"See you not? All these other sheets have the clean edge—they are single sheets. But this one—see—one side of it is ragged—it has been torn. Now do you see what I mean? *This was a double sheet,* and so, you comprehend, *one page of the letter is missing.*"

I stared stupidly, no doubt.

"But how can it be? It makes sense."

"Yes, yes, it makes sense. That is where the cleverness of the idea comes in. Read—and you will see."

I think I cannot do better than to append a facsimile of the page in question.

"You see it now?" said Poirot. "The letter breaks off where she is talking of Captain Marsh. She is sorry for him, and then she says: 'He enjoyed my show very much.' Then on the new sheet she goes on: 'He said . . .' But, *mon ami,* a page is missing. The 'He' of the new page may not be the 'he' of the old page. *In fact it is not the he* of the old page. It is another man altogether who proposed that hoax. Observe, nowhere after that is the name mentioned. Ah! *c'est épatant!* Somehow or other our murderer gets hold of this letter. It gives him away. No doubt he thinks to suppress it altogether, and then—reading it over—he sees another way of dealing with it. Remove one page, and the letter is capable of being twisted into a damning accusation of another man—a man too who has a motive for Lord Edgware's death. Ah! it was a gift! The money for the *confiture* as you say! He tears the sheet off and replaces the letter."

I looked at Poirot in some admiration. I was not perfectly convinced of the truth of this theory. It seemed to me highly possible that Carlotta had used an old half sheet that was already torn. But Poirot was so transfigured with joy that I simply had not the heart to suggest this prosaic possibility. After all, he *might* be right.

I did, however, venture to point out one or two difficulties in the way of his theory.

"But how did the man, whoever he was, get hold of the letter? Miss Adams took it straight from her handbag and gave it herself to the maid to post. The maid told us so."

The Letter

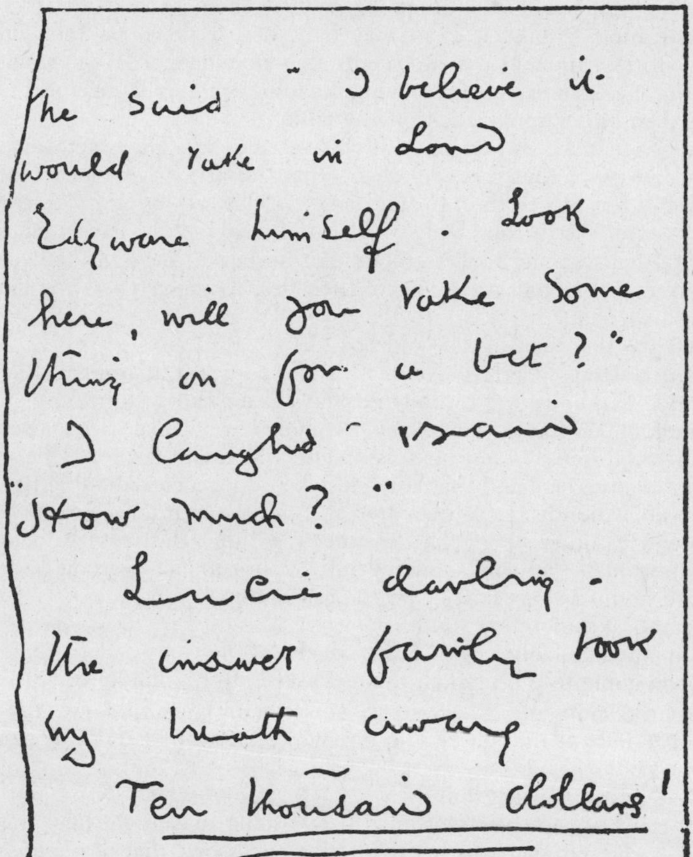

he said "I believe it would take in Lord Edgware himself. Look here, will you take some thing on for a bet?" I laughed – said "How much?" Lucie darling – the answer fairly took my breath away Ten thousand dollars!

"Therefore we must assume one of two things. Either the maid was lying, or else, during that evening, Carlotta Adams met the murderer."

I nodded.

"It seems to me that that last possibility is the most likely one. We still do not know where Carlotta Adams was between the time she left her flat and nine o'clock when she left her suitcase at Euston station. During that time, I believe myself that she met the murderer in some appointed spot—they probably had some food together. He gave her some last instructions. What happened exactly in regard to the letter we do not know. One can make a guess. She may have been carrying it in her hand meaning to post it. She may have laid it down on the table in the restaurant. He sees the address and scents a possible danger. He may have picked it up adroitly, made an excuse for leaving the table, opened it, read it, torn out the sheet, and then either replaced it on the table, or perhaps given it to her as she left, telling her that she had dropped it without noticing. The exact way of it is not important—but two things do seem clear. That Carlotta Adams met the murderer that evening either before the murder of Lord Edgware, or afterwards (there was time after she left the Corner House for a brief interview). I have a fancy, though there I am perhaps wrong, that it was the murderer who gave her the gold box—it was possibly a sentimental memento of their first meeting. *If so, the murderer is D.*"

"I don't see the point of the gold box."

"Listen, Hastings, Carlotta Adams was not addicted to veronal. Lucie Adams says so, and I, too, believe it to be true. She was a clear-eyed healthy girl with no predilection for such things. None of her friends nor her maid recognised the box. Why, then, was it found in her possession after she died? To create the impression that she *did* take veronal and that she had taken it for a considerable time—that is to say at least six months. Let us say that she met the murderer after the murder if only for a few minutes. They had a drink together, Hastings, to celebrate the success of their plan. And in the girl's drink he put sufficient veronal to ensure that there should be no waking for her on the following morning."

"Horrible," I said with a shudder.

"Yes, it was not pretty," said Poirot dryly.

"Are you going to tell Japp all this?" I asked after a minute or two.

"Not at the moment. What have I got to tell? He would say, the excellent Japp, 'another nest of the mare! The girl wrote on an odd sheet of paper!' *C'est tout.*"

I looked guiltily at the ground.

"What can I say to that? Nothing. It is a thing that might have happened. I only know it did not happen because *it is necessary that it should not have happened.*"

He paused. A dreamy expression stole across his face.

"Figure to yourself, Hastings, if only that man had had the order and the method, he would have cut that sheet—not torn it. And we should have noticed nothing. But nothing!"

"So we deduce that he is a man of careless habits," I said, smiling.

"No, no. He might have been in a hurry. You observe it is very carelessly torn. Oh! assuredly he was pressed for time."

He paused and then said:

"One thing you do remark, I hope. This man—this D—he must have had a very good alibi for that evening."

"I can't see how he could have had any alibi at all if he spent his time first at Regent Gate doing a murder and then with Carlotta Adams."

"Precisely," said Poirot. "That is what I mean. He is badly in need of an alibi, so no doubt he prepared one. Another point: Does his name really begin with D? Or does D stand for some nickname by which he was known to her?"

He paused and then said softly:

"A man whose initial or whose nickname is D. We have got to find him, Hastings. Yes, we have got to find him."

CHAPTER 24
News from Paris

On the following day we had an unexpected visit.

Geraldine Marsh was announced.

I felt sorry for her as Poirot greeted her and set a chair for her. Her large dark eyes seemed wider and darker than ever. There were black circles round them as though she had not slept. Her face looked extraordinarily haggard and weary for one so young—little more, really, than a child.

"I have come to see you, M. Poirot, because I don't know how to go on any longer. I am so terribly worried and upset."

"Yes, Mademoiselle?"

His manner was gravely sympathetic.

"Ronald told me what you said to him that day. I mean that dreadful day when he was arrested." She shivered "He told me that you came up to him suddenly, just when he had said that he supposed no one would believe him, and that you said to him: 'I believe you.' Is that true, M. Poirot?"

"It is true, Mademoiselle, that is what I said."

"I know, but I meant not was it true you said it, but were the words really true. I mean, *did* you believe his story?"

Terribly anxious she looked, leaning forward there, her hands clasped together.

"The words were true, Mademoiselle," said Poirot quietly. "I do not believe your cousin killed Lord Edgware."

"Oh!" The colour came into her face, her eyes opened big and wide. "Then you must think—that someone else did it!"

"*Evidément*, Mademoiselle." He smiled.

"I'm stupid. I say things badly. What I mean is—you think you know who that somebody is?"

She leaned forward eagerly.

"I have my little ideas, naturally—my suspicions, shall we say?"

"Won't you tell me? Please—please."

Poirot shook his head.

"It would be—perhaps—unfair."

"Then you *have* got a definite suspicion of somebody?"

Poirot merely shook his head non-committally.

"If only I knew a little more," pleaded the girl. "It would make it so much easier for me. And I might perhaps be able to help you. Yes, really I might be able to help you."

Her pleading was very disarming, but Poirot continued to shake his head.

"The Duchess of Merton is still convinced it was my stepmother," said the girl thoughtfully. She gave a slight questioning glance at Poirot.

He showed no reaction.

"But I hardly see how that can be."

"What is your opinion of her? Of your stepmother?"

"Well—I hardly know her. I was at school in Paris when my father married her. When I came home, she was quite kind. I mean, she just didn't notice I was there. I thought her very empty-headed and—well, mercenary."

Poirot nodded.

"You spoke of the Duchess of Merton. You have seen much of her?"

"Yes. She has been very kind to me. I have been with her a great deal during the last fortnight. It has been terrible—with all the talk, and the reporters, and Ronald in prison and everything." She shivered. "I feel I have no real friends. But the Duchess has been wonderful, and he has been nice too—her son, I mean."

"You like him?"

"He is shy, I think. Stiff and rather difficult to get on with. But his mother talks a lot about him, so that I feel that I know him better than I really do."

"I see. Tell me, Mademoiselle, you are fond of your cousin?"

"Of Ronald? Of course. He—I haven't seen much of him the last two years—but before that he used to live in the house. I—I always thought he was wonderful. Always joking and thinking of mad things to do. Oh! in that gloomy house of ours it made all the difference."

Poirot nodded sympathetically, but he went on to make a remark that shocked me in its crudity.

"You do not want to see him—hanged, then?"

"No, no." The girl shivered violently. "Not that. Oh! if only it were her—my stepmother. It *must* be her. The Duchess says it must."

"Ah!" said Poirot. "If only Captain Marsh had stayed in the taxi—eh?"

"Yes—at least, what do you mean?" Her brow wrinkled. "I don't understand."

"If he had not followed that man into the house. Did you hear anyone come in, by the way?"

"No, I didn't hear anything."

"What did you do when you came into the house?"

"I ran straight upstairs—to fetch the pearls, you know."

"Of course. It took you some time to fetch them."

"Yes. I couldn't find the key of my jewel-case all at once.

"So often is that the case. The more in haste, the less the speed. It was some time before you came down, and then—you found your cousin in the hall?"

"Yes, coming from the library." She swallowed.

"I comprehend. It gave you quite the turn."

"Yes, it did." She looked grateful for his sympathetic tone. "It startled me, you see."

"Quite, quite."

"Ronnie just said: 'Hello, Dina, got them?' from behind me—and it made me jump."

"Yes," said Poirot gently. "As I said before it is a pity he did not stay outside. Then the taxi-driver would have been able to swear he never entered the house."

She nodded. Her tears began to fall, splashing unheeded on her lap. She got up. Poirot took her hand.

"You want me to save him for you—is that it?"

"Yes, yes—oh! please, yes. You don't know . . ."

She stood there striving to control herself, clenching her hands.

"Life has not been easy for you, Mademoiselle," said Poirot gently. "I appreciate that. No, it has not been easy. Hastings, will you get Mademoiselle a taxi?"

I went down with the girl and saw her into the taxi. She had composed herself by now and thanked me very prettily.

I found Poirot walking up and down the room, his brows knitted in thought. He looked unhappy.

I was glad when the telephone bell rang to distract him.

"Who is that? Oh! It is Japp. *Bonjour, mon ami.*"

"What's he got to say?" I asked, drawing nearer the telephone.

Finally, after various ejaculations, Poirot spoke.

"Yes, and who called for it? Do they know?"

Whatever the answer, it was not what he expected. His face dropped ludicrously.

"Are you sure?"

". . . . ."

"No, is is a little upsetting, that is all."

". . . . ."

"Yes, I must rearrange my ideas."

". . . . ."

"*Comment?*"

". . . . ."

"All the same, I was right about it. Yes, a detail, as you say."

". . . . ."

"No, I am still of the same opinion. I would pray of you to make still further inquiries of the restaurants in the neighbourhood of Regent Gate and Euston, Tottenham Court Road and perhaps Oxford Street."

". . . . ."

"Yes, a woman and a man. And also in the neighbourhood of the Strand just before midnight. *Comment?*"

". . . . ."

"But, yes, I know that Captain Marsh was with the Dortheimers. But there are other people in the world besides Captain Marsh."

". . . . ."

"To say I have the head of the pig is not pretty. *Tout de même*, oblige me in this matter, I pray of you."

". . . . ."

He replaced the receiver.

"Well?" I asked impatiently.

"Is it well? I wonder. Hastings, that gold box *was* bought in Paris. It was ordered by letter and comes from a well-known Paris shop which specialises in such things. The letter was supposedly from a Lady Ackerly—Constance Ackerly, the letter was signed. Naturally there is no such person. The letter was received two days before the murder. It ordered the initials of (presumably) the writer in rubies and the inscription inside. It was a rush order—to be called for the following day. That is, the day before the murder."

"And it was called for?"

"Yes, it was called for and paid for in notes."

"Who called for it?" I asked excitedly. I felt we were getting near to the truth.

"A woman called for it, Hastings."

"A woman?" I said, surprised.

"*Mais oui*. A woman—short, middle-aged and *wearing pince-nez*."

We looked at each other, completely baffled.

CHAPTER 25
A Luncheon Party

It was, I think, on the day after that that we went to the Widburns' luncheon party at Claridge's.

Neither Poirot nor I were particularly anxious to go. It was, as a matter of fact, about the sixth invitation we had received. Mrs. Widburn was a persistent woman and she liked celebrities. Undaunted by refusals, she finally offered such a choice of dates that capitulation was inevitable. Under those circumstances the sooner we went and got it over the better.

Poirot had been very uncommunicative ever since the news from Paris.

To my remarks on the subject he returned always the same answer.

"There is something here I do not comprehend."

And once or twice he murmured to himself.

"Pince-nez. Pince-nez in Paris. Pince-nez in Carlotta Adams' bag."

I really felt glad of the luncheon party as a means of distraction.

Young Donald Ross was there and came up and greeted me cheerily. There were more men than women and he was put next to me at table.

Jane Wilkinson sat almost opposite us, and next to her, between her and Mrs. Widburn, sat the young Duke of Merton.

I fancied—of course it may have been only my fancy—that he looked slightly ill at ease. The company in which he found himself was, so I should imagine, little to his liking. He was a strictly conservative and somewhat reactionary young man—the kind of character that seemed to have stepped out of the Middle Ages by some regrettable mistake. His infatuation for the extremely modern Jane Wilkinson was one of those anachronistic jokes that Nature so loves to play.

Seeing Jane's beauty and appreciating the charm that her exquisitely husky voice lent to the most trite utterances, I could hardly wonder at his capitulation. But one can get used to perfect beauty and an intoxicating voice! It crossed my mind that perhaps even now a ray of common-sense was dissipating the mists of intoxicated love. It was a chance remark—a rather humiliating *gaffe* on Jane's part that gave me that impression.

Somebody—I forget who—had uttered the phrase "judgment of Paris," and straight away Jane's delightful voice was uplifted.

"Paris?" she said. "Why, Paris doesn't cut any ice nowadays. It's London and New York that count."

As sometimes happens, the words fell in a momentary lull of conversation. It was an awkward moment. On my right I heard Donald Ross draw in his breath sharply. Mrs. Widburn began to talk violently about Russian opera. Everyone hastily said something to somebody else. Jane alone looked serenely up and down the table without the least consciousness of having said anything amiss.

It was then I noticed the Duke. His lips were drawn tightly together, he had flushed, and it seemed to me as though he drew slightly away from Jane. He must have had a foretaste of the fact that for a man of his position to marry a Jane Wilkinson might lead to some awkward contretemps.

As so often happens, I made the first remark that came into my head to my left-hand neighbour, a stout titled lady who arranged children's matinées. I remember that the remark in question was: "Who is that extraordinary looking woman in purple at the other end of the table?" It was, of course, the lady's sister! Having stammered apologies, I turned and chatted to Ross, who answered in monosyllables.

It was then, rebuffed on both sides, that I noticed Bryan Martin. He must have come late for I had not seen him before.

He was a little way further down the table on my side and was leaning forward and chatting with great animation to a pretty blonde woman.

It was some time since I had seen him at close quarters, and I was struck at once by the great improvement in his looks. The haggard lines had almost disappeared. He looked younger and in every way more fit. He was laughing and chaffing his vis-à-vis and seemed in first-rate spirits.

I did not have time to observe him further, for at that moment my stout neighbour forgave me and graciously permitted me to listen to a long monologue on the beauties of a Children's Matinée which she was organising for Charity.

Poirot had to leave early as he had an appointment. He was investigating the strange disappearance of an Ambassador's boots and had a rendezvous fixed for half-past two. He charged me to make his adieus to Mrs. Widburn. While I was waiting to do so—not an easy matter, for she was at the moment closely surrounded by departing friends all breathing out "Darlings" at a great rate—somebody touched me on the shoulder.

It was young Ross.

"Isn't M. Poirot here? I wanted to speak to him."

I explained that Poirot had just departed.

Ross seemed taken aback. Looking more closely at him, I saw that something seemed to have upset him. He looked white and strained and he had a queer uncertain look in his eyes.

"Did you want to see him particularly?" I asked.

He answered slowly:

"I—don't know."

It was such a queer answer that I stared at him in surprise. He flushed.

"It sounds odd, I know. The truth is that something rather queer has happened. Something that I can't make out. I—I'd like M. Poirot's advice about it. Because, you see, I don't know what to do—I don't want to bother him, but—"

He looked so puzzled and unhappy that I hastened to reassure him.

"Poirot has gone to keep an appointment," I said. "But I know he means to be back at five o'clock. Why not ring him up then, or come and see him?"

"Thanks. Do you know, I think I will. Five o'clock?"

"Better ring up first," I said, "and make sure before coming round."

"All right. I will. Thanks, Hastings. You see, I think it might—just might—be very important."

I nodded and turned again to where Mrs. Widburn was dispensing honied words and limp handshakes.

My duty done, I was turning away when a hand was slipped through my arm.

"Don't cut me," said a merry voice.

It was Jenny Driver—looking extremely chic, by the way.

"Hello," I said. "Where have you sprung from?"

"I was lunching at the next table to you."

"I didn't see you. How is business?"

"Booming, thank you."

"The soup plates going well?"

"Soup plates, as you so rudely call them, are going very well. When everybody has got thoroughly laden up with them, there's going to be dirty work done. Something like a blister with a feather attached is going to be worn bang in the middle of the forehead."

"Unscrupulous," I said.

"Not at all. Somebody must come to the rescue of the ostriches. They're all on the dole."

She laughed and moved away.

"Good-bye. I'm taking an afternoon off from business. Going for a spin in the country."

"And very nice too," I said approvingly. "It's stifling in London to-day."

I myself walked leisurely through the Park. I reached home about four o'clock. Poirot had not yet come in. It was twenty minutes to five when he returned. He was twinkling and clearly in a good humour.

"I see, Holmes," I remarked, "that you have tracked the Ambassadorial boots."

"It was a case of cocaine smuggling. Very ingenious. For the last hour I have been in a ladies' Beauty Parlour. There was a girl there with auburn hair who would have captured your susceptible heart at once."

Poirot always has the impression that I am particularly susceptible to auburn hair. I do not bother to argue about it.

The telephone rang.

"That's probably Donald Ross," I said as I went across to the instrument.

"Donald Ross?"

"Yes. The young man we met at Chiswick. He wants to see you about something."

I took down the receiver.

"Hello. Captain Hastings speaking."

It was Ross.

"Oh! is that you, Hastings? Has M. Poirot come in?"

"Yes, he's here now. Do you want to speak to him or are you coming round?"

"It's nothing much. I can tell him just as well over the telephone."

"Right. Hold on."

Poirot came forward and took the receiver. I was so close that I could hear, faintly, Ross's voice.

"Is that M. Poirot?" The voice sounded eager—excited.

"Yes, it is I."

"Look here, I don't want to bother you, but there's something that seems to me a bit odd. It's in connection with Lord Edgware's death."

I saw Poirot's figure go taut.

"Continue, continue."

"It may seem just nonsense to you—"

"No, no. Tell me, all the same."

"It was Paris set me off. You see—" Very faintly I heard a bell trilling.

"Half a second," said Ross.

There was the sound of the receiver being laid down.

We waited. Poirot at the mouthpiece. I was standing beside him.

I say—we waited. . . .

Two minutes passed—three minutes—four minutes—five minutes.

Poirot shifted his feet uneasily. He glanced up at the clock.

Then he moved the hook up and down and spoke to the Exchange. He turned to me.

"The receiver is still off at the other end, but there is no reply. They cannot get an answer. Quick, Hastings, look up Ross's address in the telephone book. We must go there at once."

CHAPTER 26
Paris?

A few minutes later we were jumping into a taxi.

Poirot's face was very grave.

"I am afraid, Hastings," he said. "I am afraid."

"You don't mean—" I said and stopped.

"We are up against somebody who has already struck twice—that person will not hesitate to strike again. He is twisting and turning like a rat, fighting for his life. Ross is a danger. Then Ross will be eliminated."

"Was what he had to tell so important?" I asked doubtfully. "He did not seem to think so."

"Then he was wrong. Evidently what he had to tell was of supreme importance."

"But how could anyone know?"

"He spoke to you, you say. There, at Claridge's. With people all round. Madness—utter madness. Ah! why did you not bring him back with you—guard him—let no one near him till I had heard what he had to say."

"I never thought—I never dreamt—" I stammered.

Poirot made a quick gesture.

"Do not blame yourself—how could you know? I—I would have known. The murderer, you see, Hastings, is as cunning as a tiger and as relentless. Ah! shall we never arrive?"

We were there at last. Ross lived in a maisonette on the first floor of a house in a big square in Kensington. A card stuck in a little slot by the door-bell gave us the information. The hall door was open. Inside was a big flight of stairs.

"So easy to come in. None to see," murmured Poirot as he sprang up the stairs.

On the first floor was a kind of partition and a narrow door with a Yale lock. Ross's card was stuck in the centre of the door.

We paused there. Everywhere there was dead silence.

I pushed the door—to my surprise it yielded.

We entered.

There was a narrow hall and an open door one side, another in front of us opening into what was evidently the sitting-room.

Into this sitting-room we went. It was the divided half of a big front drawing-room. It was cheaply but comfortably furnished and it was empty. On a small table was the telephone, the receiver stood down beside the instrument.

Poirot took a swift step forward, looked round, then shook his head.

"Not here. Come, Hastings."

We retraced our steps and, going out into the hall, we passed through the other door. The room was a tiny dining-room. At one side of the table, fallen sideways from a chair and sprawled across the table, was Ross.

Poirot bent over him.

He straightened up—his face was white.

"He's dead. Stabbed at the base of the skull."

For long afterwards the events of that afternoon remained like a nightmare in my mind. I could not rid myself of a dreadful feeling of responsibility.

Much later, that evening, when we were alone together, I stammered out to Poirot my bitter self-reproachings. He responded quickly.

"No, no, do not blame yourself. How could you have suspected? The good God has not given you a suspicious nature to begin with."

"*You* would have suspected?"

"That is different. All my life, you see, I have tracked down murderers. I know how, each time, the impulse to kill becomes stronger, till, at last, for a trivial cause—" He broke off.

He had been very quiet ever since our ghastly discovery. All through the arrival of the police, the questioning of the other people in the house, the hundred and one details of the dreadful routine following upon a murder, Poirot had remained aloof—strangely quiet—a far-away speculative look in his eyes. Now, as he broke off his sentence, that same far-away speculative look returned.

"We have no time to waste in regrets, Hastings," he said quietly. "No time to say 'If'—The poor young man who is dead had something to tell us. And we know now that that something must have been of great importance—otherwise he would not have been killed. Since he can no longer tell us—we have got to guess. We have got to guess—with only one little clue to guide us."

"Paris," I said.

"Yes, Paris." He got up and began to stroll up and down.

"There have been several mentions of Paris in this business, but unluckily in different connections. There is the word Paris engraved in the gold box. Paris in November last. Miss Adams was there then—perhaps Ross was there also. Was there someone else there whom Ross knew? Whom he saw with Miss Adams under somewhat peculiar circumstances?"

"We can never know," I said.

"Yes, yes, we can know. We *shall* know! The power of the human brain, Hastings, is almost unlimited. What other mentions of Paris have we in connection with the case? There is the short woman with the pince-nez who called for the box at the jeweller's there. Was she known to Ross? The Duke of Merton was in Paris when the crime was committed. Paris, Paris, Paris. Lord Edgware was going to Paris—Ah! possibly we have something there. Was he killed to prevent him going to Paris?"

He sat down again, his brows drawn together. I could almost feel the waves of his furious concentration of thought.

"What happened at that luncheon?" he murmured. "Some casual word or phrase must have shown to Donald Ross the significance of the knowledge which was in his possession, but which up to then he had not known was significant. Was there some mention of France? Of Paris? Up your end of the table, I mean."

"The word Paris was mentioned but not in that connection."

I told him about Jane Wilkinson's "*gaffe*."

"That probably explains it," he said thoughtfully. "The word Paris would be sufficient—taken in conjunction with something else. But what was that something else? At what was Ross looking? Or of what had he been speaking when that word was uttered?"

"He'd been talking about Scottish superstitions."

"And his eyes were—where?"

"I'm not sure. I think he was looking towards the head of the table where Mrs. Widburn was sitting."

"Who sat next to her?"

"The Duke of Merton, then Jane Wilkinson, then some fellow I didn't know."

"M. le Duc. It is possible that he was looking at M. le Duc when the word Paris was spoken. The Duke, remember, was in Paris or was supposed to be in Paris at the time of the crime. Suppose Ross suddenly remembered something which went to show that Merton was *not* in Paris."

"My dear Poirot!"

"Yes, you consider that an absurdity. So does everyone. Had M. le Duc a motive for the crime? Yes, a very strong one. But to suppose that he committed it—oh! absurd. He is so rich, of so assured a position, of such a well-known lofty character. No one will scrutinise his alibi too carefully. And yet to fake an alibi in a big hotel is not so difficult. To go across by the afternoon service—to return—it *could* be done. Tell me, Hastings, did Ross not say anything when the word Paris was mentioned? Did he show no emotion?"

"I do seem to remember that he drew in his breath rather sharply."

"And his manner when he spoke to you afterwards. Was it bewildered. Confused?"

"That absolutely describes it."

"*Précisément*. An idea has come to him. He thinks it preposterous! Absurd! And yet—he hesitates to voice it. First he will speak to me. But alas! when he has made up his mind, I am already departed."

"If he had only said a little more to me," I lamented.

"Yes. If only— Who was near you at the time?"

"Well, everybody, more or less. They were saying good-bye to Mrs. Widburn. I didn't notice particularly."

Poirot got up again.

"Have I been all wrong?" he murmured as he began once more to pace the floor. "All the time, have I been wrong?"

I looked at him with sympathy. Exactly what the ideas were that passed through his head I did not know. "Close as an oyster," Japp had called him, and the Scotland Yard inspector's words were truly descriptive. I only knew that now, at this moment, he was at war with himself.

"At anyrate," I said, "this murder cannot be put down to Ronald Marsh."

"It is a point in his favour," my friend said absent-mindedly. "But that does not concern us for the moment."

Abruptly, as before, he sat down.

"I cannot be entirely wrong. Hastings, do you remember that I once posed to myself five questions?"

"I seem to remember dimly something of the sort."

"They were: Why did Lord Edgware change his mind on the subject of divorce? What is the explanation of the letter he said he wrote to his wife and which she said she never got? Why was there that expression of rage on his face when we left his house that day? What were a pair of pince-nez doing in Carlotta Adams' handbag? Why did someone telephone to Lady Edgware at Chiswick and immediately ring off?"

"Yes, these were the questions," I said. "I remember now."

"Hastings, I have had in mind all along a certain little idea. An idea as to who the man was—*the man behind*. Three of those questions I have answered—and the answers accord with my little idea. But two of the questions, Hastings, I cannot answer.

"You see what that means. Either I am wrong as to the person, *and it cannot be that person*. Or else the answer to the two questions that I cannot answer is there all the time. Which is it, Hastings? Which is it?"

Rising, he went to his desk, unlocked it and took out the letter Lucie Adams had sent him from America. He had asked Japp to let him keep it a day or two and Japp had agreed. Poirot laid it on the table in front of him and pored over it.

The minutes went by. I yawned and picked up a book. I did not think that Poirot would get much result from his study. We had already gone over and over the letter. Granted that it was not Ronald Marsh who was referred to, there was nothing whatever to show who else it might be.

I turned the pages of my book. . . .

Possibly I dozed off. . . .

Suddenly Poirot uttered a low cry. I sat up abruptly. He was looking at me with an indescribable expression, his eyes green and shining.

"Hastings, Hastings."

"Yes, what is it?"

"Do you remember I said to you that if the murderer had been a man of order and method he would have cut this page, not torn it?"

"Yes?"

"I was wrong. There is order and method throughout this crime. *The page had to be torn, not cut*. Look for yourself."

I looked.

"*Eh bien*, you see?"

I shook my head.

"You mean he was in a hurry?"

"Hurry or no hurry it would be the same thing. Do you not see, my friend? *The page had to be torn*. . . ."

I shook my head.

In a low voice Poirot said:

"I have been foolish. I have been blind. But *now—now*—we shall get on!"

CHAPTER 27
Concerning Pince-Nez

A minute later his mood had changed. He sprang to his feet.

I also sprang to mine—completely uncomprehending but willing.

"We will take a taxi. It is only nine o'clock. Not too late to make a visit."

I hurried after him down the stairs.

"Whom are we going to visit?"

"We are going to Regent Gate."

I judged it wisest to hold my peace. Poirot, I saw, was not in the mood for being questioned. That he was greatly excited I could see. As we sat side by side in the taxi his fingers drummed on his knee with a nervous impatience most unlike his usual calm.

I went over in my mind every word of Carlotta Adams' letter to her sister. By this time I almost knew it by heart. I repeated again and again to myself Poirot's words about the torn page.

But it was no good. As far as I was concerned, Poirot's words simply did not make sense. Why had a page *got* to be torn? No, I could not see it.

A new butler opened the door to us at Regent Gate. Poirot asked for Miss Caroll, and as we followed the butler up the stairs I wondered for the fiftieth time where the former "Greek god" could be. So far the police had failed utterly to run him to earth. A sudden shiver passed over me as I reflected that perhaps he, too, was dead. . . .

The sight of Miss Carroll, brisk and neat and eminently sane, recalled me from these fantastic speculations. She was clearly very much surprised to see Poirot.

"I am glad to find you still here, Mademoiselle," said Poirot as he bowed over her hand. "I was afraid you might be no longer in the house."

"Geraldine would not hear of my leaving," said Miss Carroll. "She begged me to stay on. And really, at a time like this, the poor child needs someone. If she needs nothing else, she needs a buffer. And I can assure you, when need be, I make a very efficient buffer, M. Poirot."

Her mouth took on a grim line. I felt that she would have a short way with reporters or news hunters.

"Mademoiselle, you have always seemed to me the pattern of efficiency. The efficiency, I admire it very much. It is rare. Mademoiselle Marsh now, she has not got the practical mind."

"She's a dreamer," said Miss Carroll. "Completely impractical. Always has been. Lucky she hasn't got her living to get."

"Yes, indeed."

"But I don't suppose you came here to talk about people being practical or impractical. What can I do for you, M. Poirot?"

I do not think Poirot quite liked to be recalled to the point in this fashion. He was somewhat addicted to the oblique approach. With Miss Carroll, however, such a thing was not practicable. She blinked at him suspiciously through her strong glasses.

"There are a few points on which I should like definite information. I know I can trust your memory, Miss Carroll."

"I wouldn't be much use as a secretary if you couldn't," said Miss Carroll grimly.

"Was Lord Edgware in Paris last November?"

"Yes."

"Can you tell me the date of his visit?"

"I shall have to look it up."

She rose, unlocked a drawer, took out a small bound book, turned the pages and finally announced:

"Lord Edgware went to Paris on November 3rd and returned on the 7th. He also went over on November 29th and returned on December 4th. Anything more?"

"Yes. For what purpose did he go?"

"On the first occasion he went to see some statuettes which he thought of purchasing and which were to be auctioned later. On the second occasion he had no definite purpose in view so far as I know."

"Did Mademoiselle Marsh accompany her father on either occasion?"

"She never accompanied her father on any occasion, M. Poirot. Lord Edgware would never have dreamed of such a thing. At that time she was at a convent in Paris, but I do not think her father went to see her or took her out—at least it would surprise me very much if he had."

"You yourself did not accompany him?"

"No."

She looked at him curiously and then said abruptly:

"Why are you asking me these questions, M. Poirot? What is the point of them?"

Poirot did not reply to this question. Instead he said:

"Miss Marsh is very fond of her cousin, is she not?"

"Really, M. Poirot, I don't see what that has got to do with you."

"She came to see me the other day! You knew that?"

"No, I did not." She seemed startled. "What did she say?"

"She told me—though not in actual words—that she was very fond of her cousin."

"Well, then, why ask me?"

"Because I seek your opinion."

This time Miss Carroll decided to answer.

"Much too fond of him in my opinion. Always has been."

"You do not like the present Lord Edgware?"

"I don't say that. I've no use for him, that's all. He's not serious. I don't deny he's got a pleasant way with him. He can talk you round. But I'd rather see Geraldine getting interested in someone with a little more backbone."

"Such as the Duke of Merton?"

"I don't know the Duke. At anyrate, he seems to take the duties of his position seriously. But he's running after that woman—that precious Jane Wilkinson."

"His mother—"

"Oh! I dare say his mother would prefer him to marry Geraldine. But what can mothers do? Sons never want to marry the girls their mothers want them to marry."

"Do you think that Miss Marsh's cousin cares for her?"

"Doesn't matter whether he does or doesn't in the position he's in."

"You think, then, that he will be condemned?"

"No, I don't. I don't think he did it."

"But he might be condemned all the same?"

Miss Carroll did not reply.

"I must not detain you." Poirot rose. "By the way, did you know Carlotta Adams?"

"I saw her act. Very clever."

"Yes, she was clever." He seemed lost in meditation. "Ah! I have put down my gloves."

Reaching forward to get them from the table where he had laid them, his cuff caught the chain of Miss Carroll's pince-nez and jerked them off. Poirot retrieved them and the gloves which he had dropped, uttering confused apologies.

"I must apologise also once more for disturbing you," he ended. "But I fancied there might be some clue in a dispute Lord Edgware had with someone last year. Hence my questions about Paris. A forlorn hope, I fear, but Mademoiselle seemed so very positive it was not her cousin who committed the crime. Remarkably positive she was. Well, good-night, Mademoiselle, and a thousand pardons for disturbing you."

We had reached the door when Miss Carroll's voice recalled us.

"M. Poirot, these aren't my glasses. I can't see through them."

"*Comment?*" Poirot stared at her in amazement. Then his face broke into smiles.

"Imbecile that I am! My own glasses fell out of my pocket as I stooped to get the gloves and pick up yours. I have mixed the two pairs. They look very alike, you see."

An exchange was made, with smiles on both sides, and we took our departure.

"Poirot," I said when we were outside. "You don't wear glasses."

He beamed at me.

"Penetrating! How quickly you see the point."

"Those were the pince-nez found in Carlotta Adams' handbag?"

"Correct."

"Why did you think they might be Miss Carroll's?"

Poirot shrugged his shoulders.

"She is the only person connected with the case who wears glasses."

"However, they are not hers," I said thoughtfully.

"So she affirms."

"You suspicious old devil."

"Not at all, not at all. Probably she spoke the truth. I think she did speak the truth. Otherwise I doubt if she would have noticed the substitution. I did it very adroitly, my friend."

We were strolling through the streets more or less at random. I suggested a taxi, but Poirot shook his head.

"I have need to think, my friend. Walking aids me."

I said no more. The night was a close one and I was in no hurry to return home.

"Were your questions about Paris mere camouflage?" I said curiously.

"Not entirely."

"We still haven't solved the mystery of the initial D," I said thoughtfully. "It's odd that nobody to do with the case has an initial D—either surname or Christian name—except—oh! yes, that's odd—except Donald Ross himself. And he's dead."

"Yes," said Poirot in a sombre voice. "He is dead."

I remembered another evening when three of us had walked at night. Remembered something else, too, and drew my breath sharpyly.

"By Jove, Poirot," I said. "Do you remember?"

"Remember what, my friend?"

"What Ross said about thirteen at table. *And he was the first to get up*."

Poirot did not answer. I felt a little uncomfortable as one always does when superstition is proved justified.

"It is queer," I said in a low voice. "You must admit it is queer."

"Eh?"

"I said it was queer—about Ross and thirteen. Poirot, what are you thinking about?"

To my utter amazement and, I must admit, somewhat to my disgust, Poirot began suddenly to shake with laughter. He shook and he shook. Something was evidently causing him the most exquisite mirth.

"What the devil are you laughing at?" I said sharply.

"Oh! Oh! Oh!" gasped Poirot. "It is nothing. It is that I think of a riddle I hear the other day. I will tell it to you. What is it that has two legs, feathers, and barks like a dog?"

"A chicken, of course," I said wearily. "I knew that in the nursery."

"You are too well-informed, Hastings. You should say, 'I do not know.' And then me, I say, 'A chicken,' and then you say, 'But a chicken does not bark like a dog,' and I say, 'Ah! I put that in to make it more difficult.' Supposing, Hastings, that there we have the explanation of the letter D?"

"What nonsense!"

"Yes, to most people, but to a certain type of mind. Oh! if I had only someone I could ask . . ."

We were passing a big cinema. People were streaming out of it discussing their own affairs, their servants, their friends of the opposite sex, and just occasionally, the picture they had just seen.

With a group of them we crossed the Euston Road.

"I loved it," a girl was sighing. "I think Bryan Martin's just wonderful. I never miss any picture he's in. The way he rode down that cliff and got there in time with the papers."

Her escort was less enthusiastic.

"Idiotic story. If they'd just had the sense to ask Ellis right away, which anyone with sense would have done—"

The rest was lost. Reaching the pavement I turned back to see Poirot standing in the middle of the road with 'buses bearing down on him from either side. Instinctively I put my hands over my eyes. There was a jarring of brakes, and some rich 'bus driver language. In a dignified manner Poirot walked to the kerb. He looked like a man walking in his sleep.

"Poirot," I said. "Were you mad?"

"No, *mon ami*. It was just that—something came to me. There, at that moment."

"A damned bad moment," I said. "And very nearly your last one."

"No matter. Ah! *mon ami*—I have been blind, deaf, insensible. Now I see the answers to all those questions—yes, all five of them. Yes—I see it all. . . . So simple, so childishly simple. . . ."

CHAPTER 28
Poirot Asks a Few Questions

We had a curious walk home.

Poirot was clearly following out some train of thought in his own mind. Occasionally he murmured a word under his breath. I heard one or two of them. Once he said: "Candles," and another time he said something that sounded like "*douzaine*." I suppose if I had been really bright I should have seen the line his thoughts were taking. It was really such a clear trail. However, at the time, it sounded to me mere gibberish.

No sooner were we at home than he flew to the telephone. He rang up the Savoy and asked to speak to Lady Edgware.

"Not a hope, old boy," I said with some amusement.

Poirot, as I have often told him, is one of the worst informed men in the world.

"Don't you know?" I went on. "She's in a new play. She'll be at the theatre. It's only half-past ten."

Poirot paid no attention to me. He was speaking to the hotel clerk who was evidently telling him exactly what I had just told him.

"Ah! is that so? I should like then, to speak to Lady Edgware's maid."

In a few minutes the connection was made.

"Is that Lady Edgware's maid? This is M. Poirot speaking. M. Hercule Poirot. You remember me, do you not?"

". . . . ."

"*Très bien*. Now, you understand, something of importance has arisen. I would like you to come and see me at once."

". . . . ."

"But yes, very important. I will give you the address. Listen carefully."

He repeated it twice, then hung up the receiver with a thoughtful face.

"What is the idea?" I asked curiously. "Have you really got a piece of information?"

"No, Hastings, it is she who will give me the information."

"What information?"

"Information about a certain person."

"Jane Wilkinson?"

"Oh! as to her, I have all the information I need. I know her back side before, as you say."

"Who, then?"

Poirot gave me one of his supremely irritating smiles and told me to wait and see.

He then busied himself in tidying up the room in a fussy manner.

Ten minutes later the maid arrived. She seemed a little nervous and uncertain. A small neat figure dressed in black, she peered about her doubtfully.

Poirot bustled forward.

"Ah! you have come. That is most kind. Sit here, will you not, Mademoiselle—Ellis, I think?"

"Yes, sir. Ellis."

She sat down on the chair Poirot had drawn forward for her.

She sat with her hands folded on her lap looking from one to the other of us. Her small bloodless face was quite composed and her thin lips were pinched together.

"To begin with, Miss Ellis, you have been with Lady Edgware how long?"

"Three years, sir."

"That is as I thought. You know her affairs well."

Ellis did not reply. She looked disapproving.

"What I mean is, you should have a good idea of who her enemies are likely to be."

Ellis compressed her lips more tightly.

"Most women have tried to do her a spiteful turn, sir. Yes, they've all been against her. Nasty jealousy."

"Her own sex did not like her?"

"No, sir. She's too good-looking. And she always gets what she wants. There's a lot of nasty jealousy in the theatrical profession."

"What about men?"

Ellis allowed a sour smile to appear on her withered countenance.

"She can do what she likes with the gentlemen, sir, and that's a fact."

"I agree with you," said Poirot, smiling. "Yet, even allowing that, I can imagine circumstances arising—" He broke off.

Then he said in a different voice:

"You know Mr. Bryan Martin, the film star?"

"Oh! yes, sir."

"Very well?"

"Very well, indeed."

"I believe I am not mistaken in saying that a little less than a year ago, Mr. Bryan Martin was very deeply in love with your mistress."

"Head over ears, sir. And it's 'is,' not 'was,' if you ask me."

"He believed at that time she would marry him—eh?"

"Yes, sir."

"Did she ever seriously consider marrying him?"

"She thought of it, sir. If she could have got her freedom from his lordship, I believe she would have married him."

"And then, I suppose, the Duke of Merton appeared on the scene?"

"Yes, sir. He was doing a tour through the States. Love at first sight it was with him."

"And so good-bye to Bryan Martin's chances?"

Ellis nodded.

"Of course Mr. Martin made an enormous amount of money," she explained. "But the Duke of Merton had position as well. And her ladyship is very keen on position. Married to the Duke, she'd have been one of the first ladies in the land."

The maid's voice held a smug complacency. It amused me.

"So Mr. Bryan Martin was—how do you say—turned down? Did he take it badly?"

"He carried on something awful, sir."

"Ah!"

"He threatened her with a revolver once. And the scenes he made. It frightened me, it did. He was drinking a lot, too. He went all to pieces."

"But in the end he calmed down."

"So it seemed, sir. But he still hung about. And I didn't like the look in his eye. I've warned her ladyship about it, but she only laughed. She's one who enjoys feeling her power, you know what I mean."

"Yes," said Poirot thoughtfully. "I think I know what you mean."

"We've not seen so much of him just lately, sir. A good thing in my opinion. He's beginning to get over it, I hope."

"Perhaps."

Something in Poirot's utterance of the word seemed to strike her. She asked anxiously:

"You don't think she's in danger, sir?"

"Yes," said Poirot gravely. "I think she is in great danger. But she has brought it on herself."

His hand, running aimlessly along the mantelshelf, caught a vase of roses and it toppled over. The water fell on Ellis's face and head. I had seldom known Poirot clumsy, and I could deduce from it that he was in a great state of mental perturbation. He was very upset—rushed for a towel—tenderly assisted the maid to dry her face and neck and was profuse in apologies.

Finally a treasury note exchanged hands and he escorted her towards the door, thanking her for her goodness in coming.

"But it is still early," he said, glancing at the clock. "You will be back before your mistress returns."

"Oh! that is quite all right, sir. She is going out to supper, I think, and anyway, she never expects me to sit up for her unless she says so special."

Suddenly Poirot flew off at a tangent.

"Mademoiselle, pardon me, but you are limping."

"That's nothing, sir. My feet are a little painful."

"The corns?" murmured Poirot in the confidential voice of one sufferer to another.

Corns, apparently, it was. Poirot expatiated upon a certain remedy which, according to him, worked wonders.

Finally Ellis departed.

I was full of curiosity.

"Well, Poirot," I said. "Well?"

He smiled at my eagerness.

"Nothing more this evening, my friend. To-morrow morning, early, we will ring up Japp. We will ask him to come round. We will also ring up Mr. Bryan Martin. I think he will be able to tell us something interesting. Also, I wish to pay him a debt that I owe him."

"Really?"

I looked at Poirot sideways. He was smiling to himself in a curious way.

"At any rate," I said, "you can't suspect *him* of killing Lord Edgware. Especially after what we've heard to-night. That would be playing Jane's game with a vengeance. To kill off the husband so as to let the lady marry someone else is a little too disinterested for any man."

"What profound judgment!"

"Now don't be sarcastic," I said with some annoyance. "And what on earth are you fiddling with all the time?"

Poirot held the object in question up.

"With the pince-nez of the good Ellis, my friend. She left them behind."

"Nonsense, she had them on her nose when she went out."

He shook his head gently.

"Wrong! Absolutely wrong! What she had on, my dear Hastings, were the pair of pince-nez we found in Carlotta Adams' handbag."

I gasped.

CHAPTER 29
Poirot Speaks

It fell to me to ring up Inspector Japp the following morning.

His voice sounded rather depressed.

"Oh! it's you, Captain Hastings. Well, what's in the wind now?"

I gave him Poirot's message.

"Come round at eleven? Well, I dare say I could. He's not got anything to help us over young Ross's death, has he? I don't mind confessing that we could do with something. There's not a clue of any kind. Most mysterious business."

"I think he's got something for you," I said non-committally. "He seems very pleased with himself at all events."

"That's more than I am, I can tell you. All right, Captain Hastings. I'll be there."

My next task was to ring up Bryan Martin. To him I said what I had been told to say: That Poirot had discovered something rather interesting which he thought Mr. Martin would like to hear. When asked what it was, I said that I had no idea. Poirot had not confided in me. There was a pause.

"All right," said Bryan at last. "I'll come."

He rang off.

Presently, somewhat to my surprise, Poirot rang up Jenny Driver and asked her, also, to be present.

He was quiet and rather grave. I asked him no questions.

Bryan Martin was the first to arrive. He looked in good health and spirits, but—or it might have been my fancy—a shade uneasy. Jenny Driver arrived almost immediately afterwards. She seemed surprised to see Bryan, and he seemed to share her surprise.

Poirot brought forward two chairs and urged them to sit down. He glanced at his watch.

"Inspector Japp will be here in one moment, I expect."

"Inspector Japp?" Bryan seemed startled.

"Yes—I have asked him to come here—informally—as a friend."

"I see."

He relapsed into silence. Jenny gave a quick glance at him then glanced away. She seemed rather preoccupied about something this morning.

A moment later, Japp entered the room.

He was, I think, a trifle surprised to find Bryan Martin and Jenny Driver there, but he made no sign. He greeted Poirot with his usual jocularity.

"Well, M. Poirot, what's it all about? You've got some wonderful theory or other, I suppose."

Poirot beamed at him.

"No, no—nothing wonderful. Just a little story quite simple—so simple that I am ashamed not to have seen it at once. I want, if you permit, to take you with me through the case from the beginning."

Japp sighed and looked at his watch.

"If you won't be more than an hour—" he said.

"Reassure yourself," said Poirot. "It will not take as long as that. See here, you want to know, do you now, who it was killed Lord Edgware, who it was killed Miss Adams, who it was killed Donald Ross?"

"I'd like to know the last," said Japp cautiously.

"Listen to me and you shall know everything. See, I am going to be humble." (Not likely! I thought unbelievingly.) "I am going to show you every step of the way—I am going to reveal how I was hoodwinked, how I displayed the gross imbecility, how it needed the conversation of my friend Hastings and a chance remark by a total stranger to put me on the right track."

He paused and then, clearing his throat, he began to speak in what I called his "lecture" voice.

"I will begin at the supper party at the Savoy. Lady Edgware accosted me and asked for a private interview. She wanted to get rid of her husband. At the close of our interview she said—somewhat unwisely, I thought—that she might have to go round in a taxi and kill him herself. Those words were heard by Mr. Bryan Martin, who came in at that moment."

He wheeled round.

"Eh? That is so, is it not?"

"We all heard," said the actor. "The Widburns, Marsh, Carlotta—all of us."

"Oh! I agree. I agree perfectly. *Eh bien,* I did not have a chance to forget those words of Lady Edgware's. Mr. Bryan Martin called on me the following morning for the express purpose of driving those words home."

"Not at all," cried Bryan Martin angrily. "I came—"

Poirot held up a hand.

"You came, ostensibly, to tell me a cock-and-bull story about being shadowed. A tale that a child might have seen through. You probably took it from an out-of-date film. A girl whose consent you had to obtain—a man whom you recognised by a gold tooth. *Mon ami,* no *young* man would have a gold tooth—it is not done in these days—and especially in America. The gold tooth it is a hopelessly old-fashioned piece of dentistry. Oh! it was all of a piece—absurd! Having told your cock-and-bull story you get down to the real purpose of your visit—to poison my mind against Lady Edgware. To put it clearly, you prepare the ground for the moment when she murders her husband."

"I don't know what you're talking about," muttered Bryan Martin. His face was deathly pale.

"You ridicule the idea that he will agree to a divorce! You think I am going to see him the following day, but actually the appointment is changed. I go to see him that morning and he *does* agree to a divorce. Any motive for a crime on Lady Edgware's part is gone. Moreover, he tells me that he has already written to Lady Edgware to that effect.

"But Lady Edgware declares that she never got that letter. Either she lies, her husband lies, or somebody has suppressed it—who?

"Now I ask myself why does M. Bryan Martin give himself the trouble to come and tell me all these lies? What inner power drives him on? And I form the idea, Monsieur, that you have been frantically in love with that lady. Lord Edgware says that his wife told him she wanted to marry an actor. Well, supposing that is so, but that the lady changes her mind. By the time Lord Edgware's letter agreeing to the divorce arrives, it is someone else she wants to marry—not you! There would be a reason, then, for you suppressing that letter."

"I never—"

"Presently you shall say all you want to say. Now you will attend to me.

"What, then, would be your frame of mind—you, a spoilt idol who has never known a rebuff? As I see it, a kind of baffled fury, a desire to do Lady Edgware as much harm as possible. And what greater harm could you do her, than to have her accused—perhaps hanged—for murder."

"Good Lord!" said Japp.

Poirot turned to him.

"But yes, that was the little idea that began to shape itself in my mind. Several things came to support it. Carlotta Adams had two principal men friends—Captain Marsh and Bryan Martin. It was possible, then, that Bryan Martin, a rich man, was the one who suggested the hoax and offered her ten thousand dollars to carry it through. It has seemed to me unlikely all along that Miss Adams could ever have believed Ronald Marsh would have the ten thousand dollars to give her. She knew him to be extremely hard up. Bryan Martin was a far more likely solution."

"I didn't—I tell you I didn't—" came hoarsely from the film actor's lips.

"When the substance of Miss Adams' letter to her sister was wired from Washington—oh! *la, la*! I was very upset. It seemed that my reasoning was wholly wrong. But later I made a discovery. The actual letter itself was sent to me and instead of being continuous, a sheet of the letter was missing. *So 'he' might refer to someone who was not Captain Marsh*.

"There was one more piece of evidence. Captain Marsh, when he was arrested, distinctly stated that he thought he saw Bryan Martin enter the house. Coming from an accused man, that carried no weight. Also M. Martin had an alibi. That naturally! It was to be expected. If M. Martin did the murder, to have an alibi was absolutely necessary.

"That alibi was vouched for by one person only—Miss Driver."

"What about it?" said the girl sharply.

"Nothing, Mademoiselle," said Poirot, smiling. "Except that the same day I noticed you lunching with M. Martin and that you presently took the trouble to come over and try to make me believe that your friend Miss Adams was specially interested in Ronald Marsh—not, as I was sure was the case—in Bryan Martin."

"Not a bit of it," said the film star stoutly.

"You may have been unaware of it, Monsieur," said Poirot quietly, "but I think it was true. It explains, as nothing else could, her feeling of dislike towards Lady Edgware. That dislike was on your behalf. You had told her all about your rebuff, had you not?"

"Well—yes—I felt I must talk to someone and she—"

"Was sympathetic. Yes, she was sympathetic, I noticed it myself. *Eh bien*, what happens next? Ronald Marsh, he is arrested. Immediately your spirits improve. Any anxiety you have had is over. Although your plan has miscarried owing to Lady Edgware's change of mind about going to a party at the last minute, yet somebody else has become the scapegoat and relieved you of all anxiety on your own account. And then—at a luncheon party—you hear Donald Ross, that pleasant, but rather stupid young man, say something to Hastings that seems to show that you are not so safe after all."

"It isn't true," the actor howled. The perspiration was running down his face. His eyes looked wild with terror. "I tell you I heard nothing—nothing—I did nothing."

Then, I think, came the greatest shock of the morning.

"That is quite true," said Poirot quietly. "And I hope you have now been sufficiently punished for coming to me—*me*, Hercule Poirot, with a cock-and-bull story."

We all gasped. Poirot continued dreamily.

"You see—I am showing you all my mistakes. There were five questions I had asked myself. Hastings knows them. The answer to three of them fitted in very well. Who had suppressed that letter? Clearly Bryan Martin answered that question very well. Another question was what had induced Lord Edgware suddenly to change his mind and agree to a divorce? Well, I had an idea as to that. Either he wanted to marry again—but I could find no evidence pointing to that—or else some kind of blackmail was involved. Lord Edgware was a man of peculiar tastes. It was possible that facts about him had come to light which, while not entitling his wife to an English divorce, might yet be used by her as a lever coupled with the threat of publicity. I think that is what happened. Lord Edgware did not want an open scandal attached to his name. He gave in, though his fury at having to do so was expressed in the murderous look on his face when he thought himself unobserved. It also explains the suspicious quickness with which he said, 'Not because of anything in the letter,' before I had even suggested that that might be the case.

"Two questions remained. The question of an odd pair of pince-nez in Miss Adams' bag which did not belong to her. And the question of why Lady Edgware was rung up on the telephone whilst she was at dinner at Chiswick. In no way could I fit in M. Bryan Martin with either of those questions.

"So I was forced to the conclusion that either I was wrong about M. Martin, or wrong about the questions. In despair I once again read that letter of Miss Adams' through very carefully. And I found something! Yes, I found something!

"See for yourselves. Here it is. You see the sheet is torn? Unevenly, as often happens. Supposing now that before the 'h' at the top there was an 's' . . .

"Ah! you have it! You see. Not *he*—but *she*! It was a *woman* who suggested this hoax to Carlotta Adams.

"Well, I made a list of all the women who had been evenly remotely connected with the case. Beside Jane Wilkinson, there were four—Geraldine Marsh, Miss Carroll, Miss Driver and the Duchess of Merton.

"Of those four, the one that interested me most was Miss Carroll. She wore glasses, she was in the house that night, she had already been inaccurate in her evidence owing to her desire to incriminate Lady Edgware, and she was also a woman of great efficiency and nerve who could have carried out such a crime. The motive was more obscure—but after all, she had worked with Lord Edgware some years and some motive might exist of which we were totally unaware.

"I also felt that I could not quite dismiss Geraldine Marsh from the case. She hated her father—she had told me so. She was a neurotic, highly-strung type. Suppose when she went into the house that night she had deliberately stabbed her father and then coolly proceeded upstairs to fetch the pearls. Imagine her agony when she found that her cousin whom she loved devotedly had not remained outside in the taxi but had entered the house!

"Her agitated manner could be well explained on these lines. It could equally well be explained by her own innocence, but by her fear that her cousin really had done the crime. There was another small point. The gold box found in Miss Adams' bag had the initial D in it. I had heard Geraldine addressed by her cousin as 'Dina.' Also, she was in a pensionnat in Paris last November and *might* possibly have met Carlotta Adams in Paris.

"You may think it fantastic to add the Duchess of Merton to the list. But she had called upon me and I recognised in her a fanatical type. The love of her whole life was centred on her son, and she might have worked herself up to contrive a plot to destroy the woman who was about to ruin her son's life.

"Then there was Miss Jenny Driver—"

He paused, looking at Jenny. She looked back at him, an impudent head on one side.

"And what have you got on me?" she asked.

"Nothing, Mademoiselle, except that you were a friend of Bryan Martin's—and that your surname begins with D."

"That's not very much."

"There's one thing more. You have the brains and the nerve to commit such a crime. I doubt if anyone else had."

The girl lit a cigarette.

"Continue," she said cheerfully.

"Was M. Martin's alibi genuine or was it not? That was what I had to decide. If it was, who was it Ronald Marsh had seen go into the house? And suddenly I remembered something. The good-looking butler at Regent Gate bore a very marked resemblance to M. Martin. It was he whom Captain Marsh had seen. And I formed a theory as to that. It is my idea that he discovered his master killed. Beside his master was an envelope containing French banknotes to the value of a hundred pounds. He took these notes, slipped out of the house, left them in safe keeping with some rascally friend and returned, letting himself in with Lord Edgware's key. He let the crime be discovered by the housemaid on the following morning. He felt in no danger himself, as he was quite convinced that Lady Edgware had done the murder, and the notes were out of the house and already changed before their loss was noticed. However, when Lady Edgware had an alibi and Scotland Yard began investigating his antecedents, he got the wind up and decamped."

Japp nodded approvingly.

"I still have the question of the pince-nez to settle. If Miss Carroll was the owner then the case seemed settled. She could have suppressed the letter, and in arranging details with Carlotta Adams, or in meeting her on the evening of the murder, the pince-nez might have inadvertently found their way into Carlotta Adams' bag.

"But the pince-nez were apparently nothing to do with Miss Carroll. I was walking home with Hastings here, somewhat depressed, trying to arrange things in my mind with order and method. And then the miracle happened!

"First Hastings spoke of things in a certain order. He mentioned Donald Ross having been one of thirteen at table at Sir Montagu Corner's and having been the first to get up. I was following out a train of thought of my own and did not pay much attention. It just flashed through my mind that, strictly speaking, that was not true. He may have got up first at the end of the dinner, but actually Lady Edgware had been the first to get up since she was called to the telephone. Thinking of her, a certain riddle occurred to me—a riddle that I fancied accorded well with her somewhat childish mentality. I told it to Hastings. He was, like Queen Victoria, not amused. I next fell to wondering who I could ask for details about M. Martin's feeling for Jane Wilkinson. She herself would not tell me, I knew. And then a passer by, as we were all crossing the road, uttered a simple sentence.

"He said to his girl companion that somebody or other 'should have asked Ellis.' And immediately the whole thing came to me in a flash!"

He looked round.

"Yes, yes, the pince-nez, the telephone call, the short woman who called for the gold box in Paris. *Ellis*, of course, Jane Wilkinson's maid. I followed every step of it—the candles—the dim light—Mrs. Van Dusen—everything. I *knew!*"

CHAPTER 30
The Story

He looked round at us.

"Come, my friends," he said gently. "Let me tell you the real story of what happened that night.

"Carlotta Adams leaves her flat at seven o'clock. From there she takes a taxi and goes to the Piccadilly Palace."

"What?" I exclaimed.

"To the Piccadilly Palace. Earlier in the day she has taken a room there as Mrs. Van Dusen. She wears a pair of strong glasses which, as we all know, alters the appearance very much. As I say, she books a room, saying that she is going by the night boat train to Liverpool and that her luggage has gone on. At eight-thirty Lady Edgware arrives and asks for her. She is shown up to her room. There they change clothes. Dressed in a fair wig, a white taffeta dress and ermine wrap, *Carlotta Adams and not Jane Wilkinson leaves the hotel and drives to Chiswick*. Yes, yes, it is perfectly possible. I have been to the house in the evening. The dinner table is lit only with candles, the lamps are dim, no one there knows Jane Wilkinson very well. There is the golden hair, the well-known husky voice and manner. Oh! it was quite easy. And if it had not been successful—if someone had spotted the fake—well, that was all arranged for, too. Lady Edgware, wearing a dark wig, Carlotta's clothes and the pince-nez, pays her bill, has her suitcase put on a taxi and drives to Euston. She removes the dark wig in the lavatory, she puts her suitcase in the cloakroom. Before going to Regent Gate she rings up Chiswick and asks to speak to Lady Edgware. This has been arranged between them. If all has gone well and Carlotta has not been spotted, she is to answer simply—'that's right.' I need hardly say Miss Adams was ignorant of the real reason for the telephone call. She goes to Regent Gate, asks for Lord Edgware, proclaims her individuality, and goes into the library. *And commits the first murder*. Of course, she did not know that Miss Carroll was watching her from above. As far as she is aware it will be the butler's word (and he has never seen her, remember—and also she wears a hat which shields her from his gaze) against the word of twelve well-known and distinguished people.

"She leaves the house, returns to Euston, changes from fair to dark again and picks up her suitcase. She has now to put in time till Carlotta Adams returns from Chiswick. They have agreed as to the approximate time. She goes to the Corner House, occasionally glancing at her watch, for the time passes slowly. Then she prepares for the second murder. She puts the small gold box she has ordered from Paris in Carlotta Adams' bag which, of course, she is carrying. Perhaps it is then she finds the letter. Perhaps it was earlier. Anyway, as soon as she sees the address, she scents danger. She opens it—her suspicions are justified.

"Perhaps her first impulse is to destroy the letter altogether. But she soon sees a better way. By removing one page of the letter it reads like an accusation of Ronald Marsh—a man who had a powerful motive for the crime. Even if Ronald has an alibi, it will still read as an accusation of a man so long as she tears off the s of 'she.' So that is what she does, then replaces it in the envelope and the envelope back in the bag.

"Then, the time having come, she walks in the direction of the Savoy Hotel. As soon as she sees the car pass, with (presumably) herself inside, she quickens her pace, enters at the same time and goes straight up the stairs. She is inconspicuously dressed in black. It is unlikely that anyone will notice her.

"Upstairs she goes to her room. Carlotta Adams has just reached it. The maid has been told to go to bed—a perfectly usual proceeding. They again change clothes and then, I fancy, Lady Edgware suggests a little drink—to celebrate. In that drink is the veronal. She congratulates her victim, says she will send her the cheque to-morrow. Carlotta Adams goes home. She is very sleepy—tries to ring up a friend—possibly M. Martin or Captain Marsh, for both have Victoria numbers—but gives it up. She is too tired. The veronal is beginning to work. She goes to bed —*and she never wakes again*. The second crime has been carried through successfully.

"Now for the third crime. It is at a luncheon party. Sir Montagu Corner makes a reference to a conversation he had with Lady Edgware on the night of the murder. That is easy. She has only to murmur some flattering phrase. But Nemesis comes upon her later. There is a mention of the 'judgment of Paris,' and she takes Paris to be the only Paris she knows—the Paris of fashions and frills!

"But opposite her is sitting a young man who was at that dinner at Chiswick—a young man who heard the Lady Edgware of that night discussing Homer and Greek civilisation generally. Carlotta Adams was a cultured well-read girl. He cannot understand. He stares. And suddenly it comes to him. *This is not the same woman*. He is terribly upset. He is not sure of himself. He must have advice. He thinks of me. He speaks to Hastings.

"But the lady overheard him. She is quick enough and shrewd enough to realise that in some way or other she has given herself away. She hears Hastings say that I will not be in till five. At twenty to five she goes to Ross's maisonette. He opens the door, is very surprised to see her, but it does not occur to him to be afraid. A strong able-bodied young man is not afraid of a woman. He goes with her into the dining-room. She pours out some story to him. Perhaps she goes on her knees and flings her arms round his neck. And then, swift and sure, she strikes—as before. Perhaps he gives a choked cry—no more. He, too, is silenced."

There was a silence. Then Japp spoke hoarsely.

"You mean—she did it all the time?"

Poirot bowed his head.

"But why, if he was willing to give her a divorce?"

"Because the Duke of Merton is a pillar of the Anglo-Catholics. Because he would not dream of marrying a woman whose husband was alive. He is a young man of fanatical principles. As a widow, she was pretty certain to be able to marry him. Doubtless she had tentatively suggested divorce, but he had not risen to the bait."

"Then why send you to Lord Edgware?"

"*Ah! parbleu.*" Poirot, from having been very correct and English, suddenly relapsed into his native self. "To pull cotton-wool over my eyes! To make me a witness to the fact that there was no motive for the murder! Yes, she dared to make me, Hercule Poirot, her catspaw! *Ma foi,* she succeeded, too! Oh! that strange brain, childlike and cunning. She can act! How well she acted surprise at being told of the letter her husband had written her which she swore she had never received. Did she feel the slightest pang of remorse for any of her three crimes? I can swear she did not."

"I told you what she was like," cried Bryan Martin. "I told you. I knew she was going to kill him. I felt it. And I was afraid that somehow she'd get away with it. She's clever—devilish clever in a kind of half-wit way. And I wanted her to suffer. I wanted her to suffer. I wanted her to hang for it."

His face was scarlet. His voice came thickly.

"Now, now," said Jenny Driver.

She spoke exactly as I have heard nursemaids speak to a small child in the park.

"And the gold box with the initial D, and Paris November inside?" said Japp.

"She ordered that by letter and sent Ellis, her maid, to fetch it. She had no idea what was inside. Also, Lady Edgware borrowed a pair of Ellis's pince-nez to help in the Van Dusen impersonation. She forgot about them and left them in Carlotta Adams' handbag—her one mistake.

"Oh! it came to me—it all came to me as I stood in the middle of the road. It was not polite what the 'bus driver said to me, but it was worth it. Ellis! Ellis's pince-nez. Ellis calling for the box in Paris. Ellis and therefore Jane Wilkinson. Very possibly she borrowed something else from Ellis besides des pince-nez."

"What?"

"A corn knife. . . ."

I shivered.

There was a momentary silence.

Then Japp said with a strange reliance in the answer:

"M. Poirot. Is this *true*?"

"It is true, *mon ami*."

Then Bryan Martin spoke, and his words were, I thought, very typical of him.

"But look here," he said peevishly. "What about *me*? Why bring *me* here to-day? Why nearly frighten me to death?"

Poirot looked at him coldly.

"To punish you, Monsieur, for being impertinent! How dare you try and make the games with Hercule Poirot?"

And then Jenny Driver laughed. She laughed and laughed.

"Serves you right, Bryan," she said at last.

She turned to Poirot.

"I'm glad as I can be that it wasn't Ronnie Marsh," she said. "I've always liked him. And I'm glad, glad, *glad* that Carlotta's death won't go unpunished! As for Bryan here, well, I'll tell you something, M. Poirot. I'm going to marry him. And if he thinks he can get divorced and married every two or three years in the approved Hollywood fashion, well, he never made a bigger mistake in his life. He's going to marry me and stick to me."

Poirot looked at her—looked at her determined chin—and at her flaming hair.

"It is very possible, Mademoiselle," he said, "that that may be so. I said that you had sufficient nerve for anything. Even to marry a film 'star.'"

CHAPTER 31
A Human Document

A day or two after that I was suddenly recalled to the Argentine. So it happened that I never saw Jane Wilkinson again and only read in the paper of her trial and condemnation. Unexpectedly, at least unexpectedly to me, she went completely to pieces when charged with the truth. So long as she was able to be proud of her cleverness and act her part she made no mistakes, but once her self-confidence failed her, owing to someone having found her out, she was as incapable as a child would be of keeping up a deception. Cross-examined, she went completely to pieces.

So, as I said before, that luncheon party was the last time I saw Jane Wilkinson. But when I think of her, I always see her the same way—standing in her room at the Savoy trying on expensive black clothes with a serious absorbed face. I am convinced that that was no pose. She was being completely natural. Her plan had succeeded and therefore she had no further qualms and doubts. Neither do I think that she ever suffered one pang of remorse for the three crimes she had committed.

I reproduce here a document which she had directed was to be sent to Poirot after her death. It is, I think, typical of that very lovely and completely conscienceless lady.

> "DEAR M. POIROT,—I have been thinking things over and I feel that I should like to write this for you. I know that you sometimes publish reports of your cases. I don't really think that you've ever published a document by the person themselves. I feel, too, that I would like everyone to know just exactly how I did it all. I still think it was all very well planned. If it hadn't been for you everything would have been quite all right. I've felt rather bitter about that, but I suppose you couldn't help it. I'm sure, if I send you this, you'll give it plenty of prominence. You will, won't you? I should like to be remembered. And I do think I am really a unique person. Everybody here seems to think so.
>
> "It began in America when I got to know Merton, I saw at once that if only I were a widow he would marry me. Unfortunately, he has got a queer sort of prejudice against divorce. I tried to overcome it but it was no good, and I had to be careful, because he was a very kinky sort of person.
>
> "I soon realised that my husband simply had got to die, but I didn't know how to set about it. You can manage things like that ever so much better in the States. I thought and I thought—but I couldn't see how to arrange it. And then, suddenly, I saw Carlotta Adams do her imitation of me and at once I began to see a way. With her help I could get an alibi. That same evening I saw you, and it suddenly struck me that it would be a good idea

to send you to my husband to ask him for a divorce. At the same time I would go about talking of killing my husband, because I've always noticed that if you speak the truth in a rather silly way nobody believes you. I've often done it over contracts. And it's also a good thing to seem stupider than you are. At my second meeting with Carlotta Adams I broached the idea. I said it was a bet—and she fell for it at once. She was to pretend to be me at some party and if she got away with it she was to have ten thousand dollars. She was very enthusiastic and several of the ideas were hers—about changing clothes and all that. You see, we couldn't do it here because of Ellis and we couldn't do it at her place because of her maid. She, of course, didn't see why we couldn't. It was a little awkward. I just said 'No.' She thought me a little stupid about it, but she gave in and we thought of the hotel plan. I took a pair of Ellis's pince-nez.

"Of course I realised quite soon that she would have to be got out of the way too. It was a pity, but after all those imitations of hers really were very impertinent. If mine hadn't happened to suit me I'd have been angry about it. I had some veronal myself, though I hardly ever take it, so that was quite easy. And then I had quite a brainwave. You see, it would be so much better if it could seem that she was in the habit of taking it. I ordered a box—the duplicate of one I'd been given and I had her initials put on it and an inscription inside. I thought if I put some odd initial and Paris, November, inside it, it would make it all much more difficult. I wrote for the box from the Ritz when I was in there lunching one day. And I sent Ellis over to fetch it. She didn't know what it was, of course.

"Everything went off quite well on the night. I took one of Ellis's corn knives, while she was over in Paris, because it was nice and sharp. She never noticed because I put it back afterwards. It was a doctor in San Francisco who showed me just where to stick it in. He'd been talking about lumbar and cistern punctures, and he said one had to be very careful, otherwise one went through the cistertia magna and into the medulla oblongata where all the vital nerve centres are, and that that would cause immediate death. I made him show me the exact place several times. I thought it might perhaps come in useful one day. I told him I wanted to use the idea in a film.

"It was very dishonourable of Carlotta Adams to write to her sister. She'd promised me to tell nobody. I do think it was clever of me to see what a good thing it would be to tear off that one page and leave he instead of she. I thought of that all by myself. I think I'm more proud of that than anything else. Everyone always says I haven't got brains—but I think it needed real brains to think of that.

"I'd thought things out very carefully and I did exactly what I'd planned when the Scotland Yard man came. I rather enjoyed that part of it. I had thought, perhaps, that he'd really arrest me. I felt quite safe, because they'd have to believe all those people at the dinner and I didn't see how they could find out about me and Carlotta changing clothes.

"After that I felt so happy and contented. My luck had held and I really felt everything was going to go right. The old Duchess was beastly to me, but Merton was sweet. He wanted to marry me as soon as possible and hadn't the least suspicion.

"I don't think I've ever been so happy as I was those few weeks. My husband's nephew being arrested made me feel just as safe as anything. And I was more proud of myself than ever for having thought of tearing that page out of Carlotta Adams' letter.

"The Donald Ross business was just sheer bad luck. I'm not quite sure now just how it was he spotted me. Something about Paris being a person and not a place. Even now I don't know who Paris was—and I think it's a silly name for a man anyway.

"It's curious how, when luck starts going against you, it keeps on going. I had to do something about Donald Ross quickly, and that did go all right. It mightn't have because I hadn't time to be clever or think of making an alibi. I did think I was safe after that.

"Of course Ellis told me you had sent for her and questioned her, but I gathered it was all something to do with Bryan Martin. I couldn't think what you were driving at. You didn't ask her whether she had called for the parcel in Paris. I suppose you thought if she repeated that to me I should smell a rat. As it was, it came as a complete surprise. I couldn't believe it. It was just uncanny the way you seemed to know everything I'd done.

"I just felt it was no good. You can't fight against luck. It *was* bad luck, wasn't it? I wonder if you are ever sorry for what you did. After all, I only wanted to be happy in my own way. And if it hadn't been for me you would never have had anything to do with the case. I never thought you'd be so horribly clever. You didn't look clever.

"It's funny, but I haven't lost my looks a bit. In spite of all that dreadful trial and the horrid things that man on the other side said to me, and the way he battered me with questions.

"I look much paler and thinner, but it suits me somehow. They all say I'm wonderfully brave. They don't hang you in public any more, do they? I think that's a pity.

"I'm sure there's never been a murderess like me before.

"I suppose I must say good-bye now. It's very queer. I don't seem to realise things a bit. I'm going to see the chaplain to-morrow.

"Yours forgivingly (because I must forgive my enemies, mustn't I?),

"JANE WILKINSON.

"P.S.—Do you think they will put me in Madame Tussauds?"

MURDER ON THE ORIENT EXPRESS

To M.E.L.M.
Arpachiyah, 1933

CONTENTS

Part One
THE FACTS

Part Two
THE EVIDENCE

Part Three
HERCULE POIROT SITS BACK AND THINKS

PART ONE
THE FACTS

CHAPTER 1
An Important Passenger on the Taurus Express

It was five o'clock on a winter's morning in Syria. Alongside the platform at Aleppo stood the train grandly designated in railway guides as the Taurus Express. It consisted of a kitchen and dining-car, a sleeping-car and two local coaches.

By the step leading up into the sleeping-car stood a young French lieutenant, resplendent in uniform, conversing with a small man, muffled up to the ears, of whom nothing was visible but a pink-tipped nose and the two points of an upward curled moustache.

It was freezingly cold, and this job of seeing off a distinguished stranger was not one to be envied, but Lieutenant Dubosc performed his part manfully. Graceful phrases fell from his lips in polished French. Not that he knew what it was all about. There had been rumours, of course, as there always were in such cases. The General—*his* General's—temper had grown worse and worse. And then there had come this Belgian stranger—all the way from England, it seemed. There had been a week—a week of curious tensity. And then certain things had happened. A very distinguished officer had committed suicide, another had resigned—anxious faces had suddenly lost their anxiety, certain military precautions were relaxed. And the General—Lieutenant Dubosc's own particular General—had suddenly looked ten years younger.

Dubosc had overheard part of a conversation between him and the stranger. "You have saved us, *mon cher*," said the General emotionally, his great white moustache trembling as he spoke. "You have saved the honour of the French Army—you have averted much bloodshed! How can I thank you for acceding to my request? To have come so far—"

To which the stranger (by name M. Hercule Poirot) had made a fitting reply including the phrase, "But indeed do I not remember that once you saved my life?" And then the General had made another fitting reply to that disclaiming any merit for that past service, and with more mention of France, of Belgium, of glory, of honour and of such kindred things they had embraced each other heartily and the conversation had ended.

As to what it had all been about, Lieutenant Dubosc was still in the dark, but to him had been delegated the duty of seeing off M. Poirot by the Taurus Express, and he was carrying it out with all the zeal and ardour befitting a young officer with a promising career ahead of him.

"Today is Sunday," said Lieutenant Dubosc. "Tomorrow, Monday evening, you will be in Stamboul."

It was not the first time he had made this observation. Conversations on the platform, before the departure of a train, are apt to be somewhat repetitive in character.

"That is so," agreed M. Poirot.

"And you intend to remain there a few days, I think?"

"*Mais oui*. Stamboul, it is a city I have never visited. It would be a pity to pass through—*comme ça*." He snapped his fingers descriptively. "Nothing presses—I shall remain there as a tourist for a few days."

"La Sainte Sophie, it is very fine," said Lieutenant Dubosc, who had never seen it.

A cold wind came whistling down the platform. Both men shivered. Lieutenant Dubosc managed to cast a surreptitious glance at his watch. Five minutes to five—only five minutes more!

Fancying that the other man had noticed his surreptitious glance, he hastened once more into speech.

"There are few people traveling this time of year," he said, glancing up at the windows of the sleeping-car above them.

"That is so," agreed M. Poirot.

"Let us hope you will not be snowed up in the Taurus!"

"That happens?"

"It has occurred, yes. Not this year, as yet."

"Let us hope, then," said M. Poirot. "The weather reports from Europe, they are bad."

"Very bad. In the Balkans there is much snow."

"In Germany too, I have heard."

"*Eh bien*," said Lieutenant Dubosc hastily as another pause seemed to be about to occur. "Tomorrow evening at seven-forty you will be in Constantinople."

"Yes," said M. Poirot, and went on desperately, "La Sainte Sophie, I have heard it is very fine."

"Magnificent, I believe."

Above their heads the blind of one of the sleeping car compartments was pushed aside and a young woman looked out.

Mary Debenham had had little sleep since she left Baghdad on the preceding Thursday. Neither in the train to Kirkuk, nor in the Rest House at Mosul, nor last night on the train had she slept properly. Now, weary of lying wakeful in the hot stuffiness of her overheated compartment, she got up and peered out.

This must be Aleppo. Nothing to see, of course. Just a long, poor-lighted platform with loud furious altercations in Arabic going on somewhere. Two men below her window were talking French. One was a French officer, the other was a little man with enormous moustaches. She smiled faintly. She had never seen anyone quite so heavily muffled up. It must be very cold outside. That was why they heated the train so terribly. She tried to force the window down lower, but it would not go.

The Wagon Lit conductor had come up to the two men. The train was about to depart, he said. Monsieur had better mount. The little man removed his hat. What an egg-shaped head he had. In spite of her preoccupations Mary Debenham smiled. A ridiculous-looking little man. The sort of little man one could never take seriously.

Lieutenant Dubosc was saying his parting speech. He had thought it out beforehand and had kept it till the last minute. It was a beautiful, polished speech.

Not to be outdone, M. Poirot replied in kind.

"En voiture, Monsieur," said the Wagon Lit conductor.

With an air of infinite reluctance M. Poirot climbed aboard the train. The conductor climbed after him. M. Poirot waved his hand. Lieutenant Dubosc came to the salute. The train, with a terrific jerk, moved slowly forward.

"Enfin!" murmured M. Hercule Poirot.

"Brrrrr," said Lieutenant Dubosc, realising to the full how cold he was. . . .

"Voila, Monsieur." The conductor displayed to Poirot with a dramatic gesture the beauty of his sleeping compartment and the neat arrangement of his luggage. "The little valise of Monsieur, I have placed it *here*."

His outstretched hand was suggestive. Hercule Poirot placed in it a folded note.

"Merci, Monsieur." The conductor became brisk and businesslike. "I have the tickets of Monsieur. I will also take the passport, please. Monsieur breaks his journey in Stamboul, I understand?"

M. Poirot assented.

"There are not many people traveling, I imagine?" he said.

"No, Monsieur. I have only two other passengers—both English. A Colonel from India, and a young English lady from Baghdad. Monsieur requires anything?"

Monsieur demanded a small bottle of Perrier.

Five o'clock in the morning is an awkward time to board a train. There were still two hours before dawn. Conscious of an inadequate night's sleep, and of a delicate mission successfully accomplished, M. Poirot curled up in a corner and fell asleep.

When he awoke it was half-past nine, and he sallied forth to the restaurant-car in search of hot coffee.

There was only one occupant at the moment, obviously the young English lady referred to by the conductor. She was tall, slim and dark—perhaps twenty-eight years of age. There was a kind of cool efficiency in the way she was eating her breakfast and in the way she called to the attendant to bring her more coffee, which bespoke a knowledge of the world and of traveling. She wore a dark-coloured traveling dress of some thin material eminently suitable for the heated atmosphere of the train.

M. Hercule Poirot, having nothing better to do, amused himself by studying her without appearing to do so.

She was, he judged, the kind of young woman who could take care of herself with perfect ease wherever she went. She had poise and efficiency. He rather liked the severe regularity of her features and the delicate pallor of her skin. He liked the burnished black head with its neat waves of hair, and her eyes, cool, impersonal and grey. But she was, he decided, just a little too efficient to be what he called *"jolie femme."*

Presently another person entered the restaurant-car. This was a tall man of between forty and fifty, lean of figure, brown of skin, with hair slightly grizzled round the temples.

"The colonel from India," said Poirot to himself.

The newcomer gave a little bow to the girl.

"Morning, Miss Debenham.

"Good-morning, Colonel Arbuthnot."

The Colonel was standing with a hand on the chair opposite her.

"Any objection?" He asked.

"Of course not. Sit down."

"Well, you know, breakfast isn't always a chatty meal."

"I should hope not. But I don't bite."

The Colonel sat down.

"Boy," he called in peremptory fashion.

He gave an order for eggs and coffee.

His eyes rested for a moment on Hercule Poirot, but they passed on indifferently. Poirot, reading the English mind correctly, knew that he had said to himself, "Only some damned foreigner."

True to their nationality, the two English people were not chatty. They exchanged a few brief remarks, and presently the girl rose and went back to her compartment.

At lunch time the other two again shared a table and again they both completely ignored the third passenger. Their conversation was more animated than at breakfast. Colonel Arbuthnot talked of the Punjab, and occasionally asked the girl a few questions about Baghdad where it became clear that she had been in a post as governess. In the course of conversation they discovered some mutual friends which had the immediate effect of making them more friendly and less stiff. They discussed old Tommy Somebody and Jerry Someone Else. The Colonel imquired whether she was going straight through to England or whether she was stopping in Stamboul.

"No, I'm going straight on."

"Isn't that rather a pity?"

"I came out this way two years ago and spent three days in Stamboul then."

"Oh, I see. Well, I may say I'm very glad you are going right through, because I am."

He made a kind of clumsy little bow, flushing a little as he did so.

"He is susceptible, our Colonel," thought Hercule Poirot to himself with some amusement. "The train, it is as dangerous as a sea voyage!"

Miss Debenham said evenly that that would be very nice. Her manner was slightly repressive.

The Colonel, Hercule Poirot noticed, accompanied her back to her compartment. Later they passed through the magnificent scenery of the Taurus. As they looked down toward the Cilician Gates, standing in the corridor side by side, a sigh came suddenly from the girl. Poirot was standing near them and heard her murmur:

"It's so beautiful! I wish—I wish——"

"Yes?"

"I wish I could enjoy it!"

Arbuthnot did not answer. The square line of his jaw seemed a little sterner and grimmer.

"I wish to Heaven you were out of all this," he said.

"Hush, please. Hush."

"Oh! it's all right." He shot a slightly annoyed glance in Poirot's direction. Then he went on. "But I don't like the idea of your being a governess—at the beck and call of tyrannical mothers and their tiresome brats."

She laughed with just a hint of uncontrol in the sound.

"Oh! you mustn't think that. The downtrodden governess is quite an exploded myth. I can assure you that it's the parents who are afraid of being bullied by *me*."

They said no more. Arbuthnot was, perhaps, ashamed of his outburst.

"Rather an odd little comedy that I watch here," said Poirot to himself thoughtfully.

He was to remember that thought of his later.

They arrived at Konya that night about half-past eleven. The two English travelers got out to stretch their legs, pacing up and down the snowy platform.

M. Poirot was content to watch the teeming activity of the station through a window pane. After about ten minutes, however, he decided that a breath of air would not perhaps be a bad thing, after all. He made careful preparations, wrapping himself in several coats and mufflers and encasing his neat boots in goloshes. Thus attired he descended gingerly to the platform and began to pace its length. He walked out beyond the engine.

It was the voices which gave him the clue to the two indistinct figures standing in the shadow of a traffic van. Arbuthnot was speaking.

"Mary——"

The girl interrupted him.

"Not now. Not now. When it's all over. When it's behind us—*then*——"

Discreetly M. Poirot turned away. He wondered.

He would hardly have recognised the cool, efficient voice of Miss Debenham. . . .

"Curious," he said to himself.

The next day he wondered whether, perhaps, they had quarreled. They spoke little to each other. The girl, he thought, looked anxious. There were dark circles under her eyes.

It was about half-past two in the afternoon when the train came to a halt. Heads were poked out of windows. A little knot of men were clustered by the side of the line looking and pointing at something under the dining-car.

Poirot leaned out and spoke to the Wagon Lit conductor who was hurrying past. The man answered and Poirot drew back his head and, turning, almost collided with Mary Debenham who was standing just behind him.

"What is the matter?" she asked rather breathlessly in French. "Why are we stopping?"

"It is nothing, Mademoiselle. It is something that has caught fire under the dining-car. Nothing serious. It is put out. They are now repairing the damage. There is no danger, I assure you."

She made a little abrupt gesture, as though she were waving the idea of danger aside as something completely unimportant.

"Yes, yes, I understand that. But the *time!*"

"The time?"

"Yes, this will delay us."

"It is possible—yes," agreed Poirot.

"But we can't afford delay! The train is due in at 6.55 and one has to cross the Bosphorus and catch the Simplon Orient Express the other side at nine o'clock. If there is an hour or two of delay we shall miss the connection."

"It is possible, yes," he admitted.

He looked at her curiously. The hand that held the window bar was not quite steady, her lips too were trembling.

"Does it matter to you very much, Mademoiselle?" he asked.

"Yes. Yes, it does. I—I must catch that train."

She turned away from him and went down the corridor to join Colonel Arbuthnot.

Her anxiety, however, was needless. Ten minutes later the train started again.

It arrived at Haydapassar only five minutes late, having made up time on the journey.

The Bosphorus was rough and M. Poirot did not enjoy the crossing. He was separated from his traveling companions on the boat, and did not see them again.

On arrival at the Galata Bridge he drove straight to the Tokatlian Hotel.

CHAPTER 2
The Tokatlian Hotel

At the Tokatlian, Hercule Poirot asked for a room with bath. Then he stepped over to the concierge's desk and inquired for letters.

There were three waiting for him and a telegram. His eyebrows rose a little at the sight of the telegram. It was unexpected.

He opened it in his usual neat, unhurried fashion. The printed words stood out clearly.

Development you predicted in Kassner Case has come unexpectedly please return immediately.

"*Voilà ce qui est embêtant,*" murmured Poirot vexedly. He glanced up at the clock.

"I shall have to go on to-night," he said to the concierge. "At what time does the Simplon Orient leave?"

"At nine o'clock, Monsieur."

"Can you get me a sleeper?"

"Assuredly, Monsieur. There is no difficulty this time of year. The trains are almost empty. First-class or second?"

"First."

"*Très bien, Monsieur*. How far are you going?"

"To London."

"*Bien, Monsieur*. I will get you a ticket to London and reserve your sleeping-car accommodation in the Stamboul-Calais coach."

Poirot glanced at the clock again. It was ten minutes to eight.

"I have time to dine?"

"But assuredly, Monsieur."

The little Belgian nodded. He went over and canceled his room order and crossed the hall to the restaurant.

As he was giving his order to the waiter a hand was placed on his shoulder.

"Ah! *mon vieux*, but this is an unexpected pleasure," said a voice behind him.

The speaker was a short, stout elderly man, his hair cut *en brosse*. He was smiling delightedly.

Poirot sprang up.

"M. Bouc."

"M. Poirot."

M. Bouc was a Belgian, a director of the Compagnie Internationale des

Wagons Lits, and his acquaintance with the former star of the Belgian Police Force dated back many years.

"You find yourself far from home, *mon cher,*" said M. Bouc.

"A little affair in Syria."

"Ah! And you return home—when?"

"To-night."

"Splendid! I, too. That is to say, I go as far as Lausanne, where I have affairs. You travel on the Simplon-Orient, I presume?"

"Yes. I have just asked them to get me a sleeper. It was my intention to remain here some days, but I have received a telegram recalling me to England on important business."

"Ah!" sighed M. Bouc. *"les affaires—les affaires!* But you—you are at the top of the tree nowadays, *mon vieux!"*

"Some little success I have had, perhaps." Hercule Poirot tried to look modest but failed signally.

Bouc laughed.

"We will meet later," he said.

Hercule Poirot addressed himself to the task of keeping his moustaches out of the soup.

That difficult task accomplished, he glanced round him whilst waiting for the next course. There were only about half a dozen people in the restaurant, and of those half-dozen there were only two that interested Hercule Poirot.

These two sat a table not far away. The younger was a likeable-looking young man of thirty, clearly an American. It was, however, not he but his companion who had attracted the little detective's attention.

He was a man of between sixty and seventy. From a little distance he had the bland aspect of a philanthropist. His slightly bald head, his domed forehead, the smiling mouth that displayed a very white set of false teeth, all seemed to speak of a benevolent personality. Only the eyes belied this assumption. They were small, deep set and crafty. Not only that. As the man, making some remark to his young companion, glanced across the room, his gaze stopped on Poirot for a moment, and just for that second there was a strange malevolence, an unnatural tensity in the glance.

Then he rose.

"Pay the bill, Hector," he said.

His voice was slightly husky in tone. It had a queer, soft, dangerous quality.

When Poirot rejoined his friend in the lounge, the other two men were just leaving the hotel. Their luggage was being brought down. The younger was supervising the process. Presently he opened the glass door and said:

"Quite ready now, Mr. Ratchett."

The elder man grunted an assent and passed out.

"Eh bien," said Poirot. "What do you think of those two?"

"They are American," said M. Bouc.

"Assuredly they are Americans. I meant what did you think of their personalities?"

"The young man seemed quite agreeable."

"And the other?"

"To tell you the truth, my friend, I did not care for him. He produced on me an unpleasant impression. And you?"

Hercule Poirot was a moment before replying.

"When he passed me in the restaurant," he said at last, "I had a curious impression. It was as though a wild animal—an animal savage, but savage! you understand—had passed me by."

"And yet he looked altogether of the most respectable."

"*Précisément!* The body—the cage—is everything of the most respectable—but through the bars, the wild animal looks out."

"You are fanciful, *mon vieux,*" said M. Bouc.

"It may be so. But I could not rid myself of the impression that evil had passed me by very close."

"That respectable American gentleman?"

"That respectable American gentleman."

"Well," said M. Bouc cheerfully. "It may be so. There is much evil in the world."

At that moment the door opened and the concierge came toward them. He looked concerned and apologetic.

"It is extraordinary, Monsieur," he said to Poirot. "There is not one first-class sleeping berth to be had on the train."

"*Comment?*" cried M. Bouc. "At this time of year? Ah, without doubt there is some party of journalists—of politicians——?"

I don't know, sir," said the concierge, turning to him respectfully. "But that's how it is."

"Well, well," M. Bouc turned to Poirot. "Have no fear, my friend. We will arrange something. There is always one compartment—the No. 16, which is not engaged. The conductor sees to that!" He smiled, then glanced up at the clock. "Come," he said, "it is time we started."

At the station M. Bouc was greeted with respectful empressement by the brown-uniformed Wagon Lit conductor.

"Good-evening, Monsieur. Your compartment is the No. I."

He called to the porters and they wheeled their load half-way along the carriage on which the tin plates proclaimed its destination:

ISTANBUL TRIESTE CALAIS

"You are full up tonight, I hear?"

"It is incredible, Monsieur. All the world elects to travel tonight!"

"All the same, you must find room for this gentleman here. He is a friend of mine. He can have the No. 16."

"It is taken, Monsieur."

"What? The No. 16?"

A glance of understanding passed between them, and the conductor smiled. He was a tall, sallow man of middle age.

"But yes, Monsieur. As I told you, we are full—full—everywhere."

"But what passes itself?" demanded M. Bouc angrily. "There is a conference somewhere? It is a party?"

"No, Monsieur. It is only chance. It just happens that many people have elected to travel tonight."

M. Bouc made a clicking sound of annoyance.

"At Belgrade," he said, "There will be the slip coach from Athens. There will also be the Bucharest-Paris coach—but we do not reach Belgrade until tomorrow evening. The problem is for tonight. There is no second-class berth free?"

"There *is* a second class berth, Monsieur—"

"Well, then—"

"But it is a lady's berth. There is already a German woman in the compartment—a lady's-maid."

"*Là, là*, that is awkward," said M. Bouc.

"Do not distress yourself, my friend," said Poirot. "I must travel in an ordinary carriage."

"Not at all. Not at all." He turned once more to the conductor. "Everyone has arrived?"

"It is true," said the man, "that there is one passenger who has not yet arrived."

He spoke slowly with hesitation.

"But speak then?"

"No. 7 berth—a second-class. The gentleman has not yet come, and it is four minutes to nine."

"Who is it?"

"An Englishman," the conductor consulted his list. "A M. Harris."

"A name of good omen," said Poirot. "I read my Dickens. M. Harris, he will not arrive."

"Put Monsieur's luggage in No. 7," said M. Bouc. "If this M. Harris arrives we will tell him that he is too late—that berths cannot be retained so long—we will arrange the matter one way or another. What do I care for a M. Harris?"

"As Monsieur pleases," said the conductor.

He spoke to Poirot's porter, directing him where to go. Then he stood aside the steps to let Poirot enter the train.

"*Tout à fait au bout, Monsieur*," he called. "The end compartment but one."

Poirot passed along the corridor, a somewhat slow progress, as most of the people traveling were standing beside their carriages.

His polite "*Pardons*" were uttered with the regularity of clockwork. At last he reached the compartment indicated. Inside it, reaching up to a suit-case, was the tall young American of the Tokatlian.

He frowned as Poirot entered.

"Excuse me," he said. "I think you've made a mistake." Then, laboriously in French, "*Je crois que vous avez un erreur*."

Poirot replied in English.

"You are Mr. Harris?"

"No, my name is MacQueen. I——"

But at that moment the voice of the Wagon Lit conductor spoke from over Poirot's shoulder. An apologetic, rather breathless voice.

"There is no other berth on the train, Monsieur. The gentleman has to come in here."

He was hauling up the corridor window as he spoke and began to lift in Poirot's luggage.

Poirot noticed the apology in his tone with some amusement. Doubtless the man had been promised a good tip if he could keep the compartment for the sole use of the other traveler. However, even the most munificent of tips lose their effect when a director of the company is on board and issues his orders.

The conductor emerged from the compartment, having swung the suit-cases up on to the racks.

"*Voilà Monsieur*," he said. "All is arranged. Yours is the upper berth, the number 7. We start in one minute."

He hurried off down the corridor. Poirot reentered the compartment.

"A phenomenon I have seldom seen," he said cheerfully. "A Wagon Lit conductor himself puts up the luggage! It is unheard of!"

His fellow traveler smiled. He had evidently got over his annoyance—had probably decided that it was no good to take the matter other than philosophically.

"The train's remarkably full," he said.

A whistle blew, there was a long, melancholy cry from the engine. Both men stepped out into the corridor.

Outside a voice shouted.

"*En voiture*."

"We're off," said MacQueen.

But they were not quite off. The whistle blew again.

"I say, sir," said the young man suddenly, "if you'd rather have the lower berth—easier, and all that—well, that's all right by me."

A likeable young fellow.

"No, no," protested Poirot. "I would not deprive you——"

"That's all right——"

"You are too amiable——"

Polite protests on both sides.

"It is for one night only," explained Poirot. "At Belgrade——"

"Oh, I see. You're getting out at Belgrade——"

"Not exactly. You see——"

There was a sudden jerk. Both men swung round to the window, looking out at the long, lighted platform as it slid slowly past them.

The Orient Express had started on its three-days' journey across Europe.

CHAPTER 3
Poirot Refuses a Case

M. Hercule Poirot was a little late in entering the luncheon-car on the following day. He had risen early, breakfasted almost alone, and had spent the morning going over the notes of the case that was recalling him to London. He had seen little of his traveling companion.

M. Bouc, who was already seated, gesticulated a greeting and summoned his friend to the empty place opposite him. Poirot sat down and soon found himself in the favoured position of the table which was served first and with the choicest morsels. The food, too, was unusually good.

It was not till they were eating a delicate cream cheese that M. Bouc allowed his attention to wander to matters other than nourishment. He was at the stage of a meal when one becomes philosophic.

"Ah!" he sighed. "If I had but the pen of a Balzac! I would depict this scene."

He waved a hand.

"It is an idea, that," said Poirot.

"Ah, you agree? It has not been done, I think? And yet—it lends itself to romance, my friend. All around us are people of all classes, of all nationalities, of all ages. For three days these people, these strangers to one another, are brought together. They sleep and eat under one roof, they cannot get away from each other.

At the end of three days they part, they go their several ways, never, perhaps, to see each other again."

"And yet," said Poirot, "suppose an accident——"

"Ah no, my friend——"

"From your point of view it would be regrettable, I agree. But nevertheless let us just for one moment suppose it. Then, perhaps, all these here are linked together—by death."

"Some more wine," said M. Bouc, hastily pouring it out. "You are morbid, *mon cher*. It is, perhaps, the digestion."

"It is true," agreed Poirot, "that the food in Syria was not, perhaps, quite suited to my stomach."

He sipped his wine. Then, leaning back, he ran his eye thoughtfully round the dining-car. There were thirteen people seated there and, as M. Bouc had said, of all classes and nationalities. He began to study them.

At the table opposite them were three men. They were, he guessed, single travelers graded and placed there by the unerring judgment of the restaurant attendants. A big, swarthy Italian was picking his teeth with gusto. Opposite him a spare, neat Englishman had the expressionless disapproving face of the well-trained servant. Next to the Englishman was a big American in a loud suit—possibly a commercial traveler.

"You've got to put it over *big*," he was saying in a loud nasal voice.

The Italian removed his toothpick to gesticulate with it freely.

"Sure," he said. "That whatta I say alla de time."

The Englishman looked out of the window and coughed.

Poirot's eye passed on.

At a small table, sitting very upright, was one of the ugliest old ladies he had ever seen. It was an ugliness of distinction—it fascinated rather than repelled. She sat very upright. Round her neck was a collar of very large pearls which, improbable though it seemed, were real. Her hands were covered with rings. Her sable coat was pushed back on her shoulders. A very small expensive black toque was hideously unbecoming to the yellow, toad-like face beneath it.

She was speaking now to the restaurant attendant in a clear, courteous but completely autocratic tone.

"You will be sufficiently amiable to place in my compartment a bottle of mineral water and a large glass of orange juice. You will arrange that I shall have chicken cooked without sauces for dinner this evening—also some boiled fish."

The attendant replied respectfully that it should be done.

She gave a slight gracious nod of the head and rose. Her glance caught Poirot's and swept over him with the nonchalance of the uninterested aristocrat.

"That is Princess Dragomiroff," said M. Bouc in a low tone. "She is a Russian. Her husband realized all this money before the Revolution and invested it abroad. She is extremely rich. A cosmopolitan."

Poirot nodded. He had heard of Princess Dragomiroff.

"She is a personality," said M. Bouc. "Ugly as sin, but she makes herself felt. You agree?"

Poirot agreed.

At another of the large tables Mary Debenham was sitting with two other women. One of them was a tall middleaged woman in a plaid blouse and tweed skirt. She had a mass of faded yellow hair unbecomingly arranged in a large bun, wore glasses, and had a long, mild, amiable face rather like a sheep. She was listening to the third woman, a stout, pleasant-faced, elderly woman who was talking in a slow clear monotone which showed no signs of pausing for breath or coming to a stop.

". . . And so my daughter said, 'Why,' she said 'you just can't apply Amurrican methods in this country. It's just natural to the folks here to be indolent,' she said. 'They just haven't got any hustle in them.' But all the same you'd be surprised to know what our college there is doing. They've gotten a fine staff of teachers. I guess there's nothing like education. We've got to apply our Western ideals and teach the East to recognize them. My daughter says——"

The train plunged into a tunnel. The calm monotonous voice was drowned.

At the next table, a small one, sat Colonel Arbuthnot—alone. His gaze was fixed upon the back of Mary Debenham's head. They were not sitting together. Yet it could easily have been managed. Why?

Perhaps, Poirot thought, Mary Debenham had demurred. A governess learns to be careful. Appearances are important. A girl with her living to get has to be discreet.

His glance shifted to the other side of the carriage. At the far end, against the wall, was a middle-aged woman dressed in black with a broad expressionless face. German or Scandinavian, he thought. Probably a German lady's maid.

After her came a couple leaning forward and talking animatedly together. The man wore English clothes of loose tweed—but he was not English. Though only the back of his head was visible to Poirot, the shape of it and the set of the shoulders betrayed him. A big man, well made. He turned his head suddenly and Poirot saw his profile. A very handsome man of thirty odd with a big fair moustache.

The woman opposite him was a mere girl—twenty at a guess. A tight-fitting little black coat and skirt, white satin blouse, small chic black toque perched at the fashionable outrageous angle. She had a beautiful foreign-looking face, dead white skin, large brown eyes, jet-black hair. She was smoking a cigarette in a long holder. Her manicured hands had deep red nails. She wore one large emerald set in platinum. There was coquetry in her glance and voice.

"*Elle est jolie—et chic,*" murmured Poirot." Husband and wife—eh?"

M. Bouc nodded.

"Hungarian Embassy, I believe," he said. "A handsome couple."

There were only two more lunchers—Poirot's fellow traveler MacQueen and his employer Mr. Ratchett. The latter sat facing Poirot, and for the second time Poirot studied that unprepossessing face, noting the false benevolence of the brow and the small, cruel eyes.

Doubtless M. Bouc saw a change in his friend's expression.

"It is at your wild animal you look?" he asked.

Poirot nodded.

As his coffee was brought to him, M. Bouc rose to his feet. Having started before Poirot, he had finished some time ago.

"I return to my compartment," he said. "Come along presently and converse with me."

"With pleasure."

Poirot sipped his coffee and ordered a liqueur. The attendant was passing from table to table with his box of money, accepting payment for bills. The elderly American lady's voice rose shrill and plaintive.

"My daughter said, 'Take a book of food tickets and you'll have no trouble—no trouble at all.' Now, that isn't so. Seems they have to have a ten per cent tip, and then there's that bottle of mineral water—and a queer sort of water too. They hadn't got any Evian or Vichy, which seems queer to me."

"It is—they must—how you say—serve the water of the country," explained the sheep-faced lady.

"Well, it seems queer to me." She looked distastefully at the heap of small change on the table in front of her. "Look at all this peculiar stuff he's given me. Dinars or something. Just a lot of rubbish, it looks. My daughter said——"

Mary Debenham pushed back her chair and left with a slight bow to the other two. Colonel Arbuthnot got up and followed her. Gathering up her despised money, the American lady followed suit, followed by the lady like a sheep. The Hungarians had already departed. The restaurant-car was empty save for Poirot and Ratchett and MacQueen.

Ratchett spoke to his companion, who got up and left the car. Then he rose himself, but instead of following MacQueen he dropped unexpectedly into the seat opposite Poirot.

"Can you oblige me with a light?" he said. His voice was soft—faintly nasal. "My name is Ratchett."

Poirot bowed slightly. He slipped his hand into his pocket and produced a matchbox which he handed to the other man, who took it but did not strike a light.

"I think," he went on, "that I have the pleasure of speaking to M. Hercule Poirot. Is that so?"

Poirot bowed again.

"You have been correctly informed, Monsieur."

The detective was conscious of those strange shrewd eyes summing him up before the other spoke again.

"In my country," he said, "we come to the point quickly. Mr. Poirot, I want you to take on a job for me."

Hercule Poirot's eyebrows went up a trifle.

"My *clientèle*, Monsieur, is limited nowadays. I undertake very few cases."

"Why, naturally, I understand that. But this, Mr. Poirot, means big money." He repeated again in his soft, persuasive voice. "Big money."

Hercule Poirot was silent a minute or two, then he said:

"What is it you wish me to do for you, M.—er—Ratchett?"

"Mr. Poirot, I am a rich man—a very rich man. Men in that position have enemies. I have an enemy."

"Only one enemy?"

"Just what do you mean by that question?" asked Ratchett sharply.

"Monsieur, in my experience when a man is in a position to have, as you say, enemies, then it does not usually resolve itself into one enemy only."

Ratchett seemed relieved by Poirot's answer. He said quickly:

"Why, yes, I appreciate that point. Enemy or enemies—it doesn't matter. What does matter is my safety."

"Safety?"

"My life has been threatened, Mr. Poirot. Now, I'm a man who can take pretty good care of himself." From the pocket of his coat his hand brought a small automatic into sight for a moment. He continued grimly. "I don't think I'm the kind of man to be caught napping. But as I look at it I might as well make assurance doubly sure. I fancy you're the man for my money, Mr. Poirot. And remember—*big* money."

Poirot looked at him thoughtfully for some minutes. His face was completely expressionless. The other could have had no clue as to what thoughts were passing in that mind.

"I regret, Monsieur," he said at length. "I cannot oblige you."

The other looked at him shrewdly.

"Name your figure, then," he said.

Poirot shook his head.

"You do not understand, Monsieur. I have been very fortunate in my profession. I have made enough money to satisfy both my needs and my caprices. I take now only such cases as—interest me."

"You've got a pretty good nerve," said Ratchett. "Will twenty thousand dollars tempt you?"

"It will not."

"If you're holding out for more, you won't get it. I know what a thing's worth to me."

"I also—M. Ratchett."

"What's wrong with my proposition?"

Poirot rose.

"If you will forgive me for being personal—I do not like your face, M. Ratchett," he said.

And with that he left the restaurant car.

CHAPTER 4
A Cry in the Night

The Simplon Orient Express arrived at Belgrade at a quarter to nine that evening. It was not due to depart again until 9.15, so Poirot descended to the platform. He did not, however, remain there long. The cold was bitter and though the platform itself was protected, heavy snow was falling outside. He returned to his compartment. The conductor, who was on the platform stamping his feet and waving his arms to keep warm, spoke to him.

"Your valises have been moved, Monsieur, to the compartment No. 1, the compartment of M. Bouc."

"But where is M. Bouc, then?"

"He has moved into the coach from Athens which has just been put on."

Poirot went in search of his friend. M. Bouc waved his protestations aside.

"It is nothing. It is nothing. It is more convenient like this. You are going through to England, so it is better that you should stay in the through coach to Calais. Me, I am very well here. It is most peaceful. This coach is empty save for myself and one little Greek doctor. Ah! my friend, what a night! They say there has not been so much snow for years. Let us hope we shall not be held up. I am not too happy about it, I can tell you."

At 9.15 punctually the train pulled out of the station, and shortly afterwards Poirot got up, said good-night to his friend and made his way along the corridor back into his own coach which was in front next to the dining-car.

On this, the second day of the journey, barriers were breaking down. Colonel Arbuthnot was standing at the door of his compartment talking to MacQueen.

MacQueen broke off something he was saying when he saw Poirot. He looked very surprised.

"Why," he cried, "I thought you'd left us. You said you were getting off at Belgrade."

"You misunderstood me," said Poirot, smiling. "I remember now, the train started from Stamboul just as we were talking about it."

"But, man, your baggage—it's gone."

"It has been moved into another compartment—that is all."

"Oh, I see."

He resumed his conversation with Arbuthnot and Poirot passed on down the corridor.

Two doors from his own compartment, the elderly American lady, Mrs. Hubbard, was standing talking to the sheeplike lady who was a Swede. Mrs. Hubbard was pressing a magazine on the other.

"No, do take it, my dear," she said. "I've got plenty other things to read. My, isn't the cold something frightful?" She nodded amicably to Poirot.

"You are most kind," said the Swedish lady.

"Not at all. I hope you'll sleep well and that your head will be better in the morning."

"It is the cold only. I make myself a cup of tea."

"Have you got some aspirin? Are you sure, now? I've got plenty. Well, good-night, my dear."

She turned to Poirot conversationally as the other woman departed.

"Poor creature, she's a Swede. As far as I can make out, she's a kind of missionary—a teaching one. A nice creature, but doesn't talk much English. She was *most* interested in what I told her about my daughter."

Poirot, by now, knew all about Mrs. Hubbard's daughter. Everyone on the train who could understand English did! How she and her husband were on the staff of a big American college in Smyrna and how this was Mrs. Hubbard's first journey to the East, and what she thought of the Turks and their slipshod ways and the condition of their roads.

The door next to them opened and the thin, pale manservant stepped out. Inside Poirot caught a glimpse of Mr. Ratchett sitting up in bed. He saw Poirot and his face changed, darkening with anger. Then the door was shut.

Mrs. Hubbard drew Poirot a little aside.

"You know, I'm dead scared of that man. Oh, not the valet—the other—his master. Master, indeed! There's something *wrong* about that man. My daughter always says I'm very intuitive. 'When Momma gets a hunch, she's dead right,' that's what my daughter says. And I've got a hunch about that man. He's next door to me, and I don't like it. I put my grips against the communicating door last night. I thought I heard him trying the handle. Do you know, I shouldn't be a bit surprised if that man turns out to be a murderer—one of these train robbers you read about. I dare say I'm foolish, but there it is. I'm downright scared of the man! My daughter said I'd have an easy journey, but somehow I don't feel happy about it. It may be foolish, but I feel anything might happen. Anything at all. And how that nice young fellow can bear to be his secretary I can't think."

Colonel Arbuthnot and MacQueen were coming toward them down the corridor.

"Come into my carriage," MacQueen was saying. "It isn't made up for the night yet. Now what I want to get right about your policy in India is this——"

The men passed and went on down the corridor to MacQueen's carriage.

Mrs. Hubbard said good-night to Poirot.

"I guess I'll go right to bed and read," she said. "Goodnight."

"Goodnight, Madame."

Poirot passed into his own compartment, which was the next one beyond Ratchett's. He undressed and got into bed, read for about half an hour and then turned out the light.

He awoke some hours later, and awoke with a start. He knew what it was that had wakened him—a loud groan, almost a cry, somewhere close at hand. At the same moment the ting of a bell sounded sharply.

Poirot sat up and switched on the light. He noticed that the train was at a standstill—presumably at a station.

That cry had startled him. He remembered that it was Ratchett who had the next compartment. He got out of bed and opened the door just as the Wagon Lit conductor came hurrying along the corridor and knocked on Ratchett's door. Poirot kept his door open a crack and watched. The conductor tapped a second time. A bell rang and a light showed over another door farther down. The conductor glanced over his shoulder.

At the same moment a voice from within the next-door compartment called out:

"*Ce n'est rien. Je me suis trompé.*"

"*Bien, Monsieur.*" The conductor scurried off again, to knock at the door where the light was showing.

Poirot returned to bed, his mind relieved, and switched off the light. He glanced at his watch. It was just twenty-three minutes to one.

CHAPTER 5
The Crime

He found it difficult to go to sleep again at once. For one thing, he missed the motion of the train. If it *was* a station outside it was curiously quiet. By contrast, the noises on the train seemed unusually loud. He could hear Ratchett moving about next door—a click as he pulled down the washbasin, the sound of the tap running, a splashing noise, then another click as the basin shut to again. Footsteps passed up the corridor outside, the shuffling footsteps of someone in bedroom slippers.

Hercule Poirot lay awake staring at the ceiling. Why was the station outside so silent? His throat felt dry. He had forgotten to ask for his usual bottle of mineral water. He looked at his watch again. Just after a quarter-past one. He would ring for the conductor and ask him for some mineral water. His finger went out to the bell, but he paused as in the stillness he heard a ting. The man couldn't answer every bell at once.

Ting . . . ting . . . ting . . . .

It sounded again and again. Where was the man? Somebody was getting impatient.

Ting. . . .

Ting. . . .

Whoever it was was keeping their finger solidly on the push.

Suddenly with a rush, his footsteps echoing up the aisle, the man came. He knocked at a door not far from Poirot's own.

Then came voices—the conductor's, deferential, apologetic, and a woman's—insistent and voluble.

Mrs. Hubbard!

Poirot smiled to himself.

The altercation—if it was one—went on for some time. Its proportions were ninety per cent of Mrs. Hubbard's to a soothing ten per cent of the conductor's. Finally the matter seemed to be adjusted. Poirot heard distinctly:

"*Bonne nuit,* Madame," a closing door.

He pressed his own finger on the bell.

The conductor arrived promptly. He looked hot and worried.

"*De l'eau minerale, s'il vous plaît.*"

"*Bien, Monsieur.*" Perhaps a twinkle in Poirot's eye led him to unburden himself.

"*La dame Americaine*——"

"Yes?"

He wiped his forehead.

"Imagine to yourself the time I have had with her! She insists—but *insists*—that there is a man in her compartment! Figure to yourself, Monsieur. In a space of this size." He swept a hand round. "Where would he conceal himself? I argue with her. I point out that it is impossible. She insists. She woke up and there was a man there. And how, I ask, did he get out and leave the door bolted behind him? But she will not listen to reason. As though, there were not enough to worry us already. This snow——"

"Snow?"

"But yes, Monsieur. Monsieur has not noticed? The train has stopped. We have run into a snowdrift. Heaven knows how long we shall be here. I remember once being snowed up for seven days."

"Where are we?"

"Between Vincovci and Brod."

"*Là, là,*" said Poirot vexedly.

The man withdrew and returned with the water.

"*Bon soir, Monsieur.*"

Poirot drank a glass of water and composed himself to sleep.

He was just dropping off when something again woke him. This time it was as though something heavy had fallen with a thud against the door.

He sprang up, opened it and looked out. Nothing. But to his right some way down the corridor a woman wrapped in a scarlet kimono was retreating from him. At the other end, sitting on his little seat, the conductor was entering up figures on large sheets of paper. Everything was deathly quiet.

"Decidedly I suffer from the nerves," said Poirot and retired to bed again. This time he slept till morning.

When he awoke the train was still at a standstill. He raised a blind and looked out. Heavy banks of snow surrounded the train.

He glanced at his watch and saw that it was past nine o'clock.

At a quarter to ten, neat spruce, and dandified as ever, he made his way to the restaurant-car, where a chorus of woe was going on.

Any barriers there might have been between the passengers had now quite broken down. All were united by a common misfortune. Mrs. Hubbard was loudest in her lamentations.

"My daughter said it would be the easiest way in the world. Just sit in the train until I got to Parrus. And now we may be here for days and days," she wailed. "And my boat sails day after tomorrow. How am I going to catch it now? Why, I can't even wire to cancel my passage. I feel too mad to talk about it."

The Italian said that he had urgent business himself in Milan. The large American said that that was "too bad, Ma'am," and soothingly expressed a hope that the train might make up time.

"My sister—her children wait me," said the Swedish lady and wept. "I get no word to them. What they think? They will say bad things have happen to me."

"How long shall we be here?" demanded Mary Debenham. "Doesn't anybody *know?*"

Her voice sounded impatient, but Poirot noted that there were no signs of that almost feverish anxiety which she had displayed during the check to the Taurus Express.

Mrs. Hubbard was off again.

"There isn't anybody knows a thing on this train. And nobody's trying to do anything. Just a pack of useless foreigners. Why, if this were at home, there'd be someone at least *trying* to do something."

Arbuthnot turned to Poirot and spoke in careful British French.

"*Vous êtes un directeur de la ligne, je crois, Monsieur. Vous pouvez nous dire——*"

Smiling, Poirot corrected him.

"No, no," he said in English. "It is not I. You confound me with my friend M. Bouc."

"Oh! I'm sorry."

"Not at all. It is most natural. I am now in the compartment that he had formerly."

M. Bouc was not present in the restaurant-car. Poirot looked about to notice who else was absent.

Princess Dragomiroff was missing and the Hungarian couple. Also Ratchett, his valet, and the German lady's-maid.

The Swedish lady wiped her eyes.

"I am foolish," she said. "I am baby to cry. All for the best, whatever happen."

This Christian spirit, however, was far from being shared.

"That's all very well," said MacQueen restlessly. "We may be here for days."

"What is this country anyway?" demanded Mrs. Hubbard tearfully.

On being told it was Yugoslavia she said:

"Oh! one of these Balkan things. What can you expect?"

"You are the only patient one, Mademoiselle," said Poirot to Miss Debenham.

She shrugged her shoulders slightly.

"What can one do?"

"You are a philosopher, Mademoiselle."

"That implies a detached attitude. I think my attitude is more selfish. I have learned to save myself useless emotion."

She was not even looking at him. Her gaze went past him, out of the window to where the snow lay in heavy masses.

"You are a strong character, Mademoiselle," said Poirot gently. "You are, I think, the strongest character amongst us."

"Oh, no. No, indeed. I know one far far stronger than I am."

"And that is——?"

She seemed suddenly to come to herself, to realize that she was talking to a stranger and a foreigner with whom, until this morning, she had only exchanged half a dozen sentences.

She laughed a polite but estranging laugh.

"Well—that old lady, for instance. You have probably noticed her. A very ugly old lady, but rather fascinating. She has only to lift a little finger and ask for something in a polite voice—and the whole train runs."

"It runs also for my friend M. Bouc," said Poirot. "But that is because he is a director of the line, not because he has a masterful character."

Mary Debenham smiled.

The morning wore away. Several people, Poirot amongst them, remained in the diningcar. The communal life was felt, at the moment, to pass the time better. He heard a good deal more about Mrs. Hubbard's daughter and he heard the lifelong habits of Mr. Hubbard, deceased, from his rising in the morning and commencing breakfast with a cereal to his final rest at night in the bedsocks that Mrs. Hubbard herself had been in the habit of knitting for him.

It was when he was listening to a confused account of the missionary aims of the Swedish lady that one of the Wagon Lit conductors came into the car and stood at his elbow.

"*Pardon, Monsieur.*"

"Yes?"

"The compliments of M. Bouc, and he would be glad if you would be so kind as to come to him for a few minutes."

Poirot rose, uttered excuses to the Swedish lady and followed the man out of the dining-car.

It was not his own conductor, but a big fair man.

He followed his guide down the corridor of his own carriage and along the corridor of the next one. The man tapped at a door, then stood aside to let Poirot enter.

The compartment was not M. Bouc's own. It was a second-class one—chosen presumably because of its slightly larger size. It certainly gave the impression of being crowded.

M. Bouc himself was sitting on the small seat in the opposite corner. In the corner next the window facing him was a small, dark man looking out at the snow. Standing up and quite preventing Poirot from advancing any farther was a big man in blue uniform (the *chef de train*) and his own Wagon Lit conductor.

"Ah, my good friend," cried M. Bouc. "Come in. We have need of you."

The little man in the window shifted along the seat, Poirot squeezed past the other two men and sat down facing his friend.

The expression on M. Bouc's face gave him, as he would have expressed it, furiously to think. It was clear that something out of the common had happened.

"What has occurred?" he asked.

"You many well ask that. First this snow—this stoppage. And now——"

He paused—and a sort of strangled gasp came from the Wagon Lit conductor.

"And now what?"

"*And now a passenger lies dead in his berth—stabbed.*"

M. Bouc spoke with a kind of calm desperation.

"An American. A man called—called—" he consulted some notes in front of him. "Ratchett—that is right—Ratchett?"

"Yes, Monsieur," the Wagon Lit man gulped.

Poirot looked at him. He was as white as chalk.

"You had better let that man sit down," he said. "He may faint otherwise."

The *chef de train* moved slightly and the Wagon Lit man sank down in the corner and buried his face in his hands.

"Brr!" said Poirot. "This is serious!"

"Certainly it is serious. To begin with, a murder—that by itself is a calamity of the first water. But not only that, the circumstances are unusual. Here we are, brought to a standstill. We may be here for hours—and not only hours—days! Another circumstance. Passing through most countries we have the police of that country on the train. But in Yugoslavia—no. You comprehend?"

"It is a position of great difficulty," said Poirot.

"There is worse to come. Dr. Constantine—I forgot, I have not introduced you—Dr. Constantine, M. Poirot."

The little dark man bowed and Poirot returned it.

"Dr. Constantine is of the opinion that death occurred at about 1 a.m."

"It is difficult to say exactly in these matters," said the doctor, "but I think I can say definitely that death occurred between midnight and two in the morning."

"When was this M. Ratchett last seen alive?" asked Poirot.

"He is known to have been alive at about twenty minutes to one, when he spoke to the conductor," said M. Bouc.

"That is quite correct," said Poirot. "I myself heard what passed. That is the last thing known?"

"Yes."

Poirot turned toward the doctor, who continued:

"The window of M. Ratchett's compartment was found wide open, leading one to suppose that the murderer escaped that way. But in my opinion that open window is a blind. Anyone departing that way would have left distinct traces in the snow. There were none."

"The crime was discovered—when?" asked Poirot.

"Michel!"

The Wagon Lit conductor sat up. His face still looked pale and frightened.

"Tell this gentleman exactly what occurred," ordered M. Bouc.

The man spoke somewhat jerkily.

"The valet of this M. Ratchett, he tapped several times at the door this morning. There was no answer. Then, half an hour ago, the restaurant-car attendant came. He wanted to know if Monsieur was taking *déjeuner*. It was eleven o'clock, you comprehend.

"I open the door for him with my key. But there is a chain, too, and that is fastened. There is no answer and it is very still in there, and cold—but cold. With the window open and snow drifting in. I thought the gentleman had had a fit, perhaps. I got the *chef de train*. We broke the chain and went in. He was—*Ah! c'était terrible!*"

He buried his face in his hands again.

"The door was locked and chained on the inside," said Poirot thoughtfully. "It was not suicide—eh?"

The Greek doctor gave a sardonic laugh.

"Does a man who commits suicide stab himself in ten—twelve—fifteen places?" he asked.

Poirot's eyes opened.

"That is great ferocity," he said.

"It is a woman," said the *chef de train*, speaking for the first time. "Depend upon it, it was a woman. Only a woman would stab like that."

Dr. Constantine screwed up his face thoughtfully.

"She must have been a very strong woman," he said. "It is not my desire to speak technically—that is only confusing—but I can assure you that one or two of the blows were delivered with such force as to drive them through hard belts of bone and muscle."

"It was not, clearly, a scientific crime," said Poirot.

"It was most unscientific," said Dr. Constantine. "The blows seem to have been delivered haphazard and at random. Some have glanced off, doing hardly any damage. It is as though somebody had shut their eyes and then in a frenzy struck blindly again and again."

"*C'est une femme,*" said the *chef de train* again. "Women are like that. When they are enraged they have great strength." He nodded so sagely that everyone suspected a personal experience of his own.

"I have, perhaps, something to contribute to your store of knowledge," said Poirot. "M. Ratchett spoke to me yesterday. He told me, as far as I was able to understand him, that he was in danger of his life."

"'Bumped off'—that is the American expression, is it not?" said M. Bouc. "Then it is not a woman. It is a 'gangster' or a 'gunman.'"

The *chef de train* looked pained at his theory having come to naught.

"If so," said Poirot, "it seems to have been done very amateurishly."

His tone expressed professional disapproval.

"There is a large American on the train," said M. Bouc, pursuing his idea—"a common-looking man with terrible clothes. He chews the gum which I believe is not done in good circles. You know whom I mean?"

The Wagon Lit conductor to whom he had appealed nodded.

"*Oui,* Monsieur, the No. 16. But it cannot have been he. I should have seen him enter or leave the compartment."

"You might not. You might not. But we will go into that presently. The question is, what to do?" He looked at Poirot.

Poirot looked back at him.

"Come, my friend," said M. Bouc. "You comprehend what I am about to ask of you. I know your powers. Take command of this investigation! No, no, do not refuse. See, to us it is serious—I speak for the Compagnie Internationale des Wagons Lits. By the time the Yugoslavian police arrive, how simple if we can present them with the solution! Otherwise delays, annoyances, a million and one inconveniences. Perhaps, who knows, serious annoyance to innocent persons. Instead—*you* solve the mystery! We say, 'A murder has occurred—*this* is the criminal!'"

"And suppose I do not solve it?"

"Ah! *mon cher.*" M. Bouc's voice became positively caressing. "I know your reputation. I know something of your methods. This is the ideal case for you. To look up the antecedents of all these people, to discover their *bona fides*—all that takes time and endless inconvenience. But have I not heard you say often that to solve a case a man has only to lie back in his chair and think? Do that. Interview the passengers on the train, view the body, examine what clues there are and then—well, I have faith in you! I am assured that it is no idle boast of yours. Lie back and think—use (as I have heard you say so often) the little grey cells of the mind—and you will *know!*"

He leaned forward, looking affectionately at his friend.

"Your faith touches me, my friend," said Poirot emotionally. "As you say, this cannot be a difficult case. I myself, last night—but we will not speak of that now. In truth, this problem intrigues me. I was reflecting, not half an hour ago, that many hours of boredom lay ahead whilst we are stuck here. And now—a problem lies ready to my hand."

"You accept then?" said M. Bouc eagerly.

"*C'est entendu*. You place the matter in my hands."

"Good—we are all at your service."

"To begin with, I should like a plan of the Istanbul-Calais coach, with a note of the people who occupied the several compartments, and I should also like to see their passports and their tickets."

"Michel will get you those."

The Wagon Lit conductor left the compartment.

"What other passengers are there on the train?" asked Poirot.

"In this coach Dr. Constantine and I are the only travelers. In the coach from Bucharest is an old gentleman with a lame leg. He is well known to the conductor. Beyond that are the ordinary carriages, but these do not concern us, since they were locked after dinner had been served last night. Forward of the Istanbul-Calais coach there is only the dining-car."

"Then it seems," said Poirot slowly, "as though we must look for our murderer in the Istanbul-Calais coach." He turned to the doctor. "That is what you were hinting, I think?"

The Greek nodded.

"At half an hour after midnight we ran into the snowdrift. No one can have left the train since then."

M. Bouc said solemnly.

"*The murderer is with us—on the train now*. . . ."

CHAPTER 6
A Woman?

"First of all," said Poirot, "I should like a word or two with young M. MacQueen. He may be able to give us valuable information."

"Certainly," said M. Bouc.

He turned to the *chef de train*.

The *chef de train* left the carriage.

The conductor returned with a bundle of passports and tickets. M. Bouc took them from him.

"Thank you, Michel. It would be best now, I think, if you were to go back to your post. We will take your evidence formally later."

"Very good, Monsieur."

Michel in his turn left the carriage.

"After we have seen young MacQueen," said Poirot, "perhaps M. le docteur will come with me to the dead man's carriage."

"Certainly."

"After we have finished there——"

But at this moment the *chef de train* returned with Hector MacQueen.

M. Bouc rose.

"We are a little cramped here," he said pleasantly. "Take my seat, M. MacQueen. M. Poirot will sit opposite you—so."

He turned to the *chef de train*.

"Clear all the people out of the restaurant-car," he said, "and let it be left free for M. Poirot. You will conduct your interviews there, *mon cher?*"

"It would be the most convenient, yes," agreed Poirot.

MacQueen had stood looking from one to the other, not quite following the rapid flow of French.

"*Qu'est ce qu'il y a?*" he began laboriously. "*Pourquoi*——?"

With a vigorous gesture Poirot motioned him to the seat in the corner. He took it and began once more.

"*Pourquoi*——?" then, checking himself and relapsing into his own tongue, "What's up on the train? Has anything happened?"

He looked from one man to another.

Poirot nodded.

"Exactly. Something has happened. Prepare yourself for a shock. *Your employer, M. Ratchett, is dead!*"

MacQueen's mouth pursed itself in a whistle. Except that his eyes grew a shade brighter, he showed no signs of shock or distress.

"So they got him after all," he said.

"What exactly do you mean by that phrase, M. MacQueen?"

MacQueen hesitated.

"You are assuming," said Poirot, "that M. Ratchett was murdered?"

"Wasn't he?" This time MacQueen did show surprise. "Why, yes," he said slowly. "That's just what I did think. Do you mean he just died in his sleep? Why, the old man was as tough as—as tough——"

"No, no," said Poirot. "Your assumption was quite right. Mr. Ratchett was murdered. Stabbed. But I should like to know why you were so sure it *was* murder, and not just—death."

MacQueen hesitated.

"I must get this clear," he said. "Who exactly are you? And where do you come in?"

"I represent the Compagnie Internationale des Wagons Lits." He paused, then added, "I am a detective. My name is Hercule Poirot."

If he expected an effect he did not get one. MacQueen said merely, "Oh, yes?" and waited for him to go on.

"You know the name, perhaps."

"Why, it does seem kind of familiar—only I always thought it was a woman's dressmaker."

Hercule Poirot looked at him with distaste.

"It is incredible!" he said.

"What's incredible?"

"Nothing. Let us advance with the matter in hand. I want you to tell me, M. MacQueen, all that you know about the dead man. You were not related to him?"

"No. I am—was—his secretary."

"For how long have you held that post?"

"Just over a year."

"Please give me all the information you can."

"Well, I met Mr. Ratchett just over a year ago when I was in Persia——"

Poirot interrupted.

"What were you doing there?"

"I had come over from New York to look into an oil concession. I don't suppose you want to hear all about that. My friends and I had been let in rather badly over it. Mr. Ratchett was in the same hotel. He had just had a row with his secretary. He offered me the job and I took it. I was at a loose end, and glad to find a well-paid job ready made, as it were."

"And since then?"

"We've traveled about. Mr. Ratchett wanted to see the world. He was hampered by knowing no languages. I acted more as a courier than as a secretary. It was a pleasant life."

"Now tell me as much as you can about your employer."

The young man shrugged his shoulders. A perplexed expression passed over his face.

"That's not so easy."

"What was his full name?"

"Samuel Edward Ratchett."

"He was an American citizen?"

"Yes."

"What part of America did he come from?"

"I don't know."

"Well, tell me what you do know."

"The actual truth is, Mr. Poirot, that I know nothing at all! Mr. Ratchett never spoke of himself, or of his life in America."

"Why do you think that was?"

"I don't know. I imagined that he might have been ashamed of his beginnings. Some men are."

"Does that strike you as a satisfactory solution?"

"Frankly, it doesn't."

"Has he any relations?"

"He never mentioned any."

Poirot pressed the point.

"You must have formed *some* theory, M. MacQueen."

"Well, yes, I did. For one thing, I don't believe Ratchett was his real name. I think he left America definitely in order to escape someone or something. I think he was successful—until a few weeks ago."

"And then?"

"He began to get letters—threatening letters."

"Did you see them?"

"Yes. It was my business to attend to his correspondence. The first letter came a fortnight ago."

"Were these letters destroyed?"

"No, I think I've got a couple still in my files—one I know Ratchett tore up in a rage. Shall I get them for you?"

"If you would be so good."

MacQueen left the compartment. He returned a few minutes later and laid down two sheets of rather dirty notepaper before Poirot.

The first letter ran as follows:

> Thought you'd doublecross us and get away with it, did you? Not on your life. We're out to GET you, Ratchett, and we WILL get you!

There was no signature.

With no comment beyond raised eyebrows, Poirot picked up the second letter.

> We're going to take you for a ride, Ratchett. Some time soon. We're going to GET you, see?

Poirot laid the letter down.

"The style is monotonous!" he said. "More so than the handwriting."

MacQueen stared at him.

"You would not observe," said Poirot pleasantly. "It requires the eye of one used to such things. This letter was not written by one person, M. MacQueen. Two or more persons wrote it—each writing a letter of a word at a time. Also, the letters are printed. That makes the task of identifying the handwriting much more difficult."

He paused, then said:

"Did you know that M. Ratchett had applied for help to me?"

"To *you?*"

MacQueen's astonished tone told Poirot quite certainly that the young man had not known of it. He nodded.

"Yes. He was alarmed. Tell me, how did he act when he received the first letter?"

MacQueen hesitated.

"It's difficult to say. He—he—passed it off with a laugh in that quiet way of his. But somehow"—he gave a slight shiver—"I felt that there was a good deal going on underneath the quietness."

Poirot nodded. Then he asked an unexpected question.

"Mr. MacQueen, will you tell me, quite honestly, exactly how you regarded your employer? Did you like him?"

Hector MacQueen took a moment or two before replying.

"No," he said at last. "I did not."

"Why?"

"I can't exactly say. He was always quite pleasant in his manner." He paused, then said, "I'll tell you the truth, Mr. Poirot. I disliked and distrusted him. He was, I am sure, a cruel and a dangerous man. I must admit, though, that I have no reasons to advance for my opinion."

"Thank you, M. MacQueen. One further question—when did you last see M. Ratchett alive?"

"Last evening about"—he thought for a minute—"ten o'clock, I should say. I went into his compartment to take down some memoranda from him."

"On what subject?"

"Some tiles and antique pottery that he bought in Persia. What was delivered was not what he had purchased. There has been a long, vexatious correspondence on the subject."

"And that was the last time M. Ratchett was seen alive?"

"Yes, I suppose so."

"Do you know when M. Ratchett received the last threatening letter?"

"On the morning of the day we left Constantinople."

"There is one more question I must ask you, M. MacQueen: were you on good terms with your employer?"

The young man's eyes twinkled suddenly.

"This is where I'm supposed to go all gooseflesby down the back. In the words of a best seller, 'You've nothing on me.' Ratchett and I were on perfectly good terms."

"Perhaps, M. MacQueen, you will give me your full name and your address in America."

MacQueen gave his name—Hector Willard MacQueen, and an address in New York.

Poirot leaned back against the cushions.

"That is all for the present, M. MacQueen," he said. "I should be obliged if you would keep the matter of M. Ratchett's death to yourself for a little time."

"His valet, Masterman, will have to know."

"He probably knows already," said Poirot dryly. "If so, try to get him to hold his tongue."

"That oughtn't to be difficult. He's a Britisher, and does what he calls 'Keeps himself to himself.' He's a low opinion of Americans and no opinion at all of any other nationality."

"Thank you, M. MacQueen."

The American left the carriage.

"Well?" demanded M. Bouc. "You believe what he says, this young man?"

"He seems honest and straightforward. He did not pretend to any affection for his employer as he probably would have done had he been involved in any way. It is true M. Ratchett did not tell him that he had tried to enlist my services and failed, but I do not think that is really a suspicious circumstance. I fancy M. Ratchett was a gentleman who kept his own counsel on every possible occasion."

"So you pronounce one person at least innocent of the crime," said M. Bouc jovially.

Poirot cast on him a look of reproach.

"Me, I suspect everybody till the last minute," he said. "All the same, I must admit that I cannot see this sober, long-headed MacQueen losing his head and stabbing his victim twelve or fourteen times. It is not in accord with his psychology—not at all."

"No," said Mr. Bouc thoughtfully. "That is the act of a man driven almost crazy with a frenzied hate—it suggests more the Latin temperament. Or else it suggests, as our friend the *chef de train* insisted, a woman."

CHAPTER 7
The Body

Followed by Dr. Constantine, Poirot made his way to the next coach and the compartment occupied by the murdered man. The conductor came and unlocked the door for them with his key.

The two men passed inside. Poirot turned inquiringly to his companion.

"How much has been disarranged in this compartment?"

"Nothing has been touched. I was careful not to move the body in making my examination."

Poirot nodded. He looked round him.

The first thing that struck the senses was the intense cold. The window was pushed down as far as it would go and the blind was drawn up.

"Brrr," observed Poirot.

The other smiled appreciatively.

"I did not like to close it," he said.

Poirot examined the window carefully.

"You are right," he announced. "Nobody left the carriage this way. Possibly the open window was intended to suggest the fact, but, if so, the snow has defeated the murderer's object."

He examined the frame of the window carefully. Taking a small case from his pocket he blew a little powder over it.

"No fingerprints at all," he said. "That means it has been wiped. Well, if there had been fingerprints it would have told us very little. They would have been those of M. Ratchett or his valet or the conductor. Criminals do not make mistakes of that kind nowadays.

"And that being so," he added cheerfully, "we might as well shut the window. Positively it is the cold storage in here!"

He suited the action to the word and then turned his attention for the first time to the motionless figure lying in the bunk.

Ratchett lay on his back. His pyjama jacket, stained with rusty patches, had been unbuttoned and thrown back.

"I had to see the nature of the wounds, you see," explained the doctor.

Poirot nodded. He bent over the body. Finally he straightened himself with a slight grimace.

"It is not pretty," he said. "Someone must have stood there and stabbed him again and again. How many wounds are there exactly?"

"I make it twelve. One or two are so slight as to be practically scratches. On the other hand, at least three would be capable of causing death."

Something in the doctor's tone caught Poirot's attention. He looked at him sharply. The little Greek was standing staring down at the body with a puzzled frown.

"Something strikes you as odd, does it not?" he asked gently. "Speak, my friend. There is something here that puzzles you?"

"You are right," acknowledged the other.

"What is it?"

"You see these two wounds—here and here,"—he pointed. "They are deep, each cut must have severed blood-vessels—and yet—the edges do not gape. They have not bled as one would have expected."

"Which suggests?"

"That the man was already dead—some little time dead—when they were delivered. But that is surely absurd."

"It would seem so," said Poirot thoughtfully. "Unless our murderer figured to himself that he had not accomplished his job properly and came back to make quite sure; but that is manifestly absurd! Anything else?"

"Well, just one thing."

"And that?"

"You see this wound here—under the right arm—near the right shoulder. Take this pencil of mine. Could you deliver such a blow?"

Poirot raised his hand.

"*Précisément,*" he said. "I see. With the *right* hand it is exceedingly difficult—

almost impossible. One would have to strike backhanded, as it were. But if the blow were struck with the *left* hand——"

"Exactly, M. Poirot. That blow was almost certainly struck with the *left* hand—"

"So that our murderer is left-handed? No, it is more difficult than that, is it not?"

"As you say, M. Poirot. Some of these other blows are just as obviously right-handed."

"Two people. We are back at two people again," murmured the detective. He asked abruptly:

"Was the electric light on?"

"It is difficult to say. You see it is turned off by the conductor every morning about ten o'clock."

"The switches will tell us," said Poirot.

He examined the switch of the top light and also the roll back bed-head light. The former was turned off. The latter was closed.

"*Eh bien,*" he said thoughtfully. "We have here a hypothesis of the First and Second Murderer, as the great Shakespeare would put it. The First Murderer stabbed his victim and left the compartment, turning off the light. The Second Murderer came in in the dark, did not see that his or her work had been done and stabbed at least twice at a dead body. *Que pensez vous de ça?*"

"Magnificent," said the little doctor with enthusiasm.

The other's eyes twinkled.

"You think so? I am glad. It sounded to me a little like the nonsense."

"What other explanation can there be?"

"That is just what I am asking myself. Have we here a coincidence or what? Are there any other inconsistencies, such as would point to two people being concerned?"

"I think I can say yes. Some of these blows, as I have already said, point to a weakness—a lack of strength, or a lack of determination. They are feeble glancing blows. But this one here—and this one——" Again he pointed. "Great strength was needed for those blows. They have penetrated the muscle."

"They were, in your opinion, delivered by a man."

"Most certainly."

"They could not have been delivered by a woman?"

"A young, vigorous athletic woman might have struck them, especially if she were in the grip of a strong emotion, but it is in my opinion highly unlikely."

Poirot was silent a moment or two.

The other said anxiously.

"You understand my point?"

"Perfectly," said Poirot. "The matter begins to clear itself up wonderfully! The murderer was a man of great strength, he was feeble, it was a woman, it was a right-handed person, it was a left-handed person—*Ah! c'est rigolo, tout ça!*"

He spoke with sudden anger.

"And the victim—what does he do in all this? Does he cry out? Does he struggle. Does he defend himself?"

He slipped his hand under the pillow and drew out the automatic pistol which Ratchett had shown him the day before.

"Fully loaded, you see," he said.

They looked round them. Ratchett's day clothing was hanging from the hooks on the wall. On the small table formed by the lid of the washing basin were various objects—false teeth in a glass of water; another glass, empty; a bottle of mineral water, a large flask and an ash-tray containing the butt of a cigar and some charred fragments of paper; also two burnt matches.

The doctor picked up the empty glass and sniffed it.

"Here is the explanation of the victim's inertia," he said quietly.

"Drugged?"

"Yes."

Poirot nodded. He picked up the two matches and scrutinized them carefully.

"You have a clue then?" demanded the little doctor eagerly.

"Those two matches are of a different shape," said Poirot. "One is flatter than the other. You see?"

"It is the kind you get on the train," said the doctor, "in paper covers."

Poirot was feeling in the pockets of Ratchett's clothing. Presently he pulled out a box of matches. He compared them carefully.

"The rounder one is a match struck by Mr. Ratchett," he said. "Let us see if he had also the flatter kind."

But a further search showed no other matches.

Poirot's eyes were darting about the compartment. They were bright and sharp like a bird's. One felt that nothing could escape their scrutiny.

With a little exclamation he bent and picked up something from the floor.

It was a small square of cambric, very dainty. In the corner was an embroidered initial—H.

"A woman's handkerchief," said the doctor. "Our friend the *chef de train* was right. There is a woman concerned in this."

"And most conveniently she leaves her handkerchief behind!" said Poirot. "Exactly as it happens in the books and on the films—and to make things even easier for us it is marked with an initial."

"What a stroke of luck for us!" exclaimed the doctor.

"Is it not?" said Poirot.

Something in his tone surprised the doctor.

But before he could ask for elucidation, Poirot had made another dive on to the floor.

This time he held out on the palm of his hand—a pipe cleaner.

"It is perhaps the property of M. Ratchett?" suggested the doctor.

"There was no pipe in any of his pockets, and no tobacco or tobacco pouch."

"Then it is a clue."

"Oh! decidedly. And again dropped most conveniently. A masculine clue this time, you note! One cannot complain of having no clues in this case. There are clues here in abundance. By the way, what have you done with the weapon?"

"There was no sign of any weapon. The murderer must have taken it away with him."

"I wonder why," mused Poirot.

"Ah!" The doctor had been delicately exploring the pyjama pockets of the dead man.

"I overlooked this," he said. "I unbuttoned the jacket and threw it straight back."

From the breast pocket he brought out a gold watch. The case was dented savagely, and the hands pointed to a quarter-past one.

"You see?" cried Constantine eagerly. "This gives us the hour of the crime. It agrees with my calculations. Between midnight and two in the morning is what I said, and probably about one o'clock, though it is difficult to be exact in these matters. *Eh bien,* here is confirmation. A quarter-past one. That was the hour of the crime."

"It is possible, yes. It is certainly possible."

The doctor looked at him curiously.

"You will pardon me, M. Poirot, but I do not quite understand you."

"I do not understand myself," said Poirot. "I understand nothing at all, and, as you perceive, it worries me."

He sighed and bent over the little table, examining the charred fragment of paper. He murmured to himself.

"What I need at this moment is an old-fashioned woman's hat-box."

Dr. Constantine was at a loss to know what to make of this singular remark. In any case, Poirot gave him no time for questions. Opening the door into the corridor, he called for the conductor.

The man arrived at a run.

"How many women are there in this coach?"

The conductor counted on his fingers.

"One, two, three—six, Monsieur. The old American lady, a Swedish lady, the young English lady, the Countess Andrenyi and Madame la Princesse Dragomiroff and her maid."

Poirot considered.

"They all have hat-boxes, yes?"

"Yes, Monsieur."

"Then bring me—let me see—yes, the Swedish lady's and that of the lady's-maid. Those two are the only hope. You will tell them it is a customs regulation—something—anything that occurs to you."

"That will be all right Monsieur. Neither lady is in her compartment at the moment."

"Then be quick."

The conductor departed. He returned with the two hatboxes. Poirot opened that of the lady's-maid and tossed it aside. Then he opened the Swedish lady's and uttered an exclamation of satisfaction. Removing the hats carefully, he disclosed round humps of wire netting.

"Ah, here is what we need. About fifteen years ago hat-boxes were made like this. You skewered through the hat with a hatpin on to this hump of wire-netting."

As he spoke he was skilfully removing two of the attachments. Then he repacked the hat-box and told the conductor to return them both where they belonged.

When the door was shut once more he turned to his companion.

"See you, my dear doctor, me, I am not one to rely upon the expert procedure. It is the psychology I seek, not the fingerprint or the cigarette ash. But in this case I would welcome a little scientific assistance. This compartment is full of clues, but can I be sure that those clues are really what they seem to be?"

"I do not quite understand you, M. Poirot."

"Well, to give you an example—we find a woman's handkerchief. Did a woman drop it? Or did a man, committing the crime, say to himself 'I will make this look like a woman's crime. I will stab my enemy an unnecessary number of times, making some of the blows feeble and ineffective, and I will drop this handkerchief where no one can miss it. That is one possibility. Then there is another. Did a woman kill him and did she deliberately drop a pipe cleaner to make it look like a man's work? Or are we seriously to suppose that two people—a man and a woman—were separately concerned, and that each was so careless as to drop a clue to their identity? It is a little too much of a coincidence, that!"

"But where does the hat-box come in?" asked the doctor, still puzzled.

"Ah! I'm coming to that. As I say, these clues, the watch stopped at a quarter-past one, the handkerchief, the pipe cleaner, they may be genuine, or they may be fake. As to that I cannot yet tell. But there is *one* clue here which I believe—though again I may be wrong—has *not* been faked. I mean this flat match, M. le docteur. *I believe that that match was used by the murderer, not by M. Ratchett.* It was used to burn an incriminating paper of some kind. Possibly a note. If so, there was something in that note, some mistake, some error, that left a possible clue to the assailant. I am going to endeavour to resurrect what that something was."

He went out of the compartment and returned a few moments later with a small spirit stove and a pair of curling tongs.

"I use them for the moustaches," he said, referring to the latter.

The doctor watched him with great interest. He flattened out the two humps of wire, and with great care wriggled the charred scrap of paper on to one of them. He clapped the other on top of it and then, holding both pieces together with the tongs, held the whole thing over the flame of the spirit lamp.

"It is a very makeshift affair, this," he said over his shoulder. "Let us hope that it will answer its purpose."

The doctor watched the proceedings attentively. The metal began to glow. Suddenly he saw faint indication of letters. Words formed themselves slowly—words of fire.

It was a very tiny scrap. Only three words and a part of another showed.

-member little Daisy Armstrong.

"Ah!" Poirot gave a sharp exclamation.

"It tells you something?" asked the doctor.

Poirot's eyes were shining. He laid down the tongs carefully.

"Yes," he said. *"I know the dead man's real name. I know why he had to leave America."*

"What was his name?"

"Cassetti."

"Cassetti." Constantine knitted his brows. "It brings back to me something. Some years ago. I cannot remember. . . . It was a case in America, was it not?"

"Yes," said Poirot. "A case in America."

Further than that Poirot was not disposed to be communicative. He looked round him as he went on:

"We will go into all that presently. Let us first make sure that we have seen all there is to be seen here."

Quickly and deftly he went once more through the pockets of the dead man's clothes but found nothing there of interest. He tried the communicating door which led through to the next compartment, but it was bolted on the other side.

"There is one thing that I do not understand," said Dr. Constantine, "if the murderer did not escape through the window, and if this communicating door was bolted on the other side, and if the door into the corridor was not only locked on the inside but chained, how then did the murderer leave the compartment?"

"That is what the audience says when a person bound hand and foot is shut into a cabinet—and disappears."

"You mean——?"

"I mean," explained Poirot, "that if the murderer intended us to believe that he had escaped by way of the window he would naturally make it appear that the other two exits were impossible. Like the 'disappearing person' in the cabinet—it is a trick. It is our business to find our how the trick is done."

He locked the communicating door on their side.

"In case," he said, "the excellent Mrs. Hubbard should take it into her head to acquire first-hand details of the crime to write to her daughter."

He looked round once more.

"There is nothing more to do here, I think. Let us rejoin M. Bouc."

CHAPTER 8
The Armstrong Kidnapping Case

They found M. Bouc finishing an omelet.

"I thought it best to have lunch served immediately in the restaurant-car" he said. "Afterward it will be cleared and M. Poirot can conduct his examination of the passengers there. In the meantime I have ordered them to bring us three some food here."

"An excellent idea," said Poirot.

Neither of the other two men was hungry, and the meal was soon eaten, but not till they were sipping their coffee did M. Bouc mention the subject that was occupying all their minds.

"*Eh bien?*" he asked.

"*Eh bien,* I have discovered the identity of the victim. I know why it was imperative he should leave America."

"Who was he?"

"Do you remember reading of the Armstrong baby? This is the man who murdered little Daisy Armstrong—Cassetti."

"I recall it now. A shocking affair—though I cannot remember the details."

"Colonel Armstrong was an Englishman—a V.C. He was half American, as his mother was a daughter of W.K. Van der Halt, the Wall Street millionaire. He married the daughter of Linda Arden, the most famous tragic American actress of her day. They lived in America and had one child—a girl—whom they idolized. When she was three years old she was kidnapped, and an impossibly high sum demanded as the price of her return. I will not weary you with all the intricacies that followed. I will come to the moment, when, after having paid over the enormous sum of two hundred thousand dollars, the child's dead body was discovered, it having been dead at least a fortnight. Public indignation rose to fever point. And there was worse to follow. Mrs. Armstrong was expecting another child. Following the shock of the discovery, she gave birth to a dead child born prematurely, and herself died. Her brokenhearted husband shot himself."

"*Mon dieu,* what a tragedy. I remember now," said M. Bouc, "There was also another death, if I remember rightly?"

"Yes—an unfortunate French or Swiss nursemaid. The police were convinced that she had some knowledge of the crime. They refused to believe her hysterical denials. Finally, in a fit of despair, the poor girl threw herself from a window and was killed. It was proved afterwards that she was absolutely innocent of any complicity in the crime."

"It is not good to think of," said M. Bouc.

"About six months later, this man Cassetti was arrested as the head of the gang who had kidnapped the child. They had used the same methods in the past. If the police seemed likely to get on their trail, they had killed their prisoner, hidden the body, and continued to extract as much money as possible before the crime was discovered.

"Now I will make it clear to you this, my friend. Cassetti was the man! But by means of the enormous wealth he had piled up and by the secret hold he had over various persons, he was acquitted on some technical inaccuracy. Notwithstanding that, he would have been lynched by the populace had he not been clever enough to give them the slip. It is now clear to me what happened. He changed his name and left America. Since then he has been a gentleman of leisure, traveling abroad and living on his *rentes*."

"*Ah! quel animal*" M. Bouc's tone was redolent of heartfelt disgust. "I cannot regret that he is dead—not at all!"

"I agree with you."

"*Tout de même,* it is not necessary that he should be killed on the Orient Express. There are other places."

"Poirot smiled a little. He realized that M. Bouc was biased in the matter.

"The question we have now to ask ourselves is this," he said. "Is this murder the work of some rival gang whom Cassetti had double-crossed in the past, or is it an act of private vengeance?"

He explained his discovery of the few words on the charred fragment of paper.

"If I am right in my assumption, then the letter was burnt by the murderer. Why? Because it mentioned the word 'Armstrong,' which is the clue to the mystery."

"Are there any members of the Armstrong family living?"

"That, unfortunately, I do not know. I think I remember reading of a younger sister of Mrs. Armstrong's."

Poirot went on to relate the joint conclusions of himself and Dr. Constantine. M. Bouc brightened at the mention of the broken watch.

"That seems to give us the time of the crime very exactly."

"Yes," said Poirot. "It is very convenient."

There was an indescribable something in his tone that made both the other two look at him curiously.

"You say that you yourself heard Ratchett speak to the conductor at twenty minutes to one?"

Poirot related just what had occurred.

"Well," said M. Bouc, "that proves at least that Cassetti—or Ratchett, as I shall continue to call him—was certainly alive at twenty minutes to one."

"Twenty-three minutes to one, to be precise."

"Then at twelve thirty-seven, to put it formally, M. Ratchett was alive. That is *one* fact, at least."

Poirot did not reply. He sat looking thoughtfully in front of him.

There was a tap on the door, and the restaurant attendant entered.

"The restaurant-car is free now, Monsieur," he said.

"We will go there," said M. Bouc, rising.

"I may accompany you?" asked Constantine.

"Certainly, my dear doctor. Unless M. Poirot has any objection?"

"Not at all. Not at all," said Poirot.

After a little politeness in the matter of procedure, "*Après vous, Monsieur.*" "*Mais non, après vous,*" they left the compartment.

PART TWO
THE EVIDENCE

CHAPTER 1
The Evidence of the Wagon Lit Conductor

In the restaurant-car all was in readiness.

Poirot and M. Bouc sat together on one side of a table. The doctor sat across the aisle.

On the table in front of Poirot was a plan of the Istanbul-Calais coach with the names of the passengers marked in in red ink.

The passports and tickets were in a pile at one side. There was writing paper, ink, pen and pencils.

"Excellent," said Poirot. "We can open our Court of Inquiry without more ado. First, I think, we should take the evidence of the Wagon Lit conductor. You probably know something about the man. What character has he? Is he a man in whose word you would place reliance?"

"I should say so most assuredly. Pierre Michel has been employed by the company for over fifteen years. He is a Frenchman—lives near Calais. Thoroughly respectable and honest. Not, perhaps, remarkable for brains."

Poirot nodded comprehendingly.

"Good," he said. "Let us see him."

Pierre Michel had recovered some of his assurance, but he was still extremely nervous.

"I hope Monsieur will not think that there has been any negligence on my part," he said anxiously, his eyes going from Poirot to M. Bouc. "It is a terrible thing that has happened. I hope Monsieur does not think that it reflects on me in any way?"

Having soothed the man's fears, Poirot began his questions. He first elicited Michel's name and address, his length of service, and the length of time he had been on this particular route. These particulars he already knew, but the routine questions served to put the man at his ease.

"And now," went on Poirot, "let us come to the events of last night. M. Ratchett retired to bed—when?"

"Almost immediately after dinner, Monsieur. Actually before we left Belgrade. So he did on the previous night. He had directed me to make up the bed while he was at dinner, and I did so."

"Did anybody go into his compartment afterward?"

"His valet, Monsieur, and the young American gentleman his secretary."

"Anyone else?"

"No, Monsieur, not that I know of."

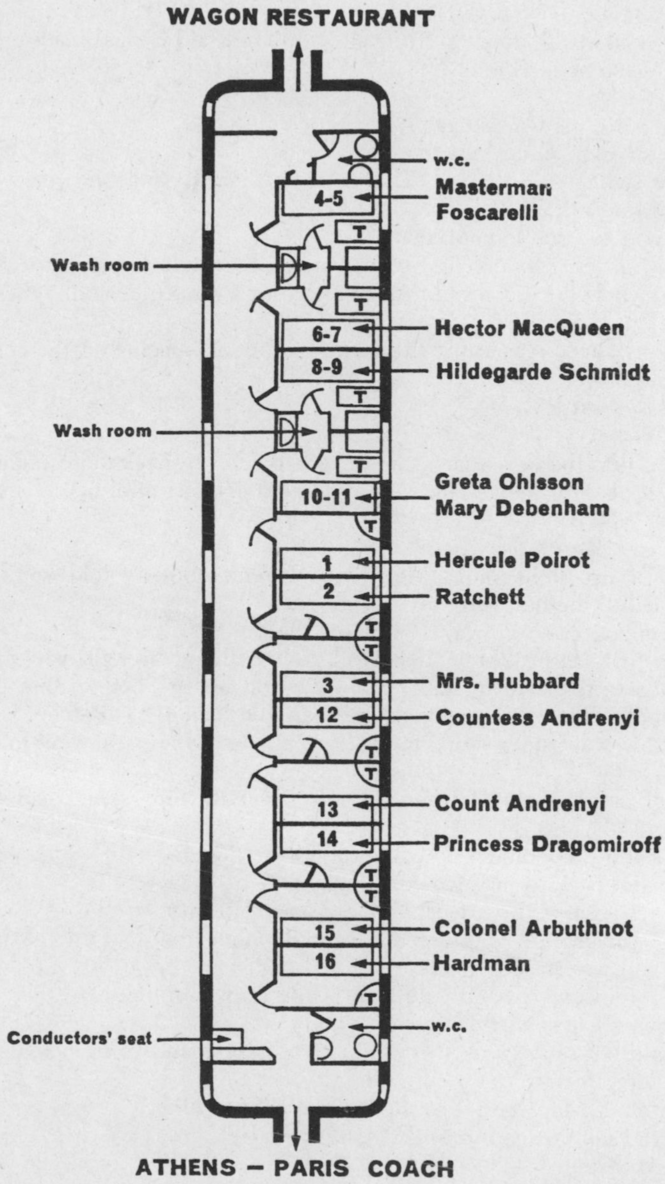
WAGON RESTAURANT
w.c.
4-5
Masterman
Foscarelli
Wash room
T
T
6-7
Hector MacQueen
8-9
Hildegarde Schmidt
Wash room
T
T
10-11
Greta Ohlsson
Mary Debenham
T
1
Hercule Poirot
2
Ratchett
T
T
3
Mrs. Hubbard
12
Countess Andrenyi
T
T
13
Count Andrenyi
14
Princess Dragomiroff
T
T
15
Colonel Arbuthnot
16
Hardman
T
w.c.
Conductors' seat
ATHENS – PARIS COACH

"Good. And that is the last you saw or heard of him?"

"No, Monsieur. You forget, he rang his bell about twenty to one—soon after we had stopped."

"What happened exactly?"

"I knocked at the door, but he called out and said he had made a mistake."

"In English or in French?"

"In French."

"What were his words exactly?"

"*Ce n'est rien. Je me suis trompé.*"

"Quite right," said Poirot. "That is what I heard. And then you went away?"

"Yes, Monsieur."

"Did you go back to your seat?"

"No, Monsieur, I went first to answer another bell that had just rung."

"Now, Michel, I am going to ask you an important question. Where were you at a quarter-past one?"

"I, Monsieur? I was at my little seat at the end—facing up the corridor."

"You are sure?"

"*Mais oui*—at least——"

"Yes?"

"I went into the next coach, the Athens coach, to speak to my colleague there. We spoke about the snow. That was at some time soon after one o'clock. I cannot say exactly."

"And you returned—when?"

"One of my bells rang, Monsieur—I remember—I told you. It was the American lady. She had rung several times."

"I recollect," said Poirot. "And after that?"

"After that, Monsieur? I answered your bell and brought you some mineral water. Then, after half an hour later, I made up the bed in one of the other compartments—that of the young American gentleman, M. Ratchett's secretary."

"Was M. MacQueen alone in his compartment when you went to make up his bed?"

"The English Colonel from No. 15 was with him. They had been sitting talking."

"What did the Colonel do when he left M. MacQueen?"

"He went back to his own compartment."

"No. 15—that is quite close to your seat, is it not?"

"Yes, Monsieur, it is the second compartment from that end of the corridor."

"His bed was already made up?"

"Yes, Monsieur. I had made it up while he was at dinner."

"What time was all this?"

"I could not say exactly, Monsieur. Not later than two o'clock, certainly."

"And after that?"

"After that, Monsieur, I sat in my seat till morning."

"You did not go again into the Athens coach?"

"No, Monsieur."

"Perhaps you slept?"

"I do not think so, Monsieur. The train being at a standstill prevented me from dozing off as I usually do."

"Did you see any of the passengers moving up or down the corridor?"

The man reflected.

"One of the ladies went to the toilet at the far end, I think."

"Which lady?"

"I do not know, Monsieur. It was far down the corridor, and she had her back to me. She had on a kimono of scarlet with dragons on it."

Poirot nodded.

"And after that?"

"Nothing, Monsieur, until the morning."

"You are sure?"

"Ah, pardon, you yourself, Monsieur, opened your door and looked out for a second."

"Good, my friend," said Poirot. "I wondered whether you would remember that. By the way, I was awakened by what sounded like something heavy falling against my door. Have you any idea what that could have been?"

The man stared at him.

"There was nothing, Monsieur. Nothing, I am positive of it."

"Then I must have had the *cauchemar*," said Poirot philosophically.

"Unless," said M. Bouc, "it was something in the compartment next door that you heard."

Poirot took no notice of the suggestion. Perhaps he did not wish to before the Wagon Lit conductor.

"Let us pass to another point," he said. "Supposing that last night an assassin joined the train. It is quite certain the he could not have left it after committing the crime?"

Pierre Michel shook his head.

"Nor that he can be concealed on it somewhere?"

"It has been well searched," said M. Bouc. "Abandon that idea, my friend."

"Besides," said Michel, "no one could get on to the sleeping-car without my seeing them."

"When was the last stop?"

"Vincovci."

"What time was that?"

"We should have left there at 11.58. But owing to the weather we were twenty minutes late."

"Someone might have come along from the ordinary part of the train?"

"No, Monsieur. After the service of dinner the door between the ordinary carriages and the sleeping-cars is locked."

"Did you yourself descend from the train at Vincovci?"

"Yes, Monsieur. I got down on to the platform as usual and stood by the step up into the train. The other conductors did the same."

"What about the forward door? The one near the restaurant-car?"

"It is always fastened on the inside."

"It is not so fastened now."

The man looked surprised, then his face cleared.

"Doubtless one of the passengers has opened it to look out on the snow."

"Probably," said Poirot.

He tapped thoughtfully on the table for a minute or two.

"Monsieur does not blame me?" said the man timidly.

Poirot smiled on him kindly.

"You have had the evil chance, my friend," he said. "Ah! One other point while I remember it. You said that another bell rang just as you were knocking at

M. Ratchett's door. In fact, I heard it myself. Whose was it?"

"It was the bell of Madame la Princesse Dragomiroff. She desired me to summon her maid."

"And you did so?"

"Yes, Monsieur."

Poirot studied the plan in front of him thoughtfully. Then he inclined his head.

"That is all," he said, "for the moment."

The man rose. He looked at M. Bouc.

"Do not distress yourself," said the latter kindly. "I cannot see that there has been any negligence on your part."

Gratified, Pierre Michel left the compartment.

CHAPTER 2
The Evidence of the Secretary

For a minute or two Poirot remained lost in thought.

"I think," he said at last, "That it would be well to have a further word with M. MacQueen, in view of what we now know."

The young American appeared promptly.

"Well," he said. "how are things going?"

"Not too badly. Since our last conversation I have learnt something—the identity of M. Ratchett."

Hector MacQueen leaned forward interestedly.

"Yes?" he said.

"Ratchett, as you suspected, was merely an alias. Ratchett was Cassetti, the man who ran the celebrated kidnapping stunts—including the famous affair of little Daisy Armstrong."

An expression of utter astonishment appeared on MacQueen's face; then it darkened.

"The damned skunk!" he exclaimed.

"You had no idea of this, M. MacQueen?"

"No, sir," said the young American decidedly. "If I had I'd have cut off my right hand before it had a chance to do secretarial work for him!"

"You feel strongly about the matter, M. MacQueen?"

"I have a particular reason for doing so. My father was the district attorney who handled the case, M. Poirot. I saw Mrs. Armstrong more than once—she was a lovely woman. So gentle and heartbroken." His face darkened. "If ever a man deserved what he got, Ratchett or Cassetti is the man. I'm rejoiced at his end. Such a man wasn't fit to live!"

"You almost feel as though you would have been willing to do the good deed yourself?"

"I do. I——" He paused, then flushed rather guiltily. "Seems I'm kind of incriminating myself."

"I should be more inclined to suspect you, M. MacQueen, if you displayed an inordinate sorrow at your employer's decease."

"I don't think I could do that, even to save myself from the chair," said MacQueen grimly.

Then he added:

"If I'm not being unduly curious, just how did you figure this out? Cassetti's identity I mean."

"By a fragment of a letter found in his compartment."

"But surely—I mean—that was rather careless of the old man?"

"That depends," said Poirot, "on the point of view."

The young man seemed to find this remark rather baffling. He stared at Poirot as though trying to make him out.

"The task before me," said Poirot, "is to make sure of the movements of everyone on the train. No offence need be taken, you understand? It is only a matter of routine."

"Sure. Get right on with it and let me clear my character if I can."

"I need hardly ask you the number of your compartment," said Poirot, smiling, "since I shared it with you for a night. It is the second-class compartment Nos. 6 and 7, and after my departure you had it to yourself."

"That's right."

"Now, M. MacQueen, I want you to describe your movements last night from the time of leaving the dining-car."

"That's quite easy. I went back to my compartment, read a bit, got out on the platform at Belgrade, decided it was too cold, and got in again. I talked for a while to a young English lady who is in the compartment next to mine. Then I fell into conversation with that Englishman, Colonel Arbuthnot—as a matter of fact I think you passed us as we were talking. Then I went in to Mr. Ratchett and, as I told you, took down some memoranda of letters he wanted written. I said goodnight to him and left him. Colonel Arbuthnot was still standing in the corridor. His compartment was already made up for the night, so I suggested that he should come along to mine. I ordered a couple of drinks and we got right down to it. Discussed world politics and the Government of India and our own troubles with the financial situation and the Wall Street crisis. I don't as a rule cotton to Britishers—they're a stiff-necked lot—but I liked this one."

"Do you know what time it was when he left you?"

"Pretty late. Getting on for two o'clock, I should say."

"You noticed that the train had stopped?"

"Oh, yes. We wondered a bit. Looked out and saw the snow lying very thick, but we didn't think it was serious."

"What happened when Colonel Arbuthnot finally said good-night?"

"He went along to his compartment and I called to the conductor to make up my bed."

"Where were you whilst he was making it?"

"Standing just outside the door in the corridor smoking a cigarette."

"And then?"

"And then I went to bed and slept till morning."

"During the evening did you leave the train at all?"

"Arbuthnot and I thought we'd get out at—what was the name of the place?—Vincovci to stretch our legs a bit. But it was bitterly cold—a blizzard on. We soon hopped back again."

"By which door did you leave the train?"

"By the one nearest to our compartment."

"The one next to the dining-car?"

"Yes."

"Do you remember if it was bolted?"

MacQueen considered.

"Why, yes, I seem to remember it was. At least there was a kind of bar that fitted across the handle. Is that what you mean?"

"Yes. On getting back into the train did you replace that bar?"

"Why, no—I don't think I did. I got in last. No, I don't seem to remember doing so."

He added suddenly:

"Is that an important point?"

"It may be. Now, I presume, Monsieur, that while you and Colonel Arbuthnot were sitting talking the door of your compartment into the corridor was open?"

Hector MacQueen nodded.

"I want you, if you can, to tell me if anyone passed along that corridor *after* the train left Vincovci until the time you parted company for the night."

MacQueen drew his brows together.

"I think the conductor passed along once," he said, "coming from the direction of the dining-car. And a woman passed the other way, going toward it."

"Which woman?"

"I couldn't say. I didn't really notice. You see, I was just arguing a point with Arbuthnot. I just seem to remember a glimpse of some scarlet silk affair passing the door. I didn't look, and anyway I wouldn't have seen the person's face. As you know, my carriage faces the dining-car end of the train, so a woman going along the corridor in that direction would have her back to me as soon as she'd passed."

Poirot nodded.

"She was going to the toilet, I presume?"

"I suppose so."

"And you saw her return?"

"Well, no, now that you mention it, I didn't notice her returning, but I suppose she must have done so."

"One more question. Do you smoke a pipe, M. MacQueen?"

"No, sir, I do not."

Poirot paused a moment.

"I think that is all at present. I should now like to see the valet of M. Ratchett. By the way, did both you and he always travel second-class?"

"He did. But I usually went first—if possible in the adjoining compartment to Mr. Ratchett. Then he had most of his baggage put in my compartment and yet could get at both it and me easily whenever he chose. But on this occasion all the first-class berths were booked except the one which he took."

"I comprehend. Thank you, M. MacQueen."

CHAPTER 3
The Evidence of the Valet

The American was succeeded by the pale Englishman with the inexpressive face whom Poirot had already noticed on the day before. He stood waiting very correctly. Poirot motioned to him to sit down.

"You are, I understand, the valet of M. Ratchett?"

"Yes, sir."

"Your name?"

"Edward Henry Masterman."

"Your age?"

"Thirty-nine."

"And your home address?"

"21 Friar Street, Clerkenwell."

"You have heard that your master has been murdered?"

"Yes, sir. A very shocking occurrence."

"Will you now tell me, please, at what hour you last saw M. Ratchett?"

The valet considered.

"It must have been about nine o'clock, sir, last night. That or a little after."

"Tell me in your own words exactly what happened."

"I went in to Mr. Ratchett as usual, sir, and attended to his wants."

"What were your duties exactly?"

"To fold or hang up his clothes, sir. Put his dental plate in water and see that he had everything he wanted for the night."

"Was his manner much the same as usual?"

The valet considered a moment.

"Well, sir, I think he was upset."

"In what way—upset?"

"Over a letter he'd been reading. He asked me if it was I who had put it in his compartment. Of course I told him I hadn't done any such thing, but he swore at me and found fault with everything I did."

"Was that unusual?"

"Oh, no, sir, he lost his temper easily—as I say, it just depended what had happened to upset him."

"Did your master ever take a sleeping draught?"

Dr. Constantine leaned forward a little.

"Always when traveling by train, sir. He said he couldn't sleep otherwise."

"Do you know what drug he was in the habit of taking?"

"I couldn't say, I'm sure, sir. There was no name on the bottle. Just *'The Sleeping Draught to be taken at bedtime.'*"

"Did he take it last night"

"Yes, sir. I poured it into a glass and put it on top of the toilet table ready for him."

"You didn't actually see him drink it?"

"No, sir."

"What happened next?"

"I asked if there was anything further, and asked what time M. Ratchett would like to be called in the morning. He said he didn't want to be disturbed till he rang."

"Was that usual?"

"Quite usual, sir. He used to ring the bell for the conductor and then send him for me when he was ready to get up."

"Was he usually an early or a late riser?"

"It depended, sir, on his mood. Sometimes he'd get up for breakfast, sometimes he wouldn't get up till just on lunch time."

"So that you weren't alarmed when the morning wore on and no summons came?"

"No, sir."

"Did you know that your master had enemies?"

"Yes, sir."

The man spoke quite unemotionally.

"How did you know?"

"I had heard him discussing some letters, sir, with Mr. MacQueen."

"Had you an affection for your employer, Masterman?"

Masterman's face became, if possible, even more inexpressive than it was normally.

"I should hardly like to say that, sir. He was a generous employer."

"But you didn't like him?"

"Shall we put it that I don't care very much for Americans, sir."

"Have you ever been in America?"

"No, sir."

"Do you remember reading in the paper of the Armstrong kidnapping case?"

A little colour came into the man's cheeks.

"Yes, indeed, sir. A little baby girl, wasn't it? A very shocking affair."

"Did you know that your employer, M. Ratchett, was the principal instigator in that affair?"

"No, indeed, sir." The valet's tone held positive warmth and feeling for the first time. "I can hardly believe it, sir."

"Nevertheless, it is true. Now, to pass to your own movements last night. A matter of routine, you understand. What did you do after leaving your master?"

"I told Mr. MacQueen, sir, that the master wanted him. Then I went to my own compartment and read."

"Your compartment was——?"

"The end second-class one, sir. Next to the diningcar." Poirot was looking at his plan.

"I see—and you had which berth?"

"The lower one, sir."

"That is No. 4?"

"Yes, sir."

"Is there anyone in with you?"

"Yes, sir. A big Italian fellow."

"Does he speak English?"

"Well, a kind of English, sir." The valet's tone was deprecating. "He's been in America—Chicago—I understand."

"Do you and he talk together much?"

"No, sir. I prefer to read."

Poirot smiled. He could visualise the scene—the large voluble Italian, and the snub direct administered by the gentleman's gentleman.

"And what, may I ask, are you reading?" he inquired.

"At present, sir, I am reading *Love's Captive*, by Mrs. Arabella Richardson."

"A good story?"

"I find it highly enjoyable, sir."

"Well, let us continue. You returned to your compartment and read *Love's Captive* till—when?"

"At about ten-thirty, sir, this Italian wanted to go to bed. So the conductor came and made the beds up."

"And then you went to bed and to sleep?"

"I went to bed, sir, but I didn't sleep."

"Why didn't you sleep?"

"I had the toothache, sir."

"Oh, *là là*—that is painful."

"Most painful, sir."

"Did you do anything for it?"

"I applied a little oil of cloves, sir, which relieved the pain a little, but I was still not able to get to sleep. I turned the light on above my head and continued to read—to take my mind off it, as it were."

"And did you not go to sleep at all?"

"Yes, sir, I dropped off about four in the morning."

"And your companion?"

"The Italian fellow? Oh, he just snored."

"He did not leave the compartment at all during the night?"

"No, sir."

"Did you?"

"No, sir."

"Did you hear anything during the night?"

"I don't think so, sir. Nothing unusual, I mean. The train being at a standstill made it all very quiet."

Poirot was silent a moment or two, then he said:

"Well, I think there is very little more to be said. You cannot throw any light upon the tragedy?"

"I'm afraid not. I'm sorry, sir."

"As far as you know, was there any quarrel or bad blood between your master and M. MacQueen?"

"Oh, no, sir. Mr. MacQueen was a very pleasant gentleman."

"Where were you in service before you came to M. Ratchett?"

"With Sir Henry Tomlinson, sir, in Grosvenor Square."

"Why did you leave him?"

"He was going to East Africa, sir, and did not require my services any longer. But I am sure he will speak for me, sir. I was with him some years."

"And you have been with M. Ratchett—how long?"

"Just over nine months, sir."

"Thank you, Masterman. By the way, are you a pipe smoker?"

"No, sir. I only smoke cigarettes—gaspers, sir."

"Thank you. That will do."

Poirot gave him a nod of dismissal.

The valet hesitated a moment.

"You'll excuse me, sir, but the elderly American lady is in what I might describe as a state, sir. She's saying she knows all about the murderer. She's in a very excitable condition, sir."

"In that case," said Poirot, smiling, "we had better see her next."

"Shall I tell her, sir? She's been demanding to see someone in authority for a long time. The conductor's been trying to pacify her."

"Send her to us, my friend," said Poirot. "We will listen to her story now."

CHAPTER 4
The Evidence of the American Lady

Mrs. Hubbard arrived in the dining-car in such a state of breathless excitement that she was hardly able to articulate her words.

"Now just tell me this. Who's in authority here? I've got some vurry important information, *vurry* important, indeed, and I just want to tell it to someone in authority as soon as may be. If you gentlemen——"

Her wavering glance fluctuated between the three men. Poirot leaned forward.

"Tell it to me, Madame," he said. "But, first, pray be seated."

Mrs. Hubbard plumped heavily down on to the seat opposite to him.

"What I've got to tell you is just this. There was a murder on the train last night, and the murderer was *right there in my compartment!*"

She paused to give dramatic emphasis to her words.

"You are sure of this, Madame?"

"Of course I'm sure! The idea! I know what I'm talking about. I'll tell you just everything there is to tell. I'd gotten into bed and gone to sleep, and suddenly I woke up—all in the dark, it was—and I knew there was a man in my compartment. I was just so scared I couldn't scream, if you know what I mean. I just lay there and thought, 'Mercy, I'm going to be killed.' I just can't describe to you how I felt. These nasty trains, I thought, and all the outrages I'd read of. And I thought, 'Well, anyway, he won't get my jewellery,' because, you see, I'd put that in a stocking and hidden it under my pillow—which isn't so mighty comfortable, by the way, kinder bumpy, if you know what I mean. But that's neither here nor there. Where was I?"

"You realized, Madame, that there was a man in your compartment."

"Yes, well, I just lay there with my eyes closed, and I thought whatever should I do, and I thought, 'Well, I'm just thankful that my daughter doesn't know the plight I'm in.' And then, somehow, I got my wits about me and I felt about with my hand and I pressed the bell for the conductor. I pressed it and I pressed it, but nothing happened, and I can tell you I thought my heart was going to stop beating. 'Mercy,' I said to myself, 'maybe they've murdered every single soul on the train.' It was at a standstill, anyhow, and a nasty quiet feel in the air. But I just went on pressing that bell, and oh! the relief when I heard footsteps coming running down the corridor and a knock on the door. 'Come in,' I screamed, and I switched on the lights at the same time. And, would you believe it, there wasn't a soul there."

This seemed to Mrs. Hubbard to be a dramatic climax rather than an anticlimax.

"And what happened next, Madame?"

"Why, I told the man what had happened, and he didn't seem to believe me. Seemed to imagine I'd dreamt the whole thing. I made him look under the seat, though he said there wasn't room for a man to squeeze himself in there. It was plain enough the man had got away, but there *had* been a man there and it just made me mad the way the conductor tried to soothe me down! I'm not one to imagine things, Mr.——I don't think I know your name?"

"Poirot, Madame, and this is M. Bouc, a director of the company, and Dr. Constantine."

Mrs. Hubbard murmured:

"Pleased to meet you, I'm sure," to all three of them in an abstracted manner, and then plunged once more into her recital.

"Now I'm just not going to pretend I was as bright as I might have been. I got it into my head that it was the man from next door—the poor fellow who's been killed. I told the conductor to look at the door between the compartments, and sure enough it wasn't bolted. Well, I soon saw to that. I told him to bolt it then and there, and after he'd gone out I got up and put a suitcase against it to make sure."

"What time was this, Mrs. Hubbard?"

"Well, I'm sure I can't tell you. I never looked to see. I was so upset."

"And what is your theory now?"

"Why, I should say it was just as plain as plain could be. The man in my compartment was the murderer. Who else could he be?"

"And you think he went back into the adjoining compartment?"

"How do I know where he went? I had my eyes tight shut."

"He must have slipped out through the door into the corridor."

"Well, I couldn't say. You see, I had my eyes tight shut."

Mrs. Hubbard sighed convulsively.

"Mercy, I was scared! If my daughter only knew——"

"You do not think, Madame, that what you heard was the noise of someone moving about next door—in the murdered man's compartment?"

"No, I do not, Mr.—what is it?—Poirot. The man was *right there in the same compartment with me*. And, what's more, I've got proof of it."

Triumphantly she hauled a large handbag into view and proceeded to burrow in its interior.

She took out in turn two large clean handkerchiefs, a pair of horn-rimmed glasses, a bottle of aspirin, a packet of Glauber's salts, a celluloid tube of bright green peppermints, a bunch of keys, a pair of scissors, a book of American Express cheques, a snapshot of an extraordinarily plain-looking child, some letters, five strings of pseudo Oriental beads and a small metal object—a button.

"You see this button? Well, it's not one of *my* buttons. It's not off anything I've got. I found it this morning when I got up."

As she placed it on the table, M. Bouc leaned forward and gave an exclamation.

"But this is a button from the tunic of a Wagon Lit attendant!"

"There may be a natural explanation for that," said Poirot.

He turned gently to the lady.

"This button, Madame, may have dropped from the conductor's uniform, either when he searched your cabin, or when he was making the bed up last night."

"I just don't know what's the matter with all you people. Seems as though you don't do anything but make objections. Now listen here. I was reading a magazine last night before I went to sleep. Before I turned the light out I placed that magazine on a little case that was standing on the floor near the window. Have you got that?"

They assured her that they had.

"Very well, then. The conductor looked under the seat from near the door and then he came in and bolted the door between me and the next compartment, but he never went up near the window. Well, this morning that button was lying right on top of the magazine. What do you call that, I should like to know?"

"That, Madame, I call evidence," said Poirot.

The answer seemed to appease the lady.

"It makes me madder than a hornet to be disbelieved," she explained.

"You have given us most interesting and valuable evidence," said Poirot soothingly. "Now, may I ask you a few questions?"

"Why, willingly."

"How was it, since you were nervous of this man Ratchett, that you hadn't already bolted the door between the compartments?"

"I had," returned Mrs. Hubbard promptly.

"Oh, you had?"

"Well, as a matter of fact, I asked that Swedish creature—a pleasant soul—if it was bolted, and she said it was."

"How was it you couldn't see for yourself?"

"Because I was in bed and my spongebag was hanging on the door handle."

"What time was it when you asked her to do this for you?"

"Now let me think. It must have been round about half-past ten or a quarter to eleven. She'd come along to see if I'd got an aspirin. I told her where to find it, and she got it out of my grip."

"You yourself were in bed?"

"Yes."

Suddenly she laughed.

"Poor soul—she was in quite a taking. You see, she'd opened the door of the next compartment by mistake."

"M. Ratchett's?"

"Yes. You know how difficult it is as you come along the train and all the doors are shut. She opened his by mistake. She was very distressed about it. He'd laughed, it seemed, and I fancy he may have said something not quite nice. Poor thing, she was all in a flutter. 'Oh! I make mistake,' she said, 'I ashamed make mistake. Not nice man,' she said, 'He say, "You too old."'"

Dr. Constantine sniggered and Mrs. Hubbard immediately froze him with a glance.

"He wasn't a nice kind of man," she said, "to say a thing like that to a lady. It's not right to laugh at such things."

Dr. Constantine hastily apologized.

"Did you hear any noise from M. Ratchett's compartment after that?" asked Poirot.

"Well—not exactly."

"What do you mean by that, Madame?"

"Well——" she paused. "He snored."

"Ah! he snored, did he?"

"Terribly. The night before it quite kept me awake."

"You didn't hear him snore after you had had the scare about a man being in your compartment?"

"Why, Mr. Poirot, how could I? He was dead."

"Ah, yes, truly," said Poirot. He appeared confused.

"Do you remember the affair of the Armstrong kidnapping, Mrs. Hubbard?" he asked.

"Yes, indeed I do. And how the wretch that did it escaped scot free! My, I'd have liked to get my hands on him."

"He has not escaped. He is dead. He died last night."

"You don't mean——?" Mrs. Hubbard half rose from her chair in excitement.

"But yes, I do. Ratchett was the man."

"*Well!* Well, to think of that! I must write and tell my daughter. Now, didn't I tell you last night that that man had an evil face? I was right, you see. My daughter always says: 'When Momma's got a hunch, you can bet your bottom dollar it's O.K.'"

"Were you acquainted with any of the Armstrong family, Mrs. Hubbard?"

"No. They moved in a very exclusive circle. But I've always heard that Mrs. Armstrong was a perfectly lovely woman and that her husband worshipped her."

"Well, Mrs. Hubbard, you have helped us very much—very much indeed. Perhaps you will give me your full name?"

"Why, certainly. Caroline Martha Hubbard."

"Will you write your address down here?"

Mrs. Hubbard did so, without ceasing to speak.

"I just can't get over it. Cassetti—on this train. I had a hunch about that man, didn't I, Mr. Poirot?"

"Yes, indeed, Madame. By the way, have you a scarlet silk dressing-gown?"

"Mercy, what an odd question! Why, no. I've got two dressing-gowns with me—a pink flannel one that's kind of cosy for on board ship, and one my daughter gave me as a present—a kind of local affair in purple silk. But what in creation do you want to know about my dressing-gowns for?"

"Well, you see, Madame, someone in a scarlet kimono entered either your or Mr. Ratchett's compartment last night. It is, as you said just now, very difficult when all the doors are shut to know which compartment is which."

"Well, no one in a scarlet dressing-gown came into my compartment."

"Then she must have gone into M. Ratchett's."

Mrs. Hubbard pursed her lips together and said grimly:

"That wouldn't surprise me any."

Poirot leaned forward.

"So you heard a woman's voice next door?"

"I don't know how you guessed that, Mr. Poirot. I don't really. But—well—as a matter of fact, I *did*."

"But when I asked you just now if you heard anything next door, you only said you heard Mr. Ratchett snoring."

"Well that was true enough. He *did* snore part of the time. As for the other ——" Mrs. Hubbard got rather pink. "It isn't a very nice thing to speak about."

"What time was it when you heard a woman's voice?"

"I can't tell you. I just woke up for a minute and heard a woman talking, and it was plain enough where she was. So I just thought, 'Well, that's the kind of man he is. Well, I'm not surprised,' and then I went to sleep again, and I'm sure I should never have mentioned anything of the kind to three strange gentlemen if you hadn't dragged it out of me."

"Was it before the scare about the man in your compartment, or after?"

"Why, that's like what you said just now! He wouldn't have had a woman talking to him if he were dead, would he?"

"*Pardon*. You must think me very stupid, Madame."

"I guess even you get kinder muddled now and then. I just can't get over it being that monster Cassetti. What my daughter will say——"

Poirot managed adroitly to help the good lady to restore the contents of her handbag and he then shepherded her toward the door.

At the last moment he said:

"You have dropped your handkerchief, Madame."

Mrs. Hubbard looked at the little scrap of cambric he held out to her.

"That's not mine, Mr. Poirot. I've got mine right here."

"*Pardon*. I thought as it had the initial H on it——"

"Well, now, that's curious, but it's certainly not mine. Mine are marked C.M.H., and they're sensible things—not expensive Paris fallals. What good is a handkerchief like that to anybody's nose?"

Neither of the three men seemed to have an answer to this question, and Mrs. Hubbard sailed out triumphantly.

CHAPTER 5
The Evidence of the Swedish Lady

M. Bouc was handling the button Mrs. Hubbard had left behind her.

"This button. I cannot understand it. Does it mean that, after all, Pierre Michel is involved in some way?" he said. He paused, then continued, as Poirot did not reply. "What have you to say, my friend?"

"That button, it suggests possibilities," said Poirot thoughtfully. "Let us interview next the Swedish lady before we discuss the evidence we have heard."

He sorted through the pile of passports in front of him.

"Ah! here we are. Greta Ohlsson, age forty-nine."

M. Bouc gave directions to the restaurant attendant, and presently the lady with the yellowish-grey bun of hair and the long mild sheep-like face was ushered in. She peered short-sightedly at Poirot through her glasses, but was quite calm.

It transpired that she understood and spoke French, so that the conversation took place in that language. Poirot first asked her the questions to which he already knew the answers—her name, age, and address. He then asked her her occupation.

She was, she told him, matron in a missionary school near Stamboul. She was a trained nurse.

"You know, of course, of what took place last night, Mademoiselle?"

"Naturally. It is very dreadful. And the American lady tells me that the murderer was actually in her compartment."

"I heard, Mademoiselle, that you were the last person to see the murdered man alive?"

"I do not know. It may be so. I opened the door of his compartment by mistake. I was much ashamed. It was a most awkward mistake."

"You actually saw him?"

"Yes. He was reading a book. I apologized quickly and withdrew."

"Did he say anything to you?"

A slight flush showed on the worthy lady's cheek.

"He laughed and said a few words. I—I did not quite catch them."

"And what did you do after that, Mademoiselle?" asked Poirot, passing from the subject tactfully.

"I went in to the American lady, Mrs. Hubbard. I asked her for some aspirin and she gave it to me."

"Did she ask you whether the communicating door between her compartment and that of M. Ratchett was bolted?"

"Yes."

"And was it?"

"Yes."

"And after that?"

"After that I go back to my own compartment, I take the aspirin and lie down."

"What time was all this?"

"When I got into bed it was five minutes to eleven, because I look at my watch before I wind it up."

"Did you go to sleep quickly?"

"Not very quickly. My head got better, but I lay awake some time."

"Had the train come to a stop before you went to sleep?"

"I do not think so. We stopped, I think, at a station, just as I was getting drowsy."

"That would be Vincovci. Now your compartment, Mademoiselle, is this one?" he indicated it on the plan.

"That is so, yes."

"You had the upper or the lower berth?"

"The lower berth, No. 10."

"And you had a companion?"

"Yes, a young English lady. Ver nice, very amiable. She had traveled from Baghdad."

"After the train left Vincovci, did she leave the compartment?"

"No, I am sure she did not."

"Why are you sure if you were asleep?"

"I sleep very lightly. I am used to waking at a sound. I am sure if she had come down from the berth above I should have awakened."

"Did you yourself leave the compartment?"

"Not until this morning."

"Have you a scarlet silk kimono, Mademoiselle?"

"No, indeed. I have a good comfortable dressing-gown of Jaeger material."

"And the lady with you, Miss Debenham? What colour is her dressing-gown?"

"A pale mauve abba such as you buy in the East."

Poirot nodded. Then he said in a friendly tone:

"Why are you taking this journey? A holiday?"

"Yes, I am going home for a holiday. But first I go to Lausanne to stay with a sister for a week or so."

"Perhaps you will be so amiable as to write me down the name and address of your sister?"

"With pleasure."

She took the paper and pencil he gave her and wrote down the name and address as requested.

"Have you ever been in America, Mademoiselle?"

"No. Very nearly once. I was to go with an invalid lady, but it was canceled at the last moment. I much regretted. They are very good, the Americans. They give much money to found schools and hospitals. They are very practical."

"Do you remember hearing of the Armstrong kidnapping case?"

"No, what was that?"

Poirot explained.

Greta Ohlsson was indignant. Her yellow bun of hair quivered with her emotion.

"That there are in the world such evil men! It tries one's faith. The poor mother. My heart aches for her."

The amiable Swede departed, her kindly face flushed, her eyes suffused with tears.

Poirot was writing busily on a sheet of paper.

"What is it you write there, my friend?" asked M. Bouc.

"*Mon cher*, it is my habit to be neat and orderly. I make here a little table of chronological events."

He finished writing and passed the paper to M. Bouc.

	9.15	Train leaves Belgrade
about	9.40	Valet leaves Ratchett with sleeping draught beside him.
about	10.0	MacQueen leaves Ratchett.
about	10.40	Greta Ohlsson sees Ratchett (last seen alive). N.B.—He was awake reading a book.
	0.10	Train leaves Vincovci (late).
	0.30	Train runs into a snowdrift.
	0.37	Ratchett's bell rings. Conductor answers it. Ratchett says, "*Ce n'est rien. Je me suis trompé.*"
about	1.17	Mrs. Hubbard thinks man is in her carriage. Rings for conductor.

M. Bouc nodded approval.

"That is very clear," he said.

"There is nothing there that strikes you as at all odd?"

"No, it seems all quite clear and above board. It seems quite plain that the crime was committed at 1.15. The evidence of the watch shows us that, and Mrs. Hubbard's story fits in. For my mind, I will make a guess at the identity of the murderer. I say, my friend, that it is the big Italian. He comes from America—from Chicago—and remember an Italian's weapon is the knife, and he stabs not once but several times."

"That is true."

"Without a doubt, that is the solution of the mystery. Doubtless he and this Ratchett were in this kidnapping business together. Cassetti is an Italian name. In some way Ratchett did on him what they call the double-cross. The Italian tracks him down, sends him warning letters first, and finally revenges himself upon him in a brutal way. It is all quite simple."

Poirot shook his head doubtfully.

"It is hardly as simple as that, I fear," he murmured.

"Me, I am convinced it is the truth," said M. Bouc, becoming more and more enamoured of his theory.

"And what about the valet with the toothache who swears that the Italian never left the compartment?"

"That is the difficulty."

Poirot twinkled.

"Yes, it is annoying, that. Unlucky for your theory, and extremely lucky for our Italian friend that M. Ratchett's valet should have had the toothache."

"It will be explained," said M. Bouc with magnificent certainty.

Poirot shook his head again.

"No, it is hardly so simple as that," he murmured again.

CHAPTER 6

The Evidence of the Russian Princess

"Let us hear what Pierre Michel has to say about this button," he said.

The Wagon Lit conductor was recalled. He looked at them inquiringly.

M. Bouc cleared his throat.

"Michel," he said. "Here is a button from your tunic. It was found in the American lady's compartment. What have you to say for yourself about it?"

The conductor's hand went automatically to his tunic.

"I have lost no button, Monsieur," he said. "There must be some mistake."

"That is very odd."

"I cannot account for it, Monsieur."

The man seemed astonished, but not in any way guilty or confused.

M. Bouc said meaningly:

"Owing to the circumstances in which it was found, it seems fairly certain that this button was dropped by the man who was in Mrs. Hubbard's compartment last night when she rang the bell."

"But, Monsieur, there was no one there. The lady must have imagined it."

"She did not imagine it, Michel. The assassin of M. Ratchett passed that way—*and dropped that button*."

As the significance of M. Bouc's word became plain to him, Pierre Michel flew into a violent state of agitation.

"It is not true, Monsieur, it is not true!" he cried. "You are accusing me of the crime. Me? I am innocent. I am absolutely innocent. Why should I want to kill a Monsieur whom I have never seen before?"

"Where were you when Mrs. Hubbard's bell rang?"

"I told you, Monsieur, in the next coach, talking to my colleague."

"We will send for him."

"Do so, Monsieur, I implore you, do so."

The conductor of the next coach was summoned. He immediately confirmed Pierre Michel's statement. He added that the conductor from the Bucharest coach had also been there. The three of them had been discussing the situation caused by the snow. They had been talking some ten minutes when Michel fancied he heard a bell. As he opened the doors connecting the two coaches, they had all heard it plainly. A bell ringing repeatedly. Michel had run post-haste to answer it.

"So you see, Monsieur, I am not guilty," cried Michel anxiously.

"And this button from a Wagon Lit tunic—how do you explain it?"

"I cannot, Monsieur. It is a mystery to me. All my buttons are intact."

Both of the other conductors also declared that they had not lost a button. Also that they had not been inside Mrs. Hubbard's compartment at any time.

"Calm yourself, Michel," said M. Bouc, "and cast your mind back to the moment when you ran to answer Mrs. Hubbard's bell. Did you meet anyone at all in the corridor?"

"No, Monsieur."

"Did you see anyone going away from you down the corridor in the other direction?"

"Again, no, Monsieur."

"Odd," said M. Bouc.

"Not so very," said Poirot. "It is a question of time. Mrs. Hubbard wakes to find someone in her compartment. For a minute or two she lies paralyzed, her eyes shut. Probably it was then that the man slipped out into the corridor. Then she starts ringing the bell. But the conductor does not come at once. It is only the third or fourth peal that he hears. I should say myself that there was ample time——"

"For what? For what, *mon cher?* Remember that there are thick drifts of snow all round the train."

"There are two courses open to our mysterious assassin," said Poirot slowly. "He could retreat into either of the toilets or he could disappear into one of the compartments."

"But they were all occupied."

"Yes."

"You mean that he could retreat into his *own* compartment?"

Poirot nodded.

"It fits, it fits," murmured M. Bouc. "During that ten minutes' absence of the conductor, the murderer comes from his own compartment, goes into Ratchett's, kills him, locks and chains the door on the inside, goes out through Mrs. Hubbard's compartment and is back safely in his own compartment by the time the conductor arrives."

Poirot murmured:

"It is not quite so simple as that, my friend. Our friend the doctor here will tell you so."

With a gesture M. Bouc signified that the three conductors might depart.

"We have still to see eight passengers," said Poirot. "Five first-class passengers—Princess Dragomiroff, Count and Countess Andrenyi, Colonel Arbuthnot and Mr. Hardman. Three second-class passengers—Miss Debenham, Antonio Foscarella and the lady's-maid Fräulein Schmidt."

"Who will you see first—the Italian?"

"How you harp on your Italian! No, we will start at the top of the tree. Perhaps Madame la Princesse will be so good as to spare us a few moments of her time. Convey that message to her, Michel."

"*Oui, Monsieur,*" said the conductor, who was just leaving the car.

"Tell her we can wait on her in her compartment if she does not wish to put herself to the trouble of coming here," called M. Bouc.

But Princess Dragomiroff declined to take this course. She appeared in the dining-car, inclined her head slightly and sat down opposite Poirot.

Her small, toad-like face looked even yellower than the day before. She was certainly ugly, and yet, like the toad, she had eyes like jewels, dark and imperious, revealing latent energy and an intellectual force that could be felt at once.

Her voice was deep, very distinct, with a slight grating quality in it.

She cut short a flowery phrase of apology from M. Bouc.

"You need not offer apologies, Messieurs. I understand a murder has taken place. Naturally, you must interview all the passengers. I shall be glad to give all the assistance in my power."

"You are most amiable, Madame," said Poirot.

"Not at all. It is my duty. What do you wish to know?"

"Your full Christian names and address, Madame. Perhaps you would prefer to write them yourself?"

Poirot proffered a sheet of paper and pencil, but the Princess waved them aside.

"You can write it," she said. "There is nothing difficult—Natalia Dragomiroff, 17 Avenue Kleber, Paris."

"You are traveling home from Constantinople, Madame?"

"Yes, I have been staying at the Austrian Embassy. My maid is with me."

"Would you be so good as to give me a brief account of your movements last night from dinner onwards?"

"Willingly. I directed the conductor to make up my bed whilst I was in the dining-car. I retired to bed immediately after dinner. I read until the hour of eleven, when I turned out my light. I was unable to sleep owing to certain rheumatic pains from which I suffer. At about a quarter to one I rang for my maid. She massaged me and then read aloud till I felt sleepy. I cannot say exactly when she left me. It may have been half an hour, it may have been later."

"The train had stopped then?"

"The train had stopped."

"You heard nothing—nothing unusual during the time, Madame?"

"I heard nothing unusual."

"What is your maid's name?"

"Hildegarde Schmidt."

"She has been with you long?"

"Fifteen years."

"You consider her trustworthy?"

"Absolutely. Her people come from an estate of my late husband's in Germany."

"You have been in America, I presume, Madame?"

The abrupt change of subject made the old lady raise her eyebrows.

"Many times."

"Were you at any time acquainted with a family of the name of Armstrong—a family in which a tragedy occurred?"

With some emotion in her voice the old lady said:

"You speak of friends of mine, Monsieur."

"You knew Colonel Armstrong well, then?"

"I knew him slightly; but his wife, Sonia Armstrong, was my god-daughter. I was on terms of friendship with her mother, the actress, Linda Arden. Linda Arden was a great genius, one of the greatest tragic actresses in the world. As Lady Macbeth, as Magda, there was no one to touch her. I was not only an admirer of her art, I was a personal friend."

"She is dead?"

"No, no, she is alive, but she lives in complete retirement. Her health is very delicate, she has to lie on a sofa most of the time."

"There was, I think, a second daughter?"

"Yes, much younger than Mrs. Armstrong."

"And she is alive?"

"Certainly."

"Where is she?"

The old woman bent an acute glance at him.

"I must ask you the reason of these questions. What have they to do with the matter in hand—the murder on this train?"

"They are connected in this way, Madame, the man who was murdered was the man responsible for the kidnapping and murder of Mrs. Armstrong's child."

"Ah!"

The straight brows drew together. Princess Dragomiroff drew herself a little more erect.

"In my view, then, this murder is an entirely admirable happening! You will pardon my slightly biased point of view."

"It is most natural, Madame. And now to return to the question you did not answer. Where is the younger daughter of Linda Arden, the sister of Mrs. Armstrong?"

"I honestly cannot tell you, Monsieur. I have lost touch with the younger generation. I believe she married an Englishman some years ago and went to England, but at the moment I cannot recollect the name."

She paused a minute and then said:

"Is there anything further you want to ask me, gentlemen?"

"Only one thing, Madame, a somewhat personal question. The colour of your dressing-gown."

She raised her eyebrows slightly.

"I must suppose you have a reason for such a question. My dressing-gown is of blue satin."

"There is nothing more, Madame. I am much obliged to you for answering my questions so promptly."

She made a slight gesture with her heavily-beringed hand.

Then, as she rose, and the others rose with her, she stopped.

"You will excuse me, Monsieur," she said, "but may I ask your name? Your face is somehow familiar to me."

"My name, Madame, is Hercule Poirot—at your service."

She was silent a minute, then:

"Hercule Poirot," she said. "Yes. I remember now. This is Destiny."

She walked away, very erect, a little stiff in her movements.

"*Voilà une grande dame,*" said M. Bouc. "What do you think of her, my friend?"

But Hercule Poirot merely shook his head.

"I am wondering," he said, "what she meant by Destiny."

CHAPTER 7
The Evidence of Count and Countess Andrenyi

Count and Countess Andrenyi were next summoned. The Count, however, entered the dining-car alone.

There was no doubt that he was a fine-looking man seen face to face. He was at least six feet in height, with broad shoulders and slender hips. He was dressed in very well-cut English tweeds, and might have been taken for an Englishman had it not been for the length of his moustache and something in the line of the cheek-bone.

"Well, Messieurs," he said, "what can I do for you?"

"You understand, Monsieur," said Poirot, "that in view of what has occurred I am obliged to put certain questions to all the passengers."

"Perfectly, perfectly," said the Count easily. "I quite understand your position. Not, I fear, that my wife and I can do much to assist you. We were asleep and heard nothing at all."

"Are you aware of the identity of the deceased, Monsieur?"

"I understand it was the big American—a man with a decidedly unpleasant face. He sat at that table at meal times."

He indicated with a nod of his head the table at which Ratchett and MacQueen had sat.

"Yes, yes, Monsieur, you are perfectly correct. I meant did you know the name of the man?"

"No." The Count looked thoroughly puzzled by Poirot's queries.

"If you want to know his name," he said, "surely it is on his passport?"

"The name on his passport is Ratchett," said Poirot. "But that, Monsieur, is not his real name. He is the man Cassetti, who was responsbile for a celebrated kidnapping outrage in America."

He watched the Count closely as he spoke, but the latter seemed quite unaffected by the piece of news. He merely opened his eyes a little.

"Ah!" he said. "That certainly should throw light upon the matter. An extraordinary country America."

"You have been there, perhaps, Monsieur le Comte?"

"I was in Washington for a year."

"You knew, perhaps, the Armstrong family?"

"Armstrong—Armstrong—it is difficult to recall—one met so many."

He smiled, shrugged his shoulders.

"But to come back to the matter in hand, gentlemen," he said. "What more can I do to assist you?"

"You retired to rest—when, Monsieur le Comte?"

Hercule Poirot's eyes stole to his plan. Count and Countess Andrenyi occupied compartments No. 12 and 13 adjoining.

"We had one compartment made up for the night whilst we were in the dining-car. On returning we sat in the other for a while——"

"What number would that be?"

"No. 13. We played picquet together. About eleven o'clock my wife retired for the night. The conductor made up my compartment and I also went to bed. I slept soundly until morning."

"Did you notice the stopping of the train?"

"I was not aware of it till this morning."

"And your wife?"

The Count smiled.

"My wife always takes a sleeping draught when traveling by train. She took her usual dose of trional."

He paused.

"I am sorry I am not able to assist you in any way."

Poirot passed him a sheet of paper and a pen.

"Thank you, Monsieur le Comte. It is a formality, but will you just let me have your name and address?"

The Count wrote slowly and carefully.

"It is just as well I should write this for you," he said pleasantly. "The spelling of my country estate is a little difficult for those unacquainted with the language."

He passed the paper across to Poirot and rose.

"It will be quite unnecessary for my wife to come here," he said. "She can tell you nothing more than I have."

A little gleam came into Poirot's eye.

"Doubtless, doubtless," he said. "But all the same I think I should like to have just one little word with Madame la Comtesse."

"I assure you it is quite unnecessary."

His voice rang out authoritatively.

Poirot blinked gently at him.

"It will be a mere formality," he said. "But you understand, it is necessary for my report."

"As you please."

The Count gave way grudgingly. He made a short, foreign bow and left the dining-car.

Poirot reached out a hand to a passport. It set out the Count's name and titles. He passed on to the further information—*accompanied by wife*. Christian name Elena Maria; maiden name Goldenberg; age twenty. A spot of grease had been dropped some time by a careless official on it.

"A diplomatic passport," said M. Bouc. "We must be careful, my friend, to give no offence. These people can have nothing to do with the murder."

"Be easy, *mon vieux*, I will be most tactful. A mere formality."

His voice dropped as the Countess Andrenyi entered the dining-car. She looked timid and extremely charming.

"You wish to see me, Messieurs?"

"A mere formality, Madame la Comtesse." Poirot rose gallantly, bowed her into the seat opposite him. "It is only to ask you if you saw or heard anything last night that may throw light upon this matter."

"Nothing at all, Monsieur. I was asleep."

"You did not hear, for instance, a commotion going on in the compartment next to yours? The American lady who occupies it had quite an attack of hysterics and rang for the conductor."

"I heard nothing, Monsieur. You see, I had taken a sleeping draught."

"Ah! I comprehend. Well, I need not detain you further." Then, as she rose swiftly, "Just one little minute—these particulars, your maiden name, age and so on, they are correct?"

"Quite correct, Monsieur."

"Perhaps you will sign this memorandum to that effect, then."

She signed quickly, a graceful slanting handwriting.

Elena Andrenyi.

"Did you accompany your husband to America, Madame?"

"No, Monsieur." She smiled, flushed a little. "We were not married then; we have only been married a year."

"Ah yes, thank you, Madame. By the way, does your husband smoke?"

She stared at him as she stood poised for departure.

"Yes."

"A pipe?"

"No. Cigarettes and cigars."

"Ah! Thank you."

She lingered; her eyes watched him curiously. Lovely eyes they were, dark and almond shaped, with very long black lashes that swept the exquisite pallor of her cheeks. Her lips, very scarlet, in the foreign fashion, were parted just a little. She looked exotic and beautiful.

"Why did you ask me that?"

"Madame," Poirot waved an airy hand, "detectives have to ask all sorts of questions. For instance, perhaps you will tell me the colour of your dressing-gown?"

She stared at him. Then she laughed.

"It is corn-coloured chiffon. Is that really important?"

"Very important, Madame."

She asked curiously:

"Are you really a detective, then?"

"At your service, Madame."

"I thought there were no detectives on the train when it passed through Yugoslavia—not until one got to Italy."

"I am not a Yugoslavian detective, Madame. I am an international detective."

"You belong to the League of Nations?"

"I belong to the world, Madame," said Poirot dramatically. He went on, "I work mainly in London. You speak English?" he added in that language.

"I speak a leetle, yes."

Her accent was charming.

Poirot bowed once more.

"We will not detain you further, Madame. You see, it was not so very terrible."

She smiled, inclined her head and departed.

"*Elle est jolie femme*," said M. Bouc appreciatively. He sighed.

"Well, that did not advance us much."

"No," said Poirot. "two people who saw nothing and heard nothing."

"Shall we now see the Italian?"

Poirot did not reply for a moment. He was studying a grease spot on a Hungarian diplomatic passport.

CHAPTER 8
The Evidence of Colonel Arbuthnot

Poirot roused himself with a slight start. His eyes twinkled a little as they met the eager ones of M. Bouc.

"Ah! my dear old friend," he said. "You see, I have become what they call the snob! The first-class, I feel it should be attended to before the second-class. Next, I think, we will interview the good-looking Colonel Arbuthnot."

Finding the Colonel's French to be of a severely limited description, Poirot conducted his interrogation in English.

Arbuthnot's name, age, home address and exact military standing were all ascertained. Poirot proceeded:

"It is that you come home from India on what is called the leave—what we call *en permission?*"

Colonel Arbuthnot, uninterested in what a pack of foreigners called anything, replied with true British brevity:

"Yes."

"But you do not come home on the P. & O. boat?"

"No."

"Why not?"

"I chose to come by the overland route for reasons of my own."

"And that," his manner seemed to say, "is one for you, you interfering little jackanapes."

"You came straight through from India?"

The Colonel replied dryly:

"I stopped for one night to see Ur of the Chaldees and for three days in Baghdad with the A.O.C., who happens to be an old friend of mine."

"You stopped three days in Baghdad. I understand that the young English lady, Miss Debenham, also comes from Baghdad. Perhaps you met her there?"

"No, I did not. I first met Miss Debenham when she and I shared the railway convoy car from Kirkuk to Nissibin."

Poirot leaned forward. He became persuasive and a little more foreign than he need have been.

"Monsieur, I am about to appeal to you. You and Miss Debenham are the only two English people on the train. It is necessary that I should ask you each your opinion of the other."

"Highly irregular," said Colonel Arbuthnot coldly.

"Not so. You see, this crime, it was most probably committed by a woman. The man was stabbed no less than twelve times. Even the *chef de train* said at once, 'It is a woman.' Well, then, what is my first task? To give all the women traveling on the Stamboul-Calais coach what Americans call the 'once over.' But to judge of an Englishwoman is difficult. They are very reserved, the English. So I appeal to you, Monsieur, in the interest of justice. What sort of a person is this Miss Debenham? What do you know about her?"

"Miss Debenham," said the Colonel with some warmth, "is a lady."

"Ah!" said Poirot with every appearance of being much gratified. "So you do not think that she is likely to be implicated in this crime?"

"The idea is absurd," said Arbuthnot. "The man was a perfect stranger—she had never seen him before."

"Did she tell you so?"

"She did. She commented at once upon his somewhat unpleasant appearance. If a woman *is* concerned, as you seem to think (to my mind without any evidence but mere assumption), I can assure you that Miss Debenham could not possibly be indicated."

"You feel warmly in the matter," said Poirot with a smile.

Colonel Arbuthnot gave him a cold stare.

"I really don't know what you mean," he said.

The stare seemed to abash Poirot. He dropped his eyes and began fiddling with the papers in front of him.

"All this is by the way," he said. "Let us be practical and come to facts. This crime, we have reason to believe, took place at a quarter-past one last night. It is part of the necessary routine to ask everyone on the train what he or she was doing at that time."

"Quite so. At a quarter-past one, to the best of my belief, I was talking to the young American fellow—secretary to the dead man."

"Ah! Were you in his compartment, or was he in yours?"

"I was in his."

"That is the young man of the name of MacQueen?"

"Yes."

"He was a friend or acquaintance of yours?"

"No, I never saw him before this journey. We fell into casual conversation yesterday and both became interested. I don't as a rule like Americans—haven't any use for 'em——"

Poirot smiled, remembering MacQueen's strictures on "Britishers."

"——But I liked this young fellow. He'd got hold of some tomfool idiotic ideas about the situation in India; that's the worst of Americans—they're so sentimental and idealistic. Well, he was interested in what I had to tell him. I've had nearly thirty years experience of the country. And I was interested in what he had to tell me about the financial situation in America. Then we got down to world politics in general. I was quite surprised to look at my watch and find it was a quarter to two."

"That is the time you broke up this conversation?"

"Yes."

"What did you do then?"

"Walked along to my own compartment and turned in."

"Your bed was made up ready?"

"Yes."

"That is the compartment—let me see—No. 15—the one next but one to the end away from the dining-car?"

"Yes."

"Where was the conductor when you went to your compartment?"

"Sitting at the end at a little table. As a matter of fact, MacQueen called him just as I went to my own compartment."

"Why did he call him?"

"To make up his bed, I suppose. The compartment hadn't been made up for the night."

"Now, Colonel Arbuthnot, I want you to think carefully. During the time you were talking to Mr. MacQueen did anyone pass along the corridor outside the door?"

"A good many people, I should think. I wasn't paying attention."

"Ah! but I am referring to—let us say the last hour and a half of your conversation. You got out at Vincovci, didn't you?"

"Yes, but only for about a minute. There was a blizzard on. The cold was something frightful. Made one quite thankful to get back to the fug, though as a rule I think the way these trains are overheated is something scandalous."

M. Bouc sighed.

"It is very difficult to please everybody," he said. "The English, they open everything—then others, they come along and shut everything. It is very difficult."

Neither Poirot nor Colonel Arbuthnot paid any attention to him.

"Now, Monsieur, cast your mind back," said Poirot encouragingly. "It was cold outside. You have returned to the train. You sit down again, you smoke—perhaps a cigarette, perhaps a pipe——"

He paused for the fraction of a second.

"A pipe for me. MacQueen smoked cigarettes."

"The train starts again. You smoke your pipe. You discuss the state of Europe—of the world. It is late now. Most people have retired for the night. Does anyone pass the door—think?"

Arbuthnot frowned in the effort of remembrance.

"Difficult to say," he said. "You see, I wasn't paying any attention."

"But you have the soldier's observation for detail. You notice without noticing, so to speak."

The Colonel thought again, but shook his head.

"I couldn't say. I don't remember anyone passing except the conductor. Wait a minute—and there was a woman, I think."

"You saw her? Was she old—young?"

"Didn't see her. Wasn't looking that way. Just a rustle and a sort of smell of scent."

"Scent? A *good* scent?"

"Well, rather fruity, if you know what I mean. I mean you'd smell it a hundred yards away. But mind you," the Colonel went on hastily, "this may have been earlier in the evening. You see, as you said just now, it was just one of those things you notice without noticing, so to speak. Some time that evening I said to myself, 'Woman—scent—got it on pretty thick.' But *when* it was I can't be sure, except that—why, yes, it must have been after Vincovci."

"Why?"

"Because I remember—sniffing, you know—just when I was talking about the utter washout Stalin's Five Year Plan was turning out. I know the idea—woman—brought the idea of the position of women in Russia into my mind. And I know we hadn't got on to Russia until pretty near the end of our talk."

"You can't pin it down more definitely than that?"

"N-no. It must have been roughly within the last half-hour."

"It was after the train had stopped?"

The other nodded.

"Yes, I'm almost sure it was."

"Did you ever know a Colonel Armstrong?"

"Armstrong—Armstrong—I've known two or three Armstrongs. There was Tommy Armstrong in the 60th—you don't mean him? And Selby Armstrong—he was killed on the Somme."

"I mean the Colonel Armstrong who married an American wife and whose only child was kidnapped and killed."

"Ah, yes, I remember reading about that—shocking affair. I don't think I actually ever came across the fellow, though, of course, I knew of him. Toby Armstrong. Nice fellow. Everybody liked him. He had a very distinguished career. Got the V.C."

"The man who was killed last night was the man responsible for the murder of Colonel Armstrong's child."

Arbuthnot's face grew rather grim.

"Then in my opinion the swine deserved what he got. Though I would have preferred to have seen him properly hanged—or electrocuted, I suppose, over there."

"In fact, Colonel Arbuthnot, you prefer law and order to private vengeance?"

"Well, you can't go about having blood feuds and stabbing each other like Corsicans or the Mafia," said the Colonel. "Say what you like, trial by jury is a sound system."

Poirot looked at him thoughtfully for a minute or two.

"Yes," he said. "I am sure that would be your view. Well, Colonel Arbuthnot, I do not think there is anything more I have to ask you. There is nothing you yourself can recall last night that in any way struck you—or shall we say strikes you now looking back—as suspicious?"

Arbuthnot considered for a moment or two.

"No," he said. "Nothing at all. Unless——" he hesitated.

"But yes, continue, I pray of you."

"Well, it's nothing really," said the Colonel slowly. "But you said *anything*."

"Yes, yes. Go on."

"Oh, it's nothing. A mere detail. But as I got back to my compartment I noticed that the door of the one beyond mine—the end one, you know——"

"Yes, No. 16."

"Well, the door of it was not quite closed. And the fellow inside peered out in a furtive sort of way. Then he pulled the door to quickly. Of course, I know there's nothing in that—but it just struck me as a bit odd. I mean, it's quite usual to open a door and stick your head out if you want to see anything. But it was the furtive way he did it that caught my attention."

"Ye-es," said Poirot doubtfully.

"I told you there was nothing to it," said Arbuthnot apologetically. "But you know what it is—early hours of the morning—everything very still—the thing had a sinister look—like a detective story. All nonsense, really."

He rose.

"Well, if you don't want me any more—"

"Thank you, Colonel Arbuthnot, there is nothing else."

The soldier hesitated for a minute. His first natural distaste for being questioned by "foreigners" had evaporated.

"About Miss Debenham," he said rather awkwardly. "You can take it from me that she's all right. She's a *pukka sahib*."

Flushing a little, he withdrew.

"What," asked Dr. Constantine with interest, "does a *pukka sahib* mean?"

"It means," said Poirot, "that Miss Debenham's father and brothers were at the same kind of school as Colonel Arbuthnot."

"Oh!" said Dr. Constantine, disappointed. "Then it has nothing to do with the crime at all."

"Exactly," said Poirot.

He fell into a reverie, beating a light tattoo on the table. Then he looked up.

"Colonel Arbuthnot smokes a pipe," he said. "In the compartment of M. Ratchett I found a pipe-cleaner. M. Ratchett smoked only cigars."

"You think——?"

"He is the only man so far who admits to smoking a pipe. And he knew of Colonel Armstrong—perhaps actually did know him though he won't admit it."

"So you think it possible——?"

"That is just it—it is *im*possible—quite impossible—that an honourable, slightly stupid, upright Englishman should stab an enemy twelve times with a knife! Do you not feel, my friends, how impossible it is?"

"That is the psychology," said M. Bouc.

"And one must respect the psychology. This crime has a signature and it is certainly not the signature of Colonel Arbuthnot. But now to our next interview."

This time M. Bouc did not mention the Italian. But he thought of him.

CHAPTER 9
The Evidence of Mr. Hardman

The last of the first-class passengers to be interviewed—Mr. Hardman—was the big flamboyant American who had shared a table with the Italian and the valet.

He wore a somewhat loud check suit, a pink shirt, a flashy tiepin, and was rolling something round his tongue as he entered the dining-car. He had a big, fleshy, coarse-featured face, with a good-humoured expression.

"Morning, gentlemen," he said. "What can I do for you?"

"You have heard of this murder, Mr.—er—Hardman?"

"Sure."

He shifted the chewing gum deftly.

"We are of necessity interviewing all the passengers on the train."

"That's all right by me. Guess that's the only way to tackle the job."

Poirot consulted the passport lying in front of him.

"You are Cyrus Bethman Hardman, United States subject, forty-one years of age, traveling salesman for typewriting ribbons?"

"O.K., that's me."

"You are traveling from Stamboul to Paris?"

"That's so."

"Reason?"

"Business."

"Do you always travel first-class, Mr. Hardman?"

"Yes, sir. The firm pays my traveling expenses."

He winked.

"Now, Mr. Hardman, we come to the events of last night."

The American nodded.

"What can you tell us about the matter?"

"Exactly nothing at all."

"Ah, that is a pity. Perhaps, Mr. Hardman, you will tell us exactly what you did last night, from dinner onwards?"

For the first time the American did not seem ready with his reply. At last he said:

"Excuse me, gentlemen, but just who are you? Put me wise."

"This is M. Bouc, a director of the Compagnie des Wagons Lits. This gentleman is the doctor who examined the body."

"And you yourself?"

"I am Hercule Poirot. I am engaged by the company to investigate this matter."

"I've heard of you," said Mr. Hardman. He reflected a minute or two longer. "Guess I'd better come clean."

"It will certainly be advisable for you to tell us all you know," said Poirot dryly.

"You'd have said a mouthful if there was anything I *did* know. But I don't. I know nothing at all—just as I said. But I *ought* to know something. That's what makes me sore. I *ought* to."

"Please explain, Mr. Hardman."

Mr. Hardman sighed, removed the chewing gum, and dived into a pocket. At the same time his whole personality seemed to undergo a change. He became less of a stage character and more of a real person. The resonant nasal tones of his voice became modified.

"That passport's a bit of bluff," he said. "That's who I really am."

Poirot scrutinised the card flipped across to him. M. Bouc peered over his shoulder.

MR. CYRUS B. HARDMAN,
McNeil's Detective Agency
New York

Poirot knew the name. It was one of the best known and most reputable private detective agencies in New York.

"Now, Mr. Hardman," he said. "Let us hear the meaning of this."

"Sure. Things came about this way. I'd come over to Europe trailing a couple of crooks—nothing to do with this business. The chase ended in Stamboul. I wired the Chief and got his instructions to return, and I would have been making my tracks back to little old New York when I got this."

He pushed across a letter.

The heading at the top was the Tokatlian Hotel.

> Dear Sir,—You have been pointed out to me as an operative of the McNeil Detective Agency. Kindly report to my suite at four o'clock this afternoon.

It was signed "S.E. Ratchett."

"*Eh bien?*"

"I reported at the time stated and Mr. Ratchett put me wise to the situation. He showed me a couple of letters he'd got."

"He was alarmed?"

"Pretended not to be, but he was rattled all right. He put up a proposition to me. I was to travel by the same train as he did to Parrus and see that nobody got him. Well, gentlemen, I *did* travel by the same train and, in spite of me, somebody *did* get him. I certainly feel sore about it. It doesn't look any too good for me."

"Did he give you any indication of the line you were to take?"

"Sure. He had it all taped out. It was his idea that I should travel in the compartment alongside his—well, that was blown upon straight away. The only place I could get was berth No. 16, and I had a bit of a job getting that. I guess the conductor likes to keep that compartment up his sleeve. But that's neither here nor there. When I looked all round the situation, it seemed to me that No. 16 was a pretty good strategic position. There was only the dining-car in front of the Stamboul sleeping-car, the door on to the platform at the front end was barred at night. The only way a thug could come was through the rear end door to the platform or along the train from the rear—in either case he'd have to pass right by my compartment."

"You had no idea, I suppose, of the identity of the possible assailant."

"Well, I knew what he looked like. Mr. Ratchett described him to me."

"What?"

All three men leaned forward eagerly.

Hardman went on:

"A small man, dark, with a womanish kind of voice—that's what the old man said. Said, too that he didn't think it would be the first night out. More likely the second or third."

"He knew something," said M. Bouc.

"He certainly knew more than he told his secretary," said Poirot thoughtfully. "Did he tell you anything about this enemy of his? Did he, for instance, say *why* his life was threatened?"

"No, he was kinder reticent about that part of it. Just said the fellow was out for his blood and meant to get it."

"A small man—dark—with a womanish voice," said Poirot thoughtfully.

Then, fixing a sharp glance on Hardman, he said:

"You know who he really was, of course?"

"Which, mister?"

"Ratchett. You recognized him?"

"I don't get you."

"Ratchett was Cassetti, the Armstrong murderer."

Mr. Hardman gave way to a prolonged whistle.

"That certainly is some surprise!" he said. "Yes, *sir!* No, I didn't recognize him. I was away out West when that case came on. I suppose I saw photos of him in the papers, but I wouldn't recognize my own mother when a press photographer had done with her. Well, I don't doubt that a few people had it in for Cassetti all right."

"Do you know of anyone connected with the Armstrong case who answers to that description—small, dark, womanish voice?"

Hardman reflected a minute or two.

"It's hard to say. Pretty nearly everyone to do with that case is dead."

"There was the girl who threw herself out of the window, remember."

"Sure. That's a good point, that. She was a foreigner of some kind. Maybe she had some wop relations. But you've got to remember that there were other cases besides the Armstrong case. Cassetti had been running this kidnapping stunt some time. You can't concentrate on that only."

"*Ah*, but we have reason to believe that this crime is connected with the Armstrong case."

Mr. Hardman cocked an inquiring eye. Poirot did not respond. The American shook his head.

"I can't call to mind anybody answering that description in the Armstrong case," he said slowly. "But of course I wasn't in it and didn't know much about it."

"Well, continue your narrative, M. Hardman."

"There's very little to tell. I got my sleep in the daytime and stayed awake on the watch at night. Nothing suspicious happened the first night. Last night was the same, as far as I was concerned. I had my door a little ajar and watched. No stranger passed."

"You are sure of that, M. Hardman?"

"I'm plumb certain. Nobody got on that train from outside and nobody came along the train from the rear carriages. I'll take my oath on that."

"Could you see the conductor from your position?"

"Sure. He sits on that little seat almost flush with my door."

"Did he leave that seat at all after the train stopped at Vincovci?"

"That was the last station? Why, yes, he answered a couple of bells—that would be just after the train came to a halt for good. Then, after that, he went past me into the rear coach—was there about a quarter of an hour. There was a bell ringing like mad and he came back running. I stepped out into the corridor to see what it was all about—felt a mite nervous, you understand—but it was only the American dame. She was raising hell about something or other. I grinned. Then he went on to another compartment and came back and got a bottle of mineral water for someone. After that he settled down in his seat till he went up to the far end to make somebody's bed up. I don't think he stirred after that until about five o'clock this morning."

"Did he doze off at all?"

"That I can't say. He may have done."

Poirot nodded. Automatically his hands straightened the papers on the table. He picked up the official card once more.

"Be so good as just to initial this," he said.

The other complied.

"There is no one, I suppose, who can confirm your story of your identity, M. Hardman?"

"On this train? Well, not exactly. Unless it might be young MacQueen. I know him well enough—seen him in his father's office in New York—but that's not to say he'll remember me from a crowd of other operatives. No, Mr. Poirot, you'll have to wait and cable New York when the snow lets up. But it's O.K., I'm not telling the tale. Well, so long, gentlemen. Pleased to have met you, Mr. Poirot."

Poirot proffered his cigarette case.

"But perhaps you prefer a pipe?"

"Not me."

He helped himself, then strode briskly off.

The three men looked at each other.

"You think he is genuine?" asked Dr. Constantine.

"Yes, yes. I know the type. Besides, it is a story that would be very easily disproved."

"He has given us a piece of very interesting evidence," said M. Bouc.

"Yes, indeed."

"A small man, dark, with a high-pitched voice," said M. Bouc thoughtfully.

"A description which applies to no one on the train, said Poirot.

CHAPTER 10
The Evidence of the Italian

"And now," said Poirot with a twinkle in his eye, "we will delight the heart of M. Bouc and see the Italian."

Antonio Foscarelli came into the dining-car with a swift, cat-like tread. His face beamed. It was a typical Italian face, sunny looking and swarthy.

He spoke French well and fluently, with only a slight accent.

"Your name is Antonio Foscarelli?"

"Yes, Monsieur."

"You are, I see, a naturalized American subject? The American grinned.

"Yes, Monsieur. It is better for my business."

"You are an agent for Ford motor cars?"

"Yes, you see——"

A voluble exposition followed. At the end of it, anything that the three men did not know about Foscarelli's business methods, his journeys, his income, and his opinion of the United States and most European countries seemed a negligible factor. This was not a man who had to have information dragged from him. It gushed out.

His good-natured childish face beamed with satisfaction as, with a last eloquent gesture, he paused and wiped his forehead with a handkerchief.

"So you see," he said, "I do big business. I am up to date. I understand salesmanship!"

"You have been in the United States, then, for the last ten years on and off?"

"Yes, Monsieur. Ah! well do I remember the day I first took the boat—to go to America, so far away! My mother, my little sister——"

Poirot cut short the flood of reminiscence.

"During your sojourn in the United States did you ever come across the deceased?"

"Never. But I know the type. Oh, yes." He snapped his fingers expressively. "It is very respectable, very well dressed, but underneath it is all wrong. Out of my experience I should say he was the big crook. I give you my opinion for what it is worth."

"Your opinion is quite right," said Poirot dryly. "Ratchett was Cassetti, the kidnapper."

"What did I tell you? I have learned to be very acute—to read the face. It is necessary. Only in America do they teach you the proper way to sell."

"You remember the Armstrong case?"

"I do not quite remember. The name, yes? It was a little girl—a baby—was it not?"

"Yes, a very tragic affair."

The Italian seemed the first person to demur to this view.

"Ah, well, these things they happen," he said philosophically, "in a great civilization such as America——"

Poirot cut him short.

"Did you ever come across any members of the Armstrong family?"

"No, I do not think so. It is difficult to say. I will give you some figures. Last year alone I sold——"

"Monsieur, pray confine yourself to the point."

The Italian's hands flung themselves out in a gesture of apology.

"A thousand pardons."

"Tell me, if you please, your exact movements last night from dinner onwards."

"With pleasure. I stay here as long as I can. It is more amusing. I talk to the American gentleman at my table. He sells typewriter ribbons. Then I go back to my compartment. It is empty. The miserable John Bull who shares it with me is away attending to his master. At last he comes back—very long face as usual. He will not talk—says yes and no. A miserable race, the English—not sympathetic. He sits in the corner, very stiff, reading a book. Then the conductor comes and makes our beds."

"Nos. 4 and 5," murmured Poirot.

"Exactly—the end compartment. Mine is the upper berth. I get up there. I smoke and read. The little Englishman has, I think, the toothache. He gets out a little bottle of stuff that smells very strong. He lies in bed and groans. Presently I sleep. Whenever I wake I hear him groaning."

"Do you know if he left the carriage at all during the night?"

"I do not think so. That, I should hear. The light from the corridor—one wakes up automatically thinking it is the Customs examination at some frontier."

"Did he ever speak of his master? Ever express any animus against him?"

"I tell you he did not speak. He was not symapthetic. A fish."

"You smoke, you say—a pipe, cigarettes, cigars?"

"Cigarettes only."

Poirot proffered him one which he accepted.

"Have you ever been in Chicago?" inquired M. Bouc.

"Oh, yes—a fine city—but I know best New York, Washington, Detroit. You have been to the States? No? You should go, it——"

Poirot pushed a sheet of paper across to him.

"If you will sign this, and put your permanent address, please."

The Italian wrote with a flourish. Then he rose—his smile was as engaging as ever.

"That is all? You do not require me further? Goodday to you, Messieurs. I wish we could get out of the snow. I have an appointment in Milan——" He shook his head sadly. "I shall lose the business."

He departed.

Poirot looked at his friend.

"He has been a long time in America," said M. Bouc, "and he is an Italian, and Italians use the knife! And they are great liars! I do not like Italians."

"*Ca se voit,*" said Poirot with a smile. "Well, it may be that you are right, but I will point out to you, my friend, that there is absolutely no evidence against the man."

"And what about the psychology? Do not Italians stab?"

"Assuredly," said Poirot. "Especially in the heat of a quarrel. But this—this is a different kind of crime. I have the little idea, my friend, that this is a crime very carefully planned and staged. It is a far-sighted, long-headed crime. It is not—how shall I express it?—a *Latin* crime. It is a crime that shows traces of a cool, resourceful, deliberate brain—I think an Anglo-Saxon brain."

He picked up the last two passports.

"Let us now," he said, "see Miss Mary Debenham."

CHAPTER 11
The Evidence of Miss Debenham

When Mary Debenham entered the dining-car she confirmed Poirot's previous estimate of her.

Very neatly dressed in a little black suit with a French grey shirt, the smooth waves of her dark head were neat and unruffled. Her manner was as calm and unruffled as her hair.

She sat down opposite Poirot and M. Bouc and looked at them inquiringly.

"Your name is Mary Hermione Debenham, and you are twenty-six years of age?" began Poirot.

"Yes."

"English?"

"Yes."

"Will you be so kind, Mademoiselle, as to write down your permanent address on this piece of paper?"

She complied. Her writing was clear and legible.

"And now, Mademoiselle, what have you to tell us of the affair last night?"

"I am afraid I have nothing to tell you. I went to bed and slept."

"Does it distress you very much, Mademoiselle, that a crime has been committed on this train?"

The question was clearly unexpected. Her grey eyes widened a little.

"I don't quite understand you."

"It was a perfectly simple question that I asked you, Mademoiselle. I will repeat it. Are you very much distressed that a crime should have been committed on this train?"

"I have not really thought about it from that point of view. No, I cannot say that I am at all distressed."

"A crime—it is all in the day's work to you, eh?"

"It is naturally an unpleasant thing to have happen," said Mary Debenham quietly.

"You are very Anglo-Saxon, Mademoiselle. *Vous n'éprouvez pas d'emotion*."

She smiled a little.

"I am afraid I cannot have hysterics to prove my sensibility. After all, people die every day."

"They die, yes. But murder is a little more rare."

"Oh, certainly."

"You were not acquainted with the dead man?"

"I saw him for the first time when lunching here yesterday."

"And how did he strike you?"

"I hardly noticed him."

"He did not impress you as an evil personality?"

She shrugged her shoulders slightly.

"Really, I cannot say I thought about it."

Poirot looked at her keenly.

"You are, I think, a little bit contemptuous of the way I prosecute my inquiries," he said with a twinkle. "Not so, you think, would an English inquiry be conducted. There everything would be cut and dried—it would be all kept to the facts—a well-ordered business. But I, Mademoiselle, have my little originalities. I look first at my witness, I sum up his or her character, and I frame my questions accordingly. Just a little minute ago I am asking questions of a gentleman who wants to tell me all his ideas on every subject. Well, him I keep strictly to the point. I want him to answer yes or no, this or that. And then you come. I see at once that you will be orderly and methodical. You will confine yourself to the matter in hand. Your answers will be brief and to the point. And because, Mademoiselle, human nature is perverse, I ask of you quite different questions. I ask what you *feel*, and what you *thought*. It does not please you this method?"

"If you will forgive my saying so, it seems somewhat of a waste of time. Whether or not I liked Mr. Ratchett's face does not seem likely to be helpful in finding out who killed him."

"Do you know who the man Ratchett really was, Mademoiselle?"

She nodded.

"Mrs. Hubbard has been telling everyone."

"And what do you think of the Armstrong affair?"

"It was quite abominable," said the girl crisply.

Poirot looked at her thoughtfully.

"You are traveling from Baghdad, I believe, Miss Debenham?"

"Yes."

"To London?"

"Yes."

"What have you been doing in Baghdad?"

"I have been acting as governess to two children."

"Are you returning to your post after your holiday?"

"I am not sure."

"Why is that?"

"Baghdad is rather out of things. I think I should prefer a post in London if I can hear of a suitable one."

"I see. I thought, perhaps, you might be going to be married."

Miss Debenham did not reply. She raised her eyes and looked Poirot full in the face. The glance said plainly, "You are impertinent."

"What is your opinion of the lady who shares your compartment—Miss Ohlsson?"

"She seems a pleasant, simple creature."

"What colour is her dressing-gown?"

Mary Debenham stared.

"A kind of brownish colour—natural wool."

"Ah! I may mention without indiscretion, I hope, that I noticed the colour of your dressing-gown on the way from Aleppo to Stamboul. A pale mauve, I believe."

"Yes, that is right."

"Have you any other dressing-gown, Mademoiselle? A scarlet dressing-gown, for example?"

"No, that is not mine."

Poirot leant forward. He was like a cat pouncing on a mouse.

"Whose, then?"

The girl drew back a little, startled.

"I don't know. What do you mean?"

"You do not say, 'No, I have no such thing.' You say, 'That is not mine'—meaning that such a thing *does* belong to someone else."

She nodded.

"Somebody else on this train?"

"Yes."

"Whose is it?"

"I told you just now. I don't know. I woke up this morning about five o'clock with the feeling that the train had been standing still for a long time. I opened the door and looked out into the corridor, thinking we might be at a station. I saw someone in a scarlet kimono some way down the corridor."

"And you don't know who it was? Was she fair or dark or grey-haired?"

"I can't say. She had on a shingle cap and I only saw the back of her head."

"And in build?"

"Tallish and slim, I should judge, but it's difficult to say. The kimono was embroidered with dragons."

"Yes, yes, that is right, dragons."

He was silent a minute. He murmured to himself:

"I cannot understand. I cannot understand. None of this makes sense."

Then, looking up, he said:

"I need not keep you further, Mademoiselle."

"Oh!" she seemed rather taken aback, but rose promptly.

In the doorway, however, she hesitated a minute and then came back.

"The Swedish lady—Miss Ohlsson, is it?—seems rather worried. She says you told her she was the last person to see this man alive. She thinks, I believe, that you suspect her on that account. Can't I tell her that she has made a mistake? Really, you know, she is the kind of creature who wouldn't hurt a fly."

She smiled a little as she spoke.

"What time was it that she went to fetch the aspirin from Mrs. Hubbard?"

"Just after half-past ten."

"She was away—how long?"

"About five minutes."

"Did she leave the compartment again during the night?"

"No."

Poirot turned to the doctor.

"Could Ratchett have been killed as early as that?"

The doctor shook his head.

"Then I think you can reassure your friend, Mademoiselle."

"Thank you." She smiled suddenly at him, a smile that invited sympathy. "She's like a sheep, you know. She gets anxious and bleats."

She turned and went out.

CHAPTER 12
The Evidence of the German Lady's-Maid

M. Bouc was looking at his friend curiously.

"I do not quite understand you, *mon vieux*. You were trying to do—what?"

"I was searching for a flaw, my friend."

"A flaw?"

"Yes—in the armour of a young lady's self-possession. I wished to shake her *sang-froid*. Did I succeed? I do not know. But I know this—she did not expect me to tackle the matter as I did."

"You suspect her," said M. Bouc slowly. "But why? She seems a very charming young lady—the last person in the world to be mixed up in a crime of this kind."

"I agree," said Constantine. "She is cold. She has not emotions. She would not stab a man; she would sue him in the law courts."

Poirot sighed.

"You must, both of you, get rid of your obsession that this is an unpremeditated and sudden crime. As for the reason why I suspect Miss Debenham, there are two. One is because of something that I overheard, and that you do not as yet know."

He retailed to them the curious interchange of phrases he had overheard on the journey from Aleppo.

"That is curious, certainly," said M. Bouc when he had finished. "It needs explaining. If it means what you suspect it means, then they are both of them in it together—she and the stiff Englishman."

Poirot nodded.

"And that is just what is not borne out by the facts," he said. "See you, if they were both in this together, what should we expect to find—that each of them would provide an alibi for the other. Is not that so? But no—that does not happen. Miss Debenham's alibi is provided by a Swedish woman whom she has never seen before, and Colonel Arbuthnot's alibi is vouched for by MacQueen, the dead man's secretary. No, that solution of the puzzle is too easy."

"You said there was another reason for your suspicions of her," M. Bouc reminded him.

Poirot smiled.

"Ah! but that is only psychological. I ask myself, is it possible for Miss Debenham to have planned this crime? Behind this business, I am convinced, there is a cool, intelligent, resourceful brain. Miss Debenhan answers to that description."

M. Bouc shook his head.

"I think you are wrong, my friend. I do not see that young English girl as a criminal."

"Ah, well," said Poirot, picking up the last passport, "to the final name on our list. Hildegarde Schmidt, lady's-maid."

Summoned by the attendant, Hildegarde Schmidt came into the restaurant-car and stood waiting respectfully.

"Poirot motioned her to sit down.

She did so, folding her hands and waiting placidly till he questioned her. She seemed a placid creature altogether—eminently respectable—perhaps not over intelligent.

Poirot's methods with Hildegarde Schmidt were a complete contrast to his handling of Mary Debenham.

He was at his kindest and most genial, setting the woman at her ease. Then, having got her to write down her name and address, he slid gently into his questions.

The interview took place in German.

"We want to know as much as possible about what happened last night," he said. "We know that you cannot give us much information bearing on the crime itself, but you may have seen or heard something that, while conveying nothing to you, may be valuable to us. You understand?"

She did not seem to. Her broad, kindly face remained set in its expression of placid stupidity as she answered:

"I do not know anything, Monsieur."

"Well, for instance, you know that your mistress sent for you last night?"

"That, yes."

"Do you remember the time?"

"I do not, Monsieur. I was asleep, you see, when the attendant came and told me."

"Yes, yes. Was it usual for you to be sent for in this way?"

"It was not unusual, Monsieur. The gracious lady often required attention at night. She did not sleep well."

"*Eh bien*, then, you received the summons and you got up. Did you put on a dressing-gown?"

"No, Monsieur, I put on a few clothes. I would not like to go in to her Excellency in my dressing-gown."

"And yet it is a very nice dressing-gown—scarlet, is it not?"

She stared at him.

"It is a dark-blue flannel dressing-gown, Monsieur."

"Ah! continue. A little pleasantry on my part, that is all. So you went along to Madame la Princesse. And what did you do when you got there?"

"I gave her massage, Monsieur, and then I read aloud. I do not read aloud very well, but her Excellency says that is all the better. So it sends her better to sleep. When she became sleepy, Monsieur, she told me to go, so I closed the book and I returned to my own compartment."

"Do you know what time that was?"

"No, Monsieur."

"Well, how long had you been with Madame la Princesse?"

"About half an hour, Monsieur."

"Good, continue."

"First, I fetched her Excellency an extra rug from my compartment. It was very cold in spite of the heating. I arranged the rug over her and she wished me good-night. I poured her out some mineral water. Then I turned out the light and left her."

"And then?"

"There is nothing more, Monsieur. I returned to my carriage and went to sleep."

"And you met no one in the corridor?"

"No, Monsieur."

"You did not, for instance, see a lady in a scarlet kimono with dragons on it?"

Her mild eyes bulged at him.

"No, indeed, Monsieur. There was nobody about except the attendant. Everyone was asleep."

"But you did see the conductor?"

"Yes, Monsieur."

"What was he doing?"

"He came out of one of the compartments, Monsieur."

"What?" M. Bouc leaned forward. "Which one?"

Hildegarde Schmidt looked frightened again and Poirot cast a reproachful glance at his friend.

"Naturally," he said. "The conductor often has to answer bells at night. Do you remember which compartment it was?"

"It was about the middle of the coach, Monsieur. Two or three doors from Madame la Princesse."

"Ah! tell us, if you please, exactly where this was and what happened."

"He nearly ran into me, Monsieur. It was when I was returning from my compartment to that of the Princess with the rug."

"And he came out of a compartment and almost collided with you? In which direction was he going?"

"Toward me, Monsieur. He apologized and passed on down the corridor toward the dining-car. A bell began ringing, but I do not think he answered it."

She paused and then said:

"I do not understand. How is it—?"

Poirot spoke reassuringly.

"It is just a question of times," he said. "All a matter of routine. This poor conductor, he seems to have had a busy night—first waking you and then answering bells."

"It was not the same conductor who woke me, Monsieur. It was another one."

"Ah, another one! Had you seen him before?"

"No, Monsieur."

"Ah! Do you think you would recognize him if you saw him?"

"I think so, Monsieur."

Poirot murmured something in M. Bouc's ear. The latter got up and went to the door to give an order.

Poirot was continuing his questions in an easy friendly manner.

"Have you ever been to America, Frau Schmidt?"

"Never, Monsieur. It must be a fine country."

"You have heard, perhaps, of who this man who was killed really was—that he was responsible for the death of a little child."

"Yes, I have heard, Monsieur. It was abominable—wicked. The good God should not allow such things. We are not so wicked as that in Germany."

Tears had come into the woman's eyes. Her strong motherly soul was moved.

"It was an abominable crime," said Poirot gravely.

He drew a scrap of cambric from his pocket and handed it to her.

"Is this your handkerchief, Frau Schmidt?"

There was a moment's silence as the woman examined it. She looked up after a minute. The colour had mounted a little in her face.

"Ah! no, indeed. It is not mine, Monsieur."

"It has the initial H, you see. That is why I thought it was yours."

"Ah! Monsieur, it is a lady's handkerchief, that. A very expensive handkerchief. Embroidered by hand. It comes from Paris, I should say."

"It is not yours and you do not know whose it is?"

"I? Oh, no, Monsieur."

Of the three listening, only Poirot caught the nuance of hesitation in the reply.

M. Bouc whispered in his ear. Poirot nodded and said to the woman:

"The three sleeping-car attendants are coming in. Will you be so kind as to tell me which is the one you met last night as you were going with the rug to the Princess?"

The three men entered. Pierre Michel, the big blond conductor of the Athens-Paris coach, and the stout burly conductor of the Bucharest one.

Hildegarde Schmidt looked at them and immediately shook her head.

"No, Monsieur," she said. "None of these is the man I saw last night."

"But these are the only conductors on the train. You must be mistaken."

"I am quite sure, Monsieur. These are all tall, big men. The one I saw was small and dark. He had a little moustache. His voice when he said *'Pardon'* was weak like a woman's. Indeed, I remember him very well, Monsieur."

CHAPTER 13
Summary of the Passengers' Evidence

"A small dark man with a womanish voice," said M. Bouc.

The three conductors and Hildegarde Schmidt had been dismissed.

M. Bouc made a despairing gesture.

"But I understand nothing—but nothing of all this! The enemy that this Ratchett spoke of, he was then on the train after all? But where is he now? How can he have vanished into thin air? My head, it whirls. Say something, then, my friend, I implore you. Show me how the impossible can be possible!"

"It is a good phrase that," said Poirot. "The impossible cannot have happened, therefore the impossible must be possible in spite of appearances."

"Explain to me then, quickly, what actually happened on the train last night."

"I am not a magician, *mon cher*. I am, like you, a very puzzled man. This affair advances in a very strange manner."

"It does not advance at all. It stays where it was."

Poirot shook his head.

"No, that is not true. We are more advanced. We know certain things. We have heard the evidence of the passengers."

"And what has that told us? Nothing at all."

"I would not say that, my friend."

"I exaggerate, perhaps. The American, Hardman, and the German maid—yes, they have added something to our knowledge. That is to say, they have made the whole business more unintelligible than it was."

"No, no, no," said Poirot soothingly.

M. Bouc turned upon him.

"Speak, then, let us hear the wisdom of Hercule Poirot."

"Did I not tell you that I was, like you, a very puzzled man? But at least we can face our problem. We can arrange such facts as we have with order and method."

"Pray continue, Monsieur," said Dr. Constantine.

Poirot cleared his throat and straightened a piece of blotting-paper.

"Let us review the case as it stands at this moment. First, there are certain indisputable facts. This man Ratchett, or Cassetti, was stabbed in twelve places and died last night. That is fact one."

"I grant it to you—I grant it, *mon vieux*," said M. Bouc with a gesture of irony.

Hercule Poirot was not at all put out. He continued calmly:

"I will pass over for the moment certain rather peculiar appearances which Dr. Constantine and I have already discussed together. I will come to them presently. The next fact of importance, to my mind, is the *time* of the crime."

"That, again, is one of the few things we do know," said M. Bouc. "The crime was committed at a quarter-past one this morning. Everything goes to show that that was so."

"Not *everything*. You exaggerate. There is, certainly, a fair amount of evidence to support that view."

"I am glad you admit that at least."

Poirot went on calmly, unperturbed by the interruption.

"We have before us three possibilities:

"One: That the crime was committed, as you say, at a quarter-past one. This is supported by the evidence of the German woman, Hildegarde Schmidt. It agrees with the evidence of Dr. Constantine.

"Possibility two: The crime was committed later and the evidence of the watch was deliberately faked.

"Possibility three: The crime was committed earlier and the evidence faked for the same reason as above."

"Now, if we accept possibility one as the most likely to have occurred and the one supported by most evidence, we must also accept certain facts arising from it. To begin with, if the crime was committed at a quarter-past one, the murderer cannot have left the train, and the question arises: Where is he? And *who* is he?

"To begin with, let us examine the evidence carefully. We first hear of the existence of this man—the small dark man with a womanish voice—from the man Hardman. He says that Ratchett told him of this person and employed him to watch out for the man. There is no *evidence* to support this—we have only Hardman's word for it. Let us next examine the question: Is Hardman the person he pretends to be—an operative of a New York Detective Agency?

"What to my mind is so interesting in this case is that we have none of the facilities afforded to the police. We cannot investigate the bona fides of any of these people. We have to rely solely on deduction. That, to me, makes the matter very much more interesting. There is no routine work. It is a matter of the intellect. I ask myself, 'Can we accept Hardman's account of himself?' I make my decision and I answer, 'Yes.' I am of the opinion that we *can* accept Hardman's account of himself."

"You rely on the intuition—what the Americans call the hunch?" said Dr. Constantine.

"Not at all. I regard the probabilities. Hardman is traveling with a false passport—that will at once make him an object of suspicion. The first thing that the police will do when they do arrive upon the scene is to detain Hardman and cable as to whether his account of himself is true. In the case of many of the passengers, to establish their bona fides will be difficult; in most cases it will probably not be attempted, especially since there seems nothing in the way of suspicion attaching to them. But in Hardman's case it is simple. Either he is the person he represents himself to be or he is not. Therefore I say that all will prove to be in order."

"You acquit him of suspicion?"

"Not at all. You misunderstand me. For all I know, any American detective might have his own private reasons for wishing to murder Ratchett. No, what I am saying is that I think we *can* accept Hardman's own account of *himself*. This story, then, that he tells of Ratchett's seeking him out and employing him, is not unlikely and is most probably, though not of course certainly, true. If we are going to accept it as true, we must see if there is any confirmation of it. We find it in rather an unlikely place—in the evidence of Hildegarde Schmidt. Her description of the man she saw in Wagon Lit uniform tallies exactly. Is there any further confirmation of these two stories? There is. There is the button found in her compartment by Mrs. Hubbard. And there is also another corroborating statement which you may not have noticed."

"What is that?"

"The fact that both Colonel Arbuthnot and Hector MacQueen mention that the conductor passed their carriage. They attached no importance to the fact, but Messieurs, *Pierre Michel has declared that he did not leave his seat except on certain specified occasions*, none of which would take him down to the far end of the coach past the compartment in which Arbuthnot and MacQueen were sitting.

"Therefore this story, the story of a small dark man with a womanish voice dressed in Wagon Lit uniform, rests on the testimony—direct or indirect—of four witnesses."

"One small point," said Dr. Constantine. "If Hildegarde Schmidt's story is true, how is it that the real conductor did not mention having seen her when he came to answer Mrs. Hubbard's bell?"

"That is explained, I think. When he arrived to answer Mrs. Hubbard, the maid was in with her mistress. When she finally returned to her own compartment, the conductor was in with Mrs. Hubbard."

M. Bouc had been waiting with difficulty until they had finished.

"Yes, yes, my friend," he said impatiently to Poirot. "But whilst I admire your caution, your method of advancing a step at a time, I submit that you have not yet touched the point at issue. We are agreed that this person exists. The point is—*where did he go?*"

Poirot shook his head reprovingly.

"You are in error. You are inclined to put the cart before the horse. Before I ask myself, *'Where did this man vanish to?'* I ask myself, *'Did such a man really exist?'* Because, you see, if the man were an invention—a fabrication—how much easier to make him disappear! So I try to establish first that there really *is* such a flesh and blood person."

"And having arrived at the fact that there is—*eh bien*—where is he now?"

"There are only two answers to that, *mon cher*. Either he is still hidden on the train in a place of such extraordinary ingenuity that we cannot even think of it, or else he is, as one might say, *two persons*. That is, he is both himself —the man feared by M. Ratchett—and a passenger on the train so well disguised that M. Ratchett did not recognize him."

"It is an idea, that," said M. Bouc, his face lighting up. Then it clouded over again. "But there is one objection——"

Poirot took the words out of his mouth.

"The height of the man. It is that you would say? With the exception of M. Ratchett's valet, all the passengers are big men—the Italian, Colonel Arbuthnot, Hector MacQueen, Count Andrenyi. Well, that leaves us the valet—not a very likely supposition. But there is another possibility. Remember the 'womanish' voice. That gives us a choice of alternatives. The man may be disguised as a woman, or, alternatively, he may actually *be* a woman. A tall woman dressed in man's clothes would look small."

"But surely Ratchett would have known——"

"Perhaps he *did* know. Perhaps, already, this woman had attempted his life wearing men's clothes the better to accomplish her purpose. Ratchett may have guessed that she would use the same trick again, so he tells Hardman to look for a man. But he mentions, however, a womanish voice."

"It is a possibility," said M. Bouc. "But——"

"Listen, my friend, I think that I should now tell you of certain inconsistencies noticed by Dr. Constantine."

He retailed at length the conclusions that he and the doctor had arrived at together from the nature of the dead man's wounds. M. Bouc groaned and held his head again.

"I know," said Poirot sympathetically. "I know exactly how you feel. The head spins, does it not?"

"The whole thing is a fantasy," cried M. Bouc.

"Exactly. It is absurd—improbable—it cannot be. So I myself have said. And yet, my friend *there it is!* One cannot escape from the facts."

"It is madness!"

"Is it not? It is so mad, my friend, that sometimes I am haunted by the sensation that really it must be very simple. . . .

"But that is only one of my 'little ideas'. . . ."

"Two murderers," groaned M. Bouc. "And on the Orient Express."

The thought almost made him weep.

"And now let us make the fantasy more fantastic," said Poirot cheerfully. "Last night on the train there are two mysterious strangers. There is the Wagon Lit attendant answering to the description given us by M. Hardman, and seen by Hildegarde Schmidt, Colonel Arbuthnot and M. MacQueen. There is also a woman in a red kimono—a tall, slim woman—seen by Pierre Michel, by Miss Debenham, by M. MacQueen and by myself—and smelt, I may say, by Colonel Arbuthnot! Who was she? No one on the train admits to having a scarlet kimono. She, too, has vanished. Was she one and the same with the spurious Wagon Lit attendant? Or was she some quite distinct personality? Where are they, these two? And, incidentally, where is the Wagon Lit uniform and the scarlet kimono?"

"Ah! that is something definite." M. Bouc sprang up eagerly. "We must search all the passengers' luggage. Yes, that will be something."

Poirot rose also.

"I will make a prophecy," he said.

"You know where they are?"

"I have a little idea."

"Where, then?"

"You will find the scarlet kimono in the baggage of one of the men and you will find the uniform of the Wagon Lit conductor in the baggage of Hildegarde Schmidt."

"Hildegarde Schmidt? You think——?"

"Not what you are thinking. I will put it like this. If Hildegarde Schmidt is guilty, the uniform *might* be found in her baggage—but if she is innocent it *certainly* will be."

"But how——" began M. Bouc and stopped.

"What is this noise that approaches?" he cried. "It resmebles a locomotive in motion."

The noise drew nearer. It consisted of shrill cries and protests in a woman's voice. The door at the end of the dining-car flew open. Mrs. Hubbard burst in.

"It's too horrible," she cried." It's just too horrible. In my sponge-bag. My sponge-bag. A great knife—all over blood."

And, suddenly toppling forward, she fainted heavily on M. Bouc's shoulder.

CHAPTER 14
The Evidence of the Weapon

With more vigour than chivalry, M. Bouc deposited the fainting lady with her head on the table. Dr. Constantine yelled for one of the restaurant attendants, who came at a run.

"Keep her head so," said the doctor. "If she revives give her a little cognac. You understand?"

Then he hurried off after the other two. His interest lay wholly in the crime—swooning middle-aged ladies did not interest him at all.

It is possible that Mrs. Hubbard revived rather quicker with these methods than she might otherwise have done. A few minutes later she was sitting up, sipping cognac from a glass proffered by the attendant, and talking once more.

"I just can't say how terrible it was. I don't suppose anybody on this train can understand my feelings. I've always been vurry, vurry sensitive ever since a child. The mere sight of blood—ugh—why even now I come over queer when I think about it."

The attendant proffered the glass again.

"*Encore un peu, Madame.*"

"D'you think I'd better? I'm a life long teetotaler. I just never touch spirits or wine at any time. All my family are abstainers. Still, perhaps as this is only medical——"

She sipped once more.

In the meantime Poirot and M. Bouc, closely followed by Dr. Constantine, had hurried out of the restaurant-car and along the corridor of the Stamboul coach toward Mrs. Hubbard's compartment.

Every traveler on the train seemed to be congregated outside the door. The conductor, a harassed look on his face, was keeping them back.

"Mais il n'y a rien à voir," he said, and repeated the sentiment in several other languages.

"Let me pass, if you please," said M. Bouc.

Squeezing his rotundity past the obstructing passengers, he entered the compartment, Poirot close behind him.

"I am glad you have come, Monsieur," said the conductor with a sigh of relief. "Everyone has been trying to enter. The American lady—such screams as she gave—*ma foi!* I thought she too had been murdered! I came at a run and there she was screaming like a mad woman, and she cried out that she must fetch you and she departed, screeching at the top of her voice and telling everybody whose carriage she passed what had occurred."

He added, with a gesture of the hand:

"*It* is in there, Monsieur. I have not touched it."

Hanging on the handle of the door that gave access to the next compartment was a large-size checked rubber spongebag. Below it on the floor, just where it had fallen from Mrs. Hubbard's hand, was a straight-bladed dagger—a cheap affair, sham Oriental, with an embossed hilt and a tapering blade. The blade was stained with patches of what looked like rust.

Poirot picked it up delicately.

"Yes," he murmured. "There is no mistake. Here is our missing weapon all right—eh, docteur?"

The doctor examined it.

"You need not be so careful," said Poirot. "There will be no fingerprints on it save those of Mrs. Hubbard."

Constantine's examination did not take long.

"It is the weapon all right," he said. "It would account for any of the wounds."

"I implore you, my friend, do not say that."

The doctor looked astonished.

"Already we are heavily overburdened by coincidence. Two people decide to stab M. Ratchett last night. It is too much of a good thing that each of them should select an identical weapon."

"As to that, the coincidence is not, perhaps, so great as it seems," said the doctor. "Thousands of these sham Eastern daggers are made and shipped to the bazaars of Constantinople."

"You console me a little, but only a little," said Poirot.

He looked thoughtfully at the door in front of him, then, lifting off the sponge-bag, he tried the handle. The door did not budge. About a foot above the handle was the door bolt. Poirot drew it back and tried again, but still the door remained fast.

"We locked it from the other side, you remember," said the doctor.

"That is true," said Poirot absently. He seemed to be thinking about something else. His brow was furrowed as though in perplexity.

"It agrees, does it not?" said M. Bouc. "The man passes through this carriage. As he shuts the communicating door behind him he feels the sponge-bag. A thought comes to him and he quickly slips the bloodstained knife inside. Then, all unwitting that he has awakened Mrs. Hubbard, he slips out through the other door into the corridor."

"As you say," murmured Poirot. "That is how it must have happened."

But the puzzled look did not leave his face.

"But what is it?" demanded M. Bouc. "There is something, is there not, that does not satisfy you?"

Poirot darted a quick look at him.

"The same point does not strike you? No, evidently not. Well, it is a small matter."

The conductor looked into the carriage.

"The American lady is coming back."

Dr. Constantine looked rather guilty. He had, he felt, treated Mrs. Hubbard rather cavalierly. But she had no reproaches for him. Her energies were concentrated on another matter.

"I'm just going to say one thing right out," she said breathlessly as she arrived in the doorway." I'm not going on any longer in this compartment! Why, I wouldn't sleep in it tonight if you paid me a million dollars."

"But, Madame——"

"I know what you are going to say, and I'm telling you right now that I won't do any such thing! Why, I'd rather sit up all night in the corridor."

She began to cry.

"Oh! if my daughter could only know—if she could see me now, why——"

Poirot interrupted firmly.

"You misunderstand, Madame. Your demand is most reasonable. Your baggage shall be changed at once to another compartment."

Mrs. Hubbard lowered her handkerchief.

"Is that so? Oh, I feel better right away. But surely it's all full up, unless one of the gentlemen——"

M. Bouc spoke.

"Your baggage, Madame, shall be moved out of this coach altogether. You shall have a compartment in the next coach which was put on at Belgrade."

"Why, that's splendid. I'm not an out of the way nervous woman, but to sleep in that compartment next door to a dead man——" She shivered. "It would drive me plumb crazy."

"Michel," called M. Bouc. "Move this baggage into a vacant compartment in the Athens-Paris coach."

"Yes, Monsieur—the same one as this—the No. 3?"

"No," said Poirot before his friend could reply. "I think it would be better for Madame to have a different number altogether. The No. 12, for instance."

"*Bien,* Monsieur."

The conductor seized the luggage. Mrs. Hubbard turned gratefully to Poirot.

"That's vurry kind and delicate of you. I appreciate it, I assure you."

"Do not mention it, Madame. We will come with you and see you comfortably installed."

Mrs. Hubbard was escorted by the three men to her new home. She looked round her happily.

"This is fine."

"It suits you, Madame? It is, you see, exactly like the compartment you have left."

"That's so—only it faces the other way. But that doesn't matter, for these trains go first one way and then the other. I said to my daughter, 'I want a carriage facing the engine,' and she said, 'Why, Momma, that'll be no good to you, for if you go to sleep one way, when you wake up the train's going the other.' And it was quite true what she said. Why, last evening we went into Belgrade one way and out the other."

"At any rate, Madame, you are quite happy and contented now?"

"Well, no, I wouldn't say that. Here we are stuck in a snowdrift and nobody doing anything about it, and my boat sailing the day after tomorrow."

"Madame," said M. Bouc, "we are all in the same case—every one of us."

"Well, that's true," admitted Mrs. Hubbard. "But nobody else has had a murderer walking right through their compartment in the middle of the night."

"What still puzzles me, Madame," said Poirot, "is how the man got into your compartment if the communicating door was bolted as you say. You are sure that it *was* bolted?"

"Why, the Swedish lady tried it before my eyes."

"Let us just reconstruct that little scene. You were lying in your bunk—so—and you could not see for yourself, you say?"

"No, because of the sponge-bag. Oh, my, I shall have to get a new sponge-bag. It makes me feel sick in my stomach to look at this one."

Poirot picked up the sponge-bag and hung it on the handle of the communicating door into the next carriage.

"*Précisément*—I see," he said. "The bolt is just underneath the handle—the sponge-bag masks it. You could not see from where you were lying whether the bolt were turned or not."

"Why, that's just what I've been telling you!"

"And the Swedish lady, Miss Ohlsson, stood so, between you and the door. She tried it and told you it was bolted."

"That's so."

"All the same, Madame, she may have made an error. You see what I mean." Poirot seemed anxious to explain. "The bolt is just a projection of metal—so. Turned to the right the door is locked, left straight, it is not. Possibly she merely tried the door, and as it was locked on the other side she may have assumed that it was locked on your side."

"Well, I guess that would be rather stupid of her."

"Madame, the most kind, the most amiable are not always the cleverest."

"That's so, of course."

"By the way, Madame, did you travel out to Smyrna this way?"

"No. I sailed right to Stamboul, and a friend of my daughter's—Mr. Johnson (a perfectly lovely man; I'd like to have you know him)—met me and showed me all round Stamboul, which I found a very disappointing city—all tumbling down. And as for those mosques and putting on those great shuffling things over your shoes—where was I?"

"You were saying that Mr. Johnson met you."

"That's so, and he saw me on board a French Messagerie boat for Smyrna, and my daughter's husband was waiting right on the quay. What he'll say when he hears about all this! My daughter said this would be just the safest, easiest way imaginable. 'You just sit in your carriage,' she said, 'and you get right to Parrus and there the American Express will meet you.' And, oh dear, what am I to do about canceling my steamship passage? I ought to let them know. I can't possibly make it now. This is just too terrible——"

Mrs. Hubbard showed signs of tears once more.

Poirot, who had been fidgeting slightly, seized his opportunity.

"You have had a shock, Madame. The restaurant attendant shall be instructed to bring you along some tea and some biscuits."

"I don't know that I'm so set on tea," said Mrs. Hubbard tearfully. "That's more an English habit."

"Coffee, then, Madame. You need some stimulant."

"That cognac's made my head feel mighty funny. I think I would like some coffee."

"Excellent. You must revive your forces."

"My, what a funny expression."

"But first, Madame, a little matter of routine. You permit that I make a search of your baggage?"

"Whatever for?"

"We are about to commence a search of all the passengers' luggage. I do not want to remind you of an unpleasant experience, but your sponge-bag—remember."

"Mercy! Perhaps you'd better! I just couldn't bear to get any more surprises of that kind."

The examination was quickly over. Mrs. Hubbard was traveling with the minimum of luggage—a hat box, a cheap suitcase, and a well-burdened traveling bag. The contents of all three were simple and straightforward, and the examination would not have taken more than a couple of minutes had not Mrs. Hubbard delayed matters by insisting on due attention being paid to photographs of "My daughter" and two rather ugly children—"My daughter's children. Aren't they cunning?"

CHAPTER 15
The Evidence of the Passengers' Luggage

Having delivered himself of various polite insincerities, and having told Mrs. Hubbard that he would order coffee to be brought to her, Poirot was able to take his leave accompanied by his two friends.

"Well, we have made a start and drawn a blank," observed M. Bouc. "Whom shall we tackle next?"

"It would be simplest, I think, just to proceed along the train carriage by carriage. That means that we start with No. 16—the amiable M. Hardman."

Mr. Hardman, who was smoking a cigar, welcomed them affably.

"Come right in, gentlemen—that is, if it's humanly possible. It's just a mite cramped in here for a party."

M. Bouc explained the object of their visit, and the big detective nodded comprehendingly.

"That's O.K. To tell the truth, I've been wondering you didn't get down to it sooner. Here are my keys, gentlemen, and if you like to search my pockets too, why, you're welcome. Shall I reach the grips down for you?"

"The conductor will do that. Michel!"

The contents of Mr. Hardman's two "grips" were soon examined and passed. They contained perhaps an undue proportion of spirituous liquor. Mr. Hardman winked.

"It's not often they search your grips at the frontiers—not if you fix the conductor. I handed out a wad of Turkish notes right away, and there's been no trouble so far."

"And at Paris?"

Mr. Hardman winked again.

"By the time I get to Paris," he said, "what's left over of this little lot will go into a bottle labeled hairwash."

"You are not a believer in Prohibition, Monsieur Hardman," said M. Bouc with a smile.

"Well," said Hardman. "I can't say Prohibition has ever worried me any."

"Ah!" said M. Bouc. "The speakeasy." He pronounced the word with care, savouring it.

"Your American terms are so quaint, so expressive," he said.

"Me, I would much like to go to America," said Poirot.

"You'd learn a few go-ahead methods over there," said Hardman. "Europe wants waking up. She's half asleep."

"It is true that America is the country of progress," agreed Poirot. "There is much that I admire about Americans. Only—I am perhaps old-fashioned—but me, I find the American woman less charming than my own countrywomen. The French or Belgian girl, coquettish, charming—I think there is no one to touch her."

Hardman turned away to peer out at the snow for a minute.

"Perhaps you're right, M. Poirot," he said. "But I guess every nation likes its own girls best."

He blinked as though the snow hurt his eyes.

"Kind of dazzling, isn't it?" he remarked. "Say, gentlemen, this business is getting on my nerves. Murder and the snow and all, and nothing *doing*. Just hanging about and killing time. I'd like to get busy after someone or something."

"The true Western spirit of hustle," said Poirot with a smile.

The conductor replaced the bags and they moved on to the next compartment. Colonel Arbuthnot was sitting in a corner smoking a pipe and reading a magazine.

Poirot explained their errand. The Colonel made no demur. He had two heavy leather suitcases.

"The rest of my kit has gone by long sea," he explained.

Like most Army men, the Colonel was a neat packer. The examination of his baggage took only a few minutes. Poirot noted a packet of pipe-cleaners.

"You always use the same kind?" he asked.

"Usually. If I can get 'em."

"Ah!" Poirot nodded.

These pipe-cleaners were identical with the one he had found on the floor of the dead man's compartment.

Dr. Constantine remarked as much when they were out in the corridor again.

"*Tout de même*," murmured Poirot, "I can hardly believe it. It is not *dans son caractère*, and when you have said that you have said everything."

The door of the next compartment was closed. It was that occupied by Princess Dragomiroff. They knocked on the door and the Princess's deep voice called, "*Entrez*."

M. Bouc was spokesman. He was very deferential and polite as he explained their errand.

The Princess listened to him in silence, her small toad-like face quite impassive.

"If it is necessary, Messieurs," she said quietly when he had finished, "that is all there is to it. My maid has the keys. She will attend to it with you."

"Does your maid always carry your keys, Madame?" asked Poirot.

"Certainly, Monsieur."

"And if during the night at one of the frontiers the Customs officials should require a piece of luggage to be opened?"

The old lady shrugged her shoulders.

"It is very unlikely. But in such a case this conductor would fetch her."

"You trust her, then, implicitly, Madame?"

"I have told you so already," said the Princess quietly. "I do not employ people whom I do not trust."

"Yes," said Poirot thoughtfully. "Trust is indeed something in these days. It is, perhaps, better to have a homely woman whom one can trust than a more *chic* maid—for example, some smart Parisienne."

He saw the dark intelligent eyes come slowly round and fasten themselves upon his face.

"What exactly are you implying, M. Poirot?"

"Nothing, Madame. I? Nothing."

"But yet. You think, do you not, that I should have a smart Frenchwoman to attend to my toilet?"

"It would be, perhaps, more usual, Madame."

She shook her head.

"Schmidt is devoted to me." Her voice dwelt lingeringly on the words. "Devotion—*c'est impayable*."

The German woman had arrived with the keys. The Princess spoke to her in her own language, telling her to open the valises and help the gentlemen in their search. She herself remained in the corridor looking out at the snow and Poirot remained with her, leaving M. Bouc to the task of searching the luggage.

She regarded him with a grim smile.

"Well, Monsieur, do you not wish to see what my valises contain?"

He shook his head.

"Madame, it is a formality, that is all."

"Are you so sure?"

"In your case, yes."

"And yet I knew and loved Sonia Armstrong. What do you think, then? That I would not soil my hands with killing such *canaille* as that man Cassetti? Well, perhaps you are right."

She was silent a minute or two, then she said:

"With such a man as that, do you know what I should have liked to have done? I should have liked to call to my servants: 'Flog this man to death and fling him out on the rubbish heap.' That is the way things were done when I was young, Monsieur."

Still he did not speak, just listened attentively.

She looked at him with a sudden impetuosity.

"You do not say anything, M. Poirot. What is it that you are thinking, I wonder?"

He looked at her with a very direct glance.

"I think, Madame, that your strength is in your will—not in your arm."

She glanced down at her thin, black-clad arms ending in those claw-like yellow hands with the rings on the fingers.

"It is true," she said. "I have no strength in these—none. I do not know if I am sorry or glad."

Then she turned abruptly back toward her carriage, where the maid was busily packing up the cases.

The Princess cut short M. Bouc's apologies.

"There is not need for you to apologize, Monsieur," she said. "A murder has been committed. Certain actions have to be performed. That is all there is to it."

"Vous êtes bien amiable, Madame."

She inclined her head slightly as they departed.

The doors of the next two carriages were shut. M. Bouc paused and scratched his head.

"Diable!" he said. "This may be awkward. These are diplomatic passports. Their baggage is exempt."

"From Customs examination, yes. But a murder is different."

"I know. All the same—we do not want to have complications——"

"Do not distress yourself, my friend. The Count and Countess will be reasonable. See how amiable Princess Dragomiroff was about it."

"She is truly *grande dame*. These two are also of the same position, but the Count impressed me as a man of somewhat truculent disposition. He was not pleased when you insisted on questioning his wife. And this will annoy him still further. Suppose—eh—we omit them. After all, they can have nothing to do with the matter. Why should I stir up needless trouble for myself."

"I do not agree with you," said Poirot. "I feel sure that Count Andrenyi will be reasonable. At any rate, let us make the attempt."

And, before M. Bouc could reply, he rapped sharply on the door of No. 13.

A voice from within cried, *"Entrez."*

The Count was sitting in the corner near the door reading a newspaper. The Countess was curled up in the opposite corner near the window. There was a pillow behind her head, and she seemed to have been asleep.

"Pardon, Monsieur le Comte," began Poirot. "Pray forgive this intrusion. It is that we are making a search of all the baggage on the train. In most cases a mere formality. But it has to be done. M. Bouc suggests that, as you have a diplomatic passport, you might reasonably claim to be exempt from such a search."

The Count considered for a moment.

"Thank you," he said. "But I do not think that I care for an exception to be made in my case. I should prefer that our baggage should be examined like that of the other passengers."

He turned to his wife.

"You do not object, I hope, Elena?"

"Not at all," said the Countess without hesitation.

A rapid and somewhat perfunctory search followed. Poirot seemed to be trying to mask an embarrassment in making various small pointless remarks, such as:

"Here is a label all wet on your suitcase, Madame," as he lifted down a blue morocco case with initials on it and a coronet.

The Countess did not reply to this observation. She seemed, indeed, rather bored by the whole proceeding, remaining curled up in her corner, staring dreamily out through the window whilst the men searched her luggage in the compartment next door.

Poirot finished his search by opening the little cupboard above the wash-basin and taking a rapid glance at its contents—a sponge, face cream, powder and a small bottle labeled "trional."

Then, with polite remarks on either side, the search party withdrew.

Mrs. Hubbard's compartment, that of the dead man, and Poirot's own came next.

They now came to the second-class carriages. The first one, Nos. 10, 11, was occupied by Mary Debenham, who was reading a book, and Greta Ohlsson, who was fast asleep but woke with a start at their entrance.

Poirot repeated his formula. The Swedish lady seemed agitated, Mary Debenham calmly indifferent.

Poirot addressed himself to the Swedish lady.

"If you permit, Mademoiselle, we will examine your baggage first, and then perhaps you would be so good as to see how the American lady is getting on. We have moved her into one of the carriages in the next coach, but she is still very upset as the result of her discovery. I have ordered coffee to be sent to her, but I think she is of those to whom someone to talk to is a necessity of the first water."

The good lady was instantly sympathetic. She would go immediately. It must have been indeed a terrible shock to the nerves, and already the poor lady was upset by the journey and leaving her daughter. Ah, yes, certainly she would go at once—her case was not locked—and she would take with her some sal ammoniac.

She bustled off. Her possessions were soon examined. They were meagre in the extreme. She had evidently not yet noticed the missing wires from the hat box.

Miss Debenham had put her book down. She was watching Poirot. When he asked her, she handed over her keys. Then, as he lifted down a case and opened it, she said:

"Why did you send her away, M. Poirot?"

"I, Mademoiselle? Why, to minister to the American lady."

"An excellent pretext—but a pretext all the same."

"I don't understand you, Mademoiselle."

"I think you understand me very well."

She smiled.

"You wanted to get me alone. Wasn't that it?"

"You are putting words into my mouth, Mademoiselle."

"And ideas into your head? No, I don't think so. The ideas are already there. That is right, isn't it?"

"Mademoiselle, we have a proverb——"

"*Qui s'excuse s'accuse;* is that what you were going to say? You must give me the credit for a certain amount of observation and common sense. For some reason or other you have got it into your head that I know something about this sordid business—this murder of a man I never saw before."

"You are imagining things, Mademoiselle."

"No, I am not imagining things at all. But it seems to me that a lot of time is wasted by not speaking the truth—by beating about the bush instead of coming straight out with things."

"And you do not like the waste of time. No, you like to come straight to the point. You like the direct method. *Eh bien,* I will give it to you, the direct method. I will ask you the meaning of certain words that I overheard on the journey from Syria. I had got out of the train to do what the English call 'stretch the legs' at the station of Konya. Your voice and the Colonel's, Mademoiselle, they came to me out of the night. You said to him, '*Not now. Not now. When it's all over. When it's behind us.*' What did you mean by those words, Mademoiselle?"

She said very quietly:

"Do you think I meant—murder?"

"It is I who am asking you, Mademoiselle."

She sighed—was lost a minute in thought. Then, as though rousing herself, she said:

"Those words had a meaning, Monsieur, but not one that I can tell you. I can only give you my solemn word of honour that I had never set eyes on this man Ratchett in my life until I saw him on this train."

"And—you refuse to explain those words?"

"Yes—if you like to put it that way—I refuse. They had to do with—with a task I had undertaken."

"A task that is now ended?"

"What do you mean?"

"It is ended, is it not?"

"Why should you think so?"

"Listen, Mademoiselle, I will recall to you another incident. There was a delay to the train on the day we were to reach Stamboul. You were very agitated, Mademoiselle. You, so calm, so self-controlled. You lost that calm."

"I did not want to miss my connection."

"So you said. But, Mademoiselle, the Orient Express leaves Stamboul every day of the week. Even if you had missed the connection it would only have been a matter of twenty-four hours' delay."

Miss Debenham for the first time showed signs of losing her temper.

"You do not seem to realize that one may have friends awaiting one's arrival in London, and that a day's delay upsets arrangements and causes a lot of annoyance."

"Ah, it is like that? There are friends awaiting your arrival? You do not want to cause them inconvenience?"

"Naturally."

"And yet—it is curious——"

"What is curious?"

"On this train—again we have a delay. And this time a more serious delay, since there is no possibility of sending a telegram to your friends or of getting them on the long—the long——"

"The long distance? The telephone, you mean."

"Ah, yes, the portmanteau call, as you say in England."

Mary Debenham smiled a little in spite of herself.

"Trunk call," she corrected. "Yes, as you say, it is extremely annoying not to be able to get any word through, either by telephone or telegraph."

"And yet, Mademoiselle, *this* time your manner is quite different. You no longer betray the impatience. You are calm and philosophical."

Mary Debenham flushed and bit her lips. She no longer felt inclined to smile.

"You do not answer, Mademoiselle?"

"I am sorry. I did not know that there was anything to answer."

"The explanation of your change of attitude, Mademoiselle."

"Don't you think that you are making rather a fuss about nothing, M. Poirot?"

Poirot spread out his hands in an apologetic gesture.

"It is perhaps a fault with us detectives. We expect the behaviour to be always consistent. We do not allow for changes of mood."

Mary Debenham made no reply.

"You know Colonel Arbuthnot well, Mademoiselle?"

He fancied that she was relieved by the change of subject.

"I met him for the first time on this journey."

"Have you any reason to suspect that he may have known this man Ratchett?"

She shook her head decisively.

"I am quite sure he didn't."

"Why are you sure?"

"By the way he spoke."

"And yet, Mademoiselle, we found a pipe-cleaner on the floor of the dead man's compartment. And Colonel Arbuthnot is the only man on the train who smokes a pipe."

He watched her narrowly, but she displayed neither surprise nor emotion, merely said:

"Nonsense. It's absurd. Colonel Arbuthnot is the last man in the world to be mixed up in a crime—especially a theatrical kind of crime like this."

It was so much what Poirot himself thought that he found himself on the point of agreeing with her. He said instead:

"I must remind you that you do not know him very well, Mademoiselle."

She shrugged her shoulders.

"I know the type well enough."

He said very gently:

"You still refuse to tell me the meaning of those words—'When it's behind us'?"

She said coldly:

"I have nothing more to say."

"It does not matter," said Hercule Poirot. "I shall find out."

He bowed and left the compartment, closing the door after him.

"Was that wise, my friend?" asked M. Bouc. "You have put her on her guard—and through her you have put the Colonel on his guard also."

"*Mon ami,* if you wish to catch a rabbit you put a ferret into the hole, and if the rabbit is there he runs. That is all I have done."

They entered the compartment of Hildegarde Schmidt.

The woman was standing in readiness, her face respectful but unemotional.

Poirot took a quick glance through the contents of the small case on the seat. Then he motioned to the attendant to get down the bigger suitcase from the rack.

"The keys?" he said.

"It is not locked, Monsieur."

Poirot undid the hasps and lifted the lid.

"Aha!" he said, and turning to M. Bouc, "You remember what I said? Look here a little moment!"

On the top of the suitcase was a hastily rolled up brown Wagon Lit uniform.

The stolidity of the German woman underwent a sudden change.

"Ach!" she cried. "That is not mine. I did not put it there. I have never looked in that case since we left Stamboul. Indeed, indeed, it is true."

She looked from one to another pleadingly.

Poirot took her gently by the arm and soothed her.

"No, no, all is well. We believe you. Do not be agitated. I am as sure you did not hide the uniform there as I am sure that you are a good cook. See. You are a good cook, are you not?"

Bewildered, the woman smiled in spite of herself.

"Yes, indeed, all my ladies have said so. I——"

She stopped, her mouth open, looking frightened again.

"No, no," said Poirot. "I assure you all is well. See, I will tell you how this happened. This man, the man you saw in Wagon Lit uniform, comes out of the dead man's compartment. He collides with you. That is bad luck for him. He has hoped that no one will see him. What to do next? He must get rid of his uniform. It is now not a safeguard, but a danger."

His glance went to M. Bouc and Dr. Constantine, who were listening attentively.

"There is the snow, you see. The snow which confuses all his plans. Where can he hide these clothes? All the compartments are full. No, he passes one where the door is open and shows it to be unoccupied. It must be the one belonging to the woman with whom he has just collided. He slips in, removes the uniform and jams it hurriedly into a suitcase on the rack. It may be some time before it is discovered."

"And then?" said M. Bouc.

"That we must discuss," said Poirot with a warning glance.

He held up the tunic. A button, the third down, was missing. Poirot slipped his hand into the pocket and took out a conductor's pass key, used to unlock the doors of the compartments.

"Here is the explanation of how our man was able to pass through locked doors," said M. Bouc. "Your questions to Mrs. Hubbard were unnecessary. Locked or not locked, the man could easily get through the communicating door. After all, if a Wagon Lit uniform, why not a Wagon Lit key?"

"Why not, indeed," said Poirot.

"We might have known it, really. You remember Michel said that the door ino the corridor of Mrs. Hubbard's compartment was locked when he came in answer to her bell."

"That is so, Monsieur," said the conductor. "That is why I thought the lady must have been dreaming."

"But now it is easy," continued M. Bouc. "Doubtless he meant to relock the communicating door also, but perhaps he heard some movement from the bed and it startled him."

"We have now," said Poirot, "only to find the scarlet kimono."

"True. And these last two compartments are occupied by men."

"We will search all the same."

"Oh! assuredly. Besides, I remember what you said."

Hector MacQueen acquiesced willingly in the search.

"I'd just as soon you did," he said with a rueful smile. "I feel I'm just definitely the most suspicious character on the train. You've only got to find a will in which the old man left me all his money, and that'll just about fix things."

M. Bouc bent a suspicious glance upon him.

"That's just my fun," said MacQueen hastily. "He'd never have left me a cent, really. I was just useful to him—languages and so on. You're apt to be done down, you know, if you don't speak anything but good American. I'm no linguist myself, but I know what I call shopping and hotel snappy bits in French and German and Italian."

His voice was a little louder than usual. It was as though he was slightly uneasy at the search in spite of his willingness.

Poirot emerged.

"Nothing," he said. "Not even a compromising bequest!"

MacQueen sighed.

"Well, that's a load off my mind," he said humorously.

They moved on to the last compartment. The examination of the luggage of the big Italian and of the valet yielded no result.

The three men stood at the end of the coach looking at each other.

"What next?" asked M. Bouc.

"We will go back to the dining-car," said Poirot. "We know now all that we can know. We have the evidence of the passengers, the evidence of their baggage, the evidence of our eyes. We can expect no further help. It must be our part now to use our brains."

He felt in his pocket for his cigarette case. It was empty.

"I will join you in a moment," he said. "I shall need the cigarettes. This is a very difficult, a very curious affair. Who wore that scarlet kimono? Where is it now? I wish I knew. There is something in this case—some factor—that escapes me! It is difficult because it has been made difficult. But we will discuss it. Pardon me a moment."

He went hurriedly along the corridor to his own compartment. He had, he knew, a further supply of cigarettes in one of his valises.

He got it down and snapped back the lock.

Then he sat back on his heels and stared.

Neatly folded on the top of the case was a thin scarlet silk kimono embroidered with dragons.

"So," he murmured. "It is like that. A defiance. Very well. I take it up."

PART THREE
HERCULE POIROT SITS BACK AND THINKS

CHAPTER 1
Which of Them?

M. Bouc and Dr. Constantine were talking together when Poirot entered the dining-car. M. Bouc was looking depressed.

"Le voilà," said the latter when he saw Poirot.

Then he added as his friend sat down:

"If you solve this case, *mon cher*, I shall indeed believe in miracles!"

"It worries you, this case?"

"Naturally it worries me. I cannot make head or tail of it."

"I agree," said the doctor.

He looked at Poirot with interest.

"To be frank," he said, "I cannot see what you are going to do next."

"No?" said Poirot thoughtfully.

He took out his cigarette case and lit one of his tiny cigarettes. His eyes were dreamy.

"That, to me, is the interest of this case," he said. "We are cut off from all the normal routes of procedure. Are these people whose evidence we have taken speaking the truth or lying? We have no means of finding out—except such means as we can devise ourselves. It is an exercise, this, of the brain."

"That is all very fine," said M. Bouc. "But what have you to go upon?"

"I told you just now. We have the evidence of the passengers and the evidence of our own eyes."

"Pretty evidence—that of the passengers! It told us just nothing at all."

Poirot shook his head.

"I do not agree, my friend. The evidence of the passengers gave us several points of interest."

"Indeed," said M. Bouc skeptically. "I did not observe it."

"That is because you did not listen."

"Well, tell me—what did I miss?"

"I will just take one instance—the first evidence we heard—that of the young MacQueen. He uttered, to my mind, one very significant phrase."

"About the letters?"

"No, not about the letters. As far as I can remember, his words were: '*We traveled about. Mr. Ratchett wanted to see the world. He was hampered by knowing no languages. I acted more as a courier than a secretary.*'"

He looked from the doctor's face to that of Mr. Bouc.

"What? You still do not see? That is inexcusable—for you had a second chance again just now when he said, *'You're apt to be done down if you speak nothing but good American.'*"

"You mean——?" M. Bouc still looked puzzled.

"Ah, it is that you want it given to you in words of one syllable. Well, here it is! *M. Ratchett spoke no French.* Yet, when the conductor came in answer to his bell last night, it was a voice speaking in *French* that told him that it was a mistake and that he was not wanted. It was moreover a perfectly idiomatic phrase that was used, not one that a man knowing only a few words of French would have selected. *'Ce n'est rien. Je me suis trompé.'*"

"It is true," cried Constantine excitedly. "We should have seen that! I remember your laying stress on the words when you repeated them to us. Now I understand your reluctance to rely upon the evidence of the dented watch. Already at twenty-three minutes to one, Ratchett was dead——"

"And it was his murderer speaking!" finished M. Bouc impressively.

Poirot raised a deprecating hand.

"Let us not go too fast. And do not let us assume more than we actually know. It is safe, I think, to say that at that time, twenty-three minutes to one, *some other person* was in Ratchett's compartment and that that person was either French, or could speak the French language fluently."

"You are very cautious, *mon vieux.*"

"One should advance only a step at a time. We have no actual *evidence* that Ratchett was dead at that time."

"There is the cry that awakened you."

"Yes, that is true."

"In one way," said M. Bouc thoughtfully, "this discovery does not affect things very much. You heard someone moving about next door. That someone was not Ratchett, but the other man. Doubtless he is washing blood from his hands, clearing up after the crime, burning the incriminating letter. Then he waits till all is still, and when he thinks it is safe and the coast is clear he locks and chains Ratchett's door on the inside, unlocks the communicating door through into Mrs. Hubbard's compartment and slips out that way. In fact it is exactly as we thought—*with the difference that Ratchett was killed about half an hour earlier*, and the watch put on to a quarter-past one to create an alibi."

"Not such a famous alibi," said Poirot. "The hands of the watch pointed to 1.15—the exact time when the intruder actually left the scene of the crime."

"True," said M. Bouc, a little confused. "What, then, does the watch convey to you?"

"If the hands were altered— say *if*—then the time at which they were set *must* have a significance. The natural reaction would be to suspect anyone who had a reliable alibi for the time indicated—in this case 1.15."

"Yes, yes," said the doctor. "That reasoning is good."

"We must also pay a little attention to the time the intruder *entered* the compartment. When had he an opportunity of doing so? Unless we are to assume the complicity of the real conductor, there was only one time when he could have done so—during the time the train stopped at Vincovci. After the train left Vincovci the conductor was sitting facing the corridor and whereas any one of the passengers would pay little attention to a Wagon Lit attendant, the *one* person who would notice an impostor would be the real conductor. But during the halt at Vincovci the conductor is out on the platform. The coast is clear."

"And, by our former reasoning, it *must* be one of the passengers," said M. Bouc. "We come back to where we were. Which of them?"

Poirot smiled.

"I have made a list," he said, "If you like to see it, it will, perhaps, refresh your memory."

The doctor and M. Bouc pored over the list together. It was written out neatly in a methodical manner in the order in which the passengers had been interviewed.

HECTOR MACQUEEN—American subject

Berth No. 6. Second Class

Motive: Possibly arising out of association with dead man?

Alibi: From midnight to 2 a.m. (Midnight to 1.30 vouched for by Col. Arbuthnot and 1.15 to 2 vouched for by conductor.)

Evidence against him: None.

Suspicious circumstances: None.

CONDUCTOR—PIERRE MICHEL—French subject

Motive: None.

Alibi: From midnight to 2 a.m. (Seen by H.P. in corridor at same time as voice spoke from Ratchett's compartment at 12.37. From 1 a.m. to 1.16 vouched for by other two conductors.)

Evidence against him: None.

Suspicious circumstances: The Wagon Lit uniform found is a point in his favour since it seems to have been intended to throw suspicion on him.

EDWARD MASTERMAN—English subject

Berth No. 4. Second Class.

Motive: Possibly arising out of connection with deceased, whose valet he was.

Alibi: From midnight to 2 a.m. (Vouched for by Antonio Foscarelli.)

Evidence against him or suspicious circumstances: None, except that he is the only man the right height or size to have worn the Wagon Lit uniform. On the other hand, it is unlikely that he speaks French well.

MRS. HUBBARD—American subject

Berth No. 3. First Class

Motive: None.

Alibi: From midnight to 2 a.m.—None.

Evidence against her or suspicious circumstances: Story of man in her compartment is substantiated by the evidence of the woman Schmidt.

GRETA OHLSSON—Swedish subject

Berth No. 10. Second Class

Motive: None.

Alibi: From midnight to 2 a.m. (Vouched for by Mary Debenham.)

Note.—Was last to see Ratchett alive.

PRINCESS DRAGOMIROFF—Naturalised French subject

Motive: Was intimately acquainted with Armstrong family, and godmother to Sonia Armstrong.

Alibi: From midnight to 2 a.m. (Vouched for by conductor and maid.)

Evidence against her or suspicious circumstances: None.

COUNT ANDRENYI—Hungarian subject

Diplomatic passport

Berth No. 13. First Class

Motive: None.

Alibi: Midnight to 2 a.m. (Vouched for by conductor—this does not cover period from 1 to 1.15.)

COUNTESS ANDRENYI—As above

Berth No. 12

Motive: None.

Alibi: Midnight to 2 a.m. Took trional and slept. (Vouched for by husband. Trional bottle in her cupboard.)

COLONEL ARBUTHNOT—British subject

Berth No. 15. First Class

Motive: None.

Alibi: Midnight to 2 a.m. Talked with MacQueen till 1.30. Went to own compartment and did not leave it. (Substantiated by MacQueen and conductor.)

Evidence against him or suspicious circumstances: Pipe-cleaner.

CYRUS HARDMAN—American subject

Berth No. 16. Second Class

Motive: None known.

Alibi: Midnight to 2 a.m. Did not leave compartment. (Substantiated by MacQueen and conductor.)

Evidence against him or suspicious circumstances: None.

ANTONIO FOSCARELLI—American subject (Italian birth)

Berth No. 5. Second Class

Motive: None known.

Alibi: Midnight to 2 a.m. (Vouched for by Edward Masterman.)

Evidence against him or suspicious circumstances: None, except that weapon used might be said to suit his temperament. (Vide B. Bouc.)

MARY DEBENHAM—British subject

Berth No. 11. Second Class

Motive: None.

Alibi: Midnight to 2 a.m. (Vouched for by Greta Ohlsson.)

Evidence against her or suspicious circumstances: Conversation overheard by H.P. and her refusal to explain same.

HILDEGARDE SCHMIDT—German subject

Berth No. 8. Second Class

Motive: None.

Alibi: Midnight to 2 a.m. (Vouched for by conductor and her mistress.) Went to bed. Was aroused by conductor at 12.38 approx. and went to mistress.

Note: The evidence of the passengers is supported by the statement of the conductor that no one entered or left Mr. Ratchett's compartment between the hours of midnight to 1 o'clock (when he himself went into the next coach) and from 1.15 to 2 o'clock.

"That document, you understand," said Poirot," is a mere précis of the evidence we heard, arranged that way for convenience."

With a grimace M. Bouc handed it back.

"It is not illuminating," he said.

"Perhaps you may find this more to your taste," said Poirot with a slight smile as he handed him a second sheet of paper.

CHAPTER 2
Ten Questions

On the paper was written:

Things needing explanation

1. The handkerchief marked with the initial H. Whose is it?
2. The pipe-cleaner. Was it dropped by Colonel Arbuthnot? Or by someone else?
3. Who wore the scarlet kimono?
4. Who was the man or woman masquerading in Wagon Lit uniform?
5. Why do the hands of the watch point to 1.15?
6. Was the murder committed at that time?
7. Was it earlier?
8. Was it later?
9. Can we be sure that Ratchett was stabbed by more than one person?
10. What other explanation of his wounds can there be?

"Well, let us see what we can do," said M. Bouc, brightening a little at this challenge to his wits. "The handkerchief to begin with. Let us by all means be orderly and methodical."

"Assuredly," said Poirot, nodding his head in a satisfied fashion.

M. Bouc continued somewhat didactically.

"The initial H is connected with three people—Mrs. Hubbard, Miss Debenham, whose second name is Hermione, and the maid Hildegarde Schmidt."

"Ah! And of those three?"

"It is difficult to say. But I *think* I should vote for Miss Debenham. For all one knows, she may be called by her second name and not her first. Also there is already some suspicion attaching to her. That conversation you overheard, *mon cher*, was certainly a little curious, and so is her refusal to explain it."

"As for me, I plump for the American," said Dr. Constantine. "It is a very expensive handkerchief that, and Americans, as all the world knows, do not care what they pay."

"So you both eliminate the maid?" asked Poirot.

"Yes. As she herself said, it is the handkerchief of a member of the upper classes."

"And the second question—the pipe-cleaner. Did Colonel Arbuthnot drop it, or somebody else?"

"That is more difficult. The English, they do not stab. You are right there. I incline to the view that someone else dropped the pipe-cleaner—and did so to incriminate the long-legged Englishman."

"As you said, M. Poirot," put in the doctor, "*Two* clues is too much carelessness. I agree with M. Bouc. The handkerchief was a genuine oversight—hence no one will admit that it is theirs. The pipe-cleaner is a faked one. In support of that theory, you notice that Colonel Arbuthnot shows no embarrassment and admits freely to smoking a pipe and using that type of cleaner."

"You reason well," said Poirot.

"Question No. 3—who wore the scarlet kimono?" went on M. Bouc. "As to that I will confess I have not the slightest idea. Have you any views on the subject, Dr. Constantine?"

"None."

"Then we confess ourselves beaten there. The next question has, at any rate, possibilities. Who was the man or woman masquerading in Wagon Lit uniform? Well, one can say with certainty a number of people whom it could *not* be. Hardman, Colonel Arbuthnot, Foscarelli, Count Andrenyi and Hector MacQueen are all too tall. Mrs. Hubbard, Hildegarde Schmidt and Greta Ohlsson are too broad. That leaves the valet, Miss Debenham, Princess Dragomiroff and Countess Andrenyi—and none of them sounds likely! Greta Ohlsson in one case and Antonio Foscarelli in the other both swear that Miss Debenham and the valet never left their compartments. Hildegarde Schmidt swears to the Princess being in hers, and Count Andrenyi has told us that his wife took a sleeping draught. Therefore it seems impossible that it can be anybody—which is absurd!"

"As our old friend Euclid says," murmured Poirot.

"It must be one of those four," said Dr. Constantine. "Unless it is someone from outside who has found a hiding-place—and that, we agreed, was impossible."

M. Bouc had passed on to the next question on the list.

"No. 5—why do the hands of the broken watch point to 1.15? I can see two explanations of that. Either it was done by the murderer to establish an alibi and afterwards he was prevented from leaving the compartment when he meant to do so by hearing people moving about, or else—wait—I have an idea coming——"

The other two waited respectfully while M. Bouc struggled in mental agony.

"I have it," he said at last. "It was *not* the Wagon Lit murderer who tampered with the watch! It was the person we have called the Second Murderer—the left-handed person—in other words the woman in the scarlet kimono. She arrives later and moves back the hands of the watch in order to make an alibi for herself."

"Bravo," said Dr. Constantine. "It is well imagined, that."

"In fact," said Poirot, "she stabbed him in the dark, not realizing that he was dead already, but somehow deduced that he had a watch in his pyjama pocket, took it out, put back the hands blindly and gave it the requisite dent."

M. Bouc looked at him coldly.

"Have you anything better to suggest yourself?" he asked.

"At the moment—no," admitted Poirot.

"All the same," he went on, "I do not think you have either of you appreciated the most interesting point about that watch."

"Does question No. 6 deal with it?" asked the doctor. "To that question—was the murder committed at that time—1.15—I answer, *No*.'"

"I agree," said M. Bouc. "'Was it earlier?' is the next question. I say yes. You, too, doctor?"

The doctor nodded.

"Yes, but the question 'Was it later?' can also be answered in the affirmative. I agree with your theory, M. Bouc, and so, I think, does M. Poirot, although he does not wish to commit himself. The First Murderer came earlier than 1.15, the Second Murderer came *after* 1.15. And as regards the question of left-handedness, ought we not to take steps to ascertain which of the passengers is left-handed?"

"I have not completely neglected that point," said Poirot. "You may have noticed that I made each passenger write either a signature or an address. That is not conclusive, because some people do certain actions with the right hand and others with the left. Some write right-handed, but play golf left-handed. Still, it is something. Every person questioned took the pen in their right hand—with the exception of Princess Dragomiroff, who refused to write."

"Princess Dragomiroff, impossible," said M. Bouc.

"I doubt if she would have had the strength to inflict that particular left-handed blow," said Dr. Constantine dubiously. "That particular wound had been inflicted with considerable force."

"More force than a woman could use?"

"No, I would not say that. But I think more force than an elderly woman could display, and Princess Dragomiroff's physique is particularly frail."

"It might be a question of the influence of mind over body," said Poirot. "Princess Dragomiroff has great personality and immense will power. But let us pass from that for the moment."

"To questions Nos. 9 and 10. Can we be sure that Ratchett was stabbed by more than one person, and what other explanation of the wounds can there be? In my opinion, medically speaking, there can *be no other* explanation of those wounds. To suggest that one man struck first feebly and then with violence, first with the right hand and then with the left, and after an interval of perhaps half an hour inflicted fresh wounds on a dead body—well, it does not make sense."

"No," said Poirot. "It does not make sense. And you think that two murderers do make sense?"

"As you yourself have said, what other explanation can there be?"

Poirot stared straight ahead of him.

"That is what I ask myself," he said. "That is what I never cease to ask myself."

He leaned back in his seat.

"From now on, it is all here," he tapped himself on the forehead. "We have thrashed it all out. The facts are all in front of us—neatly arranged with order and method. The passengers have sat here, one by one, giving their evidence. We know all that can be known—*from outside*. . . ."

He gave an affectionate smile at M. Bouc.

"It has been a little joke between us, has it not—this business of sitting back and *thinking* out the truth? Well, I am about to put my theory into practice—here before your eyes. You two must do the same. Let us all three close our eyes and think. . . ."

"One or more of those passengers killed Ratchett. *Which of them?*"

CHAPTER 3
Certain Suggestive Points

It was quite a quarter of an hour before anyone spoke.

M. Bouc and Dr. Constantine had started by trying to obey Poirot's instructions. They had endeavoured to see through a maze of conflicting particulars to a clear and outstanding solution.

M. Bouc's thoughts had run something as follows:

"Assuredly I must think. But as far as that goes I have already thought. . . . Poirot obviously thinks this English girl is mixed up in the matter. I cannot help feeling that that is most unlikely . . . . The English are extremely cold. Probably it is because they have no figures. . . . But that is not the point. I suppose the English valet is not lying when he said the other never left the compartment? But why should he? It is not easy to bribe the English, they are so unapproachable. The whole thing is most unfortunate. I wonder when we shall get out of this. There must be *some* rescue work in progress. They are so slow in these countries . . . it is hours before anyone thinks of doing anything. And the police of these countries, they will be most trying to deal with—puffed up with importance, touchy, on their dignity. They will make a grand affair of all this. It is not often that such a chance comes their way. It will be in all the newspapers. . . ."

And from there on M. Bouc's thoughts went along a well-worn course which they had already traversed some hundred times.

Dr. Constantine's thoughts ran thus:

"He is queer, this little man. A genius? Or a crank? Will he solve this mystery? Impossible. I can see no way out of it. It is all too confusing. . . . Everyone is lying, perhaps. . . . But even then that does not help one. If they are all lying it is just as confusing as if they were speaking the truth. Odd about those wounds. I cannot understand it. . . . It would be easier to understand if he had been shot—after all, the term gunman must mean that they shoot with a gun. A curious country, America. I should like to go there. It is so progressive. When I get home I must get hold of Demetrius Zagone—he has been to America, he has all the modern ideas. . . . I wonder what Zia is doing at this moment. If my wife ever finds out——"

His thoughts went on to entirely private matters.

Hercule Poirot sat very still.

One might have thought he was asleep.

And then, suddenly, after a quarter of an hour's complete immobility, his eyebrows began to move slowly up his forehead. A little sigh escaped him. He murmured beneath his breath:

"But, after all, why not? And if so—why, if so, that would explain everything."

His eyes opened. They were green like a cat's. He said softly:

"*Eh bien*. I have thought. And you?"

Lost in their reflections, both men started violently.

"I have thought also," said M. Bouc just a shade guilty. "But I have arrived at no conclusion. The elucidation of crime is your *métier*, not mine, my friend."

"I, too, have reflected with great earnestness," said the doctor unblushingly, recalling his thoughts from certain pornographic details. "I thought of many possible theories, but not one that really satisfies me."

Poirot nodded amiably. His nod seemed to say:

"Quite right. That is the proper thing to say. You have given me the cue I expected."

He sat very upright, threw out his chest, caressed his moustache and spoke in the manner of a practiced speaker addressing a public meeting.

"My friends, I have reviewed the facts in my mind, and have also gone over to myself the evidence of the passengers—with this result. I see, nebulously as yet, a certain explanation that would cover the facts as we know them. It is a very curious explanation, and I cannot be sure as yet that it is the true one. To find out definitely, I shall have to make certain experiments.

"I would like first to mention certain points which appear to me suggestive. Let us start with a remark made to me by M. Bouc in this very place on the occasion of our first lunch together on the train. He commented on the fact that we were surrounded by people of all classes, of all ages, of all nationalities. That is a fact somewhat rare at this time of year. The Athens-Paris and the Bucharest-Paris coaches, for instance, are almost empty. Remember also one passenger who failed to turn up. It is, I think, significant. Then there are some minor points that strike me as suggestive—for instance, the position of Mrs. Hubbard's sponge-bag, the name of Mrs. Armstrong's mother, the detective methods of M. Hardman, the suggestion of M. MacQueen that Ratchett himself destroyed the charred note we found, Princess Dragomiroff's Christian name, and a grease spot on a Hungarian passport."

The two men stared at him.

"Do they suggest anything to you, those points?" asked Poirot.

"Not a thing," said M. Bouc frankly.

"And M. le docteur?"

"I do not understand in the least of what you are talking."

M. Bouc, meanwhile, seizing upon the one tangible thing his friend had mentioned, was sorting through the passports. With a grunt he picked up that of Count and Countess Andrenyi and opened it.

"Is this what you mean? This dirty mark?"

"Yes. It is a fairly fresh grease spot. You notice where it occurs?"

"At the beginning of the description of the Count's wife—her Christian name, to be exact. But I confess that I still do not see the point."

"I am going to approach it from another angle. Let us go back to the handkerchief found at the scene of the crime. As we have stated not long ago—three people are associated with the letter H. Mrs. Hubbard, Miss Debenham and the maid, Hildegarde Schmidt. Now let us regard that handkerchief from another point of view. It is, my friends, an extremely expensive handkerchief—an *object de luxe*, hand made, embroidered in Paris. Which of the passengers, apart from the initial, was likely to own such a handkerchief? Not Mrs. Hubbard, a worthy woman with no pretensions to reckless extravagance in dress. Not Miss Debenham; that class of Englishwoman has a dainty linen handkerchief, but not an expensive wisp of cambric costing perhaps two hundred francs. And certainly not the maid. But there *are* two women on the train who would be likely to own such a handkerchief. Let us see if we can connect them in any way with the letter H. The two women I refer to are Princess Dragomiroff——"

"Whose Christian name is Natalia," put in M. Bouc ironically.

"Exactly. And her Christian name, as I said just now, is decidedly suggestive. The other woman is Countess Andrenyi. And at once something strikes us——"

You!"

"*Me*, then. Her Christian name on her passport is disfigured by a blob of grease. Just an accident, anyone would say. But consider that Christian name. Elena. Suppose that, instead of Elena, it were *Helena*. That capital H could be turned into a capital E and then run over the small e next to it quite easily—and then a spot of grease dropped to cover up the alteration."

"Helena," cried M. Bouc. "It is an idea, that."

"Certainly it is an idea! I look about for any confirmation, however slight, of my idea—and I find it. One of the luggage labels on the Countess's baggage is slightly damp. It is one that happens to run over the first initial on top of the case. That label has been soaked off and put on again in a different place."

"You begin to convince me," said M. Bouc. "But the Countess Andrenyi—surely——"

"Ah, now, *mon vieux*, you must turn yourself round and approach an entirely different angle of the case. How was this murder intended to appear to everybody? Do not forget that the snow has upset all the murderer's original plan. Let us imagine, for a little minute, that there is no snow, that the train proceeded on its normal course. What, then, would have happened?

"The murder, let us say, would still have been discovered in all probability at the Italian frontier early this morning. Much of the same evidence would have been given to the Italian police. The threatening letters would have been produced by M. MacQueen, M. Hardman would have told his story, Mrs. Hubbard would have been eager to tell how a man passed through her compartment, the button would have been found. I imagine that two things only would have been different. The man would have passed through Mrs. Hubbard's compartment just before one o'clock—and the Wagon Lit uniform would have been found cast off in one of the toilets."

"You mean?"

"I mean that the murder was *planned to look like an outside job*. The assassin would have been presumed to have left the train at Brod, where the train is timed to arrive at 00.58. Somebody would probably have passed a strange Wagon Lit conductor in the corridor. The uniform would be left in a conspicuous place so as to show clearly just how the trick had been played. No suspicion would have been attached to the passengers. That, my friends, was how the affair was intended to appear to the outside world.

"But the accident to the train changes everything. Doubtless we have here the reason why the man remained in the compartment with his victim so long. He was waiting for the train to go on. But at last he realized *that the train was not going on*. Different plans would have to be made. The murderer would now be *known* to be still on the train."

"Yes, yes," said M. Bouc impatiently. "I see all that. But where does the handkerchief come in?"

"I am returning to it by a somewhat circuitous route. To begin with, you must realize that the threatening letters were in the nature of a blind. They might have been lifted bodily out of an indifferently written American crime novel. They are not *real*. They are, in fact, simply intended for the police. What we have to ask ourselves, is, 'Did they deceive Ratchett?' On the face of it, the answer seems to be, 'No.' His instructions to Hardman seem to point to a definite 'private' enemy of the identity of whom he was well aware. That is if we accept Hardman's story as true. But Ratchett certainly received *one* letter of a very different character—the one containing a reference to the Armstrong baby, a fragment of which we found in his compartment. In case Ratchett had not realized it sooner, this was to make sure that he understood the reason of the threats against his life. That letter, as I have said all along, was *not* intended to be found. The murderer's first care was to destroy it. This, then, was the second hitch in his plans. The first was the snow, the second was our reconstruction of that fragment.

"That note being destroyed so carefully can only mean one thing. *There must be on the train someone so intimately connected with the Armstrong family that the finding of that note would immediately direct suspicion upon that person*.

"Now we come to the other two clues that we found. I pass over the pipe-cleaner. We have already said a good deal about that. Let us pass on to the handkerchief. Taken at its simplest, it is a clue which directly incriminates someone whose initial is H, and it was dropped there unwittingly by that person."

"Exactly," said Dr. Constantine. "She finds out that she has dropped the handkerchief and immediately takes steps to conceal her Christian name."

"How fast you go. You arrive at a conclusion much sooner than I would permit myself to do."

"Is there any other alternative?"

"Certainly there is. Suppose, for instance, that you have committed a crime and wish to cast a suspicion for it on someone else. Well, there is on the train a certain person connected intimately with the Armstrong family—a woman. Suppose, then, that you leave there a handkerchief belonging to that woman. . . . She will be questioned, her connection with the Armstrong family will be brought out—*et voilà*. Motive—*and* an incriminating article of evidence."

"But in such a case," objected the doctor, "the person indicated being innocent, would not take steps to conceal her identity."

"Ah, really? That is what you think? That is truly the opinion of the police court. But I know human nature, my friend, and I tell you that, suddenly confronted with the possibility of being tried for murder, the most innocent person will lose their head and do the most absurd things. No, no, the grease spot and the changed label do not prove guilt—they only prove that the Countess Andrenyi is anxious for some reason to conceal her identity."

"What do you think her connection with the Armstrong family can be? She has never been in America, she says."

"Exactly, and she speaks broken English, and she has a very foreign appearance which she exaggerates. But it should not be difficult to guess who she is. I mentioned just now the name of Mrs. Armstrong's mother. It was Linda Arden, and she was a very celebrated actress—among other things a Shakespearean actress. Think of *As You like It*—the Forest of Arden and Rosalind. It was there she got the inspiration for her acting name. Linda Arden, the name by which she was known all over the world, was not her real name. It may have been Goldenberg—she quite likely had central European blood in her veins—a strain of Jewish, perhaps. Many nationalities drift to America. I suggest to you, gentlemen, that that young sister of Mrs. Armstrong's, little more than a child at the time of the tragedy, was Helena Goldenberg the younger daughter of Linda Arden, and she married Count Andrenyi when he was an attaché in Washington."

"But Princess Dragomiroff says that she married an Englishman."

"Whose name she cannot remember! I ask you, my friends—is that really likely? Princess Dragomiroff loved Linda Arden as great ladies do love great artists. She was godmother to one of her daughters. Would she forget so quickly the married name of the other daughter? It is not likely. No, I think we can safely say that Princess Dragomiroff was lying. She knew Helena was on the train, she had seen her. She realized at once, as soon as she heard who Ratchett really was, that Helena would be suspected. And so, when we question her as to the sister she promptly lies—is vague, cannot remember, but 'thinks Helena married an Englishman'—a suggestion as far away from the truth as possible."

One of the restaurant attendants came through the door at the end and approached them. He addressed M. Bouc.

"The dinner, Monsieur, shall I serve it? It is ready some little time."

M. Bouc looked at Poirot. The latter nodded.

"By all means, let dinner be served."

The attendant vanished through the doors at the other end. His bell could be heard ringing and his voice upraised:

"*Premier Service. Le diner est servi. Premier diner*—First Service."

CHAPTER 4

The Grease Spot on a Hungarian Passport

Poirot shared a table with M. Bouc and the doctor.

The company assembled in the restaurant-car was a very subdued one. They spoke little. Even the loquacious Mrs. Hubbard was unnaturally quiet. She murmured as she sat:

"I don't feel as though I've got the heart to eat anything," and then partook of everything offered her, encouraged by the Swedish lady, who seemed to regard her as a special charge.

Before the meal was served Poirot had caught the chief attendant by the sleeve and murmured something to him. Constantine had a pretty good guess what the instructions had been, as he noticed that the Count and Countess Andrenyi were always served last and that at the end of the meal there was a delay in making out their bill. It therefore came about that the Count and Countess were the last left in the restaurant-car.

When they rose at length and moved in the direction of the door, Poirot sprang up and followed them.

"Pardon, Madame, you have dropped your handkerchief."

He was holding out to her the tiny monogrammed square.

She took it, glanced at it, then handed it back to him.

"You are mistaken, Monsieur, that is not my handkerchief."

"Not your handkerchief? Are you sure?"

"Perfectly sure, Monsieur."

"And yet, Madame, it has your initial—the initial H."

The Count made a sudden movement. Poirot ignored him. His eyes were fixed on the Countess's face.

Looking steadily at him she replied:

"I do not understand, Monsieur. My initials are E.A."

"I think not. Your name is Helena—not Elena. Helena Goldenberg, the younger daughter of Linda Arden—Helena Goldenberg, the sister of Mrs. Armstrong."

There was a dead silence for a minute or two. Both the Count and Countess had gone deadly white. Poirot said in a gentler tone:

"It is of no use denying. That is the truth, is it not?"

The Count burst out furiously:

"I demand, Monsieur, by what right you——"

She interrupted him, putting up a small hand toward his mouth.

"No, Rudolph. Let me speak. It is useless to deny what this gentleman says. We had better sit down and talk the matter out."

Her voice had changed. It still had the southern richness of tone, but it had become suddenly more clear cut and incisive. It was, for the first time, a definitely American voice.

The Count was silenced. He obeyed the gesture of her hand and they both sat down opposite Poirot.

"Your statement, Monsieur, is quite true," said the Countess. "I am Helena Goldenberg, the younger sister of Mrs. Armstrong."

"You did not acquaint me with that fact this morning, Madame la Comtesse."

"No."

"In fact, all that your husband and you told me was a tissue of lies."

"Monsieur," cried the Count angrily.

"Do not be angry, Rudolph. M. Poirot puts the fact rather brutally, but what he says is undeniable."

"I am glad you admit the fact so freely, Madame. Will you now tell me your reasons for so doing and also for altering your Christian name on your passport."

"That was my doing entirely," put in the Count.

Helena said quietly:

"Surely, M. Poirot, you can guess my reason—our reason. This man who was killed is the man who murdered my baby niece, who killed my sister, who broke my brother-in-law's heart. Three of the people I loved best and who made up my home—my world!"

Her voice rang out passionately. She was a true daughter of that mother, the emotional force of whose acting had moved huge audiences to tears.

She went on more quietly.

"Of all the people on the train, I alone had probably the best motive for killing him."

"And you did not kill him, Madame?"

"I swear to you, M. Poirot, and my husband knows and will swear also—that, much as I may have been tempted to do so, I never lifted a hand against that man."

"I too, gentlemen," said the Count. "I give you my word of honour that last night Helena never left her compartment. She took a sleeping draught exactly as I said. She is utterly and entirely innocent."

Poirot looked from one to the other of them.

"On my word of honour," repeated the Count.

Poirot shook his head slightly.

"And yet you took it upon yourself to alter the name in the passport?"

Monsieur Poirot," the Count spoke earnestly and passionately. "Consider my position. Do you think I could stand the thought of my wife dragged through a sordid police case. She was innocent, I knew it, but what she said was true—because of her connection with the Armstrong family she would have been immediately suspected. She would have been questioned—arrested, perhaps. Since some evil chance had taken us on the same train as this man Ratchett, there was, I felt sure, but one thing for it. I admit, Monsieur, that I lied to you—all, that is, save in one thing. My wife never left her compartment last night."

He spoke with an earnestness that it was hard to gainsay.

"I do not say that I disbelieve you, Monsieur," said Poirot slowly. "Your family is, I know, a proud and ancient one. It would be bitter indeed for you to have your wife dragged into an unpleasant police case. With that I can sympathize. But how, then, do you explain the presence of your wife's handkerchief actually in the dead man's compartment?"

"That handkerchief is not mine, Monsieur," said the Countess.

"In spite of the initial H?"

"In spite of the initial. I have handkerchiefs not unlike that, but not one that is exactly of that pattern. I know, of course that I cannot hope to make you believe me, but I assure you that it is so. That handkerchief is not mine."

"It may have been placed there by someone in order to incriminate you?"

She smiled a little.

"You are enticing me to admit that, after all, it is mine? But indeed, M. Poirot, it isn't."

She spoke with great earnestness.

"Then why, if the handkerchief was not yours, did you alter the name in the passport?"

The Count answered this.

"Because we heard that a handkerchief had been found with the initial H on it. We talked the matter over together before we came to be interviewed. I pointed out to Helena that if it were seen that her Christian name began with an H she would immediately be subjected to much more rigorous questioning. And the thing was so simple—to alter Helena to Elena was easily done."

"You have, M. le Comte, the makings of a very fine criminal," remarked Poirot dryly. "A great natural ingenuity, and an apparently remorseless determination to mislead justice."

"Oh, no, no" the girl leaned forward. "M. Poirot, he's explained to you how it was." She broke from French into English. "I was scared—absolutely dead scared, you understand. It had been so awful—that time—and to have it all raked up again. And to be suspected and perhaps thrown into prison. I was just scared stiff, M. Poirot. Can't you understand at all?"

Her voice was lovely—deep—rich—pleading, the voice of the daughter of Linda Arden the actress.

Poirot looked gravely at her.

"If I am to believe you, Madame—and I do not say that I will *not* believe you, then you must help me."

"Help you?"

"Yes. The reason for the murder lies in the past—in that tragedy which broke up your home and saddened your young life. Take me back into the past, Mademoiselle, that I may find there the link that explains the whole thing."

"What can there be to tell you? They are all dead." She repeated mournfully. "All dead—all dead—Robert, Sonia—darling, darling Daisy. She was so sweet—so happy—she had such lovely curls. We were all just crazy about her."

"There was another victim, Madame. An indirect victim, you might say."

"Poor Susanne? Yes, I had forgotten about her. The police questioned her. They were convinced she had something to do with it. Perhaps she had—but if so, only innocently. She had, I believe, chatted idly with someone, giving information as to the time of Daisy's outings. The poor thing got terribly wrought up—she thought she was being held responsible." She shuddered. "She threw herself out of the window. Oh it was horrible."

She buried her face in her hands.

"What nationality was she, Madame?"

"She was French."

"What was her last name?"

"It's absurd, but I can't remember—we all called her Susanne. A pretty laughing girl. She was devoted to Daisy."

"She was the nursery-maid, was she not?"

"Yes."

"Who was the nurse?"

"She was a trained hospital nurse. Stengelberg her name was. She, too, was devoted to Daisy—and to my sister."

"Now, Madame, I want you to think carefully before you answer this question. Have you, since you were on this train, seen anyone that you recognized?"

She stared at him.

"I? No, no one at all."

"What about Princess Dragomiroff?"

"Oh, her? I know her, of course. I thought you meant anyone—anyone from—from that time."

"So I did, Madame. Now think carefully. Some years have passed, remember. The person might have altered their appearance."

Helena pondered deeply. Then she said:

"No—I am sure—there is no one."

"You yourself—you were a young girl at the time—did you have no one to superintend your studies or to look after you?"

"Oh, yes, I had a dragon—a sort of governess to me and secretary to Sonia combined. She was English or rather Scotch—a big, red-haired woman."

"What was her name?"

"Miss Freebody."

"Young or old?"

"She seemed frightfully old to me. I suppose she couldn't have been more than forty. Susanne, of course, used to look after my clothes and maid me."

"And there were no other inmates of the house?"

"Only servants."

"And you are certain—quite certain, Madame—that you have recognized no one on the train?"

She replied earnestly:

"No one, Monsieur. No one at all."

CHAPTER 5
The Christian Name of Princess Dragomiroff

When the Count and Countess had departed, Poirot looked across at the other two.

"You see," he said, "we make progress."

"Excellent work," said M. Bouc cordially. "For my part, I should never have dreamed of suspecting Count and Countess Andrenyi. I will admit I thought them quite *hors de combat*. I suppose there is no doubt that she committed the crime? It is rather sad. Still, they will not guillotine her. There are extenuating circumstances. A few years' imprisonment—that will be all."

"In fact you are quite certain of her guilt."

"My dear friend, surely there is no doubt of it? I thought your reassuring manner was only to smooth things over till we are dug out of the snow and the police take charge."

"You do not believe the Count's positive assertion—on his word of honour—that his wife is innocent?"

"*Mon cher*—naturally—what else *could* he say? He adores his wife. He wants to save her! He tells his lie very well—quite in the grand Seigneur manner, but what else than a lie could it be?"

"Well, you know, I had the preposterous idea that it might be the truth."

"No, no. The handkerchief, remember. The handkerchief clinches the matter."

"Oh, I am not so sure about the handkerchief. You remember, I always told you that there were two possibilities as to the ownership of the handkerchief."

"All the same——"

M. Bouc broke off. The door at the end had opened, and Princess Dragomiroff entered the dining-car. She came straight to them and all three men rose to their feet.

She spoke to Poirot, ignoring the others.

"I believe, Monsieur," she said, "that you have a handkerchief of mine."

Poirot shot a glance of triumph at the other two.

"Is this it, Madame?"

He produced the little square of fine cambric.

"That is it. It has my initial in the corner."

"But, Madame la Princesse, that is the letter H," said M. Bouc. "Your Christian name—pardon me—is Natalia."

She gave him a cold stare.

"That is correct, Monsieur. My handkerchiefs are always initialed in the Russian characters. H is N in Russian."

M. Bouc was somewhat taken aback. There was something about this indomitable old lady which made him feel flustered and uncomfortable.

"You did not tell us that this handkerchief was yours at the inquiry this morning."

"You did not ask me," said the Princess dryly.

"Pray be seated, Madame," said Poirot.

She sighed.

"I may as well, I suppose."

She sat down.

"You need not make a long business of this, Messieurs. Your next question will be—how did my handkerchief come to be lying by a murdered man's body? My reply to that is that I have no idea."

"You have really no idea."

"None whatever."

"You will excuse me, Madame, but how much can we rely upon the truthfulness of your replies?"

Poirot said the words very softly. Princess Dragomiroff answered contemptuously.

"I suppose you mean because I did not tell you that Helena Andrenyi was Mrs. Armstrong's sister?"

"In fact you deliberately lied to us in the matter."

"Certainly. I would do the same again. Her mother was my friend. I believe, Messieurs, in loyalty—to one's friends and one's family and one's caste."

"You do not believe in doing your utmost to further the ends of justice?"

"In this case I consider that justice—strict justice—has been done."

Poirot leaned forward.

"You see my difficulty, Madame. In this matter of the handkerchief, even, am I to believe you? Or are you shielding your friend's daughter?"

"Oh! I see what you mean." Her face broke into a grim smile. "Well, Messieurs, this statement of mine can be easily proved. I will give you the address of the people in Paris who make my handkerchiefs. You have only to show them the one in question and they will inform you that it was made to my order over a year ago. The handkerchief is mine, Messieurs."

She rose.

"Have you anything further you wish to ask me?"

"Your maid, Madame, did she recognize this handkerchief when we showed it to her this morning?"

"She must have done so. She saw it and said nothing? Ah, well, that shows that she too can be loyal."

With a slight inclination of her head she passed out of the dining-car.

"So that was it," murmured Poirot softly. "I noticed just a trifling hesitation when I asked the maid if she knew to whom the handkerchief belonged. She was uncertain whether or not to admit that it was her mistress's. But how does that fit in with that strange central idea of mine? Yes, it might well be."

"Ah!" said M. Bouc with a characteristic gesture—"she is a terrible old lady, that!"

"Could she have murdered Ratchett?" asked Poirot of the doctor.

He shook his head.

"Those blows—the ones delivered with great force penetrating the muscle—never, never could anyone with so frail a physique inflict them."

"But the feebler ones?"

"The feebler ones, yes."

"I am thinking," said Poirot, "of the incident this morning when I said to her that the strength was in her will rather than in her arm. It was in the nature of a trap, that remark. I wanted to see if she would look down at her right or her left arm. She did neither. She looked at them both. But she made a strange reply. She said, 'No, I have no strength in these. I do not know whether to be sorry or glad.' A curious remark that. It confirms me in my belief about the crime."

"It did not settle the point about the left-handedness."

"No. By the way, did you notice that Count Andrenyi keeps his handkerchief in his right-hand breast pocket?"

M. Bouc shook his head. His mind reverted to the astonishing revelations of the last half-hour. He murmured:

"Lies—and again lies—it amazes me, the amount of lies we had told to us this morning."

"There are more still to discover," said Poirot cheerfully.

"You think so?"

"I shall be very disappointed if it is not so."

"Such duplicity is terrible," said M. Bouc. "But it seems to please you," he added reproachfully.

"It has this advantage," said Poirot. "If you confront anyone who has lied with the truth, they usually admit it—often out of sheer surprise. It is only necessary to guess *right* to produce your effect.

"That is the only way to conduct this case. I select each passenger in turn, consider their evidence and say to myself, *If* so and so is lying, on what point are they lying and what is the *reason* for the lie?' And I answer *if* they are lying—*if*, you mark—it could only be for such a reason and on such a point. We have done that once very successfully with Countess Andrenyi. We shall now proceed to try the same method on several other persons."

"And supposing, my friend, that your guess happens to be wrong?"

"Then one person, at any rate, will be completely freed from suspicion."

"Ah! A process of elimination."

"Exactly."

"And who do we tackle next?"

"We are going to tackle that *pukka sahib*, Colonel Arbuthnot."

CHAPTER 6
A Second Interview with Colonel Arbuthnot

Colonel Arbuthnot was clearly annoyed at being summoned to the dining-car for a second interview. His face wore a most forbidding expression as he sat down and said:

"Well?"

"All my apologies for troubling you a second time," said Poirot. "But there is still some information that I think you might be able to give us."

"Indeed? I hardly think so."

"To begin with, you see this pipe-cleaner?"

"Yes."

"Is it one of yours?"

"Don't know. I don't put a private mark on them, you know."

"Are you aware, Colonel Arbuthnot, that you are the only man amongst the passengers in the Stamboul-Calais carriage who smokes a pipe?"

"In that case it probably is one of mine."

"Do you know where it was found?"

"Not the least idea."

"It was found by the body of the murdered man."

Colonel Arbuthnot raised his eyebrows.

"Can you tell us, Colonel Arbuthnot, how it is likely to have got there?"

"If you mean did I drop it there myself, no, I didn't."

"Did you go into Mr. Ratchett's compartment at any time?"

"I never even spoke to the man."

"You never spoke to him and you did not murder him?"

The Colonel's eyebrows went up again sardonically.

"If I had, I should hardly be likely to acquaint you with the fact. As a matter of fact I *didn't* murder the fellow."

"Ah, well," murmured Poirot. "It is of no consquence."

"I beg your pardon?"

"I said that it was of no consequence."

"Oh!" Arbuthnot looked taken aback. He eyed Poirot uneasily.

"Because, you see," continued the little man, "the pipe-cleaner, it is of no importance. I can myself think of eleven other excellent explanations of its presence."

Arbuthnot stared at him.

"What I really wished to see you about was quite another matter," went on Poirot. "Miss Debenham may have told you, perhaps, that I overheard some words spoken to you at the station of Konya?"

Arbuthnot did not reply.

"She said, '*Not now. When it's all over. When it's behind us.*" Do you know to what those words referred?"

"I am sorry, M. Poirot, but I must refuse to answer that question."

"*Pourquoi?*"

The Colonel said stiffly:

"I suggest that you should ask Miss Debenham herself for the meaning of those words."

"I have done so."

"And she refused to tell you?"

"Yes."

"Then I should think it would have been perfectly plain—even to you—that my lips are sealed.""

"You will not give away a lady's secret?"

"You can put it that way, if you like."

"Miss Debenham told me that they referred to a private matter of her own."

"Then why not accept her word for it?"

"Because, Colonel Arbuthnot, Miss Debenham is what one might call a highly suspicious character."

"Nonsense," said the Colonel with warmth.

"It is not nonsense."

"You have nothing whatever against her."

"Not the fact that Miss Debenham was companion governess in the Armstrong household at the time of the kidnapping of little Daisy Armstrong?"

There was a minute's dead silence.

Poirot nodded his head gently.

"You see," he said, "we know more than you think. If Miss Debenham is innocent, why did she conceal that fact? Why did she tell me that she had never been in America?"

The Colonel cleared his throat.

"Aren't you possibly making a mistake?"

"I am making no mistake. Why did Miss Debenham lie to me?"

Colonel Arbuthnot shrugged his shoulders.

"You had better ask her. I still think that you are wrong."

Poirot raised his voice and called. One of the restaurant attendants came from the far end of the car.

"Go and ask the English lady in No. 11 if she will be good enough to come here."

"Bien, Monsieur."

The man departed. The four men sat in silence. Colonel Arbuthnot's face looked as though it were carved out of wood, it was rigid and impassive.

The man returned.

"The lady is just coming, Monsieur."

"Thank you."

A minute or two later Mary Debenham entered the dining-car.

CHAPTER 7
The Identity of Mary Debenham

She wore no hat. Her head was thrown back as though in defiance. The sweep of her hair back from her face, the curve of her nostril suggested the figurehead of a ship plunging gallantly into a rough sea. In that moment she was beautiful.

Her eyes went to Arbuthnot for a minute—just a minute.

She said to Poirot:

"You wished to see me?"

"I wished to ask you, Mademoiselle, why you lied to us this morning?"

"Lied to you? I don't know what you mean."

"You concealed the fact that at the time of the Armstrong tragedy you were actually living in the house. You told me that you had never been in America."

He saw her flinch for a moment and then recover herself.

"Yes," she said. "That is true."

"No, Mademoiselle, it was false."

"You misunderstood me. I mean that it is true that I lied to you."

"Ah, you admit it?"

Her lips curved into a smile.

"Certainly. Since you have found me out."

"You are at least frank, Mademoiselle."

"There does not seem anything else for me to be."

"Well, of course, that is true. And now, Mademoiselle, may I ask you the reason for these evasions?"

"I should have thought the reason leapt to the eye, M. Poirot?"

"It does not leap to mine, Mademoiselle."

She said in a quiet, even voice with a trace of hardness in it:

"I have my living to get."

"You mean——?"

She raised her eyes and looked him full in the face.

"How much do you know, M. Poirot, of the fight to get and keep decent employment? Do you think that a girl who had been detained in connection with a murder case, whose name and perhaps photographs were reproduced in the English papers—do you think that any nice ordinary middle-class Englishwoman would want to engage that girl as governess to her daughters?"

"I do not see why not—if no blame attached to you."

"Oh, blame—it is not blame—it is publicity! So far, M. Poirot, I have succeeded in life. I have had well-paid, pleasant posts. I was not going to risk the position I had attained when no good end could have been served."

"I will venture to suggest, Mademoiselle, that I would have been the best judge of that, not you."

She shrugged her shoulders.

"For instance, you could have helped me in the matter of identification."

"What do you mean?"

"Is it possible, Mademoiselle, that you did not recognize in the Countess Andrenyi Mrs. Armstrong's young sister whom you taught in New York?"

"Countess Andrenyi? No." She shook her head. "It may seem extraordinary to you, but I did not recognize her. She was not grown up, you see, when I knew her. That was over three years ago. It is true that the Countess reminded me of someone—it puzzled me. But she looks so foreign—I never connected her with the little American schoolgirl. It is true that I only glanced at her casually when coming into the restaurant-car. I noticed her clothes more than her face—" she smiled faintly—"women do! And then—well, I had my own preoccupations."

"You will not tell me your secret, Mademoiselle?"

Poirot's voice was very gentle and persuasive.

She said in a low voice:

"I can't—I can't."

And suddenly, without warning, she broke down, dropping her face down upon her outstretched arms and crying as though her heart would break.

The Colonel sprang up and stood awkwardly beside her.

"I—look here——"

He stopped and, turning round, scowled fiercely at Poirot.

"I'll break every bone in your damned body, you dirty little whipper-snapper," he said.

"Monsieur," protested M. Bouc.

Arbuthnot had turned back to the girl.

"Mary—for God's sake——"

She sprang up.

"It's nothing. I'm all right. You don't need me any more, do you, M. Poirot? If you do, you must come and find me. Oh, what an idiot—what an idiot I'm making of myself!"

She hurried out of the car. Arbuthnot, before following her, turned once more on Poirot.

"Miss Debenham's got nothing to do with this business—nothing, do you hear? And if she's worried and interfered with, you'll have me to deal with."

He strode out.

"I like to see an angry Englishman," said Poirot. "They are very amusing. The more emotional they feel the less command they have of language."

But M. Bouc was not interested in the emotional reactions of Englishmen. He was overcome by admiration of his friend.

"*Mon cher, vous êtes épatant,*" he cried. "Another miraculous guess. *C'est formidable.*"

"It is incredible how you think of these things," said Dr. Constantine admiringly.

"Oh, I claim no credit this time. It was not a guess. Countess Andrenyi practically told me."

"*Comment?* Surely not?"

"You remember I asked her about her governess or companion? I had already decided in my mind that *if* Mary Debenham were mixed up in the matter, she must have figured in the household in some such capacity."

"Yes, but the Countess Andrenyi described a totally different person."

"Exactly. A tall, middle-aged woman with red hair—in fact, the exact opposite in every respect of Miss Debenham, so much so as to be quite remarkable. But then she had to invent a name quickly, and there it was that the unconscious association of ideas gave her away. She said Miss Freebody, you remember."

"Yes?"

"*Eh bien,* you may not know it, but there is a shop in London that was called, until recently, Debenham & Freebody. With the name Debenham running in her head, the Countess clutches at another name quickly, and the first that comes is Freebody. Naturally I understood immediately."

"That is yet another lie. Why did she do it?"

"Possibly more loyalty. It makes things a little difficult."

"*Ma foi,*" said M. Bouc with violence. "But does everybody on this train tell lies?"

"That," said Poirot, "is what we are about to find out."

CHAPTER 8
Further Surprising Revelations

"Nothing would surprise me now," said M. Bouc. "Nothing! Even if everybody in the train proved to have been in the Armstrong household I should not express surprise."

"That is a very profound remark," said Poirot. "Would you like to see what your favourite suspect, the Italian, has to say for himself?"

"You are going to make another of these famous guesses of yours?"

"Precisely."

"It is really a *most* extraordinary case," said Constantine.

"No, it is most natural."

M. Bouc flung up his arms in comic despair.

"If this is what you call natural, *mon ami*——"

Words failed him.

Poirot had by this time requested the dining-car attendant to fetch Antonio Foscarelli.

The big Italian had a wary look in his eye as he came in. He shot nervous glances from side to side like a trapped animal.

"What do you want?" he said. "I have nothing to tell you—nothing, do you hear! *Per Dio*——" He struck his hand on the table.

"Yes, you have something more to tell us," said Poirot firmly. "The truth!"

"The truth?" He shot an uneasy glance at Poirot. All the assurance and geniality had gone out of his manner.

"*Mais oui*. It may be that I know it already. But it will be a point in your favour if it comes from you spontaneously."

"You talk like the American police. 'Come clean,' that is what they say—'come clean.'"

"Ah! so you have had experience of the New York police?"

"No, no, never. They could not prove a thing against me—but it was not for want of trying."

Poirot said quietly:

"That was in the Armstrong case, was it not? You were the chauffeur?"

His eyes met those of the Italian. The bluster went out of the big man. He was like a pricked balloon.

"Since you know—why ask me?"

"Why did you lie this morning?"

"Business reasons. Besides, I do not trust the Yugoslav police. They hate the Italians. They would not have given me justice."

"Perhaps it is exactly justice that they *would* have given you!"

"No, no, I had nothing to do with this business last night. I never left my carriage. The long-faced Englishman, he can tell you so. It was not I who killed this pig—this Ratchett. You cannot prove anything against me."

Poirot was writing something on a sheet of paper. He looked up and said quietly:

"Very good. You can go."

Foscarelli lingered uneasily.

"You realize that it was not I—that I could have had nothing to do with it?"

"I said that you could go."

"It is a conspiracy. You are going to frame me? All for a pig of a man who should have gone to the chair! It was an infamy that he did not. If it had been me—if I had been arrested——"

"But it was not you. You had nothing to do with the kidnapping of the child."

"What is that you are saying? Why, that little one—she was the delight of the house. Tonio, she called me. And she would sit in the car and pretend to hold the wheel. All the household worshipped her! Even the police came to understand that. Ah, the beautiful little one."

His voice had softened. The tears came into his eyes. Then he wheeled round abruptly on his heel and strode out of the dining-car.

"Pietro," called Poirot.

The dining-car attendant came at a run.

"The No. 10—the Swedish lady."

"*Bien, Monsieur*."

"Another?" cried Mr. Bouc. "Ah, no—it is not possible. I tell you it is not possible."

"*Mon cher*, we have to know. Even if in the end everybody on the train proves to have a motive for killing Ratchett, we have to know. Once we know, we can settle once for all where the guilt lies."

"My head is spinning," groaned M. Bouc.

Greta Ohlsson was ushered in sympathetically by the attendant. She was weeping bitterly.

She collapsed on the seat facing Poirot and wept steadily into a large handkerchief.

"Now do not distress yourself, Mademoiselle. Do not distress yourself." Poirot patted her on the shoulder. "Just a few little words of truth that is all. You were the nurse who was in charge of little Daisy Armstrong?"

"It is true—it is true," wept the wretched woman. "Ah, she was an angel—a little sweet, trustful angel. She knew nothing but kindness and love—and she was taken away by that wicked man—cruelly treated—and her poor mother—and the other little one who never lived at all. You cannot understand—you cannot know—if you had been there as I was—if you had seen the whole terrible tragedy—I ought to have told you the truth about myself this morning. But I was afraid. I did so rejoice that that evil man was dead—that he could not any more kill or torture little children. Ah! I cannot speak—I have no words. . . ."

She wept with more vehemence than ever.

Poirot continued to pat her gently on the shoulder.

"There—there—I comprehend—I comprehend everything—everything, I tell you. I will ask you no more questions. It is enough that you have admitted what I know to be the truth. I understand, I tell you."

By now inarticulate with sobs, Greta Ohlsson rose and groped her way blindly toward the door. As she reached it she collided with a man coming in.

It was the valet—Masterman.

He came straight up to Poirot and spoke in his usual, quiet, unemotional voice.

"I hope I'm not intruding, sir. I thought it best to come along at once, sir, and tell you the truth. I was Colonel Armstrong's batman in the war, sir, and afterwards I was his valet in New York. I'm afraid I concealed that fact this morning. It was very wrong of me, sir, and I thought I'd better come and make a clean breast of it. But I hope, sir, that you're not suspecting Tonio in any way. Old Tonio, sir, wouldn't hurt a fly. And I can swear positively that he never left the carriage all last night. So, you see, sir, he couldn't have done it. Tonio may be a foreigner, sir, but he's a very gentle creature—not like those nasty murdering Italians one reads about."

He stopped.

Poirot looked steadily at him.

"Is that all you have to say?"

"That is all, sir."

He paused, then, as Poirot did not speak, he made an apologetic little bow, and after a momentary hesitation left the dining-car in the same quiet, unobtrusive fashion as he had come.

"This," said Dr. Constantine, " is more wildly improbable than any *roman policier* I have ever read."

"I agree," said M. Bouc. "Of the twelve passengers in that coach, nine have been proved to have had a connection with the Armstrong case. What next, I ask you? Or, should I say, who next?"

"I can almost give you the answer to your question," said Poirot. "Here comes our American sleuth, M. Hardman."

"Is he, too, coming to confess?"

Before Poirot could reply, the American had reached their table. He cocked an alert eye at them and, sitting down, he drawled out:

"Just exactly what's up on this train? It seems bughouse to me."

Poirot twinkled at him:

"Are you quite sure, Mr. Hardman, that you yourself were not the gardener at the Armstrong home?"

"They didn't have a garden," replied Mr. Hardman literally.

"Or the butler?"

"Haven't got the fancy manner for a place like that. No, I never had any connection with the Armstrong house—but I'm beginning to believe I'm about the only one on this train who hadn't! Can you beat it—that's what I say? Can you beat it?"

"It is certainly a little surprising," said Poirot mildly.

"*C'est rigolo,*" burst from M. Bouc.

"Have you any ideas of your own about the crime, M. Hardman?" inquired Poirot.

"No, sir. It's got me beat. I don't know how to figure it out. They can't all be in it; but which one is the guilty party is beyond me. How did you get wise to all this, that's what I want to know?"

"I just guessed."

"Then, believe me, you're a pretty slick guesser. Yes, I'll tell the world you're a slick guesser."

Mr. Hardman leaned back and looked at Poirot admiringly.

"You'll excuse me," he said, "but no one would believe it to look at you. I take off my hat to you. I do, indeed."

"You are too kind, M. Hardman."

"Not at all. I've got to hand it to you."

"All the same," said Poirot, "the problem is not yet quite solved. Can we say with authority that we know who killed M. Ratchett?"

"Count me out," said Mr. Hardman. "I'm not saying anything at all. I'm just full of natural admiration. What about the other two you've not had a guess at yet? The old American dame and the lady's-maid? I suppose we can take it that they're the only innocent parties on the train?"

"Unless," said Poirot, smiling, "we can fit them into our little collection as—shall we say?—housekeeper and cook in the Armstrong household."

"Well, nothing in the world would surprise me now," said Mr. Hardman with quiet resignation. "Bughouse—that's what this business is—bughouse!"

"Ah, *mon cher,*" that would be indeed stretching coincidence a little too far," said M. Bouc. "They cannot all be in it."

Poirot looked at him.

"You do not understand," he said. "You do not understand at all. Tell me," he said, "do you know who killed Ratchett?"

"Do you?" countered M. Bouc.

Poirot nodded.

"Oh, yes," he said. "I have known for some time. It is so clear that I wonder you have not seen it also." He looked at Hardman and asked, "And you?"

The detective shook his head. He stared at Poirot curiously.

"I don't know," he said. "I don't know at all. Which of them was it?"

Poirot was silent a minute. Then he said:

"If you will be so good, M. Hardman, assemble everyone here. There are two possible solutions of this case. I want to lay them both before you all."

CHAPTER 9
Poirot Propounds Two Solutions

The passengers came crowding into the restaurant-car and took their seats round the tables. They all bore more or less the same expression, one of expectancy mingled with apprehension. The Swedish lady was still weeping and Mrs. Hubbard was comforting her.

"Now you must just take a hold on yourself, my dear. Everything's going to be perfectly all right. You mustn't lose your grip on yourself. If one of us is a nasty murderer we know quite well it isn't you. Why, anyone would be crazy even to think of such a thing. You sit here and I'll stay right by you; and don't you worry any."

Her voice died away as Poirot stood up.

The Wagon Lit conductor was hovering in the doorway.

"You permit that I stay, Monsieur?"

"Certainly, Michel."

Poirot cleared his throat.

"Messieurs et Mesdames, I will speak in English, since I think all of you know a little of that language. We are here to investigate the death of Samuel Edward Ratchett—alias Cassetti. There are two possible solutions of the crime. I shall put them both before you, and I shall ask M. Bouc and Dr. Constantine here to judge which solution is the right one.

"Now you all know the facts of the case. Mr. Ratchett was found stabbed this morning. He was last known to be alive at 12.37 last night, when he spoke to the Wagon Lit conductor through the door. A watch in his pyjama pocket was found to be badly dented and it had stopped at a quarter past one. Dr. Constantine, who examined the body when found, puts the time of death as having occurred between midnight and two in the morning. At half an hour after midnight, as you all know, the train ran into a snowdrift. After that time *it was impossible for anyone to leave the train*.

"The evidence of Mr. Hardman, who is a member of a New York Detective Agency" (several heads turned to look at Mr. Hardman) "shows that no one could have passed his compartment (No. 16 at the extreme end) without being seen by him. We are therefore forced to the conclusion that the murderer is to be found among the occupants of one particular coach—the Stamboul-Calais coach.

"That, I will say, *was* our theory."

Comment?" ejaculated M. Bouc, startled.

"But I will put before you an alternative theory. It is very simple. Mr. Ratchett had a certain enemy whom he feared. He gave Mr. Hardman a description of this enemy and told him that the attempt, if made at all, would most probably be made on the second night out from Stamboul.

"Now I put it to you, ladies and gentlemen, that Mr. Ratchett knew a good deal more than he told. The enemy, as Mr. Ratchett expected, joined the train at *Belgrade, or possibly at Vincovci,* by the door left open by Colonel Arbuthnot and Mr. MacQueen who had just descended to the platform. He was provided with a suit of Wagon Lit uniform, which he wore over his ordinary clothes, and a pass key which enabled him to gain access to Mr. Ratchett's compartment in spite of the door being locked. Mr. Ratchett was under the influence of a sleeping draught. This man stabbed him with great ferocity and left the compartment through the communicating door leading to Mrs. Hubbard's compartment——"

"That's so," said Mrs. Hubbard, nodding her head.

"He thrust the dagger he had used into Mrs. Hubbard's sponge-bag in passing. Without knowing it, he lost a button of his uniform. Then he slipped out of the compartment and along the corridor. He hastily thrust the uniform into a suitcase in an empty compartment, and a few minutes later, dressed in ordinary clothes, he left the train just before it started off. Again using the same means of egress—the door near the dining-car."

Everybody gasped.

"What about that watch?" demanded Mr. Hardman.

"There you have the explanation of the whole thing. *Mr. Ratchett had omitted to put his watch back an hour as he should have done* at Tzaribrod. His watch still registered Eastern European time, which is one hour *ahead* of Central European time. It was a quarter-past *twelve* when Mr. Ratchett was stabbed—not a quarter-past one."

"But it is absurd, that explanation," cried M. Bouc. "What of the voice that spoke from the compartment at twenty-three minutes to one. It was either the voice of Ratchett—or else of his murderer."

"Not necessarily. It might have been—well—a third person. One who had gone in to speak to Ratchett and found him dead. He rang the bell to summon the conductor, then, as you express it, the wind rose in him—he was afraid of being accused of the crime and he spoke pretending to be Ratchett."

C'est possible," admitted M. Bouc grudgingly.

Poirot stared at Mrs. Hubbard.

"Yes, Madame, you were going to say——?"

"Well, I don't quite know what I was going to say. Do you think I forgot to put my watch back too?"

"No, Madame. I think you heard the man pass through—but unconsciously; later you had a nightmare of a man being in your compartment and woke up with a start and rang for the conductor."

"Well, I suppose that's possible," admitted Mrs. Hubbard.

Princess Dragomiroff was looking at Poirot with a very direct glance.

"How do you explain the evidence of my maid, Monsieur?"

"Very simply, Madame. Your maid recognized the handkerchief I showed her as yours. She somewhat clumsily tried to shield you. She did encounter the man—but earlier—while the train was at Vincovci station. She pretended to have seen him at a later hour with a confused idea of giving you a watertight *alibi*."

The Princess bowed her head.

"You have thought of everything, Monsieur. I—I admire you."

There was a silence.

Then everyone jumped as Dr. Constantine suddenly hit the table a blow with his fist.

"But no," he said. "No, no, and again no! That is an explanation that will not hold water. It is deficient in a dozen minor points. The crime was not committed so—M. Poirot must know that perfectly well."

Poirot turned a curious glance on him.

"I see," he said, "that I shall have to give you my second solution. But do not abandon this one too abruptly. You may agree with it later."

He turned back again to face the others.

"There is another possible solution of the crime. This is how I arrived at it.

"When I had heard all the evidence, I leaned back and shut my eyes and began to *think*. Certain points presented themselves to me as worthy of attention. I enumerated these points to my two colleagues. Some I had already elucidated—such as a grease-spot on a passport, etc. I will run over the points that remain. The first and most important is a remark made to me by M. Bouc in the restaurant-car at lunch on the first day after leaving Stamboul—to the effect that the company assembled was interesting because it was so varied—representing as it did all classes and nationalities.

"I agreed with him, but when this particular point came into my mind, I tried to imagine whether such an assembly were ever likely to be collected under any other conditions. And the answer I made to myself was—only in America. In America there might be a household composed of just such varied nationalities—an Italian chauffeur, an English governess, a Swedish nurse, a French lady's-maid and so on. That led me to my scheme of 'guessing'—that is, casting each person for a certain part in the Armstrong drama much as a producer casts a play. Well, that gave me an extremely interesting and satisfactory result.

"I had also examined in my own mind each separate person's evidence with some curious results. Take first the evidence of Mr. MacQueen. My first interview with him was entirely satisfactory. But in my second he made rather a curious remark. I had described to him the finding of a note mentioning the Armstrong case. He said, 'But surely——' and then paused and went on, 'I mean—that was rather careless of the old man.'

"Now I could feel that that was not what he had started out to say. *Supposing what he had meant to say was, 'But surely that was burnt!'* In which case, *MacQueen knew of the note and of its destruction*— in other words, he was either the murderer or an accomplice of the murderer. Very good.

"Then the valet. He said his master was in the habit of taking a sleeping draught when traveling by train. That might be true, but *would Ratchett have taken one last night?* The automatic under his pillow gave the lie to that statement. Ratchett intended to be on the alert last night. Whatever narcotic was administered to him must have been done so without his knowledge. By whom? Obviously by MacQueen or the valet.

"Now we come to the evidence of Mr. Hardman. I believed all that he told me about his own identity, but when it came to the actual methods he had employed to guard Mr. Ratchett, his story was neither more nor less than absurd. The only way effectively to have protected Ratchett was to have passed the night actually in his compartment or in some spot where he could watch the door. The only thing that his evidence *did* show plainly was that no one *in any other part of the train could possibly have murdered Ratchett*. It drew a clear circle round the Stamboul-Calais carriage. That seemed to me a rather curious and inexplicable fact, and I put it aside to think over.

"You probably have all heard by now of the few words I overheard between Miss Debenham and Colonel Arbuthnot. The interesting thing to my mind was the fact that Colonel Arbuthnot called her *Mary* and was clearly on terms of intimacy with her. But the Colonel was only supposed to have met her a few days previously—and I know Englishmen of the Colonel's type. Even if he had fallen in love with the young lady at first sight, he would have advanced slowly and with decorum—not rushing things. Therefore I concluded that Colonel Arbuthnot and Miss Debenham were in reality well acquainted, and were for some reason pretending to be strangers. Another small point was Miss Debenham's easy familiarity with the term 'long distance' for a telephone call. Yet Miss Debenham had told me that she had never been in the States.

"To pass to another witness. Mrs. Hubbard had told us that lying in bed she was unable to see whether the communicating door was bolted or not, and so asked Miss Ohlsson to see for her. Now, though her statement would have been perfectly true if she had been occupying compartments Nos. 2, 4, 12, or any *even* number—where the bolt is directly under the handle of the door—in the *uneven* numbers, such as compartment No. 3, the bolt is well *above* the handle and could not therefore be masked by the sponge-bag in the least. I was forced to the conclusion that Mrs. Hubbard was inventing an incident that had never occurred.

"And here let me say just a word or two about *times*. To my mind, the really interesting point about the dented watch was the place where it was found—in Ratchett's pyjama pocket, a singularly uncomfortable and unlikely place to keep one's watch, especially as there is a watch 'hook' provided just by the head of the bed. I felt sure, therefore, that the watch had been deliberately placed in the pocket and faked. The crime, then, was not committed at a quarter-past one.

"Was it, then, committed earlier? To be exact, at twenty-three minutes to one? My friend M. Bouc advanced as an argument in favour of it the loud cry which awoke me from sleep. But if Ratchett were heavily drugged *he could not have cried out*. If he had been capable of crying out he would have been capable of making some kind of a struggle to defend himself, and there were no signs of any such struggle.

"I remembered that MacQueen had called attention, not once but twice (and the second time in a very blatant manner), to the fact that Ratchett could speak no French. I came to the conclusion that the whole business at twenty-three minutes to one was a comedy played for my benefit! Anyone might see through the watch business—it is a common enough device in detective stories. They assumed that I *should* see through it and that, pluming myself on my own cleverness, I would go on to assume that since Ratchett spoke no French the voice I heard at twenty-three minutes to one could not be his, and that Ratchett must be already dead. But I am convinced that at twenty-three minutes to one Ratchett was still lying in his drugged sleep.

"But the device has succeeded! I have opened my door and looked out. I have actually heard the French phrase used. If I am so unbelievably dense as not to realize the significance of that phrase, it must be brought to my attention. If necessary MacQueen can come right out in the open. He can say, 'Excuse me, M. Poirot, *that can't have been Mr. Ratchett speaking*. He can't speak French.'

"Now when was the real time of the crime? And who killed him?

"In my opinion, and this is only an opinion, Ratchett was killed at some time very close upon two o'clock, the latest hour the doctor gives us as possible.

"As to who killed him——"

He paused, looking at his audience. He could not complain of any lack of attention. Every eye was fixed upon him. In the stillness you could have heard a pin drop.

He went on slowly:

"I was particularly struck by the extraordinary difficulty of proving a case against any one person on the train and on the rather curious coincidence that in each case the testimony giving an alibi came from what I might describe as an 'unlikely' person. Thus Mr. MacQueen and Colonel Arbuthnot provided alibis for each other—two persons between whom it seemed most unlikely there should be any prior acquaintanceship. The same thing happened with the English valet and the Italian, with the Swedish lady and the English girl. I said to myself, 'This is extraordinary—they cannot *all* be in it!'

"And then, Messieurs, I saw light. They were *all* in it. For so many people connected with the Armstrong case to be traveling by the same train by a coincidence was not only unlikely, it was *impossible*. It must not be chance, but *design*. I remember a remark of Colonel Arbuthnot's about trial by jury. A jury is composed of twelve people—there were twelve passengers—Ratchett was stabbed twelve times. And the thing that had worried me all along—the extraordinary crowd traveling in the Stamboul-Calais coach at a slack time of year was explained.

"Ratchett had escaped justice in America. There was no question as to his guilt. I visualized a self-appointed jury of twelve people who condemned him to death and were forced by the exigencies of the case to be their own executioners. And immediately, on that assumption, the whole case fell into beautiful shining order.

"I saw it as a perfect mosaic, each person playing his or her allotted part. It was so arranged that if suspicion should fall on any one person, the evidence of one or more of the others would clear the accused person and confuse the issue. Hardman's evidence was necessary in case some outsider should be suspected of the crime and be unable to prove an alibi. The passengers in the Stamboul carriage were in no danger. Every minute detail of their evidence was worked out beforehand. The whole thing was a very cleverly planned jig-saw puzzle, so arranged that every fresh piece of knowledge that came to light made the solution of the whole more difficult. As my friend M. Bouc remarked, the case seemed fantastically impossible! That was exactly the impression intended to be conveyed.

"Did this solution explain everything? Yes, it did. The nature of the wounds—each inflicted by a different person. The artificial threatening letters—artificial since they were unreal, written only to be produced as evidence. (Doubtless there were real letters, warning Ratchett of his fate, which MacQueen destroyed, substituting for them these others.) Then Hardman's story of being called in by Ratchett—a lie, of course, from beginning to end—the description of the mythical 'small dark man with a womanish voice,' a convenient description, since it had the merit of not incriminating any of the actual Wagon Lit conductors and would apply equally well to a man or a woman.

"The idea of stabbing is at first sight a curious one, but on reflection nothing would fit the circumstances so well. A dagger was a weapon that could be used by everyone—strong or weak—and it made no noise. I fancy, though I may be wrong, that each person in turn entered Ratchett's darkened compartment through that of Mrs. Hubbard—and struck! They themselves would never know which blow actually killed him.

"The final letter which Ratchett had probably found on his pillow was carefully burnt. With no clue pointing to the Armstrong case, there would be absolutely no reason for suspecting any of the passengers on the train. It would be put down as an outside job, and the 'small dark man with the womanish voice' would actually have been seen by one or more of the passengers leaving the train at Brod.

"I do not know exactly what happened when the conspirators discovered that that part of their plan was impossible owing to the accident to the train. There was, I imagine, a hasty consultation, and then they decided to go through with it. It was true that now one and all of the passengers were bound to come under suspicion, but that possibility had already been foreseen and provided for. The only additional thing to be done was to confuse the issue even further. Two so-called 'clues' were dropped in the dead man's compartment—one incriminating Colonel Arbuthnot (who had the strongest alibi and whose connection with the Armstrong family was probably the hardest to prove) and the second clue, the handkerchief, incriminating Princess Dragomiroff, who by virtue of her social position, her particularly frail physique and the alibi given her by her maid and the conductor, was practically in an unassailable position. Further to confuse the issue, a 'red herring' was drawn across the trail—the mythical woman in the red kimono. Again I am to bear witness to this woman's existence. There is a heavy bang at my door. I get up and look out—and see the scarlet kimono disappearing in the distance. A judicious selection of people—the conductor, Miss Debenham and MacQueen—will also have seen her. It was, I think, someone with a sense of humour who thoughtfully placed the scarlet kimono on the top of my suitcase whilst I was interviewing people in the dining-car. Where the garment came from in the first place I do not know. I suspect it is the property of Countess Andrenyi, since her luggage contained only a chiffon negligée so elaborate as to be more a tea gown than a dressing-gown.

"When MacQueen first learned that the letter which had been so carefully burnt had in part escaped destruction, and that the word Armstrong was exactly the word remaining, he must at once have communicated his news to the others. It was at this minute that the position of Countess Andrenyi became acute and her husband immediately took steps to alter the passport. It was their second piece of bad luck!

"They one and all agreed to deny utterly any connection with the Armstrong family. They knew I had no immediate means of finding out the truth, and they did not believe that I should go into the matter unless my suspicions were aroused against one particular person.

"Now there was one further point to consider. Allowing that my theory of the crime was the correct one, and I believe that it *must* be the correct one, then obviously the Wagon Lit conductor himself must be privy to the plot. But if so, that gave us thirteen persons, not twelve. Instead of the usual formula, 'Of so many people one is guilty,' I was faced with the problem that of thirteen persons one and one only was innocent. Which was that person?

"I came to a very odd conclusion. I came to the conclusion that the person who had taken no part in the crime was the person who would be considered the most likely to do so. I refer to Countess Andrenyi. I was impressed by the earnestness of her husband when he swore to me solemnly on his honour that his wife never left her compartment that night. I decided that Count Andrenyi took, so to speak, his wife's place.

"If so, then Pierre Michel was definitely one of the twelve. But how could one explain his complicity? He was a decent man who had been many years in the employ of the Company—not the kind of man who could be bribed to assist in a crime. Then Pierre Michel must be involved in the Armstrong case. But that seemed very improbable. Then I remembered that the dead nursery-maid was French. Supposing that that unfortunate girl had been Pierre Michel's daughter.

That would explain everything—it would also explain the place chosen for the staging of the crime. Were there any others whose part in the drama was not clear? Colonel Arbuthnot I put down as a friend of the Armstrongs. They had probably been through the war together. The maid, Hildegarde Schmidt, I could guess her place in the Armstrong household. I am, perhaps, overgreedy, but I sense a good cook instinctively. I laid a trap for her—she fell into it. I said I knew she was a good cook. She answered, 'Yes, indeed, all my ladies have said so.' But if you are employed as a *lady's-maid* your employers seldom have a chance of learning whether or not you are a good cook.

"Then there was Hardman. He seemed quite definitely not to belong to the Armstrong household. I could only imagine that he had been in love with the French girl. I spoke to him of the charm of foreign women—and again I obtained the reaction I was looking for. Sudden tears came into his eyes, which he pretended were dazzled by the snow.

"There remains Mrs. Hubbard. Now Mrs. Hubbard, let me say, played the most important part in the drama. By occupying the compartment communicating with that of Ratchett she was more open to suspicion that anyone else. In the nature of things she could not have an alibi to fall back upon. To play the part she played—the perfectly natural, slightly ridiculous American fond mother—an artist was needed. But there *was* an artist connected with the Armstrong family—Mrs. Armstrong's mother—Linda Arden, the actress. . . ."

He stopped.

Then, in a soft rich dreamy voice, quite unlike the one she had used all the journey, Mrs. Hubbard said:

"I always fancied myself in comedy parts."

She went on still dreamily:

"That slip about the sponge-bag was silly. It shows you should always rehearse properly. We tried it on the way out—I was in an even number compartment then, I suppose. I never thought of the bolts being in different places."

She shifted her position a little and looked straight at Poirot.

"You know all about it, M. Poirot. You're a very wonderful man. But even you can't quite imagine what it was like—that awful day in New York. I was just crazy with grief—so were the servants—and Colonel Arbuthnot was there, too. He was John Armstrong's best friend."

"He saved my life in the war," said Arbuthnot.

"We decided then and there—perhaps we were mad—I don't know—that the sentence of death that Cassetti had escaped had got to be carried out. There were twelve of us—or rather eleven—Susanne's father was over in France, of course. First we thought we'd draw lots as to who should do it, but in the end we decided on this way. It was the chauffeur, Antonio, who suggested it. Mary worked out all the details later with Hector MacQueen. He'd always adored Sonia—my daughter—and it was he who explained to us exactly how Cassetti's money had managed to get him off.

"It took a long time to perfect our plan. We had first to track Ratchett down. Hardman managed that in the end. Then we had to try to get Masterman and Hector into his employment—or at any rate one of them. Well, we managed that. Then we had a consultation with Susanne's father. Colonel Arbuthnot was very keen on having twelve of us. He seemed to think it made it more in order. He didn't like the stabbing idea much, but he agreed that it did solve most of our difficulties. Well, Susanne's father was willing. Susanne was his only child. We knew from Hector that Ratchett would be coming back from the East sooner or later by the Orient Express. With Pierre Michel actually working on that train, the chance was too good to be missed. Besides, it would be a good way of not incriminating any outsiders.

"My daughter's husband had to know, of course, and he insisted on coming on the train with her. Hector wangled it so that Ratchett selected the right day for traveling when Michel would be on duty. We meant to engage every carriage in the Stamboul-Calais coach, but unfortunately there was one carriage we couldn't get. It was reserved long beforehand for a director of the company. Mr. Harris, of course, was a myth. But it would have been awkward to have any stranger in Hector's compartment. And then, at the last minute *you* came. . . ."

She stopped.

"Well," she said. "You know everything now, M. Poirot. What are you going to do about it? If it must all come out, can't you lay the blame upon me and me only? I would have stabbed that man twelve times willingly. It wasn't only that he was responsible for my daughter's death and her child's, and that of the other child who might have been alive and happy now. It was more than that. There had been other children before Daisy—there might be others in the future. Society had condemned him; we were only carrying out the sentence. But it's unnecessary to bring all these others into it. All these good faithful souls—and poor Michel—and Mary and Colonel Arbuthnot—they love each other. . . ."

Her voice was wonderful echoing through the crowded space—that deep, emotional, heart-stirring voice that had thrilled many a New York audience.

Poirot looked at his friend.

"You are a director of the company, M. Bouc," he said, "What do you say?"

M. Bouc cleared his throat.

"In my opinion, M. Poirot," he said, "the first theory you put forward was the correct one—decidedly so. I suggest that that is the solution we offer to the Yugoslavian police when they arrive. You agree, Doctor?"

"Certainly I agree," said Dr. Constantine. "As regards the medical evidence, I think—er—that I made one or two fantastic suggestions."

"Then," said Poirot, "having placed my solution before you, I have the honour to retire from the case. . . ."

THE ABC MURDERS

To
James Watts
One of My Most Sympathetic
Readers

Foreword

by CAPTAIN ARTHUR HASTINGS, O.B.E.

In this narrative of mine I have departed from my usual practice of relating only those incidents and scenes at which I myself was present. Certain chapters, therefore, are written in the third person.

I wish to assure my readers that I can vouch for the occurrences related in these chapters. If I have taken a certain poetic licence in describing the thoughts and feelings of various persons, it is because I believe I have set them down with a reasonable amount of accuracy. I may add that they have been 'vetted' by my friend Hercule Poirot himself.

In conclusion, I will say that if I have described at too great length some of the secondary personal relationships which arose as a consequence of this strange series of crimes, it is because the human and personal element can never be ignored. Hercule Poirot once taught me in a very dramatic manner that romance can be a by-product of crime.

As to the solving of the ABC mystery, I can only say that in my opinion Poirot showed real genius in the way he tackled a problem entirely unlike any which had previously come his way.

CONTENTS

CHAPTER 1
The Letter

It was in June of 1935 that I came home from my ranch in South America for a stay of about six months. It had been a difficult time for us out there. Like everyone else, we had suffered from world depression. I had various affairs to see to in England that I felt could only be successful if a personal touch was introduced. My wife remained to manage the ranch.

I need hardly say that one of my first actions on reaching England was to look up my old friend, Hercule Poirot.

I found him installed in one of the newest type of service flats in London. I accused him (and he admitted the fact) of having chosen this particular building entirely on account of its strictly geometrical appearance and proportions.

"But yes, my friend, it is of a most pleasing symmetry, do you not find it so?"

I said that I thought there could be too much squareness and (alluding to an old joke), I asked if in this super-modern hostelry they managed to induce hens to lay square eggs.

Poirot laughed heartily.

"Ah, you remember that? Alas! no—science has not yet induced the hens to conform to modern tastes, they still lay eggs of different sizes and colours!"

I examined my old friend with an affectionate eye. He was looking wonderfully well—hardly a day older than when I had last seen him.

"You're looking in fine fettle, Poirot," I said. "You've hardly aged at all. In fact, if it were possible, I should say that you had fewer grey hairs than when I saw you last."

Poirot beamed on me.

"And why is that not possible? It is quite true."

"Do you mean your hair is turning from grey to black instead of from black to grey?"

"Precisely."

"But surely that's a scientific impossibility!"

"Not at all."

"But that's very extraordinary. It seems against nature."

"As usual, Hastings, you have the beautiful and unsuspicious mind. Years do not change that in you! You perceive a fact and mention the solution of it in the same breath without noticing that you are doing so!"

I stared at him, puzzled.

Without a word he walked into his bedroom and returned with a bottle in his hand which he handed to me.

I took it, for the moment uncomprehending.

It bore the words:

> REVIVIT.—*To bring back the natural tone of the hair.* REVIVIT *is* NOT *a dye. In five shades, Ash, Chestnut, Titian, Brown, Black.*

"Poirot," I cried. "You have dyed your hair!"

"Ah, the comprehension comes to you!"

"So *that's* why your hair looks so much blacker than it did last time I was back."

"Exactly."

"Dear me," I said, recovering from the shock. "I suppose next time I come home I shall find you wearing false moustaches—or are you doing so now?"

Poirot winced. His moustaches had always been his sensitive point. He was inordinately proud of them. My words touched him on the raw.

"No, no, indeed, *mon ami*. That day, I pray the good God, is still far off. The false moustache! *Quel horreur!*"

He tugged at them vigorously to assure me of their genuine character.

"Well, they are very luxuriant still," I said.

"*N'est ce pas?* Never, in the whole of London, have I seen a pair of moustaches to equal mine."

A good job too, I thought privately. But I would not for the world have hurt Poirot's feelings by saying so.

Instead I asked if he still practised his profession on occasion.

"I know," I said, "that you actually retired years ago—"

"*C'est vrai*. To grow the vegetable marrows! And immediately a murder occurs—and I send the vegetable marrows to promenade themselves to the devil. And since then—I know very well what you will say—I am like the prima donna who makes positively the farewell performance! That farewell performance, it repeats itself an indefinite number of times!"

I laughed.

"In truth, it has been very like that. Each time I say: this is the end. But no, something else arises! And I will admit it, my friend, the retirement I care for it not at all. If the little grey cells are not exercised, they grow the rust."

"I see," I said. "You exercise them in moderation."

"Precisely. I pick and choose. For Hercule Poirot nowadays only the cream of crime."

"Has there been much cream about?"

"*Pas mal*. Not long ago I had a narrow escape."

"Of failure?"

"No, no." Poirot looked shocked. "But I—I, *Hercule Poirot*, was nearly exterminated."

I whistled.

"An enterprising murderer!"

"Not so much enterprising as careless," said Poirot. "Precisely that—careless. But let us not talk of it. You know, Hastings, in many ways I regard you as my mascot."

"Indeed?" I said. "In what ways?"

Poirot did not answer my question directly. He went on:

"As soon as I heard you were coming over I said to myself: something will arise. As in former days we will hunt together, we two. But if so it must be no common affair. It must be something"—he waved his hands excitedly—"something *recherché*—delicate—*fine* . . ." He gave the last untranslatable word its full flavour.

"Upon my word, Poirot," I said. "Any one would think you were ordering a dinner at the Ritz."

"Whereas one cannot command a crime to order? Very true." He sighed. "But I believe in luck—in destiny, if you will. It is your destiny to stand beside me and prevent me from committing the unforgivable error."

"What do you call the unforgivable error?"

"Overlooking the obvious."

I turned this over in my mind without quite seeing the point.

"Well," I said presently, smiling, "has this super crime turned up yet?"

"*Pas encore*. At least—that is—"

He paused. A frown of perplexity creased his forehead. His hands automatically straightened an object or two that I had inadvertently pushed awry.

"I am not sure," he said slowly.

There was something so odd about his tone that I looked at him in surprise. The frown still lingered.

Suddenly with a brief decisive nod of the head he crossed the room to a desk near the window. Its contents, I need hardly say, were all neatly docketed and pigeonholed so that he was able at once to lay his hand upon the paper he wanted.

He came slowly across to me, an open letter in his hand. He read it through himself, then passed it to me.

"Tell me, *mon ami*," he said. "What do you make of this?"

I took it from him with some interest.

It was written on thickish white notepaper in printed characters:

> MR HERCULE POIROT,—You fancy yourself, don't you, at solving mysteries that are too difficult for our poor thick-headed British police? Let us see, Mr Clever Poirot, just how clever you can be. Perhaps you'll find this not too hard to crack. Look out for Andover, on the 21st of the month.
>
> Yours, etc.,
>
> ABC.

I glanced at the envelope. That also was printed.

"Postmarked W.C.1," said Poirot as I turned my attention to the postmark. "Well, what is your opinion?"

I shrugged my shoulders as I handed it back to him.

"Some madman or other, I suppose."

"That is all you have to say?"

"Well—doesn't it sound like a madman to you?"

"Yes, my friend, it does."

His tone was grave. I looked at him curiously.

"You take this very seriously, Poirot."

"A madman, *mon ami*, is to be taken seriously. A madman is a very dangerous thing."

"Yes, of course, that is true . . . I hadn't considered that point . . . But what I meant was, it sounds more like a rather idiotic kind of hoax. Perhaps some convivial idiot who had had one over the eight."

"*Comment?* Nine? Nine what?"

"Nothing—just an expression. I meant a fellow who was tight. No, damn it, a fellow who had had a spot too much to drink."

"*Merci*, Hastings—the expression 'tight' I *am* acquainted with it. As you say, there may be nothing more to it than that . . ."

"But you think there is?" I asked, struck by the dissatisfaction of his tone.

Poirot shook his head doubtfully, but he did not speak.

"What have you done about it?" I inquired.

"What can one do? I showed it to Japp. He was of the same opinion as you—a stupid hoax—that was the expression he used. They get these things every day at Scotland Yard. I, too, have had my share . . ."

"But you take this one seriously?"

Poirot replied slowly.

"There is something about that letter, Hastings, that I do not like . . ."

In spite of myself, his tone impressed me.

"You think—what?"

He shook his head, and picking up the letter, put it away again in the desk.

"If you really take it seriously, can't you do something?" I asked.

"As always, the man of action! But what is there to do? The county police have seen the letter but they, too, do not take it seriously. There are no fingerprints on it. There are no local clues as to the possible writer."

"In fact there is only your own instinct?"

"Not instinct, Hastings. Instinct is a bad word. It is my *knowledge*—my *experience*—that tells me that something about that letter is wrong—"

He gesticulated as words failed him, then shook his head again.

"I may be making the mountain out of the anthill. In any case there is nothing to be done but wait."

"Well, the 21st is Friday. If a whacking great robbery takes place near Andover then—"

"Ah, what a comfort that would be—!"

"A *comfort?*"I stared. The word seemed to be a very extraordinary one to use. "A robbery may be a *thrill* but it can hardly be a comfort!" I protested.

Poirot shook his head energetically.

"You are in error, my friend. You do not understand my meaning. A robbery would be a relief since it would dispossess my mind of the fear of something else."

"Of what?"

"*Murder,*" said Hercule Poirot.

CHAPTER 2

(Not from Captain Hastings' Personal Narrative)

Mr Alexander Bonaparte Cust rose from his seat and peered near-sightedly round the shabby bedroom. His back was stiff from sitting in a cramped position and as he stretched himself to his full height an onlooker would have realized that he was, in reality, quite a tall man. His stoop and his near-sighted peering gave a delusive impression.

Going to a well-worn overcoat hanging on the back of the door, he took from the pocket a packet of cheap cigarettes and some matches. He lit a cigarette and then returned to the table at which he had been sitting. He picked up a railway guide and consulted it, then he returned to the consideration of a typewritten list of names. With a pen, he made a tick against one of the first names on the list.

It was Thursday, June 20th.

CHAPTER 3
Andover

I had been impressed at the time by Poirot's forebodings about the anonymous letter he had received, but I must admit that the matter had passed from my mind when the 21st actually arrived and the first reminder of it came with a visit paid to my friend by Chief Inspector Japp of Scotland Yard. The CID inspector had been known to us for many years and he gave me a hearty welcome.

"Well, I never," he exclaimed. "If it isn't Captain Hastings back from the wilds of the what do you call it! Quite like old days seeing you here with Monsieur Poirot. You're looking well, too. Just a little bit thin on top, eh? Well, that's what we're all coming to. I'm the same."

I winced slightly. I was under the impression that owing to the careful way I brushed my hair across the top of my head the thinness referred to by Japp was quite unnoticeable. However, Japp had never been remarkable for tact where I was concerned, so I put a good face upon it and agreed that we were none of us getting any younger.

"Except Monsieur Poirot here," said Japp. "Quite a good advertisement for a hair tonic, he'd be. Face fungus sprouting finer than ever. Coming out into the limelight, too, in his old age. Mixed up in all the celebrated cases of the day. Train mysteries, air mysteries, high society deaths—oh, he's here, there and everywhere. Never been so celebrated as since he retired."

"I have already told Hastings that I am like the prima donna who makes always one more appearance," said Poirot, smiling.

"Shouldn't wonder if you ended by detecting your own death," said Japp, laughing heartily. "That's an idea, that is. Ought to be put in a book."

"It will be Hastings who will have to do that," said Poirot, twinkling at me.

"Ha ha! That would be a joke, that would," laughed Japp.

I failed to see why the idea was so extremely amusing, and in any case I thought the joke was in poor taste. Poirot, poor old chap, is getting on. Jokes about his approaching demise can hardly be agreeable to him.

Perhaps my manner showed my feelings, for Japp changed the subject.

"Have you heard about Monsieur Poirot's anonymous letter?" he asked.

"I showed it to Hastings the other day," said my friend.

"Of course," I exclaimed. "It had quite slipped my memory. Let me see, what was the date mentioned?"

"The 21st," said Japp. "That's what I dropped in about. Yesterday was the 21st and just out of curiosity I rang up Andover last night. It was a hoax all right. Nothing doing. One broken shop window—kid throwing stones—and a couple of drunk and disorderlies. So just for once our Belgian friend was barking up the wrong tree."

"I am relieved, I must confess," acknowledged Poirot.

"You'd quite got the wind up about it, hadn't you?" said Japp affectionately. "Bless you, we get dozens of letters like that coming in every day! People with nothing better to do and a bit weak in the top storey sit down and write 'em. They don't mean any harm! Just a kind of excitement."

"I have indeed been foolish to take the matter so seriously," said Poirot. "It is the nest of the horse that I put my nose into there."

"You're mixing up mares and wasps," said Japp.

"*Pardon?*"

"Just a couple of proverbs. Well, I must be off. Got a little business in the next street to see to—receiving stolen jewellery. I thought I'd just drop in on my way and put your mind at rest. Pity to let those grey cells function unnecessarily."

With which words and a hearty laugh, Japp departed.

"He does not change much, the good Japp, eh?" asked Poirot.

"He looks much older," I said. "Getting as grey as a badger," I added vindictively.

Poirot coughed and said:

"You know, Hastings, there is a little device—my hairdresser is a man of great ingenuity—one attaches it to the scalp and brushes one's own hair over it—it is not a wig, you comprehend—but—"

"Poirot," I roared. "Once and for all I will have nothing to do with the beastly inventions of your confounded hairdresser. What's the matter with top of my head?"

"Nothing—nothing at all."

"It's not as though I were going *bald*."

"Of course not! Of course not!"

"The hot summers out there naturally cause the hair to fall out a bit. I shall take back a really good hair tonic."

"*Précisément*."

"And, anyway, what business is it of Japp's? He always was an offensive kind of devil. And no sense of humour. The kind of man who laughs when a chair is pulled away just as a man is about to sit down."

"A great many people would laugh at that."

"It's utterly senseless."

"From the point of view of the man about to sit, certainly it is."

"Well," I said, slightly recovering my temper. (I admit that I am touchy about the thinness of my hair.) "I'm sorry that anonymous letter business came to nothing."

"I have indeed been in the wrong over that. About that letter, there was, I thought, the odour of the fish. Instead a mere stupidity. Alas, I grow old and suspicious like the blind watch-dog who growls when there is nothing there."

"If I'm going to co-operate with you, we must look about for some other 'creamy' crime," I said with a laugh.

"You remember your remark of the other day? If you could order a crime as one orders a dinner, what would you choose?"

I fell in with his humour.

"Let me see now. Let's review the menu. Robbery? Forgery? No, I think not. Rather too vegetarian. It must be murder—red-blooded murder—with trimmings, of course."

"Naturally. The *hors d'œuvres*."

"Who shall the victim be—man or woman? Man, I think. Some big-wig. American millionaire. Prime Minister. Newspaper proprietor. Scene of the crime—well, what's wrong with the good old library? Nothing like it for atmosphere. As for the weapon—well, it might be a curiously twisted dagger—or some blunt instrument—carved stone idol—"

Poirot sighed.

"Or, of course," I said, "there's poison—but that's always so technical. Or a revolver shot echoing in the night. Then there must be a beautiful girl or two—"

"With auburn hair," murmured my friend.

"Your same old joke. One of the beautiful girls, of course, must be unjustly suspected—and there's some misunderstanding between her and the young man. And then, of course, there must be some other suspects—an older woman—dark, dangerous type—and some friend or rival of the dead man's—and a quiet secretary—dark horse—and a hearty man with a bluff manner—and a couple of discharged servants or gamekeepers or something—and a damn fool of a detective rather like Japp—and well—that's about all."

"That is your idea of the cream, eh?"

"I gather you don't agree."

Poirot looked at me sadly.

"You have made there a very pretty résumé of nearly all the detective stories that have ever been written."

"Well," I said. "What would *you* order?"

Poirot closed his eyes and leaned back in his chair. His voice came purringly from between his lips.

"A very simple crime. A crime with no complications. A crime of quiet domestic life . . . very unimpassioned—very *intime*."

"How can a crime be *intime?*"

"Supposing," murmured Poirot, "that four people sit down to play bridge and one, the odd man out, sits in a chair by the fire. At the end of the evening the man by the fire is found dead. One of the four, while he is dummy, has gone over and killed him, and intent on the play of the hand, the other three have not noticed. Ah, there would be a crime for you! *Which of the four was it?*"

"Well," I said, "I can't see *any* excitement in that!"

Poirot threw me a glance of reproof.

"No, because there are no curiously twisted daggers, no blackmail, no emerald that is the stolen eye of a god, no untraceable Eastern poisons. You have the melodramatic soul, Hastings. You would like, not one murder, but a series of murders."

"I admit," I said, "that a second murder in a book often cheers things up. If the murder happens in the first chapter, and you have to follow up everybody's alibi until the last page but one—well, it does get a bit tedious."

The telephone rang and Poirot rose to answer.

"Allo," he said. "Allo. Yes, it is Hercule Poirot speaking."

He listened for a minute or two and then I saw his face change.

His own side of the conversation was short and disjointed.

"*Mais oui* . . ."

"Yes, of course . . ."

"But yes, we will come . . ."

"Naturally . . ."

"It may be as you say . . ."

"Yes, I will bring it. *A tout à l'heure* then."

He replaced the receiver and came across the room to me.

"That was Japp speaking, Hastings."

"Yes?"

"He had just got back to the Yard. There was a message from Andover . . ."

"Andover?" I cried excitedly.

Poirot said slowly:

"An old woman of the name of Ascher who keeps a little tobacco and newspaper shop has been found murdered."

I think I felt ever so slightly damped. My interest, quickened by the sound of Andover, suffered a faint check. I had expected something fantastic—out of the way! The murder of an old woman who kept a little tobacco shop seemed, somehow, sordid and uninteresting.

Poirot continued in the same slow, grave voice:

"The Andover police believe they can put their hand on the man who did it—"

I felt a second throb of disappointment.

"It seems the woman was on bad terms with her husband. He drinks and is by way of being rather a nasty customer. He's threatened to take her life more than once.

"Nevertheless," continued Poirot, "in view of what has happened the police there would like to have another look at the anonymous letter I received. I have said that you and I will go down to Andover at once."

My spirits revived a little. After all, sordid as this crime seems to be, it was a *crime*, and it was a long time since I had had any association with crime and criminals.

I hardly listened to the next words Poirot said. But they were to come back to me with significance later.

"This is the beginning," said Hercule Poirot.

CHAPTER 4
Mrs Ascher

We were received at Andover by Inspector Glen, a tall fair-haired man with a pleasant smile.

For the sake of conciseness I think I had better give a brief résumé of the bare facts of the case.

The crime was discovered by Police Constable Dover at 1 a.m. on the morning of the 22nd. When on his round he tried the door of the shop and found it unfastened, he entered and at first thought the place was empty. Directing his torch over the counter, however, he caught sight of the huddled-up body of the old woman. When the police surgeon arrived on the spot it was elicited that the woman had been struck down by a heavy blow on the back of the head, probably while she was reaching down a packet of cigarettes from the shelf behind the counter. Death must have occurred about nine to seven hours previously.

"But we've been able to get it down a bit nearer than that," explained the inspector. "We've found a man who went in and bought some tobacco at 5:30. And a second man went in and found the shop empty, as he thought, at five minutes past six. That puts the time at between 5.30 and 6.5. So far I haven't been able to find any one who saw this man Ascher in the neighbourhood, but, of course, it's early as yet. He was in the Three Crowns at nine o'clock pretty far gone in drink. When we get hold of him he'll be detained on suspicion."

"Not a very desirable character, inspector?" asked Poirot.

"Unpleasant bit of goods."

"He didn't live with his wife?"

"No, they separated some years ago. Ascher's a German. He was a waiter at one time, but he took to drink and gradually became unemployable. His wife went into service for a bit. Her last place was as cook-housekeeper to an old lady, Miss Rose. She allowed her husband so much out of her wages to keep himself, but he was always getting drunk and coming round and making scenes at the places where she was employed. That's why she took the post with Miss Rose at The Grange. It's three miles out of Andover, dead in the country. He couldn't get at her there so well. When Miss Rose died, she left Mrs Ascher a small legacy, and the woman started this tobacco and news-agent business—quite a tiny place—just cheap cigarettes and a few newspapers—that sort of thing. She just about managed to keep going. Ascher used to come round and abuse her now and again and she used to give him a bit to get rid of him. She allowed him fifteen shillings a week regular."

"Had they any children?" asked Poirot.

"No. There's a niece. She's in service near Overton. Very superior, steady young woman."

"And you say this man Ascher used to threaten his wife?"

"That's right. He was a terror when he was in drink—cursing and swearing that he'd bash her head in. She had a hard time, did Mrs Ascher."

"What age of woman was she?"

"Close on sixty—respectable and hard-working."

Poirot said gravely:

"It is your opinion, inspector, that this man Ascher committed the crime?"

The inspector coughed cautiously.

"It's a bit early to say that, Mr Poirot, but I'd like to hear Franz Ascher's own account of how he spent yesterday evening. If he can give a satisfactory account of himself, well and good—if not—"

His pause was a pregnant one.

"Nothing was missing from the shop?"

"Nothing. Money in the till quite undisturbed. No signs of robbery."

"You think that this man Ascher came into the shop drunk, started abusing his wife and finally struck her down?"

"It seems the most likely solution. But I must confess, sir, I'd like to have another look at that very odd letter you received. I was wondering if it was just possible that it came from this man Ascher."

Poirot handed over the letter and the inspector read it with a frown.

"It doesn't read like Ascher," he said at last. "I doubt if Ascher would use the term 'our' British police—not unless he was trying to be extra cunning—and I doubt if he's got the wits for that. Then the man's a wreck—all to pieces. His hand's too shaky to print letters clearly like this. It's good quality notepaper and ink, too. It's odd that the letter should mention the 21st of the month. Of course it *might* be coincidence."

"That is possible—yes."

"But I don't like this kind of coincidence, Mr Poirot. It's a bit too pat."

He was silent for a minute or two—a frown creasing his forehead.

"ABC. Who the devil could ABC be? We'll see if Mary Drower (that's the niece) can give us any help. It's an odd business. But for this letter I'd have put my money on Franz Ascher for a certainty."

"Do you know anything of Mrs Ascher's past?"

"She's a Hampshire woman. Went into service as a girl up in London—that's where she met Ascher and married him. Things must have been difficult for them during the war. She actually left him for good in 1922. They were in London then. She came back here to get away from him, but he got wind of where she was and followed her down here, pestering her for money—" A constable came in. "Yes, Briggs, what is it?"

"It's the man Ascher, sir. We've brought him in."

"Right. Bring him in here. Where was he?"

"Hiding in a truck on the railway siding."

"He was, was he? Bring him along."

Franz Ascher was indeed a miserable and unprepossessing specimen. He was blubbering and cringing and blustering alternately. His bleary eyes moved shiftily from one face to another.

"What do you want with me? I have not done nothing. It is a shame and a scandal to bring me here! You are swine, how dare you?" His manner changed suddenly. "No, no, I do not mean that—you would not hurt a poor old man—not be hard on him. Every one is hard on poor old Franz. Poor old Franz."

Mr Ascher started to weep.

"That'll do, Ascher," said the inspector. "Pull yourself together. I'm not charging you with anything—yet. And you're not bound to make a statement unless you like. On the other hand, if you're *not* concerned in the murder of your wife—"

Ascher interrupted him—his voice rising to a scream.

"I did not kill her! I did not kill her! It is all lies! You are goddamned English pigs—all against me. I never kill her—never."

"You threatened to often enough, Ascher."

"No, no. You do not understand. That was just a joke—a good joke between me and Alice. She understood."

"Funny kind of joke! Do you care to say where you were yesterday evening, Ascher?"

"Yes, yes—I tell you everything. I did not go near Alice. I am with friends—good friends. We are at the Seven Stars—and then we are at the Red Dog—"

He hurried on, his words stumbling over each other.

"Dick Willows—he was with me—and old Curdie—and George—and Platt and lots of the boys. I tell you I do not never go near Alice. Ach Gott, it is the truth I am telling you."

His voice rose to a scream. The inspector nodded to his underling.

"Take him away. Detained on suspicion."

"I don't know what to think," he said as the unpleasant, shaking old man with the malevolent, mouthing jaw was removed. "If it wasn't for the letter, I'd say he did it."

"What about the men he mentions?"

"A bad crowd—not one of them would stick at perjury. I've no doubt he *was* with them the greater part of the evening. A lot depends on whether any one saw him near the shop between half-past five and six."

Poirot shook his head thoughtfully.

"You are sure nothing was taken from the shop?"

The inspector shrugged his shoulders.

"That depends. A packet or two of cigarettes might have been taken—but you'd hardly commit murder for that."

"And there was nothing—how shall I put it—introduced into the shop. Nothing that was odd there—incongruous?"

"There was a railway guide," said the inspector.

"A railway guide?"

"Yes. It was open and turned face downward on the counter. Looked as though someone had been looking up the trains from Andover. Either the old woman or a customer."

"Did she sell that type of thing?"

The inspector shook his head.

"She sold penny timetables. This was a big one—kind of thing only Smith's or a big stationer would keep."

A light came into Poirot's eyes. He leant forward.

A light came into the inspector's eye also.

"A railway guide, you say. A Bradshaw—*or an ABC?*"

"By the lord," he said. "It *was* an ABC."

CHAPTER 5
Mary Drower

I think that I can date my interest in the case from that first mention of the ABC railway guide. Up till then I had not been able to raise much enthusiasm. This sordid murder of an old woman in a back-street shop was so like the usual type of crime reported in the newspapers that it failed to strike a significant note. In my own mind I had put down the anonymous letter with its mention of the 21st as a mere coincidence. Mrs Ascher, I felt reasonably sure, had been the victim of her drunken brute of a husband. But now the mention of the railway guide (so familiarly known by its abbreviation of ABC, listing as it did all railway stations in their alphabetical order) sent a quiver of excitement through me. Surely—surely this could not be a second coincidence?

The sordid crime took on a new aspect.

Who was the mysterious individual who had killed Mrs Ascher and left an ABC railway guide behind him?

When we left the police station our first visit was to the mortuary to see the body of the dead woman. A strange feeling came over me as I gazed down on that wrinkled old face with the scanty grey hair drawn back tightly from the temples. It looked so peaceful, so incredibly remote from violence.

"Never knew who or what struck her," observed the sergeant. "That's what Dr Kerr says. I'm glad it was that way, poor old soul. A decent woman she was."

"She must have been beautiful once," said Poirot.

"Really?" I murmured incredulously.

"But yes, look at the line of the jaw, the bones, the moulding of the head."

He sighed as he replaced the sheet and we left the mortuary.

Our next move was a brief interview with the police surgeon.

Dr Kerr was a competent-looking middle-aged man. He spoke briskly and with decision.

"The weapon wasn't found," he said. "Impossible to say what it may have been. A weighted stick, a club, a form of sandbag—any of those would fit the case."

"Would much force be needed to strike such a blow?"

The doctor shot a keen glance at Poirot.

"Meaning, I suppose, could a shaky old man of seventy do it? Oh, yes, it's perfectly possible—given sufficient weight in the head of the weapon, quite a feeble person could achieve the desired result."

"Then the murderer could just as well be a woman as a man?"

The suggestion took the doctor somewhat aback.

"A woman, eh? Well, I confess it never occurred to me to connect a woman with this type of crime. But of course it's possible—perfectly possible. Only, psychologically speaking, I shouldn't say this was a woman's crime."

Poirot nodded his head in eager agreement.

"Perfectly, perfectly. On the fact of it, highly improbable. But one must take all possibilities into account. The body was lying—how?"

The doctor gave us a careful description of the position of the victim. It was his opinion that she had been standing with her back to the counter (and therefore to her assailant) when the blow had been struck. She had slipped down in a heap behind the counter quite out of sight of anyone entering the shop casually.

When we had thanked Dr Kerr and taken our leave, Poirot said:

"You perceive, Hastings, that we have already one further point in favour of Ascher's innocence. If he had been abusing his wife and threatening her, she would have been *facing* him over the counter. Instead she had her *back* to her assailant—obviously she is reaching down tobacco or cigarettes for a *customer*."

I gave a little shiver.

"Pretty gruesome."

Poirot shook his head gravely.

"*Pauvre femme*," he murmured.

Then he glanced at his watch.

"Overton is not, I think, many miles from here. Shall we run over there and have an interview with the niece of the dead woman?"

"Surely you will go first to the shop where the crime took place?"

"I prefer to do that later. I have a reason."

He did not explain further, and a few minutes later we were driving on the London road in the direction of Overton.

The address which the inspector had given us was that of a good-sized house about a mile on the London side of the village.

Our ring at the bell was answered by a pretty dark-haired girl whose eyes were red with recent weeping.

Poirot said gently:

"Ah! I think it is you who are Miss Mary Drower, the parlourmaid here?"

"Yes, sir, that's right. I'm Mary, sir."

"Then perhaps I can talk to you for a few minutes if your mistress will not object. It is about your aunt, Mrs Ascher."

"The mistress is out, sir. She wouldn't mind, I'm sure, if you came in here."

She opened the door of a small morning-room. We entered and Poirot, seating himself on a chair by the window, looked up keenly into the girl's face.

"You have heard of your aunt's death, of course?"

The girl nodded, tears coming once more into her eyes.

"This morning, sir. The police came over. Oh! it's terrible! Poor auntie! Such a hard life as she'd had, too. And now this—it's too awful."

"The police did not suggest your returning to Andover?"

"They said I must come to the inquest—that's on Monday, sir. But I've nowhere to go there—I couldn't fancy being over the shop—now—and what with the housemaid being away, I didn't want to put the mistress out more than may be."

"You were fond of your aunt, Mary?" said Poirot gently.

"Indeed I was, sir. Very good she's been to me always, auntie has. I went to her in London when I was eleven years old, after mother died. I started in service when I was sixteen, but I usually went along to auntie's on my day out. A lot of trouble she went through with that German fellow. 'My old devil,' she used to call him. He'd never let her be in peace anywhere. Sponging, cadging old beast."

The girl spoke with vehemence.

"Your aunt never thought of freeing herself by legal means from this persecution?"

"Well, you see, he was her husband, sir, you couldn't get away from that."

The girl spoke simply but with finality.

"Tell me, Mary, he threatened her, did he not?"

"Oh, yes, sir, it was awful the things he used to say. That he'd cut her throat, and such like: cursing and swearing too—both in German and in English. And yet auntie says he was a fine handsome figure of a man when she married him. It's dreadful to think, sir, what people come to."

"Yes, indeed. And so, I suppose, Mary, having actually heard these threats, you were not so very surprised when you learnt what had happened?"

"Oh, but I was, sir. You see, sir, I never thought for one moment that he meant it. I thought it was just nasty talk and nothing more to it. And it isn't as though auntie was afraid of him. Why, I've seen him slink away like a dog with its tail between its legs when she turned on him. *He* was afraid of *her* if you like."

"And yet she gave him money?"

"Well, he was her husband, you see, sir."

"Yes, so you said before." He paused for a minute or two. Then he said: "Suppose that, after all he did *not* kill her."

"Didn't kill her?"

She stared.

"That is what I said. Supposing some one else killed her . . . Have you any idea who that some one else could be?"

She stared at him with even more amazement.

"I've no idea, sir. It doesn't seem likely, though, does it?"

"There was no one your aunt was afraid of?"

Mary shook her head.

"Auntie wasn't afraid of people. She'd a sharp tongue and she'd stand up to anybody."

"You never heard her mention any one who had a grudge against her?"

"No, indeed, sir."

"Did she ever get anonymous letters?"

"What kind of letters did you say, sir?"

"Letters that weren't signed—or only signed by something like ABC." He watched her narrowly, but plainly she was at a loss. She shook her head wonderingly.

"Has your aunt any relations except you?"

"Not now, sir. One of ten she was, but only three lived to grow up. My Uncle Tom was killed in the war, and my Uncle Harry went to South America and no one's heard of him since, and mother's dead, of course, so there's only me."

"Had your aunt any savings? Any money put by?"

"She'd a little in the Savings Bank, sir—enough to bury her proper, that's what she always said. Otherwise she didn't more than just make ends meet—what with her old devil and all."

Poirot nodded thoughtfully. He said—perhaps more to himself than to her:

"At present one is in the dark—there is no direction—if things get clearer—" He got up. "If I want you at any time, Mary, I will write to you here."

"As a matter of fact, sir, I'm giving in my notice. I don't like the country. I stayed here because I fancied it was a comfort to auntie to have me near by. But now"—again the tears rose in her eyes—"there's no reason I should stay, and so I'll go back to London. It's gayer for a girl there."

"I wish that, when you do go, you would give me your address. Here is my card."

He handed it to her. She looked at it with a puzzled frown.

"Then you're not—anything to do with the police, sir?"

"I am a private detective."

She stood there looking at him for some moments in silence.

She said at last:

"Is there anything—queer going on, sir?"

"Yes, my child. There is—something queer going on. Later you may be able to help me."

"I—I'll do anything, sir. It—it wasn't *right*, sir, auntie being killed."

A strange way of putting it—but deeply moving.

A few seconds later we were driving back to Andover.

CHAPTER 6
The Scene of the Crime

The street in which the tragedy had occurred was a turning off the main street. Mrs Ascher's shop was situated about half-way down it on the right-hand side.

As we turned into the street Poirot glanced at his watch and I realised why he had delayed his visit to the scene of the crime until now. It was just on half-past five. He had wished to reproduce yesterday's atmosphere as closely as possible.

But if that had been his purpose it was defeated. Certainly at this moment the road bore very little likeness to its appearance on the previous evening. There were a certain number of small shops interspersed between private houses of the poorer class. I judged that ordinarily there would be a fair number of people passing up and down—mostly people of the poorer classes, with a good sprinkling of children playing on the pavements and in the road.

At this moment there was a solid mass of people standing staring at one particular house or shop and it took little perspicuity to guess which that was. What we saw was a mass of average human beings looking with intense interest at the spot where another human being had been done to death.

As we drew nearer this proved to be indeed the case. In front of a small dingy-looking shop with its shutters now closed stood a harassed-looking young policeman who was stolidly adjuring the crowd to "pass along there." By the help of a colleague, displacement took place—a certain number of people grudgingly sighed and betook themselves to their ordinary vocations, and almost immediately other persons came along and took up their stand to gaze their full on the spot where murder had been committed.

Poirot stopped a little distance from the main body of the crowd. From where we stood the legend painted over the door could be read plainly enough. Poirot repeated it under his breath.

"A. Ascher. *Oui, c'est peut-être là—*"

He broke off.

"Come, let us go inside, Hastings."

I was only too ready.

We made our way through the crowd and accosted the young policeman. Poirot produced the credentials which the inspector had given him. The constable nodded, and unlocked the door to let us pass within. We did so and entered to the intense interest of the lookers-on.

Inside it was very dark owing to the shutters being closed. The constable found and switched on the electric light. The bulb was a low-powered one so that the interior was still dimly lit.

I looked about me.

A dingy little place. A few cheap magazines strewn about, and yesterday's newspapers—all with a day's dust on them. Behind the counter a row of shelves reaching to the ceiling and packed with tobacco and packets of cigarettes. There were also a couple of jars of peppermint humbugs and barley sugar. A commonplace little shop, one of many thousand such others.

The constable in his slow Hampshire voice was explaining the *mise en scène*.

"Down in a heap behind the counter, that's where she was. Doctor says as how she never knew what hit her. Must have been reaching up to one of the shelves."

"There was nothing in her hand?"

"No, sir, but there was a packet of Player's down beside her."

Poirot nodded. His eyes swept round the small space observing—noting.

"And the railway guide was—where?"

"Here, sir." The constable pointed out the spot on the counter. "It was open at the right page for Andover and lying face down. Seems as though he must have been looking up the trains to London. If so, it mightn't have been an Andover man at all. But then, of course, the railway guide might have belonged to some one else what had nothing to do with the murder at all, but just forgot it here."

"Fingerprints?" I suggested.

The man shook his head.

"The whole place was examined straight away, sir. There weren't none."

"Not on the counter itself?" asked Poirot.

"A long sight too many, sir! All confused and jumbled up."

"Any of Ascher's among them?"

"Too soon to say, sir."

Poirot nodded, then asked if the dead woman lived over the shop.

"Yes, sir, you go through that door at the back, sir. You'll excuse me coming with you, but I've got to stay—"

Poirot passed through the door in question and I followed him. Behind the shop was a microscopic sort of parlour and kitchen combined—it was neat and clean but very dreary looking and scantily furnished. On the mantelpiece were a few photographs. I went up and looked at them and Poirot joined me.

The photographs were three in all. One was a cheap portrait of the girl we had been with that afternoon, Mary Drower. She was obviously wearing her best clothes and had the self-conscious, wooden smile on her face that so often disfigures the expression in posed photography, and makes a snapshot preferable.

The second was a more expensive type of picture—an artistically blurred reproduction of an elderly woman with white hair. A high fur collar stood up round the neck.

I guessed that this was probably the Miss Rose who had left Mrs Ascher the small legacy which had enabled her to start in business.

The third photograph was a very old one, now faded and yellow. It represented a young man and woman in somewhat old-fashioned clothes standing arm in arm. The man had a button-hole and there was an air of bygone festivity about the whole pose.

"Probably a wedding picture," said Poirot. "Regard, Hastings, did I not tell you that she had been a beautiful woman?"

He was right. Disfigured by old-fashioned hair-dressing and weird clothes, there was no disguising the handsomeness of the girl in the picture with her clear-cut features and spirited bearing. I looked closely at the second figure. It was almost impossible to recognize the seedy Ascher in this smart young man with the military bearing.

I recalled the leering drunken old man, and the worn, toil-worn face of the dead woman—and I shivered a little at the remorselessness of time . . .

From the parlour a stair led to two upstairs rooms. One was empty and unfurnished, the other had evidently been the dead woman's bedroom. After being searched by the police it had been left as it was. A couple of old worn blankets on the bed—a little stock of well-darned underwear in a drawer—cookery recipes in another—a paper-backed novel entitled *The Green Oasis*—a pair of new stockings—pathetic in their cheap shininess—a couple of china ornaments—a Dresden shepherd much broken, and a blue and yellow spotted dog—a black raincoat and a woolly jumper hanging on pegs—such were the worldly possessions of the late Alice Ascher.

If there had been any personal papers, the police had taken them.

"*Pauvre femme,*" murmured Poirot. "Come, Hastings, there is nothing for us here."

When we were once more in the street, he hesitated for a minute or two, then crossed the road. Almost exactly opposite Mrs Ascher's was a greengrocer's shop—of the type that has most of its stock outside rather than inside.

In a low voice Poirot gave me certain instructions. Then he himself entered the shop. After waiting a minute or two I followed him in. He was at the moment negotiating for a lettuce. I myself bought a pound of strawberries.

Poirot was talking animatedly to the stout lady who was serving him.

"It was just opposite you, was it not, that this murder occurred? What an affair! What a sensation it must have caused you!"

The stout lady was obviously tired of talking about the murder. She must have had a long day of it. She observed:

"It would be as well if some of that gaping crowd cleared off. What is there to look at, I'd like to know?"

"It must have been very different last night," said Poirot. "Possibly you even observed the murderer enter the shop—a tall, fair man with a beard, was he not? A Russian, so I have heard."

"What's that?" The woman looked up sharply. "A Russian did it, you say?"

"I understand that the police have arrested him."

"Did you ever now?" The woman was excited, voluble. "A foreigner."

"*Mais oui*. I thought perhaps you might have noticed him last night?"

"Well, I don't get much chance of noticing, and that's a fact. The evening's our busy time and there's always a fair few passing along and getting home after their work. A tall, fair man with a beard—no, I can't say I saw any one of that description anywhere about."

I broke in on my cue.

"Excuse me, sir," I said to Poirot. "I think you have been misinformed. A short *dark* man I was told."

An interested discussion intervened in which the stout lady, her lank husband and a hoarse-voiced shop-boy all participated. No less than four short dark men had been observed, and the hoarse boy had seen a tall fair one, "but he hadn't got no beard," he added regretfully.

Finally, our purchases made, we left the establishment, leaving our falsehoods uncorrected.

"And what was the point of all that, Poirot?" I demanded somewhat reproachfully.

"*Parbleu*, I wanted to estimate the chances of a stranger being noticed entering the shop opposite."

"Couldn't you simply have asked—without all that tissue of lies?"

"No, *mon ami*. If I had 'simply asked,' as you put it, I should have got no answer at all to my questions. You yourself are English and yet you do not seem to appreciate the quality of the English reaction to a direct question. It is invariably one of suspicion and the natural result is reticence. If I had asked those people for information they would have shut up like oysters. But by making a statement (and a somewhat out of the way and preposterous one) and by your contradiction of it, tongues are immediately loosened. We know also that that particular time was a 'busy time'—that is, that every one would be intent on their own concerns and that there would be a fair number of people passing along the pavements. Our murderer chose his time well, Hastings."

He paused and then added on a deep note of reproach:

"Is it that you have not in any degree the common sense, Hastings? I say to you: 'Make a purchase *quelconque*'—and you deliberately choose the strawberries! Already they commence to creep through their bag and endanger your good suit."

With some dismay, I perceived that this was indeed the case.

I hastily presented the strawberries to a small boy who seemed highly astonished and faintly suspicious.

Poirot added the lettuce, thus setting the seal on the child's bewilderment.

He continued to drive the moral home.

"At a cheap greengrocer's—*not* strawberries. A strawberry, unless fresh picked, is bound to exude juice. A banana—some apples—even a cabbage—but *strawberries*—"

"It was the first thing I thought of," I explained by way of excuse.

"That is unworthy of your imagination," returned Poirot sternly.

He paused on the sidewalk.

The house and shop on the right of Mrs Ascher's was empty. A "To Let" sign appeared in the windows. On the other side was a house with somewhat grimy muslin curtains.

To this house Poirot betook himself and, there being no bell, executed a series of sharp flourishes with the knocker.

The door was opened after some delay by a very dirty child with a nose that needed attention.

"Good-evening," said Poirot. "Is your mother within?"

"Ay?" said the child.

It stared at us with disfavour and deep suspicion.

"Your mother," said Poirot.

This took some twelve seconds to sink in, then the child turned and, bawling up the stairs "Mum, you're wanted," retreated to some fastness in the dim interior.

A sharp-faced woman looked over the balusters and began to descent.

"No good you wasting your time—" she began, but Poirot interrupted her.

He took off his hat and bowed magnificently.

"Good-evening, madame. I am on the staff of the *Evening Flicker*. I want to persuade you to accept a fee of five pounds and let us have an article on your late neighbour, Mrs Ascher."

The irate words arrested on her lips, the woman came down the stairs, smoothing her hair and hitching at her skirt.

"Come inside, please—on the left there. Won't you sit down, sir."

The tiny room was heavily over-crowded with a massive pseudo-Jacobean suite, but we managed to squeeze ourselves in and on to a hard-seated sofa.

"You must excuse me," the woman was saying. "I am sure I'm sorry I spoke so sharp just now, but you'd hardly believe the worry one has to put up with—fellows coming along selling this, that and the other—vacuum cleaners, stockings, lavender bags and such like foolery—and all so plausible and civil spoken. Got your name, too, pat they have, It's Mrs Fowler this, that and the other."

Seizing adroitly on the name, Poirot said:

"Well, Mrs Fowler, I hope you're going to do what I ask."

"I don't know, I'm sure." The five pounds hung alluringly before Mrs Fowler's eyes. "I *knew* Mrs Ascher, of course, but as to *writing* anything."

Hastily Poirot reassured her. No labour on her part was required. He would elicit the facts from her and the interview would be written up.

Thus encouraged, Mrs Fowler plunged willingly into reminiscence, conjecture and hearsay.

Kept herself to herself, Mrs Ascher had. Not what you'd call really *friendly*, but there, she'd had a lot of trouble, poor soul, every one knew that. And by rights Franz Ascher ought to have been locked up years ago. Not that Mrs Ascher had been afraid of him—a real tartar she could be when roused! Give as good as she got any day. But there it was—the pitcher could go to the well once too often. Again and again, she, Mrs Fowler, had said to her: "One of these days that man will do for you. Mark my words."And he had done, hadn't he? And there had she, Mrs Fowler, been right next door and never heard a sound.

In a pause Poirot managed to insert a question.

Had Mrs Ascher ever received any peculiar letters—letters without a proper signature—just something like ABC?

Regretfully, Mrs Fowler returned a negative answer.

"I know the kind of thing you mean—anonymous letters they call them—mostly full of words you'd blush to say out loud. Well, I don't know, I'm sure if Franz Ascher ever took to writing those. Mrs Ascher never let on to me if he did. What's that? A railway guide, an ABC? No, I never saw such a thing about—and I'm sure if Mrs Ascher had been sent one I'd have heard about it. I declare you could have knocked me down with a feather when I heard about this whole business. It was my girl Edie what came to me. 'Mum,' she says, 'there's ever so many policemen next door.' Gave me quite a turn it did. 'Well,' I said, when I heard about it, 'it does show that she ought never to have been alone in the house—that niece of hers ought to have been with her. A man in drink can be like a ravening wolf,' I said, 'and in my opinion a wild beast is neither more nor less than what that old devil of a husband of hers is. I've warned her,' I said, 'many times and now my words have come true. He'll do for you,' I said. And he has done for her! You can't rightly estimate what a man will do when he's in drink and this murder's a proof of it."

She wound up with a deep gasp.

"Nobody saw this man Ascher go into the shop, I believe?" said Poirot.

Mrs Fowler sniffed scornfully.

"Naturally he wasn't going to show himself," she said.

How Mr Ascher had got there without showing himself she did not deign to explain.

She agreed that there was no back way into the house and that Ascher was quite well known by sight in the district.

"But he didn't want to swing for it and he kept himself well hid."

Poirot kept the conversational ball rolling some little time longer, but when it seemed certain that Mrs Fowler had told all that she knew not once but many times over, he terminated the interview, first paying out the promised sum.

"Rather a dear five pounds' worth, Poirot," I ventured to remark when we were once more in the street.

"So far, yes."

"You think she knows more than she has told?"

"My friend, we are in the peculiar position of *not knowing what questions to ask*. We are like little children playing *cache-cache* in the dark. We stretch out our hands and grope about. Mrs Fowler has told us all that she *thinks* she knows—and has thrown in several conjectures for good measure! In the future, however, her evidence may be useful. It is for the future that I have invested that sum of five pounds."

I did not quite understand the point, but at this moment we ran into Inspector Glen.

CHAPTER 7

Mr Partridge and Mr Riddell

Inspector Glen was looking rather gloomy. He had, I gathered, spent the afternoon trying to get a complete list of persons who had been noticed entering the tobacco shop.

"And nobody has seen any one?" Poirot inquired.

"Oh, yes, they have. Three tall men with furtive expressions—four short men with black moustaches—two beards—three fat men—all strangers—and all, if I'm to believe witnesses, with sinister expressions! I wonder somebody didn't see a gang of masked men with revolvers while they were about it!"

Poirot smiled sympathetically.

"Does anybody claim to have seen the man Ascher?"

"No, they don't. And that's another point in his favour. I've just told the Chief Constable that I think this is a job for Scotland Yard. I don't believe it's a local crime."

Poirot said gravely:

"I agree with you."

The inspector said:

"You know, Monsieur Poirot, it's a nasty business—a nasty business . . . I don't like it . . ."

We had two more interviews before returning to London.

The first was with Mr James Partridge. Mr Partridge was the last person known to have seen Mrs Ascher alive. He had made a purchase from her at 5.30.

Mr Partridge was a small man, a bank clerk by profession. He wore pince-nez, was very dry and spare-looking and extremely precise in all his utterances. He lived in a small house as neat and trim as himself.

"Mr—er—Poirot," he said, glancing at the card my friend had handed to him. "From Inspector Glen? What can I do for you, Mr Poirot?"

"I understand, Mr Partridge, that you were the last person to see Mrs Ascher alive."

Mr Partridge placed his finger-tips together and looked at Poirot as though he were a doubtful cheque.

"That is a very debatable point, Mr Poirot," he said. "Many people may have made purchases from Mrs Ascher after I did so."

"If so, they have not come forward to say so."

Mr Partridge coughed.

"Some people, Mr Poirot, have no sense of public duty."

He looked at us owlishly through his spectacles.

"Exceedingly true," murmured Poirot. "You, I understand, went to the police of your own accord?"

"Certainly I did. As soon as I heard of the shocking occurrence I perceived that my statement might be helpful and came forward accordingly."

"A very proper spirit," said Poirot solemnly. "Perhaps you will be so kind as to repeat your story to me."

"By all means. I was returning to this house and at 5.30 precisely—"

"Pardon, how was it that you knew the time so accurately?"

Mr Partridge looked a little annoyed at being interrupted.

"The church clock chimed. I looked at my watch and found I was a minute slow. That was just before I entered Mrs Ascher's shop."

"Were you in the habit of making purchases there?"

"Fairly frequently. It was on my way home. About once or twice a week I was in the habit of purchasing two ounces of John Cotton mild."

"Did you know Mrs Ascher at all? Anything of her circumstances or her history?"

"Nothing whatever. Beyond my purchase and an occasional remark as to the state of the weather, I had never spoken to her."

"Did you know she had a drunken husband who was in the habit of threatening her life?"

"No, I knew nothing whatever about her."

"You knew her by sight, however. Did anything about her appearance strike you as unusual yesterday evening? Did she appear flurried or put out in any way?"

Mr Partridge considered.

"As far as I noticed, she seemed exactly as usual," he said.

Poirot rose.

"Thank you, Mr Partridge, for answering these questions. Have you, by any chance, an ABC in the house? I want to look up my return train to London."

"On the shelf just behind you," said Mr Partridge.

On the shelf in question were an ABC, a Bradshaw, the Stock Exchange Year Book, Kelly's Directory, a Who's Who and a local directory.

Poirot took down the ABC, pretended to look up a train, then thanked Mr Partridge and took his leave.

Our next interview was with Mr Albert Riddell and was of a highly different character. Mr Albert Riddell was a platelayer and our conversation took place to the accompaniment of the clattering plates and dishes by Mr Riddell's obviously nervous wife, the growling of Mr Riddell's dog and the undisguised hostility of Mr Riddell himself.

He was a big clumsy giant of a man with a broad face and small suspicious eyes. He was in the act of eating meat-pie, washed down by exceedingly black tea. He peered at us angrily over the rim of his cup.

"Told all I've got to tell once, haven't I?" he growled. "What's it to do with me, anyway? Told it to the blarsted police, I 'ave, and now I've got to spit it all out again to a couple of blarsted foreigners."

Poirot gave a quick, amused glance in my direction and then said:

"In truth I sympathize with you, but what will you? It is a question of murder, is it not? One has to be very, very careful."

"Best tell the gentleman what he wants, Bert," said the woman nervously.

"You shut your blarsted mouth," roared the giant.

"You did not, I think, go to the police of your own accord." Poirot slipped the remark in neatly.

"Why the hell should I? It were no business of mine."

"A matter of opinion," said Poirot indifferently. "There has been a murder—the police want to know who has been in the shop—I myself think it would have—what shall I say?—looked more natural if you had come forward."

"I've got my work to do. Don't say I shouldn't have come forward in my own time—"

"But as it was, the police were given your name as that of a person seen to go into Mrs Ascher's and they had to come to you. Were they satisfied with your account?"

"Why shouldn't they be?" demanded Bert truculently.

Poirot merely shrugged his shoulders.

"What are you getting at, mister? Nobody's got anything against me. Everyone knows who did the old girl in, that b— of a husband of hers."

"But he was not in the street that evening and you were."

"Trying to fasten it on me, are you? Well, you won't succeed. What reason had I got to do a thing like that? Think I wanted to pinch a tin of her bloody tobacco? Think I'm a bloody homicidal maniac as they call it? Think I—?"

He rose threateningly from his seat. His wife bleated out:

"Bert, Bert—don't say such things. Bert—they'll think—"

"Calm yourself, Monsieur," said Poirot. "I demand only your account of your visit. That you refuse it seems to me—what shall I say—a little odd?"

"Who said I refused anything?" Mr Riddell sank back again into his seat. "I don't mind."

"It was six o'clock when you entered the shop?"

"That's right—a minute or two after, as a matter of fact. Wanted a packet of Gold Flake. I pushed open the door—"

"It was closed, then?"

"That's right. I thought shop was shut, maybe. But it wasn't. I went in, there wasn't any one about. I hammered on the counter and waited a bit. Nobody came, so I went out again. That's all, and you can put it in your pipe and smoke it."

"You didn't see the body fallen down behind the counter?"

"No, no more would you have done—unless you was looking for it, maybe."

"Was there a railway guide lying about?"

"Yes, there was—face downwards. It crossed my mind like that the old woman might have had to go off sudden by train and forgot to lock shop up."

"Perhaps you picked up the railway guide or moved it along the counter?"

"Didn't touch the b— thing. I did just what I said."

"And you did not see any one leaving the shop before you yourself got there?"

"Didn't see any such thing. What I say is, why pitch on me—"

Poirot rose.

"Nobody is pitching upon you—yet. Bonsoir, Monsieur."

He left the man with his mouth open and I followed him.

In the street he consulted his watch.

"With great haste, my friend, we might manage to catch the 7.2. Let us despatch ourselves quickly."

CHAPTER 8
The Second Letter

"Well?" I demanded eagerly.

We were seated in a first-class carriage which we had to ourselves. The train, an express, had just drawn out of Andover.

"The crime," said Poirot, "was committed by a man of medium height with red hair and a cast in the left eye. He limps slightly on the right foot and has a mole just below the shoulder-blade."

"Poirot?" I cried.

For the moment I was completely taken in. Then the twinkle in my friend's eye undeceived me.

"Poirot!" I said again, this time in reproach.

"Mon ami, what will you? You fix upon me a look of doglike devotion and demand of me a pronouncement à la Sherlock Holmes! Now for the truth—*I do not know what the murderer looks like, nor where he lives, nor how to set hands upon him.*"

"If only he had left some clue," I murmured.

"Yes, the clue—it is always the clue that attracts you. Alas that he did not smoke the cigarette and leave the ash, and then step in it with a shoe that has nails of a curious pattern. No—he is not so obliging. But at least, my friend, you have the *railway guide*. The ABC, that is a clue for you!"

"Do you think he left it by mistake then?"

"Of course not. He left it on purpose. The fingerprints tell us that."

"But there weren't any on it."

"That is what I mean. What was yesterday evening? A warm June night. Does a man stroll about on such an evening in *gloves?* Such a man would certainly have attracted attention. Therefore since there are no fingerprints on the ABC, it must have been carefully wiped. An innocent man would have left prints—a guilty man would not. So our murderer left it there for a purpose—but for all that it is none the less a clue. That ABC was bought by someone—it was carried by someone—there is a possibility there."

"You think we may learn something that way?"

"Frankly, Hastings, I am not particularly hopeful. This man, this unknown X, obviously prides himself on his abilities. He is not likely to blaze a trail that can be followed straight away."

"So that really the ABC isn't helpful at all."

"Not in the sense you mean."

"In any sense?"

Poirot did not answer at once. Then he said slowly:

"The answer to that is yes. We are confronted here by an unknown personage. He is in the dark and seeks to remain in the dark. But in the very nature of things *he cannot help throwing light upon himself*. In one sense we know nothing about him—in another sense we know already a good deal. I see his figure dimly taking shape—a man who prints clearly and well—who buys good-quality paper—who is at great needs to express his personality. I see him as a child possibly ignored and passed over—I see him growing up with an inward sense of inferiority—warring with a sense of injustice . . . I see that inner urge—to assert himself—to focus attention on himself ever becoming stronger, and events, circumstances—crushing it down—heaping, perhaps, more humiliations on him. And inwardly the match is set to the powder train . . ."

"That's all pure conjecture," I objected. "It doesn't give you any practical help."

"You prefer the match end, the cigarette ash, the nailed boots! You always have. But at least we can ask ourselves some practical questions. Why the ABC? Why Mrs Ascher? Why Andover?"

"The woman's past life seems simple enough," I mused. "The interviews with those two men were disappointing. They couldn't tell us anything more than we knew already.

"To tell the truth, I did not expect much in that line. But we could not neglect two possible candidates for the murder."

"Surely you don't think—"

"There is at least a possibility that the murderer lives in or near Andover. That is a possible answer to our question: 'Why Andover?' Well, here were two men known to have been in the shop at the requisite time of day. Either of them *might* be the murderer. And there is nothing as yet to show that one or other of them is *not* the murderer."

"That great hulking brute, Riddell, perhaps," I admitted.

"Oh, I am inclined to acquit Riddell off-hand. He was nervous, blustering, obviously uneasy—"

"But surely that just shows—"

"A nature diametrically opposed to that which penned the ABC letter. Conceit and self-confidence are the characteristics that we must look for."

"Someone who throws his weight about?"

"Possibly. But some people, under a nervous and self-effacing manner, conceal a great deal of vanity and self-satisfaction."

"You don't think that little Mr Partridge—?"

"He is more *le type*. One cannot say more than that. He acts as the writer of the letter would act—goes at once to the police—pushes himself to the fore—enjoys position."

"Do you really think—?"

"No, Hastings. Personally I believe that the murderer came from outside Andover, but we must neglect no avenue of research. And although I say 'he' all the time, we must not exclude the possibility of a woman being concerned."

"Surely not!"

"The method of attack is that of a man, I agree. But anonymous letters are written by women rather than by men. We must bear that in mind."

I was silent for a few minutes, then I said:

"What do we do next?"

"My energetic Hastings," Poirot said and smiled at me.

"No, but what do we do?"

"Nothing."

"Nothing?" My disappointment rang out clearly.

"Am I the magician? The sorcerer? What would you have me do?"

Turning the matter over in my mind I found it difficult to give an answer. Nevertheless I felt convinced that something ought to be done and that we should not allow the grass to grow under our feet.

I said:

"There is the ABC—and the notepaper and envelope—"

"Naturally everything is being done in that line. The police have all the means at their disposal for that kind of inquiry. If anything is to be discovered on those lines have no fear but that they will discover it."

With that I was forced to rest content.

In the days that followed I found Poirot curiously disinclined to discuss the case. When I tried to reopen the subject he waved it aside with an impatient hand.

In my own mind I was afraid that I fathomed his motive. Over the murder of Mrs Ascher, Poirot had sustained a defeat. ABC had challenged him—and ABC had won. My friend, accustomed to an unbroken line of successes, was sensitive to his failure—so much so that he could not even endure discussion of the subject. It was, perhaps, a sign of pettiness in so great a man, but even the most sober of us is liable to have his head turned by success. In Poirot's case the head-turning process had been going on for years. Small wonder if its effects became noticeable at long last.

Understanding, I respected my friend's weakness and I made no further reference to the case. I read in the paper the account of the inquest. It was very brief, no mention was made of the ABC letter, and a verdict was returned of murder by some person or persons unknown. The crime attracted very little attention in the press. It had no popular or spectacular features. The murder of an old woman in a side street was soon passed over in the press for more thrilling topics.

Truth to tell, the affair was fading from my mind also, partly, I think, because I disliked to think of Poirot as being in anyway associated with a failure, when on July 25th it was suddenly revived.

I had not seen Poirot for a couple of days as I had been away in Yorkshire for the weekend. I arrived back on Monday afternoon and the letter came by the six o'clock post. I remember the sudden, sharp intake of breath that Poirot gave as he slit open that particular envelope.

"It has come," he said.

I stared at him—not understanding.

"What has come?"

"The second chapter of the ABC business."

For a minute I looked at him uncomprehendingly. The matter had really passed from my memory.

"Read," said Poirot and passed me over the letter.

As before, it was printed on good-quality paper.

> DEAR MR POIROT,—Well, what about it? First game to me, I think. The Andover business went with a swing, didn't it?
>
> But the fun's only just beginning. Let me draw your attention to Bexhill-on-Sea. Date, the 25th inst.
>
> What a merry time we are having! Yours, etc.,
>
> ABC.

"Good God, Poirot," I cried. "Does this mean that this fiend is going to attempt another crime?"

"Naturally, Hastings. What else did you expect? Did you think that the Andover business was an isolated case? Do you not remember my saying: 'This is the beginning'?"

"But this is horrible!"

"Yes, it is horrible."

"We're up against a homicidal maniac."

"Yes."

His quietness was more impressive than any heroics could have been. I handed back the letter with a shudder.

The following morning saw us at a conference of powers. The Chief Constable of Sussex, the Assistant Commissioner of the CID, Inspector Glen from Andover, Superintendent Carter of the Sussex police, Japp and a younger inspector called Crome, and Dr Thompson, the famous alienist, were all assembled together. The postmark on this letter was Hampstead, but in Poirot's opinion little importance could be attached to this fact.

The matter was discussed fully. Dr Thompson was a pleasant middle-aged man, who, in spite of his learning, contented himself with homely language, avoiding the technicalities of his profession.

"There's no doubt," said the Assistant Commissioner, "that the two letters are in the same hand. Both were written by the same person."

"And we can fairly assume that that person was responsible for the Andover murder."

"Quite. We've now got definite warning of a second crime scheduled to take place on the 25th—the day after tomorrow—at Bexhill. What steps can be taken?"

The Sussex Chief Constable looked at his superintendent.

"Well, Carter, what about it?"

The superintendent shook his head gravely.

"It's difficult, sir. There's not the least clue towards who the victim may be. Speaking fair and square, what steps *can* we take?"

"A suggestion," murmured Poirot.

Their faces turned to him.

"I think it possible that the surname of the intended victim will begin with the letter B."

"That would be something," said the superintendent doubtfully.

"An alphabetical complex," said Dr Thompson thoughtfully.

"I suggest it as a possibility—no more. It came into my mind when I saw the name Ascher clearly written over the shop door of the unfortunate woman who was murdered last month. When I got the letter naming Bexhill it occurred to me as a possibility that the victim as well as the place might be selected by an alphabetical system."

"It's possible," said the doctor. "On the other hand, it may be that the name Ascher was a coincidence—that the victim this time, no matter what her name is, will again be an old woman who keeps a shop. We're dealing, remember, with a madman. So far he hasn't given us any clue as to motive."

"Has a madman any motive, sir?" asked the superintendent sceptically.

"Of course he has, man. A deadly logic is one of the special characteristics of acute mania. A man may believe himself divinely appointed to kill clergymen—or doctors—or old women in tobacco shops—and there's always some perfectly coherent reason behind it. We mustn't let the alphabetical business run away with us. Bexhill succeeding to Andover *may* be a mere coincidence."

"We can at least take certain precautions, Carter, and make a special note of the B's, especially small shopkeepers, and keep a watch on all small tobacconists and newsagents looked after by a single person. I don't think there's anything more we can do than that. Naturally, keep tabs on all strangers as far as possible."

The superintendent uttered a groan.

"With the schools breaking up and the holidays beginning? People are fairly flooding into the place this week."

"We must do what we can," the Chief Constable said sharply.

Inspector Glen spoke in his turn.

"I'll have a watch kept on anyone connected with the Ascher business. Those two witnesses, Partridge and Riddell, and of course Ascher himself. If they show any sign of leaving Andover they'll be followed."

The conference broke up after a few more suggestions and a little desultory conversation.

"Poirot," I said as we walked along by the river. "Surely this crime can be prevented?"

He turned a haggard face to me.

"The sanity of a city full of men against the insanity of one man? I fear, Hastings—I very much fear. Remember the long continued successes of Jack the Ripper."

"It's horrible," I said.

"Madness, Hastings, is a terrible thing . . . *I am afraid . . . I am very much afraid . . .*"

CHAPTER 9
The Bexhill-on-Sea Murder

I still remember my awakening on the morning of the 25th of July. It must have been about seven-thirty.

Poirot was standing by my bedside gently shaking me by the shoulder. One glance at his face brought me from semi-consciousness into the full possession of my faculties.

"What is it?" I demanded, sitting up rapidly.

His answer came quite simply, but a wealth of emotion lay behind the three words he uttered.

"It has happened."

"What?" I cried. "You mean—but *today* is the 25th."

"It took place last night—or rather in the early hours of this morning."

As I sprang from bed and made a rapid toilet, he recounted briefly what he had just learnt over the telephone.

"The body of a young girl has been found on the beach at Bexhill. She has been identified as Elizabeth Barnard, a waitress in one of the cafés, who lived with her parents in a little recently built bungalow. Medical evidence gave the time of death as between 11.30 and 1 a.m."

"They're quite sure that this is *the* crime?" I asked, as I hastily lathered my face.

"An ABC open at the trains to Bexhill was found actually under the body."

I shivered.

"This is horrible!"

"*Faites attention,* Hastings. I do not want a second tragedy in my rooms!"

I wiped the blood from my chin rather ruefully.

"What is our plan of campaign?" I asked.

"The car will call for us in a few moments' time. I will bring you a cup of coffee here so that there will be no delay in starting."

Twenty minutes later we were in a fast police car crossing the Thames on our way out of London.

With us was Inspector Crome, who had been present at the conference the other day, and who was officially in charge of the case.

Crome was a very different type of officer from Japp. A much younger man, he was the silent, superior type. Well educated and well read, he was, for my taste, several shades too pleased with himself. He had lately gained kudos over a series of child murders, having patiently tracked down the criminal who was now in Broadmoor.

He was obviously a suitable person to undertake the present case, but I thought that he was just a little too aware of the fact himself. His manner to Poirot was a shade patronising. He deferred to him as a younger man to an older one—in a rather self-conscious, "public school" way.

"I've had a good long talk with Dr Thompson," he said. "He's very interested in the 'chain' or 'series' type of murder. It's the product of a particular distorted type of mentality. As a layman one can't, of course, appreciate the finer points as they present themselves to a medical point of view." He coughed. "As a matter of fact—my last case—I don't know whether you read about it—the Mabel Homer case, the Muswell Hill schoolgirl, you know—that man Capper was extraordinary. Amazingly difficult to pin the crime on to him—it was his third, too! Looked as sane as you or I. But there are various tests—verbal traps, you know—quite modern, of course, there was nothing of that kind in your day. Once you can induce a man to give himself away, you've got him! He knows that you know and his nerve goes. He starts giving himself away right and left."

"Even in my day that happened sometimes," said Poirot.

Inspector Crome looked at him and murmured conversationally:

"Oh, yes?"

There was silence between us for some time. As we passed New Cross Station, Crome said:

"If there's anything you want to ask me about the case, pray do so."

"You have not, I presume, a description of the dead girl?"

"She was twenty-three years of age, engaged as a waitress at the Ginger Cat café—"

"*Pas ça*. I wondered—if she were pretty?"

"As to that I've no information," said Inspector Crome with a hint of withdrawal. His manner said: "Really—these foreigners! All the same!"

A faint look of amusement came into Poirot's eyes.

"It does not seem to you important, that? Yet, *pour une femme*, it is of the first importance. Often it decides her destiny!"

Another silence fell.

It was not until we were nearing Sevenoaks that Poirot opened the conversation again.

"Were you informed, by any chance, how and with what the girl was strangled?"

Inspector Crome replied briefly.

"Strangled with her own belt—a thick, knitted affair, I gather."

Poirot's eyes opened very wide.

"Aha," he said. "At last we have a piece of information that is very definite. That tells one something, does it not?"

"I haven't seen it yet," said Inspector Crome coldly.

I felt impatient with the man's caution and lack of imagination.

"It gives us the hallmark of the murderer," I said. "The girl's own belt. It shows the particular beastliness of his mind!"

Poirot shot me a glance I could not fathom. On the face of it it conveyed humorous impatience. I thought that perhaps it was a warning not to be too outspoken in front of the Inspector.

I relapsed into silence.

At Bexhill we were greeted by Superintendent Carter. He had with him a pleasant-faced, intelligent-looking young inspector called Kelsey. The latter was detailed to work in with Crome over the case.

"You'll want to make your own inquiries, Crome," said the superintendent. "So I'll just give you the main heads of the matter and then you can get busy right away."

"Thank you, sir," said Crome.

"We've broken the news to her father and mother," said the superintendent. "Terrible shock to them, of course. I left them to recover a bit before questioning them, so you can start from the beginning there."

"There are other members of the family—yes?" asked Poirot.

"There's a sister—a typist in London. She's been communicated with. And there's a young man—in fact, the girl was supposed to be out with him last night, I gather."

"Any help from the ABC guide?" asked Crome.

"It's there," the superintendent nodded towards the table. "No fingerprints. Open at the page for Bexhill. A new copy, I should say—doesn't seem to have been opened much. Not bought anywhere round here. I've tried all the likely stationers."

"Who discovered the body, sir?"

"One of these fresh-air, early-morning colonels. Colonel Jerome. He was out with his dog about 6 a.m. Went along the front in the direction of Cooden, and down on to the beach. Dog went off and sniffed something. Colonel called it. Dog didn't come. Colonel had a look and thought something queer was up. Went over and looked. Behaved very properly. Didn't touch her at all and rang us up immediately."

"And the time of death was round about midnight last night?"

"Between midnight and 1 a.m.—that's pretty certain. Our homicidal joker is a man of his word. If he says the 25th, it is the 25th—though it may have been only by a few minutes."

Crome nodded.

"Yes, that's his mentality all right. There's nothing else? Nobody saw anything helpful?"

"Not as far as we know. But it's early yet. Everyone who saw a girl in white walking with a man last night will be along to tell us about it soon, and as I imagine there were about four or five hundred girls in white walking with young men last night, it ought to be a nice business."

"Well, sir, I'd better get down to it," said Crome. "There's the café and there's the girl's home. I'd better go to both of them. Kelsey can come with me."

"And Mr Poirot?" asked the superintendent.

"I will accompany you," said Poirot to Crome with a little bow.

Crome, I thought, looked slightly annoyed. Kelsey, who had not seen Poirot before, grinned broadly.

It was an unfortunate circumstance that the first time people saw my friend they were always disposed to consider him as a joke of the first water.

"What about this belt she was strangled with?" asked Crome. "Mr Poirot is inclined to think it's a valuable clue. I expect he'd like to see it."

"Du tout," said Poirot quickly. "You misunderstood me."

"You'll get nothing from that," said Carter. "It wasn't a leather belt—might have got fingerprints if it had been. Just a thick sort of knitted silk—ideal for the purpose."

I gave a shiver.

"Well," said Crome, "we'd better be getting along."

We set out forthwith.

Our first visit was to the Ginger Cat. Situated on the sea front, this was the usual type of small tearoom. It had little tables covered with orange-checked cloths and basket-work chairs of exceeding discomfort with orange cushions on them. It was the kind of place that specialized in morning coffee, five different kinds of teas (Devonshire, Farmhouse, Fruit, Carlton and Plain), and a few sparing lunch dishes for females such as scrambled eggs and shrimps and macaroni au gratin.

The morning coffees were just getting under way. The manageress ushered us hastily into a very untidy back sanctum.

"Miss—eh—Merrion?" inquired Crome.

Miss Merrion bleated out in a high, distressed gentlewoman voice:

"That is my name. This is a most distressing business. Most distressing. How it will affect our business I really cannot *think!*"

Miss Merrion was a very thin woman of forty with wispy orange hair (indeed she was astonishingly like a ginger cat herself). She played nervously with various fichus and frills that were part of her official costume.

"You'll have a boom," siad Inspector Kelsey encouragingly. "You'll see! You won't be able to serve teas fast enough!"

"Disgusting," said Miss Merrion. "Truly disgusting. It makes one despair of human nature."

But her eyes brightened nevertheless.

"What can you tell me about the dead girl, Miss Merrion?"

"Nothing," said Miss Merrion positively. "Absolutely nothing!"

"How long had she been working here?"

"This was the second summer."

"You were satisfied with her?"

"She was a good waitress—quick and obliging."

"She was pretty, yes?" inquired Poirot.

Miss Merrion, in her turn, gave him an "Oh, these foreigners" look.

"She was a nice, clean-looking girl," she said distantly.

"What time did she go off duty last night?" asked Crome.

"Eight o'clock. We close at eight. We do not serve dinners. There is no demand for them. Scrambled eggs and tea (Poirot shuddered) people come in for up to seven o'clock and sometimes after, but our rush is over by 6.30."

"Did she mention to you how she proposed to spend her evening?"

"Certainly not," said Miss Merrion emphatically. "We were not on those terms."

"No one came in and called for her? Anything like that?"

"No."

"Did she seem quite her ordinary self? Not excited or depressed?"

"Really I could not say," said Miss Merrion aloofly.

"How many waitresses do you employ?"

"Two normally, and an extra two after the 20th July until the end of August."

"But Elizabeth Barnard was not one of the extras?"

"Miss Barnard was one of the regulars."

"What about the other one?"

"Miss Higley? She is a very nice young lady."

"Were she and Miss Barnard friends?"

"Really I could not say."

"Perhaps we'd better have a word with her."

"Now?"

"If you please."

"I will send her to you," said Miss Merrion, rising. "Please keep her as short a time as possible. This is the morning coffee rush hour."

The feline and gingery Miss Merrion left the room.

"Very refined," remarked Inspector Kelsey. He mimicked the lady's mincing tone. "*Really I could not say.*"

A plump girl, slightly out of breath, with dark hair, rosy cheeks and dark eyes goggling with excitement, bounced in.

"Miss Merrion sent me," she announced breathlessly.

"Miss Higley?"

"Yes, that's me."

"You knew Elizabeth Barnard?"

"Oh, yes, I knew Betty. Isn't it *awful?* It's just too awful! I can't believe it's true. I've been saying to the girls all the morning I just *can't* believe it! 'You know, girls,' I said, 'it just doesn't seem *real*. Betty! I mean, Betty Barnard, who's been here all along, *murdered!* I just can't believe it,' I said. Five or six times I've pinched myself just to see if I wouldn't wake up. Betty murdered . . . It's—well, you know what I mean—it doesn't seem *real*."

"You knew the dead girl well?" asked Crome.

"Well, she's worked here longer than I have. I only came this March. She was here last year. She was rather quiet, if you know what I mean. She wasn't one to joke or laugh a lot. I don't mean that she was exactly *quiet*—she'd plenty of fun in her and all that—but she didn't—well, she was quiet and she wasn't quiet, if you know what I mean."

I will say for Inspector Crome that he was exceedingly patient. As a witness the buxom Miss Higley was persistently maddening. Every statement she made was repeated and qualified half a dozen times. The net result was meagre in the extreme.

She had not been on terms of intimacy with the dead girl. Elizabeth Barnard, it could be guessed, had considered herself a cut above Miss Higley. She had been friendly in working hours, but the girls had not seen much of her out of them. Elizabeth Barnard had had a "friend" who worked at the estate agents near the station. Court & Brunskill. No, he wasn't Mr Court nor Mr Brunskill. He was a clerk there. She didn't know his name. But she knew him by sight well. Good-looking—oh, very good-looking, and always so nicely dressed. Clearly, there was a tinge of jealousy in Miss Higley's heart.

In the end it boiled down to this. Elizabeth Barnard had not confided in anyone in the café as to her plans for the evening, but in Miss Higley's opinion she had been going to meet her "friend." She had had on a new white dress, "ever so sweet with one of the new necks."

We had a word with each of the other two girls but with no further results. Betty Barnard had not said anything as to her plans and no one had noticed her in Bexhill during the course of the evening.

CHAPTER 10
The Barnards

Elizabeth Barnard's parents lived in a minute bungalow, one of fifty or so recently run up by a speculative builder on the confines of the town. The name of it was Llandudno. Mr Barnard, a stout, bewildered-looking man of fifty-five or so, had noticed our approach and was standing waiting in the doorway.

"Come in, gentlemen," he said.

Inspector Kelsey took the initiative.

"This is Inspector Crome of Scotland Yard, sir," he said. "He's come down to help us over this business."

"Scotland Yard?" said Mr Barnard hopefully. "That's good. This murdering villain's got to be laid by the heels. My poor little girl—" His face was distorted by a spasm of grief.

"And this is Mr Hercule Poirot, also from London, and er—"

"Captain Hastings," said Poirot.

"Pleased to meet you, gentlemen," said Mr Barnard mechanically. "Come into the snuggery. I don't know that my poor wife's up to seeing you. All broken up, she is."

However, by the time that we were ensconced in the living-room of the bungalow, Mrs Barnard had made her appearance. She had evidently been crying bitterly, her eyes were reddened and she walked with the uncertain gait of a person who had had a great shock.

"Why, Mother, that's fine," said Mr Barnard. "You're sure you're all right—eh?"

He patted her shoulder and drew her down into a chair.

"The superintendent was very kind," said Mr Barnard. "After he'd broken the news to us, he said he'd leave any questions till later when we'd got over the first shock."

"It is too cruel. Oh, it is too cruel," cried Mrs Barnard tearfully. "The cruellest thing that ever was, it is."

Her voice had a faintly sing-song intonation that I thought for a moment was foreign till I remembered the name on the gate and realized that the "effer wass" of her speech was in reality proof of her Welsh origin.

"It's very painful, madam, I know," said Inspector Crome. "And we've every sympathy for you, but we want to know all the facts we can so as to get to work as quick as possible."

"That's sense, that is," said Mr Barnard, nodding approval.

"Your daughter was twenty-three, I understand. She lived here with you and worked at the Ginger Cat café, is that right?"

"That's it."

"This is a new place, isn't it? Where did you live before?"

"I was in the ironmongery business in Kennington. Retired two years ago. Always meant to live near the sea."

"You have two daughters?"

"Yes. My elder daughter workd in an office in London."

"Weren't you alarmed when your daughter didn't come home last night?"

"We didn't know she hadn't," said Mrs Barnard tearfully. "Dad and I always go to bed early. Nine o'clock's our time. We never knew Betty hadn't come home till the police officer came and said—and said—"

She broke down.

"Was your daughter in the habit of—er—returning home late?"

"You know what girls are nowadays, inspector," said Barnard. "Independent, that's what they are. These summer evenings they're not going to rush home. All the same, Betty was usually in by eleven."

"How did she get in? Was the door open?"

"Left the key under the mat—that's what we always did."

"There is some rumour, I believe, that your daughter was engaged to be married?"

"They don't put it as formally as that nowadays," said Mr Barnard.

"Donald Fraser his name is, and I liked him. I liked him very much," said Mrs Barnard. "Poor fellow, it'll be trouble for him—this news. Does he know yet, I wonder?"

"He works in Court & Brunskill's, I understand?"

"Yes, they're the estate agents."

"Was he in the habit of meeting your daughter most evenings after her work?"

"Not every evening. Once or twice a week would be nearer."

"Do you know if she was going to meet him yesterday?"

"She didn't say. Betty never said much about what she was doing or where she was going. But she was a good girl, Betty was. Oh, I can't believe—"

Mrs Barnard started sobbing again.

"Pull yourself together, old lady. Try to hold up, Mother," urged her husband. "We've got to get to the bottom of this."

"I'm sure Donald would never—would never—" sobbed Mrs Barnard.

"Now just you pull yourself together," repeated Mr Barnard.

"I wish to God I could give you some help—but the plain fact is I know nothing—nothing at all that can help you to find the dastardly scoundrel who did this. Betty was just a merry, happy girl—with a decent young fellow that she was—well, we'd have called it walking out with in my young days. Why anyone should want to murder her simply beats me—it doesn't make sense."

"You're very near the truth there, Mr Barnard," said Crome. "I tell you what I'd like to do—have a look over Miss Barnard's room. There may be something—letters—or a diary."

"Look over it and welcome," said Mr Barnard, rising.

He led the way. Crome followed him, then Poirot, then Kelsey, and I brought up the rear.

I stopped for a minute to retie my shoelaces, and as I did so a taxi drew up outside and a girl jumped out of it. She paid the driver and hurried up the path to the house, carrying a small suitcase. As she entered the door she saw me and stopped dead.

There was something so arresting in her pose that it intrigued me.

"Who are you?" she said.

I came down a few steps. I felt embarrassed as to how exactly to reply. Should I give my name? Or mention that I had come here with the police? The girl, however, gave me no time to make a decision.

"Oh, well," she said, "I can guess."

She pulled off the little white woollen cap she was wearing and threw it on the ground. I could see her better now as she turned a little so that the light fell on her.

My first impression was of the Dutch dolls that my sisters used to play with in my childhood. Her hair was black and cut in a straight bob and a bang across the forehead. Her cheek-bones were high and her whole figure had a queer modern angularity that was not, somehow, unattractive. She was not good-looking—plain rather—but there was an intensity about her, a forcefulness that made her a person quite impossible to overlook.

"You are Miss Barnard?" I asked.

"I am Megan Barnard. You belong to the police, I suppose?"

"Well," I said. "Not exactly—"

She interrupted me.

"I don't think I've got anything to say to you. My sister was a nice bright girl with no men friends. Good-morning."

She gave me a short laugh as she spoke and regarded me challengingly.

"That's the correct phrase, I believe?" she said.

"I'm not a reporter, if that's what you're getting at."

"Well, what are you?" She looked around. "Where's mum and dad?"

"Your father is showing the police your sister's bedroom. Your mother's in there. She's very upset."

The girl seemed to make a decision.

"Come in here," she said.

She pulled open a door and passed through. I followed her and found myself in a small, neat kitchen.

I was about to shut the door behind me—but found an unexpected resistance. The next moment Poirot had slipped quietly into the room and shut the door behind him.

"Mademoiselle Barnard?" he said with a quick bow.

"This is M. Hercule Poirot," I said.

Megan Barnard gave him a quick, appraising glance.

"I've heard of you," she said. "You're the fashionable private sleuth, aren't you?"

"Not a pretty description—but it suffices," said Poirot.

The girl sat down on the edge of the kitchen table. She felt in her bag for a cigarette. She placed it between her lips, lighted it, and then said in between two puffs of smoke:

"Somehow, I don't see what M. Hercule Poirot is doing in our humble little crime."

"Mademoiselle," said Poirot. "What you do not see and what I do not see would probably fill a volume. But all that is of no practical importance. What *is* of practical importance is something that will not be easy to find."

"What's that?"

"Death, mademoiselle, unfortunately creates a *prejudice*. A prejudice in favour of the deceased. I heard what you said just now to my friend Hastings. 'A nice bright girl with no men friends.' You said that in mockery of the newspapers. And it is very true—when a young girl is dead, that is the kind of thing that is said. She was bright. She was happy. She was sweet-tempered. She had not a care in the world. She had no undesirable acquaintances. There is a great charity always to the dead. Do you know what I should like this minute? I should like to find someone who knew Elizabeth Barnard *and who does not know she is dead!* Then, perhaps, I should hear what is useful to me—the truth."

Megan Barnard looked at him for a few minutes in silence whilst she smoked. Then, at last, she spoke. Her words made me jump.

"Betty," she said, "was an unmitigated little ass!"

CHAPTER 11
Megan Barnard

As I said, Megan Barnard's words, and still more the crisp business-like tone in which they were uttered, made me jump.

Poirot, however, merely bowed his head gravely.

"*A la bonne heure,*" he said, "You are intelligent, mademoiselle."

Megan Barnard said, still in the same detached tone:

"I was extremely fond of Betty. But my fondness didn't blind me from seeing exactly the kind of silly little fool she was—and even telling her so upon occasions! Sisters are like that."

"And did she pay any attention to your advice?"

"Probably not," said Megan cynically.

"Will you, mademoiselle, be precise."

The girl hesitated for a minute or two.

Poirot said with a slight smile:

"I will help you. I heard what you said to Hastings. That your sister was a bright, happy girl with no men friends. It was—*un peu*—the *opposite* that was true, was it not?"

Megan said slowly:

"There wasn't any harm in Betty. I want you to understand that. She'd always go straight. She's not the week-ending kind. Nothing of that sort. But she liked being taken out and dancing and—oh, cheap flattery and compliments and all that sort of thing."

"And she was pretty—yes?"

This question, the third time I had heard it, met this time with a practical response.

Megan slipped off the table, went to her suitcase, snapped it open and extracted something which she handed to Poirot.

In a leather frame was a head and shoulders of a fair-haired, smiling girl. Her hair had evidently recently been permed, it stood out from her head in a mass of rather frizzy curls. The smile was arch and artificial. It was certainly not a face that you could call beautiful, but it had an obvious and cheap prettiness.

Poirot handed it back, saying:

"You and she do not resemble each other, mademoiselle."

"Oh! I'm the plain one of the family. I've always known that." She seemed to brush aside the fact as unimportant.

"In what way exactly do you consider your sister was behaving foolishly? Do you mean, perhaps, in relation to Mr Donald Fraser?"

"That's it exactly. Don's a very quiet sort of person—but he—well, naturally he'd resent certain things—and then—"

"And then what, mademoiselle?"

His eyes were on her very steadily.

It may have been my fancy but it seemed to me that she hesitated a second before answering.

"I was afraid that he might—chuck her altogether. And that would have been a pity. He's a very steady and hard-working man and would have made her a good husband."

Poirot continued to gaze at her. She did not flush under his glance but returned it with one of her own equally steady and with something else in it—something that reminded me of her first defiant, disdainful manner.

"So it is like that," he said at last. "We do not speak the truth any longer."

She shrugged her shoulders and turned towards the door.

"Well," she said. "I've done what I could to help you."

Poirot's voice arrested her.

"Wait, mademoiselle. I have something to tell you. Come back."

Rather unwillingly, I thought, she obeyed.

Somewhat to my surprise, Poirot plunged into the whole story of the ABC letters, the murder of Andover, and the railway guide found by the bodies.

He had no reason to complain of any lack of interest on her part. Her lips parted, her eyes gleaming, she hung on his words.

"Is this all true, M. Poirot?"

"Yes, it is true."

"You really mean that my sister was killed by some horrible homicidal maniac?"

"Precisely!"

She drew a deep breath.

"You see, mademoiselle, that the information for which I ask you can give freely without wondering whether or not it will hurt anyone."

"Yes, I see that now."

"Then let us continue our conversation. I have formed the idea that this Donald Fraser has, perhaps, a violent and jealous temper, is that right?"

Megan Barnard said quietly:

"I'm trusting you now, M. Poirot. I'm going to give you the absolute truth. Don is, as I say, a very quiet person—a bottled-up person, if you know what I mean. He can't always express what he feels in words. But underneath it all he minds things terribly. And he's got a jealous nature. He was always jealous of Betty. He was devoted to her—and of course she was very fond of him, but it wasn't in Betty to be fond of one person and not notice anybody else. She wasn't made that way. She'd got a well,—an eye for any nice-looking man who'd pass the time of day with her. And of course, working in the Ginger Cat, she was always running up against men—especially in the summer holidays. She was always very pat with her tongue and if they chaffed her she'd chaff back again. And then perhaps she'd meet them and go to the pictures or something like that. Nothing serious—never anything of that kind—but she just liked her fun. She used to say that as she'd got to settle down with Don one day she might as well have her fun now while she could."

Megan paused and Poirot said:

"I understand. Continue."

"It was just that attitude of mind of hers that Don couldn't understand. If she was really keen on him he couldn't see why she wanted to go out with other people. And once or twice they had flaming big rows about it."

"M. Don, he was no longer quiet?"

"It's like all those quiet people, when they do lose their tempers they lose them with a vengeance. Don was so violent that Betty was frightened."

"When was this?"

"There was one row nearly a year ago and another—a worse one—just over a month ago. I was home for the weekend—and I got them to patch it up again, and it was then that I tried to knock a little sense into Betty—told her she was a little fool. All she would say was that there hadn't been any harm in it. Well, that was true enough, but all the same she was riding for a fall. You see, after the row a year ago, she'd got into the habit of telling a few useful lies on the principle that what the mind doesn't know the heart doesn't grieve over. This last flare-up came because she'd told Don she was going to Hastings to see a girl pal—and he found out that she'd really been over to Eastbourne with some man. He was a married man, as it happened, and he'd been a bit secretive about the business anyway—and so that made it worse. They had an awful scene—Betty saying that she wasn't married to him yet and she had a right to go about with whom she pleased and Don all white and shaking and saying that one day—one day—"

"Yes?"

"He'd commit murder—" said Megan in a lowered voice.

She stopped and stared at Poirot.

He nodded his head gravely several times.

"And so, naturally, you were afraid . . ."

"I didn't think he'd actually done it—not for a minute! But I was afraid it might be brought up—the quarrel and all that he'd said—several people knew about it."

Again Poirot nodded his head gravely.

"Just so. And I may say, mademoiselle, that but for the egoistical vanity of a killer, that is just what would have happened. If Donald Fraser escapes suspicion, it will be thanks to ABC's maniacal boasting."

He was silent for a minute or two, then he said:

"Do you know if your sister met this married man, or any other man, lately?"

Megan shook her head.

"I don't know. I've been away, you see."

"But what do you think?"

"She mayn't have met that particular man again. He'd probably sheer off if he thought there was a chance of a row, but it wouldn't surprise me if Betty had—well, been telling Don a few lies again. You see, she did so enjoy dancing and the pictures, and of course, Don couldn't afford to take her all the time."

"If so, is she likely to have confided in anyone? The girl at the café, for instance?"

"I don't think that's likely. Betty couldn't bear the Higley girl. She thought her common. And the others would be new. Betty wasn't the confiding sort anyway."

An electric bell trilled sharply above the girl's head.

She went to the window and leaned out. She drew back her head sharply.

"It's Don . . ."

"Bring him in here," said Poirot quickly. "I would like a word with him before our good inspector takes him in hand."

Like a flash Megan Barnard was out of the kitchen, and a couple of seconds later she was back again leading Donald Fraser by the hand.

CHAPTER 12
Donald Fraser

I felt sorry at once for the young man. His white haggard face and bewildered eyes showed how great a shock he had had.

He was a well-made, fine-looking young fellow, standing close on six foot, not good-looking, but with a pleasant, freckled face, high cheek-bones and flaming red hair.

"What's this, Megan?" he said. "Why in here? For God's sake, tell me—I've only just heard—Betty . . ."

His voice trailed away.

Poirot pushed forward a chair and he sank down on it.

My friend then extracted a small flask from his pocket, poured some of its contents into a convenient cup which was hanging on the dresser and said:

"Drink some of this, Mr Fraser. It will do you good."

The young man obeyed. The brandy brought a little colour back into his face. He sat up straighter and turned once more to the girl. His manner was quite quiet and self-controlled.

"It's true, I suppose?" he said. "Betty is—dead—killed?"

"It's true, Don."

He said as though mechanically:

"Have you just come down from London?"

"Yes. Dad phoned me."

"By the 9.30, I suppose?" said Donald Fraser.

His mind, shrinking from reality, ran for safety along these unimportant details.

"Yes."

There was silence for a minute or two, then Fraser said:

"The police? Are they doing anything?"

"They're upstairs now. Looking through Betty's things, I suppose."

"They've no idea who—? They don't know—?"

He stopped.

He had all a sensitive, shy person's dislike of putting violent facts into words.

Poirot moved forward a little and asked a question. He spoke in a business-like, matter-of-fact voice as though what he asked was an unimportant detail.

"Did Miss Barnard tell you where she was going last night?"

Fraser replied to the question. He seemed to be speaking mechanically:

"She told me she was going with a girl friend to St Leonards."

"Did you believe her?"

"I—" Suddenly the automaton came to life. "What the devil do you mean?"

His face then, menacing, convulsed by sudden passion, made me understand that a girl might well be afraid of rousing his anger.

Poirot said crisply:

"Betty Barnard was killed by a homicidal murderer. Only by speaking the exact truth can you help us to get on his track."

His glance for a minute turned to Megan.

"That's right, Don," she said. "It isn't a time for considering one's own feelings or anyone else's. You've got to come clean."

Donald Fraser looked suspiciously at Poirot.

"Who are you? You don't belong to the police?"

"I am better than the police," said Poirot. He said it without conscious arrogance. It was, to him, a simple statement of fact.

"Tell him" said Megan.

Donald Fraser capitulated.

"I—wasn't sure," he said. "I believed her when she said it. Never thought of doing anything else. Afterwards—perhaps it was something in her manner. I—I, well, I began to wonder."

"Yes?" said Poirot.

He had sat down opposite Donald Fraser. His eyes, fixed on the other man's, seemed to be exercising a mesmeric spell.

"I was ashamed of myself for being so suspicious. But—but I *was* suspicious . . . I thought of going to the front and watching her when she left the café. I actually went there. Then I felt I couldn't do that. Betty would see me and she'd be angry. She'd realize at once that I was watching her."

"What did you do?"

"I went over to St Leonards. Got over there by eight o'clock. Then I watched the buses—to see if she were in them . . . But there was no sign of her . . ."

"And then?"

"I—I lost my head rather. I was convinced she was with some man. I thought it probable he had taken her in his car to Hastings. I went on there—looked in hotels and restaurants, hung round cinemas—went on the pier. All damn foolishness. Even if she was there I was unlikely to find her, and anyway, there were heaps of other places he might have taken her to instead of Hastings."

He stopped. Precise as his tone had remained, I caught an undertone of that blind, bewildering misery and anger that had possessed him at the time he described.

"In the end I gave it up—came back."

"At what time?"

"I don't know. I walked. It must have been midnight or after when I got home."

"Then—"

The kitchen door opened.

"Oh, there you are," said Inspector Kelsey.

Inspector Crome pushed past him, shot a glance at Poirot and a glance at the two strangers.

"Miss Megan Barnard and Mr Donald Fraser," said Poirot, introducing them.

"This is Inspector Crome from London," he explained.

Turning to the inspector, he said:

"While you pursued your investigations upstairs I have been conversing with Miss Barnard and Mr Fraser, endeavouring if I could to find something that will throw light upon the matter."

"Oh, yes?" said Inspector Crome, his thoughts not upon Poirot but upon the two newcomers.

Poirot retreated to the hall. Inspector Kelsey said kindly as he passed:

"Get anything?"

But his attention was distracted by his colleague and he did not wait for a reply.

I joined Poirot in the hall.

"Did anything strike you, Poirot?" I inquired.

"Only the amazing magnanimity of the murderer, Hastings."

I had not the courage to say that I had not the least idea what he meant.

CHAPTER 13
A Conference

Conferences!

Much of my memories of the ABC case seem to be of conferences!

Conferences at Scotland Yard. At Poirot's rooms. Official conferences. Unofficial conferences.

This particular conference was to decide whether or not the facts relative to the anonymous letters should or should not be made public in the press.

The Bexhill murder had attracted much more attention than the Andover one.

It had, of course, far more elements of popularity. To begin with the victim was a young and good-looking girl. Also, it had taken place at a popular seaside resort.

All the details of the crime were reported fully and rehashed daily in thin disguises. The ABC railway guide came in for its share of attention. The favourite theory was that it had been bought locally by the murderer and that it was a valuable clue to his identity. It also seemed to show that he had come to the place by train and was intending to leave for London.

The railway guide had not figured at all in the meagre accounts of the Andover murder, so there seemed at present little likelihood of the two crimes being connected in the public eye.

"We've got to decide upon a policy," said the Assistant Commissioner. "The thing is—which way will give us the best results? Shall we give the public the facts—enlist their co-operation—after all, it'll be the co-operation of several million people, looking out for a madman—"

"He won't look like a madman," interjected Dr Thompson.

"—looking out for sales of ABC's—and so on. Against that I suppose there's the advantage of working in the dark—not letting our man know what we're up to, but then there's the fact that *he knows very well that we know*. He's drawn attention to himself deliberately by his letters. Eh, Crome, what's your opinion?"

"I look at it this way, sir. If you make it public, *you're playing ABC's game*. That's what he wants—publicity—notoriety. That's what he's out after. I'm right, aren't I, doctor? He wants to make a splash."

Thompson nodded.

The Assistant Commissioner said thoughtfully:

"So you're for balking him. Refusing him the publicity he's hankering after. What about you, M. Poirot?"

Poirot did not speak for a minute. When he did it was with an air of choosing his words carefully.

"It is difficult for me, Sir Lionel," he said. "I am, as you might say, an interested party. The challenge was sent to me. If I say 'Suppress that fact—do not make it public,' may it not be thought that it is my vanity that speaks? That I am afraid for my reputation? It is difficult! To speak out—to tell all—that has its advantages. It is, at least, a warning . . . On the other hand, I am as convinced as Inspector Crome *that it is what the murderer wants us to do*."

"H'm!" said the Assistant Commissioner, rubbing his chin. He looked across at Dr Thompson. "Suppose we refuse our lunatic the satisfaction of the publicity he craves. What's he likely to do?"

"Commit another crime," said the doctor promptly. "Force your hand."

"And if we splash the thing about in headlines. Then what's his reaction?"

"Same answer. One way you *feed* his megalomania, the other you *balk* it. The result's the same. Another crime."

"What do you say, M. Poirot?"

"I agree with Dr Thompson."

"A cleft stick—eh? How many crimes do you think this—lunatic has in mind?"

Dr Thompson looked across at Poirot.

"Looks like A to Z," he said cheerfully.

"Of course," he went on, "he won't get there. Not nearly. You'll have him by the heels long before that. Interesting to know how he'd have dealt with the letter X." He recalled himself guiltily from this purely enjoyable speculation. "But you'll have him long before that. G or H, let's say."

The Assistant Commissioner struck the table with his fist.

"My God, are you telling me we're going to have five more murders?"

"It won't be as much as that, sir," said Inspector Crome. "Trust me."

He spoke with confidence.

"Which letter of the alphabet do you place it at, inspector?" asked Poirot.

There was a slight ironic note in his voice. Crome, I thought, looked at him with a tinge of dislike adulterating the usual calm superiority.

"Might get him next time, M. Poirot. At any rate, I'd guarantee to get him by the time he gets to F."

He turned to the Assistant Commissioner.

"I think I've got the psychology of the case fairly clear. Dr Thompson will correct me if I'm wrong. I take it that every time ABC brings a crime off, his self-confidence increases about a hundred per cent. Every time he feels 'I'm clever—they can't catch me!' he becomes so overweeningly confident that he also becomes careless. He exaggerates his own cleverness and every one else's stupidity. Very soon he'd be hardly bothering to take any precautions at all. That's right, isn't it, doctor?"

Thompson nodded.

"That's usually the case. In non-medical terms it couldn't have been put better. You know something about such things, M. Poirot. Don't you agree?"

I don't think that Crome liked Thompson's appeal to Poirot. He considered that he and he only was the expert on this subject.

"It is as Inspector Crome says," agreed Poirot.

"Paranoia," murmured the doctor.

Poirot turned to Crome.

"Are there any material facts of interest in the Bexhill case?"

"Nothing very definite. A waiter at the Splendide at Eastbourne recognizes the dead girl's photograph as that of a young woman who dined there on the evening of the 24th in company with a middle-aged man in spectacles. It's also been recognized at a roadhouse place called the Scarlet Runner halfway between Bexhill and London. They say she was there about 9 p.m. on the 24th with a man who looked like a naval officer. They can't both be right, but either of them's probable. Of course, there's a host of other identifications, but most of them not good for much. We haven't been able to trace the ABC."

"Well, you seem to be doing all that can be done, Crome," said the Assistant Commissioner. "What do you say, M. Poirot? Does any line of inquiry suggest itself to you?"

Poirot said slowly:

"It seems to me that there is one very important clue—the discovery of the motive."

"Isn't that pretty obvious? An alphabetical complex. Isn't that what you called it, doctor?"

"*Ça, oui,*" said Poirot. "There is an alphabetical complex. But why an alphabetical complex? A madman in particular has always a very strong reason for the crimes he commits."

"Come, come, M. Poirot," said Crome. "Look at Stoneman in 1929. He ended by trying to do away with any one who annoyed him in the slightest degree."

Poirot turned to him.

"Quite so. But if you are a sufficiently great and important person, it is necessary that you should be spared small annoyances. If a fly settles on your forehead again and again, maddening you by its tickling—what do you do? You endeavour to kill that fly. You have no qualms about it. *You* are important—the fly is not. You kill the fly and the annoyance ceases. Your action appears to you sane and justifiable. Another reason for killing a fly is if you have a strong passion for hygiene. The fly is a potential source of danger to the community—the fly must go. So works the mind of the mentally deranged criminal. But consider now this case—*if the victims are alphabetically selected, then they are not being removed because they are a source of annoyance to the murderer personally*. It would be too much of a coincidence to combine the two."

"That's a point," said Dr Thompson. "I remember a case where a woman's husband was condemned to death. She started killing the members of the jury one by one. Quite a time before the crimes were connected up. They seemed entirely haphazard. But as M. Poirot says, there isn't such a thing as a murderer who commits crimes at *random*. Either he removes people who stand (however insignificantly) in his path, or else he kills by *conviction*. He removes clergymen, or policemen, or prostitutes because he firmly believes that they *should* be removed. That doesen't apply here either as far as I can see. Mrs Ascher and Betty Barnard cannot be linked as members of the same class. Of course, it's possible that there is a sex complex. Both victims have been women. We can tell better, of course, after the next crime—"

"For God's sake, Thompson, don't speak so glibly of the next crime," said Sir Lionel irritably. "We're going to do all we can to prevent another crime."

Dr Thompson held his peace and blew his nose with some violence.

"Have it your own way," the noise seemed to say. "If you won't face facts—"

The Assistant Commissioner turned to Poirot.

"I see what you're driving at, but I'm not quite clear yet."

"I ask myself," said Poirot, "what passes exactly in the mind of the murderer? He kills, it would seem from his letters, *pour le sport*—to amuse himself. Can that really be true? And even if it is true, on what principle does he select his victims *apart from the merely alphabetical one?* If he kills merely to amuse himself he would not advertise the fact, since, otherwise, he could kill with impunity. But no, he seeks, as we all agree, to make the splash in the public eye—to assert his personality. In what way has his personality been suppressed that one can connect with the two victims he has so far selected? A final suggestion: Is his motive direct personal hatred of *me*, of Hercule Poirot? Does he challenge me in public because I have (unknown to myself) vanquished him somewhere in the course of my career? Or is his animosity impersonal—directed against a *foreigner*. And if so, what again has led to that? What injury has he suffered at a foreigner's hand?"

"All very suggestive questions," said Dr Thompson.

Inspector Crome cleared his throat.

"Oh, yes? A little unanswerable at present, perhaps."

"Nevertheless, my friend," said Poirot, looking straight at him, "*It is there, in those questions, that the solution lies*. If we knew the exact reason—fantastic, perhaps, to us—but logical to him—of *why* our madman commits these crimes, we should know, perhaps, who the next victim is likely to be."

Crome shook his head.

"He selects them haphazard—that's my opinion."

"The magnanimous murderer," said Poirot.

"What's that you say?"

"I said—the magnanimous murderer! Franz Ascher woild have been arrested for the murder of his wife—Donald Fraser might have been arrested for the murder of Betty Barnard—if it had not been for the warning letters of ABC. Is he, then, so soft-hearted that he cannot bear others to suffer for something they did not do?"

"I've known stranger things happen," said Dr Thompson. "I've known men who've killed half a dozen victims all broken up because one of their victims didn't die instantaneously and suffered pain. All the same, I don't think that that is our fellow's reason. He wants the credit of these crimes for his own honour and glory. That's the explanation that fits best."

"We've come to no decision about the publicity business," said the Assistant Commissioner.

"If I may make a suggestion, sir," said Crome. "Why not wait till the receipt of the next letter? Make it public then—special editions, etc. It will make a bit of a panic in the particular town named, but it will put everyone whose name begins with C on their guard, and it'll put ABC on his mettle. He'll be determined to succeed. And that's when we'll get him."

How little we knew what the future held.

CHAPTER 14
The Third Letter

I well remember the arrival of ABC's third letter.

I may say that all precautions had been taken so that when ABC resumed his campaign there should be no unnecessary delays. A young sergeant from Scotland Yard was attached to the house and if Poirot and I were out it was his duty to open anything that came so as to be able to communicate with headquarters without loss of time.

As the days succeeded each other we had all grown more and more on edge. Inspector Crome's aloof and superior manner grew more and more aloof and superior as one by one his more hopeful clues petered out. The vague descriptions of men said to have been seen with Betty Barnard proved useless. Various cars noticed in the vicinity of Bexhill and Cooden were either accounted for or could not be traced. The investigation or purchases of ABC railway guides caused inconvenience and trouble to heaps of innocent people.

As for ourselves, each time the postman's familiar rat-tat sounded on the door, our hearts beat faster with apprehension. At least that was true for me, and I cannot but believe that Poirot experienced the same sensation.

He was, I knew, deeply unhappy over the case. He refused to leave London, preferring to be on the spot in case of emergency. In those hot dog days even his moustaches dropped—neglected for once by their owner.

It was on a Friday that ABC's third letter came. The evening post arrived about ten o'clock.

When we heard the familiar step and the brisk rat-tat, I rose and went along to the box. There were four or five letters, I remember. The last one I looked at was addressed in printed characters.

"Poirot," I cried . . . My voice died away.

"It has come? Open it, Hastings. Quickly. Every moment may be needed. We must make our plans."

I tore open the letter (Poirot for once did not reproach me with untidiness) and extracted the printed sheet.

"Read it," said Poirot.

I read aloud.

> POOR MR POIROT,—Not so good at these little criminal matters as you thought yourself, are you? Rather past your prime, perhaps? Let us see if you can do any better this time. This time it's an easy one. Churston on the 30th. Do try and do something about it! It's a bit dull having it *all* my own way, you know!
>
> Good hunting. Ever yours,
>
> ABC.

"Churston," I said, jumping to our own copy of an ABC. "Let's see where it is."

"Hastings," Poirot's voice came sharply and interrupted me. "When was that letter written? Is there a date on it?"

I glanced at the letter in my hand.

"Written on the 27th," I announced.

"Did I hear you aright, Hastings? Did he give the date of the murder as the *30th?*"

"That's right. Let me see, that's—"

"*Bon Dieu*, Hastings—do you not realize? *Today is the 30th.*"

His eloquent hand pointed to the calendar on the wall. I caught up the daily paper to confirm it.

"But why—how—" I stammered.

Poirot caught up the torn envelope from the floor. Something unusual about the address had registered itself vaguely in my brain, but I had been too anxious to get at the contents of the letter to pay more than fleeting attention to it.

Poirot was at the time living in Whitehaven Mansions. The address ran: *M. Hercule Poirot, Whitehorse Mansions;* across the corner was scrawled: *"Not known at Whitehorse Mansions, E.C.1, nor at Whitehorse Court—try Whitehaven Mansions."*

"Mon Dieu!" murmured Poirot. "Does even chance aid this madman? *Vite—vite*—we must get on to Scotland Yard."

A minute or two later we were speaking to Crome over the wire. For once the self-controlled inspector did not reply "Oh, yes?" Instead a quickly stifled curse came to his lips. He heard what we had to say, then rang off in order to get a trunk connection to Churston as rapidly as possible.

"C'est trop tard," murmured Poirot.

"You can't be sure of that," I argued, though without any great hope.

He glanced at the clock.

"Twenty minutes past ten? An hour and forty minutes to go. Is it likely that ABC will have held his hand so long?"

I opened the railway guide I had previously taken from its shelf.

"Churston, Devon," I read, "from Paddington 204¾ miles. Population 656. It sounds a fairly small place. Surely our man will be bound to be noticed there."

"Even so, another life will have been taken," murmured Poirot. "What are the trains? I imagine train will be quicker than car."

"There's a midnight train—sleeping-car to Newton Abbot—gets there 6.8 a.m., and then Churston at 7.15."

"That is from Paddington?"

"Paddington, yes."

"We will take that, Hastings."

"You'll hardly have time to get news before we start."

"If we receive bad news tonight or tomorrow morning does it matter which?"

"There's something in that."

I put a few things together in a suitcase whilst Poirot once more rang up Scotland Yard.

A few minutes later he came into the bedroom and demanded:

"Mais qu'est ce que vous faites là?"

"I was packing for you. I thought it would save time."

"Vous éprouvez trop d'émotion, Hastings. It affects your hands and your wits. Is that a way to fold a coat? And regard what you have done to my pyjamas. If the hairwash breaks what will befall them?"

"Good heavens, Poirot," I cried, "this is a matter of life and death. What does it matter what happens to our clothes?"

"You have no sense of proportion, Hastings. We cannot catch a train earlier than the time that it leaves, and to ruin one's clothes will not be the least helpful in preventing a murder."

Taking his suitcase from me firmly, he took the packing into his own hands.

He explained that we were to take the letter and envelope to Paddington with us. Some one from Scotland Yard would meet us there.

When we arrived on the platform the first person we saw was Inspector Crome.

He answered Poirot's look of inquiry.

"No news as yet. All men available are on the look-out. All persons whose name begins with C are being warned by phone when possible. There's just a chance. Where's the letter?"

Poirot gave it to him.

He examined it, swearing softly under his breath.

"Of all the damned luck. The stars in their courses fight for the fellow."

"You don't think," I suggested, "that it was done on purpose?"

Crome shook his head.

"No. He's got his rules—crazy rules—and abides by them. Fair warning. He makes a point of that. That's where his boastfulness comes in. I wonder now—I'd almost bet the chap drinks White Horse whiskey."

"Ah, c'est ingénieux, ça!" said Poirot, driven to admiration in spite of himself. "He prints the letter and the bottle is in front of him."

"That's the way of it," said Crome. "We've all of us done much the same thing one time or another, unconsciously copied something that's just under the eye. He started off White and went on horse instead of haven . . ."

The inspector, we found, was also travelling by the train.

"Even if by some unbelievable luck nothing happened, Churston is the place to be. Our murderer is there, or has been there today. One of my men is on the phone here up to the last minute in case anything comes through."

Just as the train was leaving the station we saw a man running down the platform. He reached the inspector's window and called up something.

As the train drew out of the station Poirot and I hurried along the corridor and tapped on the door of the inspector's sleeper.

"You have news—yes?" demanded Poirot.

Crome said quietly:

"It's about as bad as it can be. Sir Carmichael Clarke has been found with his head bashed in."

Sir Carmichael Clarke, although his name was not very well known to the general public, was a man of some eminence. He had been in his time a very well-known throat specialist. Retiring from his profession very comfortably off, he had been able to indulge what had been one of the chief passions of his life—a collection of Chinese pottery and porcelain. A few years later, inheriting a considerable fortune from an elderly uncle, he had been able to indulge his passion to the full, and he was now the possessor of one of the best-known collections of Chinese art. He was married but had no children and lived in a house he had built for himself near the Devon coast, only coming to London on rare occasions such as when some important sale was on.

It did not require much reflection to realize that his death, following that of the young and pretty Betty Barnard, would provide the best newspaper sensation for years. The fact that it was August and that the papers were hard up for subject matter would make matters worse.

"Eh bien," said Poirot. "It is possible that publicity may do what private efforts have failed to do. The whole country now will be looking for ABC."

"Unfortunately," I said, "that's what he wants."

"True. But it may, all the same, be his undoing. Gratified by success, he may become careless . . . That is what I hope—that he may be drunk with his own cleverness."

"How odd all this is, Poirot," I exclaimed, struck suddenly by an idea. "Do you know, this is the first crime of this kind that you and I have worked on together? All our murders have been—well, private murders, so to speak."

"You are quite right, my friend. Always, up to now, it has fallen to our lot to work from the *inside*. It has been the history of the *victim* that was important. The important points have been: 'Who benefited by the death? What opportunities had those round him to commit the crime?' It has always been the '*crime intime*.' Here, for the first time in our association, it is cold-blooded, impersonal murder. Murder from the *outside*."

I shivered.

"It's rather horrible . . ."

"Yes. I felt from the first, when I read the original letter, that there was something wrong—misshapen . . ."

He made an impatient gesture.

"One must not give way to the nerves . . . *This is no worse than any ordinary crime* . . ."

"It is . . . It is . . ."

"Is it worse to take the life or lives of strangers than to take the life of someone near and dear to you—someone who trusts and believes in you, perhaps?"

"It's worse because it's *mad* . . ."

"No, Hastings. It is not *worse*. It is only more *difficult*."

"No, no, I do not agree with you. It's infinitely more frightening."

Hercule Poirot said thoughtfully:

"It should be easier to discover because it is mad. A crime committed by someone shrewd and sane would be far more complicated. Here, if one could but hit on the *idea* . . . This alphabetical business, it has discrepancies. If I could once see the *idea*—then everything would be clear and simple . . ."

He sighed and shook his head.

"These crimes must not go on. Soon, soon, I must see the truth . . . Go, Hastings. Get some sleep. There will be much to do tomorrow."

CHAPTER 15
Sir Carmichael Clarke

Churston, lying as it does between Brixham on the one side and Paignton and Torquay on the other, occupies a position about halfway round the curve of Torbay. Until about ten years ago it was merely a golf links and below the links a green sweep of countryside dropping down to the sea with only a farmhouse or two in the way of human occupation. But of late years there had been big building developments between Churston and Paignton and the coastline is now dotted with small houses and bungalows, new roads, etc.

Sir Carmichael Clarke had purchased a site of some two acres commanding an interrupted view of the sea. The house he had built was of modern design—a white rectangle that was not unpleasing to the eye. Apart from two big galleries that housed his collection it was not a large house.

Our arrival there took place about 8 a.m. A local police officer had met us at the station and had put us *au courant* of the situation.

Sir Carmichael Clarke, it seemed, had been in the habit of taking a stroll after dinner every evening. When the police rang up—at some time after eleven—it was ascertained that he had not returned. Since his stroll usually followed the same course, it was not long before a search-party discovered his body. Death was due to a crashing blow with some heavy instrument on the back of the head. *An open ABC had been placed face downwards on the dead body.*

We arrived at Combeside (as the house was called) at about eight o'clock. The door was opened by an elderly butler whose shaking hands and disturbed face showed how much the tragedy had affected him.

"Good morning, Deveril," said the police officer.

"Good-morning, Mr Wells."

"These are the gentlemen from London, Deveril."

"This way, gentlemen." He ushered us into a long dining-room where breakfast was laid. "I'll get Mr Franklin."

A minute or two later a big fair-haired man with a sunburnt face entered the room.

This was Franklin Clarke, the dead man's only brother.

He had the resolute competent manner of a man accustomed to meeting with emergencies.

"Good-morning, gentlemen."

Inspector Wells made the introductions.

"This is Inspector Crome of the CID. Mr. Hercule Poirot and—er—Captain Hayter."

"Hastings," I corrected coldly.

Franklin Clarke shook hands with each of us in turn and in each case the handshake was accompanied by a piercing look.

"Let me offer you some breakfast," he said. "We can discuss the position as we eat."

There were no dissentient voices and we were soon doing justice to excellent eggs and bacon and coffee.

"Now for it," said Franklin Clarke. "Inspector Wells gave me a rough idea of the position last night—though I may say it seemed one of the wildest tales I have ever heard. Am I really to believe, Inspector Crome, that my poor brother is the victim of a homicidal maniac, that this is the third murder that has occurred and that *in each case an ABC railway guide has been desposited beside the body?*"

"That is substantially the position, Mr Clarke."

"But *why?* What earthly benefit can accrue from such a crime—even in the most diseased imagination?"

Poirot nodded his head in approval.

"You go straight to the point, Mr Franklin," he said.

"It's not much good looking for motives at this state, Mr Clarke," said Inspector Crome. "That's a matter for an alienist—though I may say that I've had a certain experience of criminal lunacy and that the motives are usually grossly inadequate. There is a desire to assert one's personality, to make a splash in the public eye—in fact, to be a somebody instead of a nonentity."

"Is that true, M. Poirot?"

Clarke seemed incredulous. His appeal to the older man was not too well received by Inspector Crome, who frowned.

"Absolutely true," replied my friend.

"At any rate such a man cannot escape detection long," said Clarke thoughtfully.

"*Vous croyez?* Ah, but they are cunning—*ces gens là!* And you must remember *such a type has usually all the outer signs of insignificance*—he belongs to the class of person who is usually passed over and ignored or even laughed at!"

"Will you let me have a few facts, please, Mr Clarke," said Crome, breaking in on the conversation.

"Certainly."

"Your brother, I take it, was in his usual health and spirits yesterday? He received no unexpected letters? Nothing to upset him?"

"No. I should say he was quite his usual self."

"Not upset and worried in any way."

"Excuse me, inspector. I didn't say that. To be upset and worried was my poor brother's normal condition."

"Why was that?"

"You may not know that my sister-in-law, Lady Clarke, is in very bad health. Frankly, between ourselves, she is suffering from an incurable cancer, and cannot live very much longer. Her illness has preyed terribly on my brother's mind. I myself returned from the East not long ago and I was shocked at the change in him."

Poirot interpolated a question.

"Supposing Mr Clarke, that your brother had been found shot at the foot of a cliff—or shot with a revolver beside him. What would have been your first thought?"

"Quite frankly, I should have jumped to the conclusion that it was suicide," said Clarke.

"*Encore!*" said Poirot.

"What is that?"

"A fact that repeats itself. It is of no matter."

"Anyway, it *wasn't* suicide," said Crome with a touch of curtness. "Now I believe, Mr Clarke, that it was your brother's habit to go for a stroll every evening?"

"Quite right. He always did."

"Every night?"

"Well, not if it was pouring with rain, naturally."

"And everyone in the house knew of this habit?"

"Of course."

"And outside?"

"I don't quite know what you mean by outside. The gardener may have been aware of it or not, I don't know."

"And in the village?"

"Strictly speaking, we haven't got a village. There's a post office and cottages at Churston Ferrers—but there's no village or shops."

"I suppose a stranger hanging round the place would be fairly easily noticed?"

"On the contrary. In August all this part of the world is a seething mass of strangers. They come over every day from Brixham and Torquay and Paignton in cars and buses and on foot. Broadsands, which is down there (he pointed), is a very popular beach and so is Elbury Cove—it's a well-known beauty spot and people come there and picnic. I with they didn't! You've no idea how beautiful and peaceful this part of the world is in June and the beginning of July."

"So you don't think a stranger would be noticed?"

"Not unless he looked—well, off his head."

"This man doesn't look off his head," said Crome with certainty. "You see what I'm getting at, Mr Clarke. This man must have been spying out the land beforehand and discovered your brother's habit of taking an evening stroll. I suppose, by the way, that no strange man came up to the house and asked to see Sir Carmichael yesterday?"

"Not that I know of—but we'll ask Deveril."

He rang the bell and put the question to the butler.

"No, sir, no one came to see Sir Carmichael. And I didn't notice anyone hanging about the house either. No more did the maids, because I've asked them."

The butler waited a moment, then inquired: "Is that all, sir?"

"Yes, Deveril, you can go."

The butler withdrew, drawing back in the doorway to let a young woman pass.

Franklin Clarke rose as she came in.

"This is Miss Grey, gentlemen. My brother's secretary."

My attention was caught at once by the girl's extraordinary Scandinavian fairness. She had the almost colourless ash hair—light-grey eyes—and transparent glowing pallor that one finds amongst Norwegians and Swedes. She looked about twenty-seven and seemed to be as efficient as she was decorative.

"Can I help you in any way?" she asked as she sat down.

Clarke brought her a cup of coffee, but she refused any food.

"Did you deal with Sir Carmicheal's correspondence?" asked Crome.

"Yes, all of it."

"I suppose he never received a letter or letters signed ABC?"

"ABC?" She shook her head. "No, I'm sure he didn't."

"He didn't mention having seen anyone hanging about during his evening walks lately?"

"No. He never mentioned anything of the kind."

"And you yourself have noticed no strangers?"

"Not exactly hanging about. Of course, there are a lot of people, what you might call *wandering* about at this time of year. One often meets people strolling with an aimless look across the golf links or down the lanes to the sea. In the same way, practically everyone one sees this time of year is a stranger."

Poirot nodded thoughtfully.

Inspector Crome asked to be taken over the ground of Sir Carmichael's nightly walk. Franklin Clarke led the way through the french window, and Miss Grey accompanied us.

She and I were a little behind the others.

"All this must have been a terrible shock to you all," I said.

"It seems quite unbelievable. I had gone to bed last night when the police rang up. I heard voices downstairs and at last I came out and asked what was the matter. Deveril and Mr Clarke were just setting out with lanterns."

"What time did Sir Carmichael usually come back from his walk?"

"About a quarter to ten. He used to let himself in by the side door and then sometimes he went straight to bed, sometimes to the gallery where his collections were. That is why, unless the police had rung up, he would probably not have been missed till they went to call him this morning."

"It must have been a terrible shock to his wife?"

"Lady Clarke is kept under morphia a good deal. I think she is in too dazed a condition to appreciate what goes on round her."

We had come out through a garden gate on to the golf links. Crossing a corner of them, we passed over a stile into a steep, winding lane.

"This leads down to Elbury Cove," explained Franklin Clarke. "But two years ago they made a new road leading from the main road to Broadsands and on to Elbury, so that now this lane is practically deserted."

We went on down the lane. At the foot of it a path led between brambles and bracken down to the sea. Suddenly we came out on a grassy ridge overlooking the sea and a beach of glistening white stones. All round dark green trees ran down to the sea. It was an enchanting spot—white, deep green—and sapphire blue.

"How beautiful!" I exclaimed.

Clarke turned to me eagerly.

"Isn't it? Why people want to go abroad to the Riviera when they've got this! I've wandered all over the world in my time and, honest to God, I've never seen anything as beautiful."

Then, as though ashamed of his eagerness, he said in a more matter-of-fact tone:

"This was my brother's evening walk. He came as far as here, then back up the path, and turning to the right instead of the left, went past the farm and across the fields back to the house."

We proceeded on our way till we came to a spot near the hedge, halfway across the field where the body had been found.

Crome nodded.

"Easy enough. The man stood here in the shadow. Your brother would have noticed nothing till the blow fell."

The girl at my side gave a quick shiver.

Franklin Clarke said:

"Hold up, Thora. It's pretty beastly, but it's no use shirking facts."

Thora Grey—the name suited her.

We went back to the house where the body had been taken after being photographed.

As we mounted the wide staircase the doctor came out of a room, black bag in hand.

"Anything to tell us, doctor?" inquired Clarke.

The doctor shook his head.

"Perfectly simple case. I'll keep the technicalities for the inquest. Anyway, he didn't suffer. Death must have been instantaneous."

He moved away.

"I'll just go in and see Lady Clarke."

A hospital nurse came out of a room farther along the corridor and the doctor joined her.

We went into the room out of which the doctor had come.

I came out again rather quickly. Thora Grey was still standing at the head of the stairs.

There was a queer scared expression on her face.

"Miss Grey—" I stopped. "Is anything the matter?"

She looked at me.

"I was thinking," she said, "about D."

"About D?" I stared at her stupidly.

"Yes. The next murder. Something must be done. It's got to be stopped."

Clarke came out of the room behind me.

He said:

"What's got to be stopped, Thora?"

"These awful murders."

"Yes." His jaw thrust itself out aggressively. "I want to talk to M. Poirot sometime . . . Is Crome any good?" He shot the words out unexpectedly.

I replied that he was supposed to be a very clever officer.

My voice was perhaps not as enthusiastic as it might have been.

"He's got a damned offensive manner," said Clarke. "Looks as though he knows everything—and what *does* he know? Nothing at all as far as I can make out."

He was silent for a minute or two. Then he said:

"M. Poirot's the man for my money. I've got a plan. But we'll talk of that later."

He went along the passage and tapped at the same door as the doctor had entered.

I hesitated a moment. The girl was staring in front of her.

"What are you thinking of, Miss Grey?"

She turned her eyes towards me.

"I'm wondering *where he is now* . . . the murderer, I mean. It's not twelve hours yet since it happened . . . Oh! aren't there any *real* clairvoyants who could see where he is now and what he is doing. . . ?"

"The police are searching—" I began.

My commonplace words broke the spell. Thora Grey pulled herself together.

"Yes," she said. "Of course."

In her turn she descended the staircase. I stood there a moment longer conning her words over in my mind.

ABC . . .

Where was he now. . . ?

CHAPTER 16

(Not from Captain Hastings' Personal Narrative)

Mr Alexander Bonaparte Cust came out with the rest of the audience from the Torquay Palladium, where he had been seeing and hearing that highly emotional film, *Not a Sparrow* . . .

He blinked a little as he came out into the afternoon sunshine and peered round him in that lost-dog fashion that was characteristic of him.

He murmured to himself: "It's an idea . . ."

Newsboys passed along crying out:

"Latest . . . Homicidal Maniac at Churston . . ."

They carried placards on which was written:

CHURSTON MURDER. LATEST.

Mr Cust fumbled in his pocket, found a coin, and bought a paper. He did not open it at once.

Entering the Princess Gardens, he slowly made his way to a shelter facing Torquay harbour. He sat down and opened the paper.

There were big headlines:

Sir Carmichael Clarke Murdered.
Terrible Tragedy at Churston.
Work of a Homicidal Maniac.

And below them:

> Only a month ago England was shocked and startled by the murder of a young girl, Elizabeth Barnard, at Bexhill. It may be remembered that an ABC railway guide figured in the case. An ABC was also found by the dead body of Sir Carmichael Clarke, and the police incline to the belief that both crimes were committed by the same person. Can it be possible that a homicidal murderer is going the round of our seaside resorts? . . .

A young man in flannel trousers and a bright blue Aertex shirt who was sitting beside Mr Cust remarked:

"Nasty business—eh?"

Mr Cust jumped.

"Oh, very—very—"

His hands, the young man noticed, were trembling so that he could hardly hold the paper.

"You never know with lunatics," said the young man chattily. "They don't always look balmy, you know. Often they seem just the same as you or me . . ."

"I suppose they do," said Mr Cust.

"It's a fact. Sometimes it's the war what unhinged them—never been right since."

"I—I expect you're right."

"I don't hold with wars," said the young man.

His companion turned on him.

"I don't hold with plague and sleeping sickness and famine and cancer . . . but they happen all the same!"

"War's preventable," said the young man with assurance.

Mr Cust laughed. He laughed for some time.

The young man was slightly alarmed.

"He's a bit batty himself," he thought.

Aloud he said:

"Sorry, sir, I expect you were in the war."

"I was," said Mr Cust. "It—it—unsettled me. My head's never been right since. It aches, you know. Aches terribly."

"Oh! I'm sorry about that," said the young man awkwardly.

"Sometimes I hardly know what I'm doing . . ."

"Really? Well, I must be getting along," said the young man and removed himself hurriedly. He knew what people were once they began to talk about their health.

Mr Cust remained with his paper.

He read and reread . . .

People passed to and fro in front of him.

Most of them were talking of the murder . . .

"Awful . . . do you think it was anything to do with the Chinese? Wasn't the waitress in a Chinese café . . ."

"Actually on the golf links . . ."

"I heard it was on the beach . . ."

"—but, darling, we took our tea to Elbury only *yesterday* . . ."

"—police are sure to get him . . ."

"—say he may be arrested any minute now . . ."

"—quite likely he's in Torquay . . . that other woman was who murdered the what do you call 'ems . . ."

Mr Cust folded up the paper very neatly and laid it on the seat. Then he rose and walked sedately along towards the town.

Girls passed him, girls in white and pink and blue, in summery frocks and pyjamas and shorts. They laughed and giggled. Their eyes appraised the men they passed.

Not once did their eyes linger for a second on Mr Cust . . .

He sat down at a little table and ordered tea and Devonshire cream . . .

CHAPTER 17
Marking Time

With the murder of Sir Carmichael Clarke the ABC mystery leaped into the fullest prominence.

The newspapers were full of nothing else. All sorts of "clues" were reported to have been discovered. Arrests were announced to be imminent. There were photographs of every person or place remotely connected with the murder. There were interviews with any one who would give interviews. There were questions asked in Parliament.

The Andover murder was now bracketed with the other two.

It was the belief of Scotland Yard that the fullest publicity was the best chance of laying the murderer by the heels. The population of Great Britain turned itself into an army of amateur sleuths.

The *Daily Flicker* had the grand inspiration of using the caption:

HE MAY BE IN *YOUR* TOWN!

Poirot, of course, was in the thick of things. The letters sent to him were published and facsimiled. He was abused wholesale for not having prevented the crimes and defended on the ground that he was on the point of naming the murderer.

Reporters incessantly badgered him for interviews.

What M. Poirot Says Today.

Which was usually followed by a half-column of imbecilities.

M. Poirot Takes Grave View of Situation.

M. Poirot on the Eve of Success.

Captain Hastings, the great friend of M. Poirot, told our Special Representative . . .

"Poirot," I would cry. "Pray believe me. I never said anything of the kind."

My friend would reply kindly:

"I know, Hastings—I know. The spoken word and the written—there is an astonishing gulf between them. There is a way of turning sentences that completely reverses the original meaning."

"I wouldn't like you to think I'd said—"

"But do not worry yourself. All this is of no importance. These imbecilities, even, may help."

"How?"

Eh bien," said Poirot grimly. "If our madman reads what I am supposed to have said to the *Daily Blague* today, he will lose all respect for me as an opponent!"

I am, perhaps, giving the impression that nothing practical was being done in the way of investigations. On the contrary, Scotland Yard and the local police of the various counties were indefatigable in following up the smallest clues.

Hotels, people who kept lodgings, boarding-houses—all those within a wide radius of the crimes were questioned minutely.

Hundreds of stories from imaginative people who had "seen a man looking very queer and rolling his eyes," or "noticed a man with a sinister face slinking along," were sifted to the last detail. No information, even of the vaguest character, was neglected. Trains, buses, trams, railway porters, conductors, bookstalls, stationers—there was an indefatigable round of questions and verifications.

At least a score of people were detained and questioned until they could satisfy the police as to their movements on the night in question.

The net result was not entirely a blank. Certain statements were borne in mind and noted down as of possible value, but without further evidence they led nowhere.

If Crome and his colleagues were indefatigable, Poirot seemed to me strangely supine. We argued now and again.

"But what is it that you would have me do, my friend? The routine inquiries, the police make them better than I do. Always—always you want me to run about like the dog."

"Instead of which you sit at home like—like—"

"A sensible man! My force, Hastings, is in my *brain*, not in my *feet!* All the time, whilst I seem to you idle, I am reflecting."

"Reflecting?" I cried. "Is this a time for reflection?"

"Yes, a thousand times yes."

"But what can you possibly gain by reflection? You know the facts of the three cases by heart."

"It is not the facts I reflect upon—but the mind of the murderer."

"The mind of a madman!"

"Precisely. And therefore not to be arrived at in a minute. *When I know what the murderer is like, I shall be able to find out who he is*. And all the time I learn more. After the Andover crime, what did we know about the murderer? Next to nothing at all. After the Bexhill crime? A little more. After the Churston murder? More still. I begin to see—not what *you* would like to see—the outlines of *a face and form*—but the outlines of a *mind*. A mind that moves and works in certain definite directions. After the next crime—"

"Poirot!"

My friend looked at me dispassionately.

"But, yes, Hastings, I think it is almost certain there will be another. A lot depends on *la chance* So far our *inconnu* has been lucky. This time the luck may turn against him. But in any case, after another crime, we shall know infinitely more. Crime is terribly revealing. Try and vary your methods as you will, your tastes, your habits, your attitude of mind, and your soul is revealed by your actions. There are confusing indications—sometimes it is as though there were two intelligences at work—but soon the outline will clear itself, *I shall know.*"

"Who it is?"

"No, Hastings, I shall not know his name and address! I shall know *what kind of a man he is . . .*"

"And then?"

"*Et alors, je vais à la pêche.*"

As I looked rather bewildered, he went on:

"You comprehend, Hastings, an expert fisherman knows exactly what flies to offer to what fish. I shall offer the right kind of fly."

"And then?"

"And then? And then? You are as bad as the superior Crome with his eternal 'Oh, yes?' *Eh bien,* and then he will take the bait and hook and we will reel in the line . . ."

"In the meantime people are dying right and left."

"Three people. And there are, what is it—about 120—road deaths every week?"

"That is entirely different."

"It is probably exactly the same to those who die. For the others, the relations, the friends—yes, there is a difference, but one thing at least rejoices me in this case."

"By all means let us hear anything in the nature of rejoicing."

"*Inutile* to be so sarcastic. It rejoices me that there is here no shadow of guilt to distress the innocent."

"Isn't this worse?"

"No, no, a thousand times no! There is nothing so terrible as to live in an atmosphere of suspicion—to see eyes watching you and the love in them changing to fear—nothing so terrible as to suspect those near and dear to you . . . It is poisonous—a miasma. No, the poisoning of life for the innocent, that, at least, we cannot lay at ABC's door."

"You'll soon be making excuses for the man!" I said bitterly.

"Why not? He may believe himself fully justified. We may, perhaps, end by having sympathy with his point of view."

"Really, Poirot!"

"Alas! I have shocked you. First my inertia—and then my views."

I shook my head without replying.

"All the same," said Poirot after a minute or two. "I have one project that will please you—since it is active and not passive. Also, it will entail a lot of conversation and practically no thought."

I did not quite like his tone.

"What is it?" I asked cautiously.

"The extraction from the friends, relations and servants of the victims of all they know."

"Do you suspect them of keeping things back, then?"

"Not intentionally. But telling everything you know always implies *selection*. If I were to say to you, recount me your day yesterday, you would perhaps reply: 'I rose at nine, I breakfasted at half-past, I had eggs and bacon and coffee, I went to my club, etc.' You would not include: 'I tore my nail and had to cut it. I rang for shaving water. I spilt a little coffee on the tablecloth. I brushed my hat and put it on.' One cannot tell *everything*. Therefore one *selects*. At the time of a murder people select what *they* think is important. But quite frequently they think wrong!"

"And how is one to get at the right things?"

"Simply, as I said just now, by conversation. By talking! By discussing a certain happening, or a certain person, or a certain day, over and over again, extra details are bound to arise."

"What kind of details?"

"Naturally that I do not know or I should not want to find out. But enough time has passed now for ordinary things to reassume their value. It is against all mathematical laws that in three cases of murder there is no single fact nor sentence with a bearing on the case. Some trivial happening, some trivial remark there *must* be which would be a pointer! It is looking for the needle in the haystack, I grant—*but in the haystack there is a needle*—of that I convinced!"

It seemed to me extremely vague and hazy.

"You do not see it? Your wits are not so sharp as those of a mere servant girl."

He tossed me over a letter. It was neatly written in a sloping board-school hand.

> DEAR SIR,—I hope you will forgive the liberty I take in writing to you. I have been thinking a lot since these awful two murders like poor Auntie's. It seems as though we're all in the same boat, as it were. I saw the young lady's picture in the paper, the young lady, I mean, that is the sister of the young lady that was killed at Bexhill. I made so bold as to write to her and tell her I was coming to London to get a place and asked if I could come to her or her mother as I said two heads might be better than one and I would not want much wages, but only to find out who this awful fiend is and perhaps we might get at it better if we could say what we knew something might come of it.
>
> The young lady wrote very nicely and said as how she worked in an office and lives in a hostel, but she suggested I might write you and she said she'd been thinking something of the same kind as I had. And she said we were in the same trouble and we ought to stand together. So I am writing, sir, to say I am coming to London and this is my address.
>
> Hoping I am not troubling you, Yours respectfully,
>
> MARY DROWER.

"Mary Drower," said Poirot, "is a very intelligent girl."

He picked up another letter.

"Read this."

It was a line from Franklin Clarke, saying that he was coming to London and would call upon Poirot the following day if not inconvenient.

"Do not despair, *mon ami,*" said Poirot. "Action is about to begin."

CHAPTER 18
Poirot Makes a Speech

Franklin Clarke arrived at three o'clock on the following afternoon and came straight to the point without beating about the bush.

"M. Poirot," he said, "I'm not satisfied."

"No, Mr Clarke?"

"I've no doubt that Crome is a very efficient officer, but, frankly, he puts my back up. The air of his of knowing best! I hinted something of what I had in mind to your friend here when he was down at Churston, but I've had all my brother's affairs to settle up and I haven't been free until now. My idea is, M. Poirot, that we oughtn't to let the grass grow under our feet—"

"Just what Hastings is always saying!"

"—but go right ahead. We've got to get ready for the next crime."

"So you think there will be a next crime?"

"Don't you?"

"Certainly."

"Very well, then. I want to get organized."

"Tell me your idea exactly?"

"I propose, M. Poirot, a kind of special legion—to work under your orders—composed of the friends and relatives of the murdered people."

"*Une bonne idée*."

"I'm glad you approve. By putting our heads together I feel we might get at something. Also, when the next warning comes, by being on the spot, one of us might—I don't say it's probable—but we might recognize some person as having been near the scene of a previous crime."

"I see your idea, and I approve, but you must remember, Mr Clarke, the relations and friends of the other victims are hardly in your sphere of life. They are employed persons and though they might be given a short vacation—"

Franklin Clarke interrupted.

"That's just it. I'm the only person in a position to foot the bill. Not that I'm particularly well off myself, but my brother died a rich man and it will eventually come to me. I propose, as I say, to enrol a special legion, the members to be paid for their services at the same rate as they get habitually, with, of course, the additional expenses."

"Who do you propose should form this legion?"

"I've been into that. As a matter of fact, I wrote to Miss Megan Barnard—indeed, this is partly her idea. I suggest myself, Miss Barnard, Mr Donald Fraser, who was engaged to the dead girl. Then there is a niece of the Andover woman—Miss Barnard knows her address. I don't think the husband would be of any use to us—I hear he's usually drunk. I also think the Barnards—the father and mother—are a bit old for active campaigning."

"Nobody else?"

"Well—er—Miss Grey."

He flushed slightly as he spoke the name.

"Oh! Miss Grey?"

Nobody in the world could put a gentle nuance of irony into a couple of words better than Poirot. About thirty-five years fell away from Franklin Clarke. He looked suddenly like a shy schoolboy.

"Yes. You see, Miss Grey was with my brother for over two years. She knows the countryside and the people round, and everything. I've been away for a year and a half."

Poirot took pity on him and turned the conversation.

"You have been in the East? In China?"

"Yes. I had a kind of roving commission to purchase things for my brother."

"Very interesting it must have been. *Eh bien*, Mr Clarke, I approve very highly of your idea. I was saying to Hastings only yesterday that a *rapprochement* of the people concerned was needed. It is necessary to pool reminiscences, to compare notes—*even* to talk the thing over—to talk—to talk—and again to talk. Out of some innocent phrase may come enlightenment."

A few days later the "Special Legion" met at Poirot's rooms.

As they sat round looking obediently towards Poirot, who had his place, like the chairman at a Board meeting, at the head of the table, I myself passed them, as it were, in review, confirming or revising my first impressions of them.

The three girls were all of them striking looking—the extraordinary fair beauty of Thora Grey, the dark intensity of Megan Barnard, with her strange Red Indian immobility of face—Mary Drower, neatly dressed in a black coat and skirt, with her pretty, intelligent face. Of the two men, Franklin Clarke, big, bronzed and talkative, Donald Fraser, self-contained and quiet, made an interesting contrast to each other.

Poirot, unable, of course, to resist the occasion, made a little speech.

"Mesdames and Messieurs, you know what we are here for. The police are doing their utmost to track down the criminal. I, too, in my different way. But it seems to me a reunion of those who have a personal interest in the matter—and also, I may say, a personal knowledge of the victims—might have results that an outside investigation cannot pretend to attain.

"Here we have three murders—an old woman, a young girl, an elderly man. Only one thing links these three people together—*the fact that the same person killed them*. That means that *the same person was present in three different localities* and was seen necessarily by a large number of people. That he is a madman in an advanced stage of mania goes without saying. That his appearance and behaviour give no suggestion of such a fact is equally certain. This person—and though I say *he*, remember it may be a man or a woman—has all the devilish cunning of insanity. He has succeeded so far in covering his traces completely. The police have certain vague indications but nothing upon which they can act.

"Nevertheless, there must exist indications which are not vague but certain. To take one particular point—this assassin he did not arrive at Bexhill at midnight and find conveniently on the beach a young lady whose name began with B—"

"Must we go into that?"

It was Donald Fraser who spoke—the words wrung from him, it seemed, by some inner anguish.

"It is necessary to go into everything, Monsieur," said Poirot, turning to him. "You are here, not to save your feelings by refusing to think of details, but if necessary to harrow them by going into the matter *au fond*. As I say, it was not *chance* that provided ABC with a victim in Betty Barnard. There must have been deliberate selection on his part—and therefore premeditation. That is to say, he must have reconnoitred the ground *beforehand*. There were facts of which he had informed himself—the best hour for the committing of the crime at Andover—the *mise en scène* at Bexhill—the habits of Sir Carmichael Clarke at Churston. Me, for one, I refuse to believe that there is *no* indication—no slightest hint—that might help to establish his identity.

"I make the assumption that one—or possibly *all* of you—*knows something that they do not know they know*.

"Sooner or later, by reason of your association with one another, something will come to light, will take on a significance as yet undreamed of. It is like the jigsaw puzzle—each of you may have *a piece aparently without meaning, but which when reunited may show a definite portion of the picture as a whole*."

"Words!" said Megan Barnard.

"Eh?" Poirot looked at her inquiringly.

"What you've been saying. It's just words. It doesn't mean anything."

She spoke with that kind of desperate intensity that I had come to associate with her personality.

"Words, mademoiselle, are only the outer clothing of ideas."

"Well, I think it's sense," said Mary Drower. "I do really, miss. It's often when you're talking over things that you seem to see your way clear. Your mind gets made up for you sometimes without your knowing how it's happening. Talking leads to a lot of things one way and another."

"If 'least said is soonest mended,' it's the converse we want here," said Franklin Clarke.

"What do you say, Mr Fraser?"

"I rather doubt the practical applicability of what you say, M. Poirot."

"What do you think, Thora?" asked Clarke.

"I think the principle of talking things over is always sound."

"Suppose," suggested Poirot, "that you all go over your own remembrances of the time preceding the murder. Perhaps you'll start, Mr Clarke."

"Let me see, on the morning of the day Car was killed I went off sailing. Caught eight mackerel. Lovely out there on the bay. Lunch at home. Irish stew, I remember. Slept in the hammock. Tea. Wrote some letters, missed the post, and drove into Paignton to post them. Then dinner and—I'm not ashamed to say it—reread a book of E. Nesbit's that I used to love as a kid. Then the telephone rang—"

"No further. Now reflect, Mr Clarke, did you meet anyone on your way down to the sea in the morning?"

"Lots of people."

"Can you remember anything about them?"

"Not a damned thing now."

"Sure?"

"Well—let's see—I remember a remarkably fat woman—she wore a striped silk dress and I wondered why—had a couple of kids with her . . . two young men with a fox terrier on the beach throwing stones for it—Oh, yes, a girl with yellow hair squeaking as she bathed—funny how things come back—like a photograph developing."

"You are a good subject. Now later in the day—the garden—going to the post—"

"The gardener watering . . . Going to the post? Nearly ran down a bicyclist—silly woman wobbling and shouting to a friend. That's all, I'm afraid."

Poirot turned to Thora Grey.

"Miss Grey?"

Thora Grey replied in her clear, positive voice:

"I did correspondence with Sir Carmichael in the morning—saw the housekeeper. I wrote letters and did needlework in the afternoon, I fancy. It is difficult to remember. It was quite an ordinary day. I went to bed early."

Rather to my surprise, Poirot asked no further. He said:

"Miss Barnard— can you bring back your remembrances of the last time you saw your sister?"

"It would be about a fortnight before her death. I was down for Saturday and Sunday. It was fine weather. We went to Hastings to the swimming pool."

"What did you talk about most of the time?"

"I gave her a piece of my mind," said Megan.

"And what else? She conversed of what?"

The girl frowned in an effort of memory.

"She talked about being hard up—of a hat and a couple of summer frocks she'd just bought. And a little of Don . . . She also said she disliked Milly Higley—that's the girl at the café—and we laughed about the Merrion woman who keeps the café . . . I don't remember anything else . . ."

"She didn't mention any man—forgive me, Mr Fraser—she might be meeting?"

"She wouldn't to me," said Megan dryly.

Poirot turned to the red-haired young man with the square jaw.

"Mr Fraser—I want you to cast your mind back. You went, you said, to the café on the fatal evening. Your first intention was to wait there and watch for Betty Barnard to come out. Can you remember anyone at all whom you noticed whilst you were waiting there?"

"There were a large number of people walking along the front. I can't remember any of them."

"Excuse me, but are you trying? However preoccupied the mind may be, the eye notices mechanically—unintelligently but accurately . . ."

The young man repeated doggedly:

"I don't remember anybody."

Poirot sighed and turned to Mary Drower.

"I suppose you got letters from your aunt?"

"Oh, yes, sir."

"When was the last?"

Mary thought a minute.

"Two days before the murder, sir."

"What did it say?"

"She said the old devil had been round and that she'd sent him off with a flea in the ear—excuse the expression, sir—said she expected me over on the Wednesday—that's my day out, sir—and she said we'd go to the pictures. It was going to be my birthday, sir."

Something—the thought of the little festivity perhaps, suddenly brought the tears to Mary's eyes. She gulped down a sob. Then apologized for it.

"You must forgive me, sir. I don't want to be silly. Crying's no good. It was just the thought of her—and me—looking forward to our treat. It upset me somehow, sir."

"I know just what you feel like," said Franklin Clarke. "It's always the little things that get one—and especially anything like a treat or a present—something jolly and natural. I remember seeing a woman run over once. She'd just bought some new shoes. I saw her lying there—and the burst parcel with the ridiculous little high-heeled slippers peeping out—it gave me a turn—they looked so pathetic."

Megan said with a sudden eager warmth:

"That's true—that's awfully true. The same thing happened after Betty—died. Mum had bought some stockings for her as a present—bought them the very day it happened. Poor mum, she was all broken up. I found her crying over them. She kept saying: 'I bought them for Betty—I bought them for Betty—and she never even saw them.'"

Her own voice quivered a little. She leaned forward, looking straight at Franklin Clarke. There was between them a sudden sympathy—a fraternity in trouble.

"I know," he said. "I know exactly. Those are just the sort of things that are hell to remember."

Donald Fraser stirred uneasily.

Thora Grey diverted the conversation.

"Aren't we going to make any plans—for the future?" she asked.

"Of course." Franklin Clarke resumed his ordinary manner. "I think that when the moment comes—that is, when the fourth letter arrives—we ought to join forces. Until then, perhaps we might each try our luck on our own. I don't know whether there are any points M. Poirot thinks might repay investigation?"

"I could make some suggestions," said Poirot.

"Good. I'll take them down." He produced a notebook. "Go ahead, M. Poirot. A—?"

"I consider it just possible that the waitress, Milly Higley, might know something useful."

"A—Milly Higley," wrote down Franklin Clarke.

"I suggest two methods of approach. You, Miss Barnard, might try what I call the offensive approach."

"I suppose you think that suits my style?" said Megan dryly.

"Pick a quarrel with the girl—say you knew she never liked your sister—and that your sister had told you all about *her*. If I do not err, that will provoke a flood of recrimination. She will tell you just what she thought of your sister! Some useful fact may emerge."

"And the second method?"

"May I suggest, Mr Fraser, that you should show signs of interest in the girl?"

"Is that necessary?"

"No, it is not necessary. It is just a possible line of exploration."

"Shall I try my hand?" asked Franklin. "I've—er a pretty wide experience, M. Poirot. Let me see what I can do with the young lady."

"You've got your own part of the world to attend to," said Thora Grey rather sharply.

Franklin's face fell just a little.

"Yes," he said. "I have."

"*Tout de même,* I do not think there is much you can do down there for the present," said Poirot. "Mademoiselle Grey now, she is far more fitted—"

Thora Grey interrupted him.

"But you see, M. Poirot. I have left Devon for good."

"Ah? I did not understand."

"Miss Grey very kindly stayed on to help me clear up things," said Franklin. "But naturally she prefers a post in London."

Poirot directed a sharp glance from one to the other.

"How is Lady Clarke?" he demanded.

I was admiring the faint colour in Thora Grey's cheeks and I almost missed Clarke's reply.

"Pretty bad. By the way, M. Poirot, I wonder if you could see your way to running down to Devon and paying her a visit? She expressed a desire to see you before I left. Of course, she often can't see people for a couple of days at a time, but if you would risk that—at my expense, of course."

"Certainly, Mr Clarke. Shall we say the day after tomorrow?"

"Good. I'll let nurse know and she'll arrange the dope accordingly."

"For you, my child," said Poirot, turning to Mary, "I think you might perhaps do good work in Andover. Try the children."

"The children?"

"Yes. Children will not chat readily to outsiders. But you are known in the street where your aunt lived. There were a good many children playing about. They may have noticed who went in and out of your aunt's shop."

"What about Miss Grey and myself?" asked Clarke. "That is, if I'm not to go to Bexhill."

"M. Poirot," said Thora Grey, "what was the postmark on the third letter.?"

"Putney, mademoiselle."

She said thoughtfully: "S.W.15, Putney, that is right, is it not?"

"For a wonder, the newspapers printed it correctly."

"That seems to point to ABC being a Londoner."

"On the face of it, yes."

"One ought to be able to draw him," said Clarke. "M. Poirot, how would it be if I inserted an advertisement—something after these lines: *ABC. Urgent. H.P. close on your track. A hundred for my silence. X.Y.Z.* Nothing quite so crude as that—but you see the idea. It might draw him."

"It's a possibility—yes."

"Might induce him to try and have a shot at me."

"I think it's very dangerous and silly," said Thora Grey sharply.

"What about it, M. Poirot?"

"It can do no harm to try. I think myself that ABC will be too cunning to reply." Poirot smiled a little. "I see, Mr Clarke, that you are—if I may say so without being offensive—still a boy at heart."

Franklin Clarke looked a little abashed.

"Well," he said, consulting his notebook. "We're making a start.

A.—Miss Barnard and Milly Higley.
B.—Mr Fraser and Miss Higley.
C.—Children in Andover.
D.—Advertisement.

I don't feel any of it is much good, but it will be something to do whilst waiting."

He got up and a few minutes later the meeting had dispersed.

CHAPTER 19
By Way of Sweden

Poirot returned to his seat and sat humming a little tune to himself.

"Unfortunate that she is so intelligent," he murmured.

"Who?"

"Megan Barnard. Mademoiselle Megan. 'Words,' she snaps out. At once she perceives that what I am saying means nothing at all. Everybody else was taken in."

"I thought it sounded very plausible."

"Plausible, yes. It was just that that she perceived."

"Didn't you mean what you said, then?"

"What I said could have been comprised into one short sentence. Instead I repeated myself *ad lib* without anyone but Mademoiselle Megan being aware of the fact."

"But why?"

"*Eh bien*—to get things going! To imbue everyone with the impression that there was work to be done! To start—shall we say—the conversations!"

"Don't you think any of these lines will lead to anything?"

"Oh, it is always possible."

He chuckled.

"In the midst of tragedy we start the comedy. It is so, is it not?"

"What *do* you mean?"

"The human drama, Hastings! Reflect a little minute. Here are three sets of human beings brought together by a common tragedy. Immediately a second drama commences *en tout à fait à part*. Do you remember my first case in England? Oh, so many years ago now. I brought together two people who loved one another—by the simple method of having one of them arrested for murder! Nothing less would have done it! In the midst of death we are in life, Hastings . . . Murder, I have often noticed, is a great matchmaker."

"Really, Poirot," I cried scandalized. "I'm sure none of those people was thinking of anything but—"

"Oh! my dear friend. And what about yourself?"

"I!"

"*Mais oui*, as they departed, did you not come back from the door humming a tune?"

"One may do that without being callous."

"Certainly, but that tune told me your thoughts."

"Indeed?"

"Yes. To hum a tune is extremely dangerous. It reveals the sub-conscious mind. The tune you hummed dates, I think from the days of the war. *Comme ça*," Poirot sang in an abominable falsetto voice:

> "Some of the time I love a brunette,
> Some of the time I love a blonde (Who comes
>   from Eden by way of Sweden).

"What could be more revealing? *Mais je crois que la blonde l'emporte sur la brunette!*"

"Really, Poirot," I cried, blushing slightly.

"*C'est tout naturel*. Did you observe how Franklin Clarke was suddenly at one and in sympathy with Mademoiselle Megan? How he leaned forward and looked at her? And did you also notice how very much annoyed Mademoiselle Thora Grey was about it? And Mr Donald Fraser, he—"

"Poirot," I said. "Your mind is incurably sentimental."

"That is the last thing my mind is. You are the sentimental one, Hastings."

I was about to argue the point hotly, but at that moment the door opened.

To my astonishment it was Thora Grey who entered.

"Forgive me for coming back," she said composedly. "But there was something that I think I would like to tell you, M. Poirot."

"Certainly, mademoiselle. Sit down, will you not?"

She took a seat and hesitated, for just a minute as though choosing her words.

"It is just this, M. Poirot. Mr Clarke very generously gave you to understand just now that I had left Combeside by my own wish. He is a very kind and loyal person. But as a matter of fact, it is not quite like that. I was quite prepared to stay on—there is any amount of work to be done in connection with the collections. It was Lady Clarke who wished me to leave! I can make allowances. She is a very ill woman, and her brain is somewhat muddled with the drugs they give her. It makes her suspicious and fanciful. She took an unreasoning dislike to me and insisted that I should leave the house."

I could not but admire the girl's courage. She did not attempt to gloss over facts, as so many might have been tempted to do, but went straight to the point with an admirable candour. My heart went out to her in admiration and sympathy.

"I call it splendid of you to come and tell us this," I said.

"It's always better to have the truth," she said with a little smile. "I don't want to shelter behind Mr Clarke's chivalry. He is a very chivalrous man."

There was a warm glow in her words. She evidently admired Franklin Clarke enormously.

"You have been very honest, mademoiselle," said Poirot.

"It is rather a blow to me," said Thora ruefully. "I had no idea Lady Clarke disliked me so much. In fact, I always thought she was rather fond of me." She made a wry face. "One lives and learns."

She rose.

"That is all I came to say. Goodbye."

I accompanied her downstairs.

"I call that very sporting of her," I said as I returned to the room. "She has courage, that girl."

"And calculation."

"What do you mean—calculation?"

"I mean that she has the power of looking ahead."

I looked at him doubtfully.

"She really is a lovely girl," I said.

"And wears very lovely clothes. That crêpe marocain and the silver fox collar —*dernier cri*."

"You're a man milliner, Poirot. I never notice what people have on."

"You should join a nudist colony."

As I was about to make an indignant rejoinder, he said, with a sudden change of subject:

"Do you know, Hastings, I cannot rid my mind of the impression that already, in our conversations this afternoon, something was said that was significant. It is odd—I cannot pin down exactly what it was . . . Just an impression that passed through my mind . . . *That reminds me of something I have already heard or seen or noted . . .*"

"Something at Churston?"

"No—not at Churston . . . Before that . . . No matter, presently it will come to me . . ."

He looked at me (perhaps I had not been attending very closely), laughed and began once more to hum.

"She is an angel, is she not? From Eden, by way of Sweden . . ."

"Poirot," I said. "Go to the devil!"

CHAPTER 20
Lady Clarke

There was an air of deep and settled melancholy over Combeside when we saw it again for the second time. This may, perhaps have been partly due to the weather—it was a moist September day with a hint of autumn in the air, and partly, no doubt, it was the semi-shut-up state of the house. The downstairs rooms were closed and shuttered, and the small room into which we were shown smelt damp and airless.

A capable-looking hospital nurse came to us there pulling down her starched cuffs.

"M. Poirot?" she said briskly. "I am Nurse Capstick. I got Mr Clarke's letter saying you were coming."

Poirot inquired after Lady Clarke's health.

"Not at all bad really, all things considered."

"All things considered," I presumed, meant considering she was under sentence of death.

"One can't hope for much improvement, of course, but some new treatment has made things a little easier for her. Dr Logan is quite pleased with her condition."

"But it is true, is it not, that she can never recover?"

"Oh, we never actually *say* that," said Nurse Capstick, a little shocked by this plain speaking.

"I suppose her husband's death was a terrible shock to her?"

"Well, M. Poirot, if you understand what I mean, it wasn't as much of a shock as it would have been to anyone in full possession of her health and faculties. Things are *dimmed* for Lady Clarke in her condition."

"Pardon my asking, but was she deeply attached to her husband and he to her?"

"Oh, yes, they were a very happy couple. He was very worried and upset about her, poor man. It's always worse for a doctor, you know. They can't buoy themselves up with false hopes. I'm afraid it preyed on his mind very much to begin with."

"To begin with? Not so much afterwards."

"One gets used to everything, doesn't one? And then Sir Carmichael had his collection. A hobby is a great consolation to a man. He used to run up to sales occasionally, and then he and Miss Grey were busy recataloguing and rearranging the museum on a new system."

"Oh, yes—Miss Grey. She has left, has she not?"

"Yes—I'm very sorry about it—but ladies do take these fancies sometimes when they're not well. And there's no arguing with them. It's better to give in. Miss Grey was very sensible about it."

"Had Lady Clarke always disliked her?"

"No—that is to say, not *disliked*. As a matter of fact, I think she rather liked her to begin with. But there, I mustn't keep gossiping. My patient will be wondering what has become of us."

She led us upstairs to a room on the first floor. What had at one time been a bedroom had been turned into a cheerful-looking sitting-room.

Lady Clarke was sitting in a big armchair near the window. She was painfully thin, and her face had the grey, haggard look of one who suffers much pain. She had a slightly far-away, dreamy look, and I noticed that the pupils of her eyes were mere pin-points.

"This is M. Poirot whom you wanted to see," said Nurse Capstick in her high, cheerful voice.

"Oh, yes, M. Poirot," said Lady Clarke vaguely.

She extended her hand.

"My friend Captain Hastings, Lady Clarke."

"How do you do? So good of you both to come."

We sat down as her vague gesture directed. There was a silence. Lady Clarke seemed to have lapsed into a dream. Presently with a slight effort she roused herself.

"It was about Car, wasn't it? About Car's death. Oh, yes."

She sighed, but still in a faraway manner, shaking her head.

"We never thought it would be that way round . . . I was so sure I should be the first to go . . ." She mused a minute or two. "Car was very strong—wonderful for his age. He was never ill. He was nearly sixty—but he seemed more like fifty . . . Yes, very strong . . ."

She relapsed again into her dream. Poirot, who was well acquainted with the effects of certain drugs and of how they give their taker the impression of endless time, said nothing.

Lady Clarke said suddenly:

"Yes—it was good of you to come. I told Franklin. He said he wouldn't forget to tell you. I hope Franklin isn't going to be foolish . . . he's so easily taken in, in spite of having knocked about the world so much. Men are like that . . . They remain boys . . . Franklin, in particular."

"He has an impulsive nature," said Poirot.

"Yes—yes . . . And very chivalrous. Men are so foolish that way. Even Car—" Her voice trailed off.

She shook her head with a febrile impatience.

"Everything's so dim . . . One's body is a nuisance, M. Poirot, especially when it gets the upper hand. One is conscious of nothing else—whether the pain will hold off or not—nothing else seems to matter."

"I know, Lady Clarke. It is one of the tragedies of this life."

"It makes me so stupid. I cannot even remember what it was I wanted to say to you."

"Was it something about your husband's death?"

"Car's death? Yes, perhaps . . . mad, poor creature—the murderer, I mean. It's all the noise and the speed nowadays—people can't stand it. I've always been sorry for mad people—their heads must feel so queer. And then, being shut up—it must be so terrible. But what else can one do? If they kill people . . ." She shook her head—gently pained. "You haven't caught him yet?" she asked.

"No, not yet."

"He must have been hanging round here that day."

"There were so many strangers about, Lady Clarke. It is the holiday season."

"Yes—I forgot . . . But they keep down by the beaches, they don't come up near the house."

"No stranger came to the house that day."

"Who says so?" demanded Lady Clarke, with a sudden vigour.

Poirot looked slightly taken aback.

"The servants," he said. "Miss Grey."

Lady Clarke said very distinctly:

"That girl is a liar!"

I started on my chair. Poirot threw me a glance.

Lady Clarke was going on, speaking now rather feverishly.

"I didn't like her. I never liked her. Car thought all the world of her. Used to go on about her being an orphan and alone in the world. What's wrong with being an orphan? Sometimes it's a blessing in disguise. You might have a good-for-nothing father and a mother who drank—then you would have something to complain about. Said she was so brave and such a good worker. I dare say she did her work well! I don't know where all this bravery came in!"

"Now don't excite yourself, dear," said Nurse Capstick, intervening. "We mustn't have you getting tired."

"I soon sent her packing! Franklin had the impertinence to suggest that she might be a comfort to me. Comfort to me indeed! The sooner I saw the last of her the better—that's what I said! Franklin's a fool! I didn't want him getting mixed up with her. He's a boy! No sense! 'I'll give her three months' salary, if you like,' I said. 'But out she goes. I don't want her in the house a day longer.' There's one thing about being ill—men can't argue with you. He did what I said and she went. Went like a martyr, I expect—with more sweetness and bravery!"

"Now, dear, don't get so excited. It's bad for you."

Lady Clarke waved Nurse Capstick away.

"You were as much of a fool about her as anyone else."

"Oh! Lady Clarke, you mustn't say that. I did think Miss Grey a very nice girl—so romantic looking, like someone out of a novel."

"I've no patience with the lot of you," said Lady Clarke feebly.

"Well, she's gone now, my dear. Gone right away."

Lady Clarke shook her head with feeble impatience but she did not answer.

Poirot said:

"Why did you say that Miss Grey was a liar?"

"Because she is. She told you no strangers came to the house, didn't she?"

"Yes."

"Very well, then, I saw her—with my own eyes—out of this window—talking to a perfectly strange man on the front doorstep."

"When was this?"

"In the morning of the day Car died—about eleven o'clock."

"What did this man look like?"

"An ordinary sort of man. Nothing special."

"A gentleman—or a tradesman?"

"Not a tradesman. A shabby sort of person. I can't remember."

A sudden quiver of pain shot across her face.

"Please—you must go now—I'm a little tired—Nurse."

We obeyed the cue and took our departure.

"That's an extraordinary story," I said to Poirot as we journeyed back to London. "About Miss Grey and a strange man."

"You see, Hastings? It is, as I tell you: *there is always something to be found out*."

"Why did the girl lie about it and say she had seen no one?"

"I can think of seven separate reasons—one of them an extremely simple one."

"Is that a snub?" I asked.

"It is, perhaps, an invitation to use your ingenuity. But there is no need for us to perturb ourselves. The easiest way to answer the question is to ask her."

"And suppose she tells us another lie?"

"That would indeed be interesting—and highly suggestive."

"It is monstrous to suppose that a girl like that could be in league with a madman."

"Precisely—so I do not suppose it."

I thought for some minutes longer.

"A good-looking girl has a hard time of it," I said at last with a sigh.

"*Du tout*. Disabuse your mind of that idea."

"It's true," I insisted, "everyone's hand is against her simply becuase she is good-looking."

"You speak the *bêtises*, my friend. Whose hand was against her at Combeside? Sir Carmichael's? Franklin's? Nurse Capstick's?"

"Lady Clarke was down on her, all right."

"*Mon ami,* you are full of charitable feeling towards beautiful young girls. Me, I feel charitable to sick old ladies. It may be that Lady Clarke was the clear-sighted one—and that her husband, Mr Franklin Clarke and Nurse Capstick were all as blind as bats—and Captain Hastings."

"You've got a grudge against that girl, Poirot."

To my surprise his eyes twinkled suddenly.

"Perhaps it is that I like to mount you on your romantic high horse, Hastings. You are always the true knight—ready to come to the rescue of damsels in distress—good-looking damsels, *bien entendu*."

"How ridiculous you are, Poirot," I said, unable to keep from laughing.

"Ah, well, one cannot be tragic all the time. More and more I interest myself in the human developments that arise out of this tragedy. It is three dramas of family life that we have there. First there is Andover—the whole tragic life of Mrs Ascher, her struggles, her support of her German husband, the devotion of her niece. That alone would make a novel. Then you have Bexhill—the happy, easy-going father and mother, the two daughters so widely differing from each other—the pretty fluffy fool, and the intense, strong-willed Megan with her clear intelligence and her ruthless passion for truth. And the other figure—the self-controlled young Scotsman with his passionate jealousy and his worship of the dead girl. Finally you have the Churston household—the dying wife, and the husband absorbed in his collections, but with a growing tenderness and sympathy for the beautiful girl who helps him so sympathetically, and the younger brother, vigorous, attractive, interesting, with a romantic glamour about him from his long travels.

"Realize, Hastings, that in the ordinary course of events *those three separate dramas would never have touched each other*. They would have pursued their course uninfluenced by each other. The permutations and combinations of life, Hastings—I never cease to be fascinated by them."

"This is Paddington," was the only answer I made.

It was time, I felt, that someone pricked the bubble.

On our arrival at Whitehaven Mansions we were told that a gentleman was waiting to see Poirot.

I expected it to be Franklin, or perhaps Japp, but to my astonishment it turned out to be none other than Donald Fraser.

He seemed very embarrassed and his inarticulateness was more noticeable than ever.

Poirot did not press him to come to the point of his visit, but instead suggested sandwiches and a glass of wine.

Until these made their appearance he monopolized the conversation, explaining where we had been, and speaking with kindliness and feeling of the invalid woman.

Not until we had finished the sandwiches and sipped the wine did he give the conversation a personal turn.

"You have come from Bexhill, Mr Fraser?"

"Yes."

"Any success with Milly Higley?"

"Milly Higley? Milly Higley?" Fraser repeated the name wonderingly. "Oh, that girl! No, I haven't done anything there yet. It's—"

He stopped. His hands twisted themselves together nervously.

"I don't know why I've come to you," he burst out.

"I know," said Poirot.

"You can't. How can you?"

"You have come to me because there is something that you must tell to someone. You were quite right. I am the proper person. Speak!"

Poirot's air of assurance had its effect. Fraser looked at him with a queer air of grateful obedience.

"You think so?"

"*Parbleu,* I am sure of it."

"M. Poirot, do you know anything about dreams?"

It was the last thing I had expected him to say.

Poirot, however, seemed in no wise surprised.

"I do," he replied. "You have been dreaming—?"

"Yes. I suppose you'll say it's only natural that I should—should dream about—it. But it isn't an ordinary dream."

"No?"

"I've dreamed it now three nights running, sir . . . I think I'm going mad . . ."

"Tell me—"

The man's face was livid. His eyes were staring out of his head. As a matter of face, he *looked* mad.

"It's always the same. I'm on the beach. Looking for Betty. She's lost—only lost, you understand. I've got to find her. I've got to give her her belt. I'm carrying it in my hand. And then—"

"Yes?"

"The dream changes . . . I'm not looking any more. She's there in front of me—sitting on the beach. She doesn't see me coming—It's—oh, I can't—"

"Go on."

Poirot's voice was authoritative—firm.

"I come up behind her . . . she doesn't hear me . . . I slip the belt round her neck and pull—oh—pull . . ."

The agony in his voice was frightful . . . I gripped the arms of my chair . . . The thing was too real.

"She's choking . . . she's dead . . . I've strangled her—and then her head falls back and I see her face . . . and it's *Megan*—not Betty!"

He leant back white and shaking. Poirot poured out another glass of wine and passed it over to him.

"What's the meaning of it, M. Poirot? Why does it come to me? Every night. . . ?"

"Drink up your wine," ordered Poirot.

The young man did so, then he asked in a calmer voice:

"What does it mean? I—I didn't kill her, did I?"

What Poirot answered I do not know, for at that minute I heard the postman's knock and automatically I left the room.

What I took out of the letter-box banished all my interest in Donald Fraser's extraordinary revelations.

I raced back into the siting-room.

"Poirot," I cried. "It's come. The fourth letter."

He sprang up, seized it from me, caught up his paper-knife and slit it open. He spread it out on the table.

The three of us read it together.

> Still no success? Fie! Fie! What are you and the police doing? Well, well, isn't this fun? And where shall we go next for honey?
>
> Poor Mr Poirot. I'm quite sorry for you.
>
> If at first you don't succeed; try, try, try again.
>
> We've a long way to go still.
>
> Tipperary? No—that comes farther on. Letter T.
>
> The next little incident will take place at Doncaster on September 11th.
>
> So long.
>
> ABC.

CHAPTER 21
Description of a Murder

It was at this moment, I think, that what Poirot called the human element began to fade out of the picture again. It was as though, the mind being unable to stand unadulterated horror, we had had an interval of normal human interests.

We had, one and all, felt the impossibility of doing anything until the fourth letter should come revealing the projected scene of the D murder. That atmosphere of waiting had brought a release of tension.

But now, with the printed words jeering from the white stiff paper, the hunt was up once more.

Inspector Crome had come round from the Yard, and while he was still there, Franklin Clarke and Megan Barnard came in.

The girl explained that she, too, had come up from Bexhill.

"I wanted to ask Mr Clarke something."

She seemed rather anxious to excuse and explain her procedure. I just noted the fact without attaching much importance to it.

The letter naturally filled my mind to the exclusion of all else.

Crome was not, I think, any too pleased to see the various participants in the drama. He became extremely official and non-committal.

"I'll take this with me, M. Poirot. If you care to take a copy of it—"

"No, no, it is not necessary."

"What are your plans, inspector?" asked Clarke.

"Fairly comprehensive ones, Mr Clarke."

"This time we've got to get him," said Clarke. "I may tell you, inspector, that we've formed an association of our own to deal with the matter. A legion of interested parties."

Inspector Crome said in his best manner:

"Oh, yes?"

"I gather you don't think much of amateurs, inspector?"

"You've hardly the same resources at your command, have you, Mr Clarke?"

"We've got a personal axe to grind—and that's something."

"Oh, yes?"

"I fancy your own task isn't going to be too easy, inspector. In fact, I rather fancy old ABC has done you again."

Crome, I noticed, could often be goaded into speech when other methods would have failed.

"I don't fancy the public will have much to criticize in our arrangements this time," he said. "The fool has given us ample warning. The 11th isn't till Wednesday of next week. That gives ample time for a publicity campaign in the press. Doncaster will be thoroughly warned. Every soul whose name begins with a D will be on his or her guard—that's so much to the good. Also, we'll draft police into the town on a fairly large scale. That's already been arranged for by consent of all the Chief Constables in England. The whole of Doncaster, police and civilians, will be out to catch one man—and with reasonable luck, we ought to get him!"

Clarke said quietly:

"It's easy to see you're not a sporting man, inspector."

Crome stared at him.

"What do you mean, Mr Clarke?"

"Man alive, don't you realize that on *next Wednesday the St Leger is being run at Doncaster?*"

The inspector's jaw dropped. For the life of him he could not bring out the familiar. "Oh, yes?" Instead he said:

"That's true. Yes, that complicates matters . . ."

"ABC is no fool, even if he *is* a madman."

We were all silent for a minute or two, taking in the situation. The crowds on the racecourse—the passionate, sport-loving English public—the endless complications.

Poirot murmured:

"*C'est ingénieux. Tout de même c'est bien imaginé, ça.*"

"It's my belief," said Clarke, "that the murder will take place on the racecourse—perhaps actually while the Leger is being run."

For the moment his sporting instincts took a momentary pleasure in the thought . . .

Inspector Crome rose, taking the letter with him.

"The St Leger is a complication," he allowed. "It's unfortunate."

He went out. We heard a murmur of voices in the hallway. A minute later Thora Grey entered.

She said anxiously:

"The inspector told me there is another letter. Where this time?"

It was raining outside. Thora Grey was wearing a black coat and skirt and furs. A little black hat just perched on the side of her golden head.

It was to Franklin Clarke that she spoke and she came right up to him and, with a hand on his arm, waited for his answer.

"Doncaster—and on the day of the St Leger."

We settled down to a discussion. It went without saying that we all intended to be present, but the race-meeting undoubtedly complicated the plans we had made tentatively beforehand.

A feeling of discouragement swept over me. What could this little band of six people do, after all, however strong their personal interest in the matter might be? There would be innumerable police, keen-eyed and alert, watching all likely spots. What could six more pairs of eyes do?

As though in answer to my thought, Poirot raised his voice. He spoke rather like a schoolmaster or a priest.

"*Mes enfants,*" he said. "We must not disperse the strength. We must approach this matter with method and order in our thoughts. We must look within and not without for the truth. We must say to ourselves—each one of us—what do *I* know about the murderer? And so we must build up a composite picture of the man we are going to seek."

"We know nothing about him," sighed Thora Grey helplessly.

"No, no, mademoiselle. That is not true. Each one of us knows something about him—*If we only knew what it is we know. I am convinced that the knowledge is there* if we could only get at it."

Clarke shook his head.

"We don't know anything—whether he's old or young, fair or dark! None of us has ever seen him or spoken to him! We've gone over everything we all know again and again."

"Not everything! For instance, Miss Grey here told us that she did not see or speak to any stranger on the day that Sir Carmichael Clarke was murdered."

Thora Grey nodded.

"That's quite right."

"Is it? *Lady Clarke told us, mademoiselle, that from her window she saw you standing on the front doorstep talking to a man*."

"She saw *me* talking to a strange man?" The girl seemed genuinely astonished. Surely that pure, limpid look could not be anything but genuine.

She shook her head.

"Lady Clarke must have made a mistake. I never—Oh!"

The exclamation came suddenly—jerked out of her. A crimson wave flooded her cheeks.

"I remember now! How stupid! I'd forgotten all about it. But it wasn't important. Just one of those men who came round selling stockings—you know, ex-Army people. They're very persistent. I had to get rid of him. I was just crossing the hall when he came to the door. He spoke to me instead of ringing but he was quite a harmless sort of person. I suppose that's why I forgot about him."

Poirot was swaying to and fro, his hands clasped to his head. He was muttering to himself with such vehemence that nobody else said anything, but stared at him instead.

"Stockings," he was murmuring. "Stockings . . . stockings . . . stockings . . . *ça vient* . . . stockings . . . stockings . . . it is the *motif—yes* . . . three months ago . . . and the other day . . . and now. *Bon Dieu*, I have it!"

He sat upright and fixed me with an imperious eye.

"You remember, Hastings? Andover. The shop. We go upstairs. The bedroom. On a chair. *A pair of new silk stockings*. And now I know what it was that roused my attention two days ago. It was you, mademoiselle—" He turned on Megan. "You spoke of your mother who wept *because she had bought your sister some new stockings on the very day of the murder* . . ."

He looked round on us all.

"You see? *It is the same motif* three times repeated. That cannot be coincidence. When mademoiselle spoke I had the feeling that what she said linked up with something. I know now with what. The word spoken by Mrs Ascher's next-door neighbour, Mrs Fowler. About people who were always trying to *sell* you things—and she mentioned *stockings*. Tell me, mademoiselle, it is true, is it not, that your mother bought those stockings, not at a shop, but from someone who came to the door?"

"Yes—yes—she did . . . I remember now. She said something about being sorry for these wretched men who go round and try to get orders."

"But what's the connection?" cried Franklin. "That a man came selling stockings proves nothing!"

"I tell you, my friends, it *cannot* be coincidence. Three crimes—and every time a man selling stockings and spying out the land."

He wheeled round on Thora.

"*A vous la parole!* Describe this man."

She looked at him blankly.

"I can't . . . I don't know how . . He had glasses, I think . . . and a shabby overcoat . . ."

"*Mieux que ça mademoiselle*."

"He stooped . . . I don't know. I hardly looked at him. He wasn't the sort of man you'd notice . . ."

Poirot said gravely:

"You are quite right, mademoiselle. The whole secret of the murders lies there in your description of the murderer—for without a doubt he *was* the murderer! '*He wasn't the sort of man you'd notice.*' Yes—there is no doubt about it . . . You have described the murderer!"

CHAPTER 22
(Not from Captain Hastings' Personal Narrative)

Mr Alexander Bonaparte Cust sat very still. His breakfast lay cold and untasted on his plate. A newspaper was propped up against the teapot and it was this newspaper that Mr Cust was reading with avid interest.

Suddenly he got up, paced to and fro for a minute, then sank back into a chair by the window. He buried his head in his hands with a stifled groan.

He did not hear the sound of the opening door. His landlady, Mrs Marbury, stood in the doorway.

"I was wondering, Mr Cust, if you'd fancy a nice—why, whatever is it? Aren't you feeling well?"

Mr Cust raised his head from his hands.

"Nothing. It's nothing at all, Mrs Marbury. I'm not—feeling very well this morning."

Mrs Marbury inspected the breakfast tray.

"So I see. You haven't touched your breakfast. Is it your head troubling you again?"

"No. At least, yes . . . I—I just feel a bit out of sorts."

"Well, I'm sorry, I'm sure. You'll not be going away today, then?"

Mr Cust sprang up abruptly.

"No, no. I have to go. It's business. Important. Very important."

His hands were shaking. Seeing him so agitated, Mrs Marbury tried to soothe him.

"Well, if you must—you must. Going far this time?"

"No. I'm going to"—he hesitated for a minute or two—"Cheltenham."

There was something so peculiar about the tentative way he said the word that Mrs Marbury looked at him in surprise.

"Cheltenham's a nice place," she said conversationally. "I went there from Bristol one year. The shops are ever so nice."

"I suppose so—yes."

Mrs Marbury stooped rather stiffly—for stooping did not suit her figure—to pick up the paper that was lying crumpled on the floor.

"Nothing but this murdering business in the papers nowadays," she said as she glanced at the headlines before putting it back on the table. "Gives me the creeps, it does. I don't read it. It's like Jack the Ripper all over again."

Mr Cust's lips moved, but no sound came from them.

"Doncaster—that's the place he's going to do his next murder," said Mrs Marbury. "And tomorrow! Fairly makes your flesh creep, doesn't it? If I lived in Doncaster and my name began with a D, I'd take the first train away, that I would. I'd run no risks. What did you say, Mr Cust?"

"Nothing, Mrs Marbury—nothing."

"It's the races and all. No doubt he thinks he'll get his opportunity there. Hundreds of police, they say, they're drafting in and—Why, Mr Cust, you *do* look bad. Hadn't you better have a little drop of something? Really, now, you oughtn't to go travelling today."

Mr Cust drew himself up.

"It is necessary, Mrs Marbury. I have always been punctual in my—engagements. People must have—must have confidence in you! When I have undertaken to do a thing, I carry it through. It is the only way to get on in—in—business."

"But if you're ill?"

"I am not ill, Mrs Marbury. Just a little worried over—various personal matters. I slept badly. I am really quite all right."

His manner was so firm that Mrs Marbury gathered up the breakfast things and reluctantly left the room.

Mr Cust dragged out a suitcase from under the bed and began to pack. Pyjamas, sponge-bag, spare collar, leather slippers. Then unlocking a cupboard, he transferred a dozen or so flattish cardboard boxes about ten inches by seven from a shelf to the suitcase.

He just glanced at the railway guide on the table and then left the room, suitcase in hand.

Setting it down in the hall, he put on his hat and overcoat. As he did so he sighed deeply, so deeply that the girl who came out from a room at the side looked at him in concern.

"Anything the matter, Mr Cust?"

"Nothing, Miss Lily."

"You were sighing so!"

Mr Cust said abruptly:

"Are you at all subject to premonitions, Miss Lily? To presentiments?"

"Well, I don't know that I am, really . . . Of course, there are days when you just feel everything's going wrong, and days when you feel everything's going right."

"Quite," said Mr Cust.

He sighed again.

"Well, goodbye, Miss Lily. Goodbye. I'm sure you've been very kind to me always here."

"Well, don't say goodbye as though you were going away for ever," laughed Lily.

"No, no, of course not."

"See you Friday," laughed the girl. "Where are you going this time? Seaside again."

"No, no—er—Cheltenham."

"Well, that's nice, too. But not quite as nice as Torquay. That must have been lovely. I want to go there for my holiday next year. By the way, you must have been quite near where the murder was—the ABC murder. It happened while you were down there, didn't it?"

"Er—yes. But Churston's six or seven miles away."

"All the same, it must have been exciting! Why, you may have passed the murderer in the street! You may have been quite near to him!"

"Yes, I may, of course," said Mr Cust with such a ghastly and contorted smile that Lily Marbury noticed it.

"Oh, Mr Cust, you *don't* look well."

"I'm quite all right, quite all right. Goodbye, Miss Marbury."

He fumbled to raise his hat, caught up his suitcase and fairly hastened out of the front door.

"Funny old thing," said Lily Marbury indulgently. "Looks half batty to my mind."

Inspector Crome said to his subordinate:

"Get me out a list of all stocking manufacturing firms and circularize them. I want a list of all their agents—you know, fellows who sell on commission and tout for orders."

"This the ABC case, sir?"

"Yes. One of Mr Hercule Poirot's ideas." The inspector's tone was disdainful. "Probably nothing in it, but it doesn't do to neglect any chance, however faint."

"Right, sir. Mr Poirot's done some good stuff in his time, but I think he's a bit gaga now, sir."

"He's a mountebank," said Inspector Crome. "Always posing. Takes in some people. It doesn't take in *me*. Now then, about the arrangement for Doncaster . . ."

Tom Hartigan said to Lily Marbury:

"Saw your old dugout this morning."

"Who? Mr Cust?"

"Cust it was. At Euston. Looking like a lost hen, as usual. I think the fellow's half loony. He needs someone to look after him. First he dropped his paper and then he dropped his ticket. I picked that up—he hadn't the faintest idea he'd lost it. Thanked me in an agitated sort of manner, but I don't think he recognized me."

"Oh, well," said Lily. "He's only seen you passing in the hall, and not very often at that."

They danced once round the floor.

"You dance something beautiful," said Tom.

"Go on," said Lily and wriggled yet a little closer.

They danced round again.

"Did you say Euston or Paddington?" asked Lily abruptly. Where you saw old Cust, I mean?"

"Euston."

"Are you sure?"

"Of course I'm sure. What do you think?"

"Funny. I thought you went to Cheltenham from Paddington."

"So you do. But old Cust wasn't going to Cheltenham. He was going to Doncaster."

"Cheltenham."

"Doncaster. I know, my girl! After all, I picked up his ticket, didn't I?"

"Well, he told *me* he was going to Cheltenham. I'm sure he did."

"Oh, you've got it wrong. He was going to Doncaster all right. Some people have all the luck. I've got a bit on Firefly for the Leger and I'd love to see it run."

"I shouldn't think Mr Cust went to race-meetings, he doesn't look the kind.

Oh, Tom, I hope he won't get murdered. It's Doncaster the ABC murder's going to be."

"Cust'll be all right. His name doesn't begin with a D."

"He might have been murdered last time. He was down near Churston at Torquay when the last murder happened."

"Was he? That's a bit of a coincidence, isn't it?"

He laughed.

"He wasn't at Bexhill the time before, was he?"

Lily crinkled her brows.

"He was away . . . Yes, I remember he was away . . . because he forgot his bathing-dress. Mother was mending it for him. And she said: 'There—Mr Cust went away yesterday without his bathing-dress after all,' and I said: 'Oh, never mind the old bathing-dress—there's been the most awful murder,' I said, 'a girl strangled at Bexhill.'"

"Well, if he wanted his bathing-dress, he must have been going to the seaside, I say, Lily"—his face crinkled up with amusement. "What price your old dugout being the murderer himself?"

"Poor Mr Cust? He wouldn't hurt a fly," laughed Lily.

They danced on happily—in their conscious minds nothing but the pleasure of being together.

In their unconscious minds something stirred . . .

CHAPTER 23
September 11th, Doncaster

Doncaster!

I shall, I think, remember that 11th of September all my life.

Indeed, whenever I see a mention of the St Leger my mind flies automatically not to horse-racing but to murder.

When I recall my own sensations, the thing that stands out most is a sickening sense of insufficiency. We were here—on the spot—Poirot, myself, Clarke, Fraser, Megan Barnard, Thora Grey and Mary Drower, and in the last resort *what could any of us do?*

We were building on a forlorn hope—on the chance of recognizing amongst a crowd of thousands of people a face or figure imperfectly seen on an occasion one, two or three months back.

The odds were in reality greater than that. Of us all, the only person likely to make such a recognition was Thora Grey.

Some of her serenity had broken down under the strain. Her calm, efficient manner was gone. She sat twisting her hands togehter, almost weeping, appealing incoherently to Poirot.

"I never really looked at him . . . Why didn't I? What a fool I was. You're depending on me, all of you . . . and I shall let you down. Because even if I did see him again I mightn't recognize him. I've got a bad memory for faces."

Poirot, whatever he might say to me, and however harshly he might seem to criticize the girl, showed nothing but kindness now. His manner was tender in the extreme. It struck me that Poirot was no more indifferent to beauty in distress than I was.

He patted her shoulder kindly.

"Now then, *petite*, not the hysteria. We cannot have that. If you should see this man you would recognize him."

"How do you know?"

"Oh, a great many reasons—for one, because the red succeeds the black."

"What do you mean, Poirot?" I cried.

"I speak the language of the tables. At roulette there may be a long run on the black—but in the end *red must turn up*. It is the mathematical laws of chance."

"You mean that luck turns?"

"Exactly, Hastings. And that is where the gambler (and the murderer, who is, after all, only a supreme kind of gambler since what he risks is not his money but his life) often lacks intelligent anticipation. Because he *has* won he thinks he will *continue* to win! He does not leave the tables in good time with his pocket full. So in crime the murderer who is successful *cannot conceive the possibility of not being successful!* He takes to *himself* all the credit for a successful performance—but I tell you, my friends, however carefully planned, no crime can be successful without luck!"

"Isn't that going rather far?" demurred Franklin Clarke.

Poirot waved his hands excitedly.

"No, no. It is an even chance, if you like, but it *must* be in your favour. Consider! It might have happened that someone enters Mrs Ascher's shop just as the murderer is leaving. That person might have thought of looking behind the counter, have seen the dead woman—and either laid hands on the murderer straight away or else been able to give such an accurate description of him to the police that he would have been arrested forthwith."

"Yes, of course, that's possible," admitted Clarke. "What it comes to is that a murderer's got to take a chance."

"Precisely. A murderer is always a gambler. And, like many gamblers, a murderer often does not know when to stop. With each crime his opinion of his own abilities is strengthened. His sense of proportion is warped. He does not say 'I have been clever *and lucky!*' No, he says only 'I have been clever!' And his opinion of his cleverness grows and then, *mes amis*, the ball spins, and the run of colour is over—it drops into a new number and the croupier calls out '*Rouge*'."

"You think that will happen in this case?" asked Megan, drawing her brows together in a frown.

"It *must* happen sooner or later! So far *the luck has been with the criminal*—sooner or later it must turn and be with us. I believe that it *has* turned! The clue of the stockings is the beginning. Now, instead of everything going *right* for him, everything will go *wrong* for him! And he, too, will begin to make mistakes . . ."

"I will say you're heartening," said Franklin Clarke. "We all need a bit of comfort. I've had a paralysing feeling of helplessness ever since I woke up."

"It seems to me highly problematical that we can accomplish anything of practical value," said Donald Fraser.

Megan rapped out:

"Don't be a defeatist, Don."

Mary Drower, flushing up a little, said:

"What I say is, you never know. That wicked fiend's in this place, and so are we—and after all, you do run up against people in the funniest way sometimes."

I fumed:

"If only we could do something more."

"You must remember, Hastings, that the police are doing everything reasonably possible. Special constables have been enrolled. The good Inspector Crome may have the irritating manner, but he is a very able police officer, and Colonel Anderson, the Chief Constable, is a man of action. They have taken the fullest measures for watching and patrolling the town and the racecourse. There will be plain-clothes men everywhere. There is also the press campaign. The public is fully warned."

Donald Fraser shook his head.

"He'll never attempt it, I'm thinking," he said more hopefully. "The man would just be mad!"

"Unfortunately," said Clarke dryly, "he is mad! What do you think, M. Poirot? Will he give it up or will he try to carry it through?"

"In my opinion the strength of his obsession is such that he *must* attempt to carry out his promise! Not to do so would be to admit failure, and that his insane egoism would never allow. That, I may say, is also Dr Thompson's opinion. Our hope is that he may be caught in the attempt."

Donald shook his head again.

"He'll be very cunning."

Poirot glanced at his watch. We took the hint. It had been agreed that we were to make an all-day session of it, patrolling as many streets as possible in the morning, and later, stationing ourselves at various likely points on the racecourse.

I say "we". Of course, in my own case such a patrol was of little avail since I was never likely to have set eyes on ABC. However, as the idea was to separate so as to cover as wide an area as possible I had suggested that I should act as escort to one of the ladies.

Poirot had agreed—I am afraid with somewhat of a twinkle in his eye.

The girls went off to get their hats on. Donald Fraser was standing by the window looking out, apparently lost in thought.

Franklin Clarke glanced over at him, then evidently deciding that the other was too abstracted to count as a listener, he lowered his voice a little and addressed Poirot.

"Look here, M. Poirot. You went down to Churston, I know, and saw my sister-in-law. Did she say—or hint—I mean—did she suggest at all—?"

He stopped, embarrassed.

Poirot answered with a face of blank innocence that aroused my strongest suspicions.

"*Comment?* Did your sister-in-law say, hint, or suggest—what?"

Franklin Clarke got rather red.

"Perhaps you think this isn't a time for butting in with personal things—"

"*Du tout!*"

"But I feel I'd like to get things quite straight."

"An admirable course."

This time I think Clarke began to suspect Poirot's bland face of concealing some inner amusement. He ploughed on rather heavily.

"My sister-in-law's an awfully nice woman—I've been very fond of her always—but of course, she's been ill some time—and in that kind of illness—being given drugs and all that—one tends to—well, to *fancy* things about people!"

"Ah?"

By now there was no mistaking the twinkle in Poirot's eye.

But Franklin Clarke, absorbed in his diplomatic task, was past noticing it.

"It's about Thora—Miss Grey," he said.

"Oh, it is of Miss Grey you speak?" Poirot's tone held innocent surprise.

"Yes. Lady Clarke got certain ideas in her head. You see, Thora—Miss Grey is well, rather a good-looking girl—"

"Perhaps—yes," conceded Poirot.

"And women, even the best of them, are a bit catty about other women. Of course, Thora was invaluable to my brother—he always said she was the best secretary he ever had—and he was very fond of her, too. But it was all perfectly straight and above-board. I mean, Thora isn't the sort of girl—"

"No?" said Poirot helpfully.

"But my sister-in-law got it into her head to be—well—jealous, I suppose. Not that she ever showed anything. But after Car's death, when there was a question of Miss Grey staying on—well, Charlotte cut up rough. Of course, it's partly the illness and the morphia and all that—Nurse Capstick says so—she says we mustn't blame Charlotte for getting these ideas into her head—"

He paused.

"Yes?"

"What I want you to understand, M. Poirot, is that there isn't anything in it at all. It's just a sick woman's imaginings. Look here"—he fumbled in his pocket—"here's a letter I received from my brother when I was in the Malay States. I'd like you to read it because it shows exactly what terms they were on."

Poirot took it. Franklin came over beside him and with a pointing finger read some of the extracts loud.

> "—things go on here much as usual. Charlotte is moderately free from pain. I wish one could say more. You may remember Thora Grey? She is a dear girl and a greater comfort to me than I can tell you. I should not have known what to do through this bad time but for her. Her sympathy and interest are unfailing. She has an exquisite taste and flair for beautiful things and shares my passion for Chinese art. I was indeed lucky to find her. No daughter could be a closer or more sympathetic companion. Her life had been a difficult and not always a happy one, but I am glad to feel that here she has a home and true affection.

"You see," said Franklin, "*that's* how my brother felt to her. He thought of her like a daughter. What I feel so unfair is the fact that the moment my brother is dead, his wife practically turns her out of the house! Women really are devils, M. Poirot."

"Your sister-in-law is ill and in pain, remember."

"I know. That's what I keep saying to myself. One mustn't judge her. All the same, I thought I'd show you this. I don't want you to get a false impression of Thora from anything Lady Clarke may have said."

Poirot returned the letter.

"I can assure you," he said, smiling, "that I never permit myself to get false impressions from anything anyone tells me. I form my own judgements."

"Well," said Clarke, stowing away the letter. "I'm glad I showed it to you anyway. Here come the girls. We'd better be off."

As we left the room, Poirot called me back.

"You are determined to accompany the expedition, Hastings?"

"Oh, yes. I shouldn't be happy staying here inactive."

"There is activity of mind as well as body, Hastings."

"Well, you're better at it than I am," I said.

"You are incontestably right, Hastings. Am I correct in supposing that you intend to be a cavalier to one of the ladies?"

"That was the idea."

"And which lady did you propose to honour with your company?"

"Well—I—er—hadn't considered yet."

"What about Miss Barnard?"

"She's rather the independent type," I demurred.

"Miss Grey?"

"Yes. She's better."

"I find you, Hastings, singularly though transparently dishonest! All along you had made up your mind to spend the day with your blonde angel!"

"Oh, really, Poirot!"

"I am sorry to upset your plans, but I must request you to give your escort elsewhere."

"Oh, all right. I think you've got a weakness for that Dutch doll of a girl."

"The person you are to escort is Mary Drower—and I must request you not to leave her."

"But, Poirot, why?"

"Because, my dear friend, her name begins with a D. We must take no chances."

I saw the justice of his remark. At first it seemed far-fetched. But then I realized that if ABC had a fanatical hatred of Poirot, he might very well be keeping himself informed of Poirot's movements. And in that case the elimination of Mary Drower might strike him as a very pat fourth stroke.

I promised to be faithful to my trust.

I went out leaving Poirot sitting in a chair near the window.

In front of him was a little roulette wheel. He spun it as I went out of the door and called after me:

"*Rouge*—that is a good omen, Hastings. The luck, it turns!"

CHAPTER 24

(Not from Captain Hastings' Personal Narrative)

Below his breath Mr Leadbetter uttered a grunt of impatience as his next-door neighbour got up and stumbled clumsily past him, dropping his hat over the seat in front, and leaning over to retrieve it.

All this at the culminating moment of *Not a Sparrow,* that all-star, thrilling drama of pathos and beauty that Mr Leadbetter had been looking forward to seeing for a whole week.

The golden-haired heroine, played by Katherine Royal (in Mr Leadbetter's opinion the leading film actress in the world), was just giving vent to a hoarse cry of indignation:

"Never. I would sooner starve. But I shan't starve. Remember those words: *not a sparrow falls*—"

Mr Leadbetter moved his head irritably from right to left. People! Why on earth people couldn't wait till the *end* of a film . . . And to leave at this soul-stirring moment.

Ah, that was better. The annoying gentleman had passed on and out. Mr Leadbetter had a full view of the screen and of Katherine Royal standing by the window in the Van Schreiner Mansion in New York.

And now she was boarding the train—the child in her arms . . . What curious trains they had in America—not at all like English trains.

Ah, there was Steve again in his shack in the mountains . . .

The film pursued its course to its emotional and semi-religious end.

Mr Leadbetter breathed a sigh of satisfaction as the lights went up.

He rose slowly to his feet, blinking a little.

He never left the cinema very quickly. It always took him a moment or two to return to the prosaic reality of everyday life.

He glanced round. Not many people this afternoon—naturally. They were all at the races. Mr Leadbetter did not approve of racing nor of playing cards nor of drinking nor of smoking. This left him more energy to enjoy going to the pictures.

Everyone was hurrying towards the exit. Mr Leadbetter prepared to follow suit. The man in the seat in front of him was asleep—slumped down in his chair. Mr Leadbetter felt indignant to think that anyone could sleep with such a drama as *Not a Sparrow* going on.

An irate gentleman was saying to the sleeping man whose legs were stretched out blocking the way:

"Excuse *me*, sir."

Mr Leadbetter reached the exit. He looked back.

There seemed to be some sort of commotion. A commissionaire . . . a little knot of people . . . Perhaps that man in front of him was dead drunk and not asleep . . .

He hesitated and then passed out—and in so doing missed the sensation of the day—a greater sensation even than Not Half winning the St Leger at 85 to 1.

The commissionaire was saying:

"Believe you're right, sir . . . He's ill . . . Why—what's the matter, sir?"

The other had drawn away his hand with an exclamation and was examining a red sticky smear.

"Blood . . ."

The commissionaire gave a stifled exclamation.

He had caught sight of the corner of something yellow projecting from under the seat.

"Gor blimey!" he said. *"It's ab—ABC."*

CHAPTER 25
(Not from Captain Hastings' Personal Narrative)

Mr Cust came out of the Regal Cinema and looked up at the sky.

A beautiful evening . . . A really beautiful evening . . .

A quotation from Browning came into his head.

"God's in His heaven. All's right with the world."

He had always been fond of that quotation.

Only there were times, very often, when he had felt it wasn't true . . .

He trotted along the street smiling to himself until he came to the Black Swan where he was staying.

He climbed the stairs to his bedroom, a stuffy little room on the second floor, giving over a paved inner court and garage.

As he entered the room his smile faded suddenly. There was a stain on his sleeve near the cuff. He touched it tentatively—wet and red—blood . . .

His hand dipped into his pocket and brought out something—a long slender knife. The blade of that, too, was sticky and red . . .

Mr Cust sat there a long time.

Once his eyes shot round the room like those of a hunted animal.

His tongue passed feverishly over his lips . . .

"It isn't my fault," said Mr Cust.

He sounded as though he were arguing with somebody—a schoolboy pleading to his headmaster.

He passed his tongue over his lips again . . .

Again, tentatively, he felt his coat sleeve.

His eyes crossed the room to the wash-basin.

A minute later he was pouring out water from the old-fashioned jug into the basin. Removing his coat, he rinsed the sleeve, carefully squeezing it out . . .

Ugh! The water was red now . . .

A tap on the door.

He stood there frozen into immobility—staring.

The door opened. A plump young woman—jug in hand.

"Oh, excuse me, sir. Your hot water, sir."

He managed to speak then.

"Thank you . . . I've washed in cold . . ."

Why had he said that? Immediately her eyes went to the basin.

He said frenziedly: "I—I've cut my hand . . ."

There was a pause—yes, surely a very long pause—before she said: "Yes, sir."

She went out, shutting the door.

Mr Cust stood as though turned to stone.

He listened.

It had come—at last . . .

Were there voices—exclamations—feet mounting the stairs?

He could hear nothing but the beating of his own heart . . .

Then, suddenly, from frozen immobility he leaped into activity.

He slipped on his coat, tiptoed to the door and opened it. No noises as yet except the familiar murmur arising from the bar. He crept down the stairs . . .

Still no one. That was luck. He paused at the foot of the stairs. Which way now?

He made up his mind, darted quickly along a passage and out by the door that gave into the yard. A couple of chauffeurs were there tinkering with cars and discussing winners and losers.

Mr Cust hurried across the yard and out into the street.

Round the first corner to the right—then to the left—right again . . .

Dare he risk the station?

Yes—there would be crowds there—special trains—if luck were on his side he would do it all right . . .

If only luck were with him . . .

CHAPTER 26
(Not from Captain Hastings' Personal Narrative)

Inspector Crome was listening to the excited utterances of Mr Leadbetter.

"I assure you, inspector, my heart misses a beat when I think of it. He must actually have been sitting beside me all through the programme!"

Inspector Crome, completely indifferent to the behaviour of Mr Leadbetter's heart, said:

"Just let me have it quite clear? This man went out towards the close of the big picture—"

"*Not a Sparrow*—Katherine Royal," murmured Mr Leadbetter automatically.

"He passed you and in doing so stumbled—"

"He *pretended* to stumble, I see it now. Then he leaned over the seat in front to pick up his hat. He must have stabbed the poor fellow then."

"You didn't hear anything? A cry? Or a groan?"

Mr Leadbetter had heard nothing but the loud, hoarse accents of Katherine Royal, but in the vividness of his imagination he invented a groan.

Inspector Crome took the groan at its face value and bade him proceed.

"And then he went out—"

"Can you describe him?"

"He was a very big man. Six foot at least. A giant."

"Fair or dark?"

"I—well—I'm not exactly sure. I think he was bald. A sinister-looking fellow."

"He didn't limp, did he?" asked Inspector Crome.

"Yes—yes, now you come to speak of it I think he did limp. Very dark, he might have been some kind of half-caste."

"Was he in his seat the last time the lights came up?"

"No. He came in after the big picture began."

Inspector Crome nodded, handed Mr Leadbetter a statement to sign and got rid of him.

"That's about as bad a witness as you'll find," he remarked pessimistically. "He'd say anything with a little leading. It's perfectly clear that he hasn't the faintest idea what our man looks like. Let's have the commissionaire back."

The commissionaire, very stiff and military, came in and stood to attention, his eyes fixed on Colonel Anderson.

"Now, then, Jameson, let's hear your story."

Jameson saluted.

"Yessir. Close of the performance, sir. I was told there was a gentleman taken ill, sir. Gentleman was in the two and fourpennies, slumped down in his seat like. Other gentlemen standing around. Gentleman looked bad to me, sir. One of the gentlemen standing by put his hand to the ill gentleman's coat and drew my attention. Blood sir. It was clear the gentleman was dead—stabbed, sir. My attention was drawn to an ABC railway guide, sir, under the seat. Wishing to act correctly, I did not touch same, but reported to the police immediately that a tragedy had occurred."

"Very good. Jameson, you acted very properly."

"Thank you, sir."

"Did you notice a man leaving the two and fourpennies about five minutes earlier?"

"There were several, sir."

"Could you describe them?"

"Afraid not, sir. One was Mr Geoffrey Parnell. And there was a young fellow, Sam Baker, with his young lady. I didn't notice anybody else particular."

"A pity. That'll do, Jameson."

"Yessir."

The commissionaire saluted and departed.

"The medical details we've got," said Colonel Anderson. "We'd better have the fellow that found him next."

A police constable came in and saluted.

"Mr Hercule Poirot's here, sir, and another gentleman."

Inspector Crome frowned.

"Oh, well," he said. "Better have 'em in, I suppose."

CHAPTER 27

The Doncaster Murder

Coming in hard on Poirot's heels, I just caught the fag end of Inspector Crome's remark.

Both he and the Chief Constable were looking worried and depressed.

Colonel Anderson greeted us with a nod of the head.

"Glad you've come, M. Poirot," he said politely. I think he guessed that Crome's remark might have reached our ears. "We've got it in the neck again, you see."

"Another ABC murder?"

"Yes. Damned audacious bit of work. Man leaned over and stabbed the fellow in the back."

"Stabbed this time?"

"Yes, varies his methods a bit, doesn't he? Biff on the head, strangled, now a knife. Versatile devil—what? Here are the medical details if you care to see 'em."

He shoved a paper towards Poirot.

"ABC down on the floor between the dead man's feet," he added.

"Has the dead man been identified?" asked Poirot.

"Yes. ABC's slipped up for once—if that's any satisfaction to us. Deceased's a man called Earlsfield—George Earlsfield. Barber by profession."

"Curious," commented Poirot.

"May have skipped a ltter," suggested the Colonel.

My friend shook his head doubtfully.

"Shall we have in the next witness?" asked Crome. "He's anxious to get home."

"Yes, yes,—let's get on."

A middle-aged gentleman strongly resembling the frog footman in *Alice in Wonderland* was led in. He was highly excited and his voice was shrill with emotion.

"Most shocking experience I have ever known," he squeaked. "I have a weak heart, sir—a very weak heart, it might have been the death of me."

"Your name, please," said the inspector.

"Downes. Roger Emmanuel Downes."

"Profession?"

"I am a master at Highfield School for boys."

"Now, Mr Downes, will you tell us in your own words what happened."

"I can tell you that very shortly, gentlemen. At the close of the performance I rose from my seat. The seat on my left was empty but in the one beyond a man was sitting, apparently asleep. I was unable to pass him to get out as his legs were stuck out in front of him. I asked him to allow me to pass. As he did not move I repeated my request in—a—er—slightly louder tone. He still made no response. I then took him by the shoulder to waken him. His body slumped down further and I became aware that he was either unconscious or seriously ill. I called out: 'This gentleman is taken ill. Fetch the commissionaire.' The commissionaire came. As I took my hand from the man's shoulder I found it was wet and red . . . I realized that the man had been stabbed. At the same moment the commissionaire noticed the ABC railway guide . . . I can assure you, gentlemen, the shock was terrific! Anything might have happened! For years I have suffered from cardiac weakness—"

Colonel Anderson was looking at Mr Downes with a very curious expression.

"You can consider that you're a lucky man, Mr Downes."

"I do, sir. Not even a palpitation!"

"You don't quite take my meaning, Mr Downes. You were sitting two seats away, you say?"

"Actually I was sitting at first in the next seat to the murdered man—then I moved along so as to be behind an empty seat."

"You're about the same height and build as the dead man, aren't you, and you were wearing a woollen scarf round your neck just as he was?"

"I fail to see—" began Mr Downes stiffly.

"I'm telling you, man," said Colonel Anderson, "just where your luck came in. Somehow or other, when the murderer followed you in, he got confused. *He picked on the wrong back*. I'll eat my hat, Mr Downes, if that knife wasn't meant for you!"

However well Mr Downes' heart had stood former tests, it was unable to stand up to this one. He sank on a chair, gasped, and turned purple in the face.

"Water," he gasped. "Water . . ."

A glass was brought him. He sipped it whilst his complexion gradually returned to the normal.

"Me?" he said. "Why me?"

"It looks like it," said Crome. "In fact, it's the only explanation."

"You mean that this man—this—this fiend incarnate—this bloodthirsty madman has been following *me* about waiting for an opportunity?"

"I should say that was the way of it."

"But in heaven's name, why *me?*" demanded the outraged schoolmaster.

Inspector Crome struggled with the temptation to reply:

"Why not?" and said instead: "I'm afraid it's no good expecting a lunatic to have reasons for what he does."

"God bless my soul," said Mr Downes, sobered into whispering.

He got up. He looked suddenly old and shaken.

"If you don't want me any more, gentlemen, I think I'll go home. I—I don't feel very well."

"That's quite all right, Mr Downes. I'll send a constable with you—just to see you're all right."

"Oh, no—no, thank you. That's not necessary."

"Might as well," said Colonel Anderson gruffly.

His eyes slid sideways, asking an imperceptible question of the inspector. The latter gave an equally imperceptible nod.

Mr Downes went out shakily.

"Just as well he didn't tumble to it," said Colonel Anderson. "There'll be a couple of them—eh?"

"Yes, sir. Your Inspector Rice has made arrangements. The house will be watched."

"You think," said Poirot, "that when ABC finds out his mistake he might try again?"

Anderson nodded.

"It's a possibility," he said. "Seems a methodical sort of chap, ABC. It will upset him if things don't go according to programme."

Poirot nodded thoughtfully.

"Wish we could get a description of the fellow," said Colonel Anderson irritably. "We're as much in the dark as ever."

"It may come," said Poirot.

"Think so? Well, it's possible. Damn it all, hasn't any one got eyes in their head?"

"Have patience," said Poirot.

"You seem very confident, M. Poirot. Got any reason for this optimism?"

"Yes, Colonel Anderson. Up to now, the murderer has not made a mistake. He is bound to make one soon."

"If that's all you've got to go on," began the Chief Constable with a snort, but he was interrupted.

"Mr Ball of the Black Swan is here with a young woman, sir. He reckons he's got summat to say might help you."

"Bring them along. Bring them along. We can do with anything helpful."

Mr Ball of the Black Swan was a large, slow-thinking, heavily-moving man. He exhaled a strong odour of beer. With him was a plump young woman with round eyes clearly in a state of high excitement.

"Hope I'm not intruding or wasting valuable time," said Mr Ball in a slow, thick voice. "But this wench, Mary here, reckons she's got something to tell as you ought to know."

Mary giggled in a half-hearted way.

"Well, my girl, what is it?" said Anderson. "What's your name?"

"Mary, sir, Mary Stroud."

"Well, Mary, out with it."

Mary turned her round eyes on her master.

"It's her business to take up hot water to the gents' bedrooms," said Mr Ball, coming to the rescue. "About half a dozen gentlemen we'd got staying. Some for the races and some just commercials."

"Yes, yes," said Anderson impatiently.

"Get on, lass," said Mr Ball. "Tell your tale. Nowt to be afraid of."

Mary gasped, groaned and plunged in a breathless voice into her narrative.

"I knocked on door and there wasn't no answer, otherwise I wouldn't have gone in leastways not unless the gentleman had said 'Come in,' and as he didn't say nothing I went in and he was there washing his hands."

She paused and breathed deeply.

"Go on, my girl," said Anderson.

Mary looked sideways at her master and as though receiving inspiration from his slow nod, plunged on again.

"'It's your hot water, sir,' I said, 'and I did knock,' but 'Oh,' he says, 'I've washed in cold,' he said, and so, naturally, I looks in basin, and oh! God help me, sir, *it were all red!*"

"Red?" said Anderson sharply.

Ball struck in.

"The lass told me that he had his coat off and that he was holding the sleeve of it, and it was all wet—that's right, eh, lass?"

"Yes, sir, that's right, sir."

She plunged on:

"And his face, sir, it looked queer, mortal queer it looked. Gave me quite a turn."

"When was this?" asked Anderson sharply.

"About a quarter after five, so near as I can reckon."

"Over three hours ago," snapped Anderson. "Why didn't you come at once?"

"Didn't hear about it at once," said Ball. "Not till news came along as there'd been another murder done. And then the lass she screams out as it might have been blood in the basin, and I asks her what she means, and she tells me. Well, it doesn't sound right to me and I went upstairs myself. Nobody in the room. I asks a few questions and one of the lads in the courtyard says he saw a fellow sneaking out that way and by his description it was the right one. So I says to the missus as Mary here had best go to police. She doesn't like the idea, Mary doesn't, and I says I'll come along with her."

Inspector Crome drew a sheet of paper towards him.

"Describe this man," he said. "As quick as you can. There's no time to be lost."

"Medium-sized he were," said Mary. "And stooped and wore glasses."

"His clothes?"

"A dark suit and a Homburg hat. Rather shabby looking."

She could add little to this description.

Inspector Crome did not insist unduly. The telephone wires were soon busy, but neither the inspector nor the Chief Constable were over optimistic.

Crome elicited the fact that the man, when seen sneaking across the yard, had had no bag or suitcase.

"There's a chance there," he said.

Two men were despatched to the Black Swan.

Mr Ball, swelling with pride and importance, and Mary, somewhat tearful, accompanied them.

The sergeant returned about ten minutes later.

"I've brought the register, sir," he said. "Here's the signature."

We crowded round. The writing was small and cramped—not easy to read.

"A. B. Case—or is it Cash?" said the Chief Constable.

"ABC," said Crome significantly.

"What about luggage?" asked Anderson.

"One good-sized suitcase, sir, full of small cardboard boxes."

"Boxes? What was in 'em?"

"Stockings, sir. Silk stockings."

Crome turned to Poirot.

"Congratulations," he said. "Your hunch was right."

CHAPTER 28
(Not from Captain Hastings' Personal Narrative)

Inspector Crome was in his office at Scotland Yard.

The telephone on his desk gave a discreet buzz and he picked it up.

"Jacobs speaking, sir. There's a young fellow come in with a story that I think you ought to hear."

Inspector Crome sighed. On an average twenty people a day turned up with so-called important information about the ABC case. Some of them were harmless lunatics, some of them were well-meaning persons who genuinely believed that their information was of value. It was the duty of Sergeant Jacobs to act as a human sieve—retaining the grosser matter and passing on the residue to his superior.

"Very well, Jacobs," said Crome. "Send him along."

A few minutes later there was a tap on the inspector's door and Sergeant Jacobs appeared, ushering in a tall, moderately good-looking young man.

"This is Mr Tom Hartigan, sir. He's got something to tell us which may have a possible bearing on the ABC case."

The inspector rose pleasantly and shook hands.

"Good-morning, Mr Hartigan. Sit down, won't you? Smoke? Have a cigarette?"

Tom Hartigan sat down awkwardly and looked with some awe at what he called in his own mind "One of the big-wigs." The appearance of the inspector vaguely disappointed him. He looked quite an ordinary person!

"Now then," said Crome. "You've got something to tell us that you think may have a bearing on the case. Fire ahead."

Tom began nervously.

"Of course it may be nothing at all. It's just an idea of mine. I may be wasting your time."

Again Inspector Crome sighed imperceptibly. The amount of time he had to waste in reassuring people!

"We're the best judge of that. Let's have the facts, Mr Hartigan."

"Well, it's like this, sir. I've got a young lady, you see, and her mother lets rooms. Up Camden Town way. Their second floor back has been let for over a year to a man called Cust."

"Cust—eh?"

"That's right, sir. A sort of middle-aged bloke what's rather vague and soft—and come down in the world a bit, I should say. Sort of creature who wouldn't hurt a fly you'd say—and I'd never of dreamed of anything being wrong if it hadn't been for something rather odd."

In a somewhat confused manner and repeating himself once or twice, Tom described his encounter with Mr Cust at Euston Station and the incident of the dropped ticket.

"You see, sir, look at it how you will, it's funny like. Lily—that's my young lady, sir—she was quite positive that it was Cheltenham he said, and her mother says the same—says she remembers distinct talking about it the morning he went off. Of course, I didn't pay much attention to it at the time. Lily—my young lady—said as how she hoped he wouldn't cop it from this ABC fellow going to Doncaster—and then she says it's rather a coincidence because he was down Churston way at the time of the last crime. Laughing like, I asks her whether he was at Bexhill the time before, and she says she don't know where he was, but he was away at the seaside—that she does know. And then I said to her it would be odd if he was the ABC himself and she said poor Mr Cust wouldn't hurt a fly—and that was all at the time. We didn't think no more about it. At least, in a sort of a way I did, sir, underneath like. I began wondering about this Cust fellow and thinking that, after all, harmless as he seemed, he might be a bit batty."

Tom took a breath and then went on. Inspector Crome was listening intently now.

"And then after the Doncaster murder, sir, it was in all the papers that information was wanted as to the whereabouts of a certain A. B. Case or Cash, and it gave a description that fitted well enough. First evening off I had, I went round to Lily's and asked her what her Mr Cust's initials were. She couldn't remember at first, but her mother did. Said they were A. B. right enough. Then we got down to it and tried to figure out if Cust had been away at the time of the first murder at Andover. Well, as you know, sir, it isn't too easy to remember things three months back. We had a job of it, but we got it fixed down in the end, because Mrs Marbury had a brother come from Canada to see her on June 21st. He arrived unexpected like and she wanted to give him a bed, and Lily suggested that as Mr Cust was away Bert Smith might have his bed. But Mrs Marbury wouldn't agree, because she said it wasn't acting right by her lodger, and she always liked to act fair and square. But we fixed the date all right because of Bert Smith's ship docking at Southampton that day."

Inspector Crome had listened very attentively, jotting down an occasional note.

"That's all?" he asked.

"That's all, sir. I hope you don't think I'm making a lot of nothing."

Tom flushed slightly.

"Not at all. You were quite right to come here. Of course, it's very slight evidence—these dates may be mere coincidence and the likeness of the name, too.

But it certainly warrants my having an interview with your Mr Cust. Is he at home now?"

"Yes, sir."

"When did he return?"

"The evening of the Doncaster murder, sir."

"What's he been doing since?"

"He's stayed in mostly, sir. And he's been looking very queer, Mrs Marbury says. He buys a lot of newspapers—goes out early and gets the morning ones, and then after dark he goes out and gets the evening ones. Mrs Marbury says he talks a lot to himself, too. She thinks he's getting queerer."

"What is this Mrs Marbury's address?"

Tom gave it to him.

"Thank you. I shall probably be calling round in the course of the day. I need hardly tell you to be careful of your manner if you come across this Cust."

He rose and shook hands.

"You may be quite satisfied you did the right thing in coming to us. Good-morning, Mr Hartigan."

"Well, sir?" asked Jacobs, re-entering the room a few minutes later. "Think it's the goods?"

"It's promising," said Inspector Crome. "That is, if the facts are as the boy stated them. We've had no luck with the stocking manufacturers yet. It was time we got hold of something. By the way, give me that file of the Churston case."

He spent some minutes looking for what he wanted.

"Ah, here it is. It's amongst the statements made to the Torquay police. Young man of the name of Hill. Deposes he was leaving the Torquay Palladium after the film *Not a Sparrow* and noticed a man behaving queerly. He was talking to himself. Hill heard him say 'That's an idea.' *Not a Sparrow*—that's the film that was on at the Regal in Doncaster?"

"Yes, sir."

"There may be something in that. Nothing to it at the time—but it's possible that the idea of the *modus operandi* for his next crime occurred to our man then. We've got Hill's name and address, I see. His description of the man is vague but it links up well enough with the descriptions of Mary Stroud and this Tom Hartigan . . ."

He nodded thoughtfully.

"We're getting warm," said Inspector Crome—rather inaccurately, for he himself was always slightly chilly.

"Any instructions, sir?"

"Put on a couple of men to watch this Camden Town address, but I don't want our bird frightened. I must have a word with the A.C. Then I think it would be as well if Cust was brought along here and asked if he'd like to make a statement. It sounds as though he's quite ready to get rattled."

Outside Tom Hartigan had rejoined Lily Marbury who was waiting for him on the Embankment.

"All right, Tom?"

Tom nodded.

"I saw Inspector Crome himself. The one who's in charge of the case."

"What's he like?"

"A bit quiet and ladida—not my idea of a detective."

"That's Lord Trenchard's new kind," said Lily with respect. "Some of them are ever so grand. Well, what did he say?"

Tom gave her a brief résumé of the interview.

"So they think as it really was him?"

"They think it might be. Anyway, they'll come along and ask him a question or two."

"Poor Mr Cust."

"It's no good saying poor Mr Cust, my girl. If he's ABC, he's committed four terrible murders."

Lily sighed and shook her head.

"It does seem awful," she observed.

"Well, now you're going to come and have a bite of lunch, my girl. Just you think that if we're right I expect my name will be in the papers!"

"Oh, Tom, will it?"

"Rather. And yours, too. *And* your mother's. And I dare say you'll have your picture in it, too."

"Oh, Tom." Lily squeezed his arm in an ecstasy.

"And in the meantime what do you say to a bite at the Corner House?"

Lily squeezed tighter.

"Come on then!"

"All right—half a minute. I must just telephone from the station."

"Who to?"

"A girl I was going to meet."

She slipped across the road, and rejoined him three minutes later, looking rather flushed.

"Now then, Tom."

She slipped her arm in his.

"Tell me more about Scotland Yard. You didn't see the other one there?"

"What other one?"

"The Belgian gentleman. The one that ABC writes to always."

"No. He wasn't there."

"Well, tell me all about it. What happened when you got inside? Who did you speak to and what did you say?"

Mr Cust put the receiver back very gently on the hook.

He turned to where Mrs Marbury was standing in the doorway of a room, clearly devoured with curiosity.

"Not often you have a telephone call, Mr Cust?"

"No—er—no, Mrs Marbury. It isn't."

"Not bad news, I trust?"

"No—no." How persistent the woman was. His eye caught the legend on the newspaper he was carrying.

Births—Marriages—Deaths . . .

"My sister's just had a little boy," he blurted out.

He—who had never had a sister!

"Oh, dear! Now—well, that *is* nice, I am sure. ("And never once mentioned a sister all these years," was her inward thought. "If that isn't just like a man!" I was surprised, I'll tell you, when the lady asked to speak to Mr Cust. Just at first I fancied it was my Lily's voice—something like hers, it was—but haughtier if you know what I mean—sort of high up in the air. Well, Mr Cust, my congratulations, I'm sure. Is it the first one, or have you other little nephews and nieces?"

"It's the only one," said Mr Cust. "The only one I've ever had or likely to have, and—er—I think I must go off at once. They—they want me to come. I—I think I can just catch a train if I hurry."

"Will you be away long, Mr Cust?" called Mrs Marbury as he ran up the stairs.

"Oh, no—two or three days—that's all."

He disappeared into his bedroom. Mrs Marbury retired into the kitchen, thinking sentimentally of "the dear little mite".

Her conscience gave her a sudden twinge.

Last night Tom and Lily and all the hunting back over dates! Trying to make out that Mr Cust was that dreadful monster, ABC. Just because of his initials and because of a few coincidences.

"I don't suppose they meant it seriously," she thought comfortably. "And now I hope they'll be ashamed of themselves."

In some obscure way that she could not have explained, Mr Cust's statement that his sister had had a baby had effectually removed any doubts Mrs Marbury might have had of her lodger's *bona fides*.

"I hope she didn't have too hard a time of it, poor dear," thought Mrs Marbury, testing an iron against her cheek before beginning to iron out Lily's silk slip.

Her mind ran comfortably on a well-worn obstetric track.

Mr Cust came quietly down the stairs, a bag in his hand. His eyes rested a minute on the telephone.

That brief conversation re-echoed in his brain.

"Is that you, Mr Cust? I thought you might like to know there's an inspector from Scotland Yard may be coming to see you . . ."

What had he said? He couldn't remember.

"Thank you—thank you, my dear . . . very kind of you . . ."

Something like that.

Why had she telephoned him? Could she possibly have guessed? Or did she just want to make sure he would stay in for the inspector's visit?

But how did she know the inspector was coming?

And her voice—she'd disguised her voice from her mother . . .

It looked—it looked—as though she *knew* . . .

But surely if she knew, she wouldn't . . .

She might, though. Women were very queer. Unexpectedly cruel and unexpectedly kind. He'd seen Lily once letting a mouse out of a mouse-trap.

A kind girl . . .

A kind, pretty girl . . .

He paused by the hall stand with its load of umbrellas and coats.

Should he . . . ?

A slight noise from the kitchen decided him . . .

No, there wasn't time . . .

Mrs Marbury might come out . . .

He opened the front door, passed through and closed it behind him . . .

Where . . . ?

CHAPTER 29
At Scotland Yard

Conference again.

The Assistant Commissioner, Inspector Crome, Poirot and myself.

The A.C. was saying:

"A good tip that of yours, M. Poirot, about checking a large sale of stockings."

Poirot spread out his hands.

"It was indicated. This man could not be a regular agent. He sold outright instead of touting for orders."

"Got everything clear so far, inspector?"

"I think so, sir." Crome consulted a file. "Shall I run over the position to date?"

"Yes, please."

"I've checked up with Churston, Paignton and Torquay. Got a list of people where he went and offered stockings. I must say he did the thing thoroughly. Stayed at the Pitt, small hotel near Torre Station. Returned to the hotel at 10.30 on the night of the murder. Could have taken a train from Churston at 9.57, getting to Torre at 10.20. No one answering to his description noticed on train or at station, but that Friday was Dartmouth Regatta and the trains back from Kingswear were pretty full.

"Bexhill much the same. Stayed at the Globe under his own name. Offered stockings to about a dozen addresses, including Mrs Barnard and including the Ginger Cat. Left hotel early in the evening. Arrived back in London about 11.30 the following morning. As to Andover, same procedure. Stayed at the Feathers. Offered stockings to Mrs Fowler, next door to Mrs Ascher, and to half a dozen other people in the street. The pair Mrs Ascher had I got from the niece (name of Drower)—they're identical with Cust's supply."

"So far, good," said the A.C.

"Acting on information received," said the inspector, "I went to the address given me by Hartigan, but found that Cust had left the house about half an hour previously. He received a telephone message, I'm told. First time such a thing had happened to him, so his landlady told me."

"An accomplice?" suggested the Assistant Commissioner.

"Hardly," said Poirot. "It is odd that—unless—"

We all looked at him inquiringly as he paused.

He shook his head, however, and the inspector proceeded.

"I made a thorough search of the room he had occupied. That search puts the matter beyond doubt. I found a block of notepaper similar to that on which the letters were written, a large quantity of hosiery and—at the back of the cupboard where the hosiery was stored—a parcel much the same shape and size but which turned out to contain—not hosiery—*but eight new ABC railway guides!*"

"Proof positive," said the Assistant Commissioner.

"I've found something else, too," said the inspector—his voice becoming suddenly almost human with triumph. "Only found it this morning, sir. Not had time to report yet. There was no sign of the knife in his room—"

"It would be the act of an imbecile to bring that back with him" remarked Poirot.

"After all, he's not a reasonable human being," remarked the inspector. "Anyway, it occurred to me that he might just possibly have brought it back to the house and then realized the danger of hiding it (as M. Poirot points out) in his room, and have looked about elsewhere. What place in the house would he be likely to select? I got it straight away. *The hall stand*—no one ever moves a hall stand. With a lot of trouble I got it moved out from the wall—and there it was!"

"The knife?"

"The knife. Not a doubt of it. The dried blood's still on it."

"Good work, Crome," said the A.C. approvingly. "We only need one thing more now."

"What's that?"

"The man himself."

"We'll get him, sir. Never fear."

The inspector's tone was confident.

"What do you say, M. Poirot?"

Poirot started out of a reverie.

"I beg your pardon?"

"We were saying that it was only a matter of time before we got our man. Do you agree?"

"Oh, that—yes. Without a doubt."

His tone was so abstracted that the others looked at him curiously.

"Is there anything worrying you, M. Poirot?"

"There is something that worries me very much. It is the *why?* The *motive*."

"But, my dear fellow, the man's crazy," said the Assistant Commissioner impatiently.

"I understand what M. Poirot means," said Crome, coming graciously to the rescue. "He's quite right. There's got to be some definite obsession. I think we'll find the root of the matter in an intensified inferiority complex. There may be persecution mania, too, and if so he may possibly associate M. Poirot with it. He may have the delusion that M. Poirot is a detective employed on purpose to hunt him down."

"H'm," said the A.C. "That's the jargon that's talked nowadays. In my day if a man was mad he was mad and we didn't look about for scientific terms to soften it down. I suppose a thoroughly up-to-date doctor would suggest putting a man like ABC in a nursing home, telling him what a fine fellow he was for forty-five days on end and then letting him out as a responsible member of society."

Poirot smiled but did not answer.

The conference broke up.

"Well," said the Assistant Commissioner. "As you say, Crome, pulling him in is only a matter of time."

"We'd have had him before now," said the inspector, "if he wasn't so ordinary-looking. We've worried enough perfectly inoffensive citizens as it is."

"I wonder where he is at this minute," said the Assistant Commissioner.

CHAPTER 30
(Not from Captain Hastings' Personal Narrative)

Mr Cust stood by a greengrocer's shop.

He stared across the road.

Yes, that was it.

Mrs Ascher. Newsagent and Tobacconist . . .

In the empty window was a sign.

To Let.

Empty . . .

Lifeless . . .

"Excuse me, sir."

The greengrocer's wife, trying to get at some lemons.

He apologized, moved to one side.

Slowly he shuffled away—back towards the main street of the town . . .

It was difficult—very difficult—now that he hadn't any money left . . .

Not having had anything to eat all day made one feel very queer and light-headed . . .

He looked at a poster outside a newsagent's shop.

The ABC Case. Murderer Still at Large. Interviews with M. Hercule Poirot.

Mr Cust said to himself:

"Hercule Poirot. I wonder if *he* knows . . ."

He walked on again.

It wouldn't do to stand staring at that poster . . .

He thought:

"I can't go on much longer . . ."

Foot in front of foot . . . what an odd thing walking was . . .

Foot in front of foot—ridiculous.

Highly ridiculous . . .

But man was a ridiculous animal anyway . . .

And he, Alexander Bonaparte Cust, was particularly ridiculous.

He had always been . . .

People had always laughed at him . . .

He couldn't blame them . . .

Where was he going? He didn't know. He'd come to the end. He no longer looked anywhere but at his feet.

Foot in front of foot.

He looked up. Lights in front of him. And letters . . .

Police Station.

"That's funny," said Mr Cust. He gave a little giggle.

Then he stepped inside. Suddenly, as he did so, he swayed and fell forward.

CHAPTER 31
Hercule Poirot Asks Questions

It was a clear November day. Dr Thompson and Chief Inspector Japp had come round to acquaint Poirot with the result of the police court proceedings in the case of Rex *v*. Alexander Bonaparte Cust.

Poirot himself had had a slight bronchial chill which had prevented his attending. Fortunately he had not insisted on having my company.

"Committed for trial," said Japp. "So that's that."

"Isn't it unusual?" I asked, "for a defence to be offered at this stage? I thought prisoners always reserved their defence."

"It's the usual course," said Japp. "I suppose young Lucas thought he might rush it through. He's a trier, I will say. Insanity's the only defence possible."

Poirot shrugged his shoulders.

"With insanity there can be no acquittal. Imprisonment during His Majesty's pleasure is hardly preferable to death."

"I suppose Lucas thought there was a chance," said Japp. "With a first-class *alibi* for the Bexhill murder, the whole case might be weakened. I don't think he realized how strong our case is. Anyway, Lucas goes in for originality. He's a young man, and he wants to hit the public eye."

Poirot turned to Thompson.

"What's your opinion, doctor?"

"Of Cust? Upon my soul, I don't know what to say. He's playing the sane man remarkably well. He's an epileptic, of course."

"What an amazing dénouement that was," I said.

"His falling into the Andover police station in a fit? Yes—it was a fitting dramatic curtain to the drama. ABC has always timed his effects well."

"Is it possible to commit a crime and be unaware of it?" I asked. "His denials seem to have a ring of truth in them."

Dr Thompson smiled a little.

"You mustn't be taken in by that theatrical 'I swear by God' pose. It's my opinion *that Cust knows perfectly well he committed the murders*."

"When they're as fervent as that they usually do," said Crome.

"As to your question," went on Thompson, "it's perfectly possible for an epileptic subject in a state of somnambulism to commit an action and be entirely unaware of having done so. But it is the general opinion that such an action must 'not be contrary to the will of the person in the waking state'."

He went on discussing the matter, speaking of *grand mal* and *petit mal* and, to tell the truth, confusing me hopelessly as is often the case when a learned person holds forth on his own subject.

"However, I'm against the theory that Cust committed these crimes without knowing he'd done them. You might put that theory forward if it weren't for the letters. The letters knock the theory on the head. They show premeditation and a careful planning of the crime."

"And of the letters we have still no explanation," said Poirot.

"That interests you?"

"Naturally—since they were written to me. And on the subject of the letters Cust is persistently dumb. Until I get at the reason for those letters being written to me, I shall not feel that the case is solved."

"Yes—I can understand that from your point of view. There doesn't seem to be any reason to believe that the man ever came up against you in any way?"

"None whatever."

"I might make a suggestion. Your name!"

"My name?"

"Yes. Cust is saddled—apparently by the whim of his mother (Oedipus complex there, I shouldn't wonder!)—with two extremely bombastic Christian names: Alexander and Bonaparte. You see the implications? Alexander—the popularly supposed undefeatable who sighed for more world to conquer. Bonaparte—the great Emperor of the French. He wants an adversary—an adversary, one might say, in his class. Well—there you are—Hercules the strong."

"Your words are very suggestive, doctor. They foster ideas . . ."

"Oh, it's only a suggestion. Well, I must be off."

Dr Thompson went out. Japp remained.

"Does this *alibi* worry you?" Poirot asked.

"It does a little," admitted the inspector. "Mind you, I don't believe in it, because I know it isn't true. But it is going to be a deuce to break it. This man Strange is a tough character."

"Describe him to me."

"He's a man of forty. A tough, confident, self-opinionated mining engineer. It's my opinion that it was he who insisted on his evidence being taken now. He wants to get off to Chile. He hoped the thing might be settled out of hand."

"He's one of the most positive people I've ever seen," I said.

"The type of man who would not like to admit he was mistaken," said Poirot thoughtfully.

"He sticks to his story and he's not one to be heckled. He swears by all that's blue that he picked up Cust in the Whitecross Hotel at Eastbourne on the evening of July 24th. He was lonely and wanted someone to talk to. As far as I can see, Cust made an ideal listener. He didn't interrupt! After dinner he and Cust played dominoes. It appears Strange was a whale on dominoes and to his surprise Cust was pretty hot stuff too. Queer game, dominoes. People go mad about it. They'll play for hours. That's what Strange and Cust did apparently. Cust wanted to go to bed but Strange wouldn't hear of it—swore they'd keep it up until midnight at least. And that's what they did do. They separated at ten minutes past midnight. And if Cust was in the Whitecross Hotel at Eastbourne at ten minutes past midnight on the morning of the 25th he couldn't very well be strangling Betty Barnard on the beach at Bexhill between midnight and one o'clock."

"The problem certainly seems insuperable," said Poirot thoughtfully. "Decidedly, it gives one to think."

"It's given Crome something to think about," said Japp.

"This man Strange is very positive?"

"Yes. He's an obstinate devil. And it's difficult to see just where the flaw is. Supposing Strange is making a mistake and the man wasn't Cust—why on earth should he *say* his name is Cust? And the writing in the hotel register is his all right. You can't say he's an accomplice—homicidal lunatics don't have accomplices! Did the girl die later? The doctor was quite firm in his evidence, and anyway it would take some time for Cust to get out of the hotel at Eastbourne without being seen and get over to Bexhill—about fourteen miles away—"

"It is a problem—yes," said Poirot.

"Of course, strictly speaking, it oughtn't to matter. We've got Cust on the Doncaster murder—the bloodstained coat, the knife—not a loophole there. You couldn't bounce any jury into acquitting him. He did the Churston murder. He did the Andover murder. Then, by hell, he *must* have done the Bexhill murder. But I don't see how!"

He shook his head and got up.

"Now's your chance, M. Poirot," he said. "Crome's in a fog. Exert those cellular arrangements of yours I used to hear so much about. Show us the way he did it."

Japp departed.

"What about it, Poirot?" I said. "Are the little grey cells equal to the task?"

Poirot answered my question by another.

"Tell me, Hastings, do you consider the case ended?"

"Well—yes, practically speaking. We've got the man. And we've got most of the evidence. It's only the trimmings that are needed."

Poirot shook his head.

"The case is ended! The case! The case is the *man*, Hastings. Until we know all about the man, the mystery is as deep as ever. It is not victory because we have put him in the dock!"

"We know a fair amount about him."

"We know nothing at all! We know where he was born. We know he fought in the war and received a slight wound in the head and that he was discharged from the army owing to epilepsy. We know that he lodged with Mrs Marbury for nearly two years. We know that he was quiet and retiring—the sort of man that nobody notices. We know that he invented and carried out an intensely clever scheme of systemized murder. We know that he made certain incredibly stupid blunders. We know that he killed without pity and quite ruthlessly. We know, too, that he was kindly enough not to let blame rest on any other person for the crimes he committed. If he wanted to kill unmolested—how easy to let other persons suffer for his crimes. Do you not see, Hastings, that the man is a mass of contradictions? Stupid and cunning, ruthless and magnanimous—*and that there must be some dominating factor that reconciles his two natures*."

"Of course, if you treat him like a psychological study," I began.

"What else has this case been since the beginning? All along I have been groping my way—trying *to get to know the murderer*. And now I realize, Hastings, *that I do not know him at all!* I am at sea."

"The lust for power—" I began.

"Yes—that might explain a good deal . . . But it does not satisfy me. There are things I want to know. *Why* did he commit these murders? *Why* did he choose those particular people—?"

"Alphabetically—" I began.

"Was Betty Barnard the only person in Bexhill whose name began with a B? Betty Barnard—I had an idea there . . . It ought to be true—it must be true. But if so—"

He was silent for some time. I did not like to interrupt him.

As a matter of fact, I believe I fell asleep.

I woke to find Poirot's hand on my shoulder.

"*Mon cher Hastings*," he said affectionately. "My good genius."

I was quite confused by this sudden mark of esteem.

"It is true," Poirot insisted. "Always—always—you help me—you bring me luck. You inspire me."

"How have I inspired you this time?" I asked.

"While I was asking myself certain questions I remembered a remark of yours—a remark absolutely shimmering in its clear vision. Did I not say to you once that you had a genius for stating the obvious. It is the obvious that I have neglected."

"What is this brilliant remark of mine?" I asked.

"It makes everything as clear as crystal. I see the answers to all my questions. The reason for Mrs Ascher (that, it is true, I glimpsed long ago), the reason for Sir Carmichael Clarke, the reason for the Doncaster murder, and finally and supremely important, *the reason for Hercule Poirot*."

"Could you kindly explain?" I asked.

"Not at the moment. I require first a little more information. That I can get from our Special Legion. And then—then, *when I have got the answer to a certain question, I will go and see ABC*. We will be face to face at alst—ABC and Hercule Poirot—the adversaries."

"And then?" I asked.

"And then," said Poirot. "We will talk! *Je vous assure, Hastings*—there is nothing so dangerous *for anyone who has something to hide* as conversation! Speech, so a wise old Frenchman said to me once, is an invention of man's to prevent him from thinking. It is also an infallible means of discovering that which he wishes to hide. A human being, Hastings, cannot resist the opportunity to reveal himself and express his personality which conversation gives him. Every time he will give himself away."

"What do you expect Cust to tell you?"

Hercule Poirot smiled.

"A lie," he said. "And by it, I shall know the truth!"

CHAPTER 32
And Catch a Fox

During the next few days Poirot was very busy. He made mysterious absences, talked very little, frowned to himself, and consistently refused to satisfy my natural curiosity as to the brilliance I had, according to him, displayed in the past.

I was not invited to accompany him on his mysterious comings and goings—a fact which I somewhat resented.

Towards the end of the week, however, he announced his intention of paying a visit to Bexhill and neighbourhood and suggested that I should come with him. Needless to say, I accepted with alacrity.

The invitation, I discovered, was not extended to me alone. The members of our Special Legion were also invited.

They were as intrigued by Poirot as I was. Nevertheless, by the end of the day, I had at any rate an idea as to the direction in which Poirot's thoughts were tending.

He first visited Mr and Mrs Barnard and got an exact account from her as to the hour at which Mr Cust had called on her and exactly what he had said. He then went to the hotel at which Cust had put up and extracted a minute description of that gentleman's departure. As far as I could judge, no new facts were elicited by his questions but he himself seemed quite satisfied.

Next he went to the beach—to the place where Betty Barnard's body had been discovered. Here he walked round in circles for some minutes studying the shingle attentively. I could see little point in this, since the tide covered the spot twice a day.

However I have learnt by this time that Poirot's actions are usually dictated by an idea—however meaningless they may seem.

He then walked from the beach to the nearest point at which a car could have been parked. From there again he went to the place where the Eastbourne buses waited before leaving Bexhill.

Finally he took us all to the Ginger Cat café, where we had a somewhat stale tea served by the plump waitress, Milly Higley.

Her he complimented in a flowing Gallic style on the shape of her ankles.

"The legs of the English—always they are too thin! But you, mademoiselle, have the perfect leg. It has shape—it has an ankle!"

Milly Higley giggled a good deal and told him not to go on so. She knew what French gentlemen were like.

Poirot did not trouble to contradict her mistake as to his nationality. He merely ogled her in such a way that I was startled and almost shocked.

"*Voilà,*" said Poirot, "I have finished in Bexhill. Presently I go to Eastbourne. One little inquiry there—that is all. Unnecessary for you all to accompany me. In the meantime come back to the hotel and let us have a cocktail. That Carlton tea, it was abominable!"

As we were sipping our cocktails Franklin Clarke said curiously:

"I suppose we can guess what you are after? You're out to break that alibi. But I can't see what you're so pleased about. You haven't got a new fact of any kind."

"No—that is true."

"Well, then?"

"Patience. Everything arranges itself, given time."

"You seem quite pleased with yourself anyway."

"Nothing so far has contradicted my little idea—that is why."

His face grew serious.

"My friend Hastings told me once that he had, as a young man, played a game called The Truth. It was a game where everyone in turn was asked three questions—two of which must be answered truthfully. The third one could be barred. The questions, naturally, were of the most indiscreet kind. But to begin with everyone had to swear that they would indeed speak the truth, the whole truth, and nothing but the truth."

He paused.

"Well?" said Megan.

"*Eh bien*—me, I want to play that game. Only it is not necessary to have three questions. One will be enough. One question to each of you."

"Of course," said Clarke impatiently. "We'll answer anything."

"Ah, but I want it to be more serious than that. Do you all swear to speak the truth?"

He was so solemn about it that the others, puzzled, became solemn themselves. They all swore as he demanded.

"*Bon,*" said Poirot briskly. "Let us begin—"

"I'm ready," said Thora Grey.

"Ah, but ladies first—this time it would not be the politeness. We will start elsewhere."

He turned to Franklin Clarke.

"What, *mon cher M. Clarke,* did you think of the hats the ladies wore at Ascot this year?"

Franklin Clarke stared at him.

"Is this a joke?"

"Certainly not."

"Is that seriously your question?"

"It is."

Clarke began to grin.

"Well, M. Poirot, I didn't actually go to Ascot, but from what I could see of them driving in cars, women's hats for Ascot were an even bigger joke than the hats they wear ordinarily."

"Fantastic?"

"Quite fantastic."

Poirot smiled and turned to Donald Fraser.

"When did you take your holiday this year, monsieur?"

It was Fraser's turn to stare.

"My holiday? The first two weeks in August."

His face quivered suddenly. I guessed that the question had brought the loss of the girl he loved back to him.

Poirot, however, did not seem to pay much attention to the reply. He turned to Thora Grey and I heard the slight difference in his voice. It had tightened up. His question came sharp and clear.

"Mademoiselle, in the event of Lady Clarke's death, would you have married Sir Carmichael if he had asked you?"

The girl sprang up.

"How dare you ask me such a question. It's—it's insulting!"

"Perhaps. But you have sworn to speak the truth. *Eh bien*— Yes or no?"

"Sir Carmichael was wonderfully kind to me. He treated me almost like a daughter. And that's how I felt to him—just affectionate and grateful."

"Pardon me, but that is not answering Yes or No, mademoiselle."

She hesitated.

"The answer, of course, is no!"

He made no comment.

"Thank you, mademoiselle."

He turned to Megan Barnard. The girl's face was very pale. She was breathing hard as though braced up for an ordeal.

Poirot's voice came out like the crack of a whiplash.

"Mademoiselle, what do you hope will be the result of my investigations? Do you want me to find out the truth—or not?"

Her head went back proudly. I was fairly sure of her answer. Megan, I knew, had a fanatical passion for truth.

Her answer came clearly—and it stupified me.

"No!"

We all jumped. Poirot leant forward studying her face.

"Mademoiselle Megan," he said, "you may not want the truth but—*ma foi*— you can speak it!"

He turned towards the door, then, recollecting, went to Mary Drower.

"Tell me, *mon enfant*, have you a young man?"

Mary, who had been looking apprehensive, looked startled and blushed.

"Oh, Mr Poirot. I—I—well, I'm not sure."

He smiled.

"*Alors c'est bien, mon enfant*."

He looked round for me.

"Come, Hastings, we must start for Eastbourne."

The car was waiting and soon we were driving along the coast road that leads through Pevensey to Eastbourne.

"Is it any use asking you anything, Poirot?"

"Not at this moment. Draw your own conclusions as to what I am doing."

I relapsed into silence.

Poirot, who seemed pleased with himself, hummed a little tune. As we passed through Pevensey he suggested that we stop and have a look over the castle.

As we were returning towards the car, we paused a moment to watch a ring of children—Brownies, I guessed, by their get-up—who were singing a ditty in shrill, untuneful voices . . .

"What is it that they say, Hastings? I cannot catch the words."

I listened—till I caught one refrain.

"—And catch a fox
And put him in a box
And never let him go."

"And catch a fox and put him in a box and never let him go!" repeated Poirot.

His face had gone suddenly grave and stern.

"It is very terrible that, Hastings." He was silent a minute. "You hunt the fox here?"

"I don't. I've never been able to afford to hunt. And I don't think there's much hunting in this part of the world."

"I meant in England generally. A strange sport. The waiting at the covert side—then they sound the tally-ho, do they not?—and the run begins—across the country—over the hedges and ditches—and the fox he runs—and sometimes he doubles back—but the dogs—"

"Hounds!"

"—hounds are on his trail, and at last they catch him and he dies—quickly and horribly."

"I suppose it does sound cruel, but really—"

"The fox enjoys it? Do not say *les bêtises*, my friend. *Tout de même*—it is better that—the quick, cruel death—than what those children were singing . . .

"To be shut away—in a box—for ever . . . No, it is not good, that."

He shook his head. Then he said, with a change of tone:

"Tomorrow, I am to visit the man Cust," and he added to the chauffeur:

"Back to London."

"Aren't you going to Eastbourne?" I cried.

"What need? I know—quite enough for my purpose."

CHAPTER 33

Alexander Bonaparte Cust

I was not present at the interview that took place between Poirot and that strange man—Alexander Bonaparte Cust. Owing to his association with the police and the peculiar circumstances of the case, Poirot had no difficulty in obtaining a Home Office order—but that order did not extend to me, and in any case it was essential, from Poirot's point of view, that that interview should be absolutely private—the two men face to face.

He has given me, however, such a detailed account of what passed between them, that I set it down with as much confidence on paper as though I had actually been present.

Mr Cust seemed to have shrunk. His stoop was more apparent. His fingers plucked vaguely at his coat.

For some time, I gather, Poirot did not speak.

He sat and looked at the man opposite him.

The atmosphere became restful—soothing—full of infinite leisure . . .

It must have been a dramatic moment—this meeting of the two adversaries in the long drama. In Poirot's place I should have felt the dramatic thrill.

Poirot, however, is nothing if not matter-of-fact. He was absorbed in producing a certain effect upon the man opposite him.

At last he said gently:

"Do you know who I am?"

The other shook his head.

"No—no—I can't say I do. Unless you are Mr Lucas's—what do they call it?—junior. Or perhaps you come from Mr Maynard?"

(Maynard & Cole were the defending solicitors.)

His tone was polite but not very interested. He seemed absorbed in some inner abstraction.

"I am Hercule Poirot . . ."

Poirot said the words very gently . . . and watched for the effect.

Mr Cust raised his head a little.

"Oh, yes?"

He said it as naturally as Inspector Crome might have said it—but without the superciliousness.

Then, a minute later, he repeated his remark.

"Oh, yes?" he said, and this time his tone was different—it held an awakened interest. He raised his head and looked at Poirot.

Hercule Poirot met his gaze and nodded his own head gently once or twice.

"Yes," he said. "I am the man to whom you wrote the letters."

At once the contact was broken. Mr Cust dropped his eyes and spoke irritably and fretfully.

"I never wrote to you. Those letters weren't written by me. I've said so again and again."

"I know," said Poirot. "But if you did not write them, who did?"

"An enemy. I must have an enemy. They are all against me. The police—everyone—all against me. It's a gigantic conspiracy."

Poirot did not reply.

Mr Cust said:

"Everyone's hand has been against me—always."

"Even when you were a child?"

Mr Cust seemed to consider.

"No—no—not exactly then. My mother was very fond of me. But she was ambitious—terribly ambitious. That's why she gave me those ridiculous names. She had some absurd idea that I'd cut a figure in the world. She was always urging me to assert myself—talking about will power . . . saying anyone could be master of his fate . . . she said I could do anything!"

He was silent for a minute.

"She was quite wrong, of course. I realized that myself quite soon. I wasn't the sort of person to get on in life. I was always doing foolish things—making myself look ridiculous. And I was timid—afraid of people. I had a bad time at school—the boys found out my Christian names—they used to tease me about them . . . I did very badly at school—in games and work and everything."

He shook his head.

"Just as well poor mother died. She'd have been disappointed . . . Even when I was at the Commercial College I was stupid—it took me longer to learn typing and shorthand than anyone else. And yet I didn't *feel* stupid—if you know what I mean."

He cast a sudden appealing look at the other man.

"I know what you mean," said Poirot. "Go on."

"It was just the feeling that everybody else *thought* me stupid. Very paralysing. It was the same thing later in the office."

"And later still in the war?" prompted Poirot.

Mr Cust's face lightened up suddenly.

"You know," he said, "I enjoyed the war. What I had of it, that was. I felt, for the first time, a man like anybody else. We were all in the same box. I was as good as anyone else."

His smile faded.

"And then I got that wound on the head. Very slight. But they found out I had fits . . . I'd always known of course, that there were times when I hadn't been quite sure what I was doing. Lapses, you know. And of course, once or twice I'd fallen down. But I don't really think they ought to have discharged me for that. No, I don't think it was right."

"And afterwards?" asked Poirot.

"I got a place as a clerk. Of course there was good money to be got just then. And I didn't do so badly after the war. Of course, a smaller salary . . . And—I didn't seem to get on. I was always being passed over for promotion. I wasn't go-ahead enough. It grew very difficult—really very difficult . . . Especially when the slump came. To tell you the truth, I'd got hardly enough to keep body and soul together (and you've got to look presentable as a clerk) when I got the offer of this stocking job. A salary and commission!"

Poirot said gently:

"But you are aware, are you not, that the firm whom you say employed you deny the fact?"

Mr Cust got excited again.

"That's because they're in the conspiracy—they must be in the conspiracy."

He went on:

"I've got written evidence—written evidence. I've got their letters to me, giving me instructions as to what places to go to and a list of people to call on."

"Not *written* evidence exactly—*typewritten* evidence."

"It's the same thing. Naturally a big firm of wholesale manufacturers typewrite their letters."

"Don't you know, Mr Cust, that a typewriter can be identified? All those letters were typed by one particular machine."

"What of it?"

"And that machine was your own—the one found in your room."

"It was sent me by the firm at the beginning of my job."

"Yes, but these letters were received *afterwards*. So it looks, does it not, as though *you typed them yourself and posted them to yourself?*"

"No, no! It's all part of the plot against me!"

He added suddenly:

"Besides, their letters *would* be written on the same kind of machine."

"The same *kind*, but not the same actual machine."

Mr Cust repeated obstinately:

"It's a plot!"

"And the ABC's that were found in the cupboard?"

"I know nothing about them. I thought they were all stockings."

"Why did you tick off the name of Mrs Ascher in that first list of people in Andover?"

"Because I decided to start with her. One must begin somewhere."

"Yes, that is true. *One must begin somewhere*."

"I don't mean that!" said Mr Cust. "I don't mean what you mean!"

"*But you know what I meant?*"

Mr Cust said nothing. He was trembling.

"I didn't do it!" he said. "I'm perfectly innocent! It's all a mistake. Why, look at that second crime—that Bexhill one. I was playing dominoes at Eastbourne. You've got to admit that!"

His voice was triumphant.

"Yes," said Poirot. His voice was meditative—silky. "But it's so easy, isn't it, to make a mistake of one day? And if you're an obstinate, positive man, like Mr Strange, you'll never consider the possibility of having been mistaken. What you've said you'll stick to . . . He's that kind of man. And the hotel register—it's very easy to put down the wrong date when you're signing it—probably no one will notice it at the time."

"I was playing dominoes that evening!"

"You play dominoes very well, I believe."

Mr Cust was a little flurried by this.

"I—I—well, I believe I do."

"It is a very absorbing game, is it not, with a lot of skill in it?"

"Oh, there's a lot of play in it—a lot of play! We used to play a lot in the city, in the lunch hour. You'd be surprised the way total strangers come together over a game of dominoes."

He chuckled.

"I remember one man—I've never forgotten him because of something he told me—we just got talking over a cup of coffee, and we started dominoes. Well, I felt after twenty minutes that I'd known that man all my life."

"What was it that he told you?" asked Poirot.

Mr Cust's face clouded over.

"It gave me a turn—a nasty turn. Talking of your fate being written in your hand, he was. And he showed me his hand and the lines that showed he'd have two near escapes of being drowned—and he had had two near escapes. And then he looked at mine and he told me some amazing things. Said I was going to be one of the most celebrated men in England before I died. Said the whole country would be talking about me. But he said—he said . . ."

Mr Cust broke down—faltered . . .

"Yes?"

Poirot's gaze held a quiet magnetism. Mr Cust looked at him, looked away, then back again like a fascinated rabbit.

"He said—he said—that it looked as though I might die a violent death—and he laughed and said: 'Almost looks as though you might die on the scaffold,' and then he laughed and said that was only his joke . . ."

He was silent suddenly. His eyes left Poirot's face—they ran from side to side . . .

"My head—I suffer very badly with my head . . . the headaches are something cruel sometimes. And then there are times when I don't know—when I don't know . . ."

He broke down.

Poirot leant forward. He spoke very quietly but with great assurance.

"But you do know, don't you," he said, *"that you committed the murders?"*

Mr Cust looked up. His glance was quite simple and direct. All resistance had left him. He looked strangely at peace.

"Yes," he said. "I know."

"But—I am right, am I not?—*you don't know* why *you did them?*"

Mr Cust shook his head.

"No," he said. "I don't."

CHAPTER 34
Poirot Explains

We were sitting in a state of tense attention to listen to Poirot's final explanation of the case.

"All along," he said, "I have been worried over the *why* of this case. Hastings said to me the other day that the case was ended. I replied to him that the case was the *man!* The mystery was *not the mystery of the murders,* but the *mystery of ABC*. Why did he find it necessary to commit these murders. Why did he select *me* as his adversary?

"It is no answer to say that the man was mentally unhinged. To say a man does mad things because he is mad is merely unintelligent and stupid. A madman is as logical and reasoned in his actions as a sane man—*given his peculiar biased point of view*. For example, if a man insists on going out and squatting about in nothing but a loin cloth his conduct seems eccentric in the extreme. But once you know *that the man himself is firmly convinced that he is Mahatma Gandhi,* then his conduct becomes perfectly reasonable and logical.

"What was necessary in this case was to imagine a mind so constituted *that it was logical and reasonable to commit four or more murders* and to announce them beforehand by letters written to Hercule Poirot.

"My friend Hastings will tell you that from the moment I received the first letter I was upset and disturbed. It seemed to me at once that there was something very wrong about the letter."

"You were quite right," said Franklin Clarke dryly.

"Yes. But there, at the very start, I made a grave error. I permitted my feeling—my very strong feeling about the letter to remain a mere impression. I treated it as though it had been an intuition. In a well-balanced, reasoning mind there is no such thing as an intuition—an inspired guess! You *can* guess, of course—and a guess is either right or wrong. If it is right you call it an intuition. If it is wrong you usually do not speak of it again. But what is often called an intuition is really *an impression based on logical deduction or experience*. When an expert feels that there is something wrong about a picture or a piece of furniture or the signature on a cheque he is really basing that feeling on a host of small signs and details. He has no need to go into them minutely—his experience obviates that—the net result is *the definite impression that something is wrong*. But it is not a *guess,* it is an impression based on *experience*.

"Eh bien, I admit that I did not regard that first letter in the way I should. It

just made me extremely uneasy. The police regarded it as a hoax. I myself took it seriously. I was convinced that a murder would take place in Andover as stated. As you know, a murder *did* take place.

"There was no means at that point, as I well realized, of knowing who the *person* was who had done the deed. The only course open to me was to try and understand just what kind of a person had done it.

"I had certain indications. The letter—the manner of the crime—the person murdered. What I had to discover was: the motive of the crime, the motive of the letter."

"Publicity," suggested Clarke.

"Surely an inferiority complex covers that," added Thora Grey.

"That was, of course, the obvious line to take. But why *me? Why Hercule Poirot?* Greater publicity would be ensured by sending the letters to Scotland Yard. More again by sending them to a newspaper. A newspaper might not print the first letter, but by the time the second crime took place, ABC could have been assured of all the publicity the press could give. Why, then, Hercule Poirot? Was it for some *personal* reason? There was, discernible in the letter, a slight anti-foreign bias—but not enough to explain the matter to my satisfaction.

"Then the second letter arrived—and was followed by the murder of Betty Barnard at Bexhill. It became clear now (what I had already suspected) that the murders were to proceed on an alphabetical plan, but that fact, which seemed final to most people, left the main question unaltered to my mind. Why did ABC *need* to commit these murders?"

Megan Barnard stirred in her chair.

"Isn't there such a thing as—as a blood lust?" she said.

Poirot turned to her.

"You are quite right, mademoiselle. There *is* such a thing. The lust to kill. But that did not quite fit the facts of the case. A homicidal maniac who desires to kill usually desires to kill *as many victims as possible*. It is a recurring *craving*.The great idea of such a killer is to *hide his tracks*—not to *advertise* them. When we consider the four victims selected—or at any rate three of them (for I know very little of Mr Downes or Mr Earlsfield), we realize that *if he had chosen*, the murderer could have done away with them without incurring any suspicion. Franz Ascher, Donald Fraser or Megan Barnard, possibly Mr Clarke—those are the people the police would have suspected even if they had been unable to get direct proof. An unknown homicidal murderer would not have been thought of! Why, then, did the murderer feel it necessary to call attention to himself? Was it the necessity of leaving on each body a copy of an ABC railway guide? Was *that* the compulsion? Was there some complex connected *with the railway guide?*

"I found it quite inconceivable at this point *to enter into the mind of the murderer*. Surely it could not be magnanimity? A horror of responsibility for the crime being fastened on an innocent person?

"Although I could not answer the main question, certain things I did feel I was learning about the murderer."

"Such as?" asked Fraser.

"To begin with—that he had a tabular mind. His crimes were listed by alphabetical progression—that was obviously important to him. On the other hand, he had no particular taste in victims—Mrs Ascher, Betty Barnard, Sir Carmichael Clarke, they all differed widely from each other. There was no sex complex—no particular age complex, and that seemed to me to be a very curious fact. If a man kills indiscrimately it is usually because he removes anyone who stands in his way or annoys him. *But the alphabetical progression showed that such was not the case here*. The other type of killer usually selects *a particular type of victim*—nearly always of the opposite sex. There was something haphazard about the procedure of ABC that seemed to me to be at war with the alphabetical selection.

"One slight inference I permitted myself to make. The choice of the ABC suggested to me what I may call a *railway-minded man*. This is more common in men than women. Small boys love trains better than small girls do. It might be the sign, too, of an in some ways undeveloped mind. The 'boy' motif still predominated.

"The death of Betty Barnard and the manner of it gave me certain other indications. The manner of her death was particularly suggestive. (Forgive me, Mr Fraser.) To begin with, she was strangled with her own belt—therefore she must almost certainly have been killed by someone with whom she was on friendly or affectionate terms. When I learnt something of her character a picture grew up in my mind.

"Betty Barnard was a flirt. She liked attention from a personable male. Therefore ABC, to persuade her to come out with him, must have had a certain amount of attraction—of *le sex appeal!* He must be able, as you English say, to 'get off'. He must be capable of the click! I visualize the scene on the beach thus: the man admires her belt. She takes it off, he passes it playfully round her neck—says, perhaps, 'I shall strangle you.' It is all very playful. She giggles—and he pulls—"

Donald Fraser sprang up. He was livid.

"M. Poirot—for God's sake."

Poirot made a gesture.

"It is finished. I say no more. It is over. We pass to the next murder, that of Sir Carmichael Clarke. Here the murderer goes back to his first method—the blow on the head.

"The same alphabetical complex—but one fact worries me a little. To be consistent the murderer should have chosen his towns in some definite sequence.

"If Andover is the 155th name under A, then the B crime should be the 155th also—or it should be the 156th and the C the 157th. Here again the towns seemed to be chosen in rather too *haphazard* a fashion."

"Isn't that because you're rather biased on that subject, Poirot?" I suggested. "You yourself are normally methodical and orderly. It's almost a disease with you."

"No, it is *not* a disease! *Quelle idée!* But I admit that I may be over-stressing that point. *Passons!*

"The Churston crime gave me very little extra help. We were unlucky over it, since the letter announcing it went astray, hence no preparations could be made.

"But by the time the D crime was announced, a very formidable system of defence had been evolved. It must have been obvious that ABC could not much longer hope to get away with his crimes.

"Moreover, it was at this point that the clue of the stockings came into my hand. It was perfectly clear that the presence of an individual selling stockings on and near the scene of each crime could not be a coincidence. Hence the stocking-seller must be the murderer. I may say that his description, as given me by Miss Grey, did not quite correspond with my own picture of the man who strangled Betty Barnard.

"I will pass over the next stages quickly. A fourth murder was committed—the murder of a man named George Earlsfield—it was supposed in mistake for a man named Downes, who was something of the same build and who was sitting near him in the cinema.

"*And now at last comes the turn of the tide*. Events play against ABC instead of into his hands. He is marked down—hunted—and at last arrested.

"The case, as Hastings says, is ended!

"True enough as far as the public is concerned. The man is in prison and will eventually, no doubt, go to Broadmoor. There will be no more murders! Exit! Finis! R.I.P.

"*But not for me!* I know nothing—nothing at all! Neither the *why* nor the *wherefore*.

"And there is one small vexing fact. The man Cust has an *alibi* for the night of the Bexhill crime."

"That's been worrying me all along," said Franklin Clarke.

"Yes. It worried me. For the *alibi,* it has the air of being *genuine*. But it cannot be genuine unless—and now we come to two very interesting speculations.

"Supposing, my friends, that while Cust committed *three* of the crimes—the A, C, and D crimes—*he did not commit the B crime*."

"M. Poirot. It isn't—"

Poirot silenced Megan Barnard with a look.

"Be quiet, mademoiselle. I am for the truth, I am! I have done with lies. Supposing, I say, *that ABC did not commit the second crime*. It took place, remember, in the early hours of the 25th—the day he had arrived for the crime. Supposing someone had forestalled him? What in those circumstances would he do? Commit a *second* murder, or lie low and *accept the first as a kind of macabre present?*"

"M. Poirot!" said Megan. "That's a fantastic thought! All the crimes *must* have been committed by the same person!"

He took no notice of her and went steadily on:

"Such a hypothesis had the merit of explaining one fact—*the discrepancy between the personality of Alexander Bonaparte Cust* (who could never have made the click with any girl) *and the personality of Betty Barnard's murderer*. And it has been known, before now, that would-be murderers *have* taken advantage of the crimes committed by other people. Not all the crimes of Jack the Ripper were committed by Jack the Ripper, for instance. So far, so good.

"But then I came up against a definite difficulty.

"Up to the time of the Barnard murder, *no facts about the ABC murders had been made public*. The Andover murder had created little interest. The incident of the open railway guide had not even been mentioned in the press. It therefore followed that whoever killed Betty Barnard *must have had access to facts known only to certain persons*—myself, the police, and certain relations and neighbours of Mrs Ascher.

"That line of research seemed to lead me up against a blank wall."

The faces that looked at him were blank too. Blank and puzzled.

Donald Fraser said thoughtfully:

"The police, after all, are human beings. And they're good-looking men—"

He stopped, looking at Poirot inquiringly.

Poirot shook his head gently.

"No—it is simpler than that. I told you that there was a second speculation.

"Supposing that Cust was *not* responsible for the killing of Betty Barnard? Supposing that *someone else* killed her. Could that comeone else have been responsible *for the other murders too?*"

"But that doesn't make sense!" cried Clarke.

"Doesn't it? I did then *what I ought to have done at first*. I examined the letters I had received from a totally different point of view. I had felt from the beginning that there was something wrong with them—just as a picture expert knows a picture is wrong . . .

"I had assumed, without pausing to consider, that what was wrong with them was the fact that they were written by a madman.

"Now I examined them again—and this time I came to totally different conclusion. What was wrong with them was *the fact that they were written by a sane man!*"

"What?" I cried.

"But yes—just that precisely! They were wrong as a picture is wrong—*because they were a fake!* They pretended to be the letters of a madman—of a homicidal lunatic, but in reality they were nothing of the kind."

"It doesn't make sense," Franklin Clarke repeated.

"*Mais si!* One must reason—reflect. What would be the object of writing such letters? To focus attention on the writer, to call attention to the murders! *En vérité,* it did not seem to make sense at first sight. And then I saw light. It was to focus attention on several murders—on a *group* of murders . . . Is it not your great Shakespeare who has said 'You cannot see the trees for the wood'?"

I did not correct Poirot's literary reminiscences. I was trying to see his point. A glimmer came to me. He went on:

"When do you notice a pin least? When it is in a pincushion! When do you notice an individual murder least? When it is one of *a series of related murders*.

"I had to deal with an intensely clever, resourceful murderer—reckless, daring and a thorough gambler. *Not* Mr Cust! He could never have committed these murders! No, I had to deal with a very different stamp of a man—a man with a boyish temperament (witness the schoolboy-like letters and the railway guide), an attractive man to women, and a man with a ruthless disregard for human life, a man who was necessarily a prominent person in *one* of the crimes!

"Consider when a man or woman is killed, what are the questions that the police ask? Opportunity. Where everybody was at the time of the crime? Motive. Who benefited by the deceased's death? If the motive and the opportunity are fairly obvious, what is a would-be murderer to do? Fake an alibi—that is, manipulate *time* in some way? But that is always a hazardous proceeding. Our murderer thought of a more fantastic defence. Create a *homicidal* murderer!

"I had now only to review the various crimes and find the possible guilty person. The Andover crime? The most likely suspect for that was Franz Ascher, but I could not imagine Ascher inventing and carrying out such an elaborate scheme, nor could I see him planning a premeditated murder. The Bexhill crime? Donald Fraser was a possibility. He had brains and ability, and a methodical turn of mind. But his motive for killing his sweetheart could only be jealousy—and jealousy does not tend to premeditation. Also I learned that he had his holidays *early* in August, which rendered it unlikely he had anything to do with the Churston crime. We come to the Churston crime next—and at once we are on infinitely more promising ground.

"Sir Carmichael Clarke was an immensely wealthy man. Who inherits his money? His wife, who is dying, has a life interest in it, and it then goes to *his brother Franklin*."

Poirot turned slowly round till his eyes met those of Franklin Clarke.

"I was quite sure then. The man I had known a long time in my secret mind *was the same as the man whom I had known as a person*. *ABC and Franklin Clarke were one and the same!* The daring adventurous character, the roving life, the partiality for England that had showed itself, very faintly, in the jeer at foreigners. The attractive free and easy manner—nothing easier for him than to pick up a girl in a café. The methodical tabular mind he had made a list here one day, ticked off over the headings ABC—and finally, the boyish mind—mentioned by Lady Clarke and even shown by his taste in fiction—I have ascertained that there is a book in the library called *The Railway Children* by E. Nesbit. I had no further doubt in my own mind—ABC, the man who wrote the letters and committed the crimes, was *Franklin Clarke*."

Clarke suddenly burst out laughing.

"Very ingenious! And what about our friend Cust, caught red-handed? What about the blood on his coat? And the knife he hid in his lodgings? He may deny he committed the crimes—"

Poirot interrupted.

"You are quite wrong. He admits the fact."

"What?" Clarke looked really startled.

"Oh, yes," said Poirot gently. "I had no sooner spoken to him than I was aware that Cust *believed himself to be guilty*."

"And even that didn't satisfy M. Poirot?" said Clarke.

"No. Because as soon as I saw him *I also knew that he could not be guilty!* He has neither the nerve nor the daring—nor, I may add, the *brains* to plan! All along I have been aware of the dual personality of the murderer. Now I see wherein it consisted. Two people were involved—the real murderer, cunning, resourceful and daring—and the *pseudo* murderer, stupid, vacillating and suggestible.

"Suggestible—it is in that word that the mystery of Mr Cust consists! It was not enough for you, Mr Clarke, to devise this plan of a *series* to distract attention from a *single* crime. You had also to have a stalking horse.

"I think the idea first originated in your mind as the result of a chance encounter in a city coffee den with this odd personality with his bombastic Christian names. You were at that time turning over in your mind various plans for the murder of your brother."

"Really? And why?"

"Because you were seriously alarmed for the future. I do not know whether you realize it, Mr Clarke, but you played into my hands when you showed me a certain letter written to you by your brother. In it he displayed very clearly his affection and absorption in Miss Thora Grey. His regard may have been a paternal one—or he may have preferred to think it so. Nevertheless, there was a very real danger that on the death of your sister-in-law he might, in his loneliness, turn to this beautiful girl for sympathy and comfort and it might end—as so often happens with elderly men—in his marrying her. Your fear was increased by your knowledge of Miss Grey. You are, I fancy, an excellent, if somewhat cynical judge of character. You judged, whether correctly or not, that Miss Grey was a type of young woman 'on the make'. You had no doubt that she would jump at the chance of becoming Lady Clarke. Your brother was an extremely healthy and vigorous man. There might be children and your chance of inheriting your brother's wealth would vanish.

"You have been, I fancy, in essence a disappointed man all your life. You have been the rolling stone—and you have gathered very little moss. You were bitterly jealous of your brother's wealth.

"I repeat then that, turning over various schemes in your mind, your meeting with Mr Cust gave you an idea. His bombastic Christian names, his account of his epileptic seizures and of his headaches, his whole shrinking and insignificant personality, struck you as fitting him for the tool you wanted. The whole alphabetical plan sprang into your mind—Cust's initials—the fact that your brother's name began with a C and that he lived at Churston were the nucleus of the scheme. You even went so far as to hint to Cust at his possible end—though you could hardly hope that the suggestion would bear the rich fruit that it did!

"Your arrangements were excellent. In Cust's name you wrote for a large consignment of hosiery to be sent to him. You yourself sent a number of ABC's looking like a similar parcel. You wrote to him—a typed letter purporting to be from the same firm offering him a good salary and commission. Your plans were so well laid beforehand that you typed all the letters that were sent subsequently, *and then presented him with the machine on which they had been typed*.

"You had now to look about for two victims whose names began with A and B respectively and who lived at places also beginning with those same letters.

"You hit on Andover as quite a likely spot and your preliminary reconnaissance there led you to select Mrs Ascher's shop as the scene of the first crime. Her name was written clearly over the door, and you found by experiment that she was usually alone in the shop. Her murder needed nerve, daring and reasonable luck.

"For the letter B you had to vary your tactics. Lonely women in shops might conceivably have been warned. I should imagine that you frequented a few cafés and teashops, laughing and joking with the girls there and finding out whose name began with the right letter and who would be suitable for your purpose.

"In Betty Barnard you found just the type of girl you were looking for. You took her out once or twice, explaining to her that you were a married man, and that outings must therefore take place in a somewhat hole-and-corner manner.

"Then, your preliminary plans completed, you set to work! You sent the Andover list to Cust, directing him to go there on a certain date, and you sent off the first ABC letters to me.

"On the appointed day you went to Andover—and killed Mrs Ascher—without anything occurring to damage your plans.

"Murder No. 1 was successfully accomplished.

"For the second murder, you took the precaution of committing it, in reality, *the day before*. I am fairly certain that Betty Barnard was killed well before midnight on the 24th July.

"We now come to murder No. 3—the important—in fact, the *real* murder from your point of view.

"And here a full meed of praise is due to Hastings, who made a simple and obvious remark to which no attention was paid.

"*He suggested that the third letter went astray intentionally!*

"And he was right! . . .

"In that one simple fact lies the answer to the question that has puzzled me so all along. Why were the letters addressed in the first place to Hercule Poirot, a private detective, and not to the police?

"Erroneously I imagined some personal reason.

"Not at all! The letters were sent to me because the essence of your plan was that one of them *should be wrongly addressed and go astray*—but you cannot arrange for a letter addressed to the Criminal Investigation Department of Scotland Yard to go astray! It is necessary to have a *private* address. You chose me as a fairly well-known person, and a person who was sure to take the letters to the police—and also, in your rather insular mind, you enjoyed scoring off a foreigner.

"You addressed your envelope very cleverly—Whitehaven—Whitehorse—quite a natural slip. Only Hastings was sufficiently perspicacious to disregard subtleties and go straight for the obvious!

"Of course the letter was *meant* to go astray! The police were to be set on the trail *only when the murder was safely over*. Your brother's nightly walk provided you with the opportunity. And so successfully had the ABC terror taken hold on the public mind that the possibility of your guilt never occurred to anyone.

"After the death of your brother, of course, your object was accomplished. You had no wish to commit any more murders. On the other hand, if the murders stopped without reason, a suspicion of the truth might come to someone.

"Your stalking horse, Mr Cust, had so successfully lived up to his role of the invisible—because insignificant—man, that so far no one had noticed that the same person had been seen in the vicinity of the three murders! To your annoyance, even his visit to Combeside had not been mentioned. The matter had passed completely out of Miss Grey's head.

"Always daring, you decided that one more murder must take place but this time the trail must be well blazed.

"You selected Doncaster for the scene of operations.

"Your plan was very simple. You yourself would be on the scene in the nature of things. Mr Cust would be ordered to Doncaster by his firm. Your plan was to follow him round and trust to opportunity. Everything fell out well. Mr Cust went to a cinema. That was simplicity itself. You sat a few seats away from him. When he got up to go, you did the same. You pretended to stumble, leaned over and stabbed a dozing man in the row in front, slid the ABC on to his knees and managed to collide heavily with Mr Cust in the darkened doorway, wiping the knife on his sleeve and slipping it into his pocket.

"You were not in the least at pains to choose a victim whose name began with D. Anyone would do! You assumed—and quite rightly—that it would be considered to be a *mistake*. There was sure to be someone whose name began with D not far off in the audience. It would be assumed that he had been intended to be the victim.

"And now, my friends, let us consider the matter from the point of view of the false ABC—from the point of view of Mr Cust.

"The Andover crime means nothing to him. He is shocked and surprised by the Bexhill crime—why, he himself was there about the time! Then comes the Churston crime and the headlines in the newspapers. An ABC crime at Andover when he was there, an ABC crime at Bexhill, and now another close by . . . Three crimes *and he has been at the scene of each of them*. Persons suffering from epilepsy often have blanks when they cannot remember what they have done . . . Remember that Cust was a nervous, highly neurotic subject and extremely suggestible.

"Then he receives the order to go to Doncaster.

"Doncaster! And the next ABC crime is to be in Doncaster. He must have felt as though it was fate. He loses his nerve, fancies his landlady is looking at him suspiciously, and tells her he is going to Cheltenham.

"He goes to Doncaster because it is his duty. In the afternoon he goes to a cinema. Possibly he dozes off for a minute or two.

"Imagine his feelings when on his return to his inn he discovers *that there is blood on his coat sleeve and a blood-stained knife in his pocket*. All his vague forebodings leap into certainty.

"*He—he himself—is the killer!* He remembers his headaches—his lapses of memory. He is quite sure of the truth—*he, Alexander Bonaparte Cust, is a homicidal lunatic*.

"His conduct after that is the conduct of a hunted animal. He gets back to his lodgings in London. He is safe there—known. They think he has been in Cheltenham. He has the knife with him still—a thoroughly stupid thing to do, of course. He hides it behind the hall stand.

"Then, one day, he is warned that the police are coming. It is the end! They *know!*

"The hunted animal does his last run . . .

"I don't know why he went to Andover—a morbid desire, I think, to go and look at the place where the crime was committed—the crime *he* committed though he can remember nothing about it . . .

"He has no money left—he is worn out . . . his feet lead him of his own accord to the police station.

"But even a cornered beast will fight. Mr Cust fully believes that he did the murders but he sticks strongly to his plea of innocence. And he holds with desperation to that *alibi* for the second murder. At least that cannot be laid to his door.

"As I say, when I saw him, I knew at once that he was *not* the murderer and that my name *meant* nothing to *him*. I knew, too, that he *thought* himself the murderer!

"After he had confessed his guilt to me, I knew more strongly than ever that my own theory was right."

"Your theory," said Franklin Clarke, "is absurd!"

Poirot shook his head.

"No, Mr Clarke. You were safe enough *so long as no one suspected you*. Once you *were* suspected proofs were easy to obtain."

"Proofs?"

"Yes. I found the stick that you used in the Andover and Churston murders in a cupboard at Combeside. An ordinary stick with a thick knob handle. A section of wood had been removed and melted lead poured in. Your photograph was picked out from half a dozen others by two people who saw you leaving the cinema when you were supposed to be on the racecourse at Doncaster. You were identified at Bexhill the other day by Milly Higley and a girl from the Scarlet Runner Roadhouse, where you took Betty Barnard to dine on the fatal evening. And finally—most damning of all—you *overlooked a most elementary precaution*. You left a fingerprint on Cust's typewriter—the typewriter that, if you are innocent, you *could never have handled*."

Clarke sat quite still for a minute, then he said:

"*Rouge, impair, manque!*—you win, M. Poirot! But it was worth trying!"

With an incredibly rapid motion he whipped out a small automatic from his pocket and held it to his head.

I gave a cry and involuntarily flinched as I waited for the report.

But no report came—the hammer clicked harmlessly.

Clarke stared at it in astonishment and uttered an oath.

"No, Mr Clarke," said Poirot. "You may have noticed I had a new manservant today—a friend of mine—an expert sneak thief. He removed your pistol from your pocket, unloaded it, and returned it all without you being aware of the fact."

"You unutterable little jackanapes of a foreigner!" cried Clarke, purple with rage.

"Yes, yes, that is how you feel. No, Mr Clarke, no easy death for you. You told Mr Cust that you had had near escapes from drowning. You know what that means—that you were born for another fate."

"You—"

Words failed him. His face was livid. His fists clenched menacingly.

Two detectives from Scotland Yard emerged from the next room. One of them was Crome. He advanced and uttered his time-honoured formula: "I warn you that anything you say may be used as evidence."

"He has said quite enough," said Poirot, and he added to Clarke: "You are very full of an insular superiority, but for myself I consider your crime not an English crime at all—not above board—not *sporting*—"

CHAPTER 35
Finale

I am sorry to relate that as the door closed behind Franklin Clarke I laughed hysterically.

Poirot looked at me in mild surprise.

"It's because you told him his crime was not sporting," I gasped.

"It was quite true. It was abominable—not so much the murder of his brother—but the cruelty that condemned an unfortunate man to a living death. *To catch a fox and put him in a box and never let him go!* That is not *le sport!*"

Megan Barnard gave a deep sigh.

"I can't believe it—I can't. Is it true?"

"Yes, mademoiselle. The nightmare is over."

She looked at him and her colour deepened.

Poirot turned to Fraser.

"Mademoiselle Megan, all along, was haunted by a fear that it was you who had committed the second crime."

Donald Fraser said quietly:

"I fancied so myself at one time."

"Because of your dream?" He drew a little nearer to the young man and dropped his voice confidentially. "Your dream has a very natural explanation. It is that you find that already the image of one sister fades in your memory and that its place is taken by the other sister. Mademoiselle Megan replaces her sister in your heart, but since you cannot bear to think of yourself being unfaithful so soon to the dead, you strive to stifle the thought, to kill it! That is the explanation of the dream."

Fraser's eye went towards Megan.

"Do not be afraid to forget," said Poirot gently. "She was not so well worth remembering. In Mademoiselle Megan you have one in a hundred—*un coeur magnifique!*"

Donald Fraser's eyes lit up.

"I believe you are right."

We all crowded round Poirot asking questions, elucidating this point and that.

"Those questions, Poirot? That you asked of everybody. Was there any point in them?"

"Some of them were *simplement une blague*. But I learnt one thing that I wanted to know—*that Franklin Clarke was in London when the first letter was posted*—and also I wanted to see his face when I asked my question of Mademoiselle Thora. He was off his guard. I saw all the malice and anger in his eyes."

"You hardly spared my feelings," said Thora Grey.

"I do not fancy you returned me a truthful answer, mademoiselle," said Poirot dryly. "And now your second expectation is disappointed. Franklin Clarke will not inherit his brother's money."

She flung up her head.

"Is there any need for me to stay here and be insulted?"

"None whatever," said Poirot and held the door open politely for her.

"That fingerprint clinched things, Poirot," I said thoughtfully. "He went all to pieces when you mentioned that."

"Yes, they are useful—fingerprints."

He added thoughtfully:

"I put that in to please you, my friend."

"But Poirot," I cried, "wasn't it *true?*"

"Not in the least, *mon ami,*" said Hercule Poirot.

I must mention a visit we had from Mr Alexander Bonaparte Cust a few days later. After wringing Poirot's hand and endeavouring very incoherently and unsuccessfully to thank him, Mr Cust drew himself up and said:

"Do you know, a newspaper has actually offered me a hundred pounds—*a hundred pounds*—for a brief account of my life and history. I—I really don't know what to do about it."

"I should not accept a hundred," said Poirot. "Be firm. Say five hundred is your price. And do not confine yourself to one newspaper."

"Do you really think—that I might—"

"You must realize," said Poirot smiling, "that you are a very famous man. Practically the most famous man in England today."

Mr Cust drew himself up still further. A beam of delight irradiated his face.

"Do you know, I believe you're right. Famous! In all the papers. I shall take your advice, M. Poirot. The money will be most agreeable—most agreeable. I shall have a little holiday . . . And then I want to give a nice wedding present to Lily Marbury—a dear girl—really a dear girl, M. Poirot."

Poirot patted him encouragingly on the shoulder.

"You are quite right. Enjoy yourself. And—just a little word—what about a visit to an oculist? Those headaches, it is probably that you want new glasses."

"You think that it may have been that all the time?"

"I do."

Mr Cust shook him warmly by the hand.

"You're a very great man, M. Poirot."

Poirot, as usual, did not disdain the compliment. He did not even succeed in looking modest.

When Mr Cust had strutted importantly out, my old friend smiled across at me.

"So, Hastings—we went hunting once more, did we not? *Vive le sport.*"

CARDS ON THE TABLE

Foreword by the Author

There is an idea prevalent that a detective story is rather like a big race—a number of starters—likely horses and jockeys. "You pays your money and you takes your choice!" The favorite is by common consent the opposite of a favorite on the racecourse. In other words he is likely to be a complete outsider! Spot the least likely person to have committed the crime and in nine times out of ten your task is finished.

Since I do not want my faithful readers to fling away this book in disgust, I prefer to warn them beforehand *that this is not that kind of book*. There are only *four* starters and any one of them, *given the right circumstances*, might have committed the crime. That knocks out forcibly the element of surprise. Nevertheless there should be, I think, an equal interest attached to four persons, each of whom has committed murder and is capable of committing further murders. They are four widely divergent types; the motive that drives each one of them to crime is peculiar to that person, and each one would employ a different method. The deduction must, therefore, be entirely *psychological*, but it is none the less interesting for that, because when all is said and done it is the *mind* of the murderer that is of supreme interest.

I may say, as an additional argument in favor of this story, that it was one of Hercule Poirot's favorite cases. His friend, Captain Hastings, however, when Poirot described it to him, considered it very dull! I wonder with which of them my readers will agree.

CONTENTS

CHAPTER 1
Mr. Shaitana

"My dear M. Poirot!"

It was a soft purring voice—a voice used deliberately as an instrument—nothing impulsive or unpremeditated about it.

Hercule Poirot swung round.

He bowed.

He shook hands ceremoniously.

There was something in his eye that was unusual. One would have said that this chance encounter awakened in him an emotion that he seldom had occasion to feel.

"My dear Mr. Shaitana," he said.

They both paused. They were like duellists *en garde*.

Around them a well-dressed languid London crowd eddied mildly. Voices drawled or murmured.

"Darling—exquisite!"

"Simply divine, aren't they, my dear?"

It was the Exhibition of Snuff-Boxes at Wessex House. Admission one guinea, in aid of the London hospitals.

"My dear man," said Mr. Shaitana, "how nice to see you! Not hanging or guillotining much just at present? Slack season in the criminal world? Or is there to be a robbery here this afternoon—that would be too delicious."

"Alas, Monsieur," said Poirot. "I am here in a purely private capacity."

Mr. Shaitana was diverted for a moment by a Lovely Young Thing with tight poodle curls up one side of her head and three cornucopias in black straw on the other.

He said:

"My *dear—why* didn't you come to my party? It really was a marvellous party! Quite a lot of people actually *spoke* to me! One woman even said 'How do you do,' and 'Good-bye' and 'Thank you so much'—but of course she came from a Garden City, poor dear!"

While the Lovely Young Thing made a suitable reply, Poirot allowed himself a good study of the hirsute adornment on Mr. Shaitana's upper lip.

A fine moustache—a *very* fine moustache—the only moustache in London, perhaps, that could compete with that of M. Hercule Poirot.

"But it is *not* so luxuriant," he murmured to himself. "No, decidedly it is inferior in every respect. *Tout de même*, it catches the eye."

The whole of Mr. Shaitana's person caught the eye—it was designed to do so. He deliberately attempted a Mephistophelian effect. He was tall and thin, his face was long and melancholy, his eyebrows were heavily accented and jet black, he wore a moustache with stiff waxed ends and a tiny black imperial. His clothes were works of art—of exquisite cut—but with a suggestion of the bizarre.

Every healthy Englishman who saw him longed earnestly and fervently to kick him! They said, with a singular lack of originality, "There's that damned Dago, Shaitana!"

Their wives, daughters, sisters, aunts, mothers, and even grandmothers said, varying the idiom according to their generation, words to this effect: "I know, my dear. Of course, he is *too* terrible. But *so* rich! And such marvellous parties! And he's always got something amusing and spiteful to tell you about people."

Whether Mr. Shaitana was an Argentine, or a Portuguese, or a Greek, or some other nationality rightly despised by the insular Briton, nobody knew.

But three facts were quite certain:

He existed richly and beautifully in a super flat in Park Lane.

He gave wonderful parties—large parties, small parties, *macabre* parties, respectable parties and definitely "queer" parties.

He was a man of whom nearly everybody was a little afraid.

Why this last was so can hardly be stated in definite words. There was a feeling, perhaps, that he knew a little too much about everybody. And there was a feeling, too, that his sense of humour was a curious one.

People nearly always felt that it would be better not to risk offending Mr. Shaitana.

It was his humour this afternoon to bait that ridiculous-looking little man, Hercule Poirot.

"So even a policeman needs recreation?" he said. "You study the art in your old age, M. Poirot."

Poirot smiled good-humouredly.

"I see," he said, "that you yourself have lent three snuff-boxes to the Exhibition."

Mr. Shaitana waved a deprecating hand.

"One picks up trifles here and there. You must come to my flat one day. I have some interesting pieces. I do not confine myself to any particular period or class of object."

"Your tastes are catholic," said Poirot smiling.

"As you say."

Suddenly Mr. Shaitana's eyes danced, the corners of his lips curled up, his eyebrows assumed a fantastic tilt.

"I could even show you objects in your own line, M. Poirot!"

"You have then a private 'Black Museum.'"

"Bah!" Mr. Shaitana snapped disdainful fingers. "The cup used by the Brighton murderer, the jemmy of a celebrated burglar—absurd childishness! I should never burden myself with rubbish like that. I collect only the best objects of their kind."

"And what do you consider the best objects, artistically speaking, in crime?" inquired Poirot.

Mr. Shaitana leaned forward and laid two fingers on Poirot's shoulder. He hissed his words dramatically.

"The human beings who commit them, M. Poirot."

Poirot's eyebrows rose a trifle.

"Aha, I have startled you," said Shaitana. "My dear, dear man, you and I look on these things as from poles apart! For you crime is a matter of routine: a murder, an investigation, a clue, and ultimately (for you are undoubtedly an able fellow) a conviction. Such banalities would not interest me! I am not interested in poor specimens of any kind. And the caught murderer is necessarily one of the failures. He is second-rate. No, I look on the matter from the artistic point of view. I collect only the best!"

"The best being——?" asked Poirot.

"My dear fellow—*the ones who have got away with it!* The successes! The criminals who lead an agreeable life which no breath of suspicion has ever touched. Admit that it is an amusing hobby."

"It was another word I was thinking of—not amusing."

"An idea!" cried Shaitana, paying no attention to Poirot. "A little dinner! A dinner to meet my exhibits! Really that is a most amusing thought. I cannot think why it has never occurred to me before. Yes—yes, I see it all—I see it exactly. . . . You must give me a little time—not next week—let us say the week after next. You are free? What day shall we say?"

"Any day of the week after next would suit me," said Poirot with a bow.

"Good—then let us say Friday. Friday the 18th, that will be. I will write it down at once in my little book. Really, the idea pleases me enormously."

"I am not quite sure if it pleases me," said Poirot slowly. "I do not mean that I am insensible to the kindness of your invitation—no—not that——"

Shaitana interrupted him.

"But it shocks your *bourgeois* sensibilities? My dear fellow, you *must* free yourself from the limitations of the policeman mentality."

Poirot said slowly:

"It is true that I have a thoroughly *bourgeois* attitude to murder."

"But, my dear, *why?* A stupid, bungled, butchering business—yes, I agree with you. But murder can be an *art!* A murderer can be an artist."

"Oh, I admit it."

"Well then?" Mr. Shaitana asked.

"But he is still a murderer!"

"Surely, my dear M. Poirot, to do a thing supremely well is a *justification!* You want, very unimaginatively, to take every murderer, handcuff him, shut him up, and eventually break his neck for him in the early hours of the morning. In my opinion a really successful murderer should be granted a pension out of the public funds and asked out to dinner!"

Poirot shrugged his shoulders.

"I am not as insensitive to art in crime as you think. I can admire the perfect murderer—I can also admire a tiger—that splendid tawny-striped beast. But I will admire him from outside his cage. I will not go inside. That is to say, not unless it is my duty to do so. For you see, Mr. Shaitana, the tiger might spring. . . ."

Mr. Shaitana laughed.

"I see. And the murderer?"

"Might murder," said Poirot gravely.

"My dear fellow—what an alarmist you are! Then you will not come to meet my collection of—tigers?"

"On the contrary, I shall be enchanted."

"How brave!"

"You do not quite understand me, Mr. Shaitana. My words were in the nature of a warning. You asked me just now to admit that your idea of a collection of murderers was amusing. I said I could think of another word other than amusing. That word was dangerous. I fancy, Mr. Shaitana, that your hobby might be a dangerous one!"

Mr. Shaitana laughed, a very Mephistophelian laugh.

He said:

"I may expect you, then, on the 18th?"

Poirot gave a little bow.

"You may expect me on the 18th. *Mille remerciments.*"

"I shall arrange a little party," mused Shaitana. "Do not forget. Eight o'clock."

He moved away. Poirot stood a minute or two looking after him.

He shook his head slowly and thoughtfully.

CHAPTER 2
Dinner at Mr. Shaitana's

The door of Mr. Shaitana's flat opened noiselessly. A grey-haired butler drew it back to let Poirot enter. He closed it equally noiselessly and deftly relieved the guest of his overcoat and hat.

He murmured in a low expressionless voice:

"What name shall I say?"

"M. Hercule Poirot."

There was a little hum of talk that eddied out into the hall as the butler opened a door and announced:

"M. Hercule Poirot."

Sherry-glass in hand, Shaitana came forward to meet him. He was, as usual, immaculately dressed. The Mephistophelian suggestion was heightened tonight, the eyebrows seemed accentuated in their mocking twist.

"Let me introduce you—do you know Mrs. Oliver?"

The showman in him enjoyed the little start of surprise that Poirot gave.

Mrs. Ariadne Oliver was extremely well known as one of the foremost writers of detective and other sensational stories. She wrote chatty (if not particularly grammatical) articles on *The Tendency of the Criminal; Famous Crimes Passionnels; Murder for Love v. Murder for Gain*. She was also a hot-headed feminist, and when any murder of importance was occupying space in the Press there was sure to be an interview with Mrs. Oliver, and it was mentioned that Mrs. Oliver had said, "Now if a *woman* were the head of Scotland Yard!" She was an earnest believer in woman's intuition.

For the rest she was an agreeable woman of middle age, handsome in a rather untidy fashion with fine eyes, substantial shoulders and a large quantity of rebellious grey hair with which she was continually experimenting. One day her appearance would be highly intellectual—a brow with the hair scraped back from it and coiled in a large bun in the neck—on another Mrs. Oliver would suddenly appear with Madonna loops, or large masses of slightly untidy curls. On this particular evening Mrs. Oliver was trying out a fringe.

She greeted Poirot, whom she had met before at a literary dinner, in an agreeable bass voice.

"And Superintendent Battle you doubtless know," said Mr. Shaitana.

A big square, wooden-faced man moved forward. Not only did an onlooker feel that Superintendent Battle was carved out of wood—he also managed to convey the impression that the wood in question was the timber out of a battleship.

Superintendent Battle was supposed to be Scotland Yard's best representative. He always looked stolid and rather stupid.

"I know M. Poirot," said Superintendent Battle.

And his wooden face creased into a smile and then returned to its former unexpressiveness.

"Colonel Race," went on Mr. Shaitana.

Poirot had not previously met Colonel Race, but he knew something about him. A dark, handsome, deeply bronzed man of fifty, he was usually to be found in some outpost of empire—especially if there were trouble brewing. Secret Service is a melodramatic term, but it described pretty accurately to the lay mind the nature and scope of Colonel Race's activities.

Poirot had by now taken in and appreciated the particular essence of his host's humorous intentions.

"Our other guests are late," said Mr. Shaitana. "My fault, perhaps. I believe I told them 8:15."

But at that moment the door opened and the butler announced:

"Dr. Roberts."

The man who came in did so with a kind of parody of a brisk bedside manner. He was a cheerful, highly-coloured individual of middle age. Small twinkling eyes, a touch of baldness, a tendency to *embonpoint* and a general air of well-scrubbed and disinfected medical practitioner. His manner was cheerful and confident. You felt that his diagnosis would be correct and his treatments agreeable and practical—"a little champagne in convalescence perhaps." A man of the world!

"Not late, I hope?" said Dr. Roberts genially.

He shook hands with his host and was introduced to the others. He seemed particularly gratified at meeting Battle.

"Why, you're one of the big noises at Scotland Yard, aren't you? This *is* interesting! Too bad to make you talk shop but I warn you I shall have a try at it. Always been interested in crime. Bad thing for a doctor, perhaps. Mustn't say so to my nervous patients—ha ha!"

Again the door opened.

"Mrs. Lorrimer."

Mrs. Lorrimer was a well-dressed woman of sixty. She had finely-cut features, beautifully arranged grey hair, and a clear, incisive voice.

"I hope I'm not late," she said, advancing to her host.

She turned from him to greet Dr. Roberts, with whom she was acquainted.

The butler announced:

"Major Despard."

Major Despard was a tall, lean, handsome man, his face slightly marred by a scar on the temple. Introductions completed, he gravitated naturally to the side of Colonel Race—and the two men were soon talking sport and comparing their experiences on *safari*.

For the last time the door opened and the butler announced:

"Miss Meredith."

A girl in the early twenties entered. She was of medium height and pretty. Brown curls clustered in her neck, her grey eyes were large and wide apart. Her face was powdered but not made-up. Her voice was slow and rather shy.

She said:

"Oh dear, am I the last?"

Mr. Shaitana descended on her with sherry and an ornate and complimentary reply. His introductions were formal and almost ceremonious.

Miss Meredith was left sipping her sherry by Poirot's side.

"Our friend is very punctilious," said Poirot with a smile.

The girl agreed.

"I know. People rather dispense with introductions nowadays. They just say 'I expect you know everybody' and leave it at that."

"Whether you do or you don't?"

"Whether you do or don't. Sometimes it makes it awkward—but I think this is more awe-inspiring."

She hesitated and then said:

"Is that Mrs. Oliver, the novelist?"

Mrs. Oliver's bass voice rose powerfully at that minute, speaking to Dr. Roberts.

"You can't get away from a woman's instinct, doctor. Women know these things."

Forgetting that she no longer had a brow she endeavoured to sweep her hair back from it but was foiled by the fringe.

"That is Mrs. Oliver," said Poirot.

"The one who wrote *The Body in the Library?*"

"That identical one."

Miss Meredith frowned a little.

"And that wooden-looking man—a *superintendent* did Mr. Shaitana say?"

"From Scotland Yard."

"And you?"

"And me?"

"I know all about you, M. Poirot. It was you who really solved the A.B.C. Crimes."

"Mademoiselle, you cover me with confusion."

Miss Meredith drew her brows together.

"Mr. Shaitana," she began and then stopped. "Mr. Shaitana——"

Poirot said quietly:

"One might say he was 'crime-minded.' It seems so. Doubtless he wishes to hear us dispute ourselves. He is already egging on Mrs. Oliver and Dr. Roberts. They are now discussing untraceable poisons."

Miss Meredith gave a little gasp as she said:

"What a queer man he is!"

"Dr. Roberts?"

"No, Mr. Shaitana."

She shivered a little and said:

"There's always something a little frightening about him, I think. You never know what would strike him as amusing. It might—it might be something *cruel*."

"Such as fox-hunting, eh?"

Miss Meredith threw him a reproachful glance.

"I meant—oh! something *Oriental!*"

"He has perhaps the tortuous mind," admitted Poirot.

"Torturer's?"

"No, no, tortuous, I said."

"I don't think I like him frightfully," confided Miss Meredith, her voice dropping.

"You will like his dinner, though," Poirot assured her. "He has a marvellous cook."

She looked at him doubtfully and then laughed.

"Why," she exclaimed, "I believe you are quite human."

"But certainly I am human!"

"You see," said Miss Meredith, "all these celebrities are rather intimidating."

"Mademoiselle, you should not be intimidated—you should be thrilled! You should have all ready your autograph book and your fountain-pen."

"Well, you see, I'm not really terribly interested in crime. I don't think women are: it's always men who read detective stories."

Hercule Poirot sighed affectedly.

"Alas!" he murmured. "What would I not give at this minute to be even the most minor of film stars!"

The butler threw the door open.

"Dinner is served," he murmured.

Poirot's prognostication was amply justified. The dinner was delicious and its serving perfection. Subdued light, polished wood, the blue gleam of Irish glass. In the dimness, at the head of the table, Mr. Shaitana looked more than ever diabolical.

He apologised gracefully for the uneven number of the sexes.

Mrs. Lorrimer was on his right hand, Mrs. Oliver on his left. Miss Meredith was between Superintendent Battle and Major Despard. Poirot was between Mrs. Lorrimer and Dr. Roberts.

The latter murmured facetiously to him.

"You're not going to be allowed to monopolise the only pretty girl all the evening. You French fellows, you don't waste your time, do you?"

"I happen to be Belgian," murmured Poirot.

"Same thing where the ladies are concerned, I expect, my boy," said the doctor cheerfully.

Then, dropping the facetiousness, and adopting a professional tone, he began to talk to Colonel Race on his other side about the latest developments in the treatment of sleeping sickness.

Mrs. Lorrimer turned to Poirot and began to talk of the latest plays. Her judgments were sound and her criticisms apt. They drifted on to books and then to world politics. He found her a well-informed and thoroughly intelligent woman.

On the opposite side of the table Mrs. Oliver was asking Major Despard if he knew of any unheard-of out-of-the-way poisons.

"Well, there's *curare*."

"My *dear* man, *vieux jeu!* That's been done hundreds of times. I mean something *new!*"

Major Despard said dryly:

"Primitive tribes are rather old-fashioned. They stick to the good old stuff their grandfathers and great-grandfathers used before them."

"Very tiresome of them," said Mrs. Oliver. "I should have thought they were always experimenting with pounding up herbs and things. Such a chance for explorers, I always think. They could come home and kill off all their rich old uncles with some new drug that no one's ever heard of."

"You should go to civilisation, not to the wilds for that," said Despard. "In the modern laboratory, for instance. Cultures of innocent-looking germs that will produce bona fide diseases."

"That wouldn't do for *my* public," said Mrs. Oliver. "Besides one is so apt to get the names wrong—staphylococcus and streptococcus and all those things—so difficult for my secretary and anyway rather dull, don't you think so? What do *you* think, Superintendent Battle?"

"In real life people don't bother about being too subtle, Mrs. Oliver," said the superintendent. "They usually stick to arsenic because it's nice and handy to get hold of."

"Nonsense," said Mrs. Oliver. "That's simply because there are lots of crimes you people at Scotland Yard never find out. Now if you had a woman there——"

"As a matter of fact we have——"

"Yes, those dreadful policewomen in funny hats who bother people in parks. I mean a woman at the head of things. Women *know* about crime."

"They're usually very successful criminals," said Superintendent Battle. "Keep their heads well. It's amazing how they'll brazen things out."

Mr. Shaitana laughed gently.

"Poison is a woman's weapon," he said. "There must be many secret women poisoners—never found out."

"Of course there are," said Mrs. Oliver happily, helping herself lavishly to a *mousse* of *foie gras*.

"A doctor, too, has opportunities," went on Mr. Shaitana thoughtfully.

"I protest," cried Dr. Roberts. "When we poison our patients it's entirely by accident." He laughed heartily.

"But if I were to commit a crime," went on Mr. Shaitana.

He stopped; something in that pause compelled attention.

All faces were turned to him.

"I should make it very simple, I think. There's always accident—a shooting accident, for instance—or the domestic kind of accident."

Then he shrugged his shoulders and picked up his wine-glass.

"But who am I to pronounce—with so many experts present. . . ."

He drank. The candlelight threw a red shade from the wine on to his face with its waxed moustache, its little imperial, its fantastic eyebrows. . . .

There was a momentary silence.

Mrs. Oliver said:

"Is it twenty-to or twenty-past? An angel passing. . . . My feet aren't crossed—it must be a black angel!"

CHAPTER 3
A Game of Bridge

When the company returned to the drawing-room a bridge table had been set out. Coffee was handed round.

"Who plays bridge?" asked Mr. Shaitana. "Mrs. Lorrimer, I know. And Dr. Roberts. Do you play, Miss Meredith?"

"Yes. I'm not frightfully good, though."

"Excellent. And Major Despart? Good. Supposing you four play here."

"Thank goodness there's to be bridge," said Mrs. Lorrimer in an aside to Poirot. "I'm one of the worst bridge fiends that ever lived. It's growing on me. I simply will *not* go out to dinner now if there's no bridge afterwards! I just fall asleep. I'm ashamed of myself, but there it is."

They cut for partners. Mrs. Lorrimer was partnered with Anne Meredith against Major Despard and Dr. Roberts.

"Women against men," said Mrs. Lorrimer as she took her seat and began shuffling the cards in an expert manner. "The blue cards, don't you think, partner? I'm a forcing two."

"Mind you win," said Mrs. Oliver, her feminist feelings rising. "Show the men they can't have it all their own way."

"They haven't got a hope, the poor dears," said Dr. Roberts cheerfully as he started shuffling the other pack. "Your deal, I think, Mrs. Lorrimer."

Major Despard sat down rather slowly. He was looking at Anne Meredith as though he had just made the discovery that she was remarkably pretty.

"Cut, please," said Mrs. Lorrimer impatiently. And with a start of apology he cut the pack she was presenting to him.

Mrs. Lorrimer began to deal with a practised hand.

"There is another bridge table in the other room," said Mr. Shaitana.

He crossed to a second door and the other four followed him into a small comfortably furnished smoking-room where a second bridge table was set ready.

"We must cut out," said Colonel Race.

Mr. Shaitana shook his head.

"I do not play," he said. "Bridge is not one of the games that amuse me."

The others protested that they would much rather not play, but he overruled them firmly and in the end they sat down. Poirot and Mrs. Oliver against Battle and Race.

Mr. Shaitana watched them for a little while, smiled in a Mephistophelian manner as he observed on what hand Mrs. Oliver declared Two No Trumps, and then went noiselessly through into the other room.

There they were well down to it, their faces serious, the bids coming quickly. "One heart." "Pass." "Three clubs." "Three spades." "Four diamonds." "Double." "Four hearts."

Mr. Shaitana stood watching a moment, smiling to himself.

Then he crossed the room and sat down in a big chair by the fireplace. A tray of drinks had been brought in and placed on an adjacent table. The firelight gleamed on the crystal stoppers.

Always an artist in lighting, Mr. Shaitana had simulated the appearance of a merely firelit room. A small shaded lamp at his elbow gave him light to read by if he so desired. Discreet floodlighting gave the room a subdued glow. A slightly stronger light shone over the bridge table, from whence the monotonous ejaculations continued.

"One no trump"—an aggressive note in the voice—Dr. Roberts.

"No bid"—a quiet voice—Anne Meredith's.

A slight pause always before Despard's voice came. Not so much a slow thinker as a man who liked to be sure before he spoke.

"Four hearts."

"Double."

His face lit up by the flickering firelight, Mr. Shaitana smiled.

He smiled and he went on smiling. His eyelids flickered a little. . . .

His party was amusing him.

"Five diamonds. Game and rubber," said Colonel Race.

"Good for you, partner," he said to Poirot. "I didn't think you'd do it. Lucky they didn't lead a spade."

"Wouldn't have made much difference, I expect," said Superintendent Battle, a man of gentle magnanimity.

He had called spades. His partner, Mrs. Oliver, had had a spade, but "something had told her" to lead a club—with disastrous results.

Colonel Race looked at his watch.

"Ten-past-twelve. Time for another?"

"You'll excuse me," said Superintendent Battle. "But I'm by way of being an 'early-to-bed' man."

"I, too," said Hercule Poirot.

"We'd better add up," said Race.

The result of the evening's five rubbers was an overwhelming victory for the male sex. Mrs. Oliver had lost three pounds and seven shillings to the other three. The biggest winner was Colonel Race.

Mrs. Oliver, though a bad bridge player, was a sporting loser. She paid up cheerfully.

"Everything went wrong for me tonight," she said. "It is like that sometimes. I held the most beautiful cards yesterday. A hundred and fifty honours three times running."

She rose and gathered up her embroidered evening bag, just refraining in time from stroking her hair off her brow.

"I suppose our host is next door," she said.

She went through the communicating door, the others behind her.

Mr. Shaitana was in his chair by the fire. The bridge players were absorbed in their game.

"Double five clubs," Mrs. Lorrimer was saying in her cool, incisive voice.

"Five No Trumps."

Mrs. Oliver came up to the bridge table. This was likely to be an exciting hand.

Superintendent Battle came with her.

Colonel Race went towards Mr. Shaitana, Poirot behind him.

"Got to be going, Shaitana," said Race.

Mr. Shaitana did not answer. His head had fallen forward, and he seemed to be asleep. Race gave a momentary whimsical glance at Poirot and went a little nearer. Suddenly he uttered a muffled ejaculation, bent forward. Poirot was beside him in a minute, he, too, looking where Colonel Race was pointing—something that might have been a particularly ornate shirt stud—but it was not. . . .

Poirot bent, raised one of Mr. Shaitana's hands, then let it fall. He met Race's inquiring glance and nodded. The latter raised his voice.

"Superintendent Battle, just a minute."

The superintendent came over to them. Mrs. Oliver continued to watch the play of Five No Trumps doubled.

Superintendent Battle, despite his appearance of stolidity, was a very quick man. His eyebrows went up and he said in a low voice as he joined them:

"Something wrong?"

With a nod Colonel Race indicated the silent figure in the chair.

As Battle bent over it, Poirot looked thoughtfully at what he could see of Mr.

Shaitana's face. Rather a silly face it looked now, the mouth drooping open—the devilish expression lacking. . . .

Hercule Poirot shook his head.

Superintendent Battle straightened himself. He had examined, without touching, the thing which looked like an extra stud in Mr. Shaitana's shirt—and it was not an extra stud. He had raised the limp hand and let it fall.

Now he stood up, unemotional, capable, soldierly—prepared to take charge efficiently of the situation.

"Just a minute, please," he said.

And the raised voice was his official voice, so different that all the heads at the bridge table turned to him, and Anne Meredith's hand remained poised over an ace of spades in dummy.

"I'm sorry to tell you all," he said, "that our host, Mr. Shaitana, is dead."

Mrs. Lorrimer and Dr. Roberts rose to their feet. Despard stared and frowned. Anne Meredith gave a little gasp.

"Are you sure, man?"

Dr. Roberts, his professional instincts aroused, came briskly across the floor with a bounding medical "in-at-the-death" step.

Without seeming to, the bulk of Superintendent Battle impeded his progress.

"Just a minute, Dr. Roberts. Can you tell me first who's been in and out of this room this evening?"

Roberts stared at him.

"In and out? I don't understand you. Nobody has."

The superintendent transferred his gaze.

"Is that right, Mrs. Lorrimer?"

"Quite right."

"Not the butler nor any of the servants?"

"No. The butler brought in that tray as we sat down to bridge. He has not been in since."

Superintendent Battle looked at Despard.

Despard nodded in agreement.

Anne said rather breathlessly, "Yes—yes, that's right."

"What's all this, man," said Roberts impatiently. "Just let me examine him; may be just a fainting fit."

"It isn't a fainting fit, and I'm sorry—but *nobody's going to touch him until the divisional surgeon comes. Mr. Shaitana's been murdered, ladies and gentlemen*."

"Murdered?" A horrified incredulous sigh from Anne.

A stare—a very blank stare—from Despard.

A sharp incisive "Murdered?" from Mrs. Lorrimer.

A "Good God!" from Dr. Roberts.

Superintendent Battle nodded his head slowly. He looked rather like a Chinese porcelain mandarin. His expression was quite blank.

"Stabbed," he said. "That's the way of it. Stabbed."

Then he shot out a question:

"Any of you leave the bridge table during the evening?"

He saw four expressions break up—waver. He saw fear—comprehension—indignation—dismay—horror; but he saw nothing definitely helpful.

"Well?"

There was a pause, and then Major Despard said quietly (he had risen now and was standing like a soldier on parade, his narrow, intelligent face turned to Battle):

"I think every one of us, at one time or another, moved from the bridge table—either to get drinks or to put wood on the fire. I did both. When I went to the fire Shaitana was asleep in the chair."

"Asleep?"

"I thought so—yes."

"He may have been," said Battle. "Or he may have been dead then. We'll go into that presently. I'll ask you now to go into the room next door." He turned to the quiet figure at his elbow: "Colonel Race, perhaps you'll go with them?"

Race gave a quick nod of comprehension.

"Right, superintendent."

The four bridge players went slowly through the doorway.

Mrs. Oliver sat down in a chair at the far end of the room and began to sob quietly.

Battle took up the telephone receiver and spoke. Then he said:

"The local police will be round immediately. Orders from headquarters are that I'm to take on the case. Divisional surgeon will be here almost at once. How long should you say he's been dead, M. Poirot? I'd say well over an hour myself."

"I agree. Alas, that one cannot be more exact—that one cannot say, 'This man has been dead one hour, twenty-five minutes and forty seconds.'"

Battle nodded absently.

"He was sitting right in front of the fire. That makes a slight difference. Over an hour—not more than two and a half: that's what our doctor will say, I'll be bound. And nobody heard anything and nobody saw anything. Amazing! What a desperate chance to take. He might have cried out."

"But he did not. The murderer's luck held. As you say, *mon ami*, it was a very desperate business."

"Any idea, M. Poirot, as to motive? Anything of that kind?"

Poirot said slowly:

"Yes, I have something to say on that score. Tell me, M. Shaitana—he did not give you any hint of what kind of a party you were coming to tonight?"

Superintendent Battle looked at him curiously.

"No, M. Poirot. He didn't say anything at all. Why?"

A bell whirred in the distance and a knocker was plied.

"That's our people," said Superintendent Battle. "I'll go and let 'em in. We'll have your story presently. Must get on with the routine work."

Poirot nodded.

Battle left the room.

Mrs. Oliver continued to sob.

Poirot went over to the bridge table. Without touching anything, he examined the scores. He shook his head once or twice.

"The stupid little man! Oh, the stupid little man," murmured Hercule Poirot. "To dress up as the devil and try to frighten people. *Quel enfantillage!*"

The door opened, The divisional surgeon came in, bag in hand. He was followed by the divisional inspector, talking to Battle. A camera man came next. There was a constable in the hall.

The routine of the detection of crime had begun.

CHAPTER 4
First Murderer?

Hercule Poirot, Mrs. Oliver, Colonel Race and Superintendent Battle sat round the dining-room table.

It was an hour later. The body had been examined, photographed and removed. A fingerprint expert had been and gone.

Superintendent Battle looked at Poirot.

"Before I have those four in, I want to hear what you've got to tell me. According to you there was something behind this party tonight?"

Very deliberately and carefully Poirot retold the conversation he had held with Shaitana at Wessex House.

Superintendent Battle pursed his lips. He very nearly whistled.

"Exhibits—eh? Murderers all alive oh! And you think he *meant* it? You don't think he was pulling your leg?"

Poirot shook his head.

"Oh, no, he meant it. Shaitana was a man who prided himself on his Mephistophelian attitude to life. He was a man of great vanity. He was also a stupid man—that is why he is dead."

"I get you," said Superintendent Battle, following things out in his mind. "A party of eight and himself. Four 'sleuths,' so to speak—and four murderers!"

"It's impossible!" cried Mrs. Oliver. "Absolutely impossible. None of those people can be *criminals*."

Superintendent Battle shook his head thoughtfully.

"I wouldn't be so sure of that, Mrs. Oliver. Murderers look and behave very much like everybody else. Nice, quiet, well-behaved, reasonable folk very often."

"In that case, it's Dr. Roberts," said Mrs. Oliver firmly. "I felt instinctively that there was something wrong with that man as soon as I saw him. My instincts never lie."

Battle turned to Colonel Race.

"What do you think, sir?"

Race shrugged his shoulders. He took the question as referring to Poirot's statement and not to Mrs. Oliver's suspicions.

"It could be," he said. "It could be. It shows that Shaitana was right in *one* case at least! After all, he can only have *suspected* that these people were murderers—he can't have been *sure*. He *may* have been right in all four cases, he may have been right in only one case—but he was right in *one* case; his death proved that."

"One of them got the wind up. Think that's it, M. Poirot?"

Poirot nodded.

"The late Mr. Shaitana had a reputation," he said. "He had a dangerous sense of humour, and was reputed to be merciless. The victim thought that Shaitana was giving himself an evening's amusement, leading up to a moment when he'd hand the victim over to the police—*you!* He (or she) must have thought that Shaitana had definite evidence."

"Had he?"

Poirot shrugged his shoulders.

"That we shall never know."

"Dr. Roberts!" repeated Mrs. Oliver firmly. "Such a hearty man. Murderers are often hearty—as a disguise! If I were you, Superintendent Battle, I should arrest him at once."

"I dare say we would if there was a Woman at the Head of Scotland Yard," said Superintendent Battle, a momentary twinkle showing in his unemotional eye. "But, you see, mere men being in charge, we've got to be careful. We've got to get there slowly."

"Oh, men—men," sighed Mrs. Oliver, and began to compose newspaper articles in her head.

"Better have them in now," said Superintendent Battle. "It won't do to keep them hanging about too long."

Colonel Race half rose.

"If you'd like us to go——"

Superintendent Battle hesitated a minute as he caught Mrs. Oliver's eloquent eye. He was well aware of Colonel Race's official position, and Poirot had worked with the police on many occasions. For Mrs. Oliver to remain was decidedly stretching a point. But Battle was a kindly man. He remembered that Mrs. Oliver had lost three pounds and seven shillings at bridge, and that she had been a cheerful loser.

"You can all stay," he said, "as far as I'm concerned. But no interruptions, please (he looked at Mrs. Oliver), and there mustn't be a hint of what M. Poirot has just told us. That was Shaitana's little secret, and to all intents and purposes it died with him. Understand?"

"Perfectly," said Mrs. Oliver.

Battle strode to the door and called the constable who was in duty in the hall.

"Go to the little smoking-room. You'll find Anderson there with the four guests. Ask Dr. Roberts if he'll be so good as to step this way."

"I should have kept him to the end," said Mrs. Oliver. "In a book, I mean," she added apologetically.

"Real life's a bit different," said Battle.

"I know," said Mrs. Oliver. "Badly constructed."

Dr. Roberts entered with the springiness of his step slightly subdued.

"I say, Battle," he said. "This is the devil of a business! Excuse me, Mrs. Oliver, but it is. Professionally speaking, I could hardly have believed it! To stab a man with three other people a few yards away." He shook his head. "Whew! I wouldn't like to have done it!" A slight smile twitched up the corners of his mouth. "What can I say or do to convince you that I *didn't* do it?"

"Well, there's motive, Dr. Roberts."

The doctor nodded his head emphatically.

"That's all clear. I hadn't the shadow of a motive for doing away with poor Shaitana. I didn't even know him very well. He amused me—he was such a fantastic fellow. Touch of the Oriental about him. Naturally, you'll investigate my relations with him closely—I expect that. I'm not a fool. But you won't find anything. I'd no reason for killing Shaitana, and I didn't kill him."

Superintendent Battle nodded woodenly.

"That's all right, Dr. Roberts. I've got to investigate, as you know. You're a sensible man. Now, can you tell me anything about the other three people?"

"I'm afraid I don't know very much. Despard and Miss Meredith I met for the first time tonight. I knew *of* Despard before—read his travel book, and a jolly good yarn it is."

"Did you know that he and Mr. Shaitana were acquainted?"

"No. Shaitana never mentioned him to me. As I say, I'd heard of him, but never met him. Miss Meredith I've never seen before. Mrs. Lorrimer I know slightly."

"What do you know about her?"

Roberts shrugged his shoulders.

"She's a widow. Moderately well off. Intelligent, well-bred woman—first-class bridge player. That's where I've met her, as a matter of fact—playing bridge."

"And Mr. Shaitana never mentioned her, either?"

"No."

"H'm—that doesn't help us much. Now, Dr. Roberts, perhaps you'll be so kind as to tax your memory carefully and tell me how often you yourself left your seat at the bridge table, and all you can remember about the movements of the others."

Dr. Roberts took a few minutes to think.

"It's difficult," he said frankly. "I can remember my own movements, more or less. I got up three times—that is, on three occasions when I was dummy I left my seat and made myself useful. Once I went over and put wood on the fire. Once I brought drinks to the two ladies. Once I poured out a whisky and soda for myself."

"Can you remember the times?"

"I could only say very roughly. We began to play about nine-thirty, I imagine. I should say it was about an hour later that I stoked the fire, quite a short time after that I fetched the drinks (next hand but one, I think), and perhaps half-past eleven when I got myself a whisky and soda—but those times are quite approximate. I couldn't answer for their being correct."

"The table with the drinks was beyond Mr. Shaitana's chair?"

"Yes. That's to say, I passed quite near him three times."

"And each time, to the best of your belief, he was asleep?"

"That's what I thought the first time. The second time I didn't even look at him. Third time I rather fancy the thought just passed through my mind: 'How the beggar does sleep.' But I didn't really look closely at him."

"Very good. Now, when did your fellow-players leave their seats?"

Dr. Roberts frowned.

"Difficult—very difficult. Despard went and fetched an extra ash-tray, I think. And he went for a drink. That was before me, for I remember he asked me if I'd have one, and I said I wasn't quite ready."

"And the ladies?"

"Mrs. Lorrimer went over to the fire once. Poked it, I think. I rather fancy she spoke to Shaitana, but I don't know. I was playing a rather tricky no trump at the time."

"And Miss Meredith?"

"She certainly left the table once. Came round and looked at my hand—I was her partner at the time. Then she looked at the other people's hands, and then she wandered round the room. I don't know what she was doing exactly. I wasn't paying attention."

Superintendent Battle said thoughtfully:

"As you were sitting at the bridge-table, no one's chair was directly facing the fireplace?"

"No, sort of sideways on, and there was a big cabinet between—Chinese piece, very handsome. I can see, of course, that it would be perfectly *possible* to stab the old boy. After all, when you're playing bridge, you're playing bridge. You're not looking round you and noticing what is going on. The only person who's likely to be doing that is dummy. And in this case—"

"In this case, undoubtedly, dummy was the murderer," said Superintendent Battle.

"All the same," said Dr. Roberts, "it wanted nerve, you know. After all, who is to say that somebody won't look up just at the critical moment?"

"Yes," said Battle. "It was a big risk. The motive must have been a strong one. I wish we knew what it was," he added with unblushing mendacity.

"You'll find out, I expect," said Roberts. "You'll go through his papers, and all that sort of thing. There will probably be a clue."

"We'll hope so," said Superintendent Battle gloomily.

He shot a keen glance at the other.

"I wonder if you'd oblige me, Dr. Roberts, by giving me a personal opinion—as man to man."

"Certainly."

"Which do you fancy yourself of the three?"

Dr. Roberts shrugged his shoulders.

"That's easy. Off-hand, I'd say Despard. The man's got plenty of nerve; he's used to a dangerous life where you've got to act quickly. He wouldn't mind taking a risk. It doesn't seem to me likely the women are in on this. Take a bit of strength, I should imagine."

"Not so much as you might think. Take a look at this."

Rather like a conjurer, Battle suddenly produced a long thin instrument of gleaming metal with a small round jewelled head.

Dr. Roberts leaned forward, took it, and examined it with rich professional appreciation. He tried the point and whistled.

"What a tool! What a tool! Absolutely made for murder, this little toy. Go in like butter—absolutely like butter. Brought it with him, I suppose."

Battle shook his head.

"No. It was Mr. Shaitana's. It lay on the table near the door with a good many other knick-knacks."

"So the murderer helped himself. A bit of luck finding a tool like that."

"Well, that's one way of looking at it," said Battle slowly.

"Well, of course, it wasn't luck for Shaitana, poor fellow."

"I didn't mean that, Dr. Roberts. I meant that there was another angle of looking at the business. It occurs to me that it was noticing this weapon that put the idea of murder into our criminal's mind."

"You mean it was a sudden inspiration—that the murder wasn't premeditated? He conceived the idea after he got here? Er—anything to suggest that idea to you?"

He glanced at him searchingly.

"It's just an idea," said Superintendent Battle stolidly.

"Well, it might be so, of course," said Dr. Roberts slowly.

Superintendent Battle cleared his throat.

"Well, I won't keep you any longer, doctor. Thank you for your help. Perhaps you'll leave your address."

"Certainly. 200 Gloucester Terrace, W.2. Telephone No. Bayswater 23896."

"Thank you. I may have to call upon you shortly."

"Delighted to see you any time. Hope there won't be too much in the papers. I don't want my nervous patients upset."

Superintendent Battle looked round at Poirot.

"Excuse me, M. Poirot. If you'd like to ask any questions, I'm sure the doctor wouldn't mind."

"Of course not. Of course not. Great admirer of yours, M. Poirot. Little grey cells—order and method. I know all about it. I feel sure you'll think of something most intriguing to ask me."

Hercule Poirot spread out his hands in his most foreign manner.

"No, no. I just like to get all the details clear in my mind. For instance, how many rubbers did you play?"

"Three," said Roberts promptly. "We'd got to one game all, in the fourth rubber, when you came in."

"And who played with who?"

"First rubber, Despard and I against the ladies. They beat us, God bless 'em. Walk over; we never held a card.

"Second rubber, Miss Meredith and I against Despard and Mrs. Lorrimer. Third rubber, Mrs. Lorrimer and I against Miss Meredith and Despard. We cut each time, but it worked out like a pivot. Fourth rubber, Miss Meredith and I again."

"Who won and who lost?"

"Mrs. Lorrimer won every rubber. Miss Meredith won the first and lost the next two. I was a bit up and Miss Meredith and Despard must have been down."

Poirot said, smiling, "The good superintendent has asked you your opinion of your companions as candidates for murder. I now ask you for your opinion of them as bridge players."

"Mrs. Lorrimer's first class," Dr. Roberts replied promptly. "I'll bet she makes a good income a year out of bridge. Despard's a good player, too—what I call a *sound* player—long-headed chap. Miss Meredith you might describe as quite a safe player. She doesn't make mistakes, but she isn't brilliant."

"And you yourself, doctor?"

Roberts' eyes twinkled.

"I overcall my hand a bit, or so they say. But I've always found it pays."

Poirot smiled.

Dr. Roberts rose.

"Anything more?"

Poirot shook his head.

"Well, good-night, then. Good-night, Mrs. Oliver. You ought to get some copy out of this. Better than your untraceable poisons, eh?"

Dr. Roberts left the room, his bearing springy once more. Mrs. Oliver said bitterly as the door closed behind him:

"Copy! Copy, indeed! People are so unintelligent. I could invent a better murder *any* day than anything *real*. I'm *never* at a loss for a plot. And the people who read my books *like* untraceable poisons!"

CHAPTER 5
Second Murderer?

Mrs. Lorrimer came into the dining-room like a gentlewoman. She looked a little pale, but composed.

"I'm sorry to have to bother you," Superintendent Battle began.

"You must do your duty, of course," said Mrs. Lorrimer quietly. "It is, I agree, an unpleasant position in which to be placed, but there is no good shirking it. I quite realise that one of the four people in that room must be guilty. Naturally, I can't expect you to take my word that I am not the person."

She accepted the chair that Colonel Race offered her and sat down opposite the superintendent. Her intelligent grey eyes met his. She waited attentively.

"You knew Mr. Shaitana well?" began the superintendent.

"Not very well. I have known him over a period of some years, but never intimately."

"Where did you meet him?"

"At a hotel in Egypt—the Winter Palace at Luxor, I think."

"What did you think of him?"

Mrs. Lorrimer shrugged her shoulders slightly.

"I thought him—I may as well say so—rather a charlatan."

"You had—excuse me for asking—no motive for wishing him out of the way?"

Mrs. Lorrimer looked slightly amused.

"Really, Superintendent Battle, do you think I should admit it if I had?"

"You might," said Battle. "A really intelligent person might know that a thing was bound to come out."

Mrs. Lorrimer inclined her head thoughtfully.

"There is that, of course. No, Superintendent Battle, I had no motive for wishing Mr. Shaitana out of the way. It is really a matter of indifference to me whether he is alive or dead. I thought him a *poseur*, and rather theatrical, and sometimes he irritated me. That is—or rather was—my attitude towards him."

"That is that, then. Now, Mrs. Lorrimer, can you tell me anything about your three companions?"

"I'm afraid not. Major Despard and Miss Meredith I met for the first time tonight. Both of them seem charming people. Dr. Roberts I know slightly. He's a very popular doctor, I believe."

"He is not your own doctor?"

"Oh, no."

"Now, Mrs. Lorrimer, can you tell me how often you got up from your seat tonight, and will you also describe the movements of the other three?"

Mrs. Lorrimer did not take any time to think.

"I thought you would probably ask me that. I have been trying to think it out. I got up once myself when I was dummy. I went over to the fire. Mr. Shaitana was alive then. I mentioned to him how nice it was to see a wood fire."

"And he answered?"

"That he hated radiators."

"Did any one overhear your conversation?"

"I don't think so. I lowered my voice, not to interrupt the players." She added dryly: "In fact you have only my word for it that Mr. Shaitana *was* alive and spoke to me."

Superintendent Battle made no protest. He went on with his quiet methodical questioning.

"What time was that?"

"I should think we had been playing a little over an hour."

"What about the others?"

"Dr. Roberts got me a drink. He also got himself one—that was later. Major Despard also went to get a drink—at about 11:15, I should say."

"Only once?"

"No—twice, I think. The men moved about a fair amount—but I didn't notice what they did. Miss Meredith left her seat once only, I think. She went round to look at her partner's hand."

"But she remained near the bridge-table?"

"I couldn't say at all. She may have moved away."

Battle nodded.

"It's all very vague," he grumbled.

"I am sorry."

Once again Battle did his conjuring trick and produced the long delicate stiletto.

"Will you look at this, Mrs. Lorrimer?"

Mrs. Lorrimer took it without emotion.

"Have you ever seen that before?"

"Never."

"Yet it was lying on a table in the drawing-room."

"I didn't notice it."

"You realise, perhaps, Mrs. Lorrimer, that with a weapon like that a woman could do the trick just as easily as a man."

"I suppose she could," said Mrs. Lorrimer quietly.

She leaned forward and handed the dainty little thing back to him.

"But all the same," said Superintendent Battle, "the woman would have to be pretty desperate. It was a long chance to take."

He waited a minute, but Mrs. Lorrimer did not speak.

"Do you know anything of the relations between the other three and Mr. Shaitana?"

She shook her head.

"Nothing at all."

"Would you care to give me an opinion as to which of them you consider the most likely person?"

Mrs. Lorrimer drew herself up stiffly.

"I should not care to do anything of the kind. I consider that a most improper question."

The superintendent looked like an abashed little boy who had been reprimanded by his grandmother.

"Address, please," he mumbled, drawing his notebook towards him.

"111 Cheyne Lane, Chelsea."

"Telephone number?"

"Chelsea 45632."

Mrs. Lorrimer rose.

"Anything you want to ask, M. Poirot?" said Battle hurriedly.

Mrs. Lorrimer paused, her head slightly inclined.

"Would it be a *proper* question, Madame, to ask you your opinion of your companions, not as potential murderers but as bridge players?"

Mrs. Lorrimer answered coldly:

"I have no objection to answering that—if it bears upon the matter at issue in any way—though I fail to see how it can."

"I will be the judge of that. Your answer, if you please, Madame."

In the tone of a patient adult humouring an idiot child, Mrs. Lorrimer replied:

"Major Despard is a good sound player. Dr. Roberts overcalls, but plays his hand brilliantly. Miss Meredith is quite a nice little player, but a bit too cautious. Anything more?"

In his turn doing a conjuring trick, Poirot produced four crumpled bridge scores.

"These scores, Madame, is one of these yours?"

She examined them.

"This is my writing. It is the score of the third rubber."

"And this score?"

"That must be Major Despard's. He cancels as he goes."

"And this one?"

"Miss Meredith's. The first rubber."

"So this unfinished one is Dr. Roberts'?"

"Yes."

"Thank you, Madame, I think that is all."

Mrs. Lorrimer turned to Mrs. Oliver.

"Good-night, Mrs. Oliver. Good-night, Colonel Race."

Then, having shaken hands with all four of them, she went out.

CHAPTER 6
Third Murderer?

"Didn't get any extra change out of her," commented Battle. "Put me in my place, too. She's the old-fashioned kind, full of consideration for others, but arrogant as the devil! I can't believe she did it, but you never know! She's got plenty of resolution. What's the idea of the bridge scores, M. Poirot?"

Poirot spread them out on the table.

"They are illuminating, do you not think? What do we want in this case? A clue to character. And a clue not to one character, but to four characters. And this is where we are most likely to find it—in these scribbled figures. Here is the first rubber, you see— a tame business, soon over. Small neat figures—careful addition and subtraction—that is Miss Meredith's score. She was playing with Mrs. Lorrimer. They had the cards, and they won.

"In this next one it is not so easy to follow the play, since it is kept in the cancellation style. But it tells us perhaps something about Major Despard—a man who likes the whole time to know at a glance where he stands. The figures are small and full character.

"This next score is Mrs. Lorrimer's—she and Dr. Roberts against the other two—a Homeric combat—figures mounting up above the line each side. Overcalling on the doctor's part, and they go down; but, since they are both first-class players, they never go down very much. If the doctor's overcalling induces rash bidding on the other side there is the chance seized of doubling. See—these figures here are doubled tricks gone down. A characteristic handwriting, graceful, very legible, firm.

"Here is the last score—the unfinished rubber. I collected one score in each person's handwriting, you see. Figures rather flamboyant. Not such high scores as the preceding rubber. That is probably because the doctor was playing with Miss Meredith, and she is a timid player. His calling would make her more so!

"You think, perhaps, that they are foolish, these questions that I ask? But it is not so. I want to get at the characters of these four players, and when it is only about bridge I ask, every one is ready and willing to speak."

"I never think your questions foolish, M. Poirot," said Battle. "I've seen too much of your work. Every one's got their own ways of working. I know that. I give my inspectors a free hand always. Every one's got to find out for themselves what method suits them best. But we'd better not discuss that now. We'll have the girl in."

Anne Meredith was upset. She stopped in the doorway. Her breath came unevenly.

Superintendent Battle was immediately fatherly. He rose, set a chair for her at a slightly different angle.

"Sit down, Miss Meredith, sit down. Now, don't be alarmed. I know all this seems rather dreadful, but it's not so bad, really."

"I don't think anything could be worse," said the girl in a low voice. "It's so awful—*so awful*—to think that *one* of us—that one of *us*——"

"You let me do the thinking," said Battle kindly. "Now, then, Miss Meredith, suppose we have your address first of all."

"Wendon Cottage, Wallingford."

"No address in town?"

"No, I'm staying at my club for a day or two."

"And your club is?"

"Ladies' Naval and Military."

"Good. Now, then, Miss Meredith, how well did you know Mr. Shaitana?"

"I didn't know him well at all. I always thought he was a most frightening man."

"Why?"

"Oh, well, he *was!* That awful smile! And a way he had of bending over you. As though he might bite you."

"Had you known him long?"

"About nine months. I met him in Switzerland during the winter sports."

"I should never have thought he went in for winter sports," said Battle, surprised.

"He only skated. He was a marvellous skater. Lots of figures and tricks."

"Yes, that sounds more like him. And did you see much of him after that?"

"Well—a fair amount. He asked me to parties and things like that. They were rather fun."

"But you didn't like him himself?"

"No, I thought he was a shivery kind of man."

Battle said gently:

"But you'd no special reason for being afraid of him?"

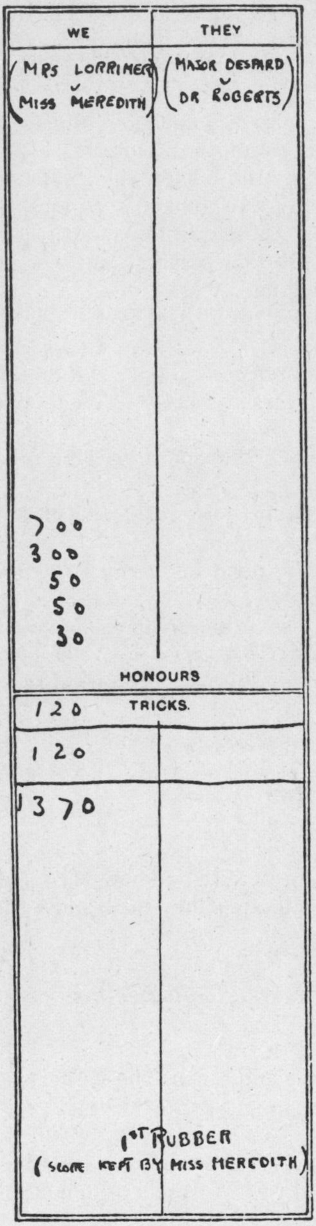
WE
THEY
MRS LORRIMER
MISS MEREDITH
MAJOR DESPARD
DR ROBERTS
700
300
50
50
30
HONOURS
TRICKS.
120
120
1370
1ST RUBBER
(SCORE KEPT BY MISS MEREDITH)

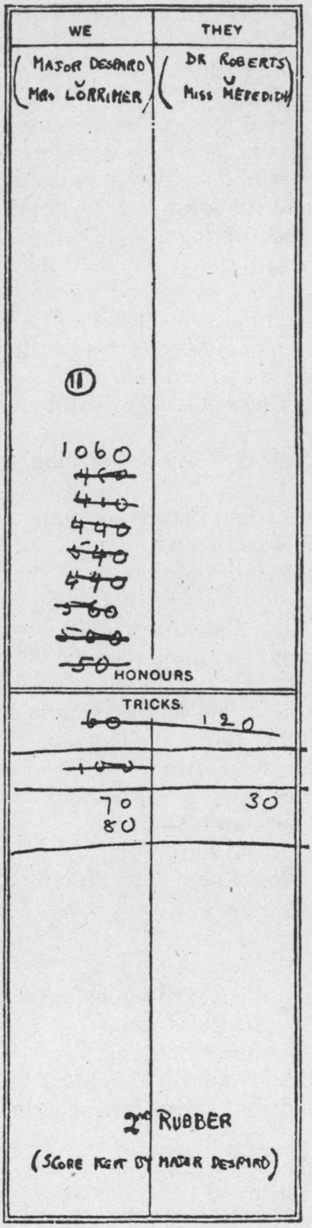
WE
THEY
MAJOR DESPARD
MRS LORRIMER
DR ROBERTS
MISS MEREDITH
11
1060
410
440
540
440
500
50
HONOURS
TRICKS.
60
120
100
70
80
30
2ND RUBBER
(SCORE KEPT BY MAJOR DESPARD)

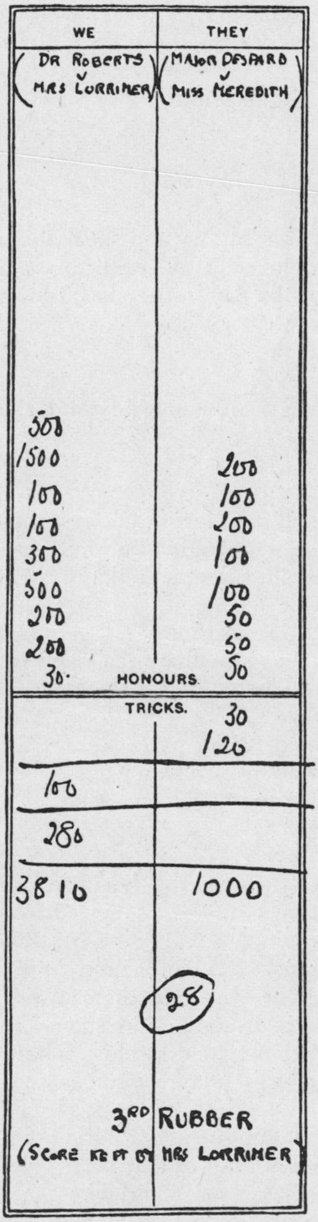
WE
THEY
DR ROBERTS v MRS LORRIMER
MAJOR DESPARD v MISS MEREDITH
500
1500
100
100
300
500
200
200
30.
200
100
200
100
100
50
50
50
HONOURS
TRICKS.
30
120
100
280
3810
1000
28
3RD RUBBER
(SCORE KEPT BY MRS LORRIMER)

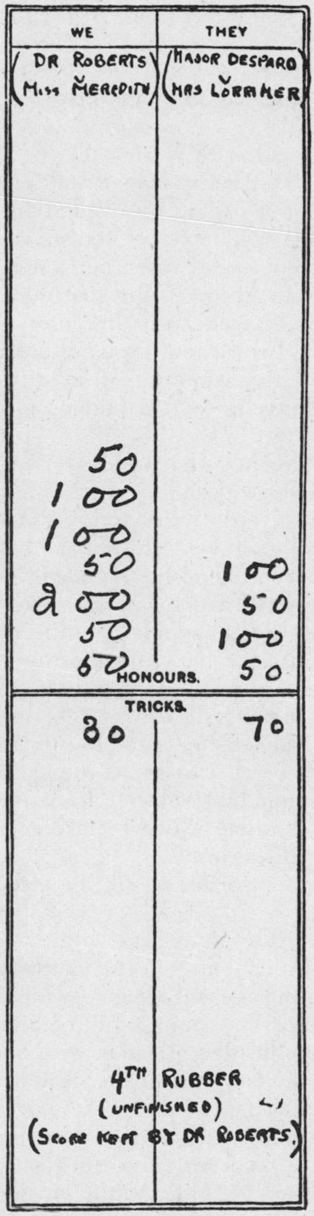
WE
THEY
DR ROBERTS v MISS MEREDITH
MAJOR DESPARD v MRS LORRIMER
50
100
100
50
200
50
50
100
50
100
50
HONOURS.
TRICKS.
80
70
4TH RUBBER
(UNFINISHED)
(SCORE KEPT BY DR ROBERTS)

Anne Meredith raised wide limpid eyes to his.

"Special reason? Oh, no."

"That's all right, then. Now about tonight. Did you leave your seat at all?"

"I don't think so. Oh, yes, I may have done once. I went round to look at the others' hands."

"But you stayed by the bridge-table all the time?"

"Yes."

"Quite sure, Miss Meredith?"

The girl's cheeks flamed suddenly.

"No—no, I think I walked about."

"Right. You'll excuse me, Miss Meredith, but try and speak the truth. I know you're nervous, and when one's nervous one's apt to—well, to say the thing the way you want it to be. But that doesn't really pay in the end. You walked about. Did you walk over in the direction of Mr. Shaitana?"

The girl was silent for a minute, then she said:

"Honestly—*honestly*—I don't remember."

"Well, we'll leave it that you may have done. Know anything about the other three?"

The girl shook her head.

"I've never seen any of them before."

"What do you think of them? Any likely murderers amongst them?"

"I can't believe it. I just can't believe it. It couldn't be Major Despard. And I don't believe it could be the doctor—after all, a doctor could kill any one in much easier ways. A drug—something like that."

"Then, if it's any one, you think it's Mrs. Lorrimer."

"Oh, I *don't*. I'm sure she wouldn't. She's so charming—and so kind to play bridge with. She's so good herself, and yet she doesn't make one feel nervous, or point out one's mistakes."

"Yet you left her name to the last," said Battle.

"Only because stabbing seems somehow more like a woman."

Battle did his conjuring trick. Anne Meredith shrank back.

"Oh, horrible. Must I—take it?"

"I'd rather you did."

He watched her as she took the stiletto gingerly, her face contracted with repulsion.

"With this tiny thing—with this——"

"Go in like butter," said Battle with gusto. "A child could do it."

"You mean—you mean"—wide, terrified eyes fixed themselves on his face—"that *I* might have done it? But I didn't. Oh, I didn't. Why should I?"

"That's just the question we'd like to know," said Battle. "What's the motive? Why did any one want to kill Shaitana? He was a picturesque person, but he wasn't dangerous, as far as I can make out."

Was there a slight indrawing of her breath—a sudden lifting of her breast?

"Not a blackmailer, for instance, or anything of that sort?" went on Battle. "And anyway, Miss Meredith, you don't look the sort of girl who's got a lot of guilty secrets."

For the first time she smiled, reassured by his geniality.

"No, indeed I haven't. I haven't got any secrets at all."

"Then don't you worry, Miss Meredith. We shall have to come round and ask you a few more questions, I expect, but it will be all a matter of routine."

He got up.

"Now you go off. My constable will get you a taxi; and don't you lie awake worrying yourself. Take a couple of aspirins."

He ushered her out. As he came back Colonel Race said in a low, amused voice:

"Battle, what a really accomplished liar you are! Your fatherly air was unsurpassed."

"No good dallying about with her, Colonel Race. Either the poor kid is dead scared—in which case it's cruelty, and I'm not a cruel man; I never have been—or she's a highly accomplished little actress, and we shouldn't get any further if we were to keep her here half the night."

Mrs. Oliver gave a sigh and ran her hands freely through her fringe until it stood upright and gave her a wholly drunken appearance.

"Do you know," she said, "I rather believe now that she did it! It's lucky it's not in a book. They don't really like the young and beautiful girl to have done it. All the same, I rather think she did. What do *you* think, M. Poirot?"

"Me, I have just made a discovery."

"In the bridge scores again?"

"Yes. Miss Anne Meredith turns her score over, draws lines and uses the back."

"And what does that mean?"

"It means she has the habit of poverty or else is of a naturally economical turn of mind."

"She's expensively dressed," said Mrs. Oliver.

"Send in Major Despard," said Superintendent Battle.

CHAPTER 7
Fourth Murderer?

Despard entered the room with a quick springing step—a step that reminded Poirot of something or some one.

"I'm sorry to have kept you waiting all this while, Major Despard," said Battle. "But I wanted to let the ladies get away as soon as possible."

"Don't apologise. I understand."

He sat down and looked inquiringly at the superintendent.

"How well did you know Mr. Shaitana?" began the latter.

"I've met him twice," said Despard crisply.

"Only twice?"

"That's all."

"On what occasions?"

"About a month ago we were both dining at the same house. Then he asked me to a cocktail party a week later."

"A cocktail party here?"

"Yes."

"Where did it take place—this room or the drawing-room?"

"In all the rooms."

"See this little thing lying about?"

Battle once more produced the stilleto.

Major Despard's lip twisted slightly.

"No," he said. "I didn't mark it down on that occasion for future use."

"There's no need to go ahead of what I say, Major Despard."

"I beg your pardon. The inference was fairly obvious."

There was a moment's pause, then Battle resumed his inquiries.

"Had you any motive for disliking Mr. Shaitana?"

"Every motive."

"Eh?" The superintendent sounded startled.

"For disliking him—not for killing him," said Despard. "I hadn't the least wish to kill him, but I would thoroughly have enjoyed kicking him. A pity. It's too late now."

"Why did you want to kick him, Major Despard?"

"Because he was the sort of Dago who needed kicking badly. He used to make the toe of my boot fairly itch."

"Know anything about him—to his discredit, I mean?"

"He was too well dressed—he wore his hair too long—and he smelt of scent."

"Yet you accepted his invitation to dinner," Battle pointed out.

"If I were only to dine in houses where I thoroughly approved of my host I'm afraid I shouldn't dine out very much, Superintendent Battle," said Despard dryly.

"You like society, but you don't approve of it?" suggested the other.

"I like it for very short periods. To come back from the wilds to lighted rooms and women in lovely clothes, to dancing and good food and laughter—yes, I enjoy that—for a time. And then the insincerity of it all sickens me, and I want to be off again."

"It must be a dangerous sort of life that you lead, Major Despard, wandering about in these wild places."

Despard shrugged his shoulders. He smiled slightly.

"Mr. Shaitana didn't lead a dangerous life—but he is dead, and I am alive!"

"He may have led a more dangerous life than you think," said Battle meaningly.

"What do you mean?"

"The late Mr. Shaitana was a bit of a Nosey Parker," said Battle.

The other leaned forward.

"You mean that he meddled with other people's lives—that he discovered—what?"

"I really meant that perhaps he was the sort of man who meddled—er—well, with women."

Major Despard leant back in his chair. He laughed, an amused but indifferent laugh.

"I don't think women would take a mountebank like that seriously."

"What's your theory of who killed him, Major Despard?"

"Well, I know I didn't. Little Miss Meredith didn't. I can't imagine Mrs. Lorrimer doing so—she reminds me of one of my more God-fearing aunts. That leaves the medical gentleman."

"Can you describe your own and other people's movements this evening?"

"I got up twice—once for an ash-tray, and I also poked the fire—and once for a drink——"

"At what times?"

"I couldn't say. First time might have been about half-past ten, the second time eleven, but that's pure guesswork. Mrs. Lorrimer went over to the fire once and said something to Shaitana. I didn't actually hear him answer, but then, I wasn't paying attention. I couldn't swear he didn't. Miss Meredith wandered about the room a bit, but I don't think she went over near the fireplace. Roberts was always jumping up and down—three or four times at least."

"I'll ask you M. Poirot's question," said Battle with a smile. "What did you think of them as bridge players?"

"Miss Meredith's quite a good player. Roberts overcalls his hand disgracefully. He deserves to go down more than he does. Mrs. Lorrimer's damned good."

Battle turned to Poirot.

"Anything else, M. Poirot?"

Poirot shook his head.

Despard gave his address as the Albany, wished them good-night and left the room.

As he closed the door behind him, Poirot made a slight movement.

"What is it?" demanded Battle.

"Nothing," said Poirot. "It just occurred to me that he walked like a tiger—yes, just so—lithe, easy, does the tiger move along."

"H'm!" said Battle. "Now, then"—his eye glanced round at his three companions—*"which of 'em did it?"*

CHAPTER 8
Which of Them?

Battle looked from one face to another. Only one person answered his question. Mrs. Oliver, never averse to giving her views, rushed into speech.

"The girl or the doctor," she said.

Battle looked questioningly at the other two. But both the men were unwilling to make a pronouncement. Race shook his head. Poirot carefully smoothed his crumpled bridge scores.

"One of 'em did it," said Battle musingly. "One of 'em's lying like hell. But which? It's not easy—no, it's not easy."

He was silent for a minute or two, then he said:

"If we're to go by what they *say*, the medico thinks Despard did it, Despard thinks the medico did it, the girl thinks Mrs. Lorrimer did it—and Mrs. Lorrimer won't say! Nothing very illuminating there."

"Perhaps not," said Poirot.

Battle shot him a quick glance.

"You think there is?"

Poirot waved an airy hand.

"A *nuance*—nothing more! Nothing to go upon."

Battle continued:

"You two gentlemen won't say what you think——"

"No evidence," said Race curtly.

"Oh, you *men!*" sighed Mrs. Oliver, despising such reticence.

"Let's look at the rough possibilities," said Battle. He considered a minute. "I put the doctor first, I think. Specious sort of customer. Would know the right spot to shove the dagger in. But there's not much more than that to it. Then take Despard. There's a man with any amount of nerve. A man accustomed to quick decisions and a man who's quite at home doing dangerous things. Mrs. Lorrimer? She's got any amount of nerve, too, and she's the sort of woman who might have a secret in her life. She looks as though she's known trouble. On the other hand, I'd say she's what I call a high-principled woman—sort of woman who might be headmistress of a girls' school. It isn't easy to think of her sticking a knife into any one. In fact, I don't think she did. And lastly, there's little Miss Meredith. We don't know anything about her. She seems an ordinary good-looking, rather shy girl. But one doesn't know, as I say, anything about her."

"We know that Shaitana believed she had committed murder," said Poirot.

"The angelic face masking the demon," mused Mrs. Oliver.

"This getting us anywhere, Battle?" asked Colonel Race.

"Unprofitable speculation, you think, sir? Well, there's bound to be speculation in a case like this."

"Isn't it better to find out something about these people?"

Battle smiled.

"Oh, we shall be hard at work on that. I think you could help us there."

"Certainly. How?"

"As regards Major Despard. He's been abroad a lot—in South America, in East Africa, in South Africa—you've means of knowing those parts. You could get information about him."

Race nodded.

"It shall be done. I'll get all available data."

"Oh," cried Mrs. Oliver. "I've got a plan. There are four of us—four sleuths, as you might say—and four of *them!* How would it be if we each took one. Backed our fancy! Colonel Race takes Major Despard, Superintendent Battle takes Dr. Roberts, I'll take Anne Meredith, and M. Poirot takes Mrs. Lorrimer. Each of us to follow our own line!"

Superintendent Battle shook his head decisively.

"Couldn't quite do that, Mrs. Oliver. This is official, you see. I'm in charge. I've got to investigate *all* lines. Besides, it's all very well to say back your fancy. Two of us might want to back the same horse! Colonel Race hasn't said he suspects Major Despard. And M. Poirot mayn't be putting his money on Mrs. Lorrimer."

Mrs. Oliver sighed.

"It was such a good plan," she sighed regretfully. "So *neat*." Then she cheered up a little. "But you don't mind me doing a little investigating on my own, do you?"

"No," said Superintendent Battle slowly. "I can't say I object to that. In fact, it's out of my power to object. Having been at this party tonight, you're naturally free to do anything your own curiosity or interest suggests. But I'd like to point out to you, Mrs. Oliver, that you'd better be a little careful."

"Discretion itself," said Mrs. Oliver. "I shan't breathe a word of—of anything——" she ended a little lamely.

"I do not think that was quite Superintendent Battle's meaning," said Hercule Poirot. "He meant that you will be dealing with a person who has already, to the best of our belief, killed twice. A person, therefore, who will not hesitate to kill a third time—if he considers it necessary."

Mrs. Oliver looked at him thoughtfully. Then she smiled—an agreeable engaging smile, rather like that of an impudent small child.

"You Have Been Warned," she quoted. "Thank you, M. Poirot. I'll watch my step. But I'm not going to be out of this."

Poirot bowed gracefully.

"Permit me to say—you are the sport, Madame."

"I presume," said Mrs. Oliver, sitting up very straight and speaking in a business-like committee-meeting manner, "that all information we receive will be pooled—that is, that we will not keep any knowledge to ourselves. Our own deductions and impressions, of course, we are entitled to keep up our sleeves."

Superintendent Battle sighed.

"This isn't a detective story, Mrs. Oliver," he said.

Race said:

"Naturally, all information must be handed over to the police."

Having said this in his most "Orderly Room" voice, he added with a slight twinkle in his eye: "I'm sure you'll play fair, Mrs. Oliver—the stained glove, the fingerprint on the tooth-glass, the fragment of burnt paper—you'll turn them over to Battle here."

"You may laugh," said Mrs. Oliver. "But a woman's intuition——"

She nodded her head with decision.

Race rose to his feet.

"I'll have Despard looked up for you. It may take a little time. Anything else I can do?"

"I don't think so, thank you, sir. You've no hints? I'd value anything of that kind."

"H'm. Well—I'd keep a special lookout for shooting or poison or accidents, but I expect you're on to that already."

"I'd made a note of that—yes, sir."

"Good man, Battle. You don't need me to teach you your job. Good-night, Mrs. Oliver. Good-night, M. Poirot."

And, with a final nod to Battle, Colonel Race left the room.

"Who is he?" asked Mrs. Oliver.

"Very fine Army record," said Battle. "Travelled a lot, too. Not many parts of the world he doesn't know about."

"Secret Service, I suppose," said Mrs. Oliver. "You can't tell me so—I know; but he wouldn't have been asked otherwise this evening. The four murderers and the four sleuths—Scotland Yard. Secret Service. Private. Fiction. A clever idea."

Poirot shook his head.

"You are in error, Madame. It was a very *stupid* idea. The tiger was alarmed—and the tiger sprang."

"The tiger? Why the tiger?"

"By the tiger I mean the murderer," said Poirot.

Battle said bluntly:

"What's *your* idea of the right line to take, M. Poirot? That's one question. And I'd also like to know what you think of the psychology of these four people. You're rather hot on that."

Still smoothing his bridge scores, Poirot said:

"You are right—psychology is very important. We know the *kind* of murder that has been committed, the *way* it was committed. If we have a person who from the psychological point of view could not have committed that particular type of murder, then we can dismiss that person from our calculations. We know *something* about these people. We have our own impression of them, we know the line that each has elected to take, and we know something about their minds and their characters from what we have learned about them as card players and from the study of their handwriting and of these scores. But alas! it is not too easy to give a definite pronouncement. This murder required audacity and nerve—a person who was willing to take a risk. Well, we have Dr. Roberts—a bluffer—an overcaller of his hand—a man with complete confidence in his own powers to pull off a risky thing. His psychology fits very well with the crime. One might say, then, that that automatically wipes out Miss Meredith. She is timid, frightened of overcalling her hand, careful, economical, prudent and lacking in self-confidence. The last type of person to carry out a bold and risky coup. But a timid person will murder out of fear. A frightened nervous person can be made desperate, can turn like a rat at bay if driven into a corner. If Miss Meredith had committed a crime in the past, and if she believed that Mr. Shaitana knew the circumstances of that crime and was about to deliver her up to justice she would be wild with terror—she would stick at nothing to save herself. It would be the same result, though brought about through a different reaction—not cool nerve and daring, but desperate panic. Then take Major Despard—a cool, resourceful man willing to try a long shot if he believed it absolutely necessary. He would weigh the pros and cons and might decide that there was a sporting chance in his favour—and he is the type of man to prefer action to inaction, and a man who would never shrink from taking the dangerous way if he believed there was a reasonable chance of success. Finally, there is Mrs. Lorrimer, an elderly woman, but a woman in full possession of her wits and faculties. A cool woman. A woman with a mathematical brain. She has probably the best brain of the four. I confess that if Mrs. Lorrimer committed a crime, I should expect it to be a *premeditated* crime. I can see her planning a crime slowly and carefully, making sure that there were no flaws in her scheme. For that reason she seems to me slightly more unlikely than the other three. She is, however, the most dominating personality, and whatever she undertook she would probably carry through without a flaw. She is a thoroughly efficient woman."

He paused.

"So, you see, that does not help us much. No—there is only one way in this crime. We must go back into the past."

Battle signed.

"You've said it," he murmured.

"In the opinion of Mr. Shaitana, each of those four people had committed murder. Had he evidence? Or was it a guess? We cannot tell. It is unlikely, I think, that he could have had actual evidence in all four cases——"

"I agree with you there," said Battle, nodding his head. "That would be a bit too much of a coincidence."

"I suggest that it might come about this way—murder or a certain form of murder is mentioned, and Mr. Shaitana surprised a look on some one's face. He was very quick—very sensitive to expression. It amuses him to experiment—to probe gently in the course of apparently aimless conversation—he is alert to notice a wince, a reservation, a desire to turn the conversation. Oh, it is easily done. If you suspect a certain secret, nothing is easier than to confirm your suspicion. Every time a word goes home you notice it—*if you are watching for such a thing*."

"It's the sort of game would have amused our late friend," said Battle, nodding.

"We may assume, then, that such was the procedure in one or more cases. He may have come across a piece of actual evidence in another case and followed it up.

I doubt whether, in any of the cases, he had sufficient actual knowledge with which, for instance, to have gone to the police."

"Or it mayn't have been the kind of case," said Battle. "Often enough there's a fishy business—we suspect foul play, but we can't ever prove it. Anyway, the course is clear. We've got to go through the records of all these people—and note any deaths that may be significant. I expect you noticed, just as the Colonel did, what Shaitana said at dinner."

"The black angel," murmured Mrs. Oliver.

"A neat little reference to poison, to accidents, to a doctor's opportunities, to shooting accidents. I shouldn't be surprised if he signed his death-warrant when he said those words."

"It was a nasty sort of pause," said Mrs. Oliver.

"Yes," said Poirot. "Those words went home to one person at least—that person probably thought that Shaitana knew far more than he really did. That listener thought that they were the prelude to the end—that the party was a dramatic entertainment arranged by Shaitana leading up to arrest for murder as its climax! Yes, as you say, he signed his death-warrant when he baited his guests with these words."

There was a moment's silence.

"This will be a long business," said Battle with a sigh. "We can't find out all we want in a moment—and we've got to be careful. We don't want any of the four to suspect what we're doing. All our questioning and so on must seem to have to do with *this* murder. There mustn't be a suspicion that we've got any idea of the motive for the crime. And the devil of it is we've got to check up on four possible murders in the past, not one."

Poirot demurred.

"Our friend Mr. Shaitana was not infallible," he said. "He may—it is just possible—have made a mistake."

"About all four?"

"No—he was more intelligent than that."

"Call it fifty-fifty?"

"Not even that. For me, I say one in four."

"One innocent and three guilty? That's bad enough. And the devil of it is, even if we get at the truth it mayn't help us. Even if somebody did push their great-aunt down the stairs in 1912, it won't be much use to us in 1937."

"Yes, yes, it will be of use to us." Poirot encouraged him. "You know that. You know it as well as I do."

Battle nodded slowly.

"I know what you mean," he said. "Same hallmark."

"Do you mean," said Mrs. Oliver, "that the former victim will have been stabbed with a dagger too?"

"Not quite as crude as that, Mrs. Oliver," said Battle turning to her. "But I don't doubt it will be essentially the same *type* of crime. The *details* may be different, but the essentials underlying them will be the same. It's odd, but a criminal gives himself away every time by that."

"Man is an unoriginal animal," said Hercule Poirot.

"Women," said Mrs. Oliver, "are capable of infinite variation. I should never commit the same type of murder twice running."

"Don't you ever write the same plot twice running?" asked Battle.

"The Lotus Murder," murmured Poirot. "The Clue of the Candle Wax."

Mrs. Oliver turned on him, her eyes beaming appreciation.

"That's clever of you—that's really very clever of you. Because, of course, those two are exactly the same plot—but nobody else has seen it. One is stolen papers at an informal week-end party of the Cabinet, and the other's a murder in Borneo in a rubber planter's bungalow."

"But the essential point on which the story turns is the same," said Poirot. "One of your neatest tricks. The rubber planter arranges his own murder—the Cabinet Minister arranges the robbery of his own papers. At the last minute the third person steps in and turns deception into reality."

"I enjoyed your last, Mrs. Oliver," said Superintendent Battle kindly. "The one where all the Chief Constables were shot simultaneously. You just slipped up once or twice on official details. I know you're keen on accuracy, so I wondered if—"

Mrs. Oliver interrupted him.

"As a matter of fact I don't care two pins about accuracy. Who is accurate? Nobody nowadays. If a reporter writes that a beautiful girl of twenty-two dies by turning on the gas after looking out over the sea and kissing her favourite labrador, Bob, good-bye, does anybody make a fuss because the girl was twenty-six, the room faced inland, and the dog was a Sealyham terrier called Bonnie? If a journalist can do that sort of thing, I don't see that it matters if I mix up police ranks and say a revolver when I mean an automatic, and a dictograph when I mean a phonograph, and use a poison that just allows you to gasp one dying sentence and no more. What really matters is plenty of *bodies!* If the thing's getting a little dull, some more blood cheers it up. Somebody is going to tell something—and then they're killed first! That always goes down well. It comes in all my books—camouflaged different ways, of course. And people *like* untraceable poisons, and idiotic police inspectors and girls tied up in cellars with sewer gas or water pouring in (such a troublesome way of killing any one really) and a hero who can dispose of anything from three to seven villains single-handed. I've written thirty-two books by now—and of course they're all exactly the same really, as M. Poirot seems to have noticed—but nobody else has—and I only regret one thing—making my detective a Finn. I don't really know anything about Finns and I'm always getting letters from Finland pointing out something impossible that he's said or done. They seem to read detective stories a good deal in Finland. I suppose it's the long winters with no daylight. In Bulgaria and Roumania they don't seem to read at all. I'd have done better to have made him a Bulgar."

She broke off.

"I'm so sorry. I'm talking shop. And this is a real murder." Her face lit up. "What a good idea it would be if *none* of them had murdered him. If he'd asked them all, and then quietly committed suicide just for the fun of making a schemozzle."

Poirot nodded approvingly.

"An admirable solution. So neat. So ironic. But, alas, Mr. Shaitana was not that sort of man. He was very fond of life."

"I don't think he was really a nice man," said Mrs. Oliver slowly.

"He was not nice, no," said Poirot. "But he was alive—and now he is dead, and as I told him once, I have a *bourgeois* attitude to murder. I disapprove of it."

He added softly:

"And so—I am prepared to go inside the tiger's cage. . . ."

CHAPTER 9
Dr. Roberts

"Good-morning, Superintendent Battle."

Dr. Roberts rose from his chair and offered a large pink hand smelling of a mixture of good soap and faint carbolic.

"How are things going?" he went on.

Superintendent Battle glanced round the comfortable consulting-room before answering.

"Well, Dr. Roberts, strictly speaking, they're not going. They're standing still."

"There's been nothing much in the papers, I've been glad to see."

"*Sudden death of the well-known Mr. Shaitana at an evening party in his own house*. It's left at that for the moment. We've had the autopsy—I brought a report of the findings along—thought it might interest you——"

"That's very kind of you—it would—h'm—h'm. Yes, very interesting."

He handed it back.

"And we've interviewed Mr. Shaitana's solicitor. We know the terms of his will. Nothing of interest there. He has relatives in Syria, it seems. And then, of course, we've been through all his private papers."

Was it fancy or did that broad, clean-shaven countenance look a little strained—a little wooden?

"And?" said Dr. Roberts.

"Nothing," said Superintendent Battle, watching him.

There wasn't a sigh of relief. Nothing so blatant as that. But the doctor's figure seemed to relax just a shade more comfortably in his chair.

"And so you've come to me?"

"And so, as you say, I've come to you."

The doctor's eyebrows rose a little and his shrewd eyes looked into Battle's.

"Want to go through *my* private papers—eh?"

"That was my idea."

"Got a search-warrant?"

"No."

"Well, you could get one easily enough, I suppose. I'm not going to make difficulties. It's not very pleasant being suspected of murder but I suppose I can't blame you for what's obviously your duty."

"Thank you, sir," said Superintendent Battle with real gratitude. "I appreciate your attitude, if I may say so, very much. I hope all the others will be as reasonable, I'm sure."

"What can't be cured must be endured," said the doctor good-humouredly.

He went on:

"I've finished seeing my patients here. I'm just off on my rounds. I'll leave you my keys and just say a word to my secretary and you can rootle to your heart's content."

"That's all very nice and pleasant, I'm sure," said Battle. "I'd like to ask you a few more questions before you go."

"About the other night? Really, I told you all I know."

"No, not about the other night. About yourself."

"Well, man, ask away, what do you want to know?"

"I'd just like a rough sketch of your career, Dr. Roberts. Birth, marriage, and so on."

"It will get me into practice for *Who's Who,*" said the doctor dryly. "My career's a perfectly straightforward one. I'm a Shropshire man, born at Ludlow. My father was in practice there. He died when I was fifteen. I was educated at Shrewsbury and went in for medicine like my father before me. I'm a St. Christopher's man—but you'll have all the medical details already, I expect."

"I looked you up, yes, sir. You an only child or have you any brothers or sisters?"

"I'm an only child. Both my parents are dead and I'm unmarried. Will that do to get on with? I came into partnership here with Dr. Emery. He retired about fifteen years ago. Lives in Ireland. I'll give you his address if you like. I live here with a cook, a parlourmaid and a housemaid. My secretary comes in daily. I make a good income and I only kill a reasonable number of my patients. How's that?"

Superintendent Battle grinned.

"That's fairly comprehensive, Dr. Roberts. I'm glad you've got a sense of humour. Now I'm going to ask you one more thing."

"I'm a strictly moral man, superintendent."

"Oh, that wasn't my meaning. No, I was just going to ask you if you'd give me the names of four friends—people who've known you intimately for a number of years. Kind of references, if you know what I mean."

"Yes, I think so. Let me see now. You'd prefer people who are actually in London now?"

"It would make it a bit easier, but it doesn't really matter."

The doctor thought for a minute or two, then with his fountain-pen he scribbled four names and addresses on a sheet of paper and pushed it across the desk to Battle.

"Will those do? They're the best I can think of on the spur of the moment."

Battle read carefully, nodded his head in satisfaction and put the sheet of paper away in an inner pocket.

"It's just a question of elimination," he said. "The sooner I can get one person eliminated and go on to the next, the better it is for every one concerned. I've got to make perfectly certain that you weren't on bad terms with the late Mr. Shaitana, that you had no private connections or business dealings with him, that there was no question of his having injured you at any time and your bearing resentment. *I* may believe you when you say you only knew him slightly—but it isn't a question of *my* belief. I've got to say I've made *sure*."

"Oh, I understand perfectly. You've got to think everybody's a liar till he's proved he's speaking the truth. Here are my keys, superintendent. That's the drawers of the desk—that's the bureau—that little one's the key of the poison cupboard. Be sure you lock it up again. Perhaps I'd better just have a word with my secretary."

He pressed a button on his desk.

Almost immediately the door opened and a competent-looking young woman appeared.

"You rang, doctor?"

"This is Miss Burgess—Superintendent Battle from Scotland Yard."

Miss Burgess turned a cool gaze on Battle. It seemed to say:

"Dear me, what sort of an animal is this?"

"I should be glad, Miss Burgess, if you will answer any questions Superintendent Battle may put to you, and give him any help he may need."

"Certainly, if you say so, doctor."

"Well," said Roberts, rising, "I'll be off. Did you put the morphia in my case? I shall need it for the Lockheart case."

He bustled out, still talking, and Miss Burgess followed him.

She returned a minute or two later to say:

"Will you press that button when you want me, Superintendent Battle?"

Superintendent Battle thanked her and said he would do so. Then he set to work.

His search was careful and methodical, though he had no great hopes of finding anything of importance. Roberts' ready acquiescence dispelled the chance of that. Roberts was no fool. He would realise that a search would be bound to come and he would make provisions accordingly. There was, however, a faint chance that Battle might come across a hint of the information he was really after, since Roberts would not know the real object of his search.

Superintendent Battle opened and shut drawers, rifled pigeon-holes, glanced through a cheque-book, estimated the unpaid bills—noted what those same bills were for, scrutinised Roberts' pass-book, ran through his case notes and generally left no written document unturned. The result was meagre in the extreme. He next took a look through the poison cupboard, noted the wholesale firms with which the doctor dealt, and the system of checking, relocked the cupboard and passed on to the bureau. The contents of the latter were of a more personal nature, but Battle found nothing germane to his search. He shook his head, sat down in the doctor's chair and pressed the desk button.

Miss Burgess appeared with commendable promptitude.

Superintendent Battle asked her politely to be seated and then sat studying her for a moment, before he decided which way to tackle her. He had sensed immediately her hostility and he was uncertain whether to provoke her into unguarded speech by increasing that hostility or whether to try a softer method of approach.

"I suppose you know what all this is about, Miss Burgess?" he said at last.

"Dr. Roberts told me," said Miss Burgess shortly.

"The whole thing's rather delicate," said Superintendent Battle.

"Is it?" said Miss Burgess.

"Well, it's rather a nasty business. Four people are under suspicion and one of them must have done it. What I want to know is whether you've ever seen this Mr. Shaitana?"

"Never."

"Ever heard Dr. Roberts speak of him?"

"Never—no, I am wrong. About a week ago Dr. Roberts told me to enter up a dinner appointment in his engagement-book. Mr. Shaitana, 8:15, on the 18th."

"And that is the first you ever heard of this Mr. Shaitana?"

"Yes."

"Never seen his name in the papers? He was often in the fashionable news."

"I've got better things to do than reading the fashionable news."

"I expect you have. Oh, I expect you have," said the superintendent mildly.

"Well," he went on. "There it is. All four of these people will only admit to knowing Mr. Shaitana slightly. But one of them knew him well enough to kill him. It's my job to find out which of them it was."

There was an unhelpful pause. Miss Burgess seemed quite uninterested in the performance of Superintendent Battle's job. It was her job to obey her employer's orders and sit here listening to what Superintendent Battle chose to say and answer any direct questions he might choose to put to her.

"You know, Miss Burgess," the superintendent found it uphill work but he persevered, "I doubt if you appreciate half the difficulties of our job. People say things, for instance. Well, we mayn't believe a word of it, but we've got to take notice of it all the same. It's particularly noticeable in a case of this kind. I don't want to say anything against your sex but there's no doubt that a woman, when she's rattled, is apt to lash out with her tongue a bit. She makes unfounded accusations, hints this, that and the other, and rakes up all sorts of old scandals that have probably nothing whatever to do with the case."

"Do you mean," demanded Miss Burgess, "that one of these other people have been saying things against the doctor?"

"Not exactly *said* anything," said Battle cautiously. "But all the same, I'm bound to take notice. Suspicious circumstances about the death of a patient. Probably all a lot of nonsense. I'm ashamed to bother the doctor with it."

"I suppose some one's got hold of that story about Mrs. Graves," said Miss Burgess wrathfully. "The way people talk about things they know nothing whatever about is disgraceful. Lots of old ladies get like that—they think everybody is poisoning them—their relations and their servants and even their doctors. Mrs. Graves had had three doctors before she came to Dr. Roberts and then when she got the same fancies about him he was quite willing for her to have Dr. Lee instead. It's the only thing to do in these cases, he said. And after Dr. Lee she had Dr. Steele, and then Dr. Farmer—until she died, poor old thing."

"You'd be surprised the way the smallest thing starts a story," said Battle. "Whenever a doctor benefits by the death of a patient somebody has something ill-natured to say. And yet why shouldn't a grateful patient leave a little something, or even a big something to her medical attendant."

"It's the relations," said Miss Burgess. "I always think there's nothing like death for bringing out the meanness of human nature. Squabbling over who's to have what before the body's cold. Luckily, Dr. Roberts has never had any trouble of that kind. He always says he hopes his patients won't leave him anything. I believe he once had a legacy of fifty pounds and he's had two walking-sticks and a gold watch, but nothing else."

"It's a difficult life, that of a professional man," said Battle with a sigh. "He's always open to blackmail. The most innocent occurrences lend themselves sometimes to a scandalous appearance. A doctor's got to avoid even the appearance of evil—that means he's got to have his wits about him good and sharp."

"A lot of what you say is true," said Miss Burgess. "Doctors have a difficult time with hysterical women."

"Hysterical women. That's right. I thought, in my own mind, that that was all it amounted to."

"I suppose you mean that dreadful Mrs. Craddock?"

Battle pretended to think.

"Let me see, was it three years ago? No, more."

"Four or five, I think. She was a *most* unbalanced woman! I was glad when she went abroad and so was Dr. Roberts. She told her husband the most frightful lies—they always do, of course. Poor man, he wasn't quite himself—he'd begun to be ill. He died of anthrax, you know, an infected shaving brush."

"I'd forgotten that," said Battle untruthfully.

"And then she went abroad and died not long afterwards. But I always thought she was a nasty type of woman—man-mad, you know."

"I know the kind," said Battle. "Very dangerous, they are. A doctor's got to give them a wide berth. Whereabouts did she die abroad—I don't seem to remember."

"Egypt, I think it was. She got blood-poisoning—some native infection."

"Another thing that must be difficult for a doctor," said Battle, making a conversational leap, "is when he suspects that one of his patients is being poisoned by one of their relatives. What's he to do? He's got to be sure—or else hold his tongue. And if he's done the latter, then it's awkward for him if there's talk of foul play afterwards. I wonder if any case of that kind has ever come Dr. Roberts' way?"

"I really don't think it has," said Miss Burgess, considering. "I've never heard of anything like that."

"From the statistical point of view, it would be interesting to know how many deaths occur among a doctor's practice per year. For instance now, you've been with Dr. Roberts some years——"

"Seven."

"Seven. Well, how many deaths have there been in that time off-hand?"

"Really, it's difficult to say." Miss Burgess gave herself up to calculation. She was by now quite thawed and unsuspicious. "Seven, eight—of course, I can't remember exactly—I shouldn't say more than thirty in the time."

"Then I fancy Dr. Roberts must be a better doctor than most," said Battle genially. "I suppose, too, most of his patients are upper-class. They can afford to take care of themselves."

"He's a very popular doctor. He's so good at diagnosis."

Battle sighed and rose to his feet.

"I'm afraid I've been wandering from my duty, which is to find out a connection between the doctor and this Mr. Shaitana. You're quite sure he wasn't a patient of the doctor's?"

"Quite sure."

"Under another name, perhaps?" Battle handed her a photograph. "Recognise him at all?"

"What a very theatrical-looking person. No, I've never seen him here at any time."

"Well, that's that." Battle sighed. "I'm much obliged to the doctor, I'm sure, for being so pleasant about everything. Tell him so from me, will you? Tell him I'm passing on to No. 2. Good-bye, Miss Burgess, and thank you for your help."

He shook hands and departed. Walking along the street he took a small notebook from his pocket and made a couple of entries in it under the letter R.

Mrs. Graves? unlikely.
Mrs. Craddock?
No legacies.
No wife. (Pity.)
Investigate deaths of patients. Difficult.

He closed the book and turned into the Lancaster Gate branch of the London & Wessex Bank.

The display of his official card brought him to a private interview with the manager.

"Good-morning, sir. One of your clients is a Dr. Geoffrey Roberts, I understand."

"Quite correct, superintendent."

"I shall want some information about that gentleman's account going back over a period of years."

"I will see what I can do for you."

A complicated half-hour followed. Finally Battle, with a sigh, tucked away a sheet of pencilled figures.

"Got what you want?" inquired the bank manager curiously.

"No, I haven't. Not one suggestive lead. Thank you all the same."

At the same moment, Dr. Roberts, washing his hands in his consulting-room, said over his shoulder to Miss Burgess:

"What about our stolid sleuth, eh? Did he turn the place upside down and you inside out?"

"He didn't get much out of me, I can tell you," said Miss Burgess, setting her lips tightly.

"My dear girl, no need to be an oyster. I told you to tell him all he wanted to know. What did he want to know, by the way?"

"Oh, he kept harping on your knowing that man Shaitana—suggested even that he might have come here as a patient under a different name. He showed me his photograph. Such a theatrical-looking man!"

"Shaitana? Oh, yes, fond of posing as a modern Mephistopheles. It went down rather well on the whole. What else did Battle ask you?"

"Really nothing very much. Except—oh, yes somebody had been telling him some absurd nonsense about Mrs. Graves—you know the way she used to go on."

"Graves? Graves? Oh, yes, old Mrs. Graves! That's rather funny!" The doctor laughed with considerable amusement. "That's really very funny indeed."

And in high good humour he went in to lunch.

CHAPTER 10
Dr. Roberts (continued)

Superintendent Battle was lunching with M. Hercule Poirot.

The former looked downcast, the latter sympathetic.

"Your morning, then, has not been entirely successful," said Poirot thoughtfully.

Battle shook his head.

"It's going to be uphill work, M. Poirot."

"What do you think of him?"

"Of the doctor? Well, frankly, I think Shaitana was right. He's a killer. Reminds me of Westaway. And of that lawyer chap in Norfolk. Same hearty, self-confident manner. Same popularity. Both of them were clever devils—so's Roberts. All the same, it doesn't follow that Roberts killed Shaitana—and as a matter of fact I don't think he did. He'd know the risk too well—better than a layman would—that Shaitana might wake and cry out. No, I don't think Roberts murdered him."

"But you think he has murdered some one?"

"Possibly quite a lot of people. Westaway had. But it's going to be hard to get at. I've looked over his bank account—nothing suspicious there—no large sums suddenly paid in. At any rate, in the last seven years he's not had any legacy from a patient. That wipes out murder for direct gain. He's never married—that's a pity—so ideally simple for a doctor to kill his own wife. He's well-to-do, but then he's got a thriving practice among well-to-do people."

"In fact he appears to lead a thoroughly blameless life—and perhaps does do so."

"Maybe. But I prefer to believe the worst."

He went on:

"There's the hint of a scandal over a woman—one of his patients—name of Craddock. That's worth looking up, I think. I'll get some one on to that straightaway. Woman actually died out in Egypt of some local disease, so I don't think there's anything in that—but it might throw a light on his general character and morals."

"Was there a husband?"

"Yes. Husband died of anthrax."

"Anthrax?"

"Yes, there were a lot of cheap shaving brushes on the market just then—some of them infected. There was a regular scandal about it."

"Convenient," suggested Poirot.

"That's what I thought. If her husband were threatening to kick up a row—— But there, it's all conjecture. We haven't a leg to stand upon."

"Courage, my friend. I know your patience. In the end, you will have perhaps as many legs as a centipede."

"And fall into the ditch as a result of thinking about them," grinned Battle.

Then he asked curiously:

"What about you, M. Poirot? Going to take a hand?"

"I too, might call on Dr. Roberts."

"Two of us in one day. That ought to put the wind up him."

"Oh, I shall be very discreet. I shall not inquire into his past life."

"I'd like to know just exactly what line you'll take," said Battle curiously, "but don't tell me unless you want to."

"Du tout—du tout. I am most willing. I shall talk a little of bridge, that is all."

"Bridge again. You harp on that, don't you, M. Poirot?"

"I find the subject very useful."

"Well, every man to his taste. I don't deal much in these fancy approaches. They don't suit my style."

"What is your style, superintendent?"

The superintendent met the twinkle in Poirot's eye with an answering twinkle in his own.

"A straightforward, honest, zealous officer doing his duty in the most laborious manner—that's my style. No frills. No fancy work. Just honest perspiration. Stolid and a bit stupid—that's my ticket."

Poirot raised his glass.

"To our respective methods—and may success crown our joint efforts."

"I expect Colonel Race may get us something worth having about Despard," said Battle. "He's got a good many sources of information."

"And Mrs. Oliver?"

"Bit of a toss-up there. I rather like that woman. Talks a lot of nonsense, but she's a sport. And women get to know things about other women that men can't get at. She may spot something useful."

They separated. Battle went back to Scotland Yard to issue instructions for certain lines to be followed up. Poirot betook himself to 200 Gloucester Terrace.

Dr. Roberts' eyebrows rose comically as he greeted his guest.

"Two sleuths in one day," he asked. "Handcuffs by this evening, I suppose."

Poirot smiled.

"I can assure you, Dr. Roberts, that my attentions are being equally divided between all four of you."

"That's something to be thankful for, at all events. Smoke?"

"If you permit, I prefer my own."

Poirot lighted one of his tiny Russian cigarettes.

"Well, what can I do for you?" asked Roberts.

Poirot was silent for a minute or two puffing, then he said:

"Are you a keen observer of human nature, doctor?"

"I don't know. I suppose I am. A doctor has to be."

"That was exactly my reasoning. I said to myself, 'A doctor has always to be studying his patients—their expressions, their colour, how fast they breathe, any signs of restlessness—a doctor notices these things automatically almost without noticing he notices! Dr. Roberts is the man to help me.'"

"I'm willing enough to help. What's the trouble?"

Poirot produced from a neat little pocket-case three carefully folded bridge scores.

"These are the first three rubbers the other evening," he explained. "Here is the first one—in Miss Meredith's handwriting. Now can you tell me—with this to refresh your memory—exactly what the calling was and how each hand went?"

Roberts stared at him in astonishment.

"You're joking, M. Poirot. How can I possibly remember?"

"Can't you? I should be so very grateful if you could. Take this first rubber. The first game must have resulted in a game call in hearts or spades, or else one or other side must have gone down fifty."

"Let me see—that was the first hand. Yes, I think they went out in spades."

"And the next hand?"

"I suppose one or other of us went down fifty—but I can't remember which or what it was in. Really, M. Poirot, you can hardly expect me to do so."

"Can't you remember any of the calling or the hands?"

"I got a grand slam—I remember that. It was doubled too. And I also remember going down a nasty smack—playing three no trumps, I think it was—went down a packet. But that was later on."

"Do you remember with whom you were playing?"

"Mrs. Lorrimer. She looked a bit grim, I remember. Didn't like my overcalling, I expect."

"And you can't remember any other of the hands or the calling?"

Roberts laughed.

"My dear M. Poirot, did you really expect I could. First there was the murder—enough to drive the most spectacular hands out of one's mind—and in addition I've played at least half a dozen rubbers since then."

Poirot sat looking rather crestfallen.

"I'm sorry," said Roberts.

"It does not matter very much," said Poirot slowly. "I hoped that you might remember one or two, at least, of the hands, because I thought they might be valuable landmarks in remembering other things."

"What other things?"

"Well, you might have noticed, for instance, that your partner made a mess of playing a perfectly simple no trumper, or that an opponent, say, presented you with a couple of unexpected tricks by failing to lead an obvious card."

Dr. Roberts became suddenly serious. He leaned forward in his chair.

"Ah," he said. "Now I see what you're driving at. Forgive me. I thought at first you were talking pure nonsense. You mean that the murder—the successful accomplishment of the murder—might have made a definite difference in the guilty party's play?"

Poirot nodded.

"You have seized the idea correctly. It would be a clue of the first excellence if you had been four players who knew each other's game well. A variation, a sudden lack of brilliance, a missed opportunity—that would have been immediately noticed. Unluckily, you were all strangers to each other. Variation in play would not be so noticeable. But think, M. le docteur, I beg of you to *think*. Do you remember any inequalities—any sudden glaring mistakes—in the play of any one?"

There was silence for a minute or two, then Dr. Roberts shook his head.

"It's no good. I can't help you," he said frankly. "I simply don't remember. All I can tell you is what I told you before: Mrs. Lorrimer is a first-class player—she never made a slip that I noticed. She was brilliant from start to finish. Despard's play was uniformly good too. Rather a conventional player—that is, his bidding is strictly conventional. He never steps outside the rules. Won't take a long chance. Miss Meredith——" He hesitated.

"Yes? Miss Meredith?" Poirot prompted him.

"She did make mistakes—once or twice—I remember—towards the end of the evening, but that may simply have been because she was tired—not being a very experienced player. Her hand shook, too——"

He stopped.

"When did her hand shake?"

"When was it now? I can't remember. . . . I think she was just nervous. M. Poirot, you're making me imagine things."

"I apologise. There is another point on which I seek your help."

"Yes?"

Poirot said slowly:

"It is difficult. I do not, you see, wish to ask you a leading question. If I say, did you notice so and so—well, I have put the thing into your head. Your answer will not be so valuable. Let me try to get at the matter another way. If you will be so kind, Dr. Roberts, describe to me the contents of the room in which you played."

Roberts looked thoroughly astonished.

"The contents of the room?"

"If you will be so good."

"My dear fellow, I simply don't know where to begin."

"Begin anywhere you choose."

"Well, there was a good deal of furniture——"

"*Non, non, non,* be precise, I pray of you."

Dr. Roberts sighed.

He began facetiously after the manner of an auctioneer.

"One large settee upholstered in ivory brocade—one ditto in green ditto—

four or five large chairs. Eight or nine Persian rugs—a set of twelve small gilt Empire chairs. William and Mary bureau. (I feel just like an auctioneer's clerk.) Very beautiful Chinese cabinet. Grand piano. There was other furniture but I'm afraid I didn't notice it. Six first-class Japanese prints. Two Chinese pictures on looking-glass. Five or six very beautiful snuff-boxes. Some Japanese ivory netsuke figures on a table by themselves. Some old silver—Charles I. tazzas, I think. One or two pieces of Battersea enamel——"

"Bravo, bravo!" Poirot applauded.

"A couple of old English slipware birds—and, I think, a Ralph Wood figure. Then there was some Eastern stuff—intricate silver work. Some jewellery, I don't know much about that. Some Chelsea birds, I remember. Oh, and some miniatures in a case—pretty good ones, I fancy. That's not all by a long way—but it's all I can think of for the minute."

"It is magnificent," said Poirot with due appreciation. "You have the true observer's eye."

The doctor asked curiously:

"Have I included the object you had in mind?"

"That is the interesting thing about it," said Poirot. "If you had mentioned the object I had in mind it would have been extremely surprising to me. As I thought, you would not mention it."

"Why?"

Poirot twinkled.

"Perhaps—because it was not there to mention."

Roberts stared.

"That seems to remind me of something."

"It reminds you of Sherlock Holmes, does it not? The curious incident of the dog in the night. The dog did not howl in the night. That is the curious thing! Ah, well, I am not above stealing the tricks of others."

"Do you know, M. Poirot, I am completely at sea as to what you are driving at."

"That is excellent, that. In confidence, that is how I get my little effects."

Then, as Dr. Roberts still looked rather dazed, Poirot said with a smile as he rose to his feet:

"You may at least comprehend this, what you have told me is going to be very helpful to me in my next interview."

The doctor rose also.

"I can't see how, but I'll take your work for it," he said.

They shook hands.

Poirot went down the steps of the doctor's house, and hailed a passing taxi.

"111 Cheyne Lane, Chelsea," he told the driver.

CHAPTER 11
Mrs. Lorrimer

111 Cheyne Lane was a small house of very neat and trim appearance standing in a quiet street. The door was painted black and the steps were particularly well whitened, the brass of the knocker and handle gleamed in the afternoon sun.

The door was opened by an elderly parlourmaid with an immaculate white cap and apron.

In answer to Poirot's inquiry she said that her mistress was at home.

She preceded him up the narrow staircase.

"What name, sir?"

"M. Hercule Poirot."

He was ushered into a drawing-room of the usual L shape. Poirot looked about him, noting details. Good furniture, well polished, of the old family type. Shiny chintz on the chairs and settees. A few silver photograph frames about in the old-fashioned manner. Otherwise an agreeable amount of space and light, and some really beautiful chrysanthemums arranged in a tall jar.

Mrs. Lorrimer came forward to meet him. She shook hands without showing any particular surprise at seeing him, indicated a chair, took one herself and remarked favourably on the weather.

There was a pause.

"I hope, Madame," said Hercule Poirot, "that you will forgive this visit."

Looking directly at him, Mrs. Lorrimer asked:

"Is this a professional visit?"

"I confess it."

"You realise, I suppose, M. Poirot, that though I shall naturally give Superintendent Battle and the official police any information and help they may require, I am by no means bound to do the same for any unofficial investigator?"

"I am quite aware of that fact, Madame. If you show me the door, me, I march to that door with complete submission."

Mrs. Lorrimer smiled very slightly.

"I am not yet prepared to go to those extremes, M. Poirot. I can give you ten minutes. At the end of that time I have to go out to a bridge party."

"Ten minutes will be ample for my purpose. I want you to describe to me, madame, the room in which you played bridge the other evening—the room in which Mr. Shaitana was killed."

Mrs. Lorrimer's eyebrows rose.

"What an extraordinary question! I do not see the point of it."

"Madame, if when you were playing bridge, some one were to say to you—why do you play that ace or why do you put on the knave that is taken by the queen and not the king which would take the trick? If people were to ask you such questions, the answers would be rather long and tedious, would they not?"

Mrs. Lorrimer smiled slightly.

"Meaning that in this game you are the expert and I am the novice. Very well." She reflected a minute. "It was a large room. There were a good many things in it."

"Can you describe some of those things?"

"There were some glass flowers—modern—rather beautiful. . . . And I think there were some Chinese or Japanese pictures. And there was a bowl of tiny red tulips—amazingly early for them."

"Anything else?"

"I'm afraid I didn't notice anything in detail."

"The furniture—do you remember the colour of the upholstery?"

"Something silky, I think. That's all I can say."

"Did you notice any of the small objects?"

"I'm afraid not. There were so many. I know it struck me as quite a collector's room."

There was a silence for a minute. Mrs. Lorrimer said with a faint smile:

"I'm afraid I have not been very helpful."

"There is something else." He produced the bridge scores. "Here are the first three rubbers played. I wondered if you could help me with the aid of these scores to reconstruct the hands."

"Let me see." Mrs. Lorrimer looked interested. She bent over the scores.

"That was the first rubber. Miss Meredith and I were playing against the two men. The first game was played in four spades. We made it and an over trick. Then the next hand was left at two diamonds and Dr. Roberts went down one trick on it. There was quite a lot of bidding on the third hand, I remember. Miss Meredith passed. Major Despard went a heart. I passed. Dr. Roberts gave a jump bid of three clubs. Miss Meredith went three spades. Major Despard bid four diamonds. I doubled. Dr. Roberts took it into four hearts. They went down one."

"Epatant," said Poirot. "What a memory!"

Mrs. Lorrimer went on, disregarding him:

"On the next hand Major Despard passed and I bid a no trump. Dr. Roberts bid three hearts. My partner said nothing. Despard put his partner to four. I doubled and they went down two tricks. Then I dealt and we went out on a four-spade call."

She took up the next score.

"It is difficult, that," said Poirot. "Major Despard scores in the cancellation manner."

"I rather fancy both sides went down fifty to start with—then Dr. Roberts went down to five diamonds and we doubled and got him down three tricks. Then we made three clubs, but immediately after the others went game in spades. We made the second game in five clubs. Then we went down a hundred. The others made one heart, we made two no trumps and we finally won the rubber with a four-club call."

She picked up the next score.

"This rubber was rather a battle, I remember. It started tamely. Major Despard and Miss Meredith made a one-heart call. Then we went down a couple of fifties trying for four hearts and four spades. Then the others made game in spades—no use trying to stop them. We went down three hands running after that but undoubled. Then we won the second game in no trumps. Then a battle royal started. Each side went down in turn. Dr. Roberts overcalled but though he went down badly once or twice, his calling paid, for more than once he frightened Miss Meredith out of bidding her hand. Then he bid an original two spade, I gave him three diamonds, he bid four no trumps, I bid five spades and he suddenly jumped to seven diamonds. We were doubled, of course. He had no business to make such a call. By a kind of miracle we got it. I never thought we should when I saw his hand go down. If the others led a heart we would have been three tricks down. As it was they led the king of clubs and we got it. It was really very exciting."

"Je crois bien—a Grand Slam Vulnerable doubled. It causes the emotions, that! Me, I admit it, I have not the nerve to go for the slams. I content myself with the game."

"Oh, but you shouldn't," said Mrs. Lorrimer with energy. "You must play the game properly."

"Take risks, you mean?"

"There is no risk if the bidding is correct. It should be a mathematical certainty. Unfortunately, few people really bid well. They know the opening bids but later they lose their heads. They cannot distinguish between a hand with winning cards in it and a hand without losing cards—but I mustn't give you a lecture on bridge, or on the losing count, M. Poirot."

"It would improve my play, I am sure, Madame."

Mrs. Lorrimer resumed her study of the score.

"After that excitement the next hands were rather tame. Have you the fourth score there? Ah, yes. A ding-dong battle—neither side able to score below."

"It is often like that as the evening wears on."

"Yes, one starts tamely and then the cards get worked up."

Poirot collected the scores and made a little bow.

"Madame, I congratulate you. Your card memory is magnificent—but magnificent! You remember, one might say, every card that was played!"

"I believe I do."

"Memory is a wonderful gift. With it the past is never the past—I should imagine, Madame, that to you the past unrolls itself, every incident clear as yesterday. Is that so?"

She looked at him quickly. Her eyes were wide and dark.

It was only for a moment, then she had resumed her woman-of-the-world manner, but Hercule Poirot did not doubt. That shot had gone home.

Mrs. Lorrimer rose.

"I'm afraid I shall have to leave now. I am so sorry—but I really mustn't be late."

"Of course not—of course not. I apologise for trespassing on your time."

"I'm sorry I haven't been able to help you more."

"But you have helped me," said Hercule Poirot.

"I hardly think so."

She spoke with decision.

"But yes. You have told me something I wanted to know."

She asked no question as to what that something was.

He held out his hand.

"Thank you, Madame, for your forbearance."

As she shook hands with him she said:

"You are an extraordinary man, M. Poirot."

"I am as the good God made me, Madame."

"We are all that, I suppose."

"Not all, Madame. Some of us have tried to improve on His pattern. Mr. Shaitana, for instance."

"In what way do you mean?"

"He had a very pretty taste in *objets de virtu* and *bric-à-brac*—he should have been content with that. Instead, he collected other things."

"What sort of things?"

"Well—shall we say—sensations?"

"And don't you think that was *dans son caractère?*"

Poirot shook his head gravely.

"He played the part of the devil too successfully. But he was not the devil. *Au fond*, he was a stupid man. And so—he died."

"Because he was stupid?"

"It is the sin that is never forgiven and always punished, Madame."

There was a silence. Then Poirot said:

"I take my departure. A thousand thanks for your amiability, Madame. I will not come again unless you send for me."

Her eyebrows rose.

"Dear me, M. Poirot, why should I send for you?"

"You might. It is just an idea. If so, I will come. Remember that."

He bowed once more and left the room.

In the street he said to himself.

"I am right. . . . I am sure I am right. . . . It *must* be that!"

CHAPTER 12
Anne Meredith

Mrs. Oliver extricated herself from the driving-seat of her little two-seater with some difficulty. To begin with, the makers of modern motor-cars assume that only a pair of sylph-like knees will ever be under the steering-wheel. It is also the fashion to sit low. That being so, for a middle-aged woman of generous proportions it requires a good deal of superhuman wriggling to get out from under the steering-wheel. In the second place, the seat next to the driving-seat was encumbered by several maps, a hangbag, three novels and a large bag of apples. Mrs. Oliver was partial to apples and had indeed been known to eat as many as five pounds straight off whilst composing the complicated plot of *The Death in the Drain Pipe*—coming to herself with a start and an incipient stomach-ache an hour and ten minutes after she was due at an important luncheon party given in her honour.

With a final determined heave and a sharp shove with the knee against a recalcitrant door, Mrs. Oliver arrived a little too suddenly on the sidewalk outside the gate of Wendon Cottage, showering apple cores freely round her as she did so.

She gave a deep sigh, pushed back her country hat to an unfashionable angle, looked down with approval at the tweeds she had remembered to put on, frowned a little when she saw that she had absent-mindedly retained her London high-heeled patent leather shoes, and pushing open the gate of Wendon Cottage walked up the flagged path to the front door. She rang the bell and executed a cheerful little rat-a-tat-tat on the knocker—a quaint conceit in the form of a toad's head.

As nothing happened she repeated the performance.

After a further pause of a minute and a half, Mrs. Oliver stepped briskly round the side of the house on a voyage of exploration.

There was a small old-fashioned garden with Michaelmas daisies and straggling chrysanthemums behind the cottage, and beyond it a field. Beyond the field was the river. For an October day the sun was warm.

Two girls were just crossing the field in the direction of the cottage. As they came through the gate into the garden, the foremost of the two stopped dead.

Mrs. Oliver came forward.

"How do you do, Miss Meredith? You remember me, don't you?"

"Oh—oh, of course." Anne Meredith extended her hand hurriedly. Her eyes looked wide and startled. Then she pulled herself together.

"This is my friend who lives with me—Miss Dawes. Rhoda, this is Mrs. Oliver."

The other girl was tall, dark, and vigorous-looking. She said excitedly:

"Oh, are you the Mrs. Oliver? Ariadne Oliver?"

"I am," said Mrs. Oliver, and she added to Anne, "Now let us sit down somewhere, my dear, because I've got a lot to say to you."

"Of course. And we'll have tea——"

"Tea can wait," said Mrs. Oliver.

Anne led the way to a little group of deck and basket chairs, all rather dilapidated. Mrs. Oliver chose the strongest-looking with some care, having had various unfortunate experiences with flimsy summer furniture.

"Now, my dear," she said briskly. "Don't let's beat about the bush. About this murder the other evening. We've got to get busy and do something."

"Do something?" queried Anne.

"Naturally," said Mrs. Oliver. "I don't know what *you* think, but I haven't the least doubt who did it. That doctor. What was his name? Roberts. That's it! Roberts. A Welsh name! I never trust the Welsh! I had a Welsh nurse and she took me to Harrogate one day and went home having forgotten all about me. Very unstable. But never mind about her. Roberts did it—that's the point and we must put our heads together and prove he did."

Rhoda Dawes laughed suddenly—then she blushed.

"I beg your pardon. But you're—you're so different from what I would have imagined."

"A disappointment, I expect," said Mrs. Oliver serenely. "I'm used to that. Never mind. What we must do is prove that Roberts did it!"

"How can we?" said Anne.

"Oh, don't be so defeatist, Anne," cried Rhoda Dawes. "I think Mrs. Oliver's splendid. Of course, she knows all about these things. She'll do just as Sven Hjerson does."

Blushing slightly at the name of her celebrated Finnish detective, Mrs. Oliver said:

"It's got to be done, and I'll tell you why, child. You don't want people thinking *you* did it?"

"Why should they?" asked Anne, her colour rising.

"You know what people are!" said Mrs. Oliver. "The three who didn't do it will come in for just as much suspicion as the one who did."

Anne Meredith said slowly:

"I still don't quite see why you came to *me*, Mrs. Oliver?"

"Because in my opinion the other two don't matter! Mrs. Lorrimer is one of those women who play bridge at bridge clubs all day. Women like that *must* be made of armour-plating—they can look after themselves all right! And anyway she's old. It wouldn't matter if any one thought she'd done it. A girl's different. She's got her life in front of her."

"And Major Despard?" asked Anne.

"Pah!" said Mrs. Oliver. "He's a man. I never worry about men. Men can look after themselves. Do it remarkably well, if you ask me. Besides, Major Despard enjoys a dangerous life. He's getting his fun at home instead of on the Irrawaddy—or do I mean the Limpopo? You know what I mean—that yellow African river that men like so much. No, I'm not worrying my head about either of those two."

"It's very kind of you," said Anne slowly.

"It was a beastly thing to happen," said Rhoda. "It's broken Anne up, Mrs. Oliver. She's awfully sensitive. And I think you're quite right. It would be ever so much better to do something than just to sit here thinking about it all."

"Of course it would," said Mrs. Oliver. "To tell you the truth, a real murder has never come my way before. And, to continue telling the truth, I don't believe real murder is very much in my line. I'm so used to loading the dice—if you understand what I mean. But I wasn't going to be out of it and let those three men have all the fun to themselves. I've always said that if a woman were the head of Scotland Yard——"

"Yes?" said Rhoda, leaning forward with parted lips. "If you were head of Scotland Yard, what would you do?"

"I should arrest Dr. Roberts straight away——"

"Yes?"

"However, I'm not the head of Scotland Yard," said Mrs. Oliver, retreating from dangerous ground. "I'm a private individual——"

"Oh, you're not that," said Rhoda, confusedly complimentary.

"Here we are," continued Mrs. Oliver, "three private individuals—all women. Let us see what we can do by putting our heads together."

Anne Meredith nodded thoughtfully. Then she said:

"Why do you think Dr. Roberts did it?"

"He's that sort of man," replied Mrs. Oliver promptly.

"Don't you think, though——" Anne hesitated. "Wouldn't a doctor——? I mean, something like poison would be so much easier for him."

"Not at all. Poison—drugs of any kind would point straight to a doctor. Look how they are always leaving cases of dangerous drugs in cars all over London and getting them stolen. No, just because he *was* a doctor he'd take special care not to use anything of a medical kind."

"I see," said Anne doubtfully.

Then she said:

"But why do you think he wanted to kill Mr. Shaitana? Have you any idea?"

"Idea? I've got any amount of ideas. In fact, that's just the difficulty. It always is my difficulty. I can never think of even one plot at a time. I always think of at least five, and then it's agony to decide between them. I can think of six beautiful reasons for the murder. The trouble is I've no earthly means of knowing which is right. To begin with, perhaps Shaitana was a moneylender. He had a very oily look. Roberts was in his clutches, and killed him because he couldn't get the money to repay the loan. Or perhaps Shaitana ruined his daughter or his sister. Or perhaps Roberts is a bigamist, and Shaitana knew it. Or possibly Roberts married Shaitana's second cousin, and will inherit all Shaitana's money through her. Or—— How many have I got to?"

"Four," said Rhoda.

"Or—and this is a really good one—suppose Shaitana knew some secret in Roberts' past. Perhaps you didn't notice, my dear, but Shaitana said something rather peculiar at dinner—just before a rather queer pause."

Anne stooped to tickle a caterpillar. She said, "I don't think I remember."

"What did he say?" asked Rhoda.

"Something about—what was it?—an accident and poison. Don't you remember?"

Anne's left hand tightened on the basketwork of her chair.

"I do remember something of the kind," she said composedly.

Rhoda said suddenly, "Darling, you ought to have a coat. It's not summer, remember. Go and get one."

Anne shook her head.

"I'm quite warm."

But she gave a queer little shiver as she spoke.

"You see my theory," went on Mrs. Oliver. "I dare say one of the doctor's patients poisoned himself by accident; but, of course, really, it was the doctor's own doing. I dare say he's murdered lots of people that way."

A sudden colour came into Anne's cheeks. She said, "Do doctors usually want to murder their patients wholesale? Wouldn't it have rather a regrettable effect on their practice?"

"There would be a reason, of course," said Mrs. Oliver vaguely.

"I think the idea is absurd," said Anne crisply. "Absolutely absurdly melodramatic."

"Oh, Anne!" cried Rhoda in an agony of apology. She looked at Mrs. Oliver. Her eyes, rather like those of an intelligent spaniel, seemed to be trying to say something. "Try and understand. Try and understand," those eyes said.

"I think it's a splendid idea, Mrs. Oliver," Rhoda said earnestly. "And a doctor could get hold of something quite untraceable, couldn't he?"

"Oh!" exclaimed Anne.

The other two turned to look at her.

"I remember something else," she said. "Mr. Shaitana said something about a doctor's opportunities in a laboratory. He must have meant something by that."

"It wasn't Mr. Shaitana who said that." Mrs. Oliver shook her head. "It was Major Despard."

A footfall on the garden walk made her turn her head.

"Well!" she exclaimed. "Talk of the devil!"

Major Despard had just come round the corner of the house.

CHAPTER 13
Second Visitor

At the sight of Mrs. Oliver, Major Despard looked slightly taken aback. Under his tan his face flushed a rich brick-red. Embarrassment made him jerky. He made for Anne.

"I apologise, Miss Meredith," he said. "Been ringing your bell. Nothing happened. Was passing this way. Thought I might just look you up."

"I'm so sorry you've been ringing," said Anne. "We haven't got a maid—only a woman who comes in the mornings."

She introduced him to Rhoda.

Rhoda said briskly:

"Let's have some tea. It's getting chilly. We'd better go in."

They all went into the house. Rhoda disappeared into the kitchen. Mrs. Oliver said:

"This is quite a coincidence—our all meeting here."

Despard said slowly, "Yes."

His eyes rested on her thoughtfully—appraising eyes.

"I've been telling Miss Meredith," said Mrs. Oliver, who was thoroughly enjoying herself, "that we ought to have a plan of campaign. About the murder, I mean. Of course, that doctor did it. Don't you agree with me?"

"Couldn't say. Very little to go on."

Mrs. Oliver put on her "How like a man!" expression.

A certain air of constraint had settled over the three. Mrs. Oliver sensed it quickly enough. When Rhoda brought in tea she rose and said she must be getting back to town. No, it was ever so kind of them, but she wouldn't have any tea.

"I'm going to leave you my card," she said. "Here it is, with my address on it. Come and see me when you come up to town, and we'll talk everything over and see if we can't think of something ingenious to get to the bottom of things."

"I'll come out to the gate with you," said Rhoda.

Just as they were walking down the path to the front gate, Anne Meredith ran out of the house and overtook them.

"I've been thinking things over," she said.

Her pale face looked unusually resolute.

"Yes, my dear?"

"It's extraordinarily kind of you, Mrs. Oliver, to have taken all this trouble. But I'd really rather not do anything at all. I mean—it was all so horrible. I just want to forget about it."

"My dear child, the question is, will you be *allowed* to forget about it?"

"Oh, I quite understand that the police won't let it drop. They'll probably come here and ask me a lot more questions. I'm prepared for that. But privately, I mean, I don't want to think about it—or be reminded of it in any way. I dare say I'm a coward, but that's how I feel about it."

"Oh, Anne!" cried Rhoda Dawes.

"I can understand your feeling, but I'm not at all sure that you're wise," said Mrs. Oliver. "Left to themselves, the police will probably never find out the truth."

Anne Meredith shrugged her shoulders.

"Does that really matter?"

"Matter?" cried Rhoda. "Of course it matters. It *does* matter, doesn't it, Mrs. Oliver?"

"I should certainly say so," said Mrs. Oliver dryly.

"I don't agree," said Anne obstinately. "Nobody who knows me would ever think I'd done it. I don't see any reason for interfering. It's the business of the police to get at the truth."

"Oh, Anne, you *are* spiritless," said Rhoda.

"That's how I feel, anyway," said Anne. She held out her hand. "Thank you very much, Mrs. Oliver. It's very good of you to have bothered."

"Of course, if you feel that way, there's nothing more to be said," said Mrs. Oliver cheerfully. "I, at any rate, shall not let the grass grow under my feet. Goodbye, my dear. Look me up in London if you change your mind."

She climbed into the car, started it, and drove off, waving a cheerful hand at the two girls.

Rhoda suddenly made a dash after the car and leapt on the running-board.

"What you said—about looking you up in London," she said breathlessly. "Did you only mean Anne, or did you mean me, too?"

Mrs. Oliver applied the brake.

"I meant both of you, of course."

"Oh, thank you. Don't stop. I—perhaps I might come one day. There's something—— No, don't stop. I can jump off."

She did so and, waving a hand, ran back to the gate, where Anne was standing.

"What on earth——?" began Anne.

"Isn't she a duck?" asked Rhoda enthusiastically. "I do like her. She had on odd stockings, did you notice? I'm sure she's frightfully clever. She must be—to write all those books. What fun if she found out the truth when the police and every one were baffled."

"Why did she come here?" asked Anne.

Rhoda's eyes opened wide.

"Darling—she told you——"

Anne made an impatient gesture.

"We must go in. I forgot. I've left him all alone."

Major Despard was standing by the mantelpiece, teacup in hand.

He cut short Anne's apologies for leaving him.

"Miss Meredith, I want to explain why I've butted in like this."

"Oh—but——"

"I said that I happened to be passing—that wasn't strictly true. I came here on purpose."

"How did you know my address?" asked Anne slowly.

"I got it from Superintendent Battle."

He saw her shrink slightly at the name.

He went on quickly:

"Battle's on his way here now. I happened to see him at Paddington. I got my car out and came down here. I knew I could beat the train easily."

"But why?"

Despard hesitated just for a minute.

"I may have been presumptuous—but I had the impression that you were, perhaps, what is called 'alone in the world.'"

"She's got me," said Rhoda.

Despard shot a quick glance at her, rather liking the gallant boyish figure that leant against the mantelpiece and was following his words so intensely. They were an attractive pair, these two.

"I'm sure she couldn't have a more devoted friend than you, Miss Dawes," he said courteously; "but it occurred to me that, in the peculiar circumstances, the advice of some one with a good dash of worldly wisdom might not be amiss. Frankly, the situation is this: Miss Meredith is under suspicion of having committed murder. The same applies to me and to the two other people who were in the room last night. Such a situation is not agreeable—and it has its own peculiar difficulties and dangers which some one as young and inexperienced as you are, Miss Meredith, might not recognise. In my opinion, you ought to put yourself in the hands of a thoroughly good solicitor. Perhaps you have already done so?"

Anne Meredith shook her head.

"I never thought of it."

"Exactly as I suspected. Have you got a good man—a London man, for choice?"

Again Anne shook her head.

"I've hardly ever needed a solicitor."

"There's Mr. Bury," said Rhoda. "But he's about a hundred-and-two, and quite gaga."

"If you'll allow me to advise you, Miss Meredith, I recommend your going to Mr. Myherne, my own solicitor. Jacobs, Peel & Jacobs is the actual name of the firm. They're first-class people, and they know all the ropes."

Anne had got paler. She sat down.

"Is it really necessary?" she asked in a low voice.

"I should say emphatically so. There are all sorts of legal pitfalls."

"Are these people very—expensive?"

"That doesn't matter a bit," said Rhoda. "That will be *quite* all right, Major Despard. I think everything you say is quite true. Anne ought to be protected."

"Their charges will, I think, be quite reasonable," said Despard. He added seriously: "I really do think it's a wise course, Miss Meredith."

"Very well," said Anne slowly. "I'll do it if you think so."

"Good."

Rhoda said warmly:

"I think it's awfully nice of you, Major Despard. Really frightfully nice."

Anne said, "Thank you."

She hesitated, and then said:

"Did you say Superintendent Battle was coming here?"

"Yes. You mustn't be alarmed by that. It's inevitable."

"Oh, I know. As a matter of fact, I've been expecting him."

Rhoda said impulsively:

"Poor darling—it's nearly killing her, this business. It's such a shame—so frightfully unfair."

Despard said:

"I agree—it's a pretty beastly business—dragging a young girl into an affair of this kind. If any one wanted to stick a knife into Shaitana, they ought to have chosen some other place or time."

Rhoda asked squarely:

"Who do you think did it? Dr. Roberts or that Mrs. Lorrimer?"

A very faint smile stirred Despard's moustache.

"May have done it myself, for all you know."

"Oh, no," cried Rhoda. "Anne and I know *you* didn't do it."

He looked at them both with kindly eyes.

A nice pair of kids. Touchingly full of faith and trust. A timid little creature, the Meredith girl. Never mind, Myherne would see her through. The other was a fighter. He doubted if she would have crumpled up in the same way if she'd been in her friend's place. Nice girls. He'd like to know more about them.

These thoughts passed through his mind. Aloud he said:

"Never take anything for granted, Miss Dawes. I don't set as much value on human life as most people do. All this hysterical fuss about road deaths, for instance. Man is always in danger—from traffic, from germs, from a hundred-and-one things. As well be killed one way as another. The moment you begin being careful of yourself—adopting as your motto 'Safety First'—you might as well be dead, in my opinion."

"Oh, I do agree with you," cried Rhoda. "I think one ought to live frightfully dangerously—if one gets the chance, that is. But life, on the whole, is terribly tame."

"It has its moments."

"Yes, for *you*. You go to out-of-the-way places and get mauled by tigers and shoot things and jiggers bury themselves in your toes and insects sting you, and everything's terribly uncomfortable but frightfully thrilling."

"Well, Miss Meredith has had her thrill, too. I don't suppose it often happens that you've actually *been in the room* while a murder was committed——"

"Oh, don't!" cried Anne.

He said quickly:

"I'm sorry."

But Rhoda said with a sigh:

"Of course it was awful—but it was exciting, too! I don't think Anne appreciates that side of it. You know, I think that Mrs. Oliver is thrilled to the core to have been there that night."

"Mrs——? Oh, your fat friend who writes the books about the unpronounceable Finn. Is she trying her hand at detection in real life?"

"She wants to."

"Well, let's wish her luck. It would be amusing if she put one over on Battle and Co."

"What is Superintendent Battle like?" asked Rhoda curiously.

Major Despard said gravely:

"He's an extraordinarily astute man. A man of remarkable ability."

"Oh!" said Rhoda. "Anne said he looked rather stupid."

"That, I should imagine, is part of Battle's stock-in-trade. But we mustn't make any mistakes. Battle's no fool."

He rose.

"Well, I must be off. There's just one other thing I'd like to say."

Anne had risen also.

"Yes?" she said as she held out her hand.

Despard paused a minute, picking his words carefully. He took her hand and retained it in his. He looked straight into the wide, beautiful grey eyes.

"Don't be offended with me," he said. "I just want to say this: It's humanly possible that there may be some feature of your acquaintanceship with Shaitana that you don't want to come out. If so—don't be angry, please" (he felt the instinctive pull of her hand)—"you are perfectly within your rights in refusing to answer any questions Battle may ask unless your solicitor is present."

Anne tore her hand away. Her eyes opened, their grey darkening with anger.

"There's nothing—*nothing*. . . . I hardly knew the beastly man."

"Sorry," said Major Despard. "Thought I ought to mention it."

"It's quite true," said Rhoda. "Anne barely knew him. She didn't like him much, but he gave frightfully good parties."

"That," said Major Despard grimly, "seems to have been the only justification for the late Mr. Shaitana's existence."

Anne said in a cold voice:

"Superintendent Battle can ask me anything he likes. I've nothing to hide—*nothing*."

Despard said very gently, "Please forgive me."

She looked at him. Her anger dwindled. She smiled—it was a very sweet smile.

"It's all right," she said. "You meant it kindly, I know."

She held out her hand again. He took it and said:

"We're in the same boat, you know. We ought to be pals. . . ."

It was Anne who went with him to the gate. When she came back Rhoda was staring out of the window and whistling. She turned as her friend entered the room.

"He's frightfully attractive, Anne."

"He's nice, isn't he?"

"A great deal more than nice. . . . I've got an absolute passion for him. Why wasn't I at that damned dinner instead of you? I'd have enjoyed the excitement—the net closing round me—the shadow of the scaffold——"

"No, you wouldn't. You're talking nonsense, Rhoda."

Anne's voice was sharp. Then it softened as she said:

"It was nice of him to come all this way—for a stranger—a girl he's only met once."

"Oh, he fell for you. Obviously. Men don't do purely disinterested kindnesses. He wouldn't have come toddling down if you'd been cross-eyed and covered with pimples!"

"Don't you think so?"

"I do not, my good idiot. Mrs. Oliver's a *much* more disinterested party."

"I don't like her," said Anne abruptly. "I had a sort of feeling about her. . . . I wonder what she really came for?"

"The usual suspicions of your own sex. I dare say Major Despard had an axe to grind, if it comes to that."

"I'm sure he hadn't," cried Anne hotly.

Then she blushed as Rhoda Dawes laughed.

CHAPTER 14
Third Visitor

Superintendent Battle arrived at Wallingford about six o'clock. It was his intention to learn as much as he could from innocent local gossip before interviewing Miss Anne Meredith.

It was not difficult to glean such information as there was. Without committing himself definitely to any statement, the superintendent nevertheless gave several different impressions of his rank and calling in life.

At least two people would have said confidently that he was a London builder come down to see about a new wing to be added to the cottage, from another you would have learned that he was "one of these weekenders wanting to take a furnished cottage," and two more would have said they knew positively, and for a fact, that he was the representative of a hardcourt tennis firm.

The information that the superintendent gathered was entirely favourable.

"Wendon Cottage? Yes, that's right—on the Marlbury Road. You can't miss it. Yes, two young ladies. Miss Dawes and Miss Meredith. Very nice young ladies, too. The quiet kind.

"Here for years? Oh, no, not that long. Just over two years. September quarter they came in. Mr. Pickersgill they bought it from. Never used it much, he didn't, after his wife died."

Superintendent Battle's informant had never heard they came from Northumberland. London, *he* thought they came from. Popular in the neighbourhood, though some people were old-fashioned and didn't think two young ladies ought to be living alone. But very quiet, they were. None of this cocktail-drinking week-end lot. Miss Rhoda, she was the dashing one. Miss Meredith was the quiet one. Yes, it was Miss Dawes what paid the bills. She was the one had got the money.

The superintendent's researches at last led him inevitably to Mrs. Astwell—who "did" for the ladies at Wendon Cottage.

Mrs. Astwell was a loquacious lady.

"Well, no, sir. I hardly think they'd want to sell. Not so soon. They only got in two years ago. I've done for them from the beginning, yes, sir. Eight o'clock till twelve—those are my hours. Very nice, lively young ladies, always ready for a joke or a bit of fun. Not stuck-up at all."

"Well, of course, I couldn't say if it's the same Miss Dawes *you* knew, sir—the same *family,* I mean. It's my fancy her home's in Devonshire. She gets the cream sent her now and again, and says it reminds her of home; so I think it must be.

"As you say, sir, it's sad for so many young ladies having to earn their livings nowadays. These young ladies aren't what you'd call rich, but they have a very pleasant life. It's Miss Dawes has got the money, of course. Miss Anne's her companion, in a manner of speaking, I suppose you might say. The cottage belongs to Miss Dawes.

"I couldn't really say what part Miss Anne comes from. I've heard her mention the Isle of Wight, and I know she doesn't like the North of England; and she and Miss Rhoda were together in Devonshire, because I've heard them joke about the hills and talk about the pretty coves and beaches."

The flow went on. Every now and then Superintendent Battle made a mental note. Later, a cryptic word or two was jotted down in his little book.

At half-past eight that evening he walked up the path to the door of Wendon Cottage.

It was opened to him by a tall, dark girl wearing a frock of orange cretonne.

"Miss Meredith live here?" inquired Superintendent Battle.

He looked very wooden and soldierly.

"Yes, she does."

"I'd like to speak to her, please. Superintendent Battle."

He was immediately favoured with a piercing stare.

"Come in," said Rhoda Dawes, drawing back from the doorway.

Anne Meredith was sitting in a cosy chair by the fire, sipping coffee. She was wearing embroidered crêpe-de-chine pyjamas.

"It's Superintendent Battle," said Rhoda, ushering in the guest.

Anne rose and came forward with outstretched hand.

"A bit late for a call," said Battle. "But I wanted to find you in, and it's been a fine day."

Anne smiled.

"Will you have some coffee, superintendent? Rhoda, fetch another cup."

"Well, it's very kind of you, Miss Meredith."

"We think we make rather good coffee," said Anne.

She indicated a chair, and Superintendent Battle sat down. Rhoda brought a cup, and Anne poured out his coffee. The fire crackled and the flowers in the vases made an agreeable impression upon the superintendent.

It was a pleasant homey atmosphere. Anne seemed self-possessed and at her ease, and the other girl continued to stare at him with devouring interest.

"We've been expecting you," said Anne.

Her tone was almost reproachful. "Why have you neglected me?" it seemed to say.

"Sorry, Miss Meredith. I've had a lot of routine work to do."

"Satisfactory?"

"Not particularly. But it all has to be done. I've turned Dr. Roberts inside out, so to speak. And the same for Mrs. Lorrimer. And now I've come to do the same for you, Miss Meredith."

Anne smiled.

"I'm ready."

"What about Major Despard?" asked Rhoda.

"Oh, he won't be overlooked. I can promise you that," said Battle.

He set down his coffee-cup and looked towards Anne. She sat up a little straighter in her chair.

"I'm quite ready, superintendent. What do you want to know?"

"Well, roughly, all about yourself, Miss Meredith."

"I'm quite a respectable person," said Anne, smiling.

"She's led a blameless life, too," said Rhoda. "I can answer for that."

"Well, that's very nice," said Superintendent Battle cheerfully. "You've known Miss Meredith a long time, then?"

"We were at school together," said Rhoda. "What ages ago it seems, doesn't it, Anne?"

"So long ago, you can hardly remember it, I suppose," said Battle with a chuckle. "Now, then, Miss Meredith, I'm afraid I'm going to be rather like those forms you fill up for passports."

"I was born——" began Anne.

"Of poor but honest parents," Rhoda put in.

Superintendent Battle held up a slightly reproving hand.

"Now, now, young lady," he said.

"Rhoda, darling," said Anne gravely. "It's serious, this."

"Sorry," said Rhoda.

"Now, Miss Meredith, you were born—where?"

"At Quetta, in India."

"Ah, yes. Your people were Army folk?"

"Yes—my father was Major John Meredith. My mother died when I was eleven. Father retired when I was fifteen and went to live in Cheltenham. He died when I was eighteen and left practically no money."

Battle nodded his head sympathetically.

"Bit of a shock to you, I expect."

"It was, rather. I always knew that we weren't well off, but to find there was practically nothing—well, that's different."

"What did you do, Miss Meredith?"

"I had to take a job. I hadn't been particularly well educated and I wasn't clever. I didn't know typing or shorthand, or anything. A friend in Cheltenham found me a job with friends of hers—two small boys home in the holidays, and general help in the house."

"Name, please?"

"That was Mrs. Eldon, The Larches, Ventnor. I stayed there for two years, and then the Eldons went abroad. Then I went to a Mrs. Deering."

"My aunt," put in Rhoda.

"Yes, Rhoda got me the job. I was very happy. Rhoda used to come and stay sometimes, and we had great fun."

"What were you there—companion?"

"Yes—it amounted to that."

"More like under-gardener," said Rhoda.

She explained:

"My Aunt Emily is just mad on gardening. Anne spent most of her time weeding or putting in bulbs."

"And you left Mrs. Deering?"

"Her health got worse, and she had to have a regular nurse."

"She's got cancer," said Rhoda. "Poor darling, she has to have morphia and things like that."

"She had been very kind to me. I was very sorry to go," went on Anne.

"I was looking about for a cottage," said Rhoda, "and wanting some one to share it with me. Daddy's married again—not my sort at all. I asked Anne to come here with me, and she's been here ever since."

"Well, that certainly seems a most blameless life," said Battle. "Let's just get the dates clear. You were with Mrs. Eldon two years, you say. By the way, what is her address now?"

"She's in Palestine. Her husband has some Government appointment out there—I'm not sure what."

"Ah, well, I can soon find out. And after that you went to Mrs. Deering?"

"I was with her three years," said Anne quickly. "Her address is Marsh Dene, Little Hembury, Devon."

"I see," said Battle. "So you are now twenty-five, Miss Meredith. Now, there's just one thing more—the name and address of a couple of people in Cheltenham who knew you and your father."

Anne supplied him with these.

"Now, about this trip to Switzerland—where you met Mr. Shaitana. Did you go alone there—or was Miss Dawes here with you?"

"We went out together. We joined some other people. There was a party of eight."

"Tell me about your meeting with Mr. Shaitana."

Anne crinkled her brows.

"There's really nothing to tell. He was just there. We knew him in the way you do know people in a hotel. He got first prize at the Fancy Dress Ball. He went as Mephistopheles."

Superintendent Battle sighed.

"Yes, that always was his favourite effect."

"He really was marvellous," said Rhoda. "He hardly had to make-up at all."

The superintendent looked from one girl to the other.

"Which of you two young ladies knew him best?"

Anne hesitated. It was Rhoda who answered.

"Both the same to begin with. Awfully little, that is. You see, our crowd was the skiing lot, and we were off doing runs most days and dancing together in the evenings. But then Shaitana seemed to take rather a fancy to Anne. You know, went out of his way to pay her compliments, and all that. We ragged her about it, rather."

"I just think he did it to annoy me," said Anne. "Because I didn't like him. I think it amused him to make me feel embarrassed."

Rhoda said, laughing:

"We told Anne it would be a nice rich marriage for her. She got simply wild with us."

"Perhaps," said Battle, "you'd give me the names of the other people in your party?"

"You aren't what I'd call a trustful man," said Rhoda. "Do you think that every word we're telling you is downright lies?"

Superintendent Battle twinkled.

"I'm going to make quite sure it isn't, anyway," he said.

"You *are* suspicious," said Rhoda.

She scribbled some names on a piece of paper and gave it to him.

Battle rose.

"Well, thank you very much, Miss Meredith," he said. "As Miss Dawes says, you seem to have led a particularly blameless life. I don't think you need worry much. It's odd the way Mr. Shaitana's manner changed to you. You'll excuse my asking, but he didn't ask you to marry him—or—er—pester you with attentions of another kind?"

"He didn't try to seduce her," said Rhoda helpfully. "If that's what you mean."

Anne was blushing.

"Nothing of the kind," she said. "He was always most polite and—and—formal. It was just his elaborate manners that made me uncomfortable."

"And little things he said or hinted?"

"Yes—at least—no. He never hinted things."

"Sorry. These lady-killers do sometimes. Well, good-night, Miss Meredith. Thank you very much. Excellent coffee. Good-night, Miss Dawes."

"There," said Rhoda as Anne came back into the room after shutting the front door after Battle. "That's over, and not so very terrible. He's a nice fatherly man, and he evidently doesn't suspect you in the least. It was all ever so much better than I expected."

Anne sank down with a sigh.

"It was really quite easy," she said. "It was silly of me to work myself up so. I thought he'd try to browbeat me—like K.C.s on the stage."

"He looks sensible," said Rhoda. "He'd know well enough you're not a murdering kind of female."

She hesitated and then said:

"I say, Anne, you didn't mention being at Croftways. Did you forget?"

Anne said slowly:

"I didn't think it counted. I was only there a few months. And there's no one to ask about me there. I can write and tell him if you think it matters; but I'm sure it doesn't. Let's leave it."

"Right, if you say so."

Rhoda rose and turned on the wireless.

A raucous voice said:

"You have just heard the Black Nubians play 'Why do you tell me lies, Baby?'"

CHAPTER 15
Major Despard

Major Despard came out of the Albany, turned sharply into Regent Street and jumped on a bus.

It was the quiet time of day—the top of the bus had very few seats occupied. Despard made his way forward and sat down on the front seat.

He had jumped on the bus while it was going. Now it came to a halt, took up passengers and made its way once more up Regent Street.

A second traveller climbed the steps, made his way forward and sat down in the front seat on the other side.

Despard did not notice the new-comer, but after a few minutes a tentative voice murmured:

"It is a good view of London, is it not, that one gets from the top of a bus?"

Despard turned his head. He looked puzzled for a moment, then his face cleared.

"I beg your pardon, M. Poirot. I didn't see it was you. Yes, as you say, one has a good bird's-eye view of the world from here. It was better, though, in the old days, when there wasn't all this caged-in glass business."

Poirot sighed.

"*Tout de même*, it was not always agreeable in the wet weather when the inside was full. And there is much wet weather in this country."

"Rain? Rain never did any harm to any one."

"You are in error," said Poirot. "It leads often to a *fluxion de poitrine*."

Despard smiled.

"I see you belong to the well-wrapped-up school, M. Poirot."

Poirot was indeed well equipped against any treachery of an autumn day. He wore a greatcoat and a muffler.

"Rather odd, running into you like this," said Despard.

He did not see the smile that the muffler concealed. There was nothing odd in this encounter. Having ascertained a likely hour for Despard to leave his rooms, Poirot had been waiting for him. He had prudently not risked leaping on the bus, but he had trotted after it to its next stopping-place and boarded it there.

"True. We have not seen each other since the evening at Mr. Shaitana's," he replied.

"Aren't you taking a hand in that business?" asked Despard.

Poirot scratched his ear delicately.

"I reflect," he said. "I reflect a good deal. To run to and fro, to make the investigations, that, no. It does not suit my age, my temperament, or my figure."

Despard said unexpectedly:

"Reflect, eh? Well, you might do worse. There's too much rushing about nowadays. If people sat tight and thought about a thing before they tackled it, there'd be less mess-ups than there are."

"Is that your procedure in life, Major Despard?"

"Usually," said the other simply. "Get your bearings, figure out your route, weigh up the pros and cons, make your decision—and stick to it."

His mouth set grimly.

"And, after that, nothing will turn you from your path, eh?" asked Poirot.

"Oh, I don't say that. No use in being pig-headed over things. If you've made a mistake, admit it."

"But I imagine that you do not often make a mistake, Major Despard."

"We all make mistakes, M. Poirot."

"Some of us," said Poirot with a certain coldness, possibly due to the pronoun the other had used, "make less than others."

Despard looked at him, smiled slightly and said:

"Don't you ever have a failure, M. Poirot?"

"The last time was twenty-eight years ago," said Poirot with dignity. "And even then, there were circumstances—but no matter."

"That seems a pretty good record," said Despard.

He added: "What about Shaitana's death? That doesn't count, I suppose, since it isn't officially your business."

"It is not my business—no. But, all the same, it offends my *amour propre*. I consider it an impertinence, you comprehend, for a murder to be committed under my very nose—by some one who mocks himself at my ability to solve it!"

"Not under *your* nose only," said Despard dryly. "Under the nose of the Criminal Investigation Department also."

"That was probably a bad mistake," said Poirot gravely. "The good square Superintendent Battle, he may look wooden, but he is not wooden in the head—not at all."

"I agree," said Despard. "That stolidity is a pose. He's a very clever and able officer."

"And I think he is very active in the case."

"Oh, he's active enough. See a nice quiet soldierly-looking fellow on one of the back seats?"

Poirot looked over his shoulder.

"There is no one here now but ourselves."

"Oh, well, he's inside, then. He never loses me. Very efficient fellow. Varies his appearance, too, from time to time. Quite artistic about it."

"Ah, but that would not deceive you. You have the very quick and accurate eye."

"I never forget a face—even a black one—and that's a lot more than most people can say."

"You are just the person I need," said Poirot. "What a chance, meeting you today! I need some one with a good eye and a good memory. *Malheureusement* the two seldom go together. I have asked the Dr. Roberts a question, without result, and the same with Madame Lorrimer. Now, I will try you and see if I get what I want. Cast your mind back to the room in which you played cards at Mr. Shaitana's, and tell me what you remember of it."

Despard looked puzzled.

"I don't quite understand."

"Give me a description of the room—the furnishings—the objects in it."

"I don't know that I'm much of a hand at that sort of thing," said Despard slowly. "It was a rotten sort of room—to my mind. Not a man's room at all. A lot of brocade and silk and stuff. Sort of room a fellow like Shaitana would have."

"But to particularise——"

Despard shook his head.

"Afraid I didn't notice. . . . He'd got some good rugs. Two Bokharas and three or four really good Persian ones, including a Hamadan and a Tabriz. Rather a good eland head—no, that was in the hall. From Rowland Ward's, I expect."

"You do not think that the late Mr. Shaitana was one to go out and shoot wild beasts?"

"Not he. Never potted anything but sitting game, I'll bet. What else was there? I'm sorry to fail you, but I really can't help much. Any amount of knick-knacks lying about. Tables were thick with them. Only thing I noticed was a rather jolly idol. Easter Island, I should say. Highly polished wood. You don't see many of them. There was some Malay stuff, too. No, I'm afraid I can't help you."

"No matter," said Poirot, looking slightly crestfallen.

He went on:

"Do you know, Mrs. Lorrimer, she has the most amazing card memory! She could tell me the bidding and play of nearly every hand. It was astonishing."

Despard shrugged his shoulders.

"Some women are like that. Because they play pretty well all day long, I suppose."

"You could not do it, eh?"

The other shook his head.

"I just remember a couple of hands. One where I could have got game in diamonds—and Roberts bluffed me out of it. Went down himself, but we didn't double him, worse luck. I remember a no trumper, too. Tricky business—every card wrong. We went down a couple—lucky not to have gone down more."

"Do you play much bridge, Major Despard?"

"No, I'm not a regular player. It's a good game, though."

"You prefer it to poker?"

"I do personally. Poker's too much of a gamble."

Poirot said thoughtfully:

"I do not think Mr. Shaitana played any game—any card game, that is."

"There's only one game that Shaitana played consistently," said Despard grimly.

"And that?"

"A lowdown game."

Poirot was silent for a minute, then he said:

"Is it that you *know* that? Or do you just *think* it?"

Despard went brick red.

"Meaning one oughtn't to say things without giving chapter and verse? I suppose that's true. Well, it's accurate enough. I happen to *know*. On the other hand, I'm not prepared to give chapter and verse. Such information as I've got came to me privately."

"Meaning a woman or women are concerned?"

"Yes. Shaitana, like the dirty dog he was, preferred to deal with women."

"You think he was a blackmailer? That is interesting."

Despard shook his head.

"No, no, you've misunderstood me. In a way, Shaitana was a blackmailer, but not the common or garden sort. He wasn't after money. He was a spiritual blackmailer, if there can be such a thing."

"And he got out of it—what?"

"He got a kick out of it. That's the only way I can put it. He got a thrill out of seeing people quail and flinch. I suppose it made him feel less of a louse and more of a man. And it's a very effective pose with women. He'd only got to hint that he knew everything—and they'd start telling him a lot of things that perhaps he didn't know. That would tickle his sense of humour. Then he'd strut about in his Mephistophelian attitude of 'I know everything! I am the great Shaitana!' The man was an ape!"

"So you think that he frightened Miss Meredith that way," said Poirot slowly.

"Miss Meredith?" Despard stared. "I wasn't thinking of her. She isn't the kind to be afraid of a man like Shaitana."

"*Pardon*. You meant Mrs. Lorrimer."

"No, no, no. You misunderstand me. I was speaking generally. It wouldn't be easy to frighten Mrs. Lorrimer. And she's not the kind of woman who you can imagine having a guilty secret. No, I was not thinking of any one in particular."

"It was the general method to which you referred?"

"Exactly."

"There is no doubt," said Poirot slowly, "that what you call a Dago often has a very clever understanding of women. He knows how to approach them. He worms secrets out of them——"

He paused.

Despard broke in impatiently:

"It's absurd. The man was a mountebank—nothing really dangerous about him. And yet women were afraid of him. Ridiculously so."

He started up suddenly.

"Hallo, I've overshot the mark. Got too interested in what we were discussing. Good-bye, M. Poirot. Look down and you'll see my faithful shadow leave the bus when I do."

He hurried to the back and down the steps. The conductor's bell jangled. But a double pull sounded before it had time to stop.

Looking down to the street below, Poirot noticed Despard striding back along the pavement. He did not trouble to pick out the following figure. Something else was interesting him.

"No one in particular," he murmured to himself. "Now, I wonder."

CHAPTER 16
The Evidence of Elsie Batt

Sergeant O'Connor was unkindly nicknamed by his colleagues at the Yard: "The Maidservant's Prayer."

There was no doubt that he was an extremely handsome man. Tall, erect, broad-shouldered, it was less the regularity of his features than the roguish and daredevil spark in his eye which made him so irresistible to the fair sex. It was indubitable that Sergeant O'Connor got results, and got them quickly.

So rapid was he, that only four days after the murder of Mr. Shaitana, Sergeant O'Connor was sitting in the three-and-sixpenny seats at the *Willy Nilly Revue* side by side with Miss Elsie Batt, late parlourmaid to Mrs. Craddock of 117 North Audley Street.

Having laid his line of approach carefully, Sergeant O'Connor was just launching the great offensive.

"——Reminds me," he was saying, "of the way one of my old governors used to carry on. Name of Craddock. He was an odd cuss, if you like."

"Craddock," said Elsie. "I was with some Craddocks once."

"Well, that's funny. Wonder whether they were the same?"

"Lived in North Audley Street, they did," said Elsie.

"My lot were going to London when I left them," said O'Connor promptly. "Yes, I believe it *was* North Audley Street. Mrs. Craddock was rather a one for the gents."

Elsie tossed her head.

"I'd no patience with her. Always finding fault and grumbling. Nothing you did right."

"Her husband got some of it, too, didn't he?"

"She was always complaining he neglected her—that he didn't understand her. And she was always saying how bad her health was and gasping and groaning. Not ill at all, if you ask *me*."

O'Connor slapped his knee.

"Got it. Wasn't there something about her and some doctor? A bit too thick or something?"

"You mean Dr. Roberts? He was a nice gentleman, he was."

"You girls, you're all alike," said Sergeant O'Connor. "The moment a man's a bad lot, all the girls stick up for him. I know his kind."

"No, you don't, and you're all wrong about him. There wasn't anything of that kind about him. Wasn't his fault, was it, if Mrs. Craddock was always sending for him? What's a doctor to do? If you ask me, he didn't think nothing of her at all, except as a patient. It was all her doing. Wouldn't leave him alone, she wouldn't."

"That's all very well, Elsie. Don't mind me calling you Elsie, do you? Feel as though I'd known you all my life."

"Well, you haven't! Elsie, indeed."

She tossed her head.

"Oh, very well, Miss Batt." He gave her a glance. "As I was saying, that's all very well, but the husband, he cut up rough, all the same, didn't he?"

"He was a bit ratty one day," admitted Elsie. "But, if you ask me, he was ill at the time. He died just after you know."

"I remember—died of something queer, didn't he?"

"Something Japanese, it was—all from a new shaving brush he'd got. Seems awful, doesn't it, that they're not more careful? I've not fancied anything Japanese since."

"Buy British, that's my motto," said Sergeant O'Connor sententiously. "And you were saying he and the doctor had a row?"

Elsie nodded, enjoying herself as she re-lived past scandals.

"Hammer and tongs, they went at it," she said. "At least, the master did. Dr. Roberts was ever so quiet. Just said, 'Nonsense.' And, 'What have you got into your head?'"

"This was at the house, I suppose?"

"Yes. She'd sent for him. And then she and the master had words, and in the middle of it Dr. Roberts arrived, and the master went for him."

"What did he say exactly?"

"Well, of course, I wasn't supposed to hear. It was all in the Missus's bedroom. I thought something was up, so I got the dustpan and did the stairs. I wasn't going to miss anything."

Sergeant O'Connor heartily concurred in this sentiment, reflecting how fortunate it was that Elsie was being approached unofficially. On interrogation by Sergeant O'Connor of the Police, she would have virtuously protested that she had not overheard anything at all.

"As I say," went on Elsie, "Dr. Roberts, he was very quiet—the master was doing all the shouting."

"What was he saying?" asked O'Connor, for the second time approaching the vital point.

"Abusing of him proper," said Elsie with relish.

"How do you mean?"

Would the girl never come to actual words and phrases?

"Well, I didn't understand a lot of it," admitted Elsie. "There were a lot of long words, 'unprofessional conduct,' and 'taking advantage,' and things like that—and I heard him say he'd get Dr. Roberts struck off the—Medical Register, would it be? Something like that."

"That's right," said O'Connor. "Complain to the Medical Council."

"Yes, he said something like that. And the Missus was going on in sort of hysterics, saying, 'You never cared for me. You neglected me. You left me alone.' And I heard her say that Dr. Roberts had been an angel of goodness to her.

"And then the doctor, he came through into the dressing-room with the master and shut the door of the bedroom—I heard it—and he said quite plain:

"'My good man, don't you realise your wife's hysterical? She doesn't know what she's saying. To tell you the truth, it's been a very difficult and trying case, and I'd have thrown it up long ago if I'd thought it was con—con—some long word; oh, yes, consistent—that was it—consistent with my duty.' That's what he said. He said something about not overstepping a boundary, too—something between doctor and patient. He got the master quietened a bit, and then he said:

"'You'll be late at your office, you know. You'd better be off. Just think things over quietly. I think you'll realise that the whole business is a mare's nest. I'll just wash my hands here before I go on to my next case. Now, you think it over, my dear fellow. I can assure you that the whole thing arises out of your wife's disordered imagination.'

"And the master, he said, 'I don't know what to think.'

"And he come out—and, of course, I was brushing hard—but he never even noticed me. I thought afterwards he looked ill. The doctor, he was whistling quite cheerily and washing his hands in the dressing-room, where there was hot and cold laid on. And presently he came out, too, with his bag, and he spoke to me very nicely and cheerily, as he always did, and he went down the stairs, quite cheerful and gay and his usual self. So, you see, I'm quite sure as he hadn't done anything wrong. It was all her."

"And then Craddock got this anthrax?"

"Yes, I think he'd got it already. The mistress, she nursed him very devoted, but he died. Lovely wreaths there was at the funeral."

"And afterwards? Did Dr. Roberts come to the house again?"

"No, he didn't, Nosey! You've got some grudge against him. I tell you there was nothing in it. If there were he'd have married her when the master was dead, wouldn't he? And he never did. No such fool. He'd taken her measure all right. She used to ring him up, though, but somehow he was never in. And then she sold the house, and we all got our notices, and she went abroad to Egypt."

"And you didn't see Dr. Roberts in all that time?"

"No. *She* did, because she went to him to have this—what do you call it?—'noculation against the typhoid fever. She came back with her arm ever so sore with it. If you ask me, he made it clear to her then that there was nothing doing. She didn't ring him up no more, and she went off very cheerful with a lovely lot of new clothes—all light colours, although it was the middle of winter, but she said it would be all sunshine and hot out there."

"That's right," said Sergeant O'Connor. "It's too hot sometimes, I've heard. She died out there. You know that, I suppose?"

"No, indeed I didn't. Well, fancy that! She may have been worse than I thought, poor soul."

She added with a sigh:

"I wonder what they did with all that lovely lot of clothes. They're blacks out there, so they couldn't wear them."

"You'd have looked a treat in them, I expect," said Sergeant O'Connor.

"Impudence," said Elsie.

"Well, you won't have my impudence much longer," said Sergeant O'Connor. "I've got to go away on business for my firm."

"You going for long?"

"May be going abroad," said the Sergeant.

Elsie's face fell.

Though unacquainted with Lord Byron's famous poem, "I never loved a dear gazelle," etc., its sentiments were at that moment hers. She thought to herself:

"Funny how all the really attractive ones never come to anything. Oh, well, there's always Fred."

Which is gratifying, since it shows that the sudden incursion of Sergeant O'Connor into Elsie's life did not affect it permanently. "Fred" may even have been the gainer!

CHAPTER 17
The Evidence of Rhoda Dawes

Rhoda Dawes came out of Debenham's and stood meditatively upon the pavement. Indecision was written all over her face. It was an expressive face; each fleeting emotion showed itself in a quickly varying expression.

Quite plainly at this moment Rhoda's face said, "Shall I or shan't I? I'd like to. . . . But perhaps I'd better not. . . ."

The commissionaire said, "Taxi, Miss?" to her, hopefully.

Rhoda shook her head.

A stout woman carrying parcels with an eager "shopping early for Christmas" expression on her face, cannoned into her severly, but still Rhoda stood stockstill, trying to make up her mind.

Chaotic odds and ends of thought flashed through her mind.

"After all, why shouldn't I? She asked me to—but perhaps it's just a thing she says to every one. . . . She doesn't mean it to be taken seriously. . . . Well, after all, Anne didn't want me. She made it quite clear she'd rather go with Major Despard to the solicitor man alone. . . . And why shouldn't she? I mean, three *is* a crowd. . . . And it isn't really any business of mine. . . . It isn't as though I particularly *wanted* to see Major Despard. . . . He is nice, though. . . . I think he must have fallen for Anne. Men don't take a lot of trouble unless they have. . . . I mean, it's never just kindness. . . ."

A messenger boy bumped into Rhoda and said, "Beg pardon, Miss," in a reproachful tone.

"Oh, dear," thought Rhoda. "I can't go on standing here all day. Just because I'm such an idiot that I can't make up my mind. . . . I think that coat and skirt's going to be awfully nice. I wonder if brown would have been more useful than green? No, I don't think so. Well, come on, shall I go, or shan't I? Half-past three—it's quite a good time—I mean, it doesn't look as though I'm cadging a meal or anything. I might just go and look, anyway."

She plunged across the road, turned to the right, and then to the left, up Harley Street, finally pausing by the block of flats always airily described by Mrs. Oliver as "all among the nursing homes."

"Well, she can't eat me," thought Rhoda, and plunged boldly into the building.

Mrs. Oliver's flat was on the top floor. A uniformed attendant whisked her up in a lift and decanted her on a smart new mat outside a bright green door.

"This is awful," thought Rhoda. "Worse than dentists. I must go through with it now, though."

Pink with embarrassment, she pushed the bell.

The door was opened by an elderly maid.

"Is—could I—is Mrs. Oliver at home?" asked Rhoda.

The maid drew back, Rhoda entered, she was shown into a very untidy drawing-room. The maid said:

"What name shall I say, please?"

"Oh—er—Miss Dawes—Miss Rhoda Dawes."

The maid withdrew. After what seemed to Rhoda about a hundred years, but was really exactly a minute and forty-five seconds, the maid returned.

"Will you step this way, miss?"

Pinker than ever, Rhoda followed her. Along a passage, round a corner, a door was opened. Nervously she entered into what seemed at first to her startled eyes to be an African forest!

Birds—masses of birds, parrots, macaws, birds unknown to ornithology, twined themselves in and out of what seemed to be a primeval forest. In the middle of this riot of bird and vegetable life, Rhoda perceived a battered kitchen-table with a typewriter on it, masses of typescript littered all over the floor and Mrs. Oliver, her hair in wild confusion, rising from a somewhat rickety-looking chair.

"My dear, how nice to see you," said Mrs. Oliver, holding out a carbon-stained hand and trying with her other hand to smooth her hair, a quite impossible proceeding.

A paper bag, touched by her elbow, fell from the desk, and apples rolled energetically all over the floor.

"Never mind, my dear, don't bother, some one will pick them up some time."

Rather breathless, Rhoda rose from a stooping position with five apples in her grasp.

"Oh, thank you—no, I shouldn't put them back in the bag. I think it's got a hole in it. Put them on the mantelpiece. That's right. Now, then, sit down and let's talk."

Rhoda accepted a second battered chair and focused her eyes on her hostess.

"I say, I'm terribly sorry. Am I interrupting, or anything?" she asked breathlessly.

"Well, you are and you aren't," said Mrs. Oliver. "I *am* working, as you see. But that dreadful Finn of mine has got himself terribly tangled up. He did some awfully clever deduction with a dish of French beans, and now he's just detected deadly poison in the sage-and-onion stuffing of the Michaelmas goose, and I've just remembered that French beans are over by Michaelmas."

Thrilled by this peep into the inner world of creative detective fiction, Rhoda said breathlessly, "They might be tinned."

"They might, of course," said Mrs. Oliver doubtfully. "But it would rather spoil the point. I'm always getting tangled up in horticulture and things like that. People write to me and say I've got the wrong flowers all out together. As though it mattered—and, anyway, they are all out together in a London shop."

"Of course it doesn't matter," said Rhoda loyally. "Oh, Mrs. Oliver, it must be marvellous to write."

Mrs. Oliver rubbed her forehead with a carbonny finger and said:

"Why?"

"Oh," said Rhoda, a little taken aback. "Because it must. It must be wonderful just to sit down and write off a whole book."

"It doesn't happen exactly like that," said Mrs. Oliver. "One actually has to *think*, you know. And thinking is always a bore. And you have to plan things. And then one gets stuck every now and then, and you feel you'll never get out of the mess—but you do! Writing's not particularly enjoyable. It's hard work, like everything else."

"It doesn't seem like work," said Rhoda.

"Not to *you*," said Mrs. Oliver, "because you don't have to do it! It feels very like work to me. Some days I can only keep going by repeating over and over to myself the amount of money I might get for my next serial rights. That spurs you on, you know. So does your bank-book when you see how much overdrawn you are."

"I never imagined you actually typed your books yourself," said Rhoda. "I thought you'd have a secretary."

"I did have a secretary, and I used to try and dictate to her, but she was so competent that it used to depress me. I felt she knew so much more about English and grammar and full stops and semi-colons than I did, that it gave me a kind of inferiority complex. Then I tried having a thoroughly incompetent secretary, but, of course, that didn't answer very well, either."

"It must be so wonderful to be able to think of things," said Rhoda.

"I can always think of things," said Mrs. Oliver happily. "What is so tiring is writing them down. I always think I've finished, and then when I count up I find I've only written thirty thousand words instead of sixty thousand, and so then I have to throw in another murder and get the heroine kidnapped again. It's all very boring."

Rhoda did not answer. She was staring at Mrs. Oliver with the reverence felt by youth for celebrity—slightly tinged by disappointment.

"Do you like the wall-paper?" asked Mrs. Oliver, waving an airy hand. "I'm frightfully fond of birds. The foliage is supposed to be tropical. It makes me feel it's a hot day, even when it's freezing. I can't do anything unless I feel very, very warm. But Sven Hjerson breaks the ice on his bath every morning!"

"I think it's all marvellous," said Rhoda. "And it's awfully nice of you to say I'm not interrupting you."

"We'll have some coffee and toast," said Mrs. Oliver. "Very black coffee and very hot toast. I can always eat that any time."

She went to the door, opened it and shouted. Then she returned and said:

"What brings you to town—shopping?"

"Yes, I've been doing some shopping."

"Is Miss Meredith up, too?"

"Yes, she's gone with Major Despard to a solicitor."

"Solicitor, eh?"

Mrs. Oliver's brows rose inquiringly.

"Yes. You see, Major Despard told her she ought to have one. He's been awfully kind—he really has."

"I was kind, too," said Mrs. Oliver, "but it didn't seem to go down very well, did it? In fact, I think your friend rather resented my coming."

"Oh, she didn't—really she didn't." Rhoda wriggled on her chair in a paroxysm of embarrassment. "That's really one reason why I wanted to come to-day—to explain. You see, I saw you had got it all wrong. She did seem very ungracious, but it wasn't that, really. I mean, it wasn't your coming. It was something you said."

"Something I *said?*"

"Yes. You couldn't tell, of course. It was just unfortunate."

"What did I say?"

"I don't expect you remember, even. It was just the way you put it. You said something about an accident and poison."

"Did I?"

"I knew you'd probably not remember. Yes. You see, Anne, had a ghastly experience once. She was in a house where a woman took some poison—hat paint, I think it was—by mistake for something else. And she died. And, of course, it was an awful shock to Anne. She can't bear thinking of it or speaking of it. And your saying that reminded her, of course, and she dried up and got all stiff and queer like she does. And I saw you noticed it. And I couldn't say anything in front of her. But I did want you to know that it wasn't what you thought. She wasn't ungrateful."

Mrs. Oliver looked at Rhoda's flushed eager face. She said slowly:

"I see."

"Anne's awfully sensitive," said Rhoda. "And she's bad about—well, facing things. If anything's upset her, she'd just rather not talk about it, although that isn't any good, really—at least, I don't think so. Things are there just the same—whether you talk about them or not. It's only running away from them to pretend they don't exist. I'd rather have it all out, however painful it would be."

"Ah," said Mrs. Oliver quietly. "But you, my dear, are a soldier. Your Anne isn't."

Rhoda flushed.

Mrs. Oliver smiled.

"Anne's a darling."

She said, "I didn't say she wasn't. I only said she hadn't got your particular brand of courage."

She sighed, then said rather unexpectedly to the girl:

"Do you believe in the value of truth, my dear, or don't you?"

"Of course I believe in the truth," said Rhoda, staring.

"Yes, you say that—but perhaps you haven't thought about it. The truth hurts sometimes—and destroys one's illusions."

"I'd rather have it, all the same," said Rhoda.

"So would I. But I don't know that we're wise."

Rhoda said earnestly:

"Don't tell Anne, will you, what I've told you? She wouldn't like it."

"I certainly shouldn't dream of doing any such thing. Was this long ago?"

"About four years ago. It's odd, isn't it, how the same things happen again and again to people. I had an aunt who was always in shipwrecks. And here's Anne mixed up in two sudden deaths—only, of course, this one's much worse. Murder's rather awful, isn't it?"

"Yes, it is."

The black coffee and the hot buttered toast appeared at this minute.

Rhoda ate and drank with childish gusto. It was very exciting to her thus to be sharing an intimate meal with a celebrity.

When they had finished she rose and said:

"I do hope I haven't interrupted you too terribly. Would you mind—I mean, would it bother you awfully—if I sent one of your books to you, would you sign it for me?"

Mrs. Oliver laughed.

"Oh, I can do better than that for you." She opened a cupboard at the far end of the room. "Which would you like? I rather fancy *The Affair of the Second Goldfish* myself. It's not quite such frightful tripe as the rest."

A little shocked at hearing an authoress thus describe the children of her pen, Rhoda accepted eagerly. Mrs. Oliver took the book, opened it, inscribed her name with a superlative flourish and handed it to Rhoda.

"There you are."

"Thank you very much. I have enjoyed myself. Sure you didn't mind my coming?"

"I wanted you to," said Mrs. Oliver.

She added after a moment's pause:

"You're a nice child. Good-bye. Take care of yourself, my dear."

"Now, why did I say that?" she murmured to herself as the door closed behind her guest.

She shook her head, ruffled her hair, and returned to the masterly dealings of Sven Hjerson with the sage-and-onion stuffing.

CHAPTER 18
Tea Interlude

Mrs. Lorrimer came out of a certain door in Harley Street.

She stood for a minute at the top of the steps, and then she descended them slowly.

There was a curious expression on her face—a mingling of grim determination and of strange indecision. She bent her brows a little, as though to concentrate on some all-absorbing problem.

It was just then that she caught sight of Anne Meredith on the opposite pavement.

Anne was standing staring up at a big block of flats just on the corner.

Mrs. Lorrimer hesitated a moment, then she crossed the road.

"How do you do, Miss Meredith?"

Anne started and turned.

"Oh, how do you do?"

"Still in London?" said Mrs. Lorrimer.

"No. I've only come up for the day. To do some legal business."

Her eyes were still straying back to the big block of flats.

Mrs. Lorrimer said:

"Is anything the matter?"

Anne started guiltily.

"The matter? Oh, no, what should be the matter?"

"You were looking as though you had something on your mind."

"I haven't—well, at least I have, but it's nothing important, something quite silly." She laughed a little.

She went on:

"It's only that I thought I saw my friend—the girl I live with—go in there, and I wondered if she'd gone to see Mrs. Oliver."

"Is that where Mrs. Oliver lives? I didn't know."

"Yes. She came to see us the other day and she gave us her address and asked us to come and see her. I wondered if it was Rhoda I saw or not."

"Do you want to go up and see?"

"No, I'd rather not do that."

"Come and have tea with me," said Mrs. Lorrimer. "There is a shop quite near here that I know."

"It's very kind of you," said Anne, hesitating.

Side by side they walked down the street and turned into a side street. In a small pastrycook's they were served with tea and muffins.

They did not talk much. Each of them seemed to find the other's silence restful.

Anne asked suddenly:

"Has Mrs. Oliver been to see you?"

Mrs. Lorrimer shook her head.

"No one has been to see me except M. Poirot."

"I didn't mean——" began Anne.

"Didn't you? I think you did," said Mrs. Lorrimer.

The girl looked up—a quick, frightened glance. Something she saw in Mrs. Lorrimer's face seemed to reassure her.

"He hasn't been to see me," she said slowly.

There was a pause.

"Hasn't Superintendent Battle been to see you?" asked Anne.

"Oh, yes, of course," said Mrs. Lorrimer.

Anne said hesitatingly:

"What sort of things did he ask you?"

Mrs. Lorrimer sighed wearily.

"The usual things, I suppose. Routine inquiries. He was very pleasant over it all."

"I suppose he interviewed every one."

"I should think so."

There was another pause.

Anne said:

"Mrs. Lorrimer, do you think—they will ever find out who did it?"

Her eyes were bent on her plate. She did not see the curious expression in the older woman's eyes as she watched the downcast head.

Mrs. Lorrimer said quietly:

"I don't know. . . ."

Anne murmured:

"It's not—very nice, is it?"

There was that same curious appraising and yet sympathetic look on Mrs. Lorrimer's face, as she asked:

"How old are you, Anne Meredith?"

"I—I?" the girl stammered. "I'm twenty-five."

"And I am sixty-three," said Mrs. Lorrimer.

She went on slowly:

"Most of your life is in front of you. . . ."

Anne shivered.

"I might be run over by a bus on the way home," she said.

"Yes, that is true. And I—might not."

She said it in an odd way. Anne looked at her in astonishment.

"Life is a difficult business," said Mrs. Lorrimer. "You'll know that when you come to my age. It needs infinite courage and a lot of endurance. And in the end one wonders: 'Was it worth while?'"

"Oh, *don't*," said Anne.

Mrs. Lorrimer laughed, her old competent self again.

"It's rather cheap to say gloomy things about life," she said.

She called the waitress and settled the bill.

As they got to the shop door a taxi crawled past, and Mrs. Lorrimer hailed it.

"Can I give you a lift?" she asked. "I am going south of the park."

Anne's face had lighted up.

"No, thank you. I see my friend turning the corner. Thank you so much, Mrs. Lorrimer. Good-bye."

"Good-bye. Good luck," said the older woman.

She drove away and Anne hurried forward.

Rhoda's face lit up when she saw her friend, then changed to a slightly guilty expression.

"Rhoda, have you been to see Mrs. Oliver?" demanded Anne.

"Well, as a matter of fact, I have."

"And I just caught you."

"I don't know what you mean by caught. Let's go down here and take a bus. You'd gone off on your own ploys with the boy friend. I thought at least he'd give you tea."

Anne was silent for a minute—a voice ringing in her ears.

"Can't we pick up your friend somewhere and all have tea together?"

And her own answer—hurried, without taking time to think:

"Thanks awfully, but we've got to go out to tea together with some people."

A lie—and such a silly lie. The stupid way one said the first thing that came into one's head instead of just taking a minute or two to think. Perfectly easy to have said "Thanks, but my friend has got to go out to tea." That is, if you didn't, as she hadn't, wanted to have Rhoda too.

Rather odd, that, the way she hadn't wanted Rhoda. She had wanted, definitely, to keep Despard to herself. She had felt jealous. Jealous of Rhoda. Rhoda was so bright, so ready to talk, so full of enthusiasm and life. The other evening Major Despard had looked as though he thought Rhoda nice. But it was her, Anne Meredith, he had come down to see. Rhoda was like that. She didn't mean it, but she reduced you to the background. No, definitely she hadn't wanted Rhoda there.

But she had managed it very stupidly, getting flurried like that. If she'd managed better, she might be sitting now having tea with Major Despard at his club or somewhere.

She felt definitely annoyed with Rhoda. Rhoda was a nuisance. And what had she been doing going to see Mrs. Oliver?

Out loud she said:

"Why did you go and see Mrs. Oliver?"

"Well, she asked us to."

"Yes, but I didn't suppose she really meant it. I expect she always has to say that."

"She did mean it. She was awfully nice—couldn't have been nicer. She gave me one of her books. Look."

Rhoda flourished her prize.

Anne said suspiciously:

"What did you talk about? Not me?"

"Listen to the conceit of the girl!"

"No, but did you? Did you talk about the—the murder?"

"We talked about her murders. She's writing one where there's poison in the sage and onions. She was frightfully human—and said writing was awfully hard work and said how she got into tangles with plots, and we had black coffee and hot buttered toast," finished Rhoda in a triumphant burst.

Then she added:

"Oh, Anne, you want your tea."

"No, I don't. I've had it. With Mrs. Lorrimer."

"Mrs. Lorrimer? Isn't that the one—the one who was there?"

Anne nodded.

"Where did you come across her? Did you go and see her?"

"No. I ran across her in Harley Street."

"What was she like?"

Anne said slowly:

"I don't know. She was—rather queer. Not at all like the other night."

"Do you still think she did it?" asked Rhoda.

Anne was silent for a minute or two. Then she said:

"I don't know. Don't let's talk of it, Rhoda! You know how I hate talking of things."

"All right, darling. What was the solicitor like? Very dry and legal?"

"Rather alert and Jewish."

"Sounds all right." She waited a little and then said:

"How was Major Despard?"

"Very kind."

"He's fallen for you, Anne. I'm sure he has."

"Rhoda, don't talk nonsense."

"Well, you'll see."

Rhoda began humming to herself. She thought:

"Of course he's fallen for her. Anne's awfully pretty. But a bit wishy-washy. . . . She'll never go on treks with him. Why, she'd scream if she saw a snake. . . . Men always do take fancies to unsuitable women."

Then she said aloud.

"That bus will take us to Paddington. We'll just catch the 4:48."

CHAPTER 19
Consultation

The telephone rang in Poirot's room and a respectful voice spoke.

"Sergeant O'Connor. Superintendent Battle's compliments and would it be convenient for Mr. Hercule Poirot to come to Scotland Yard at 11:30?"

Poirot replied in the affirmative and Sergeant O'Connor rang off.

It was 11:30 to the minute when Poirot descended from his taxi at the door of New Scotland Yard—to be at once seized upon by Mrs. Oliver.

"M. Poirot. How splendid! Will you come to my rescue?"

"*Enchanté,* madame. What can I do?"

"Pay my taxi for me. I don't know how it happened but I brought out the bag I keep my going-abroad money in and the man simply won't take francs or liras or marks!"

Poirot gallantly produced some loose change, and he and Mrs. Oliver went inside the building together.

They were taken to Superintendent Battle's own room. The superintendent was sitting behind a table and looking more wooden than ever. "Just like a piece of modern sculpture," whispered Mrs. Oliver to Poirot.

Battle rose and shook hands with them both and they sat down.

"I thought it was about time for a little meeting," said Battle. "You'd like to hear how I've got on, and I'd like to hear how you've got on. We're just waiting for Colonel Race and then——"

But at that moment the door opened and the colonel appeared.

"Sorry I'm late, Battle. How do you do, Mrs. Oliver. Hallo, M. Poirot. Very sorry if I've kept you waiting. But I'm off to-morrow and had a lot of things to see to."

"Where are you going to?" asked Mrs. Oliver.

"A little shooting trip—Baluchistan way."

Poirot said, smiling ironically:

"A little trouble, is there not, in that part of the world? You will have to be careful."

"I mean to be," said Race gravely—but his eyes twinkled.

"Got anything for us, sir?" asked Battle.

"I've got you your information re Despard. Here it is——"

He pushed over a sheaf of papers.

"There's a mass of dates and places there. Most of it quite irrelevant, I should imagine. Nothing against him. He's a stout fellow. Record quite unblemished. Strict disciplinarian. Liked and trusted by the natives everywhere. One of their cumbrous names for him in Africa, where they go in for such things, is 'The man who keeps his mouth shut and judges fairly.' General opinion of the white races that Despard is a Pukka Sahib. Fine shot. Cool head. Generally long-sighted and dependable."

Unmoved by this eulogy, Battle asked:

"Any sudden deaths connected with him?"

"I laid special stress on that point. There's one fine rescue to his credit. Pal of his was being mauled by a lion."

Battle sighed.

"It's not rescues I want."

"You're a persistent fellow, Battle. There's only one incident I've been able to rake up that might suit your book. Trip into the interior in South America. Despard accompanied Professor Luxmore, the celebrated botanist, and his wife. The professor died of fever and was buried somewhere up the Amazon."

"Fever—eh?"

"Fever. But I'll play fair with you. One of the native bearers (who was sacked for stealing, incidentally) had a story that the professor didn't die of fever, but was shot. The rumour was never taken seriously."

"About time it was, perhaps."

Race shook his head.

"I've given you the facts. You asked for them and you're entitled to them, but I'd lay long odds against its being Despard who did the dirty work the other evening. He's a white man, Battle."

"Incapable of murder, you mean?"

Colonel Race hesitated.

"Incapable of what I'd call murder—yes," he said.

"But not incapable of killing a man for what would seem to him good and sufficient reasons, is that it?"

"If so, they *would* be good and sufficient reasons!"

Battle shook his head.

"You can't have human beings judging other human beings and taking the law into their own hands."

"It happens, Battle—it happens."

"It shouldn't happen—that's my point. What do you say, M. Poirot?"

"I agree with you, Battle. I have always disapproved of murder."

"What a delightfully droll way of putting it," said Mrs. Oliver. "Rather as though it were fox-hunting or killing ospreys for hats. Don't you think there are people who ought to be murdered?"

"That, very possibly."

"Well, then!"

"You do not comprehend. It is not the victim who concerns me so much. It is the effect on the character of the slayer."

"What about war?"

"In war you do not exercise the right of private judgment. *That* is what is so dangerous. Once a man is imbued with the idea that he knows who ought to be allowed to live and who ought not—then he is half-way to becoming the most dangerous killer there is—the arrogant criminal who kills not for profit—but for an idea. He has usurped the functions of *le bon Dieu*."

Colonel Race rose:

"I'm sorry I can't stop with you. Too much to do. I'd like to see the end of this business. Shouldn't be surprised if there never was an end. Even if you find out who did it, it's going to be next to impossible to prove. I've given you the facts you wanted, but in my opinion Despard's not the man. I don't believe he's ever committed murder. Shaitana may have heard some garbled rumour of Professor Luxmore's death, but I don't believe there's more to it than that. Despard's a white man, and I don't believe he's ever been a murderer. That's my opinion. And I know something of men."

"What's Mrs. Luxmore like?" asked Battle.

"She lives in London, so you can see for yourself. You'll find the address among those papers. Somewhere in South Kensington. But I repeat, Despard isn't the man."

Colonel Race left the room, stepping with the springy noiseless tread of a hunter.

Battle nodded his head thoughtfully as the door closed behind him.

"He's probably right," he said. "He knows men. Colonel Race does. But all the same, one can't take anything for granted."

He looked through the mass of documents Race had deposited on the table, occasionally making a pencil note on the pad beside him.

"Well, Superintendent Battle," said Mrs. Oliver. "Aren't you going to tell us what you have been doing?"

He looked up and smiled, a slow smile that creased his wooden face from side to side.

"This is all very irregular, Mrs. Oliver. I hope you realise that."

"Nonsense," said Mrs. Oliver. "I don't suppose for a moment you'll tell us anything you don't want to."

Battle shook his head.

"No," he said decidedly. "Cards on the table. That's the motto for this business. I mean to play fair."

Mrs. Oliver hitched her chair nearer.

"Tell us," she begged.

Superintendent Battle said slowly:

"First of all, I'll say this. As far as the actual murder of Mr. Shaitana goes, I'm not a penny the wiser. There's no hint nor clue of any kind to be found in his papers. As for the four others, I've had them shadowed, naturally, but without any tangible result. That was only to be expected. No, as M. Poirot said, there's only one hope—the past. Find out what crime exactly (if any, that is to say—after all, Shaitana may have been talking through his hat to make an impression on M. Poirot) these people have committed—and it may tell you who committed this crime."

"Well, have you found out anything?"

"I've got a line on one of them."

"Which?"

"Dr. Roberts."

Mrs. Oliver looked at him with thrilled expectation.

"As M. Poirot here knows, I tried out all kinds of theories. I established the fact pretty clearly that none of his immediate family had met with a sudden death. I've explored every alley as well as I could, and the whole thing boils down to one possibility—and rather an outside possibility at that. A few years ago Roberts must have been guilty of indiscretion, at least, with one of his lady patients. There may have been nothing in it—probably wasn't. But the woman was the hysterical, emotional kind who likes to make a scene, and either the husband got wind of what was going on, or his wife 'confessed.' Anyway, the fat was in the fire as far as the doctor was concerned. Enraged husband threatening to report him to the General Medical Council—which would probably have meant the ruin of his professional career."

"What happened?" demanded Mrs. Oliver breathlessly.

"Apparently Roberts managed to calm down the irate gentleman temporarily—and he died of anthrax almost immediately afterwards."

"Anthrax? But that's a cattle disease?"

The superintendent grinned.

"Quite right, Mrs. Oliver. It isn't the untraceable arrow poison of the South American Indian! You may remember that there was rather a scare about infected shaving brushes of cheap make about that time. Craddock's shaving brush was proved to have been the cause of infection."

"Did Dr. Roberts attend him?"

"Oh, no. Too canny for that. Dare say Craddock wouldn't have wanted him in any case. The only evidence I've got—and that's precious little—is that among the doctor's patients there *was* a case of anthrax at the time."

"You mean the doctor infected the shaving brush?"

"That's the big idea. And mind you, it's only an idea. Nothing whatever to go on. Pure conjecture. But it could be."

"He didn't marry Mrs. Craddock afterwards?"

"Oh, dear me, no, I imagine the affection was always on the lady's side. She tended to cut up rough, I hear, but suddenly went off to Egypt quite happily for the winter. She died there. A case of some obscure blood-poisoning. It's got a long name, but I don't expect it would convey much to you. Most uncommon in this country, fairly common amongst the natives in Egypt."

"So the doctor couldn't have poisoned her?"

"I don't know," said Battle slowly. "I've been chatting to a bacteriologist friend of mine—awfully difficult to get straight answers out of these people. They never can say yes or no. It's always 'that might be possible under certain conditions'—'it would depend on the pathological condition of the recipient'—'such cases have been known'—'a lot depends on individual idiosyncrasy'— all that sort of stuff. But as far as I could pin my friend down I got at this—the germ, or germs, I suppose, might have been introduced into the blood before leaving England. The symptoms would not make their appearance for some time to come."

Poirot asked:

"Was Mrs. Craddock inoculated for typhoid before going to Egypt? Most people are, I fancy."

"Good for you, M. Poirot."

"And Dr. Roberts did the inoculation?"

"That's right. There you are again—we can't prove anything. She had the usual two inoculations—and they may have been typhoid inoculations for all we know. Or one of them may have been typhoid inoculation and the other—something else. We don't know. We never shall know. The whole thing is pure hypothesis. All we can say is: it might be."

Poirot nodded thoughtfully.

"It agrees very well with some remarks made to me by Mr. Shaitana. He was exalting the successful murderer—the man against whom his crime could never be brought home."

"How did Mr. Shaitana know about it, then?" asked Mrs. Oliver.

Poirot shrugged his shoulders.

"That we shall never learn. He himself was in Egypt at one time. We know that, because he met Mrs. Lorrimer there. He may have heard some local doctor comment on curious features of Mrs. Craddock's case—a wonder as to how the infection arose. At some other time he may have heard gossip about Roberts and Mrs. Craddock. He might have amused himself by making some cryptic remark to the doctor and noted the startled awareness in his eye—all that one can never know. Some people have an uncanny gift of divining secrets. Mr. Shaitana was one of those people. All that does not concern us. We have only to say—he guessed. Did he guess right?"

"Well, I think he did," said Battle. "I've a feeling that our cheerful, genial doctor wouldn't be too scrupulous. I've known one or two like him—wonderful how certain types resemble each other. In my opinion he's a killer all right. He killed Craddock. He may have killed Mrs. Craddock if she was beginning to be a nuisance and cause a scandal. *But did he kill Shaitana?* That's the real question. And comparing the crimes, I rather doubt it. In the case of the Craddocks he used medical methods each time. The deaths appeared to be due to natural causes. In my opinion if he had killed Shaitana, he would have done so in a medical way. He'd have used the germ and not the knife."

"I never thought it was him," said Mrs. Oliver. "Not for a minute. He's too obvious, somehow."

"Exit Roberts," murmured Poirot. "And the others?"

Battle made a gesture of impatience.

"I've pretty well drawn a blank. Mrs. Lorrimer's been a widow for twenty years now. She's lived in London most of the time, occasionally going abroad in the winter. Civilised places—the Riviera, Egypt, that sort of thing. Can't find any mysterious deaths associated with her. She seems to have led a perfectly normal, respectable life—the life of a woman of the world. Every one seems to respect her and to have the highest opinion of her character. The worst that they can say about her is that she doesn't suffer fools gladly! I don't mind admitting I've been beaten all along the line there. And yet there must be *something!* Shaitana thought there was."

He sighed in a dispirited manner.

"Then there's Miss Meredith. I've got her history taped out quite clearly. Usual sort of story. Army officer's daughter. Left with very little money. Had to earn her living. Not properly trained for anything. I've checked up on her early days at Cheltenham. All quite straightforward. Every one very sorry for the poor little thing. She went first to some people in the Isle of Wight—kind of nursery-governess and mother's help. The woman she was with is out in Palestine but I've talked with her sister and she says Mrs. Eldon liked the girl very much. Certainly no mysterious deaths nor anything of that kind.

"When Mrs. Eldon went abroad, Miss Meredith went to Devonshire and took a post as companion to an aunt of a school friend. The school friend is the girl she is living with now—Miss Rhoda Dawes. She was there over two years until Miss Dawes got too ill and had to have a regular trained nurse. Cancer, I gather. She's alive still, but very vague. Kept under morphia a good deal, I imagine. I had an interview with her. She remembered 'Anne,' said she was a nice child. I also talked to a neighbour of hers who would be better able to remember the happenings of the last few years. No deaths in the parish except one or two of the older villagers, with whom, as far as I can make out, Anne Meredith never came into contact.

"Since then there's been Switzerland. Thought I might get on the track of some fatal accident there, but nothing doing. And there's nothing in Wallingford either."

"So Anne Meredith is acquitted?" asked Poirot.

Battle hesitated.

"I wouldn't say that. There's *something*. . . . There's a scared look about her that can't quite be accounted for by panic over Shaitana. She's too watchful. Too much on the alert. I'd swear there was *something*. But there it is—she's led a perfectly blameless life."

Mrs. Oliver took a deep breath—a breath of pure enjoyment.

"And yet," she said, "Anne Meredith was in the house when a woman took poison by mistake and died."

She had nothing to complain of in the effect her words produced.

Superintendent Battle spun round in his chair and stared at her in amazement.

"Is this true, Mrs. Oliver? How do you know?"

"I've been sleuthing," said Mrs. Oliver. "I get on with girls. I went down to see those two and told them a cock-and-bull story about suspecting Dr. Roberts. The Rhoda girl was friendly—oh, and rather impressed by thinking I was a celebrity. The little Meredith hated my coming and showed it quite plainly. She was suspicious. Why should she be if she hadn't got anything to hide? I asked either of them to come and see me in London. The Rhoda girl did. And she blurted the whole thing out. How Anne had been rude to me the other day because something I'd said had reminded her of a painful incident, and then she went on to describe the incident."

"Did she say when and where it happened?"

"Three years ago in Devonshire."

The superintendent muttered something under his breath and scribbled on his pad. His wooden calm was shaken.

Mrs. Oliver sat enjoying her triumph. It was a moment of great sweetness to her.

Battle recovered his temper.

"I take off my hat to you, Mrs. Oliver," he said. "You've put one over on us this time. That is very valuable information. And it just shows how easily you can miss a thing."

He frowned a little.

"She can't have been there—wherever it was—long. A couple of months at most. It must have been between the Isle of Wight and going to Miss Dawes. Yes, that could be it right enough. Naturally Mrs. Eldon's sister only remembers she went off to a place in Devonshire—she doesn't remember exactly who or where."

"Tell me," said Poirot, "was this Mrs. Eldon an untidy woman?"

Battle bent a curious gaze upon him.

"It's odd your saying that, M. Poirot. I don't see how you could have known. The sister was rather a precise party. In talking I remember her saying 'My sister is so dreadfully untidy and slapdash.' But how did *you* know?"

"Because she needed a mother's-help," said Mrs. Oliver.

Poirot shook his head.

"No, no, it was not that. It is of no moment. I was only curious. Continue, Superintendent Battle."

"In the same way," went on Battle, "I took it for granted that she went to Miss Dawes straight from the Isle of Wight. She's sly, that girl. She deceived me all right. Lying the whole time."

"Lying is not always a sign of guilt," said Poirot.

"I know that, M. Poirot. There's the natural liar. I should say she was one, as a matter of fact. Always says the thing that sounds best. But all the same it's a pretty grave risk to take, suppressing facts like that."

"She wouldn't know you had any idea of past crimes," said Mrs. Oliver.

"That's all the more reason for not suppressing that little piece of information. It must have been accepted as a bona fide case of accidental death, so she'd nothing to fear—*unless she were guilty*."

"Unless she were guilty of the Devonshire death, yes," said Poirot.

Battle turned to him.

"Oh, I know. Even if that accidental death turns out to be not so accidental, *it doesn't follow that she killed Shaitana*. But these other murders are murders too. I want to be able to bring home a crime to the person responsible for it."

"According to Mr. Shaitana, that is impossible," remarked Poirot.

"It is in Roberts' case. It remains to be seen if it is in Miss Meredith's. I shall go down to Devon to-morrow."

"Will you know where to go?" asked Mrs. Oliver. "I didn't like to ask Rhoda for more details."

"No, that was wise of you. I shan't have much difficulty. There must have been an inquest. I shall find it in the coroner's records. That's routine police work. They'll have it all taped out for me by to-morrow morning."

"What about Major Despard?" asked Mrs. Oliver. "Have you found out anything about him?"

"I've been waiting for Colonel Race's report. I've had him shadowed, of course. One rather interesting thing, he went down to see Miss Meredith at Wallingford. You remember he said he'd never met her until the other night."

"But she is a very pretty girl," murmured Poirot.

Battle laughed.

"Yes, I expect that's all there is to it. By the way, Despard's taking no chances. He's already consulted a solicitor. That looks as though he's expecting trouble."

"He is a man who looks ahead," said Poirot. "He is a man who prepared for every contingency."

"And therefore not the kind of man to stick a knife into a man in a hurry," said Battle with a sigh.

"Not unless it was the only way," said Poirot. "He can act quickly, remember."

Battle looked across the table at him.

"Now, M. Poirot, what about your cards? Haven't seen your hand down on the table yet."

Poirot smiled.

"There is so little in it. You think I conceal facts from you? It is not so. I have not learned many facts. I have talked with Dr. Roberts, with Mrs. Lorrimer, with Major Despard (I have still to talk to Miss Meredith) and what have I learnt? This! That Dr. Roberts is a keen observer, that Mrs. Lorrimer on the other hand has a most remarkable power of concentration but is, in consequence, almost blind to her surroundings. But she is fond of flowers. Despard notices only those things which appeal to him—rugs, trophies of sport. He has neither what I call the outward vision (seeing details all around you—what is called an observant person) nor the inner vision—concentration, the focusing of the mind on one object. He has a purposefully limited vision. He sees only what blends and harmonises with the bent of his mind."

"So those are what you call facts—eh?" said Battle curiously.

"They *are* facts. Very small fry—perhaps."

"What about Miss Meredith?"

"I have left her to the end. But I shall question her too as to what she remembers in that room."

"It's an odd method of approach," said Battle thoughtfully. "Purely psychological. Suppose they're leading you up the garden path?"

Poirot shook his head with a smile.

"No, that would be impossible. Whether they try to hinder or to help, they necessarily reveal their *type of mind*."

"There's something in it, no doubt," said Battle thoughtfully. "I couldn't work that way myself, though."

Poirot said, still smiling:

"I feel I have done very little in comparison with you and with Mrs. Oliver—and with Colonel Race. My cards, that I place on the table, are very low ones."

Battle twinkled at him.

"As to that, M. Poirot, the two of trumps is a low card, but it can take any one of three aces. All the same, I'm going to ask you to do a practical job of work."

"And that is?"

"I want you to interview Professor Luxmore's widow."

"And why do you not do that yourself?"

"Because, as I said just now, I'm off to Devonshire."

"Why do you not do that yourself?" repeated Poirot.

"Won't be put off, will you? Well, I'll speak the truth. I think you'll get more out of her than I shall."

"My methods being less straightforward?"

"You can put it that way if you like," said Battle, grinning. "I've heard Inspector Japp say that you've got a tortuous mind."

"Like the late Mr. Shaitana?"

"You think he would have been able to get things out of her?"

Poirot said slowly:

"I rather think he *did* get things out of her!"

"What makes you think so?" asked Battle sharply.

"A chance remark of Major Despard's."

"Gave himself away, did he? That sounds unlike him."

"Oh, my dear friend, it is impossible *not* to give oneself away—unless one never opens one's mouth! Speech is the deadliest of revealers."

"Even if people tell lies?" asked Mrs. Oliver.

"Yes, madame, because it can be seen at once that you tell a *certain kind of lie*."

"You make me feel quite uncomfortable," said Mrs. Oliver, getting up.

Superintendent Battle accompanied her to the door and shook her warmly by the hand.

"You've been the goods, Mrs. Oliver," he said. "You're a much better detective than that long lanky Laplander of yours."

"Finn," corrected Mrs. Oliver. "Of course he's idiotic. But people like him. Good-bye."

"I, too, must depart," said Poirot.

Battle scribbled an address on a piece of paper and shoved it into Poirot's hand.

"There you are. Go and tackle her."

Poirot smiled.

"And what do you want me to find out?"

"The truth about Professor Luxmore's death."

"*Mon cher* Battle! Does anybody know the truth about anything?"

"I'm going to about this business in Devonshire," said the superintendent with decision.

Poirot murmured:

"I wonder."

CHAPTER 20

The Evidence of Mrs. Luxmore

The maid who opened the door at Mrs. Luxmore's South Kensington address looked at Hercule Poirot with deep disapproval. She showed no disposition to admit him into the house.

Unperturbed, Poirot gave her a card.

"Give that to your mistress. I think she will see me."

It was one of his more ostentatious cards. The words "Private Detective" were printed in one corner. He had had them specially engraved for the purpose of obtaining interviews with the so-called fair sex. Nearly every woman, whether conscious of innocence or not, was anxious to have a look at a private detective and find out what he wanted.

Left ignominiously on the mat, Poirot studied the door-knocker with intense disgust at its unpolished condition.

"Ah! for some Brasso and a rag," he murmured to himself.

Breathing excitedly the maid returned and Poirot was bidden to enter.

He was shown into a room on the first floor—a rather dark room smelling of stale flowers and unemptied ashtrays. There were large quantities of silk cushions of exotic colours all in need of cleaning. The walls were emerald green and the ceiling was of pseudo copper.

A tall, rather handsome woman was standing by the mantelpiece. She came forward and spoke in a deep husky voice.

"M. Hercule Poirot?"

Poirot bowed. His manner was not quite his own. He was not only foreign but ornately foreign. His gestures were positively baroque. Faintly, very faintly, it was the manner of the late Mr. Shaitana.

"What did you want to see me about?"

Again Poirot bowed.

"If I might be seated? It will take a little time——"

She waved him impatiently to a chair and sat down herself on the edge of a sofa.

"Yes? Well?"

"It is, madame, that I make the inquiries—the private inquiries, you understand?"

The more deliberate his approach, the greater her eagerness.

"Yes—yes?"

"I make inquiries into the death of the late Professor Luxmore."

She gave a gasp. Her dismay was evident.

"But why? What do you mean? What has it got to do with you?"

Poirot watched her carefully before proceeding.

"There is, you comprehend, a book being written. A life of your eminent husband. The writer, naturally, is anxious to get all his facts exact. As to your husband's death, for instance——"

She broke in at once:

"My husband died of fever—on the Amazon."

Poirot leaned back in his chair. Slowly, very, very slowly, he shook his head to and fro—a maddening, monotonous motion.

"Madame, madame——" he protested.

"But I know! I was there at the time."

"Ah, yes, certainly. You were *there*. Yes, my information says so."

She cried out:

"What information?"

Eyeing her closely Poirot said:

"Information supplied to me by the late Mr. Shaitana."

She shrank back as though flicked with a whip.

"Shaitana?" she muttered.

"A man," said Poirot, "possessed of vast stores of knowledge. A remarkable man. That man knew many secrets."

"I suppose he did," she murmured, passing a tongue over her dry lips.

Poirot leaned forward. He achieved a little tap on her knee.

"He knew, for instance, that your husband did not die of fever."

She stared at him. Her eyes looked wild and desperate.

He leaned back and watched the effect of his words.

She pulled herself together with an effort.

"I don't—I don't know what you mean."

It was very unconvincingly said.

"Madame," said Poirot, "I will come out into the open. I will," he smiled, "place my cards upon the table. Your husband did not die of a fever. *He died of a bullet!*"

"Oh!" she cried.

She covered her face with her hands. She rocked herself to and fro. She was in terrible distress. But somewhere, in some remote fibre of her being, she was enjoying her own emotions. Poirot was quite sure of that.

"And therefore," said Poirot in a matter-of-fact tone, "you might just as well tell me the whole story."

She uncovered her face and said:

"It wasn't in the least the way you think."

Again Poirot leaned forward—again he tapped her knee.

"You misunderstand me—you misunderstand me utterly," he said. "I know very well that it was not you who shot him. It was Major Despard. But you were the cause."

"I don't know. I don't know. I suppose I was. It was all too terrible. There is a sort of fatality that pursues me."

"Ah, how true that is," cried Poirot. "How often have I not seen it? There are some women like that. Wherever they go, tragedies follow in their wake. It is not their fault. These things happen in spite of themselves."

Mrs. Luxmore drew a deep breath.

"You understand. I see you understand. It all happened so naturally."

"You travelled together into the interior, did you not?"

"Yes. My husband was writing a book on various rare plants. Major Despard was introduced to us as a man who knew the conditions and would arrange the necessary expedition. My husband liked him very much. We started."

There was a pause. Poirot allowed it to continue for about a minute and a half and then murmured as though to himself.

"Yes, one can picture it. The winding river—the tropical night—the hum of the insects—the strong soldierly man—the beautiful woman. . . ."

Mrs. Luxmore sighed.

"My husband was, of course, years older than I was. I married as a mere child before I knew what I was doing. . . ."

Poirot shook his head sadly.

"I know. I know. How often does that not occur?"

"Neither of us would admit what was happening," went on Mrs. Luxmore. "John Despard never said anything. He was the soul of honour."

"But a woman always knows," prompted Poirot.

"How right you are. . . . Yes, a woman knows. . . . But I never showed him that I knew. We were Major Despard and Mrs. Luxmore to each other right up to the end. . . . We were both determined to play the game."

She was silent, lost in admiration of that noble attitude.

"True," murmured Poirot. "One must play the cricket. As one of your poets so finely says, 'I could not love thee, dear, so much, loved I not cricket more.'"

"Honour," corrected Mrs. Luxmore with a slight frown.

"Of course—of course—honour. 'Loved I not honour more.'"

"Those words might have been written for us," murmured Mrs. Luxmore. "No matter what it cost us, we were both determined never to say the fatal word. And then——"

"And then——" prompted Poirot.

"That ghastly night." Mrs. Luxmore shuddered.

"Yes?"

"I suppose they must have quarrelled—John and Timothy, I mean. I came out of my tent. . . . I came out of my tent . . ."

"Yes—yes?"

Mrs. Luxmore's eyes were wide and dark. She was seeing the scene as though it were being repeated in front of her.

"I came out of my tent," she repeated. "John and Timothy were—— Oh!" she shuddered. "I can't remember it all clearly. I came between them. . . . I said 'No—no, it isn't *true!*' Timothy wouldn't listen. He was threatening John. John had to fire—in self-defence. Ah!" She gave a cry and covered her face with her hands. "He was dead—stone dead—shot through the heart."

"A terrible moment for you, madame."

"I shall never forget it. John was noble. He was all for giving himself up. I refused to hear of it. We argued all night. 'For my sake,' I kept saying. He saw that in the end. Naturally he couldn't let me suffer. The awful publicity. Think of the headlines. *Two Men and a Woman in the Jungle. Primeval Passions*.

"I put it all to John. In the end he gave in. The boys had seen and heard nothing. Timothy had been having a bout of fever. We said he had died of it. We buried him there beside the Amazon."

A deep, tortured sigh shook her form.

"And then—back to civilisation—and to part for ever."

"Was it necessary, madame?"

"Yes, yes. Timothy dead stood between us just as Timothy alive had done—more so. We said good-bye to each other—for ever. I meet John Despard sometimes—out in the world. We smile, we speak politely—no one would ever guess that there was anything between us. But I see in his eyes—and he in mine—that we will never forget. . . ."

There was a long pause. Poirot paid tribute to the curtain by not breaking the silence.

Mrs. Luxmore took out a vanity case and powdered her nose—the spell was broken.

"What a tragedy," said Poirot, but in a more everyday tone.

"You can see, M. Poirot," said Mrs. Luxmore earnestly, "that the truth must never be told."

"It would be painful——"

"It would be impossible. This friend, this writer—surely he would not wish to blight the life of a perfectly innocent woman?"

"Or even to hang a perfectly innocent man?" murmured Poirot.

"You see it like that? I am so glad. He *was* innocent. A *crime passionnel* is not really a crime. And in any case it was in self-defence. He *had* to shoot. So you do understand, M. Poirot, that the world must continue to think Timothy died of fever?"

Poirot murmured.

"Writers are sometimes curiously callous."

"Your friend is a woman-hater? He wants to make us suffer? But you must not allow that. I shall not allow it. If necessary I shall take the blame on myself. I shall say *I* shot Timothy."

She had risen to her feet. Her head was thrown back.

Poirot also rose.

"Madame," he said as he took her hand, "such splendid self-sacrifice is unnecessary. I will do my best so that the true facts shall never be known."

A sweet womanly smile stole over Mrs. Luxmore's face. She raised her hand slightly, so that Poirot, whether he had meant to do so or not, was forced to kiss it.

"An unhappy woman thanks you, M. Poirot," she said.

It was the last word of a persecuted queen to a favoured courtier—clearly an exit line. Poirot duly made his exit.

Once out in the street, he drew a long breath of fresh air.

CHAPTER 21
Major Despard

"Quelle femme," murmured Hercule Poirot. *"Ce pauvre Despard! Ce qu'il a du souffrir! Quel voyage épouvantable!"*

Suddenly he began to laugh.

He was now walking along the Brompton Road. He paused, took out his watch, and made a calculation.

"But yes, I have the time. In any case to wait will do him no harm. I can now attend to the other little matter. What was it that my friend in the English police force used to sing—how many years—forty years ago? 'A little piece of sugar for the bird.'"

Humming a long-forgotten tune, Hercule Poirot entered a sumptuous-looking shop mainly devoted to the clothing and general embellishment of women and made his way to the stocking counter.

Selecting a sympathetic-looking and not too haughty damsel he made known his requirements.

"Silk stockings? Oh, yes, we have a very nice line here. Guaranteed pure silk."

Poirot waved them away. He waxed eloquent once more.

"French silk stockings? With the duty, you know, they are very expensive."

A fresh lot of boxes was produced.

"Very nice, mademoiselle, but I had something of a finer texture still in mind."

"These are a hundred gauge. Of course, we have some extra fine, but I'm afraid they come out at about thirty-five shillings a pair. And no durability, of course. Just like cobwebs."

"C'est ça, exactement."

A prolonged absence of the young lady this time.

She returned at last.

"I'm afraid they are actually thirty-seven and sixpence a pair. But beautiful, aren't they?"

She slid them tenderly from a gauzy envelope—the finest, gauziest wisps of stockings.

"*Enfin*—that is it exactly!"

"Lovely, aren't they? How many pairs, sir?"

"I want—let me see, nineteen pairs."

The young lady very nearly fell down behind the counter, but long training in scornfulness just kept her erect.

"There would be a reduction on two dozen," she said faintly.

"No, I want nineteen pairs. Of slightly different colours, please."

The girl sorted them out obediently, packed them up and made out the bill.

As Poirot departed with his purchase, the next girl at the counter said:

"Wonder who the lucky girl is? Must be a nasty old man. Oh, well, she seems to be stringing him along good and proper. Stockings at thirty-seven and sixpence indeed!"

Unaware of the low estimate formed by the young ladies of Messrs. Harvey Robinson's upon his character, Poirot was trotting homewards.

He had been in for about half an hour when he heard the door-bell ring. A few minutes later Major Despard entered the room.

He was obviously keeping his temper with difficulty.

"What the devil did you want to go and see Mrs. Luxmore for?" he asked.

Poirot smiled.

"I wished, you see, for the true story of Professor Luxmore's death."

"True story? Do you think that woman's capable of telling the truth about anything?" demanded Despard wrathfully.

"*Eh bien*, I did wonder now and then," admitted Poirot.

"I should think you did. That woman's crazy."

Poirot demurred.

"Not at all. She is a romantic woman, that is all."

"Romantic be damned. She's an out-and-out liar. I sometimes think she even believes her own lies."

"It is quite possible."

"She's an appalling woman. I had the hell of a time with her out there."

"That also I can well believe."

Despard sat down abruptly.

"Look here, M. Poirot, I'm going to tell you the truth."

"You mean you are going to give me your version of the story?"

"My version will be the true version."

Poirot did not reply.

Despard went on dryly:

"I quite realise that I can't claim any merit in coming out with this now. I'm telling the truth because it's the only thing to be done at this stage. Whether you believe me or not is up to you. I've no kind of proof that my story is the correct one."

He paused for a minute and then began.

"I arranged the trip for the Luxmores. He was a nice old boy quite batty about mosses and plants and things. She was a——well, she was what you've no doubt observed her to be! That trip was a nightmare. I didn't care a damn for the woman—rather disliked her, as a matter of fact. She was the intense, soulful kind that always makes me feel prickly with embarrassment. Everything went all right for the first fortnight. Then we all had a go of fever. She and I had it slightly. Old Luxmore was pretty bad. One night—now you've got to listen to this carefully—I was sitting outside my tent. Suddenly I saw Luxmore in the distance staggering off into the bush by the river. He was absolutely delirious and quite unconscious of what he was doing. In another minute he would be in the river—and at that particular spot it would have been the end of him. No chance of a rescue. There wasn't time to rush after him—only one thing to be done. My rifle was beside me as usual. I snatched it up. I'm a pretty accurate shot. I was quite sure I could bring the old boy down—get him in the leg. And then, just as I fired, that idiotic fool of a woman flung herself from somewhere upon me, yelping out, 'Don't shoot. For God's sake, don't shoot.' She caught my arm and jerked it ever so slightly just as the rifle went off—with the result that the bullet got him in the back and killed him dead!

"I can tell you that was a pretty ghastly moment. And that damned fool of a woman still didn't understand what she'd done. Instead of realising that she'd been responsible for her husband's death, she firmly believed that I'd been trying to shoot the old boy in cold blood—for love of her, if you please! We had the devil of a scene—she insisting that we should say he'd died of fever. I was sorry for her—especially as I saw she didn't realise what she'd done. But she'd have to realise it if the truth came out! And then her complete certainty that I was head over heels in love with her gave me a bit of a jar. It was going to be a pretty kettle of fish if she went about giving that out. In the end I agreed to do what she wanted—partly for the sake of peace, I'll admit. After all, it didn't seem to matter much. Fever or accident. And I didn't want to drag a woman through a lot of unpleasantness—even if she was a damned fool. I gave it out next day that the professor was dead of fever and we buried him. The bearers knew the truth, of course, but they were all devoted to me and I knew that what I said they'd swear to if need be. We buried poor old Luxmore and got back to civilisation. Since then I've spent a good deal of time dodging the woman."

He paused, then said quietly:

"That's my story, M. Poirot."

Poirot said slowly:

"It was to that incident that Mr. Shaitana referred, or so you thought, at dinner that night?"

Despard nodded.

"He must have heard it from Mrs. Luxmore. Easy enough to get the story out of her. That sort of thing would have amused him."

"It might have been a dangerous story—to you—in the hands of a man like Shaitana."

Despard shrugged his shoulders.

"I wasn't afraid of Shaitana."

Poirot didn't answer.

Despard said quietly:

"That again you have to take my word for. It's true enough, I suppose, that I had a kind of motive for Shaitana's death. Well, the truth's out now—take it or leave it."

Poirot held out a hand.

"I will take it, Major Despard. I have no doubt at all that things in South America happened exactly as you have described."

Despard's face lit up.

"Thanks," he said laconically.

And he clasped Poirot's hand warmly.

CHAPTER 22
Evidence from Combeacre

Superintendent Battle was in the police station of Combeacre.

Inspector Harper, rather red in the face, talked in a slow, pleasing Devonshire voice.

"That's how it was, sir. Seemed all as right as rain. The doctor was satisfied. Every one was satisfied. Why not?"

"Just give me the facts about the two bottles again. I want to get it quite clear."

"Syrup of Figs—that's what the bottle was. She took it regular, it seems. Then there was this hat paint she'd been using—or rather the young lady, her companion, had been using for her. Brightening up a garden hat. There was a good deal left over, and the bottle broke, and Mrs. Benson herself said, 'Put it in that old bottle—the Syrup of Figs bottle.' That's all right. The servants heard her. The young lady, Miss Meredith, and the housemaid and the parlourmaid—they all agree on that. The paint was put into the old Syrup of Figs bottle and it was put up on the top shelf in the bathroom with other odds and ends."

"Not re-labelled?"

"No. Careless, of course; the coroner commented on that."

"Go on."

"On this particular night the deceased went into the bathroom, took down a Syrup of Figs bottle, poured herself out a good dose and drank it. Realised what she'd done and they sent off at once for the doctor. He was out on a case and it was some time before they could get at him. They did all they could, but she died."

"She herself believed it to be an accident?"

"Oh, yes—every one thought so. It seems clear the bottles must have got mixed up somehow. It was suggested the housemaid did it when she dusted, but she swears she didn't."

Superintendent Battle was silent—thinking. Such an easy business. A bottle taken down from an upper shelf, put in place of the other. So difficult to trace a mistake like that to its source. Handled it with gloves, possibly, and anyway, the last prints would be those of Mrs. Benson herself. Yes, so easy—so simple. But, all the same, murder! The perfect crime.

But why? That still puzzled him—why?

"This young lady-companion, this Miss Meredith, she didn't come into money at Mrs. Benson's death?" he asked.

Inspector Harper shook his head.

"No. She'd only been there about six weeks. Difficult place, I should imagine. Young ladies didn't stay long as a rule."

Battle was still puzzled. Young ladies didn't stay long. A difficult woman, evidently. But if Anne Meredith had been unhappy, she could have left as her predecessors had done. No need to kill—unless it were sheer unreasoning vindictiveness. He shook his head. That suggestion did not ring true.

"Who did get Mrs. Benson's money?"

"I couldn't say, sir, nephews and nieces, I believe. But it wouldn't be very much—not when it was divided up, and I heard as how most of her income was one of these annuities."

Nothing there then. But Mrs. Benson had died. And Anne Meredith had not told him that she had been at Combeacre.

It was all profoundly unsatisfactory.

He made diligent and painstaking inquiries. The doctor was quite clear and emphatic. No reason to believe it was anything but an accident. Miss—couldn't remember her name—nice girl but rather helpless—had been very upset and distressed. There was the vicar. He remembered Mrs. Benson's last companion—a modest-looking girl. Always came to church with Mrs. Benson. Mrs. Benson had been—not difficult—but a trifle severe toward young people. She was the rigid type of Christian.

Battle tried one or two other people but learned nothing of value. Anne Meredith was hardly remembered. She had lived among them a few months—that was all—and her personality was not sufficiently vivid to make a lasting impression. A nice little thing seemed to be the accepted description.

Mrs. Benson loomed out a little more clearly. A self-righteous grenadier of a woman, working her companions hard and changing her servants often. A disagreeable woman—but that was all.

Nevertheless Superintendent Battle left Devonshire under the firm impression that, for some reason unknown, Anne Meredith had deliberately murdered her employer.

CHAPTER 23
The Evidence of a Pair of Silk Stockings

As Superintendent Battle's train rushed eastwards through England, Anne Meredith and Rhoda Dawes were in Hercule Poirot's sitting-room.

Anne had been unwilling to accept the invitation that had reached her by the morning's post, but Rhoda's counsel had prevailed.

"Anne—you're a coward—yes, a coward. It's no good going on being an ostrich, burying your head in the sand. There's been a murder and you're one of the suspects—the least likely one perhaps——"

"That would be the worst," said Anne with a touch of humour. "It's always the least likely person who did it."

"But you are one," continued Rhoda, undisturbed by the interruption. "And so it's no use putting your nose in the air as though murder was a nasty smell and nothing to do with you."

"It *is* nothing to do with me," Anne persisted. "I mean, I'm quite willing to answer any questions the police want to ask me, but this man, this Hercule Poirot, he's an outsider."

"And what will he think if you hedge and try to get out of it? He'll think you're bursting with guilt."

"I'm certainly not bursting with guilt," said Anne coldly.

"Darling, I know that. You couldn't murder anybody if you tried. But horrible suspicious foreigners don't know that. I think we ought to go nicely to his house. Otherwise he'll come down here and try to worm things out of the servants."

"We haven't got any servants."

"We've got Mother Astwell. She can wag a tongue with anybody! Come on, Anne, let's go. It will be rather fun really."

"I don't see why he wants to see me." Anne was obstinate.

"To put one over on the official police, of course," said Rhoda impatiently. "They always do—the amateurs, I mean. They make out that Scotland Yard are all boots and brainlessness."

"Do you think this man Poirot is clever?"

"He doesn't look a Sherlock," said Rhoda. "I expect he has been quite good in his day. He's gaga now, of course. He must be at least sixty. Oh, come on, Anne, let's go and see the old boy. He may tell us dreadful things about the others."

"All right," said Anne, and added, "You do *enjoy* all this so, Rhoda."

"I suppose because it isn't my funeral," said Rhoda. "You were a noodle, Anne, not just to have looked up at the right minute. If only you had, you could live like a duchess for the rest of your life on blackmail."

So it came about that at three o'clock of that same afternoon, Rhoda Dawes and Anne Meredith sat primly on their chairs in Poirot's neat room and sipped blackberry *sirop* (which they disliked very much but were too polite to refuse) from old-fashioned glasses.

"It was most amiable of you to accede to my request, mademoiselle," Poirot was saying.

"I'm sure I shall be glad to help you in any way I can," murmured Anne vaguely.

"It is a little matter of memory."

"Memory?"

"Yes, I have already put these questions to Mrs. Lorrimer, to Dr. Roberts and to Major Despard. None of them, alas, have given me the response that I hoped for."

Anne continued to look at him inquiringly.

"I want you, mademoiselle, to cast your mind back to that evening in the drawing-room of Mr. Shaitana."

A weary shadow passed over Anne's face. Was she never to be free of that nightmare?

Poirot noticed the expression.

"I know, mademoiselle, I know," he said kindly. "*C'est pénible, n'est ce pas?* That is very natural. You, so young as you are, to be brought in contact with horror for the first time. Probably you have never known or seen a violent death."

Rhoda's feet shifted a little uncomfortably on the floor.

"Well?" said Anne.

"Cast your mind back. I want you to tell me what you remember of that room?"

Anne stared at him suspiciously.

"I don't understand?"

"But, yes. The chairs, the tables, the ornaments, the wallpaper, the curtains, the fire-irons. You saw them all. Can you not then describe them?"

"Oh, I see." Anne hesitated, frowning. "It's difficult. I don't really think I remember. I couldn't say what the wallpaper was like. I think the walls were painted—some inconspicuous colour. There were rugs on the floor. There was a piano." She shook her head. "I really couldn't tell you any more."

"But you are not trying, mademoiselle. You must remember some object, some ornament, some piece of *bric-à-brac?*"

"There was a case of Egyptian jewellery, I remember," said Anne slowly. "Over by the window."

"Oh, yes, at the extreme other end of the room from the table on which lay the little dagger."

Anne looked at him.

"I never heard which table that was on."

"Pas si bête," commented Poirot to himself. "But then, no more is Hercule Poirot! If she knew me better she would realise I would never lay a *piege* as gross as that!"

Aloud he said:

"A case of Egyptian jewellery, you say?"

Anne answered with some enthusiasm.

"Yes—some of it was lovely. Blues and red. Enamel. One or two lovely rings. And scarabs—but I don't like them so much."

"He was a great collector, Mr. Shaitana," murmured Poirot.

"Yes, he must have been," Anne agreed. "The room was full of stuff. One couldn't begin to look at it all."

"So that you cannot mention anything else that particularly struck your notice?"

Anne smiled a little as she said:

"Only a vase of chrysanthemums that badly wanted their water changed."

"Ah, yes, servants are not always too particular about that."

Poirot was silent for a moment or two.

Anne asked timidly.

"I'm afraid I didn't notice—whatever it is you wanted me to notice."

Poirot smiled kindly.

"It does not matter, *mon enfant*. It was, indeed, an outside chance. Tell me, have you seen the good Major Despard lately?"

He saw the delicate pink colour come up in the girl's face. She replied:

"He said he would come and see us again quite soon."

Rhoda said impetuously:

"*He* didn't do it, anyway! Anne and I are quite sure of that."

Poirot twinkled at them.

"How fortunate—to have convinced two such charming young ladies of one's innocence."

"Oh, dear," thought Rhoda. "He's going to be French, and it does embarrass me so."

She got up and began examining some etchings on the wall.

"These are awfully good," she said.

"They are not bad," said Poirot.

He hesitated, looking at Anne.

"Mademoiselle," he said at last. "I wonder if I might ask you to do me a great favour—oh, nothing to do with the murder. This is an entirely private and personal matter."

Anne looked a little surprised. Poirot went on speaking in a slightly embarrassed manner.

"It is, you understand, that Christmas is coming on. I have to buy presents for many nieces and grand-nieces. And it is a little difficult to choose what young ladies like in this present time. My tastes, alas, are rather old-fashioned."

"Yes?" said Anne kindly.

"Silk stockings, now—are silk stockings a welcome present to receive?"

"Yes, indeed. It's always nice to be given stockings."

"You relieve my mind. I will ask my favour. I have obtained some different colours. There are, I think, about fifteen or sixteen pairs. Would you be so amiable as to look through them and set aside half a dozen pairs that seem to you the most desirable?"

"Certainly I will," said Anne, rising, with a laugh.

Poirot directed her towards a table in an alcove—a table whose contents were strangely at variance, had she but known it, with the well-known order and neatness of Hercule Poirot. There were stockings piled up in untidy heaps—some fur-lined gloves—calendars and boxes of bonbons.

"I send off my parcels very much *à l'avance,*" Poirot explained. "See, mademoiselle, here are the stockings. Select me, I pray of you, six pairs."

He turned, intercepting Rhoda, who was following him.

"As for mademoiselle here, I have a little treat for her—a treat that would be no treat to you, I fancy, Mademoiselle Meredith."

"What is it?" cried Rhoda.

He lowered his voice.

"A knife, mademoiselle, with which twelve people once stabbed a man. It was given me as a souvenir by the Compagnie Internationale des Wagons Lits."

"Horrible," cried Anne.

"Ooh! Let me see," said Rhoda.

Poirot led her through into the other room, talking as he went.

"It was given me by the Compagnie Internationale des Wagons Lits because——"

They passed out of the room.

They returned three minutes later. Anne came towards them.

"I think these six are the nicest, M. Poirot. Both these are very good evening shades, and this lighter colour would be nice when summer comes and it's daylight in the evening."

"Mille remercîments, mademoiselle."

He offered them more sirop, which they refused, and finally accompanied them to the door, still talking genially.

When they had finally departed he returned to the room and went straight to the littered table. The pile of stockings still lay in a confused heap. Poirot counted the six selected pairs and then went on to count the others.

He had bought nineteen pairs. There were now only seventeen.

He nodded his head slowly.

CHAPTER 24

Elimination of Three Murderers?

On arrival in London, Superintendent Battle came straight to Poirot. Anne and Rhoda had then been gone an hour or more.

Without more ado, the superintendent recounted the result of his researches in Devonshire.

"We're on to it—not a doubt of it," he finished. "That's what Shaitana was aiming at—with his 'domestic accident' business. But what gets me is the motive. Why did she want to kill the woman?"

"I think I can help you there, my friend."

"Go ahead, M. Poirot."

"This afternoon I conducted a little experiment. I induced mademoiselle and her friend to come here. I put to them my usual questions as to what there was in the room that night."

Battle looked at him curiously.

"You're very keen on that question."

"Yes, it's useful. It tells me a good deal. Mademoiselle Meredith was suspicious—very suspicious. She takes nothing for granted, that young lady. So that good dog, Hercule Poirot, he does one of his best tricks. He lays a clumsy amateurish trap. Mademoiselle mentions a case of jewellery. I say was not that at the opposite end of the room from the table with the dagger. Mademoiselle does not fall into the trap. She avoids it cleverly. And after that she is pleased with herself, and her vigilance relaxes. So that is the object of this visit—to get her to admit that she knew where the dagger was, and that she noticed it! Her spirits rise when she has, as she thinks, defeated me. She talked quite freely about the jewellery. She has noticed many details of it. There is nothing else in the room that she remembers—except that a vase of chrysanthemums needed its water changing."

"Well?" said Battle.

"Well, it is significant, that. Suppose we knew nothing about this girl. Her words would give us a clue to her character. She notices flowers. She is, then, fond of flowers? No, since she does not mention a very big bowl of early tulips which would at once have attracted the attention of a flower lover. No, it is the paid companion who speaks—the girl whose duty it has been to put fresh water in the vases—and, allied to that, there is a girl who loves and notices jewellery. Is not that, at least, suggestive?"

"Ah," said Battle. "I'm beginning to see what you're driving at."

"Precisely. As I told you the other day, I place my cards on the table. When you recounted her history the other day, and Mrs. Oliver made her startling announcement, my mind went at once to an important point. The murder could not have been committed for gain, since Miss Meredith had still to earn her living after it happened. Why, then? I considered Miss Meredith's temperament as it appeared superficially. A rather timid young girl, poor, but well-dressed, fond of pretty things. . . . The temperament, is it not, of a *thief*, rather than a murderer. And I asked immediately if Mrs. Eldon had been a tidy woman. You replied that no, she had not been tidy. I formed a hypothesis. Supposing that Anne Meredith was a girl with a weak streak in her character—the kind of girl who takes little things from the big shops. Supposing that, poor, and yet loving pretty things, she helped herself once or twice to things from her employer. A brooch, perhaps, an odd half-crown or two, a string of beads. Mrs. Eldon, careless, untidy, would put down these disappearances to her own carelessness. She would not suspect her gentle little mother's-help. But, now, suppose a different type of employer—an employer who *did* notice—accused Anne Meredith of theft. That would be a possible motive for murder. As I said the other evening, Miss Meredith would only commit a murder through fear. She knows that her employer will be able to prove the theft. There is only one thing that can save her: her employer must die. And so she changes the bottles, and Mrs. Benson dies—ironically enough convinced that the mistake is her own, and not suspecting for a minute that the cowed, frightened girl has had a hand in it."

"It's possible," said Superintendent Battle. "It's only a hypothesis, but it's possible."

"It is a little more than possible, my friend—it is also probable. For this afternoon I laid a little trap nicely baited—the real trap—after the sham one had been circumvented. If what I suspect is true, Anne Meredith will never, never be able to resist a really expensive pair of stockings! I ask her to aid me. I let her know carefully that I am not sure exactly how many stockings there are, I go out of the room, leaving her alone—and the result, my friend, is that I have now seventeen pairs of stockings, instead of nineteen, and that two pairs have gone away in Anne Meredith's handbag."

"Whew!" Superintendent Battle whistled. "What a risk to take, though."

"*Pas du tout*. What does she think I suspect her of? Murder. What is the risk, then, in stealing a pair, or two pairs, of silk stockings? I am not looking for a thief. And, besides, the thief, or the kleptomaniac, is always the same—convinced that she can get away with it."

Battle nodded his head.

"That's true enough. Incredibly stupid. The pitcher goes to the well time after time. Well, I think between us we've arrived fairly clearly at the truth. Anne Meredith was caught stealing. Anne Meredith changed a bottle from one shelf to another. We know that was murder—but I'm damned if we could ever prove it. Successful crime No. 2. Roberts gets away with it. Anne Meredith gets away with it. But what about Shaitana? Did Anne Meredith kill Shaitana?"

He remained silent for a moment or two, then he shook his head.

"It doesn't work out right," he said reluctantly. "She's not one to take a risk. Change a couple of bottles, yes. She knew no one could fasten that on her. It was absolutely safe—because any one might have done it! Of course, it mightn't have worked. Mrs. Benson might have noticed before she drank the stuff, or she mightn't have died from it. It was what I call a *hopeful* kind of murder. It might work or it mightn't. Actually, it did. But Shaitana was a very different pair of shoes. That was deliberate, audacious, purposeful murder."

Poirot nodded his head.

"I agree with you. The two types of crime are not the same."

Battle rubbed his nose.

"So that seems to wipe her out as far as he's concerned. Roberts and the girl, both crossed off our list. What about Despard? Any luck with the Luxmore woman?"

Poirot narrated his adventures of the preceding afternoon.

Battle grinned.

"I know that type. You can't disentangle what they remember from what they invent."

Poirot went on. He described Despard's visit, and the story the latter had told.

"Believe him?" Battle asked abruptly.

"Yes, I do."

Battle sighed.

"So do I. Not the type to shoot a man because he wanted the man's wife. Anyway, what's wrong with the divorce court? Every one flocks there. And he's not a professional man; it wouldn't ruin him, or anything like that. No, I'm of the opinion that our late lamented Mr. Shaitana struck a snag there. Murderer No. 3 wasn't a murderer, after all."

He looked at Poirot.

"That leaves——?"

"Mrs. Lorrimer," said Poirot.

The telephone rang. Poirot got up and answered it. He spoke a few words, waited, spoke again. Then he hung up the receiver and returned to Battle.

His face was very grave.

"That was Mrs. Lorrimer speaking," he said. "She wants me to come round and see her—now."

He and Battle looked at each other. The latter shook his head slowly.

"Am I wrong?" he said. "Or were you expecting something of the kind?"

"I wondered," said Hercule Poirot. "That was all. I wondered."

"You'd better get along," said Battle. "Perhaps you'll manage to get at the truth at last."

CHAPTER 25
Mrs. Lorrimer Speaks

The day was not a bright one, and Mrs. Lorrimer's room seemed rather dark and cheerless. She herself had a grey look, and seemed much older than she had done on the occasion of Poirot's last visit.

She greeted him with her usual smiling assurance.

"It is very nice of you to come so promptly, M. Poirot. You are a busy man, I know."

"At your service, madame," said Poirot with a little bow.

Mrs. Lorrimer pressed the bell by the fireplace.

"We will have tea brought in. I don't know what you feel about it, but I always think it's a mistake to rush straight into confidences without any decent paving of the way."

"There are to be confidences, then, madame?"

Mrs. Lorrimer did not answer, for at that moment her maid answered the bell. When she had received the order and gone again, Mrs. Lorrimer said dryly:

"You said, if you remember, when you were last here, that you would come if I sent for you. You had an idea, I think, of the reason that should prompt me to send."

There was no more just then. Tea was brought. Mrs. Lorrimer dispensed it, talking intelligently on various topics of the day.

Taking advantage of a pause, Poirot remarked:

"I hear you and little Mademoiselle Meredith had tea together the other day."

"We did. You have seen her lately?"

"This very afternoon."

"She is in London, then, or have you been down to Wallingford?"

"No. She and her friend were so amiable as to pay me a visit."

"Ah, the friend. I have not met her."

Poirot said, smiling a little:

"This murder—it has made for a *rapprochement*. You and Mademoiselle Meredith have tea together. Major Despard, he, too, cultivates Miss Meredith's acquaintance. The Dr. Roberts, he is perhaps the only one out of it."

"I saw him out at bridge the other day," said Mrs. Lorrimer. "He seemed quite his usual cheerful self."

"As fond of bridge as ever?"

"Yes—still making the most outrageous bids—and very often getting away with it."

She was silent for a moment or two, then said:

"Have you seen Superintendent Battle lately?"

"Also this afternoon. He was with me when you telephoned."

Shading her face from the fire with one hand, Mrs. Lorrimer asked:

"How is he getting on?"

Poirot said gravely:

"He is not very rapid, the good Battle. He gets there slowly, but he does get there in the end, madame."

"I wonder." Her lips curved in a faintly ironical smile.

She went on:

"He has paid me quite a lot of attention. He has delved, I think, into my past history right back to my girlhood. He has interviewed my friends, and chatted to my servants—the ones I have now and the ones who have been with me in former years. What he hoped to find I do not know, but he certainly did not find it. He might as well have accepted what I told him. It was the truth. I knew Mr. Shaitana very slightly. I met him at Luxor, as I said, and our acquaintanceship was never more than an acquaintanceship. Superintendent Battle will not be able to get away from these facts."

"Perhaps not," said Poirot.

"And you, M. Poirot? Have not you made any inquiries?"

"About you, madame?"

"That is what I meant."

Slowly the little man shook his head.

"It would have been of no avail."

"Just exactly what do you mean by that, M. Poirot?"

"I will be quite frank, madame. I have realised from the beginning that, of the four persons in Mr. Shaitana's room that night, the one with the best brains, with the coolest, most logical head, was you, madame. If I had to lay money on the chance of one of those four planning a murder and getting away with it successfully, it is on you that I should place my money."

Mrs. Lorrimer's brows rose.

"Am I expected to feel flattered?" she asked dryly.

Poirot went on, without paying any attention to her interruption.

"For a crime to be successful, it is usually necessary to think every detail of it out beforehand. All possible contingencies must be taken into account. The *timing* must be accurate. The *placing* must be scrupulously correct. Dr. Roberts might bungle a crime through haste and over-confidence; Major Despard would probably be too prudent to commit one; Miss Meredith might lose her head and give herself away. You, madame, would do none of these things. You would be clear-headed and cool, you are sufficiently resolute of character, and could be sufficiently obsessed with an idea to the extent of overruling prudence, you are not the kind of woman to lose her head."

Mrs. Lorrimer sat silent for a minute or two, a curious smile playing round her lips. At last she said:

"So that is what you think of me, M. Poirot. That I am the kind of woman to commit an ideal murder."

"At least you have the amiability not to resent the idea."

"I find it very interesting. So it is your idea that I am the only person who could successfully have murdered Shaitana?"

Poirot said slowly:

"There is a difficulty there, madame."

"Really? Do tell me?"

"You may have noticed that I said just now a phrase something like this: 'For a crime to be successful it is usually necessary to plan every detail of it carefully beforehand.' 'Usually' is the word to which I want to draw your attention. For there *is* another type of successful crime. Have you ever said suddenly to any one, 'Throw a stone and see if you can hit that tree,' and the person obeys quickly, without thinking—and surprisingly often he *does* hit the tree? But when he comes to repeat the throw it is not so easy—for he has begun to *think*. 'So hard—no harder—a little more to the right—to the left.' The first was an almost unconscious action, the body obeying the mind as the body of an animal does. *Eh bien*, madame, there is a type of crime like that—a crime committed on the spur of the moment—an inspiration—a flash of genius—without time to pause or think. And that, madame, was the kind of crime that killed Mr. Shaitana. A sudden dire necessity, a flash of inspiration, rapid execution."

He shook his head.

"And that, madame, is not your type of crime at all. If you killed Mr. Shaitana, it should have been a premeditated crime."

"I see." Her hand waved softly to and fro, keeping the heat of the fire from her face. "And, of course, it wasn't a premeditated crime, so I couldn't have killed him—eh, M. Poirot?"

Poirot bowed.

"That is right, madame."

"And yet——" She leaned forward, her waving hand stopped. *"I did kill Shaitana, M. Poirot. . . ."*

CHAPTER 26
The Truth

There was a pause—a very long pause.

The room was growing dark. The firelight leaped and flickered.

Mrs. Lorrimer and Hercule Poirot looked not at each other, but at the fire. It was as though time was momentarily in abeyance.

Then Hercule Poirot sighed and stirred.

"So it was that—all the time. . . . *Why* did you kill him, madame?"

"I think you know why, M. Poirot."

"Because he knew something about you—something that had happened long ago?"

"Yes."

"And that something was—another death, madame?"

She bowed her head.

Poirot said gently:

"Why did you tell me? What made you send for me to-day?"

"You told me once that I should do so some day."

"Yes—that is, I hoped. . . . I knew, madame, that there was only one way of learning the truth as far as you were concerned—and that was by your own free will. If you did not choose to speak, you would not do so, and you would never give yourself away. But there was a chance—that you yourself might *wish* to speak."

Mrs. Lorrimer nodded.

"It was clever of you to foresee that—the weariness—the loneliness——"

Her voice died away.

Poirot looked at her curiously.

"So it has been like that? Yes, I can understand it might be. . . ."

"Alone—quite alone," said Mrs. Lorrimer. "No one knows what that means unless they have lived, as I have lived, with the knowledge of what one has done."

Poirot said gently:

"Is it an impertinence, madame, or may I be permitted to offer my sympathy?"

She bent her head a little.

"Thank you, M. Poirot."

There was another pause, then Poirot said, speaking in a slightly brisker tone:

"Am I to understand, madame, that you took the words Mr. Shaitana spoke at dinner as a direct menace aimed at you?"

She nodded.

"I realised at once that he was speaking so that one person should understand him. That person was myself. The reference to a woman's weapon being poison was meant for me. He *knew*. I had suspected it once before. He had brought the conversation round to a certain famous trial, and I saw his eyes watching me. There was a kind of uncanny knowledge in them. But, of course, that night I was quite sure."

"And you were sure, too, of his future intentions?"

Mrs. Lorrimer said dryly:

"It was hardly likely that the presence of Superintendent Battle and yourself was an accident. I took it that Shaitana was going to advertise his own cleverness by pointing out to you both that he had discovered something that no one else had suspected."

"How soon did you make up your mind to act, madame?"

Mrs. Lorrimer hesitated a little.

"It is difficult to remember exactly when the idea came into my mind," she said. "I had noticed the dagger before going in to dinner. When we returned to the drawing-room I picked it up and slipped it into my sleeve. No one saw me do it. I made sure of that."

"It would be dexterously done, I have no doubt, madame."

"I made up my mind then exactly what I was going to do. I had only to carry it out. It was risky, perhaps, but I considered that it was worth trying."

"That is your coolness, your successful weighing of chances, coming into play. Yes, I see that."

"We started to play bridge," continued Mrs. Lorrimer. Her voice was cool and unemotional. "At last an opportunity arose. I was dummy. I strolled across the room to the fireplace. Shaitana had dozed off to sleep. I looked over at the others. They were all intent on the game. I leant over and—and did it——"

Her voice shook just a little, but instantly it regained its cool aloofness.

"I spoke to him. It came into my head that that would make a kind of alibi for me. I made some remark about the fire, and then pretended he had answered me and went on again, saying something like: 'I agree with you. I do not like radiators, either.'"

"He did not cry out at all?"

"No. I think he made a little grunt—that was all. It might have been taken for words from a distance."

"And then?"

"And then I went back to the bridge-table. The last trick was just being played."

"And you sat down and resumed play?"

"Yes."

"With sufficient interest in the game to be able to tell me nearly all the calling and the hands two days later?"

"Yes," said Mrs. Lorrimer simply.

"*Epatant!*" said Hercule Poirot.

He leaned back in his chair. He nodded his head several times. Then, by way of a change, he shook it.

"But there is still something, madame, that I do not understand."

"Yes?"

"It seems to me that there is some factor I have missed. You are a woman who considers and weighs everything carefully. You decide that, for a certain reason, you will run an enormous risk. You do run it—successfully. And then, not two weeks later, you change your mind. Frankly, madame, that does not seem to me to ring true."

A queer little smile twisted her lips.

"You are quite right, M. Poirot, there is one factor that you do not know. Did Miss Meredith tell you where she met me the other day?"

"It was, I think she said, near Mrs. Oliver's flat."

"I believe that is so. But I meant the actual name of the street. Anne Meredith met me in Harley Street."

"Ah!" He looked at her attentively. "I begin to see."

"Yes, I thought you would. I had been to see a specialist there. He told me what I already half suspected."

Her smile widened. It was no longer twisted and bitter. It was suddenly sweet.

"I shall not play very much more bridge, M. Poirot. Oh, he didn't say so in so many words. He wrapped up the truth a little. With great care, etc., etc., I might live several years. But I shall not take any great care. I am not that kind of a woman."

"Yes, yes, I begin to understand," said Poirot.

"It made a difference, you see. A month—two months, perhaps—not more. And then, just as I left the specialist, I saw Miss Meredith. I asked her to have tea with me."

She paused, then went on:

"I am not, after all, a wholly wicked woman. All the time we were having tea I was thinking. By my action the other evening I had not only deprived the man Shaitana of life (that was done, and could not be undone), I had also, to a varying degree, affected unfavourably the lives of three other people. Because of what I had done, Dr. Roberts, Major Despard and Anne Meredith, none of whom had injured me in any way, were passing through a very grave ordeal, and might even be in danger. That, at least, I could undo. I don't know that I felt particularly moved by the plight of either Dr. Roberts or Major Despard—although both of them had presumably a much longer span of life in front of them than I had. They were men, and could, to a certain extent, look after themselves. But when I looked at Anne Meredith——"

She hesitated, then continued slowly:

"Anne Meredith was only a girl. She had the whole of her life in front of her. This miserable business might ruin that life. . . .

"I didn't like the thought of that. . . .

"And then, M. Poirot, with these ideas growing in my mind, I realised that what you had hinted had come true. I was not going to be able to keep silence. This afternoon I rang you up. . . ."

Minutes passed.

Hercule Poirot leaned forward. He stared, deliberately stared through the gathering gloom, at Mrs. Lorrimer. She returned that intent gaze quietly and without any nervousness.

He said at last:

"Mrs. Lorrimer, are you sure—are you *positive* (you will tell me the truth, will you not?)—*that the murder of Mr. Shaitana was not premeditated?* Is it not a fact that you planned the crime *beforehand*—that you went to that dinner with the murder already all mapped out in your mind?"

Mrs. Lorrimer stared at him for a moment, then she shook her head sharply.

"No," she said.

"You did not plan the murder beforehand?"

"Certainly not."

"Then—then. . . . Oh, you are lying to me—you must be lying! . . ."

Mrs. Lorrimer's voice cut into the air like ice.

"Really, M. Poirot, you forget yourself."

The little man sprang to his feet. He paced up and down the room, muttering to himself, uttering ejaculations.

Suddenly he said:

"Permit me?"

And, going to the switch, he turned on the electric lights.

He came back, sat down in his chair, placed both hands on his knees and stared straight at his hostess.

"The question is," he said, "can Hercule Poirot possibly be wrong?"

"No one can always be right," said Mrs. Lorrimer coldly.

"I am," said Poirot. "Always I am right. It is so invariable that it startles me. But now it looks, it very much looks, as though I am wrong. And that upsets me. Presumably, you know what you are saying. It is your murder! Fantastic, then, that Hercule Poirot should know better than you do how you committed it."

"Fantastic and very absurd," said Mrs. Lorrimer still more coldly.

"I am, then, mad. Decidedly I am mad. No—*sacré nom d'un petit bonhomme*—I am *not* mad! I am right. I *must* be right. I am willing to believe that you killed Mr. Shaitan—*but you cannot have killed him in the way you say you did*. No one can do a thing that is not *dans son caractère!*"

He paused. Mrs. Lorrimer drew in an angry breath and bit her lips. She was about to speak, but Poirot forestalled her.

"Either the killing of Shaitana was planned beforehand—*or you did not kill him at all!*"

"I really believe you *are* mad, M. Poirot. If I am willing to admit I committed the crime, I should not be likely to lie about the way I did it. What would be the point of such a thing?"

Poirot got up again and took one turn round the room. When he came back to his seat his manner had changed. He was gentle and kindly.

"You did not kill Shaitana," he said softly. "I see that now. I see everything. Harley Street. And little Anne Meredith standing forlorn on the pavement. I see, too, another girl—a very long time ago, a girl who has gone through life always alone—terribly alone. Yes, I see all that. But one thing I do not see—why are you so certain that Anne Meredith did it?"

"Really, M. Poirot——"

"Absolutely useless to protest—to lie further to me, madame. *I tell you, I know the truth*. I know the very emotions that swept over you that day in Harley Street. You would not have done it for Major Despard, *non plus*. You would not have done it for Dr. Roberts—oh, no! But Anne Meredith is different. You have compassion for her, *because she has done what you once did*. You do not know even—or so I imagine—what *reason* she had for the crime. But you are quite sure she did it. You were sure that first evening—the evening it happened—when Superintendent Battle invited you to give your views on the case. Yes, I know it all, you see. It is quite useless to lie further to me. You see that, do you not?"

He paused for an answer, but none came. He nodded his head in satisfaction.

"Yes, you are sensible. That is good. It is a very noble action that you perform there, madame, to take the blame on yourself and to let this child escape."

"You forget," said Mrs. Lorrimer in a dry voice, "I am not an innocent woman. Years ago, M. Poirot, I killed my husband. . . ."

There was a moment's silence.

"I see," said Poirot. "It is justice. After all, only justice. You have the logical mind. You are willing to suffer for the act you committed. Murder is murder—it does not matter who the victim is. Madame, you have courage, and you have clear-sightedness. But I ask of you once more: *How can you be so sure?* How do you *know* that it was Anne Meredith who killed Mr. Shaitana?"

A deep sigh broke from Mrs. Lorrimer. Her last resistance had gone down before Poirot's insistence. She answered his question quite simply like a child.

"Because," she said, "I saw her."

CHAPTER 27
The Eye-Witness

Suddenly Poirot laughed. He could not help it. His head went back, and his high Gallic laugh filled the room.

"Pardon, madame," he said, wiping his eyes. "I could not help it. Here we argue and we reason! We ask questions! We invoke the psychology—and all the time *there was an eye-witness of the crime*. Tell me, I pray of you."

"It was fairly late in the evening. Anne Meredith was dummy. She got up and looked over her partner's hand, and then she moved about the room. The hand wasn't very interesting—the conclusion was inevitable. I didn't need to concentrate on the cards. Just as we got to the last three tricks I looked over towards the fireplace. Anne Meredith was bent over Mr. Shaitana. As I watched, she straightened herself—her hand had been actually on his breast—a gesture which awakened my surprise. She straightened herself, and I saw her face and her quick look over towards us. Guilt and fear—that is what I saw on her face. Of course, I didn't know what had happened then. I only wondered what on earth the girl could have been doing. Later—I knew."

Poirot nodded.

"But *she* did not know that you knew. *She* did not know that you had seen her?"

"Poor child," said Mrs. Lorrimer. "Young, frightened—her way to make in the world. Do you wonder that I—well, held my tongue?"

"No, no, I do not wonder."

"Especially knowing that I—that I myself——" She finished the sentence with a shrug. "It was certainly not my place to stand accuser. It was up to the police."

"Quite so—but to-day you have gone further than that."

Mrs. Lorrimer said grimly:

"I've never been a very soft-hearted or compassionate woman, but I suppose these qualities grow upon one in one's old age. I assure you, I'm not often actuated by pity."

"It is not always a very safe guide, madame. Mademoiselle Anne is young, she is fragile, she looks timid and frightened—oh, yes, she seems a very worthy subject for compassion. But I, *I do not agree*. Shall I tell you, madame, why Miss Anne Meredith killed Mr. Shaitana? It was because he knew that she had previously killed an elderly lady to whom she was companion—because that lady had found her out in a petty theft."

Mrs. Lorrimer looked a little startled.

"Is that true, M. Poirot?"

"I have no doubt of it, whatsoever. She is so soft—so gentle—one would say. Pah! She is dangerous, madame, that little Mademoiselle Anne! Where her own safety, her own comfort, is concerned, she will strike wildly—treacherously. With Mademoiselle Anne *those two crimes will not be the end*. She will gain confidence from them. . . ."

Mrs. Lorrimer said sharply:

"What you say is horrible, M. Poirot. Horrible!"

Poirot rose.

"Madame, I will now take my leave. Reflect on what I have said."

Mrs. Lorrimer was looking a little uncertain of herself. She said with an attempt at her old manner:

"If it suits me, M. Poirot, I shall deny this whole conversation. You have no witnesses, remember. What I have just told you that I saw on that fatal evening is—well, private between ourselves."

Poirot said gravely.

"Nothing shall be done without your consent, madame. And be at peace; I have my own methods. Now that I know what I am driving at——"

He took her hand and raised it to his lips.

"Permit me to tell you, madame, that you are a most remarkable woman. All my homage and respects. Yes, indeed, a woman in a thousand. Why, you have not even done what nine hundred and ninety-nine women out of a thousand could not have resisted doing."

"What is that?"

"Told me just why you killed your husband—and how entirely justified such a proceeding really was."

Mrs. Lorrimer drew herself up.

"Really, M. Poirot," she said stiffly. "My reasons were entirely my own business."

"Magnifique!" said Poirot, and, once more raising her hand to his lips, he left the room.

It was cold outside the house, and he looked up and down for a taxi, but there was none in sight.

He began to walk in the direction of King's Road.

As he walked he was thinking hard. Occasionally he nodded his head; once he shook it.

He looked back over his shoulder. Some one was going up the steps of Mrs. Lorrimer's house. In figure it looked very like Anne Meredith. He hesitated for a minute, wondering whether to turn back or not, but in the end he went on.

On arrival at home, he found that Battle had gone without leaving any message.

He proceeded to ring the superintendent up.

"Hallo." Battle's voice can through. "Got anything?"

"Je crois bien. Mon ami, we must get after the Meredith girl—and quickly."

"I'm getting after her—but why quickly?"

"Because, my friend, she may be dangerous."

Battle was silent for a minute or two. Then he said:

"I know what you mean. But there's no one. . . . Oh, well, we mustn't take chances. As a matter of fact, I've written her. Official note, saying I'm calling to see her to-morrow. I thought it might be a good thing to get her rattled."

"It is a possibility, at least. I may accompany you?"

"Naturally. Honoured to have your company, M. Poirot."

Poirot hung up the receiver with a thoughtful face.

His mind was not quite at rest. He sat for a long time in front of his fire, frowning to himself. At last, putting his fears and doubts aside, he went to bed.

"We will see in the morning," he murmured.

But of what the morning would bring he had no idea.

CHAPTER 28
Suicide

The summons came by telephone at the moment when Poirot was sitting down to his morning coffee and rolls.

He lifted the telephone receiver, and Battle's voice spoke:

"That M. Poirot?"

"Yes, it is I. *Qu'est ce qu'il y a?"*

The mere inflection of the superintendent's voice had told him that something had happened. His own vague misgivings came back to him.

"But quickly, my friend, tell me."

"It's Mrs. Lorrimer."

"Lorrimer—yes?"

"What the devil did you say to her—or did she say to you—yesterday? You never told me anything; in fact, you let me think that the Meredith girl was the one we were after."

Poirot said quietly:

"What has happened?"

"Suicide."

"Mrs. Lorrimer has committed suicide?"

"That's right. It seems she has been very depressed and unlike herself lately. Her doctor had ordered her some sleeping stuff. Last night she took an overdose."

Poirot drew a deep breath.

"There is no question of—accident?"

"Not the least. It's all cut and dried. She wrote to the three of them."

"Which three?"

"The other three. Roberts, Despard and Miss Meredith. All fair and square—no beating about the bush. Just wrote that she would like them to know that she was taking a short-cut out of all the mess—that it was she who had killed Shaitana—and that she apologised—apologised!—to all three of them for the inconvenience and annoyance they had suffered. Perfectly calm, business-like letter. Absolutely typical of the woman. She was a cool customer all right."

For a minute or two Poirot did not answer.

So this was Mrs. Lorrimer's final word. She had determined, after all, to shield Anne Meredith. A quick painless death instead of a protracted painful one, and her last action an altruistic one—the saving of the girl with whom she felt a secret bond of sympathy. The whole thing planned and carried out with quite ruthless efficiency—a suicide carefully announced to the three interested parties. What a woman! His admiration quickened. It was like her—like her clear-cut determination, her insistence on what she had decided being carried out.

He had thought to have convinced her—but evidently she had preferred her own judgment. A woman of very strong will.

Battle's voice cut into his meditations.

"What the devil did you say to her yesterday? You must have put the wind up her, and this is the result. But you implied that the result of your interview was definite suspicion of the Meredith girl."

Poirot was silent a minute or two. He felt that, dead, Mrs. Lorrimer constrained him to her will, as she could not have done if she were living.

He said at last slowly:

"I was in error. . . ."

There were unaccustomed words on his tongue, and he did not like them.

"You made a mistake, eh?" said Battle. "All the same, she must have thought you were on to her. It's a bad business—letting her slip through our fingers like this."

"You could not have proved anything against her," said Poirot.

"No—I suppose that's true. . . . Perhaps it's all for the best. You—er—didn't mean this to happen, M. Poirot?"

Poirot's disclaimer was indignant. Then he said:

"Tell me exactly what has occurred."

"Roberts opened his letters just before eight o'clock. He lost no time, dashed off at once in his car, leaving his parlourmaid to communicate with us, which she did. He got to the house to find that Mrs. Lorrimer hadn't been called yet, rushed up to her bedroom—but it was too late. He tried artificial respiration, but there was nothing doing. Our divisional surgeon arrived soon after and confirmed his treatment."

"What was the sleeping stuff?"

"Veronal, I think. One of the Barbituric group, at any rate. There was a bottle of tablets by her bed."

"What about the other two? Did they not try to communicate with you?"

"Despard is out of town. He hasn't had this morning's post."

"And—Miss Meredith?"

"I've just rung her up."

"*Eh bien?*"

"She had just opened the letter a few moments before my call came through. Post is later there."

"What was her reaction?"

"A perfectly proper attitude. Intense relief decently veiled. Shocked and grieved—that sort of thing."

Poirot paused a moment, then he said:

"Where are you now, my friend?"

"At Cheyne Lane."

"*Bien*. I will come round immediately."

In the hall at Cheyne Lane he found Dr. Roberts on the point of departure. The doctor's usual florid manner was rather in abeyance this morning. He looked pale and shaken.

"Nasty business this, M. Poirot. I can't say I'm not relieved—from my own point of view—but, to tell you the truth, it's a bit of a shock. I never really thought for a minute that it was Mrs. Lorrimer who stabbed Shaitana. It's been the greatest surprise to me."

"I, too, am surprised."

"Quiet, well-bred, self-contained woman. Can't imagine her doing a violent thing like that. What was the motive, I wonder? Oh, well, we shall never know now. I confess I'm curious, though."

"It must take a load off your mind—this occurrence."

"Oh, it does, undoubtedly. It would be hypocrisy not to admit it. It's not very pleasant to have a suspicion of murder hanging over you. As for the poor woman herself—well, it was undoubtedly the best way out."

"So she thought herself."

Roberts nodded.

"Conscience, I suppose," he said as he let himself out of the house.

Poirot shook his head thoughtfully. The doctor had misread the situation. It was not remorse that had made Mrs. Lorrimer take her life.

On his way upstairs he paused to say a few words of comfort to the elderly parlourmaid, who was weeping quietly.

"It's so dreadful, sir. So very dreadful. We were all so fond of her. And you having tea with her yesterday so nice and quiet. And now to-day she's gone. I shall never forget this morning—never as long as I live. The gentleman pealing at the bell. Rang three times, he did, before I could get to it. And, 'Where's your mistress?' he shot out at me. I was so flustered, I couldn't hardly answer. You see, we never went in to the mistress till she rang—that was her orders. And I just couldn't get out anything. And the doctor, he says, 'Where's her room?' and ran up the stairs, and me behind him, and I showed him the door, and he rushes in, not so much as knocking, and takes one look at her lying there, and, 'Too late,' he says. She was dead, sir. But he sent me for brandy and hot water, and he tried desperate to bring her back, but it couldn't be done. And then the police coming and all—it isn't—it isn't—decent, sir. Mrs. Lorrimer wouldn't have liked it. And why the police? It's none of their business, surely, even if an accident has occurred and the poor mistress did take an overdose by mistake."

Poirot did not reply to her question.

He said:

"Last night, was your mistress quite as usual? Did she seem upset or worried at all?"

"No, I don't think so, sir. She was tired—and I think she was in pain. She hasn't been well lately, sir."

"No, I know."

The sympathy in his tone made the woman go on.

"She was never one for complaining, sir, but both cook and I had been worried about her for some time. She couldn't do as much as she used to do, and things tired her. I think, perhaps, the young lady coming after you left was a bit too much for her."

With his foot on the stairs, Poirot turned back.

"The young lady? Did a young lady come here yesterday evening?"

"Yes, sir. Just after you left, it was. Miss Meredith, her name was."

"Did she stay long?"

"About an hour, sir."

Poirot was silent for a minute or two, then he said:

"And afterwards?"

"The mistress went to bed. She had dinner in bed. She said she was tired."

Again Poirot was silent; then he said:

"Do you know if your mistress wrote any letters yesterday evening?"

"Do you mean after she went to bed? I don't think so, sir."

"But you are not sure?"

"There were some letters on the hall table ready to be posted, sir. We always took them last thing before shutting up. But I think they had been lying there since earlier in the day."

"How many were there?"

"Two or three—I'm not quite sure, sir. Three, I think."

"You—or cook—whoever posted them—did not happen to notice to whom they were addressed? Do not be offended at my question. It is of the utmost importance."

"I went to the post myself with them, sir. I noticed the top one—it was to Fortnum and Mason's. I couldn't say as to the others."

The woman's tone was earnest and sincere.

"Are you sure there were not more than three letters?"

"Yes, sir, I'm quite certain of that."

Poirot nodded his head gravely. Once more he started up the staircase. Then he said:

"You knew, I take it, that your mistress took medicine to make her sleep?"

"Oh, yes, sir, it was the doctor's orders. Dr. Lang."

"Where was this sleeping medicine kept?"

"In the little cupboard in the mistress's room."

Poirot did not ask any further questions. He went upstairs. His face was very grave.

On the upper landing Battle greeted him. The superintendent looked worried and harassed.

"I'm glad you've come, M. Poirot. Let me introduce you to Dr. Davidson."

The divisional surgeon shook hands. He was a tall, melancholy man.

"The luck was against us," he said. "An hour or two earlier, and we might have saved her."

"H'm," said Battle. "I mustn't say so officially, but I'm not sorry. She was a—well, she was a lady. I don't know what her reasons were for killing Shaitana, but she may just conceivably have been justified."

"In any case," said Poirot, "it is doubtful if she would have lived to stand her trial. She was a very ill woman."

The surgeon nodded in agreement.

"I should say you were quite right. Well, perhaps it is all for the best."

He started down the stairs.

Battle moved after him.

"One minute, doctor."

Poirot, his hand on the bedroom door, murmured, "I may enter—yes?"

Battle nodded over his shoulder. "Quite all right. We're through." Poirot passed into the room, closing the door behind him. . . .

He went over to the bed and stood looking down at the quiet, dead face.

He was very disturbed.

Had the dead woman gone to the grave in a last determined effort to save a young girl from death and disgrace—or was there a different, a more sinister explanation?

There were certain facts. . . .

Suddenly he bent down, examining a dark, discoloured bruise on the dead woman's arm.

He straightened himself up again. There was a strange, cat-like gleam in his eyes that certain close associates of his would have recognised.

He left the room quickly and went downstairs. Battle and a subordinate were at the telephone. The latter laid down the receiver and said:

"He hasn't come back, sir."

Battle said:

"Despard. I've been trying to get him. There's a letter for him with the Chelsea postmark all right."

Poirot asked an irrelevant question.

"Had Dr. Roberts had his breakfast when he came here?"

Battle stared.

"No," he said, "I remember he mentioned that he'd come out without it."

"Then he will be at his house now. We can get him."

"But why——?"

But Poirot was already busy at the dial. Then he spoke:

"Dr. Roberts? It is Dr. Roberts speaking? *Mais oui,* it is Poirot here. Just one question. Are you well acquainted with the handwriting of Mrs. Lorrimer?"

"Mrs. Lorrimer's handwriting? I—no, I don't know that I'd ever seen it before."

"Je vous remercie."

Poirot laid down the receiver quickly.

Battle was staring at him.

"What's the big idea, M. Poirot?" he asked quietly.

Poirot took him by the arm.

"Listen, my friend. A few minutes after I left this house yesterday Anne Meredith arrived. I actually saw her going up the steps, though I was not quite sure of her identity at the time. Immediately after Anne Meredith left Mrs. Lorrimer went to bed. As far as the maid knows, *she did not write any letters then*. And, for reasons which you will understand when I recount to you our interview, *I do not believe that she wrote those three letters before my visit*. When did she write them, then?"

"After the servants had gone to bed?" suggested Battle. "She got up and posted them herself."

"That is possible, yes, but there is another possibility—*that she did not write them at all*."

Battle whistled.

"My God, you mean——"

The telephone trilled. The sergeant picked up the receiver. He listened a minute, then turned to Battle.

"Sergeant O'Connor speaking from Despard's flat, sir. There's reason to believe that Despard's down at Wallingford-on-Thames."

Poirot caught Battle by the arm.

"Quickly, my friend. We, too, must go to Wallingford. I tell you, I am not easy in my mind. This may not be the end. I tell you again, my friend, this young lady, she is dangerous."

CHAPTER 29
Accident

"Anne," said Rhoda.

"Mmm?"

"No, really, Anne, don't answer with half your mind on a crossword puzzle. I want you to attend to me."

"I am attending."

Anne sat bolt upright and put down the paper.

"That's better. Look here, Anne." Rhoda hesitated. "About this man coming."

"Superintendent Battle?"

"Yes. Anne, I wish you'd tell him—about being at the Bensons'."

Anne's voice grew rather cold.

"Nonsense. Why should I?"

"Because—well, it might look—as though you'd been keeping something back. I'm sure it would be better to mention it."

"I can't very well now," said Anne coldly.

"I wish you had in the first place."

"Well, it's too late to bother about that now."

"Yes." Rhoda did not sound convinced.

Anne said rather irritably:

"In any case, I can't see *why*. It's got nothing to do with all this."

"No, of course not."

"I was only there about two months. He only wants these things as—well—references. Two months doesn't count."

"No, I know. I expect I'm being foolish, but it does worry me rather. I feel you ought to mention it. You see, if it came out some other way, it might look rather bad—your keeping dark about it, I mean."

"I don't see how it can come out. Nobody knows but you."

"N-no?"

Anne pounced on the slight hesitation in Rhoda's voice.

"Why, who does know?"

"Well, every one at Combeacre," said Rhoda after a moment's pause.

"Oh, that!" Anne dismissed it with a shrug. "The superintendent isn't likely to come up against any one from there. It would be an extraordinary coincidence if he did."

"Coincidences happen."

"Rhoda, you're being extraordinary about this. Fuss, fuss, fuss."

"I'm terribly sorry, darling. Only you know what the police might be like if they thought you were—well—hiding things."

"They won't know. Who's to tell them? Nobody knows but you."

It was the second time she had said those words. At this second repetition her voice changed a little—something queer and speculative came into it.

"Oh, dear, I wish you would," sighed Rhoda unhappily.

She looked guiltily at Anne, but Anne was not looking at her. She was sitting with a frown on her face, as though working out some calculation.

"Rather fun, Major Despard turning up," said Rhoda.

"What? Oh, yes."

"Anne, he *is* attractive. If you don't want him, *do, do, do* hand him over to me!"

"Don't be absurd, Rhoda. He doesn't care tuppence for me."

"Then why does he keep on turning up? Of course he's keen on you. You're just the sort of distressed damsel that he'd enjoy rescuing. You look so beautifully helpless, Anne."

"He's equally pleasant to both of us."

"That's only his niceness. But if you don't want him, I could do the sympathetic friend act—console his broken heart, etc., etc., and in the end I might get him. Who knows?" Rhoda concluded inelegantly.

"I'm sure you're quite welcome to him, my dear," said Anne, laughing.

"He's got such a lovely back to his neck," sighed Rhoda. "Very brick red and muscular."

"Darling, must you be so mawkish?"

"Do you like him, Anne?"

"Yes, very much."

"Aren't we prim and sedate? I think he likes me a little—not as much as you, but a little."

"Oh, but he does like you," said Anne.

Again there was an unusual note in her voice, but Rhoda did not hear it.

"What time is our sleuth coming?" she asked.

"Twelve," said Anne. She was silent for a minute or two, then she said, "It's only half-past ten now. Let's go out on the river."

"But isn't—didn't Despard say he'd come round about eleven?"

"Why should we wait in for him? We can leave a message with Mrs. Astwell which way we've gone, and he can follow us along the towpath."

"In fact, don't make yourself cheap, dear, as mother always said!" laughed Rhoda. "Come on, then."

She went out of the room and through the garden door. Anne followed her.

* * *

Major Despard called at Wendon Cottage about ten minutes later. He was before his time, he knew, so he was a little surprised to find both girls had already gone out.

He went through the garden and across the fields and turned to the right along the towpath.

Mrs. Astwell remained a minute or two looking after him, instead of getting on with her morning chores.

"Sweet on one or other of 'em, he is," she observed to herself. "I think it's Miss Anne, but I'm not certain. He don't give away much by his face. Treats 'em both alike. I'm not sure they ain't both sweet on him, too. If so, they won't be such dear friends so much longer. Nothing like a gentleman for coming between two young ladies."

Pleasurably excited by the prospect of assisting at a budding romance, Mrs. Astwell turned indoors to her task of washing up the breakfast things, when once again the door-bell rang.

"Drat that door," said Mrs. Astwell. "Do it on purpose, they do. Parcel, I suppose. Or might be a telegram."

She moved slowly to the front door.

Two gentlemen stood there, a small foreign gentleman and an exceedingly English, big, burly gentleman. The latter she had seen before, she remembered.

"Miss Meredith at home?" asked the big man.

Mrs. Astwell shook her head.

"Just gone out."

"Really? Which way? We didn't meet her."

Mrs. Astwell, secretly studying the amazing moustache of the other gentleman and deciding that they looked an unlikely pair to be friends, volunteered further information.

"Gone out on the river," she explained.

The other gentleman broke in:

"And the other lady? Miss Dawes?"

"They've both gone."

"Ah, thank you," said Battle. "Let me see, which way does one get to the river?"

"First turning to the left, down the lane," Mrs. Astwell replied promptly. "When you get to the towpath, go right. I heard them say that's the way they were going," she added helpfully. "Not above a quarter of an hour ago. You'll soon catch 'em up."

"And I wonder," she added to herself as she unwillingly closed the front door, having stared inquisitively at their retreating backs, "who you two may be. Can't place you, somehow."

Mrs. Astwell returned to the kitchen sink, and Battle and Poirot duly took the first turning to the left—a straggling lane which soon ended abruptly at the towpath.

Poirot was hurrying along, and Battle eyed him curiously.

"Anything the matter, M. Poirot? You seem in a mighty hurry."

"It is true. I am uneasy, my friend."

"Anything particular?"

Poirot shook his head.

"No. But there are possibilities. You never know. . . ."

"You've something in your head," said Battle. "You were urgent that we should come down here this morning without losing a moment—and, my word, you made Constable Turner step on the gas! What are you afraid of? The girl's shot her bolt."

Poirot was silent.

"What are you afraid of?" Battle repeated.

"What is one always afraid of in these cases?"

Battle nodded.

"You're quite right. I wonder——"

"You wonder what, my friend?"

Battle said slowly:

"I'm wondering if Miss Meredith knows that her friend told Mrs. Oliver a certain fact."

Poirot nodded his head in vigorous appreciation.

"Hurry, my friend," he said.

They hastened along the river bank. There was no craft visible on the water's surface, but presently they rounded a bend, and Poirot suddenly stopped dead. Battle's quick eyes saw also.

"Major Despard," he said.

Despard was about two hundred yards ahead of them, striding along the river bank.

A little farther on the two girls were in view in a punt on the water, Rhoda punting—Anne lying and laughing up at her. Neither of them were looking towards the bank.

And then—*it happened*. Anne's hand outstretched, Rhoda's stagger, her plunge overboard—her desperate grasp at Anne's sleeve—the rocking boat—then an overturned punt and two girls struggling in the water.

"See it?" cried Battle as he started to run. "Little Meredith caught her round the ankle and tipped her in. My God, that's her fourth murder!"

They were both running hard. But some one was ahead of them. It was clear that neither girl could swim, but Despard had run quickly along the path to the nearest point, and now he plunged in and swam towards them.

"*Mon Dieu*, this is interesting," cried Poirot. He caught at Battle's arm. "Which of them will he go for first?"

The two girls were not together. About twelve yards separated them.

Despard swam powerfully towards them—there was no check in his stroke. He was making straight for Rhoda.

Battle, in his turn, reached the nearest bank and went in. Despard had just brought Rhoda successfully to shore. He hauled her up, flung her down and plunged in again, swimming towards the spot where Anne had just gone under.

"Be careful," called Battle. "Weeds."

He and Battle got to the spot at the same time, but Anne had gone under before they reached her.

They got her at last and between them towed her to the shore.

Rhoda was being ministered to by Poirot. She was sitting up now, her breath coming unevenly.

Despard and Battle laid Anne Meredith down.

"Artificial respiration," said Battle. "Only thing to do. But I'm afraid she's gone."

He set to work methodically. Poirot stood by, ready to relieve him.

Despard dropped down by Rhoda.

"Are you all right?" he asked hoarsely.

She said slowly:

"You saved me. You saved *me*. . . ." She held out her hands to him, and as he took them she burst suddenly into tears.

He said, "Rhoda. . . ."

Their hands clung together. . . .

He had a sudden vision—of African scrub, and Rhoda, laughing and adventurous, by his side. . . .

CHAPTER 30
Murder

"Do you mean to say," said Rhoda incredulously, "that Anne *meant* to push me in? I know it *felt* like it. And she knew I can't swim. But—but was it *deliberate?*"

"It was quite deliberate," said Poirot.

They were driving through the outskirts of London.

"But—but—why?"

Poirot did not reply for a minute or two. He thought he knew one of the motives that had led Anne to act as she had done, and that motive was sitting next to Rhoda at the minute.

Superintendent Battle coughed.

"You'll have to prepare yourself, Miss Dawes, for a bit of a shock. This Mrs. Benson, your friend lived with, her death wasn't quite the accident that it appeared—at least, so we've reason to suppose."

"What *do* you mean?"

"We believe," said Poirot, "that Anne Meredith changed two bottles."

"Oh, no—no, how horrible! It's *impossible*. Anne? Why should she?"

"She had her reasons," said Superintendent Battle. "But the point is, Miss Dawes, that, as far as Miss Meredith knew, *you were the only person who could give us a clue to that incident*. You didn't tell her, I suppose, that you'd mentioned it to Mrs. Oliver?"

Rhoda said slowly:

"No. I thought she'd be annoyed with me."

"She would. Very annoyed," said Battle grimly. "But she thought that the only danger could come from *you*, and that's why she decided to—er—eliminate you."

"Eliminate? *Me?* Oh, how beastly! It *can't* be all true."

"Well, she's dead now," said Superintendent Battle, "so we might as well leave it at that; but she wasn't a nice friend for you to have, Miss Dawes—and that's a fact."

The car drew up in front of a door.

"We'll go in to M. Poirot's," said Superintendent Battle, "and have a bit of a talk about it all."

In Poirot's sitting-room they were welcomed by Mrs. Oliver, who was entertaining Dr. Roberts. They were drinking sherry. Mrs. Oliver was wearing one of the new horsy hats and a velvet dress with a bow on the chest on which reposed a large piece of apple core.

"Come in. Come in," said Mrs. Oliver hospitably and quite as though it were her house and not Poirot's. "As soon as I got your telephone call I rang up Dr. Roberts, and we came round here. And all his patients are dying, but he doesn't care. They're probably getting better, really. We want to hear all about everything."

"Yes, indeed, I'm thoroughly fogged," said Roberts.

"Eh bien," said Poirot. "The case is ended. The murderer of Mr. Shaitana is found at last."

"So Mrs. Oliver told me. That pretty little thing, Anne Meredith. I can hardly believe it. A most unbelievable murderess."

"She was a murderess all right," said Battle. "Three murders to her credit—and not her fault that she didn't get away with a fourth one."

"Incredible!" murmured Roberts.

"Not at all," said Mrs. Oliver. "Least likely person. It seems to work out in real life just the same as in books."

"It's been an amazing day," said Roberts. "First Mrs. Lorrimer's letter. I suppose that was a forgery, eh?"

"Precisely. A forgery written in triplicate."

"She wrote one to herself, too?"

"Naturally. The forgery was quite skilful—it would not deceive an expert, of course—but, then, it was highly unlikely that an expert would have been called in. All the evidence pointed to Mrs. Lorrimer's having committed suicide."

"You will excuse my curiosity, M. Poirot, but what made you suspect that she had not committed suicide?"

"A little conversation that I had with a maidservant at Cheyne Lane."

"She told you of Anne Meredith's visit the former evening?"

"That among other things. And then, you see, I had already come to a conclusion in my own mind as to the identity of the guilty person—that is, the person who killed Mr. Shaitana. That person was not Mrs. Lorrimer."

"What made you suspect Miss Meredith?"

Poirot raised his hand.

"A little minute. Let me approach this matter in my own way. Let me, that is to say, eliminate. The murderer of Mr. Shaitana was not Mrs. Lorrimer, nor was it Major Despard, and, curiously enough, it was not Anne Meredith. . . ."

He leaned forward. His voice purred, soft and cat-like.

"You see, Dr. Roberts, *you were the person who killed Mr. Shaitana;* and you also killed Mrs. Lorrimer. . . ."

There was at least three minutes' silence. Then Roberts laughed a rather menacing laugh.

"Are you quite mad, M. Poirot? I certainly did not murder Mr. Shaitana, and I could not possibly have murdered Mrs. Lorrimer. My dear Battle"—he turned to the Scotland Yard man—"are *you* standing for this?"

"I think you'd better listen to what M. Poirot has to say," said Battle quietly.

Poirot said:

"It is true that though I have known for some time that you—and only you—could have killed Shaitana, it would not be an easy matter to prove it. But Mrs. Lorrimer's case is quite different." He leaned forward. "It is not a case of my knowing. It is much simpler than that—for we have *an eye-witness who saw you do it.*"

Roberts grew very quiet. His eyes glittered. He said sharply:

"You are talking rubbish!"

"Oh, no, I am not. It was early in the morning. You bluffed your way into Mrs. Lorrimer's room, where she was still heavily asleep under the influence of the drug she had taken the night before. You bluff again—pretend to see at a glance that she is dead! You pack the parlourmaid off for brandy—hot water—all the rest of it. You are left alone in the room. The maid has only had the barest peep. And then what happens?

"You may not be aware of the fact, Dr. Roberts, *but certain firms of window cleaners specialise in early morning work*. A window cleaner with his ladder arrived at the same time as you did. He placed his ladder against the side of the house and began his work. The first window he tackled was that of Mrs. Lorrimer's room. When, however, he saw what was going on, he quickly retired to another window, *but he had seen something first*. He shall tell us his own story."

Poirot stepped lightly across the floor, turned a door handle, called:

"Come in, Stephens," and returned.

A big awkward-looking man with red hair entered. In his hand he held a uniformed hat bearing the legend "Chelsea Window Cleaners' Association" which he twirled awkwardly.

Poirot said:

"Is there anybody you recognise in this room?"

The man looked round, then gave a bashful nod of the head towards Dr. Roberts.

"Him," he said.

"Tell us when you saw him last and what he was doing."

"This morning it was. Eight o'clock job at a lady's house in Cheyne Lane. I started on the windows there. Lady was in bed. Looked ill she did. She was just turning her head round on the pillow. This gent I took to be a doctor. He shoved her sleeve up and jabbed something into her arm just about here——" he gestured. "She just dropped back on the pillow again. I thought I'd better hop it to another window, so I did. Hope I didn't do wrong in any way?"

"You did admirably, my friend," said Poirot.

He said quietly:

"*Eh bien,* Dr. Roberts?"

"A—a simple restorative—" stammered Roberts. "A last hope of bringing her round. It's monstrous——"

Poirot interrupted him.

"A simple restorative?—N-methyl-cyclo-hexenyl-methyl-malonyl urea," said Poirot. He rolled out the syllables unctuously. "Known more simply as Evipan. Used an as anaesthetic for short operations. Injected intravenously in large doses it produces instant unconsciousness. It is dangerous to use it after veronal or any barbiturates have been given. I noticed the bruised place on her arm where something had obviously been injected into a vein. A hint to the police surgeon and the drug was easily discovered by no less a person than Sir Charles Imphrey, the Home Office Analyst."

"That about cooks your goose, I think," said Superintendent Battle. "No need to prove the Shaitana business, though, of course, if necessary we can bring a further charge as to the murder of Mr. Charles Craddock—and possibly his wife also."

The mention of those two names finished Roberts. He leaned back in his chair.

"I throw in my hand," he said. "You've got me! I suppose that sly devil Shaitana put you wise before you came that evening. And I thought I'd settled his hash so nicely."

"It isn't Shaitana you've got to thank," said Battle. "The honours lie with M. Poirot here."

He went to the door and two men entered.

Superintendent Battle's voice became official as he made the formal arrest.

As the door closed behind the accused man Mrs. Oliver said happily, if not quite truthfully:

"I always *said* he did it!"

CHAPTER 31
Cards on the Table

It was Poirot's moment, every face was turned to his in eager anticipation.

"You are very kind," he said, smiling. "You know, I think, that I enjoy my little lecture. I am a prosy old fellow.

"This case, to my mind, has been one of the most interesting cases I have ever come across. There was *nothing*, you see, to go upon. There were four people, one of whom *must* have committed the crime but which of the four? Was there anything to tell one? In the material sense—no. There were no tangible clues—no fingerprints—no incriminating papers or documents. There were only—the people themselves.

"And one tangible clue—the bridge scores.

"You may remember that from the beginning I showed a particular interest in those scores. They told me something about the various people who had kept them and they did more. They gave me one valuable hint. I noticed at once, in the third rubber, the figure of 1500 above the line. That figure could only represent one thing—a call of grand slam. Now if a person were to make up their minds to commit a crime under these somewhat unusual circumstances (that is, during a rubber game of bridge) that person was clearly running two serious risks. The first was that the victim might cry out and the second was that even if the victim did not cry out some one of the other three might chance to look up at the psychological moment and *actually witness the deed*.

"Now as to the first risk, nothing could be done about it. It was a matter of a gambler's luck. But something could be done about the second. It stands to reason that during an interesting or an exciting hand the attention of the three players would be wholly on the game, whereas during a dull hand they were more likely to be looking about them. Now a bid of grand slam is always exciting. It is very often (as in this case it was) doubled. Every one of the three players is playing with close attention—the declarer to get his contract, the adversaries to discard correctly and to get him down. It was, then, a distinct possibility that the murder was committed during this particular hand and I determined to find out, if I could, exactly how the bidding had gone. I soon discovered that dummy during this particular hand had been Dr. Roberts. I bore that in mind and approached the matter from my second angle—psychological probability. Of the four suspects Mrs.

Lorrimer struck me as by far the most likely to plan and carry out a successful murder—but I could not see her as committing any crime that had to be improvised on the spur of the moment. On the other hand her manner that first evening puzzled me. It suggested either that she had committed the murder herself or that she knew who had committed it. Miss Meredith, Major Despard and Dr. Roberts were all psychological possibilities, though, as I have already mentioned, each of them would have committed the crime from an entirely different *angle*.

"I next made a second test. I got every one in turn to tell me just what they remembered of the room. From that I got some very valuable information. First of all, by far the most likely person to have noticed the dagger was Dr. Roberts. He was a natural observer of trifles of all kinds—what is called an observant man. Of the bridge hands, however, he remembered practically nothing at all. I did not expect him to remember much, but his complete forgetfulness looked as though he had had something else on his mind all the evening. Again, you see, Dr. Roberts was indicated.

"Mrs. Lorrimer I found to have a marvellous card memory, and I could well imagine that with any one of her powers of concentration a murder could easily be committed close at hand and she would never notice anything. She gave me a valuable piece of information. The grand slam was bid by Dr. Roberts (quite unjustifiably)—and he bid it in her suit, not his own, so that she necessarily played the hand.

"The third test, the test on which Superintendent Battle and I built a good deal, was the discovery of the earlier murders so as to establish a similarity of method. Well, the credit for those discoveries belongs to Superintendent Battle, to Mrs. Oliver and to Colonel Race. Discussing the matter with my friend Battle, he confessed himself disappointed because there were no points of similarity between any of the three earlier crimes and that of the murder of Mr. Shaitana. But actually that was not true. The two murders attributed to Dr. Roberts, when examined closely, *and from the psychological points of view and not the material one,* proved to be *almost exactly the same*. They, too, had been what I might describe as *public* murders. A shaving brush boldly infected in the victim's own dressing-room while the doctor officially washes his hands after a visit. The murder of Mrs. Craddock under cover of a typhoid inoculation. Again done quite openly—in the sight of the world, as you might say. And the reaction of the man is the same. Pushed into a corner, he seizes a chance and acts at once—sheer bold audacious bluff—exactly like his play at bridge. As at bridge, so in the murder of Shaitana, he took a long chance and played his cards well. The blow was perfectly struck and at exactly the right moment.

"Now just at the moment that I had decided quite definitely that Roberts was the man, Mrs. Lorrimer asked me to come and see her—and quite convincingly accused herself of the crime! I nearly believed her! For a minute or two I *did* believe her—and then my little grey cells reasserted their mastery. It could not be—so it was not!

"But what she told me was more difficult still.

"She assured me that she had actually *seen* Anne Meredith commit the crime.

"It was not till the following morning—when I stood by a dead woman's bed—that I saw how I could still be right and Mrs. Lorrimer still have spoken the truth.

"Anne Meredith went over to the fireplace—*and saw that Mr. Shaitana was dead!* She stopped over him—perhaps stretched out her hand to the gleaming head of the jewelled pin.

"Her lips part to call out, but she does not call out. She remembers Shaitana's talk at dinner. Perhaps he has left some record. She, Anne Meredith, has a motive for desiring his death. Every one will say that she has killed him. She dare not call out. Trembling with fear and apprehension she goes back to her seat.

"So Mrs. Lorrimer is right, since she, as she thought, saw the crime committed—but I am right too, for actually she did not see it.

"If Roberts had held his hand at this point, I doubt if we could have ever brought his crimes home to him. We *might* have done so—by a mixture of bluff and various ingenious devices. I would at any rate have *tried*.

"But he lost his nerve and once again overbid his hand. And this time the cards lay wrong for him and he came down heavily.

"No doubt he was uneasy. He knew that Battle was nosing about. He foresaw the present situation going on indefinitely, the police still searching—and perhaps, by some miracle—coming on traces of his former crimes. He hit upon the brilliant idea of making Mrs. Lorrimer the scapegoat for the party. His practised eye guessed, no doubt, that she was ill and that her life could not be very much prolonged. How natural in those circumstances for her to choose a quick way out, and before taking it, confess to the crime! So he manages to get a sample of her handwriting—forges three identical letters and arrives at the house hot-foot in the morning with his story of the letter he has just received. His parlourmaid quite correctly is instructed to ring up the police. All he needs is a start. And he gets it. By the time the police surgeon arrives it is all over. Dr. Roberts is ready with his story of artificial respiration that has failed. It is all perfectly plausible—perfectly straightforward.

"In all this he has no idea of throwing suspicion on Anne Meredith. He does not even know of her visit the night before. It is suicide and security only that he is aiming at.

"It is in fact an awkward moment for him when I ask if he is acquainted with Mrs. Lorrimer's handwriting. If the forgery has been detected he must save himself by saying that he has never seen her handwriting. His mind works quickly, but not quickly enough.

"From Wallingford I telephone to Mrs. Oliver. She plays her part by lulling his suspicions and bringing him here. And then when he is congratulating himself that all is well, though not exactly in the way he has planned, the blow falls. Hercule Poirot springs! And so—the gambler will gather in no more tricks. He has thrown his cards upon the table. *C'est fini*."

There was silence. Rhoda broke it with a sigh.

"What amazing luck that window-cleaner happened to be there," she said.

"Luck? Luck? That was not luck, mademoiselle. That was the grey cells of Hercule Poirot. And that reminds me——"

He went to the door.

"Come in—come in, my dear fellow. You acted your part *à merveille*."

He returned accompanied by the window cleaner, who now held his red hair in his hand and who looked somehow a very different person.

"My friend Mr. Gerald Hemmingway, a very promising young actor."

"Then there was no window-cleaner?" cried Rhoda. "Nobody saw him?"

"I saw," said Poirot. "With the eyes of the mind one can see more than with the eyes of the body. One leans back and closes the eyes——"

Despard said cheerfully:

"Let's stab him, Rhoda, and see if his ghost can come back and find out who did it."

DEATH ON THE NILE

To Sybil Burnett
who also loves wandering about the world

PART ONE

CHAPTER 1

Linnet Ridgeway!

"That's *Her!*" said Mr. Burnaby, the landlord of the Three Crowns.

He nudged his companion.

The two men stared with round bucolic eyes and slightly open mouths.

A big scarlet Rolls-Royce had just stopped in front of the local post office.

A girl jumped out, a girl without a hat and wearing a frock that looked (but only *looked*) simple. A girl with golden hair and straight autocratic features—a girl with a lovely shape—a girl such as was seldom seen in Malton-under-Wode.

With a quick imperative step she passed into the post office.

"That's her!" said Mr. Burnaby again. And he went on in a low awed voice. "Millions she's got. . . . Going to spend thousands on the place. Swimming pools there's going to be, and Italian gardens and a ballroom and a half of the house pulled down and rebuilt . . ."

"She'll bring money into the town," said his friend.

He was a lean seedy-looking man. His tone was envious and grudging.

Mr. Burnaby agreed.

"Yes, it's a great thing for Malton-under-Wode. A great thing it is."

Mr. Burnaby was complacent about it.

"Wake us all up proper," he added.

"Bit of a difference from Sir George," said the other.

"Ah, it was the 'orses did for him," said Mr. Burnaby indulgently. "Never 'ad no luck."

"What did he get for the place?"

"A cool sixty thousand, so I've heard."

The lean man whistled.

Mr. Burnaby went on triumphantly:

"And they say she'll have spent another sixty thousand before she's finished!"

"Wicked!" said the lean man. "Where'd she *get* all that money from?"

"America, so I've heard. Her mother was the only daughter of one of those millionaire blokes. Quite like the pictures, isn't it?"

The girl came out of the post office and climbed into the car.

As she drove off the lean man followed her with his eyes.

He muttered:

"It seems all wrong to me—her looking like that. Money *and* looks—it's too much! If a girl's as rich as that she's no right to be a good-looker as well. And she *is* a good-looker . . . Got everything that girl has. Doesn't seem fair . . ."

ii

Extract from the social column of the *Daily Blague*.

"Among those supping at Chez Ma Tante I noticed beautiful Linnet Ridgeway. She was with the Hon. Joanna Southwood, Lord Windlesham and Mr. Toby Bryce. Miss Ridgeway, as everyone knows, is the daughter of Melhuish Ridgeway who married Anna Hartz. She inherits from her grandfather, Leopold Hartz, an immense fortune. The lovely Linnet is the sensation of the moment, and it is rumoured that an engagement may be announced shortly. Certainly Lord Windlesham seemed very épris!"

iii

The Hon. Joanna Southwood said:

"Darling, I think it's going to be all perfectly *marvellous!*"

She was sitting in Linnet Ridgeway's bedroom at Wode Hall.

From the window the eye passed over the gardens to open country with blue shadows of woodlands.

"It's rather perfect, isn't it?" said Linnet.

She leaned her arms on the window-sill. Her face was eager, alive, dynamic. Beside her, Joanna Southwood seemed, somehow, a little dim—a tall, thin young woman of twenty-seven, with a long clever face and freakishly plucked eyebrows.

"And you've done so much in the time! Did you have lots of architects and things?"

"Three."

"What are architects like? I don't think I've ever met any."

"They were all right. I found them rather unpractical sometimes."

"Darling, you soon put *that* right! You are the *most* practical creature!"

Joanna picked up a string of pearls from the dressing-table.

"I suppose these are real, aren't they, Linnet?"

"Of course."

"I know it's 'of course' to you, my sweet, but it wouldn't be to most people. Heavily cultured or even Woolworth! Darling, they really are *incredible*, so exquisitely matched. They must be worth the *most* fabulous sums!"

"Rather vulgar, you think?"

"No, not at all—just pure beauty. What *are* they worth?"

"About fifty thousand."

"What a lovely lot of money! Aren't you afraid of having them stolen?"

"No, I always wear them—and anyway they're insured."

"Let me wear them till dinner-time, will you, darling? It would give me such a thrill."

Linnet laughed.

"Of course, if you like."

"You know, Linnet, I really do envy you. You've simply got *everything*. Here you are at twenty, your own mistress, with any amount of money, looks, superb health. You've even got *brains!* When are you twenty-one?"

"Next June. I shall have a grand coming-of-age party in London."

"And then are you going to marry Charles Windlesham? All the dreadful little gossip writers are getting so excited about it. And he really is frightfully devoted."

Linnet shrugged her shoulders.

"I don't know. I don't really want to marry any one yet."

"Darling, how right you are! It's never quite the same afterwards, is it?"

The telephone shrilled and Linnet went to it.

"Yes? Yes?"

The butler's voice answered her.

"Miss de Bellefort is on the line. Shall I put her through?"

"Bellefort? Oh, of course, yes, put her through."

A click and a voice, an eager, soft, slightly breathless voice.

"Hallo, is that Miss Ridgeway? *Linnet!*"

"*Jackie darling!* I haven't heard anything of you for ages and *ages!*"

"I know. It's awful. Linnet, I want to see you terribly."

"Darling, can't you come down here? My new toy. I'd love to show it to you."

"That's just what I want to do."

"Well, jump into a train or a car."

"Right, I will. A frightfully dilapidated two-seater. I bought it for fifteen pounds and some days it goes beautifully. But it has moods. If I haven't arrived by tea-time you'll know it's had a mood. So long, my sweet."

Linnet replaced the receiver. She crossed back to Joanna.

"That's my oldest friend, Jacqueline de Bellefort. We were together at a convent in Paris. She's had the most terribly bad luck. Her father was a French Count, her mother was American—a Southerner. The father went off with some woman, and her mother lost all her money in the Wall Street crash. Jackie was left absolutely broke. I don't know how she's managed to get along the last two years."

Joanna was polishing her deep blood-coloured nails with her friend's nail pad. She leant back with her head on one side scrutinising the effect.

"Darling," she drawled, "won't that be rather *tiresome?* If any misfortunes happen to my friends I always drop them *at once!* It sounds heartless, but it saves such a lot of trouble later! They always want to borrow money off you, or else they start a dress-making business and you have to get the most terrible clothes from them. Or they paint lampshades, or do Batik scarves."

"So if I lost all my money, you'd drop me to-morrow?"

"Yes, darling, I would. You can't say I'm not honest about it! I only like successful people. And you'll find that's true of nearly everybody—only most people won't admit it. They just say that 'really they can't put up with Mary or Emily or Pamela any more! Her troubles have made her so *bitter* and peculiar, poor dear!'"

"How beastly you are, Joanna!"

"I'm only on the make, like every one else."

"*I'm* not on the make!"

"For obvious reasons! You don't have to be sordid when good-looking, middle-aged American trustees pay you over a vast allowance every quarter."

"And you're wrong about Jacqueline," said Linnet. "She's not a sponge. I've wanted to help her but she won't let me. She's as proud as the devil."

"What's she in such a hurry to see you for? I'll bet she wants something! You just wait and see."

"She sounded excited about something," admitted Linnet. "Jackie always did get frightfully worked up over things. She once stuck a penknife into some one!"

"Darling, how thrilling!"

"A boy who was teasing a dog. Jackie tried to get him to stop. He wouldn't. She pulled him and shook him but he was much stronger than she was, and at last she whipped out a penknife and plunged it right into him. There was the *most* awful row!"

"I should think so. It sounds most uncomfortable!"

Linnet's maid entered the room. With a murmured word of apology, she took down a dress from the wardrobe and went out of the room with it.

"What's the matter with Marie?" asked Joanna. "She's been crying."

"Poor thing. You know I told you she wanted to marry a man who has a job in Egypt. She didn't know much about him so I thought I'd better make sure he was all right. It turned out that he had a wife already—and three children."

"What a lot of enemies you must make, Linnet."

"Enemies?" Linnet looked surprised.

Joanna nodded and helped herself to a cigarette.

"Enemies, my sweet. You're so devastatingly efficient. And you're so frightfully good at doing the right thing."

Linnet laughed.

"Why, I haven't got an enemy in the world!"

iv

Lord Windlesham sat under the cedar tree. His eyes rested on the graceful proportions of Wode Hall. There was nothing to mar its old-world beauty, the new buildings and additions were out of sight round the corner. It was a fair and peaceful sight bathed in the autumn sunshine. Nevertheless, as he gazed, it was no longer Wode Hall that Charles Windlesham saw. Instead, he seemed to see a more imposing Elizabethan mansion, a long sweep of park, a bleaker background. . . . It was his own family seat, Charltonbury, and in the foreground stood a figure—a girl's figure with bright golden hair and an eager confident face . . . Linnet as mistress of Charltonbury!

He felt very hopeful. That refusal of hers had not been at all a definite refusal. It had been little more than a plea for time. Well, he could afford to wait a little . . .

How amazingly suitable the whole thing was. It was certainly advisable that he should marry money, but not such a matter of necessity that he could regard himself as forced to put his own feelings on one side. And he loved Linnet. He would have wanted to marry her even if she had been practically penniless instead of one of the richest girls in England. Only, fortunately, she *was* one of the richest girls in England. . . .

His mind played with attractive plans for the future. The Mastership of the Roxdale perhaps, the restoration of the west wing, no need to let the Scotch shooting. . . .

Charles Windlesham dreamed in the sun.

v

It was four o'clock when the dilapidated little two-seater stopped with a sound of crunching gravel. A girl got out of it—a small slender creature with a mop of dark hair. She ran up the steps and tugged at the bell.

A few minutes later she was being ushered into the long stately drawing-room, and an ecclesiastical butler was saying with the proper mournful intonation:

"Miss de Bellefort."

"Linnet!"

"Jackie!"

Windlesham stood a little aside, watching sympathetically as this fiery little creature flung herself open-armed upon Linnet.

"Lord Windlesham—Miss de Bellefort—my best friend."

A pretty child, he thought—not really pretty but decidedly attractive with her dark curly hair and her enormous eyes. He murmured a few tactful nothings and then managed unobtrusively to leave the two friends together.

Jacqueline pounced—in a fashion that Linnet remembered as being characteristic of her.

"Windlesham? Windlesham? *That's* the man the papers always say you're going to marry! Are you, Linnet? *Are* you?"

Linnet murmured:

"Perhaps."

"Darling—I'm so glad! He looks nice."

"Oh, don't make up your mind about it—I haven't made up my own mind yet."

"Of course not! Queens always proceed with due deliberation to the choosing of a consort!"

"Don't be ridiculous, Jackie."

"But you *are* a queen, Linnet! You always were. *Sa Majesté, la reine Linette. Linette la blonde!* And I—*I'm* the queen's confidante! The trusted Maid of Honour."

"What nonsense you talk, Jackie, darling. Where have you been all this time? You just disappear. And you never write."

"I hate writing letters. Where have I been? Oh, about three parts submerged, darling. In JOBS, you know. Grim jobs with grim women!"

"Darling, I wish you'd—"

"Take the queen's bounty? Well, frankly darling, that's what I'm here for. No, not to borrow money. It's not got to that yet! But I've come to ask a great big important favour!"

"Go on."

"If you're going to marry the Windlesham man you'll understand, perhaps."

Linnet looked puzzled for a minute, then her face cleared.

"Jackie, do you mean—"

"Yes, darling, *I'm engaged!*"

"So that's it! I thought you were looking particularly alive somehow. You always do, of course, but even more than usual."

"That's just what I feel like."

"Tell me all about him."

"His name's Simon Doyle. He's big and square and incredibly simple and boyish and utterly adorable! He's poor—got no money. He's what you call 'county' all right—but very impoverished county—a younger son and all that. His people come from Devonshire. He loves country and country things. And for the last five years he's been in the city in a stuffy office. And now they're cutting down and he's out of a job. Linnet, I shall *die* if I can't marry him! I shall die! I shall die! I shall *die. . . !*"

"Don't be ridiculous, Jackie."

"I shall die, I tell you! I'm crazy about him. He's crazy about me. We can't live without each other."

"Darling, you *have* got it badly!"

"I know. It's awful, isn't it? This love business gets hold of you and you can't do anything about it."

She paused for a minute. Her dark eyes dilated, looked suddenly tragic. She gave a little shiver.

"It's—even frightening sometimes! Simon and I were made for each other. I shall never care for any one else. And *you've* got to help us, Linnet. I heard you'd bought this place and it put an idea into my head. Listen, you'll have to have a land agent—perhaps two. I want you to give the job to Simon."

"Oh!" Linnet was startled.

Jacqueline rushed on.

"He's got all that sort of thing at his finger-tips. He knows all about estates—was brought up on one. And he's got his business training too. Oh, Linnet, you will give him a job, won't you, for love of me? If he doesn't make good, sack him. But he will. And we can live in a little house and I shall see lots of you and everything in the garden will be too, too divine."

She got up.

"Say you will, Linnet. Say you will. Beautiful Linnet! Tall golden Linnet! My own very special Linnet! Say you will."

"Jackie—"

"You will?"

Linnet burst out laughing.

"Ridiculous Jackie! Bring along your young man and let me have a look at him and we'll talk it over."

Jackie darted at her, kissing her exuberantly:

"*Darling* Linnet—you're a real friend! I knew you were. You wouldn't let me down—ever. You're just the loveliest thing in the world. Good-bye."

"But, Jackie, you're *staying*."

"Me? No, I'm not. I'm going back to London and tomorrow I'll come back and bring Simon and we'll settle it all up. You'll adore him. He really is a *pet*."

"But can't you wait and just have tea?"

"No, I can't wait, Linnet. I'm too excited. I must get back and tell Simon. I know I'm mad, darling, but I can't help it. Marriage will cure me, I expect. It always seems to have a very sobering effect on people."

She turned at the door, stood a moment, then rushed back for a last quick bird-like embrace.

"Dear Linnet—there's no one like you."

vi

M. Gaston Blondin, the proprietor of that modish little restaurant *Chez Ma Tante*, was not a man who delighted to honour many of his clientèle. The rich, the beautiful, the notorious and the well-born might wait in vain to be signalled out and paid special attention. Only in the rarest cases did M. Blondin, with gracious condescension, greet a guest, accompany him to a privileged table, and exchange with him suitable and apposite remarks.

On this particular night, M. Blondin had exercised his royal prerogative three times—once for a duchess, once for a famous racing peer, and once for a little man of comical appearance with immense black moustaches and who, a casual onlooker would have thought, could bestow no favour on *Chez Ma Tante* by his presence there.

M. Blondin, however, was positively fulsome in his attentions.

Though clients had been told for the last half-hour that a table was not to be had, one now mysteriously appeared, placed in a most favourable position. M. Blondin conducted the client to it with every appearance of *empressement*.

"But, naturally, for *you* there is *always* a table, M. Poirot! How I wish that you would honour us oftener."

Hercule Poirot smiled, remembering that past incident wherein a dead body, a waiter, M. Blondin, and a very lovely lady had played a part.

"You are too amiable, M. Blondin," he said.

"And you are alone, M. Poirot?"

"Yes, I am alone."

"Oh, well, Jules here will compose for you a little meal that will be a poem—positively a poem! Women, however charming, have this disadvantage, they distract the mind from food! You will enjoy your dinner, M. Poirot, I promise you that. Now, as to wine—"

A technical conversation ensued. Jules, the *maître d'hôtel,* assisting.

Before departing, M. Blondin lingered a moment, lowering his voice confidentially.

"You have grave affairs on hand?"

Poirot shook his head.

"I am, alas, a man of leisure," he said sadly. "I have made the economies in my time and I have now the means to enjoy a life of idleness."

"I envy you."

"No, no, you would be unwise to do so. I can assure you, it is not so gay as it sounds." He sighed. "How true is the saying that man was forced to invent work in order to escape the strain of having to think."

M. Blondin threw up his hands.

"But there is so much! There is travel!"

"Yes, there is travel. Already I have done not so badly. This winter I shall visit Egypt, I think. The climate, they say, is superb! One will escape from the fogs, the greyness, the monotony of the constantly falling rain."

"Ah! Egypt," breathed M. Blondin.

"One can even voyage there now, I believe, by train, escaping all sea travel except the Channel."

"Ah, the sea, it does not agree with you?"

Hercule Poirot shook his head and shuddered slightly.

"I, too," said M. Blondin with sympathy. "Curious the effect it has upon the stomach."

"But only upon certain stomachs! There are people on whom the motion makes no impression whatever. They actually *enjoy* it!"

"An unfairness of the good God," said M. Blondin.

He shook his head sadly, and brooding on the impious thought, withdrew.

Smooth-footed, deft-handed waiters ministered to the table. Toast Melba, butter, an ice-pail, all the adjuncts to a meal of quality.

The negro orchestra broke into an ecstasy of strange discordant noise. London danced.

Hercule Poirot looked on, registering impressions in his neat orderly mind.

How bored and weary most of the faces were! Some of those stout men, however, were enjoying themselves . . . whereas a patient endurance seemed to be the sentiment exhibited on their partners' faces. The fat woman in purple was looking radiant. . . . Undoubtedly the fat had certain compensations in life . . . a zest—a gusto—denied to those of more fashionable contours.

A good sprinkling of young people—some vacant looking—some bored—some definitely unhappy. How absurd to call youth the time of happiness—youth the time of greatest vulnerability!

His glance softened as it rested on one particular couple. A well-matched pair, tall broad-shouldered man, slender delicate girl. Two bodies that moved in a perfect rhythm of happiness. Happiness in the place, the hour, and in each other.

The dance stopped abruptly. Hands clapped and it started again. After a second encore the couple returned to their table close by Poirot.

The girl was flushed, laughing. As she sat, he could study her face as it was lifted laughing to her companion.

There was something else beside laughter in her eyes.

Hercule Poirot shook his head doubtfully.

"She cares too much, that little one," he said to himself. "It is not safe. No, it is not safe."

And then a word caught his ear. *Egypt*.

Their voices came to him clearly—the girl's young, fresh, arrogant with just a trace of soft-sounding foreign Rs, and the man's pleasant, low-toned, well-bred English.

"I'm *not* counting my chickens before they're hatched, Simon. I tell you Linnet won't let us down!"

"I might let *her* down."

"Nonsense—it's just the right job for you."

"As a matter of fact I think it is . . . I haven't really any doubts as to my capability. And I mean to make good—for *your* sake!"

The girl laughed softly, a laugh of pure happiness.

"We'll wait three months—to make sure you don't get the sack. And then—"

"And then I'll endow thee with my worldly goods—that's the hang of it, isn't it?"

"And as I say, we'll go to Egypt for our honeymoon. Damn the expense! I've always wanted to go to Egypt all my life. The Nile and the pyramids and the sand . . ."

He said, his voice slightly indistinct:

"We'll see it together, Jackie . . . together. Won't it be marvellous?"

"I wonder. Will it be as marvellous to you as it is to me? Do you really care—as much as I do?"

Her voice was suddenly sharp—her eyes dilated—almost with fear.

The man's answer came with an equal sharpness:

"Don't be absurd, Jackie."

But the girl repeated:

"I wonder . . ."

Then she shrugged her shoulders:

"Let's dance."

Hercule Poirot murmured to himself:

"*Un qui aime et un qui se laisse aimer*. Yes, I wonder too."

vii

Joanna Southwood said:

"And suppose he's a terrible tough?"

Linnet shook her head.

"Oh, he won't be. I can trust Jacqueline's taste."

Joanna murmured:

"Ah, but people don't run true to form in love affairs."

Linnet shook her head impatiently. Then she changed the subject.

"I must go and see Mr. Pierce about those plans."

"Plans?"

"Yes, some dreadful insanitary old cottages. I'm having them pulled down and the people moved."

"How sanitary and public-spirited of you, darling."

"They'd have had to go anyway. Those cottages would have overlooked my new swimming pool."

"Do the people who live in them like going?"

"Most of them are delighted. One or two are being rather stupid about it—really tiresome, in fact. They don't seem to realise how vastly improved their living conditions will be!"

"But you're being quite high-handed about it, I presume."

"My dear Joanna, it's to their advantage really."

"Yes, dear, I'm sure it is. Compulsory benefit."

Linnet frowned. Joanna laughed.

"Come now, you *are* a tyrant, admit it. A beneficent tyrant if you like!"

"I'm not the least bit a tyrant."

"But you like your own way!"

"Not especially."

"Linnet Ridgeway, you can look me in the face and tell me of *any one occasion* on which you've failed to do exactly as you wanted?"

"Heaps of times."

"Oh, yes, 'heaps of times'—just like that—but no concrete example. And you simply can't think up one, darling, however hard you try! The triumphal progress of Linnet Ridgeway in her golden car."

Linnet said sharply:

"You think I'm selfish?"

"No—just irresistible. The combined effect of money and charm. Everything goes down before you—what you can't buy with cash you buy with a smile. Result: Linnet Ridgeway, the Girl Who Has Everything."

"Don't be ridiculous, Joanna!"

"Well, haven't you got everything?"

"I suppose I have. . . . It sounds rather disgusting somehow!"

"Of course it's disgusting, darling! You'll probably get terribly bored and blasé by and by. In the meantime enjoy the triumphal progress in the golden car. Only I wonder, I really do wonder, what will happen when you want to go down a street which has a board up saying No Thoroughfare."

"Don't be idiotic, Joanna." As Lord Windlesham joined them Linnet said, turning to him. "Joanna is saying the nastiest things to me."

"All spite," said Joanna vaguely as she got up from her seat.

She made no apology for leaving them. She had caught the glint in Windlesham's eye.

He was silent for a minute or two. Then he went straight to the point.

"Have you come to a decision, Linnet?"

Linnet said slowly:

"Am I being a brute? I suppose, if I'm not sure, I ought to say No—"

He interrupted her.

"Don't say it. You shall have time—as much time as you want. But I think, you know, we should be happy together."

"You see," Linnet's tone was apologetic, almost childish, "I'm enjoying myself so much—especially with all this." She waved a hand. "I wanted to make Wode Hall into my real ideal of a country house and I do think I've got it nice, don't you?"

"It's beautiful. Beautifully planned. Everything perfect. You're very clever, Linnet."

He paused a minute and went on:

"And you like Charltonbury, don't you? Of course it wants modernising and all that—but you're so clever at that sort of thing. You'd enjoy it."

"Why, of course, Charltonbury's divine."

She spoke with a ready enthusiasm, but inwardly she was conscious of a sudden chill. An alien note had sounded, disturbing her complete satisfaction with life.

She did not analyse the feeling at the moment, but later, when Windlesham had gone into the house, she tried to probe into the recesses of her mind.

Charltonbury—yes, that was it—she had resented the mention of Charltonbury. But why? Charltonbury was modestly famous. Windlesham's ancestors had held it since the time of Elizabeth. To be mistress of Charltonbury was a position unsurpassed in society. Windlesham was one of the most desirable partis in England.

Naturally he wouldn't take Wode seriously. . . . It was not in any way to be compared with Charltonbury.

Ah, but Wode was *hers!* She had seen it, acquired it, rebuilt and redressed it, lavished money on it. It was her own possession, her kingdom.

But in a sense it wouldn't count if she married Windlesham. What would they want with two country places? And of the two naturally Wode Hall would be the one to be given up.

She, Linnet Ridgeway, wouldn't exist any longer. She would be Countess of Windlesham, bringing a fine dowry to Charltonbury and its master. She would be queen consort, not queen any longer.

"I'm being ridiculous," said Linnet to herself.

But it was curious how she did hate the idea of abandoning Wode. . . .

And wasn't there something else nagging at her?

Jackie's voice with that queer blurred note in it saying, *"If I don't marry him I'll die. I shall die. I shall die. . . ."*

So positive, so earnest. Did she, Linnet, feel like that about Windlesham? Assuredly she didn't. Perhaps she could never feel like that about any one. It must be—rather wonderful—to feel like that . . .

The sound of a car came through the open window.

Linnet shook herself impatiently. That must be Jackie and her young man. She'd go out and meet them.

She was standing in the open doorway as Jacqueline and Simon Doyle got out of the car.

"Linnet," Jackie ran to her. "This is Simon. Simon, here's Linnet. She's just the most wonderful person in the world."

Linnet saw a tall broad-shouldered young man with very dark blue eyes, crisply curling brown hair, a square chin and a boyish appealing simple smile . . .

She stretched out a hand. The hand that clasped hers was firm and warm. . . . She liked the way he looked at her, the *naïve* genuine admiration.

Jackie had told him she was wonderful and he clearly thought that she was wonderful. . . .

A warm sweet feeling of intoxication ran through her veins.

"Isn't this all lovely?" she said. "Come in, Simon, and let me welcome my new land agent properly."

And as she turned to lead the way she thought:

"I'm frightfully—frightfully happy. I like Jackie's young man. . . . I like him enormously. . . ."

And then with a sudden pang:

"Lucky Jackie. . . ."

viii

Tim Allerton leant back in his wicker chair and yawned as he looked out over the sea. He shot a quick sidelong glance at his mother.

Mrs. Allerton was a good-looking white-haired woman of fifty. By imparting an expression of pinched severity to her mouth every time she looked at her son, she sought to disguise the fact of her intense affection for him. Even total strangers were seldom deceived by this device and Tim himself saw through it perfectly.

He said:

"Do you really like Majorca, Mother?"

"Well—" Mrs. Allerton considered. "It's cheap."

"And cold," said Tim with a slight shiver.

He was a tall, thin young man with dark hair and a rather narrow chest. His mouth had a very sweet expression, his eyes were sad and his chin was indecisive. He had long delicate hands.

Threatened by consumption some years ago, he had never displayed a really robust physique. He was popularly supposed "to write," but it was understood among his friends that inquiries as to literary output were not encouraged.

"What are you thinking of, Tim?"

Mrs. Allerton was alert. Her bright dark brown eyes looked suspicious.

Tim Allerton grinned at her.

"I was thinking of Egypt."

"Egypt?"

Mrs. Allerton sounded doubtful.

"Real warmth, darling. Lazy golden sands. The Nile. I'd like to go up the Nile, wouldn't you?"

"Oh, I'd *like* it." Her tone was dry. "But Egypt's expensive, my dear. Not for those who have to count the pennies."

Tim laughed. He rose, stretched himself. Suddenly he looked alive and eager. There was an excited note in his voice.

"The expense will be my affair. Yes, darling. A little flutter on the Stock Exchange. With thoroughly satisfactory results. I heard this morning."

"This morning?" said Mrs. Allerton sharply. "You only had one letter and that—"

She stopped and bit her lip.

Tim looked momentarily undecided whether to be amused or annoyed. Amusement gained the day.

"And that was from Joanna," he finished coolly. "Quite right, Mother. What a queen of detectives you'd make! The famous Hercule Poirot would have to look to his laurels if you were about."

Mrs. Allerton looked rather cross.

"I just happened to see the handwriting—"

"And knew it wasn't that of a stockbroker? Quite right. As a matter of fact it was yesterday I heard from them. Poor Joanna's handwriting *is* rather noticeable—sprawls about all over the envelope like an inebriated spider."

"What does Joanna say? Any news?"

Mrs. Allerton strove to make her voice sound casual and ordinary. The friendship between her son and his second cousin, Joanna Southwood, always irritated her. Not, as she put it to herself, that there was "anything in it." She was quite sure there wasn't. Tim had never manifested a sentimental interest in Joanna, nor she in him. Their mutual attraction seemed to be founded on gossip and the possession of a large number of friends and acquaintances in common. They both liked people and discussing people. Joanna had an amusing if caustic tongue.

It was not because Mrs. Allerton feared that Tim might fall in love with Joanna that she found herself alway becoming a little stiff in manner if Joanna were present or when letters from her arrived.

It was some other feeling hard to define—perhaps an unacknowledged jealousy in the unfeigned pleasure Tim always seemed to take in Joanna's society. He and his mother were such perfect companions that the sight of him absorbed and interested in another woman always startled Mrs. Allerton slightly. She fancied, too, that her own presence on these occasions set some barrier between the two members of the younger generation. Often she had come upon them eagerly absorbed in some conversation, and at sight of her their talk had wavered, had seemed to include her rather too purposefully and as in duty bound. Quite definitely, Mrs. Allerton did not like Joanna Southwood. She thought her insincere, affected and essentially superficial. She found it very hard to prevent herself saying so in unmeasured tones.

In answer to her question, Tim pulled the letter out of his pocket and glanced through it. It was quite a long letter, his mother noted.

"Nothing much," he said. "The Devenishes are getting a divorce. Old Monty's been had up for being drunk in charge of a car. Windlesham's gone to Canada. Seems he was pretty badly hit when Linnet Ridgeway turned him down. She's definitely going to marry this land agent person."

"How extraordinary! Is he very dreadful?"

"No, no, not at all. He's one of the Devonshire Doyles. No money, of course—and he was actually engaged to one of Linnet's best friends. Pretty thick, that."

"I don't think it's at all nice," said Mrs. Allerton flushing.

Tim flashed her a quick affectionate glance.

"I know, darling. You don't approve of snaffling other people's husbands and all that sort of thing."

"In my day we had our standards," said Mrs. Allerton. "And a very good thing too! Nowadays young people seem to think they can just go about doing anything they choose."

Tim smiled.

"They don't only think it. They do it. *Vide* Linnet Ridgeway!"

"Well, I think it's horrid!"

Tim twinkled at her.

"Cheer up, you old die-hard! Perhaps I agree with you. Anyway, *I* haven't helped myself to any one's wife or fiancée yet."

"I'm sure you'd never do such a thing," said Mrs. Allerton. She added with spirit, "I've brought you up properly."

"So the credit is yours, not mine."

He smiled teasingly at her as he folded the letter and put it away again. Mrs. Allerton let the thought just flash across her mind:

"Most letters he shows to me. He only reads me snippets from Joanna's."

But she put the unworthy thought away from her, and decided, as ever, to behave like a gentlewoman.

"Is Joanna enjoying life?" she asked.

"So so. Says she thinks of opening a delicatessen shop in Mayfair."

"She always talks about being hard up," said Mrs. Allerton with a tinge of spite. "But she goes about everywhere and her clothes must cost her a lot. She's always beautifully dressed."

"Ah, well," said Tim. "She probably doesn't pay for them. No, Mother, I don't mean what your Edwardian mind suggests to you. I just mean quite literally that she leaves her bills unpaid."

Mrs. Allerton sighed.

"I never know how people manage to do that."

"It's a kind of special gift," said Tim. "If only you have sufficiently extravagant tastes, and absolutely no sense of money values, people will give you any amount of credit."

"Yes, but you come to the Bankruptcy Court in the end like poor Sir George Wode."

"You have a soft spot for that old horse coper—probably because he called you a rosebud in 1879 at a dance."

"I wasn't born in 1879," Mrs. Allerton retorted with spirit. "Sir George has charming manners and I won't have you calling him a horse coper."

"I've heard funny stories about him from people that know."

"You and Joanna don't mind what you say about people—anything will do so long as it's sufficiently ill-natured."

Tim raised his eyebrows.

"My dear, you're quite heated. I didn't know old Wode was such a favourite of yours."

"You don't realise how hard it is for him—having to sell Wode Hall. He cared terribly about that place."

Tim suppressed the easy retort. After all, who was he to judge? Instead he said thoughtfully:

"You know, I think you're not far wrong there. Linnet asked him to come down and see what she'd done to the place and he refused quite rudely."

"Of course. She ought to have known better than to ask him."

"And I believe he's quite venomous about her—mutters things under his breath whenever he sees her. Can't forgive her for having giving him an absolutely top price for the wormeaten family estate."

"And you can't understand that?" Mrs. Allerton spoke sharply.

"Frankly," said Tim calmly, "I can't. Why live in the past? Why cling on to things that have been?"

"What are you going to put in their place?"

He shrugged his shoulders.

"Excitement, perhaps. Novelty. The joy of never knowing what may turn up from day to day. Instead of inheriting a useless tract of land, the pleasure of making money for yourself—by your own brains and skill."

"A successful deal on the Stock Exchange in fact!"

He laughed:

"Why not?"

"And what about an equal *loss* on the Stock Exchange?"

"That, dear, is rather tactless. And quite inappropriate to-day. . . . What about this Egypt plan?"

"Well—"

He cut in, smiling at her.

"That's settled. We've both always wanted to see Egypt."

"When do you suggest?"

"Oh, next month. January's about the best time there. We'll enjoy the delightful society in this hotel a few weeks longer."

"Tim!" said Mrs. Allerton reproachfully. Then she added guiltily. "I'm afraid I promised Mrs. Leech that you'd go with her to the police station. She doesn't understand any Spanish."

Tim made a grimace.

"About her ring? The blood red ruby of the horseleech's daughter? Does she still persist in thinking it's been stolen? I'll go if you like, but it's a waste of time. She'll only get some wretched chambermaid into trouble. I distinctly saw it on her finger when she went into the sea that day. It came off in the water and she never noticed."

"She says she is quite sure she took it off and left it on her dressing-table."

"Well, she didn't. I saw it with my own eyes. The woman's a fool. Any woman's a fool who goes prancing into the sea in December pretending the water's quite warm just because the sun happens to be shining rather brightly at the moment. Stout women oughtn't to be allowed to bathe anyway. They look so revolting in bathing dresses."

Mrs. Allerton murmured:

"I really feel I ought to give up bathing."

Tim gave a shout of laughter.

"You? You can give most of the young things points and to spare."

Mrs. Allerton sighed and said:

"I wish there were a few more young people for you here."

Tim Allerton shook his head decidedly.

"I don't. You and I get along rather comfortably without outside distractions."

"You'd like it if Joanna were here."

"I wouldn't."His tone was unexpectedly resolute. "You're all wrong there. Joanna amuses me, but I don't really like her, and to have her around much gets on my nerves. I'm thankful she isn't here. I should be quite resigned if I were never to see Joanna again."

He added, almost below his breath:

"There's only one woman in the world I've got a real respect and admiration for. And I think, Mrs. Allerton, you know very well who that woman is."

His mother blushed and looked quite confused.

Tim said gravely:

"There aren't very many really nice women in the world. You happen to be one of them."

ix

In an apartment overlooking Central Park in New York, Mrs. Robson exclaimed:

"If that isn't just too lovely! You really are the luckiest girl, Cornelia."

Cornelia Robson flushed responsively.

She was a big clumsy-looking girl with brown dog-like eyes.

"Oh, it will be wonderful," she gasped.

Old Miss Van Schuyler inclined her head in a satisfied fashion at this correct attitude on the part of poor relations.

"I've always dreamed of a trip to Europe," sighed Cornelia. "But I just didn't feel I'd ever get there."

"Miss Bowers will come with me as usual, of course," said Miss Van Schuyler. "But as a social companion I find her limited—very limited. There are many little things that Cornelia can do for me."

"I'd just love to, Cousin Marie," said Cornelia eagerly.

"Well, well, then that's settled," said Miss Van Schuyler. "Just run and find Miss Bowers, my dear. It's time for my egg nog."

Cornelia departed.

Her mother said:

"My dear Marie, I'm really *most* grateful to you! You know I think Cornelia suffers a lot from not being a social success. It makes her feel kind of mortified. If I could afford to take her to places—but you know how it's been since Ned died."

"I'm very glad to take her," said Miss Van Schuyler. "Cornelia has always been a nice handy girl, willing to run errands, and not so selfish as some of these young people nowadays."

Mrs. Robson rose and kissed her rich relative's wrinkled and slightly yellow face.

"I'm just ever so grateful," she declared.

On the stairs she met a tall capable looking woman who was carrying a glass containing a yellow foamy liquid.

"Well, Miss Bowers, so you're off to Europe?"

"Why, yes, Mrs. Robson."

"What a lovely trip!"

"Why, yes, I should think it would be very enjoyable."

"But you've been abroad before?"

"Oh yes, Mrs. Robson. I went over to Paris with Miss Van Schuyler last Fall. But I've never been to Egypt before."

Mrs. Robson hesitated.

"I do hope—there won't be any—trouble."

She had lowered her voice.

Miss Bowers, however, replied in her usual tone.

"Oh, *no*, Mrs. Robson, I shall take good care of *that*. I keep a very sharp look out always."

But there was still a faint shadow on Mrs. Robson's face as she slowly continued down the stairs.

x

In his office down town Mr. Andrew Pennington was opening his personal mail.

Suddenly his fist clenched itself and came down on his desk with a bang, his face crimsoned and two big veins stood out on his forehead.

He pressed a buzzer on his desk and a smart-looking stenographer appeared with commendable promptitude.

"Tell Mr. Rockford to step in here."

"Yes, Mr. Pennington."

A few minutes later, Sterndale Rockford, Pennington's partner, entered the office. The two men were not unlike—both tall, spare with grey hair and clean-shaven clever faces.

"What's up, Pennington?"

Pennington looked up from the letter he was re-reading.

He said:

"Linnet's married. . . ."

"*What?*"

"You heard what I said! Linnet Ridgeway's *married!*"

"How? When? Why didn't we hear about it?"

Pennington glanced at the calendar on his desk.

"She wasn't married when she wrote this letter, but she's married now. Morning of the 4th. That's to-day."

Rockford dropped into a chair.

"Whew! No warning? Nothing? Who's the man?"

Pennington referred again to the letter.

"Doyle. Simon Doyle."

"What sort of a fellow is he? Ever heard of him?"

"No. She doesn't say much. . . ." He scanned the lines of clear upright handwriting. "Got an idea there's something hole and corner about the business. . . . That doesn't matter. The whole point is, she's married."

The eyes of the two men met. Rockford nodded.

"This needs a bit of thinking out," he said quietly.

"What are we going to do about it?"

"I'm asking you."

The two men sat silent.

Then Rockford said:

"Got any plan?"

Pennington said slowly:

"The *Normandie* sails to-day. One of us could just make it."

"You're crazy! What's the big idea?"

Pennington said:

"Those British lawyers—" and stopped.

"What about 'em? Surely you're not going over to tackle 'em? You're mad!"

"I'm not suggesting you—or I—should go to England."

"What's the big idea, then?"

Pennington smoothed out the letter on the table.

"Linnet's going to Egypt for her honeymoon. Expects to be there a month or more. . . ."

"Egypt—eh?"

Rockford considered. Then he looked up and met the other's glance.

"Egypt," he said, "*that's* your idea!"

"Yes—a chance meeting. Over on a trip. Linnet and her husband—honeymoon atmosphere. It might be done."

Rockford said doubtfully:

"She's sharp, Linnet is . . . but—"

Pennington said softly:

"I think there might be ways of—managing it."

Again their eyes met.

Rockford nodded.

"All right, big boy."

Pennington looked at the clock.

"We'll have to hustle—whichever of us is going."

"You go," said Rockford promptly. "You always made a hit with Linnet. Uncle Andrew. That's the ticket!"

Pennington's face had hardened.

He said:

"I hope I can pull it off."

His partner said:

"You've got to pull it off. The situation's critical. . . ."

xi

William Carmichael said to the thin weedy youth who opened the door inquiringly:

"Send Mr. Jim to me, please."

Jim Fanthorp entered the room and looked inquiringly at his uncle. The older man looked up with a nod and a grunt.

"Humph, there you are."

"You asked for me?"

"Just cast an eye over this."

The young man sat down and drew the sheaf of papers towards him. The elder man watched him.

"Well?"

The answer came promptly.

"Looks fishy to me, sir."

Again the senior partner of Carmichael, Grant & Carmichael uttered his characteristic grunt.

Jim Fanthorp re-read the letter which had just arrived by Air Mail from Egypt.

> ". . . It seems wicked to be writing business letters on such a day. We have spent a week at Mena House and made an expedition to the Fayum. The day after tomorrow we are going up the Nile to Luxor and Assuan by steamer, and perhaps on to Khartoum. When we went into Cook's this morning to see about our tickets who do you think was the first person I saw—my

> American trustee Andrew Pennington. I think you met him two years ago when he was over. I had no idea he was in Egypt and he had no idea that I was! Nor that I was married! My letter, telling him of my marriage, must have just missed him. He is actually going up the Nile on the same trip that we are. Isn't it a coincidence? Thank you so much for all you have done in this busy time. I . . ."

As the young man was about to turn the page, Mr. Carmichael took the letter from him.

"That's all," he said. "The rest doesn't matter. Well, what do you think?"

His nephew considered for a moment—then he said:

"Well—I think—not a coincidence. . . ."

The other nodded approval.

"Like a trip to Egypt?" he barked out.

"You think that's advisable?"

"I think there's no time to lose."

"But why me?"

"Use your brains, boy, use your brains. Linnet Ridgeway has never met you, no more has Pennington. If you go by air you may get there in time."

"I—I don't like it, sir. What am I to do?"

"Use your eyes. Use your ears. Use your brains—if you've got any. And, if necessary—act."

"I—I don't like it."

"Perhaps not—but you've got to do it."

"It's—necessary?"

"In my opinion," said Mr. Carmichael, "it's absolutely vital."

xii

Mrs. Otterbourne, readjusting the turban of native material that she wore draped round her head, said fretfully:

"I really don't see why we shouldn't go on to Egypt. I'm sick and tired of Jerusalem."

As her daughter made no reply, she said:

"You might at least answer when you're spoken to."

Rosalie Otterbourne was looking at a newspaper reproduction of a face. Below it was written:

> "Mrs. Simon Doyle, who before her marriage was the well-known society beauty, Miss Linnet Ridgeway. Mr. and Mrs. Doyle are spending their honeymoon in Egypt."

Rosalie said:

"You'd like to move on to Egypt, Mother?"

"Yes, I would," Mrs. Otterbourne snapped. "I consider they've treated us in a most cavalier fashion here. My being here is an advertisement—I ought to get a special reduction in terms. When I hinted as much I consider they were most impertinent—*most* impertinent. I told them exactly what I thought of them."

The girl sighed. She said:

"One place is very like another. I wish we could get right away."

"And this morning," went on Mrs. Otterbourne, "the manager actually had the impertinence to tell me that all the rooms had been booked in advance and that he would require ours in two days' time."

"So we've got to go somewhere."

"Not at all. I'm quite prepared to fight for my rights."

Rosalie murmured: "I suppose we might as well go on to Egypt. It doesn't make any difference."

"It's certainly not a matter of life or death," said Mrs. Otterbourne.

But there she was quite wrong—for a matter of life and death was exactly what it was.

PART TWO
EGYPT

CHAPTER 1

"That's Hercule Poirot, the detective," said Mrs. Allerton.

She and her son were sitting in brightly painted scarlet basket chairs outside the Cataract Hotel at Assuan.

They were watching the retreating figures of two people—a short man dressed in a white silk suit and a tall slim girl.

Tim Allerton sat up in an unusually alert fashion.

"That funny little man?" he asked incredulously.

"That funny little man!"

Tim said: "What on earth's he doing out here?"

His mother laughed.

"Darling, you sound quite excited. Why do men enjoy crime so much? I hate detective stories and never read them. But I don't think M. Poirot is here with any ulterior motive. He's made a good deal of money and he's seeing life, I fancy."

"Seems to have an eye for the best-looking girl in the place."

Mrs. Allerton tilted her head a little on one side as she considered the retreating backs of M. Poirot and his companion.

The girl by his side overtopped him by some three inches. She walked well, neither stiffly nor slouchingly.

"I suppose she *is* quite good-looking?" said Mrs. Allerton.

She shot a little glance sideways at Tim. Somewhat to her amusement the fish rose at once.

"She's more than quite. Pity she looks so bad-tempered and sulky."

"Perhaps that's just expression, dear."

"Unpleasant young devil, I think. But she's pretty enough."

The subject of these remarks was walking slowly by Poirot's side. Rosalie Otterbourne was twirling an unopened parasol, and her expression certainly bore out what Tim had just said. She looked both sulky and bad-tempered. Her eyebrows were drawn together in a frown and the scarlet line of her mouth was drawn downwards.

They turned to the left out of the hotel gate and entered the cool shade of the public gardens.

Hercule Poirot was prattling gently, his expression that of beatific good humour. He wore a white silk suit, carefully pressed, a panama hat and carried a highly ornamental fly whisk with a sham amber handle.

"—it enchants me," he was saying. "The black rocks of Elephantine, and the sun, the little boats on the river. Yes, it is good to be alive."

He paused and then added:

"You do not find it so, Mademoiselle?"

Rosalie Otterbourne said shortly:

"It's all right, I suppose. I think Assuan's a gloomy sort of place. The hotel's half empty, and every one's about a hundred—"

She stopped—biting her lip.

Hercule Poirot's eyes twinkled.

"It is true, yes, I have one leg in the grave."

"I—I wasn't thinking of you," said the girl. "I'm sorry. That sounded rude."

"Not at all. It is natural you should wish for young companions of your own age. Ah, well, there is *one* young man, at least."

"The one who sits with his mother all the time? I like *her*—but I think he looks dreadful—so conceited!"

Poirot smiled.

"And I—am I conceited?"

"Oh, I don't think so."

She was obviously uninterested—but the fact did not seem to annoy Poirot. He merely remarked with placid satisfaction:

"My best friend says that I am very conceited."

"Oh, well," said Rosalie vaguely, "I suppose you have something to be conceited about. Unfortunately crime doesn't interest me in the least."

Poirot said solemnly:

"I am delighted to learn that you have no guilty secret to hide."

Just for a moment the sulky mask of her face was transformed as she shot him a swift questioning glance. Poirot did not seem to notice it as he went on.

"Madame, your mother was not at lunch to-day. She is not indisposed, I trust?"

"This place doesn't suit her," said Rosalie briefly. "I shall be glad when we leave."

"We are fellow-passengers, are we not? We both make the excursion up to Wâdi Halfa and the Second Cataract?"

"Yes."

They came out from the shade of the garden on to a dusty stretch of road bordered by the river. Five watchful bead sellers, two vendors of postcards, three sellers of plaster scarabs, a couple of donkey boys and some detached but hopeful infantile riff-raff closed in upon them.

"You want beads, sir? Very good, sir. Very cheap. . . ."

"Lady, you want scarab. Look—great queen—very lucky. . . ."

"You look, sir—real lapis. Very good, very cheap. . . ."

"You want ride donkey, sir? This very good donkey. This donkey Whisky and Soda, sir. . . ."

"You want to go granite quarries, sir? This very good donkey. Other donkey very bad, sir, that donkey fall down. . . ."

"You want postcard—very cheap—very nice. . . ."

"Look, lady. . . . Only ten piastres—very cheap—lapis—this ivory. . . ."

"This very good fly whisk—this all amber. . . ."

"You go out in boat, sir? I got very good boat, sir. . . ."

"You ride back to hotel, lady? This first-class donkey. . . ."

Hercule Poirot made vague gestures to rid himself of this human cluster of flies. Rosalie stalked through them like a sleep walker.

"It's best to pretend to be deaf and blind," she remarked.

The infantile riff-raff ran alongside murmuring plaintively.

"Bakshish? Bakshish? Hip, hip, hurrah—very good, very nice. . . ."

Their gaily coloured rags trailed picturesquely and the flies lay in clusters on their eyelids.

They were the most persistent. The others fell back and launched a fresh attack on the next comer. Now Poirot and Rosalie only ran the gauntlet of the shops—suave persuasive accents here. . . .

"You visit my shop to-day, sir?" "You want that ivory crocodile, sir?" "You not been in my shop yet, sir? I show you very beautiful things."

They turned into the fifth shop and Rosalie handed over several rolls of films—the object of the walk.

Then they came out again and walked towards the river's edge.

One of the Nile steamers was just mooring. Poirot and Rosalie looked interestedly at the passengers.

"Quite a lot, aren't there?" commented Rosalie.

She turned her head as Tim Allerton came up and joined them. He was a little out of breath as though he had been walking fast.

They stood there for a moment or two and then Tim spoke:

"An awful crowd as usual, I suppose," he remarked disparagingly, indicating the disembarking passengers.

"They're usually quite terrible," agreed Rosalie.

All three wore the air of superiority assumed by people who are already in a place when studying new arrivals.

"Hallo!" said Tim, his voice suddenly excited. "I'm damned if that isn't Linnet Ridgeway."

If the information left Poirot unmoved, it stirred Rosalie's interest. She leaned forward and her sulkiness quite dropped from her as she asked:

"Where? That one in white?"

"Yes, there with the tall man. They're coming ashore now. He's the new husband, I suppose. Can't remember her name now."

"Doyle," said Rosalie. "Simon Doyle. It was in all the newspapers. She's simply rolling, isn't she?"

"Only about the richest girl in England," said Tim cheerfully.

The three lookers-on were silent watching the passengers come ashore. Poirot gazed with interest at the subject of the remarks of his companions. He murmured:

"She is beautiful."

"Some people have got everything," said Rosalie bitterly.

There was a queer grudging expression on her face as she watched the other girl come up the gang-plank.

Linnet Doyle was looking as perfectly turned out as if she was stepping on the centre of the stage in a Revue. She had something too of the assurance of a famous actress. She was used to being looked at, to being admired, to being the centre of the stage wherever she went.

She was aware of the keen glances bent upon her—and at the same time almost unaware of them, such tributes were part of her life.

She came ashore playing a rôle, even though she played it unconsciously. The rich, beautiful society bride on her honeymoon. She turned with a little smile and a light remark to the tall man by her side. He answered and the sound of his voice seemed to interest Hercule Poirot. His eyes lit up and he drew his brows together.

The couple passed close to him. He heard Simon Doyle say:

"We'll try and make time for it, darling. We can easily stay a week or two if you like it here."

His face was turned towards her, eager, adoring, a little humble.

Poirot's eyes ran over him thoughtfully—the square shoulders, the bronzed face, the dark blue eyes, the rather childlike simplicity of the smile.

"Lucky devil," said Tim after they had passed. "Fancy finding an heiress who hasn't got adenoids and flat feet!"

"They look frightfully happy," said Rosalie with a note of envy in her voice. She said suddenly but so low that Tim did not catch the words: "It isn't fair."

Poirot heard, however. He had been frowning somewhat perplexedly but now he flashed a quick glance towards her.

Tim said:

"I must collect some stuff for my mother now."

He raised his hat and moved off. Poirot and Rosalie retraced their steps slowly in the direction of the hotel, waving aside fresh proffers of donkeys.

"So it is not fair, Mademoiselle?" said Poirot gently.

The girl flushed angrily.

"I don't know what you mean."

"I am repeating what you said just now under your breath. Oh, yes, you did."

Rosalie Otterbourne shrugged her shoulders.

"It really seems a little too much for one person. Money, good looks, marvellous figure and—"

She paused and Poirot said:

"And love? Eh? And love? But you do not know—she may have been married for her money!"

"Didn't you see the way he looked at her?"

"Oh, yes, Mademoiselle. I saw all there was to see—indeed I saw something that you did not."

"What was that?"

Poirot said slowly:

"I saw, Mademoiselle, dark lines below a woman's eyes. I saw a hand that clutched a sunshade so tight that the knuckles were white. . . ."

Rosalie was staring at him.

"What do you mean?"

"I mean that all is not the gold that glitters—I mean that though the lady is rich and beautiful and beloved, there is all the same *something* that is not right. And I know something else."

"Yes?"

"I know," said Poirot frowning, "that somewhere, at some time, *I have heard that voice before*—the voice of M. Doyle—and I wish I could remember where."

But Rosalie was not listening. She had stopped dead. With the point of her sunshade she was tracing patterns in the loose sand. Suddenly she broke out fiercely:

"I'm odious. I'm quite odious. I'm just a beast through and through. I'd like to tear the clothes off her back and stamp on her lovely arrogant self-confident face. I'm just a jealous cat—but that's what I feel like. She's so horribly successful and poised and assured."

Hercule Poirot looked a little astonished by the outburst. He took her by the arm and gave her a friendly little shake.

"*Tenez*—you will feel better for having said that!"

"I just hate her. I've never hated any one so much at first sight."

"Magnificent."

Rosalie looked at him doubtfully. Then her mouth twitched and she laughed.

"*Bien*," said Poirot, and laughed too.

They proceeded amicably back to the hotel.

"I must find mother," said Rosalie, as they came into the cool dim hall.

Poirot passed out on the other side on to the terrace overlooking the Nile. Here were little tables set for tea, but it was early still. He stood for a few moments looking down on to the river then strolled down through the gardens.

Some people were playing tennis in the hot sun. He paused to watch them for a while, then went on down the steep path. It was there, sitting on a bench overlooking the Nile, that he came upon the girl of *Chez Ma Tante*. He recognised her at once. Her face, as he had seen it that night, was securely etched upon his memory. The expression on it now was very different. She was paler, thinner, and there were lines that told of a great weariness and misery of spirit.

He drew back a little. She had not seen him, and he watched her for a while without her suspecting his presence. Her small foot tapped impatiently on the ground. Her eyes, dark with a kind of smouldering fire, had a queer kind of suffering dark triumph in them. She was looking out across the Nile where the white-sailed boats glided up and down the river.

A face—and a voice. He remembered them both. This girl's face and the voice he had heard just now, the voice of a newly made bridegroom. . . .

And even as he stood there considering the unconscious girl, the next scene in the drama was played.

Voices sounded above. The girl on the seat started to her feet. Linnet Doyle and her husband came down the path. Linnet's voice was happy and confident. The look of strain and tenseness of muscle had quite disappeared. Linnet was happy.

The girl who was standing there took a step or two forward.

The other two stopped dead.

"Hallo, Linnet," said Jacqueline de Bellefort. "So here you are! We never seem to stop running into each other. Hallo, Simon, how are you?"

Linnet Doyle had shrunk back against the rock with a little cry. Simon Doyle's good-looking face was suddenly convulsed with rage. He moved forward as though he would have liked to strike the slim girlish figure.

With a quick birdlike turn of her head she signalled her realisation of a stranger's presence. Simon turned his head and noticed Poirot.

He said awkwardly:

"Hallo, Jacqueline, we didn't expect to see you here."

The words were unconvincing in the extreme.

The girl flashed white teeth at them.

"Quite a surprise?" she asked.

Then, with a little nod, she walked up the path.

Poirot moved delicately in the opposite direction.

As he went he heard Linnet Doyle say:

"Simon—for God's sake—Simon—what can we do?"

CHAPTER 2

Dinner was over.

The terrace outside the Cataract Hotel was softly lit. Most of the guests staying at the hotel were there sitting at little tables.

Simon and Linnet Doyle came out, a tall distinguished-looking grey-haired man with a keen clean-shaven American face beside them.

As the little group hesitated for a moment in the doorway, Tim Allerton rose from his chair nearby and came forward.

"You don't remember me, I'm sure," he said pleasantly to Linnet. "But I'm Joanna Southwood's cousin."

"Of course—how stupid of me. You're Tim Allerton. This is my husband"—a faint tremor in the voice—pride—shyness? "and this is my American trustee, Mr. Pennington."

Tim said:

"You must meet my mother."

A few minutes later they were sitting together in a party. Linnet in the corner, Tim and Pennington each side of her, both talking to her, vying for her attention. Mrs. Allerton talked to Simon Doyle.

The swing doors revolved. A sudden tension came into the beautiful upright figure sitting in the corner between the two men. Then it relaxed as a small man came out and walked across the terrace.

Mrs. Allerton said:

"You're not the only celebrity here, my dear. That funny little man is Hercule Poirot."

She had spoken lightly, just out of instinctive social tact to bridge an awkward pause, but Linnet seemed struck by the information.

"Hercule Poirot? Of course—I've heard of him. . . ."

She seemed to sink into a fit of abstraction. The two men on either side of her were momentarily at a loss.

Poirot had strolled across to the edge of the terrace, but his attention was immediately solicited.

"Sit down, M. Poirot. What a lovely night."

He obeyed.

"*Mais oui, Madame,* it is indeed beautiful."

He smiled politely at Mrs. Otterbourne. What draperies of black ninon and that ridiculous turban effect!

Mrs. Otterbourne went on in her high complaining voice.

"Quite a lot of notabilities here now, aren't there? I expect we shall see a paragraph about it in the papers soon. Society beauties, famous novelists—"

She paused with a slight mock modest laugh.

Poirot felt, rather than saw, the sulky frowning girl opposite him flinch and set her mouth in a sulkier line than before.

"You have a novel on the way at present, Madame?" he inquired.

Mrs. Otterbourne gave her little self-conscious laugh again.

"I'm being dreadfully lazy. I really must set to. My public is getting terribly impatient—and my publisher—poor man! Appeals by every post! Even cables!"

Again he felt the girl shift in the darkness.

"I don't mind telling you, M. Poirot, I am partly here for local colour. *Snow On The Desert's Face*—that is the title of my new book. Powerful—Suggestive. Snow—on the desert—melted in the first flaming breath of passion."

Rosalie got up, muttering something, and moved away down into the dark garden.

"One must be strong," went on Mrs. Otterbourne, wagging the turban emphatically. "Strong meat—that is what my books are. Libraries may ban them—no matter! I speak the truth. Sex—ah! M. Poirot—why is every one so afraid of sex? The pivot of the universe! You have read my books?"

"Alas, Madame! You comprehend, I do not read many novels. My work—"

Mrs. Otterbourne said firmly:

"I must give you a copy of *Under The Fig Tree*. I think you will find it significant. It is outspoken—but it is *real!*"

"That is most kind of you, Madame. I will read it with pleasure."

Mrs. Otterbourne was silent a minute or two. She fidgeted with a long chain of beads that was wound twice round her neck.

She looked swiftly from side to side.

"Perhaps—I'll just slip up and get it for you now."

"Oh, Madame, pray do not trouble yourself. Later—"

"No, no. It's no trouble." She rose. "I'd like to show you—"

"What is it, Mother?"

Rosalie was suddenly at her side.

"Nothing, dear. I was just going up to get a book for M. Poirot."

"The *Fig Tree*? I'll get it."

"You don't know where it is, dear. I'll go."

"Yes, I do."

The girl went swiftly across the terrace and into the hotel.

"Let me congratulate you, Madame, on a very lovely daughter," said Poirot, with a bow.

"Rosalie? Yes, yes—she is good-looking. But she's very *hard*, M. Poirot. And no sympathy with illness. She always thinks she knows best. She imagines she knows more about my health than I do myself—"

Poirot signalled to a passing waiter.

"A liqueur, Madame? A chartreuse? A crème de menthe?"

Mrs. Otterbourne shook her head vigorously.

"No, no. I am practically a teetotaller. You may have noticed I never drink anything but water—or perhaps lemonade. I cannot bear the taste of spirits."

"Then may I order you a lemon squash, Madame?"

He gave the order—one lemon squash and one benedictine.

The swing door revolved. Rosalie passed through and came towards them, a book in her hand.

"Here you are," she said. Her voice was quite expressionless—almost remarkably so.

"M. Poirot has just ordered me a lemon squash," said her mother.

"And you, Mademoiselle, what will you take?"

"Nothing." She added, suddenly conscious of the curtness, "Nothing, thank you."

Poirot took the volume which Mrs. Otterbourne held out to him. It still bore its original jacket, a gaily coloured affair representing a lady with smartly shingled hair and scarlet fingernails sitting on a tiger skin in the traditional costume of Eve.

Above her was a tree with the leaves of an oak, bearing large and improbably coloured apples.

It was entitled *Under the Fig Tree* by Salome Otterbourne. On the inside was a publisher's blurb. It spoke enthusiastically of the superb courage and realism of this study of a modern woman's love life. Fearless, unconventional, realistic, were the adjectives used.

Poirot bowed and murmured:

"I am honoured, Madame."

As he raised his head, his eyes met those of the authoress's daughter. Almost involuntarily he made a little movement. He was astonished and grieved at the eloquent pain they revealed.

It was at that moment that the drinks arrived and created a welcome diversion.

Poirot lifted his glass gallantly.

"A votre santé, Madame—Mademoiselle."

Mrs. Otterbourne, sipping her lemonade murmured:

"So refreshing—delicious."

Silence fell on the three of them. They looked down to the shining black rocks in the Nile. There was something fantastic about them in the moonlight. They were like vast prehistoric monsters lying half out of the water. A little breeze came up suddenly and as suddenly died away.

There was a feeling in the air of hush—of expectancy.

Hercule Poirot brought his gaze to the terrace and its occupants. Was he wrong, or was there the same hush of expectancy there? It was like a moment on the stage when one is waiting for the entrance of the leading lady.

And just at that moment the swing doors began to revolve once more. This time it seemed as though they did so with a special air of importance. Every one had stopped talking and was looking towards them.

A dark slender girl in a wine coloured evening frock came through. She paused for a minute, then walked deliberately across the terrace and sat down at an empty table. There was nothing flaunting, nothing out of the way about her demeanour and yet it had somehow the studied effect of a stage entrance.

"Well!" said Mrs. Otterbourne. She tossed her turbaned head. "She seems to think she is somebody, that girl!"

Poirot did not answer. He was watching. The girl had sat down in a place where she could look deliberately across at Linnet Doyle. Presently, Poirot noticed, Linnet Doyle leant forward and said something and a moment later got up and changed her seat. She was now sitting facing in the opposite direction.

Poirot nodded thoughtfully to himself.

It was about five minutes later that the other girl changed her seat to the opposite side of the terrace. She sat smoking and smiling quietly, the picture of contented ease. But always, as though unconsciously, her meditative gaze was on Simon Doyle's wife.

After a quarter of an hour Linnet Doyle got up abruptly and went into the hotel. Her husband followed her almost immediately.

Jacqueline de Bellefort smiled and twisted her chair round. She lit a cigarette and stared out over the Nile. She went on smiling to herself.

CHAPTER 3

"M. Poirot."

Poirot got hastily to his feet. He had remained sitting out on the terrace alone after every one else had left. Lost in meditation, he had been staring at the smooth shiny black rocks when the sound of his name recalled him to himself.

It was a well-bred assured voice, a charming voice, although, prehaps, a trifle arrogant.

Hercule Poirot, rising quickly, looked into the commanding eyes of Linnet Doyle.

She wore a wrap of rich purple velvet over her white satin gown and she looked more lovely and more regal than Poirot had imagined possible.

"You are M. Hercule Poirot?" said Linnet.

It was hardly a question.

"At your service, Madame."

"You know who I am, perhaps?"

"Yes, Madame. I have heard your name. I know exactly who you are."

Linnet nodded. That was only what she had expected. She went on in her charming autocratic manner.

"Will you come with me into the card-room, M. Poirot? I am very anxious to speak to you."

"Certainly, Madame."

She led the way into the hotel. He followed. She led him into the deserted card-room and motioned him to close the door. Then she sank down on a chair at one of the tables and he sat down opposite her.

She plunged straightaway into what she wanted to say. There were no hesitations. Her speech came flowingly.

"I have heard a great deal about you, M. Poirot, and I know that you are a very clever man. It happens that I am urgently in need of some one to help me—and I think very possibly that you are the man who could do it."

Poirot inclined his head.

"You are very amiable, Madame. But you see, I am on holiday, and when I am on holiday I do not take cases."

"That could be arranged."

It was not offensively said—only with the quiet confidence of a young woman who had always been able to arrange matters to her satisfaction.

Linnet Doyle went on:

"I am the subject, M. Poirot, of an intolerable persecution. That persecution has got to stop! My own idea was to go to the police about it, but my—my husband seems to think that the police would be powerless to do anything."

"Perhaps—if you would explain a little further?" murmured Poirot politely.

"Oh yes, I will do so. The matter is perfectly simple."

There was still no hesitation—no faltering. Linnet Doyle had a clear-cut business-like mind. She only paused a minute so as to present the facts as concisely as possible.

"Before I met my husband, he was engaged to a Miss de Bellefort. She was also a friend of mine. My husband broke off his engagement to her—they were not suited in any way. She, I am sorry to say, took it rather hard. . . . I—am very sorry about that—but these things cannot be helped. She made certain—well, threats—to which I paid very little attention and which, I may say, she has not attempted to carry out. But instead she has adopted the extraordinary course of—of following us about wherever we go."

Poirot raised his eyebrows.

"Ah—rather an unusual—er—revenge."

"Very unusual—and very ridiculous! But also—annoying."

She bit her lip.

Poirot nodded.

"Yes, I can imagine that. You are, I understand, on your honeymoon?"

"Yes. It happened—the first time—at Venice. She was there—at Danielli's. I thought it was just coincidence. Rather embarrassing, but that was all. Then, we found her on board the boat at Brindisi. We—we understood that she was going on to Palestine. We left her, as we thought, on the boat. But—but when we got to Mena House she was there—waiting for us."

Poirot nodded.

"And now!"

"We came up the Nile by boat. I—I was half expecting to find her on board. When she wasn't there I thought she had stopped being so—so childish. But when we got here—she—she was here—waiting."

Poirot eyed her keenly for a moment. She was still perfectly composed, but the knuckles of the hand that was gripping the table were white with the force of her grip.

He said:

"And you are afraid this state of things may continue?"

"Yes." She paused. "Of course the whole thing is idiotic! Jacqueline is making herself utterly ridiculous. I am surprised she hasn't got more pride—more dignity."

Poirot made a slight gesture.

"There are times, Madame, when pride and dignity—they go by the board! There are other—stronger emotions."

"Yes, possibly." Linnet spoke impatiently. "But what on earth can she hope to *gain* by all this?"

"It is not always a question of gain, Madame."

Something in his tone struck Linnet disagreeably. She flushed and said quickly:

"You are right. A discussion of motives is beside the point. The crux of the matter is that this has got to be stopped."

"And how do you propose that that should be accomplished, Madame?" Poirot asked.

"Well—naturally—my husband and I cannot continue being subjected to this annoyance. There must be some kind of legal redress against such a thing."

She spoke impatiently. Poirot looked at her thoughtfully as he asked:

"Has she threatened you in actual words in public? Used insulting language? Attempted any bodily harm?"

"No."

"Then, frankly, Madame, *I do not see what you can do*. If it is a young lady's pleasure to travel in certain places and those places are the same where you and your husband find yourselves—*eh bien*— what of it? The air is free to all! There is no question of her forcing herself upon your privacy? It is always in public that these encounters take place?"

"You mean there is nothing that I can do about it?"

Linnet sounded incredulous.

Poirot said placidly:

"Nothing at all as far as I can see. Mademoiselle de Bellefort is within her rights."

"But—but it is maddening! It is *intolerable* that I should have to put up with this!"

Poirot said dryly:

"I sympathise with you, Madame—especially as I imagine that you have not often had to put up with things."

Linnet was frowning.

"There *must* be some way of stopping it," she murmured.

Poirot shrugged his shoulders.

"You can always leave—move on somewhere else," he suggested.

"Then she will follow!"

"Very possibly—yes."

"It's absurd!"

"Precisely."

"Anyway why should I—we—run away? As though—as though—"

She stopped.

"Exactly, Madame. As though—! It is all there, is it not?"

Linnet lifted her head and stared at him.

"What do you mean?"

Poirot altered his tone. He leant forward, his voice was confidential, appealing. He said very gently:

"Why do you mind so much, Madame?"

"Why? But it's maddening! Irritating to the last degree! I've told you why!"

Poirot shook his head.

"Not altogether."

Linnet said again:

"What do you mean?"

Poirot leant back, folded his arms and spoke in a detached impersonal manner.

"*Ecoutez,* Madame, I will recount to you a little history. It is that one day a month or two ago I am dining in a restaurant in London. At the table next to me are two people, a man and a girl. They are very happy, so it seems, very much in love. They talk with confidence of the future. It is not that I listen to what is not meant for me—they are quite oblivious of who hears them and who does not. The man's back is to me, but I can watch the girl's face. It is very intense. She is in love—heart, soul and body, and she is not of those who love lightly and often. With her it is clearly the life and the death. They are engaged to be married, these two, that is what I gather, and they talk of where they shall pass the days of their honeymoon. They plan to go to Egypt."

He paused. Linnet said sharply.

"Well?"

Poirot went on.

"That is a month or two ago, but the girl's face—I do not forget it. I know that I shall remember if I see it again. And I remember too the man's voice. And I think you can guess, Madame, when it is I see the one and hear the other again. It is here in Egypt. The man is on his honeymoon yes—but he is on his honeymoon *with another woman*."

Linnet said sharply:

"What of it? I had already mentioned the facts."

"The facts—yes."

"Well then?"

Poirot said slowly:

"The girl in the restaurant mentioned a friend—a friend whom she was very positive would not let her down. That friend, I think, was you, Madame."

Linnet flushed.

"Yes. I told you we had been friends."

"And she trusted you?"

"Yes."

She hesitated for a moment, biting her lip impatiently, then as Poirot did not seem disposed to speak she broke out.

"Of course, the whole thing was very unfortunate. But these things happen, M. Poirot."

"Ah! yes, they happen, Madame." He paused. "You are of the Church of England, I presume?"

"Yes." Linnet looked slightly bewildered.

"Then you have heard portions of the Bible read aloud in church. You have heard of King David and of the rich man who had many flocks and herds and the poor man who had one ewe lamb—and of how the rich man took the poor man's one ewe lamb. That was something that happened, Madame."

Linnet sat up. Her eyes flashed angrily.

"I see perfectly what you are driving at, M. Poirot! You think, to put it vulgarly, that I stole my friend's young man. Looking at the matter sentimentally—which is, I suppose, the way people of your generation cannot help looking at things—that is possibly true. But the real hard truth is different. I don't deny that Jackie was passionately in love with Simon, but I don't think you take into account that he may not have been equally devoted to her. He was very fond of her, but I think that even before he met me he was beginning to feel that he had made a mistake. Look at it clearly, M. Poirot. Simon discovers that it is I he loves, not Jackie. What is he to do? Be heroically noble and marry a woman he does not care for—and thereby probably ruin three lives—for it is doubtful whether he could make Jackie happy under these circumstances—? If he were actually married to her when he met me I agree that it *might* be his duty to stick to her—though I'm not really sure of that. If one person is unhappy the other suffers too. But an engagement is not really binding. If a mistake has been made, then surely it is better to face the fact before it is too late. I admit that it was very hard on Jackie and I'm terribly sorry about it—but there it is. It was inevitable."

"I wonder."

She stared at him.

"What do you mean?"

"It is very sensible, very logical—all that you say! But it does not explain one thing."

"What is that?"

"Your own attitude, Madame. See you, this pursuit of you, you might take it in two ways—it might cause you annoyance—yes, or it might stir your pity—that your friend should have been so deeply hurt as to throw all regard for the conventions aside. But that is not the way you react—no, to you this persecution is *intolerable*—and why? It can be for one reason only—*that you feel a sense of guilt*."

Linnet sprang to her feet.

"How dare you? Really, M. Poirot, this is going too far."

"But I do dare, Madame! I am going to speak to you quite frankly. I suggest to you that, although you may have endeavoured to gloss over the fact to yourself, *you deliberately set about taking your husband from your friend*. I suggest that you felt strongly attracted to him at once. But I suggest that there was a moment when you hesitated, when you realised that there was a *choice*—that you could refrain or go on. I suggest that the initiative rested with *you*—not with Mr. Doyle. You are beautiful, Madame, you are rich, you are clever, intelligent—and you have charm. You could have exercised that charm or you could have restrained it. You had everything, Madame, that life can offer. Your friend's life was bound up in one person. You knew that—but though you hesitated, you did not hold your hand. You stretched it out and like King David you took the poor man's one ewe lamb."

There was a silence. Linnet controlled herself with an effort and said in a cold voice:

"All this is quite beside the point!"

"No, it is not beside the point. I am explaining to you just why the unexpected appearances of Mademoiselle de Bellefort have upset you so much. It is because, though she may be unwomanly and undignified in what she is doing, you have the inner conviction that she has right on her side."

"That's not true!"

Poirot shrugged his shoulders.

"You refuse to be honest with yourself."

"Not at all."

Poirot said gently:

"I should say, Madame, that you have had a happy life, that you have been generous and kindly in your attitude towards others."

"I have tried to be," said Linnet.

The impatient anger died out of her face. She spoke simply—almost forlornly.

"And that is why the feeling that you have deliberately caused injury to some one upsets you so much, and why you are so reluctant to admit the fact. Pardon me if I have been impertinent, but the psychology it is the most important factor in a case."

Linnet said slowly:

"Even supposing what you say were true—and I don't admit it, mind—what can be done about it now? One can't alter the past—one must deal with things as they are."

Poirot nodded.

"You have the clear brain. Yes, one cannot go back over the past. One must accept things as they are. And sometimes, Madame, that is all one can do—accept the consequences of one's past deeds."

"You mean," said Linnet incredulously, "that I can do nothing—*nothing?*"

"You must have courage, Madame, that is what it seems like to me."

Linnet said slowly:

"Couldn't you—talk to Jackie—to Miss de Bellefort? Reason with her?"

"Yes, I could do that. I will do that if you would like me to do so. But do not expect much result. I fancy that Mademoiselle de Bellefort is so much in the grip of a fixed idea that nothing will turn her from it."

"But surely we can do *something* to extricate ourselves?"

"You could, of course, return to England and establish yourself in your own house."

"Even then, I suppose, Jacqueline is capable of planting herself in the village, so that I should see her every time I went out of the grounds."

"True."

"Besides," said Linnet slowly, "I don't think that Simon would agree to run away."

"What is his attitude in this?"

"He's furious—simply furious."

Poirot nodded thoughtfully.

Linnet said appealingly:

"You will—talk to her?"

"Yes, I will do that. But is is my opinion that I shall not be able to accomplish anything."

Linnet said violently:

"Jackie is extraordinary! One can't tell what she will do!"

"You spoke just now of certain threats she had made. Would you tell me what those threats were?"

Linnet shrugged her shoulders.

"She threatened to—well—kill us both. Jackie can be rather—Latin sometimes."

"I see." Poirot's tone was grave.

Linnet turned to him appealingly:

"You will act for me?"

"No, Madame." His tone was firm. "I will not accept a commission from you. I will do what I can in the interests of humanity. That, yes. There is here a situation that is full of difficulty and danger. I will do what I can to clear it up—but I am not very sanguine as to my chance of success."

Linnet Doyle said slowly:

"But you will not act for *me?*"

"No, Madame," said Hercule Poirot.

CHAPTER 4

Hercule Poirot found Jacqueline de Belleforte sitting on the rocks directly overlooking the Nile. He had felt fairly certain that she had not retired for the night and that he would find her somewhere about the grounds of the hotel.

She was sitting with her chin cupped in the palms of her hands, and she did not turn her head or look round at the sound of his approach.

"Mademoiselle de Bellefort?" said Poirot. "You permit that I speak to you for a little moment?"

Jacqueline turned her head slightly. A faint smile played round her lips.

"Certainly," she said. "You are M. Hercule Poirot, I think? Shall I make a guess? You are acting for Mrs. Doyle who has promised you a large fee if you succeed in your mission."

Poirot sat down on a bench near her.

"Your assumption is partially correct," he said, smiling. "I have just come from Mrs. Doyle. But I am not accepting any fee from her and strictly speaking I am not acting for her."

"Oh!"

Jacqueline studied him attentively.

"Then why have you come?" she asked abruptly.

Hercule Poirot's reply was in the form of another question.

"Have you ever seen me before, Mademoiselle?"

She shook her head.

"No, I do not think so."

"Yet I have seen you. I sat next to you once at *Chez Ma Tante*. You were there with Mr. Simon Doyle."

A strange masklike expression came over the girl's face. She said:

"I remember that evening . . ."

"Since then," said Poirot, "many things have occurred."

"As you say, many things have occurred."

Her voice was hard with an undertone of desperate bitterness.

"Mademoiselle, I speak as a friend. *Bury your dead!*"

She looked startled.

"What do you mean?"

"Give up the past! Turn to the future! What is done is done. Bitterness will not undo it."

"I'm sure that that would suit dear Linnet admirably."

Poirot made a gesture.

"I am not thinking of her at this moment! I am thinking of *you*. You have suffered—yes—but what you are doing now will only prolong that suffering."

She shook her head.

"You're wrong. There are times—when I almost enjoy myself."

"And that, Mademoiselle, is the worst of all."

She looked up swiftly.

"You're not stupid," she said. She added slowly, "I believe you mean to be kind."

"Go home, Mademoiselle. You are young, you have brains—the world is before you."

Jacqueline shook her head slowly.

"You don't understand—or you won't. Simon is my world."

"Love is not everything, Mademoiselle." Poirot said gently, "It is only when we are young that we think it is."

But the girl still shook her head.

"You don't understand." She shot him a quick look. "You know all about it, of course? You've talked to Linnet? And you were in the restaurant that night. . . . Simon and I loved each other."

"I know that you loved him."

She was quick to perceive the inflection of his words. She repeated with emphasis:

"*We loved each other*. And I loved Linnet . . . I trusted her. She was my best friend. All her life Linnet has been able to buy everything she wanted. She's never denied herself anything. When she saw Simon she wanted him—and she just took him."

"And he allowed himself to be—bought?"

Jacqueline shook her dark head slowly.

"No, it's not quite like that. If it were I shouldn't be here now. . . . You're suggesting that Simon isn't worth caring for . . . If he'd married Linnet for her money that would be true. But he didn't marry her for her money. It's more complicated than that. There's such a thing as *glamour*, M. Poirot. And money helps that. Linnet had an 'atmosphere,' you see. She was the queen of a kingdom—the young princess—luxurious to her fingertips. It was like a stage setting. She had the world at her feet. One of the richest and most sought after peers in England wanting to marry her. And she stoops instead to the obscure Simon Doyle. . . . Do you wonder it went to his head?" She made a sudden gesture. "Look at the moon up there. You see her very plainly, don't you? She's very real. *But if the sun were to shine you wouldn't be able to see her at all*. It was rather like that. I was the moon. . . . When the sun came out, Simon couldn't see me any more. . . . He was dazzled. He couldn't see anything but the sun—Linnet."

She paused and then went on:

"So you see it was—glamour. She went to his head. And then there's her complete assurance—her habit of command. She's so sure of herself that she makes other people sure. Simon was—weak, perhaps, but then he's a very simple person. He would have loved me and me only if Linnet hadn't come along and snatched him up in her golden chariot. And I know—I know perfectly—that he wouldn't have ever fallen in love with her if she hadn't made him."

"That is what you think—yes."

"I *know* it. He loved me—he will always love me."

Poirot said:

"Even now—?"

A quick answer seemed to rise to her lips, then be stifled. She looked at Poirot and a deep burning colour spread over her face. She looked away, her head dropped down. She said in a low stifled voice:

"Yes, I know. He hates me now. Yes, hates me. . . . He'd better be careful."

With a quick gesture she fumbled in a little silk bag that lay on the seat. Then she held out her hand. On the palm of it was a small pearl-handled pistol—a dainty toy it looked.

"Nice little thing, isn't it?" she said. "Looks too foolish to be real, but it is real! One of those bullets would kill a man or a woman. And I'm a good shot." She smiled a faraway reminiscent smile. "When I went home as a child with my mother to South Carolina, my grandfather taught me to shoot. He was the old-fashioned kind that believes in shooting—espeically where honour is concerned. My father, too, he fought several duels as a young man. He was a good swordsman. He killed a man once. That was over a woman. So you see, M. Poirot—" she met his eyes squarely, "I've hot blood in me! I bought this when it first happened. I meant to kill one or other of them—the trouble was I couldn't decide which. Both of them would have been unsatisfactory. If I'd thought Linnet would have looked afraid—but she's got plenty of physical courage. She can stand up to physical action. And then I thought I'd—wait! That appealed to me more and more. After all I could do it any time—it would be more fun to wait and—think about it! And then this idea came to my mind—to follow them! Whenever they arrived at some faraway spot and were together and happy—they should see—*me!* And it worked! It got Linnet badly—in a way nothing else could have done! It got right under her skin. . . . That was when I began to enjoy myself. . . . And there's nothing she can do about it! I'm always perfectly pleasant and polite! There's not a word they can take hold of! It's poisoning everything—everything—for them."

Her laugh rang out—clear and silvery.

Poirot grasped her arm.

"Be quiet. Quiet, I tell you."

Jacqueline looked at him.

"Well?" she said.

Her smile was definitely challenging.

"Mademoiselle, I beseech you, do not do what you are doing."

"Leave dear Linnet alone, you mean?"

"It is deeper than that. Do not open your heart to evil."

Her lips fell apart, a look of bewilderment came into her eyes.

Poirot went on gravely:

"Because—if you do—*evil will come*. . . . Yes, very surely evil will come. . . . It will enter in and make its home within you and after a while it will no longer be possible to drive it out."

Jacqueline stared at him. Her glance seemed to waver, to flicker uncertainly.

She said, "I—don't know—"

Then she cried out defiantly:

"You can't stop me."

"No," said Hercule Poirot. "I cannot stop you."

His voice was sad.

"Even if I were to—kill her, you couldn't stop me."

"No—not if you were willing—to pay the price."

Jacqueline de Bellefort laughed.

"Oh, I'm not afraid of death! What have I got to live for, after all? I suppose you believe it's very wrong to kill a person who has injured you—even if they've taken away everything you had in the world?"

Poirot said steadily:

"Yes, Mademoiselle. I believe it is the unforgivable offence—to kill."

Jacqueline laughed again.

"Then you ought to approve of my present scheme of revenge. Because you see, *as long as it works,* I shan't use that pistol. . . . But I'm afraid—yes, afraid sometimes—it all goes red—I want to hurt her—to stick a knife into her, to put my dear little pistol close against her head and then—just press with my finger—*Oh!*"

The exclamation startled him.

"What is it, Mademoiselle?"

She had turned her head and was staring into the shadows.

"Some one—standing over there. He's gone now."

Hercule Poirot looked round sharply.

The place seemed quite deserted.

"There seems no one here but outselves, Mademoiselle."

He got up.

"In any case I have said all I came to say. I wish you good-night."

Jacqueline got up too. She said almost pleadingly:

"You do understand—that I can't do what you ask me to do?"

Poirot shook his head.

"No—for *you could do it!* There is always a moment! Your friend Linnet—there was a moment too, in which she could have held her hand. . . . She let it pass by. And if one does that, then one is committed to the enterprise and there comes no second chance."

"No second chance . . ." said Jacqueline de Bellefort.

She stood brooding for a moment, then she lifted her head defiantly.

"Good-night, M. Poirot."

He shook his head sadly and followed her up the path to the hotel.

CHAPTER 5

On the following morning Simon Doyle joined Hercule Poirot as the latter was leaving the hotel to walk down to the town.

"Good-morning, M. Poirot."

"Good-morning, M. Doyle."

"You going to the town? Mind if I stroll along with you?"

"But certainly. I shall be delighted."

The two men walked side by side, passed out through the gateway and turned into the cool shade of the gardens. Then Simon removed his pipe from his mouth and said:

"I understand, M. Poirot, that my wife had a talk with you last night?"

"That is so."

Simon Doyle was frowning a little. He belonged to that type of men of action who find it difficult to put thoughts into words and who have trouble in expressing themselves clearly.

"I'm glad of one thing," he said. "You've made her realise that we're more or less powerless in the matter."

"There is clearly no legal redress," agreed Poirot.

"Exactly. Linnet didn't seem to understand that." He gave a faint smile. "Linnet's been brought up to believe that every annoyance can automatically be referred to the police."

"It would be pleasant if such were the case," said Poirot.

There was a pause. Then Simon said suddenly, his face going very red as he spoke:

"It's—it's infamous that she should be victimised like this! She's done nothing! If any one likes to say I behaved like a cad they're welcome to say so! I suppose I did. But I won't have the whole thing visited on Linnet. She had nothing whatever to do with it."

Poirot bowed his head gravely but said nothing.

"Did you—er—have you—talked to Jackie—Miss de Bellefort?"

"Yes, I have spoken with her."

"Did you get her to see sense?"

"I'm afraid not."

Simon broke out irritably.

"Can't she see what an ass she's making of herself? Doesn't she realise that no decent woman would behave as she is doing? Hasn't she got any pride or self-respect?"

Poirot shrugged his shoulders.

"She has only a sense of—injury, shall we say?" he replied.

"Yes, but damn it all, man, decent girls don't behave like this! I admit I was entirely to blame. I treated her damned badly and all that. I should quite understand her being thoroughly fed up with me and never wishing to see me again. But this following me round—it's—it's *indecent!* Making a show of herself! What the devil does she hope to get out of it?"

"Perhaps—revenge!"

"Idiotic! I'd really understand better if she'd tried to do something melodramatic—like taking a pot shot at me."

"You think that would be more like her—yes?"

"Frankly I do. She's hot-blooded—and she's got an ungovernable temper. I shouldn't be surprised at her doing anything while she was in a white-hot rage. But this spying business—" he shook his head.

"It is more subtle—yes! It is intelligent!"

Doyle stared at him.

"You don't understand. It's playing hell with Linnet's nerves."

"And yours?"

Simon looked at him with momentary surprise.

"Me? I'd like to wring the little devil's neck."

"There is nothing, then, of the old feeling left?"

"My dear M. Poirot—how can I put it? It's like the moon when the sun comes out. You don't know it's there any more. When once I'd met Linnet—Jackie didn't exist."

"*Tiens, c'est drôle ça!*" muttered Poirot.

"I beg your pardon."

"Your simile interested me, that is all."

Again flushing, Simon said, "I suppose Jackie told you that I'd only married Linnet for her money? Well, that's a damned lie! I wouldn't marry any woman for money! What Jackie doesn't understand is that it's difficult for a fellow when—when—a woman cares for him as she cared for me."

"Ah?"

Poirot looked up sharply.

Simon blundered on.

"It—it—sounds a caddish thing to say—but Jackie was *too* fond of me!"

"*Un qui aime et un qui se laisse aimer,*" murmured Poirot.

"Eh? What's that you say? You see a man doesn't want to feel that a woman cares more for him than he does for her." His voice grew warm as he went on. "He doesn't want to feel *owned,* body and soul. It's that damned *possessive* attitude! This man is *mine*—he *belongs* to me! That's the sort of thing I can't stick—no man could stick! He wants to get away—to get free. He wants to own his woman—he doesn't want *her* to own *him*."

He broke off, and with fingers that trembled slightly he lit a cigarette.

Poirot said:

"And it is like that that you felt with Mademoiselle Jacqueline?"

"Eh?" Simon stared and then admitted:

"Er—yes—well, yes, as a matter of fact I did. She doesn't realise that, of course. And it's not the sort of thing I could ever tell her. But I *was* feeling restless—and then I met Linnet—and she just swept me off my feet! I'd never seen anything so lovely. It was all so amazing. Every one kow-towing to her—and then her singling out a poor chump like me."

His tone held boyish awe and astonishment.

"I see," said Poirot. He nodded thoughtfully. "Yes—I see."

"Why can't Jackie take it like a man?" demanded Simon resentfully.

A very faint smile twitched Poirot's upper lip.

"Well, you see, M. Doyle, to begin with she is *not* a man."

"No, no—but I meant take it like a good sport! After all you've got to take your medicine when it comes to you. The fault's all mine, I admit. But there it is! If you no longer care for a girl it's simply madness to marry her. And now I see what

Jackie's really like and the lengths she is likely to go to, I feel I've had rather a lucky escape."

"The lengths she is likely to go to," Poirot repeated thoughtfully. "Have you an idea, M. Doyle, what those lengths are?"

Simon looked at him, rather startled.

"No—at least, what do you mean?"

"You know she carries a pistol about with her."

Simon frowned, then shook his head.

"I don't believe she'll use that—now. She might have done earlier on. But I believe it's got past that. She's just spiteful now—trying to take it out of us both."

Poirot shrugged his shoulders.

"It may be so," he said doubtfully.

"It's Linnet I'm worrying about," said Simon somewhat unnecessarily.

"I quite realise that," said Poirot.

"I'm not really afraid of Jackie doing any melodramatic shooting stuff, but this spying and following business has absolutely got Linnet on the raw. I'll tell you the plan I've made and perhaps you can suggest improvements on it. To begin with I've announced fairly openly that we're going to stay here ten days. But to-morrow—the steamer *Karnak* starts from Shellal to Wâdi Halfa. I propose to book passages on that under an assumed name. To-morrow we'll go an excursion to Philæ. Linnet's maid can take the luggage. We'll join the *Karnak* at Shellal. When Jackie finds we don't come back it will be too late—we shall be well on our way. She'll assume we have given her the slip and gone back to Cairo. In fact I might even bribe the porter to say so. Inquiry at the tourist offices won't help her, because our names won't appear. How does that strike you?"

"It is well imagined, yes. And suppose she waits here till you return?"

"We may not return. We could go on to Khartoum and then perhaps by air to Kenya. She can't follow us all over the globe."

"No, there must come a time when financial reasons forbid. She has very little money, I understand."

Simon looked at him with admiration.

"That's clever of you. Do you know, I hadn't thought of that. Jackie's as poor as they make them."

"And yet she has managed to follow you so far?"

Simon said doubtfully:

"She's got a small income, of course. Something under two hundred a year, I imagine. I suppose—yes, I suppose she must have sold out the capital to do what she's doing."

"So that the time will come when she has exhausted her resources and is quite penniless?"

"Yes . . ."

Simon wriggled uneasily. The thought seemed to make him uncomfortable. Poirot watched him attentively.

"No," he remarked. "No, it is not a pretty thought. . . ."

Simon said rather angrily:

"Well, *I* can't help it!" Then he added, "What do you think of my plan?"

"I think it may work, yes. But it is, of course, a *retreat*."

"Simon flushed.

"You mean, we're running away? Yes, that's true. . . . But Linnet—"

Poirot watched him, then gave a short nod.

"As you say, it may be the best way. But remember, Mademoiselle de Bellefort has brains."

Simon said sombrely:

"Some day, I feel, we've got to make a stand and fight it out. Her attitude isn't reasonable."

"Reasonable, *mon Dieu!*" cried Poirot.

"There's no reason why women shouldn't behave like rational beings," said Simon stolidly.

Poirot said dryly:

"Quite frequently they do. That is even more upsetting!" He added, "I too, shall be on the *Karnak*. It is part of my itinerary."

"Oh!" Simon hesitated, then said, choosing his words with some embarrassment. "That isn't—isn't—er—on our account in any way? I mean I wouldn't like to think—"

Poirot disabused him quickly.

"Not at all. It was all arranged before I left London. I always make my plans well in advance."

"You don't just move on from place to place as the fancy takes you? Isn't the latter really pleasanter?"

"Perhaps. But to succeed in life every detail should be arranged well beforehand."

Simon laughed and said:

"That is how the more skilful murderer behaves, I suppose."

"Yes—though I must admit that the most brilliant crime I remember and one of the most difficult to solve was committed on the spur of the moment."

Simon said boyishly:

"You must tell us something about your cases on board the *Karnak*."

"No, no, that would be to talk—what do you call it—the shop."

"Yes, but your kind of shop is rather thrilling. Mrs. Allerton thinks so. She's longing to get a chance to cross-question you."

"Mrs. Allerton? That is the charming grey-haired woman who has such a devoted son?"

"Yes. She'll be on the *Karnak*, too."

"Does she know that you—?"

"Certainly not," said Simon with emphasis. "Nobody knows. I've gone on the principle that it's better not to trust anybody."

"An admirable sentiment—and one which I always adopt. By the way, the third member of your party, the tall grey-haired man—"

"Pennington?"

"Yes. He is travelling with you?"

Simon said grimly:

"Not very usual on a honeymoon, you were thinking? Pennington is Linnet's American trustee. We ran across him by chance in Cairo."

"*Ah vraiment!* You permit a question? She is of age, Madame your wife?"

Simon looked amused.

"She isn't actually twenty-one yet—but she hadn't got to ask any one's consent before marrying me. It was the greatest surprise to Pennington. He left New York on the *Carmanic* two days before Linnet's letter got there telling him of our marriage. So he knew nothing about it."

"The *Carmanic*—" murmured Poirot.

"It was the greatest surprise to him when we ran into him at Shepheard's in Cairo."

"That was indeed the coincidence!"

"Yes, and we found that he was coming on this Nile trip—so naturally we foregathered—couldn't have done anything else decently. Besides that, it's been—well, a relief in some ways." He looked embarrassed again. "You see Linnet's been all strung up—expecting Jackie to turn up anywhere and everywhere. While we were alone together the subject kept coming up. Andrew Pennington's a help that way—we have to talk of outside matters."

"Your wife has not confided in Mr. Pennington?"

"No." Simon's jaw looked aggressive. "It's nothing to do with any one else. Besides, when we started on this Nile trip we thought we'd seen the end of the business."

Poirot shook his head.

"You have not seen the end of it yet. No—the end is not yet at hand. I am very sure of that."

"I must say, M. Poirot, you're not very encouraging."

Poirot looked at him with a slight feeling of irritation. He thought to himself:

"The Anglo Saxon, he takes nothing seriously but playing games! He does not grow up."

Linnet Doyle—Jacqueline de Bellefort—both of them took the business seriously enough. But in Simon's attitude he could find nothing but male impatience and annoyance.

He said:

"You will permit me an impertinent question? Was it *your* idea to come to Egypt for your honeymoon?"

Simon flushed.

"No, of course not. As a matter of fact I'd rather have gone anywhere else. But Linnet was absolutely set upon it. And so—and so—"

He stopped rather lamely.

"Naturally," said Poirot gravely.

He appreciated the fact that if Linnet Doyle was set upon anything, that thing had to happen.

He thought to himself:

"I have now heard three separate accounts of the affair. Linnet Doyle's—Jacqueline de Bellefort's—Simon Doyle's. Which of them is nearest to the truth?"

CHAPTER 6

Simon and Linnet Doyle set off on their expedition to Philæ about eleven o'clock the following morning. Jacqueline de Bellefort, sitting on the hotel balcony, watched them set off in the picturesque sailing boat. What she did not see was the departure of a car laden with luggage and in which sat a demure-looking maid from the front door of the hotel and which turned to the right in the direction of Shellal.

Hercule Poirot decided to pass the remaining two hours before lunch on the island of Elephantine immediately opposite the hotel.

He went down to the landing stage. There were two men just stepping into one of the hotel boats and Poirot joined them. The men were obviously strangers to each other. The younger of them had arrived by train the day before. He was a tall dark-haired young man with a thin face and a pugnacious chin. He was wearing an extremely dirty pair of grey flannel trousers and a high-necked polo jumper singularly unsuited to the climate. The other was a slightly podgy middle-aged man who lost no time in entering into conversation with Poirot in idiomatic but slightly broken English. Far from taking part in the conversation, the younger man merely scowled at them both and then deliberately turned his back on them and proceeded to admire the agility with which the Nubian boatman steered the boat with his toes as he manipulated the sail with his hands.

It was very peaceful on the water, the great smooth slippery black rocks gliding by and the soft breeze fanning their faces. Elephantine was reached very quickly and on going ashore Poirot and his loquacious acquaintance made straight for the museum. By this time the latter had produced a card which he handed to Poirot with a little bow. It bore the inscription:

Signor Guido Richetti, Archeologo.

Not to be outdone, Poirot returned the bow and extracted his own card. These formalities completed, the two men stepped into the museum together, the Italian pouring forth a stream of erudite information. They were by now conversing in French.

The young man in the flannel trousers strolled listlessly round the museum yawning from time to time and then escaped to the outer air.

Poirot and Signor Richetti at last followed him. The Italian was energetic in examining the ruins, but presently Poirot, espying a green-lined sunshade which he recognised on the rocks down by the river, escaped in that direction.

Mrs. Allerton was sitting on a large rock, a sketchbook by her side and a book on her lap.

Poirot removed his hat politely and Mrs. Allerton at once entered into conversation.

"Good-morning," she said. "I suppose it would be quite impossible to get rid of some of these awful children."

A group of small black figures surrounded her, all grinning and posturing and holding out imploring hands as they lisped "Bakshish" at intervals hopefully.

"I thought they'd get tired of me," said Mrs. Allerton sadly. "They've been watching me for over two hours now—and they close in on me little by little, and then I yell 'Imshi' and brandish my sunshade at them and they scatter for a minute or two, and then they come back and stare and stare and their eyes are simply disgusting and so are their noses, and I don't believe I really like children, not unless they're more or less washed and have the rudiments of manners."

She laughed ruefully.

Poirot gallantly attempted to disperse the mob for her but without avail. They scattered and then reappeared, closing in once more.

"If there were only any peace in Egypt I should like it better," said Mrs. Allerton. "But you can never be alone anywhere—some one is always pestering you for money, or offering you donkeys, or beads, or expeditions to native villages, or duck shooting."

"It is the great disadvantage, that is true," agreed Poirot.

He spread his handkerchief cautiously on the rock and sat somewhat gingerly upon it.

"Your son is not with you this morning?" he went on.

"No, Tim had some letters to get off before we leave. We're doing the trip to the Second Cataract, you know."

"I, too."

"I'm so glad. I want to tell you that I'm quite thrilled to meet you. When we were in Majorca, there was a Mrs. Leech there and she was telling us the most wonderful things about you. She'd lost a ruby ring bathing and she was just lamenting that you weren't there to find it for her."

"Ah, *parbleu*, but I am not the diving seal!"

They both laughed.

Mrs. Allerton went on:

"I saw you from my window walking down the drive with Simon Doyle this morning. Do tell me what you make of him? We're all so excited about him."

"Ah? Truly?"

"Yes. You know his marriage to Linnet Ridgeway was the greatest surprise. She was supposed to be going to marry Lord Windlesham and then suddenly she gets engaged to this man no one had ever heard of!"

"You know her well, Madame?"

"No, but a cousin of mine, Joanna Southwood, is one of her best friends."

"Ah, yes, I have read that name in the papers." He was silent a moment and then went on, "She is a young lady very much in the news, Mademoiselle Joanna Southwood."

"Oh, she knows how to advertise herself all right," snapped Mrs. Allerton.

"You do not like her, Madame?"

"That was a nasty remark of mine." Mrs. Allerton looked penitent. "You see, I'm old-fashioned. I don't like her much. Tim and she are the greatest friends, though."

"I see," said Poirot.

His companion shot a quick look at him. She changed the subject.

"How very few young people there are out here! That pretty girl with the chestnut hair and the appalling mother in the turban is almost the only young creature in the place. You have talked to her a good deal, I notice. She interests me, that child."

"Why is that, Madame?"

"I feel sorry for her. You can suffer so much when you are young and sensitive. I think she is suffering."

"Yes, she is not happy, poor little one."

"Tim and I call her the 'sulky girl.' I've tried to talk to her once or twice, but she's snubbed me on each occasion. However, I believe she's going on this Nile trip too, and I expect we'll have to be more or less all matey together, shan't we?"

"It is a possible contingency, Madame."

"I'm very matey really—people interest me enormously. All the different types." She paused, then said, "Tim tells me that that dark girl—her name is de Bellefort—is the girl who was engaged to Simon Doyle. It's rather awkward for them—meeting like this."

"It is awkward—yes," agreed Poirot.

Mrs. Allerton shot a quick glance at him.

"You know, it may sound foolish, but she almost frightened me. She looked so—intense."

Poirot nodded his head slowly.

"You were not far wrong, Madame. A great force of emotion is always frightening."

"Do people interest you too, M. Poirot? Or do you reserve your interest for potential criminals."

"Madame—that category would not leave many people outside it."

Mrs. Allerton looked a trifle startled.

"Do you really mean that?"

"Given the particular incentive—that is to say," Poirot added.

"Which would differ?"

"Naturally."

Mrs. Allerton hesitated—a little smile on her lips.

"Even I, perhaps?"

"Mothers, Madame, are particularly ruthless when their children are in danger."

She said gravely:

"I think that's true—yes, you're quite right."

She was silent a minute or two, then she said smiling:

"I'm trying to imagine motives for crime suitable for every one in the hotel. It's quite entertaining. Simon Doyle for instance?"

Poirot said smiling:

"A very simple crime—a direct short-cut to his objective. No subtlety about it."

"And therefore very easily detected?"

"Yes—he would not be ingenious."

"And Linnet?"

"That would be like the queen in your *Alice in Wonderland*, 'Off with her head.'"

"Of course. The divine right of monarchy! Just a little bit of the Naboth's vineyard touch. And the dangerous girl—Jacqueline de Bellefort—could *she* do a murder?"

Poirot hesitated for a minute or two, then he said doubtfully:

"Yes, I think she could."

"But you're not sure?"

"No. She puzzles me, that little one."

"I don't think Mr. Pennington could do one, do you? He looks so desiccated and dyspeptic—with no red blood in him."

"But possibly a strong sense of self-preservation."

"Yes, I suppose so. And poor Mrs. Otterbourne in her turban?"

"There is always vanity."

"As a motive for murder?" Mrs. Allerton asked doubtfully.

"Motives for murder are sometimes very trivial, Madam."

"What are the most usual motives, M. Poirot?"

"Most frequent—money. That is to say gain in its various ramifications. Then there is revenge, and love, and fear—and pure hate, and beneficence—"

"M. Poirot!"

"Oh, yes, Madame. I have known of—shall we say A?—being removed by B solely in order to benefit C. Political murders often come under that heading. Some one is considered to be harmful to civilisation and is removed on that account. Such people forget that life and death are the affair of the good God."

He spoke gravely.

Mrs. Allerton said quietly:

"I am glad to hear you say that. All the same, God chooses his instruments."

"There is danger in thinking like that, Madame."

She adopted a lighter tone:

"After this conversation, M. Poirot, I shall wonder that there is any one left alive!"

She got up.

"We must be getting back. We have to start immediately after lunch."

When they reached the landing stage they found the young man in the polo jumper just taking his place in the boat. The Italian was already waiting. As the Nubian boatman cast the sail loose and they started Poirot addressed a polite remark to the stranger:

"There are very wonderful things to be seen in Egypt, are there not?"

The young man was now smoking a somewhat noisome pipe. He removed it from his mouth and remarked briefly and emphatically in astonishingly well-bred accents:

"They make me sick."

Mrs. Allerton put on her pince-nez and surveyed him with pleasurable interest. Poirot said:

"Indeed? And why is that?"

"Take the Pyramids. Great blocks of useless masonry. Put up to minister to the egoism of a despotic bloated king. Think of the sweated masses who toiled to build them and died doing it. It makes me sick to think of the suffering and torture they represent."

Mrs. Allerton said cheerfully:

"You'd rather have no Pyramids, no Parthenon, no beautiful tombs or temples—just the solid satisfaction of knowing that people got three meals a day and died in their beds."

The young man directed his scowl in her direction.

"I think human beings matter more than stones."

"But they do not endure as well," remarked Hercule Poirot.

"I'd rather see a well-fed worker than any so-called work of art. What matters is the future—not the past."

This was too much for Signor Richetti who burst into a torrent of impassioned speech not too easy to follow.

The young man retorted by telling everybody exactly what he thought of the capitalist system. He spoke with the utmost venom.

When the tirade was over they had arrived at the hotel landing stage.

Mrs. Allerton murmured cheerfully, "Well, well," and stepped ashore. The young man directed a baleful glance after her.

In the hall of the hotel Poirot encountered Jacqueline de Bellefort. She was dressed in riding clothes. She gave him an ironical little bow.

"I'm going donkey riding. Do you recommend the native villages, M. Poirot?"

"Is that your excursion to-day, Mademoiselle? *Eh bien,* they are picturesque—but do not spend large sums on native curios."

"Which are shipped here from Europe? No, I am not so easy to deceive as that."

With a little nod she passed out into the brilliant sunshine.

Poirot completed his packing—a very simple affair since his possessions were always in the most meticulous order. Then he repaired to the dining-room and ate an early lunch.

After lunch the hotel bus took the passengers for the Second Cataract to the station where they were to catch the daily express from Cairo on to Shellal—a ten minutes' run.

The Allertons, Poirot, the young man in the dirty flannel trousers and the Italian were the passengers. Mrs. Otterbourne and her daughter had made the expedition to the dam and to Philæ and would join the steamer at Shellal.

The train from Cairo and Luxor was about twenty minutes late. However, it arrived at last, and the usual scenes of wild activity occurred. Native porters taking suitcases out of the train collided with other porters putting them in.

Finally, somewhat breathless, Poirot found himself with an assortment of his own, the Allertons' and some totally unknown luggage in one compartment while Tim and his mother were elsewhere with the remains of the assorted baggage.

The compartment in which Poirot found himself was occupied by an elderly lady with a very wrinkled face, a stiff white stock, a good many diamonds and an expression of reptilian contempt for the majority of mankind.

She treated Poirot to an aristocratic glare and retired behind the pages of an American magazine. A big, rather clumsy young woman of under thirty was sitting opposite her. She had eager brown eyes rather like a dog's, untidy hair, and a terrific air of willingness to please. At intervals the old lady looked over the top of her magazine and snapped an order at her.

"Cornelia, collect the rugs. When we arrive look after my dressing-case. On no account let any one else handle it. Don't forget my paper-cutter."

The train run was brief. In ten minutes' time they came to rest on the jetty where the *S.S. Karnak* was awaiting them. The Otterbournes were already on board.

The *Karnak* was a smaller steamer than the *Papyrus* and the *Lotus*, the First Cataract steamers which are too large to pass through the locks of the Assuan dam. The passengers went on board and were shown their accommodation. Since the boat was not full most of the passengers had cabins on the promenade deck. The entire forward part of this deck was occupied by an observation saloon all glass enclosed where the passengers could sit and watch the river unfold before them. On the deck below was a smoking-room and small drawing-room and on the deck below that, the dining-saloon.

Having seen his possessions disposed in his cabin, Poirot came out on the deck again to watch the process of departure. He joined Rosalie Otterbourne who was leaning over the side.

"So now we journey into Nubia. You are pleased, Mademoiselle?"

The girl drew a deep breath.

"Yes. I feel that one's really getting away from things at last."

She made a gesture with her hand. There was a savage aspect about the sheet of water in front of them, the masses of rock without vegetation that came down to the water's edge—here and there a trace of houses abandoned and ruined as a result of the damming up of the waters. The whole scene had a melancholy, almost sinister charm.

"Away from *people*," said Rosalie Otterbourne.

"Except those of our own number, Mademoiselle?"

She shrugged her shoulders. Then she said:

"There's something about this country that makes me feel—wicked. It brings to the surface all the things that are boiling inside one. Everything's so unfair—so unjust."

"I wonder. You cannot judge by material evidence."

Rosalie muttered:

"Look at—at some people's mothers—and look at mine. There is no God but Sex and Salome Otterbourne is its Prophet." She stopped. "I shouldn't have said that, I suppose."

Poirot made a gesture with his hands.

"Why not say it—to me? I am one of those who hear many things. If, as you say, you boil inside—like the jam—*Eh bien*, let the scum come to the surface—and then one can take it off with a spoon, so."

He made the gesture of dropping something into the Nile.

"There, it has gone."

Rosalie said:

"What an extraordinary man you are!" Her sulky mouth twisted into a smile. Then she suddenly stiffened as she exclaimed. "Why, here are Mrs. Doyle and her husband! I had no idea *they* were coming on this trip!"

Linnet had just emerged from a cabin half-way along the deck. Simon was behind her. Poirot was almost startled by the look of her—so radiant, so assured. She looked positively arrogant with happiness. Simon Doyle, too, was a transformed being. He was grinning from ear to ear and looking like a happy schoolboy.

"This is grand," he said as he too leaned on the rail. "I'm really looking forward to this trip, aren't you, Linnet? It feels somehow, so much less touristy—as though we were really going into the heart of Egypt."

His wife responded quickly.

"I know. It's so much—wilder, somehow."

Her hand slipped through his arm. He pressed it close to his side.

"We're off, Lin," he murmured.

The steamer was drawing away from the jetty. They had started on their seven days' journey to the Second Cataract and back.

Behind them a light silvery laugh rang out. Linnet whipped round.

Jacqueline de Bellefort was standing there. She seemed amused.

"Hallo, Linnet! I didn't expect to find you here. I thought you said you were staying at Assuan another ten days. This is a surprise!"

"You—you didn't—" Linnet's tongue stammered. She forced a ghastly conventional smile. "I didn't expect to see you either."

"No?"

Jacqueline moved away to the other side of the boat. Linnet's grasp on her husband's arm tightened.

"Simon—Simon—"

All Doyle's good-natured pleasure had gone. He looked furious. His hands clenched themselves in spite of his effort at self-control.

The two of them moved a little away. Without turning his head Poirot caught scraps of disjointed words.

". . . turn back . . . impossible . . . we could . . ." and then slightly louder, Doyle's voice, despairing but grim:

"We can't run away forever, Lin. *We've got to go through with it now* . . ."

It was some hours later. Daylight was just fading. Poirot stood in the glass-enclosed saloon looking straight ahead. The *Karnak* was going through a narrow gorge. The rocks came down with a kind of sheer ferocity to the river flowing deep and swift between them. They were in Nubia now.

He heard a movement and Linnet Doyle stood by his side.

Her fingers twisted and untwisted themselves, she looked as he had never yet seen her look. There was about her the air of a bewildered child. She said:

"M. Poirot, I'm afraid—I'm afraid of everything. I've never felt like this before. All these wild rocks and the awful grimness and starkness. Where are we going? What's going to happen? I'm afraid, I tell you. Every one hates me. I've never felt like that before. I've always been nice to people—I've done things for them—and they hate me—lots of people hate me—except for Simon I'm surrounded by enemies. . . . It's terrible to feel—that there are people who hate you . . ."

"But what is all this, Madame?"

She shook her head.

"I suppose—it's nerves . . . I just feel that—everything's unsafe all around me."

She cast a quick nervous glance over her shoulder. Then she said abruptly:

"How will all this end? We're caught here. Trapped. There's no way out. We've got to go on. I—I don't know where I am."

She slipped down on to a seat. Poirot looked down on her gravely; his glance was not untinged with compassion.

She said:

"How did she know we were coming on this boat? How could she have known?"

Poirot shook his head as he answered.

"She has brains, you know."

"I feel as though I shall never escape from her."

Poirot said:

"There is one plan you might have adopted. In fact I am surprised that it did not occur to you. After all, with you, Madame, money is no object. Why did you not engage your own private dahabiyah?"

Linnet shook her head rather helplessly.

"If we'd known about all this—but you see we didn't—then. And it was difficult . . ." She flashed out with sudden impatience. "Oh! you don't understand half my difficulties. I've got to be careful with Simon. . . . He's—he's absurdly sensitive—about money. About my having so much! He wanted me to go to some little place in Spain with him—he—wanted to pay all our honeymoon expenses himself. As if it *mattered!* Men are stupid! He's got to get used to—to—living comfortably. The mere idea of a dahabiyah upset him—the—the needless expense. I've got to educate him—gradually."

She looked up, bit her lip vexedly, as though feeling that she had been led into discussing her difficulties rather too unguardedly.

She got up.

"I must change. I'm sorry, M. Poirot, I'm afraid I've been talking a lot of foolish nonsense."

CHAPTER 7

Mrs. Allerton, looking quiet and distinguished in her simple black lace evening gown, descended two decks to the dining-room. At the door of it her son caught her up.

"Sorry, darling. I thought I was going to be late."

"I wonder where we sit." The saloon was dotted with little tables. Mrs. Allerton paused till the steward, who was busy seating a party of people, could attend to them.

"By the way," she added. "I asked little Hercule Poirot to sit at our table."

"Mother, you didn't!" Tim sounded really taken aback and annoyed.

His mother stared at him in surprise. Tim was usually so easy going.

"My dear, do you mind?"

"Yes, I do. He's an unmitigated little bounder!"

"Oh, no, Tim! I don't agree with you."

"Anyway, what do we want to get mixed up with an outsider for? Cooped up like this on a small boat that sort of thing is always a bore. He'll be with us morning, noon and night."

"I'm sorry, dear." Mrs. Allerton looked distressed. "I thought really it would amuse you. After all, he must have had a varied experience. And you love detective stories."

Tim grunted:

"I wish you wouldn't have these bright ideas, Mother. We can't get out of it now, I suppose?"

"Really, Tim, I don't see how we can."

"Oh, well, we shall have to put up with it, I suppose."

The steward came to them at this minute and led them to a table. Mrs. Allerton's face wore rather a puzzled expression as she followed him. Tim was usually so easy going and good-tempered. This outburst was quite unlike him. It wasn't as though he had the ordinary Britisher's dislike, and mistrust of, foreigners. Tim was very cosmopolitan. Oh, well—she sighed. Men were incomprehensible! Even one's nearest and dearest had unsuspected reactions and feelings.

As they took their places, Hercule Poirot came quickly and silently into the dining-saloon. He paused with his hand on the back of the third chair.

"You really permit, Madame, that I avail myself of your kind suggestion?"

"Of course. Sit down, M. Poirot."

"You are most amiable."

She was uneasily conscious that as he seated himself he shot a swift glance at Tim and that Tim had not quite succeeded in masking a somewhat sullen expression.

Mrs. Allerton set herself to produce a pleasant atmosphere. As they drank their soup, she picked up the passenger list which had been placed beside her plate.

"Let's try and identify everybody," she said cheerfully. "I always think that's rather fun."

She began reading.

"Mrs. Allerton, Mr. T. Allerton. That's easy enough! Miss de Bellefort. They've put her at the same table as the Otterbournes, I see. I wonder what she and Rosalie will make of each other. Who comes next? Dr. Bessner. Dr. Bessner? Who can identify Dr. Bessner?"

She bent her glance on a table at which four men sat together.

"I think he must be the fat one with the closely-shaved head and the moustache. A German, I should imagine. He seems to be enjoying his soup very much."

Certain succulent noises floated across to them.

Mrs. Allerton continued:

"Miss Bowers? Can we make a guess at Miss Bowers? There are three or four women—no, we'll leave her for the present. Mr. and Mrs. Doyle. Yes, indeed, the lions of this trip. She really is very beautiful and what a perfectly lovely frock she is wearing."

Tim turned round in his chair. Linnet and her husband and Andrew Pennington had been given a table in the corner. Linnet was wearing a white dress and pearls.

"It looks frightfully simple to me," said Tim. "Just a length of stuff with a kind of cord round the middle."

"Yes, darling," said his mother. "A very nice manly description of an eighty-guinea model."

Tim said: "I can't think why women pay so much for their clothes. It seems absurd to me."

Mrs. Allerton proceeded with her study of her fellow-passengers.

"Mr. Fanthorp must be the intensely quiet young man who never speaks at the same table as the German. Rather a nice face, cautious but intelligent."

Poirot agreed:

"He is intelligent—yes. He does not talk, but he listens very attentively and he also watches. Yes, he makes good use of his eyes. Not quite the type you would expect to find travelling for pleasure in this part of the world. I wonder what he is doing here."

"Mr. Ferguson," read Mrs. Allerton. "I feel that Ferguson must be our anti-capitalist friend. Mrs. Otterbourne, Miss Otterbourne. We know all about them. Mr. Pennington? Alias Uncle Andrew. He's a good-looking man, I think—"

"Now, Mother," said Tim.

"I think he's very good-looking in a dry sort of way," said Mrs. Allerton. "Rather a ruthless jaw. Probably the kind of man one reads about in the paper who operates on Wall Street—or is it *in* Wall Street? I'm sure he must be extremely rich. Next—M. Hercule Poirot—whose talents are really being wasted. Can't you get up a crime for M. Poirot, Tim?"

But her well-meant banter only seemed to annoy her son anew.

He scowled and Mrs. Allerton hurried on. "Mr. Richetti. Our Italian archæological friend. Then Miss Robson and last of all Miss Van Schuyler. The last's easy. The very ugly old American lady who obviously feels herself the queen of the boat and who is clearly going to be very exclusive and speak to nobody who doesn't come up to the most exacting standards! She's rather marvellous, isn't she, really? A kind of period piece. The two women with her must be Miss Bowers and Miss Robson—perhaps a secretary—the thin one with pince-nez—and a poor relation—the rather pathetic young woman who is obviously enjoying herself in spite of being treated like a black slave. I think Robson's the secretary woman and Bowers is the poor relation."

"Wrong, Mother," said Tim grinning. He had suddenly recovered his good humour.

"How do you know?"

"Because I was in the lounge before dinner and the old bean said to the companion woman, 'Where's Miss Bowers? Fetch her at once, Cornelia,' and away trotted Cornelia like an obedient dog."

"I shall have to talk to Miss Van Schuyler," mused Mrs. Allerton.

Tim grinned again.

"She'll snub you, Mother."

"Not at all. I shall pave the way by sitting near her and conversing in low (but penetrating) well-bred tones about any titled relations and friends I can remember. I think a casual mention of your second cousin once removed the Duke of Glasgow would probably do the trick."

"How unscrupulous you are, Mother."

Events after dinner were not without their amusing side to a student of human nature.

The socialist young man (who turned out to be Mr. Ferguson as deduced) retired to the smoking-room, scorning the assemblage of passengers in the observation saloon on the top deck.

Miss Van Schuyler duly secured the best and most undraughty position there by advancing firmly on a table at which Mrs. Otterbourne was sitting and saying:

"You'll excuse me, I am sure, but I *think* my knitting was left here!"

Fixed by a hypnotic eye the turban rose and gave ground. Miss Van Schuyler established herself and her suite. Mrs. Otterbourne sat down near by and hazarded various remarks which were met with such chilling politeness that she soon gave up. Miss Van Schuyler then sat in glorious isolation. The Doyles sat with the Allertons. Dr. Bessner retained the quiet Mr. Fanthorp as a companion. Jacqueline de Bellefort sat by herself with a book. Rosalie Otterbourne was restless. Mrs. Allerton spoke to her once or twice and tried to draw her into their group but the girl responded ungraciously.

M. Hercule Poirot spent his evening listening to an account of Mrs. Otterbourne's mission as a writer.

On his way to his cabin that night he encountered Jacqueline de Bellefort. She was leaning over the rail and as she turned her head he was struck by the look of acute misery on her face. There was now no insouciance, no malicious defiance, no dark flaming triumph.

"Good-night, Mademoiselle."

"Good-night, M. Poirot." She hesitated, then said, "You were surprised to find me here?"

"I was not so much surprised as sorry—very sorry . . ." He spoke gravely.

"You mean sorry—for *me?*"

"That is what I meant. You have chosen, Mademoiselle, the dangerous course. . . . As we here in this boat have embarked on a journey so you too have embarked on your own private journey—a journey on a swift-moving river, between dangerous rocks and heading for who knows what currents of disaster . . ."

"Why do you say all this?"

"Because it is true. . . . You have cut the bonds that moored you to safety. I doubt now if you could turn back if you would."

She said very slowly:

"That *is* true . . ."

Then she flung her head back.

"Ah, well—one must follow one's star—wherever it leads."

"Beware, Mademoiselle, that it is not a false star . . ."

She laughed and mimicked the parrot cry of the donkey boys:

"That very bad star, sir! That star fall down . . ."

He was just dropping off to sleep when the murmur of voices awoke him.

It was Simon Doyle's voice he heard, repeating the same words he had used when the steamer left Shellal.

"We've got to go through with it now . . ."

"Yes," thought Hercule Poirot to himself, "we have got to go through with it now . . ."

He was not happy.

CHAPTER 8

The steamer arrived early next morning at Es-Sabûa. Cornelia Robson, her face beaming, a large flapping hat on her head, was one of the first to hurry on shore. Cornelia was not good at snubbing people. She was of an amiable disposition and disposed to like all her fellow creatures. The sight of Hercule Poirot in a white suit, pink shirt, large black bow tie and a white topee did not make her wince as the aristocratic Miss Van Schuyler would assuredly have winced.

As they walked together up an avenue of sphinxes she responded readily to his conventional opening.

"Your companions are not coming ashore to view the temple?"

"Well, you see, Cousin Marie—that's Miss Van Schuyler—never gets up very early. She has to be very, very careful of her health. And, of course, she wanted Miss Bowers, that's her hospital nurse, to do things for her. And she said too that this isn't one of the best temples—but she was frightfully kind and said it would be quite all right for me to come."

"That was very gracious of her," said Poirot dryly.

The ingenuous Cornelia agreed unsuspectingly.

"Oh, she's very kind. It's simply wonderful of her to bring me on this trip. I do feel I'm a lucky girl. I just could hardly believe it when she suggested to Mother that I should come too."

"And you have enjoyed it—yes?"

"Oh, it's been wonderful. I've seen Italy—Venice and Padua and Pisa—and then Cairo—only Cousin Marie wasn't very well in Cairo so I couldn't get around much, and now this wonderful trip up to Wâdi Halfa and back."

Poirot said, smiling:

"You have the happy nature, Mademoiselle."

He looked thoughtfully from her to the silent frowning Rosalie who was walking ahead by herself.

"She's very nice looking, isn't she?" said Cornelia, following his glance. "Only kind of scornful looking. She's very English, of course. She's not as lovely as Mrs. Doyle. I think Mrs. Doyle's the loveliest, the most elegant woman I've ever seen! And her husband just worships the ground she walks on, doesn't he? I think that grey-haired lady is kind of distinguished looking, don't you? She's cousin to a duke, I believe. She was talking about him right near us last night. But she isn't actually titled herself, is she?"

She prattled on until the dragoman in charge called a halt and began to intone.

"This temple was dedicated to Egyptian God Amun and the Sun God Ré-Harakhte—whose symbol was hawk's head . . ."

It droned on. Dr. Bessner, Bædeker in hand, mumbled to himself in German. He preferred the written word.

Tim Allerton had not joined the party. His mother was breaking the ice with the reserved Mr. Fanthorp. Andrew Pennington, his arm through Linnet Doyle's, was listening attentively, seemingly most interested in the measurements as recited by the guide.

"Sixty-five feet high, is that so? Looks a little less to me. Great fellow, this Rameses. An Egyptian live wire."

"A big business man, Uncle Andrew."

Andrew Pennington looked at her appreciatively.

"You look fine this morning, Linnet. I've been a mite worried about you lately. You've looked kind of peaky."

Chatting together, the party returned to the boat. Once more the *Karnak* glided up the river. The scenery was less stern now. There were palms, cultivation.

It was as though the change in the scenery had relieved some secret oppression that had brooded over the passengers. Tim Allerton had got over his fit of moodiness, Rosalie looked less sulky. Linnet seemed almost light-hearted. Pennington said to her:

"It's tactless to talk business to a bride on her honeymoon, but there are just one or two things—"

"Why, of course, Uncle Andrew." Linnet at once became businesslike. "My marriage has made a difference of course."

"That's just it. Some time or other I want your signature to several documents."

"Why not now?"

Andrew Pennington glanced round. Their corner of the observation saloon was quite untenanted. Most of the people were outside on the deck space between the observation saloon and the cabins. The only occupants of the saloon were Mr. Ferguson who was drinking beer at a small table in the middle, his legs encased in their dirty flannel trousers stuck out in front of him, whilst he whistled to himself in the intervals of drinking, M. Hercule Poirot who was sitting close up to the front glass intent on the panorama unfolding before him, and Miss Van Schuyler who was sitting in a corner reading a book on Egypt.

"That's fine," said Andrew Pennington.

He left the saloon.

Linnet and Simon smiled at each other—a slow smile that took a few minutes to come to full fruition.

He said:

"All right, sweet?"

"Yes, still all right. . . . Funny how I'm not rattled any more."

Simon said with a deep conviction in his tone:

"You're marvellous."

Pennington came back. He brought with him a sheaf of closely-written documents.

"Mercy!" cried Linnet. "Have I got to sign all these?"

Andrew Pennington was apologetic.

"It's tough on you, I know. But I'd just like to get your affairs put in proper shape. First of all there's the lease of the Fifth Avenue property . . . then there are the Western Lands Concessions. . . ."

He talked on, rustling and sorting the papers. Simon yawned.

The door to the deck swung open and Mr. Fanthorp came in. He gazed aimlessly round, then strolled forward and stood by Poirot looking out at the pale blue water and the yellow enveloping sands. . . .

"—you sign just there," concluded Pennington, spreading a paper before Linnet and indicating a space.

Linnet picked up the document and glanced through it. She turned back once to the first page, then taking up the fountain-pen Pennington had laid beside her she signed her name, *Linnet Doyle*. . . .

Pennington took away the paper and spread out another.

Fanthorp wandered over in their direction. He peered out through the side window at something that seemed to interest him on the bank they were passing.

"That's just the transfer," said Pennington. "You needn't read it."

But Linnet took a brief glance through it. Pennington laid down a third paper. Again Linnet perused it carefully.

"They're all quite straightforward," said Andrew. "Nothing of interest. Only legal phraseology."

Simon yawned again.

"My dear girl, you're not going to read the whole lot through, are you? You'll be at it till lunch time and longer."

"I always read everything through," said Linnet. "Father taught me to do that. He said there might be some clerical error."

Pennington laughed rather harshly.

"You're a grand woman of business, Linnet."

"She's much more conscientious than I'd be," said Simon laughing. "I've never read a legal document in my life. I sign where they tell me to sign on the dotted line—and that's that."

"That's frightfully slipshod," said Linnet disapprovingly.

"I've no business head," said Simon cheerfully. "Never had. A fellow tells me to sign—I sign. It's much the simplest way."

Andrew Pennington was looking at him thoughtfully. He said dryly, stroking his upper lip:

"A little risky sometimes, Doyle?"

"Nonsense," said Simon. "I'm not one of those people who believe the whole world is out to do one down. I'm a trusting kind of fellow—and it pays, you know, I've hardly ever been let down."

Suddenly, to every one's surprise, the silent Mr. Fanthorp swung round and addressed Linnet.

"I hope I'm not butting in, but you must let me say how much I admire your businesslike capacity. In my profession—er—I am a lawyer—I find ladies sadly unbusinesslike. Never to sign a document before you read it through is admirable—altogether admirable."

He gave a little bow. Then, rather red in the face, he turned once more to contemplate the banks of the Nile.

Linnet said rather uncertainly, "er—thank you. . . ." She bit her lip to repress a giggle. The young man had looked so preternaturally solemn.

Andrew Pennington looked seriously annoyed.

Simon Doyle looked uncertain whether to be annoyed or amused.

The backs of Mr. Fanthorp's ears were bright crimson.

"Next, please," said Linnet smiling up at Pennington.

But Pennington was looking decidedly ruffled.

"I think perhaps some other time would be better," he said stiffly. "As—er—Doyle says if you have to read through all these we shall be here till lunch time. We mustn't miss enjoying the scenery. Anyway those first two papers were the only urgent ones. We'll settle down to business later."

Linnet said:

"It's frightfully hot in here. Let's go outside."

The three of them passed through the swing door. Hercule Poirot turned his head. His gaze rested thoughtfully on Mr. Fanthorp's back, then it shifted to the lounging figure of Mr. Ferguson who had his head thrown back and was still whistling softly to himself.

Finally Poirot looked over at the upright figure of Miss Van Schuyler in her corner. Miss Van Schuyler was glaring at Mr. Ferguson.

The swing door on the port side opened and Cornelia Robson hurried in.

"You've been a long time," snapped the old lady. "Where've you been?"

"I'm so sorry, Cousin Marie. The wool wasn't where you said it was. It was in another case altogether—"

"My dear child, you are perfectly hopeless at finding anything! You are willing, I know, my dear, but you must try to be a little cleverer and quicker. It only needs *concentration*."

"I'm so sorry, Cousin Marie. I'm afraid I am very stupid."

"Nobody need be stupid if they *try*, my dear. I have brought you on this trip and I expect a little attention in return."

Cornelia flushed.

"I'm very sorry, Cousin Marie."

"And where is Miss Bowers? It was time for my drops ten minutes ago. Please go and find her at once. The doctor said it was most important—"

But at this stage Miss Bowers entered, carrying a small medicine glass.

"Your drops, Miss Van Schuyler."

"I should have had them at eleven," snapped the old lady. "If there's one thing I detest it's unpunctuality."

"Quite," said Miss Bowers. She glanced at her wristwatch. "It's exactly half a minute to eleven."

"By my watch it's ten past."

"I think you'll find my watch is right. It's a perfect timekeeper. It never loses or gains."

Miss Bowers was quite imperturbable.

Miss Van Schuyler swallowed the contents of the medicine glass.

"I feel definitely worse," she snapped.

"I'm sorry to hear that, Miss Van Schuyler."

Miss Bowers did not sound sorry. She sounded completely uninterested. She was obviously making the correct reply mechanically.

"It's too hot in here," snapped Miss Van Schuyler. "Find me a chair on the deck, Miss Bowers. Cornelia, bring my knitting. Don't be clumsy or drop it. And then I shall want you to wind some wool."

The procession passed out.

Mr. Ferguson sighed, stirred his legs and remarked to the world at large:

"Gosh, I'd like to scrag that dame."

Poirot asked interestedly:

"She is a type you dislike, eh?"

"Dislike? I should say so. What good has that woman ever been to any one or anything? She's never worked or lifted a finger. She's just battened on other people. She's a parasite—and a damned unpleasant parasite. There are a lot of people on this boat I'd say the world could do without."

"Really?"

"Yes. That girl in here just now, signing share transfers and throwing her weight about. Hundreds and thousands of wretched workers slaving for a mere pittance to keep her in silk stockings and useless luxuries. One of the richest women in England, so some one told me—and never done a hand's turn in her life."

"Who told you she was one of the richest women in England?"

Mr. Ferguson cast a belligerent eye at him.

"A man you wouldn't be seen speaking to! A man who works with his hands and isn't ashamed of it! Not one of your dressed-up foppish good for nothings."

His eyes rested unfavourably on the bow tie and pink shirt.

"Me, I work with my brains and am not ashamed of it," said Poirot, answering the glance.

Mr. Ferguson merely snorted.

"Ought to be shot up—the lot of them!" he snorted.

"My dear young man," said Poirot. "What a passion you have for violence!"

"Can you tell me of any good that can be done without it? You've got to break down and destroy before you can build up."

"It is certainly much easier and much noisier and much more spectacular."

"What do *you* do for a living? Nothing at all, I bet. Probably call yourself a middle man."

"I am not a middle man. I am a top man," said Hercule Poirot with slight arrogance.

"What *are* you?"

"I am a detective," said Hercule Poirot with the modest air of one who says, "I am a King."

"Good God," the young man seemed seriously taken aback. "Do you mean that girl actually totes about a dumb dick? Is she as careful of her precious skin as *that?*"

"I have no connection whatever with Mr. and Mrs. Doyle," said Poirot stiffly. "I am on a holiday."

"Enjoying a vacation—eh?"

"And you? Is it not that you are on a holiday also?"

"Holiday!" Mr. Ferguson snorted. Then he added cryptically, "I'm studying conditions."

"Very interesting," murmured Poirot and moved gently out on to the deck.

Miss Van Schuyler was established in the best corner. Cornelia knelt in front of her, her arms outstretched with a skein of grey wool upon them. Miss Bowers was sitting very upright reading the *Saturday Evening Post*.

Poirot wandered gently onward down the starboard deck. As he passed round the stern of the boat he almost ran into a woman who turned a startled face towards him—a dark piquant Latin face. She was neatly dressed in black and had been standing talking to a big burly man in uniform—one of the engineers by the look of him. There was a queer expression on both their faces—guilt and alarm. Poirot wondered what they had been talking about.

He rounded the stern and continued his walk along the port side. A cabin door opened and Mrs. Otterbourne emerged and nearly fell into his arms. She was wearing a scarlet satin dressing-gown.

"So sorry," she apologised. "Dear Mr. Poirot—so very sorry. The motion—just the motion, you know. Never did have any sea legs. If the boat would only keep still. . . ." She clutched at his arm. "It's the pitching I can't stand. . . . Never really happy at sea. . . . And left all alone here hour after hour. That girl of mine—no sympathy—no understanding of her poor old mother who's done everything for her . . ." Mrs. Otterbourne began to weep. "Slaved for her I have—worn myself to the bone—to the bone. A *grande amoureuse*—that's what I might have been—a *grande amoureuse*—sacrificed everything—everything . . . and nobody cares! But I'll tell every one—I'll tell them now—how she neglects me—how hard she is—making me come on this journey—bored to death. . . . I'll go and tell them now—"

She surged forward. Poirot gently repressed the action.

"I will send her to you, Madame. Re-enter your cabin. It is best that way—"

"No. I want to tell every one—every one on the boat—"

"It is too dangerous, Madame. The sea is too rough. You might be swept overboard."

Mrs. Otterbourne looked at him doubtfully.

"You think so. You really think so?"

"I do."

He was successful. Mrs. Otterbourne wavered, faltered and re-entered her cabin.

Poirot's nostrils twitched once or twice. Then he nodded and walked on to where Rosalie Otterbourne was sitting between Mrs. Allerton and Tim.

"Your mother wants you, Mademoiselle."

She had been laughing quite happily. Now her face clouded over. She shot a quick suspicious look at him and hurried along the deck.

"I can't make that child out," said Mrs. Allerton. "She varies so. One day she's friendly—the next day she's positively rude."

"Thoroughly spoilt and bad-tempered," said Tim.

Mrs. Allerton shook her head.

"No. I don't think it's that. I think she's unhappy."

Tim shrugged his shoulders.

"Oh, well, I suppose we've all got our private troubles."

His voice sounded hard and curt.

A booming noise was heard.

"Lunch," cried Mrs. Allerton delightedly. "I'm starving."

That evening Poirot noticed that Mrs. Allerton was sitting talking to Miss Van Schuyler. As he passed Mrs. Allerton closed one eye and opened it again.

She was saying: "Of course at Calfries Castle—the dear Duke—"

Cornelia, released from attendance, was out on the deck. She was listening to Dr. Bessner who was instructing her somewhat ponderously in Egyptology as culled from the pages of Bædeker. Cornelia listened with rapt attention.

Leaning over the rail Tim Allerton was saying:

"Anyhow, it's a rotten world. . . ."

Rosalie Otterbourne answered:

"It's unfair. . . . Some people have everything."

Poirot sighed.

He was glad that he was no longer young.

CHAPTER 9

On the Monday morning various expressions of delight and appreciation were heard on the deck of the *Karnak*. The steamer was moored to the bank and a few hundred yards away, the morning sun just striking it, was a great temple carved out of the face of the rock. Four colossal figures, hewn out of the cliff, look out eternally over the Nile and face the rising sun.

Cornelia Robson said incoherently:

"Oh, M. Poirot, isn't it wonderful? I mean they're so big and so peaceful—and looking at them makes one feel that one's so small and—and rather like an insect—and that nothing matters very much really, does it?"

Mr. Fanthorp who was standing near by, murmured:

"Very—er—impressive."

"Grand, isn't it?" said Simon Doyle, strolling up. He went on confidentially to Poirot. "You know, I'm not much of a fellow for temples and sight-seeing and all that, but a place like this sort of gets you, if you know what I mean. Those old Pharoahs must have been wonderful fellows."

The others had drifted away. Simon lowered his voice.

"I'm no end glad we came on this trip. It's—well, it's cleared things up. Amazing why it should—but there it is. Linnet's got her nerve back. She says it's because she's actually *faced* the business at last."

"I think that is very probable," said Poirot.

"She says that when she actually saw Jackie on the boat she felt terrible—and then—suddenly—it didn't matter any more. We're both agreed that we won't try and dodge her any more. We'll just meet her on her own ground and show her that this ridiculous stunt of hers doesn't worry us a bit. It's just damned bad form—that's all. She thought she'd get us badly rattled—but now, well, we just aren't rattled any more. That ought to show her."

"Yes," said Poirot thoughtfully.

"So that's splendid, isn't it?"

"Oh yes, yes."

Linnet came along the deck. She was dressed in a soft shade of apricot linen. She was smiling.

She greeted Poirot with no particular enthusiasm, just gave him a cool nod and then drew her husband away.

Poirot realised with a momentary flicker of amusement that he had not made himself popular by his critical attitude. Linnet was used to unqualified admiration of all she was or did. Hercule Poirot had sinned noticeably against this creed.

Mrs. Allerton, joining him, murmured: "What a difference in that girl! She looked worried and not very happy at Assuan. To-day she looks so happy that one might almost be afraid she was fey."

Before Poirot could respond as he meant the party was called to order. The official dragoman took charge and the party was led ashore to visit Abu Simbel.

Poirot himself fell into step with Andrew Pennington.

"It is your first visit to Egypt—yes?" he asked.

"Why, no, I was here in 1923. That is to say, I was in Cairo. I've never been this trip up the Nile before."

"You came over on the *Carmanic*, I believe—at least so Mrs. Doyle was telling me."

Pennington shot a shrewd glance in his direction.

"Why yes, that is so," he admitted.

"I wondered if you had happened to come across some friends of mine who were aboard—the Rushington Smiths."

"I can't recall any one of that name. The boat was full and we had bad weather. A lot of passengers hardly appeared and in any case the voyage is so short one doesn't get to know who is on board and who isn't."

"Yes, that is very true. What a pleasant surprise your running into Mrs. Doyle and her husband. You had no idea they were married?"

"No. Mrs. Doyle had written me, but the letter was forwarded on and I only received it some days after our unexpected meeting in Cairo."

"You have known her for very many years, I understand?"

"Why, I should say I have, M. Poirot. I've known Linnet Ridgeway since she was just a cute little thing so high—" He made an illustrating gesture. "Her father and I were lifelong friends. A very remarkable man, Melhuish Ridgeway—and a very successful one."

"His daughter comes into a considerable fortune, I understand. . . . Ah, *pardon*—perhaps it is not delicate what I say there."

Andrew Pennington seemed slightly amused.

"Oh, that's pretty common knowledge. Yes, Linnet's a wealthy woman."

"I suppose, though, that the recent slump is bound to affect any stock, however sound it may be?"

Pennington took a moment or two to answer. He said at last:

"That, of course, is true to a certain extent. The position is very difficult in these days."

Poirot murmured.

"I should imagine, however, that Mrs. Doyle has a keen business head."

"That is so. Yes, that is so. Linnet is a clever practical girl."

They came to a halt. The guide proceeded to instruct them on the subject of the temple built by the great Rameses. The four colossi of Rameses himself, one pair on each side of the entrance, hewn out of the living rock looked down on the straggling little party of tourists.

Signor Richetti, disdaining the remarks of the dragoman, was busy examining the reliefs of negro and Syrian captives on the bases of the colossi on either side of the entrance.

When the party entered the temple, a sense of dimness and peace came over them. The still vividly coloured reliefs on some of the inner walls were pointed out, but the party tended to break up into groups.

Dr. Bessner read sonorously in German from a Bædeker, pausing every now and then to translate for the benefit of Cornelia who walked in a docile manner beside him. This was not to continue, however. Miss Van Schuyler, entering on the arm of the phlegmatic Miss Bowers, uttered a commanding "Cornelia, come here," and the instruction had perforce to cease. Dr. Bessner beamed after her vaguely through his thick lenses.

"A very nice maiden, that," he announced to Poirot. "She does not look so starved as some of these young women—no, she has the nice curves— She listens, too, very intelligently—it is a pleasure to instruct her."

It fleeted across Poirot's mind that it seemed to be Cornelia's fate either to be bullied or instructed. In any case she was always the listener, never the talker.

Miss Bowers, momentarily released by the peremptory summons of Cornelia, was standing in the middle of the temple looking about her with her cool incurious gaze. Her reaction to the wonders of the past was succinct.

"The guide says the name of one of these gods or goddesses was Mut. Can you beat it?"

There was an inner sanctuary where sat four figures eternally presiding, strangely dignified in their dim aloofness.

Before them stood Linnet and her husband. Her arm was in his, her face lifted—a typical face of the new civilisation, intelligent, curious, untouched by the past.

Simon said suddenly:

"Let's get out of here. I don't like these four fellows—especially the one in the high hat."

"That's Amon, I suppose. And that one is Rameses. Why don't you like them? I think they're very impressive."

"They're a damned sight too impressive—there's something uncanny about them. Come out into the sunlight."

Linnet laughed, but yielded.

They came out of the temple into the sunshine with the sand yellow and warm about their feet. Linnet began to laugh. At their feet in a row, presenting a momentarily gruesome appearance as though sawn from their bodies, were the heads of half a dozen Nubian boys. The eyes rolled, the heads moved rhythmically from side to side, the lips chanted a new invocation.

"Hip, hip, *hurray!* Hip, hip, *hurray!* Very good, very nice. Thank you very much."

"How absurd! How do they do it? Are they really buried very deep?"

Simon produced some small change.

"Very good, very nice, very expensive," he mimicked.

Two small boys in charge of the "show" picked up the coins neatly.

Linnet and Simon passed on.

They had no wish to return to the boat, and they were weary of sight-seeing. They settled themselves with their backs to the cliff and let the warm sun bake them through. . . .

"How lovely the sun is," thought Linnet. "How warm—how safe. . . . How lovely it is to be happy. . . . How lovely to be me—me—me—Linnet—"

Her eyes closed. She was half asleep, half awake, drifting in the midst of thought that was like the sand drifting and blowing.

Simon's eyes were open. They, too, held contentment. What a fool he'd been to be rattled that first night. . . . There was nothing to be rattled about. . . . Everything was all right. . . . After all, one could trust Jackie—

There was a shout—some one running towards him waving their arms—shouting. . . .

Simon stared stupidly for a moment. Then he sprang to his feet and dragged Linnet with him.

Not a minute too soon. A big boulder hurtling down the cliff crashed past them. If Linnet had remained where she was she would have been crushed to atoms.

White-faced they clung together. Hercule Poirot and Tim Allerton ran up to them.

"*Ma foi,* Madame, that was a near thing."

All four instinctively looked up at the cliff. There was nothing to be seen. But there was a path along the top. Poirot remembered seeing some natives walking along there when they had first come ashore.

He looked at the husband and wife. Linnet looked dazed still—bewildered. Simon, however, was inarticulate with rage.

"God damn her," he ejaculated.

He checked himself with a quick glance at Tim Allerton.

The latter said:

"Phew, that was near! Did some fool bowl that thing over, or did it get detached on its own?"

Linnet was very pale. She said with difficulty:

"I think—some fool must have done it."

"Might have crushed you like an eggshell. Sure you haven't got an enemy, Linnet?"

Linnet swallowed twice and found difficulty in answering the light-hearted raillery.

Poirot said quickly:

"Come back to the boat, Madame. You must have a restorative."

They walked there silently, Simon still full of pent-up rage, Tim trying to talk cheerfully and distract Linnet's mind from the danger she had run, Poirot with a grave face.

And then, just as they reached the gang-plank, Simon stopped dead. A look of amazement spread over his face.

Jacqueline de Bellefort was just coming ashore. Dressed in blue gingham she looked childish this morning.

"Good God," said Simon under his breath. "So it *was* an accident, after all."

The anger went out of his face. An overwhelming relief showed so plainly that Jacqueline noticed something amiss.

"Good-morning," she said. "I'm afraid I'm a little on the late side."

She gave them all a nod and stepped ashore and proceeded in the direction of the temple.

Simon clutched Poirot's arm. The other two had gone on.

"My God, that's a relief. I thought—I thought—"

Poirot nodded.

"Yes, yes, I know what you thought."

But he himself still looked grave and preoccupied.

He turned his head and noted carefully what had become of the rest of the party from the ship.

Miss Van Schuyler was slowly returning on the arm of Miss Bowers.

A little farther away Mrs. Allerton was standing laughing at the little Nubian row of heads. Mrs. Otterbourne was with her.

The others were nowhere in sight.

Poirot shook his head as he followed Simon slowly on to the boat.

CHAPTER 10

"Will you explain to me, Madame, the meaning of the word fey?"

Mrs. Allerton looked slightly surprised.

She and Poirot were toiling slowly up to the rock overlooking the Second Cataract. Most of the others had gone up on camels, but Poirot had felt that the motion of the camel was slightly reminiscent of that of a ship. Mrs. Allerton had put it on the grounds of personal dignity.

They had arrived at Wâdi Halfa the night before. This morning two launches had conveyed all the party to the Second Cataract with the exception of Signor Richetti, who had insisted on making an excursion of his own to a remote spot called Semna, which he explained was of paramount interest as being the gateway of Nubia in the time of Amenemhet III, and where there was a stele recording the fact that on entering Egypt negroes must pay custom duties. Everything had been done to discourage this example of individuality but with no avail. Signor Richetti was determined and had waved aside each objection—(1) that the expedition was not worth making—(2) that the expedition could not be made owing to the impossibility of getting a car there—(3) that no car could be obtained to do the trip—(4) that a car would be a prohibitive price. Having scoffed at 1, expressed incredulity at 2, offered to find a car himself to 3, and bargained fluently in Arabic for 4, Signor Richetti had at last departed—his departure being arranged in a secret and furtive manner in case some of the other tourists should take it into their heads to stray from the appointed paths of sight-seeing.

"Fey?" Mrs. Allerton put her head on one side as she considered her reply. "Well, it's a Scotch word, really. It means the kind of exalted happiness that comes before disaster. You know—it's too good to be true."

She enlarged on the theme. Poirot listened attentively.

"I thank you, Madame. I understand now. It is odd that you should have said that yesterday—when Madame Doyle was to escape death so shortly afterwards."

Mrs. Allerton gave a little shiver.

"It must have been a very near escape. Do you think some of those little black wretches rolled that stone over for fun? It's the sort of thing boys might do all over the world—not perhaps really meaning any harm."

Poirot shrugged his shoulders.

"It may be, Madame."

He changed the subject, talking of Majorca and asking various practical questions from the point of view of a possible visit.

Mrs. Allerton had grown to like the little man very much—partly, perhaps, out of a contradictory spirit. Tim, she felt, was always trying to make her less friendly to Hercule Poirot whom he had summarised firmly as "the worst kind of bounder." But she herself did not call him a bounder—she supposed it was his somewhat foreign exotic clothing which roused her son's prejudices. She herself found him an intelligent and stimulating companion. He was also extremely sympathetic. She found herself suddenly confiding in him her dislike of Joanna Southwood. It eased her to talk of the matter. And, after all, why not? He did not know Joanna—would probably never meet her. Why should she not ease herself of that constantly borne burden of jealous thought.

At that same moment Tim and Rosalie Otterbourne were talking of her.

Tim had just been half jestingly abusing his luck. His rotten health, never bad enough to be really interesting—yet not good enough for him to have led the life he would have chosen. Very little money—no congenial occupation.

"A thoroughly lukewarm tame existence," he finished discontentedly.

Rosalie said abruptly:

"You've got something heaps of people would envy you."

"What's that?"

"Your mother."

Tim was surprised and pleased.

"Mother? Yes, of course she is quite unique. It's nice of you to see it."

"I think she's marvellous. She looks so lovely—so composed and calm—as though nothing could ever touch her and yet—and yet somehow she's always ready to be funny about things too. . . ."

Rosalie was stammering slightly in her earnestness.

Tim felt a rising warmth towards the girl. He wished he could return the compliment, but lamentably Mrs. Otterbourne was his idea of the world's greatest menace. The inability to respond in kind made him embarrassed.

Miss Van Schuyler had stayed in the launch. She could neither risk the ascent on a camel nor on her legs. She had said snappily:

"I'm sorry to have to ask you to stay with me, Miss Bowers. I intended you to go and Cornelia to stay, but girls are so selfish. She rushed off without a word to me. And I actually saw her talking to that very unpleasant and ill-bred young man, Ferguson. Cornelia has disappointed me sadly. She has absolutely no social sense."

Miss Bowers replied in her usual matter-of-fact fashion:

"That's quite all right, Miss Van Schuyler. It would have been a hot walk up there and I don't fancy the look of those saddles on the camels. Fleas as likely as not."

She adjusted her glasses, screwed up her eyes to look at the party descending the hill and remarked:

"Miss Robson isn't with that young man any more. She's with Dr. Bessner."

Miss Van Schuyler grunted.

Since she had discovered that Dr. Bessner had a large clinic in Czecho-Slovakia and a European reputation as a fashionable physician she was disposed to be gracious to him. Besides, she might need his professional services before the journey was over.

When the party returned to the *Karnak*, Linnet gave a cry of surprise.

"A telegram for me."

She snatched it off the board and tore it open.

"Why—I don't understand—potatoes—beetroots—what does it mean, Simon?"

Simon was just coming to look over her shoulder when a furious voice said:

"Excuse me, that telegram is for me."

And Signor Richetti snatched it rudely from her hand, fixing her with a furious glare as he did so.

Linnet stared in surprise for a moment, then turned over the envelope.

"Oh, Simon, what a fool I am. It's Richetti—not Ridgeway—and anyway, of course, my name isn't Ridgeway now. I must apologise."

She followed the little archæologist up to the stern of the boat.

"I am so sorry, Signor Richetti. You see my name was Ridgeway before I married and I haven't been married very long and so—"

She paused, her face dimpled with smiles, inviting him to smile upon a young bride's *faux pas*.

But Richetti was obviously "not amused." Queen Victoria at her most disapproving could not have looked more grim.

"Names should be read carefully. It is inexcusable to be careless in these matters."

Linnet bit her lip and her colour rose. She was not accustomed to have her apologies received in this fashion. She turned away and, rejoining Simon, she said angrily, "These Italians are really insupportable."

"Never mind, darling, let's go and look at that big ivory crocodile you liked."

They went ashore together.

Poirot, watching them walk up the landing-stage, heard a sharp indrawn breath. He turned to see Jacqueline de Bellefort at his side. Her hands were clenched on the rail. The expression on her face as she turned it towards him quite startled him. It was no longer gay or malicious. She looked devoured by some inner consuming fire.

"They don't care any more." The words came low and fast. "They've got beyond me. I can't reach them. . . . They don't mind if I'm here or not . . . I can't—I can't hurt them any more. . . ."

Her hands on the rail trembled.

"Mademoiselle—"

She broke in.

"Oh, it's too late now—too late for warning. . . . You were right. I ought not to have come. Not on this journey. What did you call it? A journey of the soul? I can't go back—I've got to go on. And I'm going on. They shan't be happy together—they shan't. I'd kill him sooner. . . ."

She turned abruptly away. Poirot staring after her, felt a hand on his shoulder.

"Your girl friend seems a trifle upset, M. Poirot."

Poirot turned. He stared in surprise, seeing an old acquaintance.

"Colonel Race."

The tall bronzed man smiled.

"Bit of a surprise—eh?"

Hercule Poirot had come across Colonel Race a year previously in London. They had been fellow-guests at a very strange dinner party—a dinner party that had ended in death for that strange man, their host.

Poirot knew that Race was a man of unadvertised goings and comings. He was usually to be found in one of the outposts of Empire where trouble was brewing.

"So you are here at Wâdi Halfa," Poirot remarked thoughtfully.

"I am here on this boat."

"You mean?"

"That I am making the return journey with you to Shellal."

Hercule Poirot's eyebrows rose.

"That is very interesting. Shall we, perhaps, have a little drink."

They went into the observation saloon, now quite empty. Poirot ordered a whisky for the colonel and a double orangeade full of sugar for himself.

"So you make the return journey with us," said Poirot as he sipped. "You would go faster, would you not, on the Government steamer which travels by night as well as day?"

Colonel Race's face creased appreciatively.

"You're right on the spot as usual, M, Poirot," he said pleasantly.

"It is, then, the passengers?"

"One of the passengers."

"Now which one, I wonder?" Hercule Poirot asked of the ornate ceiling.

"Unfortunately I don't know myself," said Race ruefully.

Poirot looked interested.

Race said:

"There's no need to be mysterious to you. We've had a good deal of trouble out here—one way and another. It isn't the people who ostensibly lead the rioters that we're after. It's the men who very cleverly put the match to the gunpowder. There were three of them. One's dead. One's in prison. I want the third man—a man with five or six cold-blooded murders to his credit. He's one of the cleverest paid agitators that ever existed. . . . He's on this boat. I know that from a passage in a letter that passed through our hands. Decoded it said: 'X will be on the *Karnak* trip Feb. 7th-13th. . . .' It didn't say under what name X would be passing."

"Have you any description of him?"

"No. American, Irish and French descent. Bit of a mongrel. That doesn't help us much. Have you got any ideas?"

"An idea—it is all very well," said Poirot meditatively.

Such was the understanding betwen them that Race pressed him no further. He knew that Hercule Poirot did not ever speak unless he were sure.

Poirot rubbed his nose and said unhappily:

"There passes itself something on this boat that causes me much inquietude."

Race looked at him inquiringly.

"Figure to yourself," said Poirot, "a person A who has grievously wronged a person B. The person B desires the revenge. The person B makes the threats."

"A and B being both on this boat?"

Poirot nodded.

"Precisely."

"And B, I gather, being a woman?"

"Exactly."

Race lit a cigarette.

"I shouldn't worry. People who go about talking of what they are going to do don't usually do it."

"And particularly is that the case with *les femmes*, you would say! Yes, that is true."

But he still did not look happy.

"Anything else?" asked Race.

"Yes, there is something. Yesterday the person A had a very near escape from death. The kind of death that might very conveniently be called an accident."

"Engineered by B?"

"No, that is just the point. B could have had nothing to do with it."

"Then it *was* an accident."

"I suppose so—but I do not like such accidents."

"You're quite sure B could have had no hand in it?"

"Absolutely."

"Oh well, coincidences do happen. Who is A, by the way? A particularly disagreeable person?"

"On the contrary. A is a charming, rich and beautiful young lady."

Race grinned.

"Sounds quite like a novelette."

"*Peut-être*. But I tell you, I am not happy, my friend. If I am right, and after all I am constantly in the habit of being right—"

Race smiled into his moustache at this typical utterance.

"—then there is matter for grave inquietude. And now, *you* come to add yet another complication. You tell me that there is a man on the *Karnak* who kills."

"He doesn't usually kill charming young ladies.

Poirot shook his head in a dissatisfied manner.

"I am afraid, my friend," he said. "I am afraid. . . . To-day, I advised this lady, Mrs. Doyle, to go with her husband to Khartoum, not to return on this boat. But they would not agree. I pray to Heaven that we may arrive at Shellal without catastrophe."

"Aren't you taking rather a gloomy view?"

Poirot shook his head.

"I am afraid," he said simply. "Yes I, Hercule Poirot, am afraid. . . ."

CHAPTER 11

Cornelia Robson stood inside the temple of Abu Simbel. It was the evening of the following day—a hot still evening. The *Karnak* was anchored once more at Abu Simbel to permit a second visit to be made to the temple—this time by artificial light. The difference this made was considerable and Cornelia commented wonderingly on the fact to Mr. Ferguson who was standing by her side.

"Why, you see it ever so much better now!" she exclaimed. "All those enemies having their heads cut off by the king—they just stand right out. That's a cute kind of castle there that I never noticed before. I wish Dr. Bessner was here, he'd tell me what it was."

"How you can stand that old fool beats me," said Ferguson gloomily.

"Why, he's just one of the kindest men I've ever met!"

"Pompous old bore."

"I don't think you ought to speak that way."

The young man gripped her suddenly by the arm. They were just emerging from the temple into the moonlight.

"Why do you stick being bored by fat old men—and bullied and snubbed by a vicious old harridan?"

"Why, Mr. Ferguson!"

"Haven't you got any spirit? Don't you know you're just as good as she is?"

"But I'm not!" Cornelia spoke with honest conviction.

"You're not as rich—that's all you mean."

"No, it isn't. Cousin Marie's very very cultured, and—"

"Cultured—" the young man let go of her arm as suddenly as he had taken it. "That word makes me sick."

Cornelia looked at him in alarm.

"She doesn't like you talking to me, does she?" said the young man.

Cornelia blushed and looked embarrassed.

"Why—? Because she thinks I'm not her social equal! Pah—doesn't that make you see red?"

Cornelia faltered out:

"I wish you wouldn't get so mad about things."

"Don't you realise—and you an American—that every one is born free and equal?"

"They're not," said Cornelia with calm certainty.

"My good girl—it's part of your constitution!"

"Cousin Marie says politicians aren't gentlemen," said Cornelia. "And of course people aren't equal. It doesn't make sense. I know I'm kind of homely looking and I used to feel mortified about it sometimes, but I've got over that. I'd like to have been born elegant and beautiful like Mrs. Doyle, but I wasn't, so I guess it's no use worrying."

"Mrs. Doyle!" said Ferguson with deep contempt. "She's the sort of woman who ought to be shot as an example."

Cornelia looked at him anxiously.

"I believe it's your digestion," she said kindly. "I've got a special kind of pepsin that Cousin Marie tried once. Would you like to try it?"

Mr. Ferguson said:

"You're impossible!"

He turned and strode away. Cornelia went on towards the boat. Just as she was crossing on to the gangway, he caught her up once more.

"You're the nicest person on the boat," he said. "And mind you remember it."

Blushing with pleasure Cornelia repaired to the observation saloon.

Miss Van Schuyler was conversing with Dr. Bessner—an agreeable conversation dealing with certain royal patients of his.

Cornelia said guiltily:

"I do hope I haven't been a long time, Cousin Marie."

Glancing at her watch the old lady snapped:

"You haven't exactly hurried, my dear. And what have you done with my velvet stole?"

Cornelia looked round.

"Shall I see if it's in the cabin, Cousin Marie?"

"Of course it isn't! I had it just after dinner in here, and I haven't moved out of the place. It was on that chair."

Cornelia made a desultory search.

"I can't see it anywhere, Cousin Marie."

"Nonsense," said Miss Van Schuyler. "Look about." It was an order such as one might give to a dog and in her doglike fashion Cornelia obeyed. The quiet Mr. Fanthorp who was sitting at a table near by rose and assisted her. But the stole could not be found.

The day had been such an unusually hot and sultry one that most people had retired early after going ashore to view the temple. The Doyles were playing bridge with Pennington and Race at a table in a corner. The only other occupant of the saloon was Hercule Poirot, who was yawning his head off at a small table near the door.

Miss Van Schuyler, making a Royal Progress bedwards with Cornelia and Miss Bowers in attendance, paused by his chair, and he sprang politely to his feet, stifling a yawn of gargantuan dimensions.

Miss Van Schuyler said:

"I have only just realised who you are, M. Poirot. I may tell you that I have heard of you from my old friend Rufus Van Aldin. You must tell me about your cases some time."

With a kindly but condescending nod she passed on.

Poirot, his eyes twinkling a little through their sleepiness, bowed in an exaggerated manner.

Then he yawned once more. He felt heavy and stupid with sleep and could hardly keep his eyes open. He glanced over at the bridge players, absorbed in their game, then at young Fanthorp who was deep in a book. Apart from them the saloon was empty.

He passed through the swinging door out on to the deck. Jacqueline de Bellefort, coming precipitately along the deck, almost collided with him.

"Pardon, Mademoiselle."

She said:

"You look sleepy, M. Poirot."

He admitted it frankly.

"*Mais oui*—I am consumed with sleep. I can hardly keep my eyes open. It has been a day very close and oppressive."

"Yes." She seemed to brood over it. "It's been the sort of day when things—snap! Break! When one can't go on. . . ."

Her voice was low and charged with passion.

She looked not at him, but towards the sandy shore. Her hands were clenched, rigid. . . .

Suddenly the tension relaxed. She said:

"Good-night, M. Poirot."

"Good-night, Mademoiselle."

Her eyes met his, just for a swift moment. Thinking it over next day he came to the conclusion that there had been appeal in that glance. He was to remember it afterwards. . . .

Then he passed on to his cabin and she went towards the saloon.

Cornelia, having dealt with Miss Van Schuyler's many needs and fantasies, took some needlework with her back to the saloon. She herself did not feel in the least sleepy. On the contrary she felt wide awake and slightly excited.

The bridge four were still at it. In another chair the quiet Fanthorp read a book. Cornelia sat down to her needlework.

Suddenly the door opened and Jacqueline de Bellefort came in. She stood in the doorway, her head thrown back. Then she pressed a bell and sauntered across to Cornelia and sat down.

"Been ashore?" she asked.

"Yes. I thought it was just fascinating in the moonlight."

Jacqueline nodded.

"Yes, lovely night. . . . A real honeymoon night."

Her eyes went to the bridge table—rested a moment on Linnet Doyle.

The boy came in answer to the bell.

Jacqueline ordered a double gin. As she gave the order Simon Doyle shot a quick glance at her. A faint line of anxiety showed between his eyebrows.

His wife said:

"Simon, we're waiting for you to call."

Jacqueline hummed a little tune to herself.

When the drink came, she picked it up, said, "Well, here's to crime," drank it off and ordered another.

Again Simon looked across from the bridge table. His calls became slightly absent-minded. His partner, Pennington, took him to task.

Jacqueline began to hum again, at first under her breath, then louder.

"He was her man and he did her wrong. . . ."

"Sorry," said Simon to Pennington. "Stupid of me not to return your lead. That gives 'em rubber."

Linnet rose to her feet.

"I'm sleepy. I think I'll go to bed."

"About time to turn in," said Colonel Race.

"I'm with you," agreed Pennington.

"Coming, Simon?"

Doyle said slowly:

"Not just yet. I think I'll have a drink first."

Linnet nodded and went out. Race followed her. Pennington finished his drink and then followed suit.

Cornelia began to gather up her embroidery.

"Don't go to bed, Miss Robson," said Jacqueline. "Please don't. I feel like making a night of it. Don't desert me."

Cornelia sat down again.

"We girls must stick together," said Jacqueline.

She threw back her head and laughed—a shrill laugh without merriment.

The second drink came.

"Have something," said Jacqueline.

"No, thank you very much," said Cornelia.

Jacqueline tilted back her chair. She hummed now loudly. . . .

"He was her man and he did her wrong. . . ."

Mr. Fanthorp turned a page of *Europe from Within*.

Simon Doyle picked up a magazine.

"Really, I think I'll go to bed," said Cornelia. "It's getting very late."

"You can't go to bed yet," said Jacqueline. "I forbid you to. Tell me all about yourself."

"Well—I don't know—there isn't much to tell," Cornelia faltered. "I've just lived at home and I haven't been around much. This is my first trip to Europe. I'm just loving every minute of it."

Jacqueline laughed.

"You're a happy sort of person, aren't you? God, I'd like to be you."

"Oh! would you? But I mean—I'm sure—"

Cornelia felt flustered.

Undoubtedly Miss de Bellefort was drinking too much. That wasn't exactly a novelty to Cornelia. She had seen plenty of drunkenness during Prohibition years. But there was something else. . . . Jacqueline de Bellefort was talking to her—was looking at her—and yet, Cornelia felt—it was as though, somehow, she was talking to some one else. . . .

But there were only two other people in the room, Mr. Fanthorp and Mr. Doyle. Mr. Fanthorp seemed quite absorbed in his book. Mr. Doyle was looking rather odd—a queer sort of watchful look on his face. . . .

Jacqueline said again:

"Tell me all about yourself."

Always obedient, Cornelia tried to comply. She talked rather heavily, going into unnecessary small details about her daily life. She was so unused to being the talker. Her rôle was so constantly that of listener.

And yet Miss de Bellefort seemed to want to know. When Cornelia faltered to a standstill, the other girl was quick to prompt her.

"Go on—tell me more."

And so Cornelia went on ("Of course, mother's very delicate—some days she touches nothing but cereals—") unhappily conscious that all she said was supremely uninteresting, yet flattered by the other girl's seeming interest. But was she interested? Wasn't she, somehow, listening to something else—or perhaps—*for* something else? She was looking at Cornelia, yes, but wasn't there really *someone else,* sitting in the room. . . .

"And of course we get very good art classes and last winter I had a course of—"

(How late was it? Surely very late. She had been talking and talking. If only something definite would happen. . . .)

And immediately, as though in answer to the wish, something did happen. Only, at the moment, it seemed very natural.

Jacqueline turned her head and spoke to Simon Doyle:

"Ring the bell, Simon. I want another drink."

Simon Doyle looked up from his magazine and said quietly:

"The stewards have gone to bed. It's after midnight."

"I tell you I want another drink."

Simon said:

"You've had quite enough drinks, Jackie."

She swung round at him.

"What damned business is it of yours?"

He shrugged his shoulders.

"None."

She watched him for a minute or two. Then she said:

"What's the matter, Simon? Are you afraid?"

Simon did not answer. Rather elaborately he picked up his magazine again.

Cornelia murmured.

"Oh, dear—as late as that—I must—"

She began to fumble, dropped a thimble. . . .

Jacqueline said:

"Don't go to bed. I'd like another woman here—to support me." She began to laugh again. "Do you know what Simon over there is afraid of? He's afraid *I'm* going to tell you the story of *my* life."

"Oh—er—" Cornelia spluttered a little.

Jacqueline said clearly:

"You see, he and I were once engaged."

"Oh, really?"

Cornelia was the prey of conflicting emotions. She was deeply embarrassed but at the same time pleasurably thrilled. How—how *black* Simon Doyle was looking.

"Yes, it's a very sad story," said Jacqueline, her soft voice was low and mocking. "He treated me rather badly, didn't you, Simon?"

Simon Doyle said brutally.

"Go to bed, Jackie. You're drunk."

"If you're embarrassed, Simon dear, you'd better leave the room."

Simon Doyle looked at her. The hand that held the magazine shook a little, but he spoke bluntly.

"I'm staying," he said.

Cornelia murmured for the third time:

"I really must—it's so late—"

"You're not to go," said Jacqueline. Her hand shot out and held the other girl in her chair. "You're to stay and hear what I've got to say."

"Jackie," said Simon sharply. "you're making a fool of yourself! For God's sake, go to bed."

Jacqueline sat up suddenly in her chair. Words poured from her in a soft hissing stream.

"You're afraid of a scene, aren't you? That's because you're so English—so reticent! You want me to behave 'decently,' don't you? But I don't care whether I behave decently or not! You'd better get out of here quickly—because I'm going to talk—a lot."

Jim Fanthorp carefully shut his book, yawned, glanced at his watch, got up and strolled out. It was a very British and utterly unconvincing performance.

Jacqueline swung round in her chair and glared at Simon.

"You damned fool," she said thickly, "do you think you can treat me as you have done and get away with it?"

Simon Doyle opened his lips, then shut them again. He sat quite still as though he were hoping that her outburst would exhaust itself if he said nothing to provoke her further.

Jacqueline's voice came thick and blurred. It fascinated Cornelia, totally unused to naked emotions of any kind.

"I told you," said Jacqueline, "that I'd kill you sooner than see you go to another woman. . . . You don't think I meant that? *You're wrong*. I've only been waiting! You're *my* man! Do you hear? You belong to me. . . ."

Still Simon did not speak. Jacqueline's hand fumbled a moment or two on her lap. She leaned forward.

"I told you I'd kill you and I meant it. . . ." Her hand came up suddenly with something in it that gleamed. "I'll shoot you like a dog—like the dirty dog you are. . . ."

Now at last Simon acted. He sprang to his feet, but at the same moment she pulled the trigger. . . .

Simon half twisted—fell across a chair. . . . Cornelia screamed and rushed to the door. Jim Fanthorp was on the deck leaning over the rail. She called to him.

"Mr. Fanthorp. . . . Mr. Fanthorp. . . ."

He ran to her, she clutched at him incoherently. . . .

"She's shot him! Oh! She's shot him. . . ."

Simon Doyle still lay as he had fallen half into and across a chair. . . . Jacqueline stood as though paralysed. She was trembling violently, and her eyes, dilated and frightened, were staring at the crimson stain slowly soaking through Simon's trouser leg just below the knee where he held a handkerchief close against the wound. . . .

She stammered out:

"I didn't mean. . . . Oh, my God, I didn't really mean . . ."

The pistol dropped from her nervous fingers with a clatter on the floor. She kicked it away with her foot. It slid under one of the settees.

Simon, his voice faint, murmured:

"Fanthorp, for Heaven's sake—there's some one coming. . . . Say it's all right—an accident—something—there mustn't be a scandal over this."

Fanthorp nodded in quick comprehension. He wheeled round to the door where a startled Nubian face showed. He said:

"All right—all right—just fun!"

The black face looked doubtful, puzzled, then reassured. The teeth showed in a wide grin. The boy nodded and went off.

Fanthorp turned back.

"That's all right. Don't think anybody else heard. Only sounded like a cork, you know. Now the next thing—"

He was startled. Jacqueline suddenly began to weep hysterically.

"Oh, God, I wish I were dead. . . . I'll kill myself. I'll be better dead. . . . Oh, what have I done—what have I done?"

Cornelia hurried to her.

"Hush, dear, hush."

Simon, his brow wet, his face twisted with pain, said urgently:

"Get her away. For God's sake, get her out of here! Get her to her cabin, Fanthorp. Look here, Miss Robson, get that hospital nurse of yours." He looked appealingly from one to the other of them.

"Don't leave her. Make quite sure she's safe with the nurse looking after her. Then get hold of old Bessner and bring him here. For God's sake, don't let any news of this get to my wife."

Jim Fanthorp nodded comprehendingly. The quiet young man was cool and competent in an emergency.

Between them he and Cornelia got the weeping, struggling girl out of the saloon and along the deck to her cabin. There they had more trouble with her. She fought to free herself, her sobs redoubled.

"I'll drown myself. . . . I'll drown myself. . . . I'm not fit to live. . . . Oh, Simon—Simon."

Fanthorp said to Cornelia:

"Better get hold of Miss Bowers. I'll stay while you get her."

Cornelia nodded and hurried out.

As soon as she left Jacqueline clutched Fanthorp.

"His leg—it's bleeding—broken. . . . He may bleed to death. I must go to him. . . . Oh, Simon—Simon—how could I?"

Her voice rose. Fanthorp said urgently:

"Quietly—quietly. . . . He'll be all right."

She began to struggle again.

"Let me go. Let me throw myself overboard. . . . Let me kill myself."

Fanthorp, holding her by the shoulders, forced her back on to the bed.

"You must stay here. Don't make a fuss. Pull yourself together. It's all right, I tell you."

To his relief, the distraught girl did manage to control herself a little, but he was thankful when the curtains were pushed aside and the efficient Miss Bowers, neatly dressed in a hideous kimono, entered accompanied by Cornelia.

"Now then," said Miss Bowers briskly. "What's all this?"

She took charge without any sign of surprise and alarm.

Fanthorp thankfully left the overwrought girl in her capable hands and hurried along to the cabin occupied by Dr. Bessner.

He knocked and entered on the top of the knock.

"Dr. Bessner?"

A terrific snore resolved itself, and a startled voice said:

"So? What is it?"

By this time Fanthorp had switched the light on. The doctor blinked up at him, looking rather like a large owl.

"It's Doyle. He's been shot. Miss de Bellefort shot him. He's in the saloon. Can you come?"

The stout doctor reacted promptly. He asked a few curt questions, pulled on his bedroom slippers and a dressing-gown, picked up a little case of necessities and accompanied Fanthorp to the lounge.

Simon had managed to get the window beside him open. He was leaning his head against it, inhaling the air. His face was a ghastly colour.

Dr. Bessner came over to him.

"Ha? So? What have we here?"

A handkerchief sodden with blood lay on the carpet and on the carpet itself was a dark stain.

The doctor's examination was punctuated with Teutonic grunts and exclamations.

"Yes, it is bad this. . . . The bone is fractured. And a big loss of blood. Herr Fanthorp, you and I must get him to my cabin. So—like this. He cannot walk. We must carry him, thus."

As they lifted him Cornelia appeared in the doorway.

Catching sight of her, the doctor uttered a grunt of satisfaction.

"Ach, it is you? Goot. Come with us. I have need of assistance. You will be better than my friend here. He looks a little pale already."

Fanthorp emitted a rather sickly smile.

"Shall I get Miss Bowers?" he asked.

Dr. Bessner threw a considering glance over Cornelia.

"You will do very well, young lady," he announced. "You will not faint or be foolish, hein?"

"I can do what you tell me," said Cornelia eagerly.

Bessner nodded in a satisfied fashion.

The procession passed along the deck.

The next ten minutes was purely surgical and Mr. Jim Fanthorp did not enjoy it at all. He felt secretly ashamed of the superior fortitude exhibited by Cornelia.

"So, that is the best I can do," announced Dr. Bessner at last. "You have been a hero, my friend." He patted Simon approvingly on the shoulder.

Then he rolled up his sleeve and produced a hypodermic needle.

"And now I will give you something to make you sleep. Your wife, what about her?"

Simon said weakly:

"She needn't know till the morning. . . ." He went on: "I—you mustn't blame Jackie. . . . It's been all my fault. I treated her disgracefully . . . poor kid—she didn't know what she was doing. . . ."

Dr. Bessner nodded comprehendingly.

"Yes, yes—I understand. . . ."

"My fault—" Simon urged. His eyes went to Cornelia. "Some one—ought to—stay with her—she might—hurt herself—"

Dr. Bessner injected the needle. Cornelia said with quiet competence:

"It's all right, Mr. Doyle. Miss Bowers is going to stay with her all night. . . ."

A grateful look flashed over Simon's face.

His body relaxed. His eyes closed. Suddenly he jerked them open.

"Fanthorp?"

"Yes, Doyle."

"The pistol. . . . Ought not to leave it . . . lying about . . . the boys will find it in the morning. . . ."

Fanthorp nodded.

"Quite right. I'll go and get hold of it now."

He went out of the cabin and along the deck. Miss Bowers appeared at the door of Jacqueline's cabin.

"She'll be all right now," she announced. "I've given her a morphine injection."

"But you'll stay with her?"

"Oh, yes. Morphia excites some people. I shall stay all night."

Fanthorp went on to the lounge.

Some three minutes later there was a tap on Bessner's cabin door.

"Dr. Bessner?"

"Yes?" The stout man appeared.

Fanthorp beckoned him out on the deck.

"Look here—I can't find that pistol. . . ."

"What is that?"

"The pistol. It dropped out of the girl's hand. She kicked it away and it went under a settee. *It isn't under that settee now.*"

They stared at each other.

"But who can have taken it?"

Fanthorp shrugged his shoulders.

"Bessner said:

"It is curious, that. But I do not see what we can do about it."

Puzzled and vaguely alarmed, the two men separated.

CHAPTER 12

Hercule Poirot was just wiping the lather from his freshly shaved face when there was a quick tap on the door and hard on top of it Colonel Race entered unceremoniously.

He closed the door behind him.

He said:

"Your instinct was quite correct. It's happened."

Poirot straightened up and asked sharply:

"What has happened?"

"Linnet Doyle's dead—shot through the head last night."

Poirot was silent for a minute, two memories vividly before him—a girl in a garden at Assuan saying in a hard breathless voice, "I'd like to put my dear little pistol against her head and just press the trigger,"—and another more recent memory, the same voice saying, "One feels one can't go on—the kind of day when something breaks,"—and that strange momentary flash of appeal in her eyes. What had been the matter with him not to respond to that appeal? He had been blind, deaf, stupid with his need for sleep. . . .

Race went on:

"I've got some slight official standing—they sent for me. Put it in my hands. The boat's due to start in half an hour but it will be delayed till I give the word. There's a possibility, of course, that the murderer came from the shore."

Poirot shook his head.

Race acquiesced in the gesture.

"I agree. One can pretty well rule that out. Well, man, it's up to you. This is your show."

Poirot had been attiring himself with a neat-fingered celerity. He said now:

"I am at your disposal."

The two men stepped out on the deck.

Race said:

"Bessner should be there by now. I sent the steward for him."

There were four cabins de luxe with bathrooms on the boat. Of the two on the port side one was occupied by Dr. Bessner, the other by Andrew Pennington. On the starboard side the first was occupied by Miss Van Schuyler, and the one next to it by Linnet Doyle. Her husband's dressing cabin was next door.

A white-faced steward was standing outside the door of Linnet Doyle's cabin. He opened the door for them and they passed inside. Dr. Bessner was bending over the bed. He looked up and grunted as the other two entered.

"What can you tell us, doctor, about this business?" asked Race.

Bessner rubbed his unshaven jaw meditatively.

"Ach! She was shot—shot at close quarters. See—here just above the ear—this is where the bullet entered. A very little bullet—I should say a .22. The pistol it was held close against her head—see there is blackening here, the skin is scorched."

Again in a sick wave of memory Poirot thought of those words uttered at Assuan.

S.S. KARNAK

PROMENADE DECK

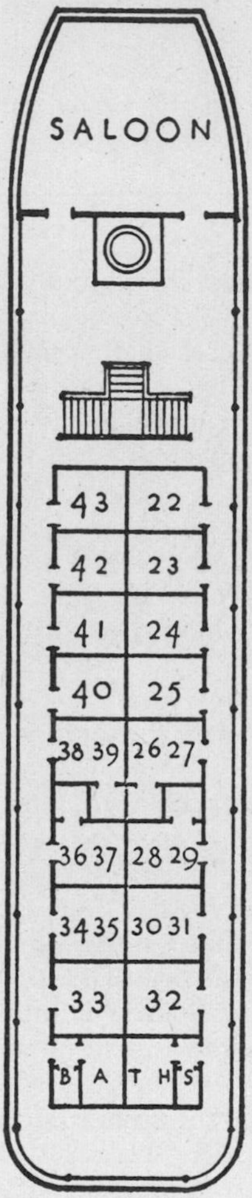

PLAN

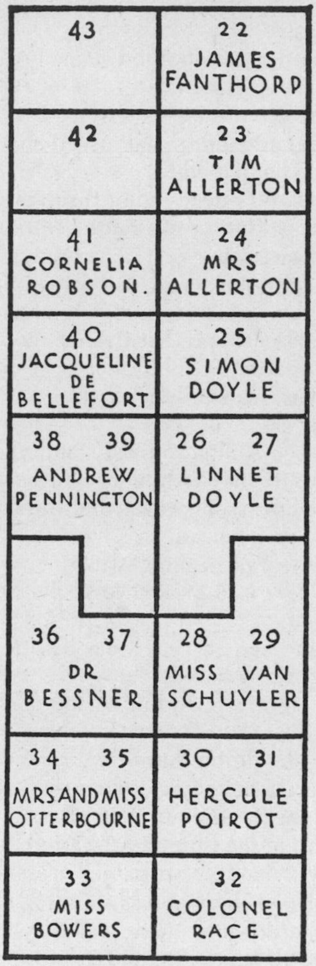

CABINS

Bessner went on.

"She was asleep—there was no struggle—the murderer crept up in the dark and shot her as she lay there."

"Ah! non!" Poirot cried out. His sense of psychology was outraged. Jacqueline de Bellefort creeping into a darkened cabin, pistol in hand—no, it did not "fit," that picture.

Bessner stared at him through his thick lenses.

"But that is what happened, I tell you."

"Yes, yes. I did not mean what you thought. I was not contradicting you."

Bessner gave a satisfied grunt.

Poirot came up and stood beside him. Linnet Doyle was lying on her side. Her attitude was natural and peaceful. But above the ear was a tiny hole with an incrustation of dried blood round it.

Poirot shook his head sadly.

Then his gaze fell on the white painted wall just in front of him and he drew in his breath sharply.

Its white neatness was marred by a big wavering letter J scrawled in some brownish-red medium.

Poirot stared at it, then he leaned over the dead girl and very gently picked up her right hand. One finger of it was stained a brownish-red.

"Nom d'un nom d'un nom!" ejaculated Hercule Poirot.

"Eh? What is that?"

Dr. Bessner looked up.

"Ach! *That*."

Race said:

"Well, I'm damned. What do you make of that, Poirot?"

Poirot swayed a little on his toes.

"You ask me what I make of it. *Eh bien,* it is very simple, is it not? Mrs. Doyle is dying, she wishes to indicate her murderer, and so she writes with her finger dipped in her own blood the initial letter of her murderer's name. Oh yes, it is astonishingly simple."

"Ach! but—"

Dr. Bessner was about to break out, but a peremptory gesture from Race silenced him.

"So it strikes you like that?" he said slowly.

Poirot turned round on him, nodding his head.

"Yes, yes. It is, as I say, of an astonishing simplicity! It is so familiar, is it not? *It has been done so often,* in the pages of the romance of crime! It is now, indeed, a little *vieux jeu!* It leads one to suspect that our murderer is—old fashioned!"

Race drew a long breath.

"I see," he said. "I thought at first—"

He stopped.

Poirot said with a very faint smile:

"That I believed in all the old clichés of melodrama? But pardon, Dr. Bessner, you were about to say—?"

Bessner broke out gutturally:

"What do I say? Pah! I say it is absurd—it is the nonsense! The poor lady she died instantaneously. To dip her finger in the blood (and as you see, there is hardly any blood) and write the letter J upon the wall. Bah—it is the nonsense—the melodramatic nonsense!"

"C'est l'enfantillage," agreed Poirot.

"But it was done with a purpose," suggested Race.

"That—naturally," said Poirot and his face was grave.

Race said:

"What does J stand for?"

Poirot replied promptly:

"J stands for Jacqueline de Bellefort, a young lady who declared to me less than a week ago that she would like nothing better than to—" he paused and then deliberately quoted, "—to put my dear little pistol close against her head and then just press with my finger. . . ."

"*Gott im Himmel!*" said Dr. Bessner.

There was a momentary silence. Then Race drew a deep breath and said:

"*Which is just what was done here?*"

Bessner nodded.

"That is so, yes. It was a pistol of very small calibre—as I say probably a .22. The bullet has got to be extracted, of course, before we can say definitely."

Race nodded in swift comprehension. Then he said:

"What about time of death?"

Bessner stroked his jaw again. His finger made a rasping sound.

"I would not care to be too precise. It is now eight o'clock. I will say, with due regard to the temperature last night, that she has been dead certainly six hours and probably not longer than eight."

"That puts it between midnight and 2 a.m."

"That is so."

There was a pause. Race looked round.

"What about her husband? I suppose he sleeps in the cabin next door."

"At the moment," said Dr. Bessner, "he is asleep in my cabin."

Both men looked very surprised.

Bessner nodded his head several times.

"Ach, so. I see you have not been told about that. Mr. Doyle was shot last night in the saloon."

"Shot? By whom?"

"By the young lady Jacqueline de Bellefort."

Race asked sharply:

"Is he badly hurt?"

"Yes, the bone was splintered. I have done all that is possible at the moment but it is necessary, you understand, that the fracture should be X-rayed as soon as possible and proper treatment given such as is impossible on this boat."

Poirot murmured:

"Jacqueline de Bellefort."

His eyes went again to the J on the wall.

Race said abruptly:

"If there is nothing more we can do here for the moment, let's go below. The management has put the smoking-room at our disposal. We must get the details of what happened last night."

They left the cabin. Race locked the door and took the key with him.

"We can come back later," he said. "The first thing to do is to get all the facts clear."

They went down to the deck below where they found the manager of the *Karnak* waiting uneasily in the doorway of the smoking-room.

The poor man was terribly upset and worried over the whole business, and was eager to leave everything in Colonel Race's hands.

"I feel I can't do better than leave it to you, sir, seeing your official position. I'd had orders to put myself at your disposal in the—er—other matter. If you will take charge, I'll see that everything is done as you wish."

"Good man. To begin with I'd like this room kept clear for me and for M. Poirot during the inquiry."

"Certainly, sir."

"That's all at present. Go on with your own work. I know where to find you."

Looking slightly relieved the manager left the room.

Race said:

"Sit down, Bessner, and let's have the whole story of what happened last night."

They listened in silence to the doctor's rumbling voice.

"Clear enough," said Race, when he had finished. "The girl worked herself up, helped by a drink or two, and finally took a pot shot at the man with a .22 pistol. Then she went along to Linnet Doyle's cabin and shot her as well."

But Dr. Bessner was shaking his head.

"No, no. I do not think so. I do not think that was *possible*. For one thing she would not write her own initial on the wall—it would be ridiculous, *nicht wahr?*"

"She might," Race declared, "if she were as blindly mad and jealous as she sounds, she might want to—well—sign her name to the crime, so to speak."

Poirot shook his head.

"No, no, I do not think she would be as—as *crude* as that."

"Then there's only one reason for that J. It was put there by some one else deliberately to throw suspicion on her."

The doctor said:

"Yes, and the criminal was unlucky—because you see, it is not only *unlikely* that the young Fräulein did the murder—it is also I think *impossible*."

"How's that?"

Bessner explained Jacqueline's hysterics and the circumstances which had led Miss Bowers to take charge of her.

"And I think—I am sure—that Miss Bowers stayed with her all night."

Race said:

"If that's so, it's going to simplify matters very much."

Poirot asked:

"Who discovered the crime?"

"Mrs. Doyle's maid, Louise Bourget. She went to call her mistress as usual, found her dead, and came out and flopped into the steward's arms in a dead faint. He went to the manager, who came to me. I got hold of Bessner and then came for you."

Poirot nodded.

Race said:

"Doyle's got to know. You say he's asleep still."

The doctor said:

"Yes, he's still asleep in my cabin. I gave him a strong opiate last night."

Race turned to Poirot.

"Well," he said, "I don't think we need detain the doctor any longer, eh? Thank you, doctor."

Bessner rose.

"I will have my breakfast, yes. And then I will go back to my cabin and see if Mr. Doyle is ready to wake."

"Thanks."

Bessner went out. The two men looked at each other.

"Well, what about it, Poirot?" Race said. "You're the man in charge. I'll take my orders from you. You say what's to be done."

Poirot bowed.

"Eh bien," he said, "we must hold the court of inquiry. First of all, I think we must verify the story of the affair last night. That is to say, we must question Fanthorp and Miss Robson who were the actual witnesses of what occurred. The disappearance of the pistol is very significant."

Race rang a bell and sent a message by the steward.

Poirot sighed and shook his head.

"It is bad, this," he murmured. "It is bad."

"Have you any ideas?" asked Race curiously.

"My ideas conflict. They are not well arranged—they are not orderly. There is, you see, the big fact that this girl hated Linnet Doyle and wanted to kill her."

"You think she's capable of it?"

"I think so—yes." Poirot sounded doubtful.

"But not in this way? That's what's worrying you, isn't it? Not to creep into her cabin in the dark and shoot her while she was sleeping. It's the cold-bloodedness that strikes you as not ringing true?"

"In a sense, yes."

"You think that this girl, Jacqueline de Bellefort, is incapable of a premeditated cold-blooded murder."

Poirot said slowly:

"I am not sure, you see. She would have the brains—yes. But I doubt if, physically, she could bring herself to do the *act*. . . ."

Race nodded.

"Yes, I see. . . . Well, according to Bessner's story, it would also have been physically impossible.

"If that is true it clears the ground considerably. Let us hope it is true." He paused and then added simply: "I shall be glad if it is so, for I have for that little one much sympathy."

The door opened and Fanthorp and Cornelia came in. Bessner followed them.

Cornelia gasped out:

"Isn't this just awful? Poor, poor Mrs. Doyle. And she was so lovely too. It must have been a real *fiend* who could hurt her! And poor Mr. Doyle, he'll just go half crazy when he knows! Why even last night he was so frightfully worried lest she should hear about his accident."

"That is just what we want you to tell us about, Miss Robson," said Race. "We want to know exactly what happened last night."

Cornelia began a little confusedly, but a question or two from Poirot helped matters.

"Ah, yes, I understand. After the bridge, Madame Doyle went to her cabin. Did she really go to her cabin, I wonder?"

"She did," said Race. "I actually saw her. I said good-night to her at the door."

"And the time?"

"Mercy, I couldn't say," said Cornelia.

"It was twenty past eleven," said Race.

"*Bien*. Then at twenty past eleven, Madame Doyle was alive and well. At that moment there was in the saloon—who?"

Fanthorp answered.

"Doyle was there. And Miss de Bellefort. Myself and Miss Robson."

"That's so," agreed Cornelia. "Mr. Pennington had a drink and then went off to bed."

"That was how much later?"

"Oh, about three or four minutes."

"Before half-past eleven, then?"

"Oh, yes."

"So that there were left in the saloon you, Miss Robson, Miss de Bellefort, Mr. Doyle and Mr. Fanthorp. What were you all doing?"

"Mr. Fanthorp was reading a book. I'd got some embroidery. Miss de Bellefort was—she was—"

Fanthorp came to the rescue.

"She was drinking pretty heavily."

"Yes," agreed Cornelia. "She was talking to me mostly and asking me about things at home. And she kept saying things—to me mostly, but I think they were kind of meant for Mr. Doyle. He was getting kind of mad at her but he didn't say anything. I think he thought if he kept quiet she might simmer down."

"But she didn't?"

Cornelia shook her head.

"I tried to go once or twice, but she made me stop and I was getting very uncomfortable. And then Mr. Fanthorp got up and went out—"

"It was a little embarrassing," said Fanthorp. "I thought I'd make an unobtrusive exit. Miss de Bellefort was clearly working up for a scene."

"And then she pulled out the pistol," went on Cornelia. "And Mr. Doyle jumped up to try and get it away from her, and it went off and shot him through the leg, and then she began to sob and cry—and I was scared to death and ran out after Mr. Fanthorp and he came back with me, and Mr. Doyle said not to make a fuss, and one of the Nubian boys heard the noise of the shot and came along, but Mr. Fanthorp told him it was all right and then we got Jacqueline away to her cabin and Mr. Fanthorp stayed with her while I got Miss Bowers."

Cornelia paused breathless.

"What time was this?" asked Race.

Cornelia said again: "Mercy, I don't know," but Fanthorp answered promptly:

"It must have been about twenty minutes past twelve. I know that it was actually half-past twelve when I finally got to my cabin."

"Now let me be quite sure on one or two points," said Poirot. "After Mrs. Doyle left the saloon did any of you four leave it?"

"No."

"You are quite certain Miss de Bellefort did not leave the saloon at all?"

Fanthorp answered promptly:

"Positive. Neither Doyle, Miss de Bellefort, Miss Robson, nor myself left the saloon."

"Good. That establishes the fact that Miss de Bellefort could not possibly have shot Mrs. Doyle before—let us say—twenty past twelve. Now, Miss Robson, you went to fetch Miss Bowers. Was Miss de Bellefort alone in her cabin during that period?"

"No, Mr. Fanthorp stayed with her."

"Good. So far, Miss de Bellefort has a perfect alibi. Miss Bowers is the next person to interview, but before I send for her I should like to have your opinion on one or two points. Mr. Doyle, you say, was very anxious that Miss de Bellefort should not be left alone. Was he afraid, do you think, that she was contemplating some further rash act?"

"That is my opinion," said Fanthorp.

"He was definitely afraid she might attack Mrs. Doyle?"

"No." Fanthorp shook his head. "I don't think that was his idea at all. I think he was afraid she might—er—do something rash to herself."

"Suicide?"

"Yes. You see, she seemed completely sobered and heartroken at what she had done. She was full of self-reproach. She kept saying she would be better dead."

Cornelia said timidly:

"I think he was rather upset about her. He spoke—quite nicely. He said it was all his fault—that he'd treated her badly. He—he was really very nice."

Hercule Poirot nodded thoughtfully.

"Now about the pistol," he went on. "What happened to that?"

"She dropped it," said Cornelia.

"And afterwards?"

Fanthorp explained how he had gone back to search for it, but had not been able to find it.

"Aha," said Poirot. "Now we begin to arrive. Let us, I pray you, be very precise. Describe to me exactly what happened."

"Miss de Bellefort let it fall. Then she kicked it away from her with her foot."

"She sort of hated it," explained Cornelia. "I know just what she felt."

"And it went under a settee, you say. Now be very careful. Miss de Bellefort did not recover that pistol before she left the saloon?"

Both Fanthorp and Cornelia were positive on that point.

"*Précisément*. I seek only to be very exact, you comprehend. Then we arrive at this point. When Miss de Bellefort leaves the saloon the pistol is under the settee. And since Miss de Bellefort is not left alone, Mr. Fanthorp, Miss Robson or Miss Bowers being with her, she has no opportunity to get back the pistol after she left the saloon. What time was it, Mr. Fanthorp, when you went back to look for it?"

"It must have been just before half-past twelve."

"And how long would have elapsed between the time you and Dr. Bessner carried Mr. Doyle out of the saloon until you returned to look for the pistol?"

"Perhaps five minutes—perhaps a little more."

"Then in that five minutes *some one removes that pistol from where it lay out of sight under the settee*. That some one was *not* Miss de Bellefort. Who was it? It seems highly probable that the person who removed it was the murderer of Mrs. Doyle. We may assume, too, that that person had overheard or seen something of the events immediately preceding."

"I don't see how you make that out," objected Fanthorp.

"Because," said Hercule Poirot. "You have just told us *that the pistol was out of sight under the settee*. Therefore it is hardly credible that it was discovered by *accident*. It was taken by *some one who knew it was there*. Therefore that some one must have assisted at the scene."

Fanthorp shook his head.

"I saw no one when I went out on the deck just before the shot was fired."

"Ah, but you went out by the door on the starboard side."

"Yes. The same side as my cabin."

"Then if there had been anybody at the port door looking through the glass you would not have seen them?"

"No," admitted Fanthorp.

"Did any one hear the shot except the Nubian boy?"

"Not as far as I know."

Fanthorp went on:

"You see, the windows in here were all closed. Miss Van Schuyler felt a draught earlier in the evening. The swing doors were shut. I doubt if the shot would be at all closely heard. It would only sound like the pop of a cork."

Race said:

"As far as I know no one seems to have heard the other shot—the shot that killed Mrs. Doyle."

"That we will inquire into presently," said Poirot. "For the moment we still concern ourselves with Mademoiselle de Bellefort. We must speak to Miss Bowers. But first, before you go"—he arrested Fanthorp and Cornelia with a gesture "—you will give me a little information about yourselves. Then it will not be necessary to call you again later. You first, Monsieur—your full name."

"James Lechdale Fanthorp."

"Address?"

"Glasmore House, Market Donnington, Northamptonshire."

"Your profession?"

"I am a lawyer."

"And your reasons for visiting this country."

There was a pause. For the first time the impassive Mr. Fanthorp seemed taken aback. He said at last—almost mumbling the words:

"Er—pleasure."

"Aha," said Poirot. "You take the holiday, that is it, yes?"

"Er—yes."

"Very well, Mr. Fanthorp. Will you just give me a brief account of your own movements last night after the events we have just been narrating."

"I went straight to bed."

"That was at—?"

"Just after half-past twelve."

"Your cabin is No. 22 on the starboard side—the one nearest the saloon?"

"Yes."

"I will ask you one more question. Did you hear anything—anything at all after you went to your cabin?"

Fanthorp considered.

"I turned in very quickly. I *think* I heard a kind of splash just as I was dropping off to sleep. Nothing else."

"You heard a kind of splash? Near at hand?"

Fanthorp shook his head.

"Really, I couldn't say. I was half asleep."

"And what time would that be?"

"It might have been about one o'clock. I can't really say."

"Thank you, Mr. Fanthorp. That is all."

Poirot turned his attention to Cornelia.

"And now, Miss Robson? Your full name?"

"Cornelia Ruth. And my address is The Red House, Bellfield, Connecticut."

"What brought you to Egypt?"

"Cousin Marie, Miss Van Schuyler, brought me along on a trip."

"Had you ever met Mrs. Doyle previous to this journey?"

"No, never."

"And what did you do last night?"

"I went right to bed after helping Dr. Bessner with Mr. Doyle's leg."

"Your cabin is—?"

"41 on the port side—right next door to Miss de Bellefort."

"And did you hear anything?"

Cornelia shook her head.

"I didn't hear a thing."

"No splash?"

"No, but then I wouldn't, because the boat's against the bank on my side."

Poirot nodded.

"Thank you, Miss Robson. Now perhaps you will be so kind as to ask Miss Bowers to come here."

Fanthorp and Cornelia went out.

"That seems clear enough," said Race. "Unless three independent witnesses are lying, Jacqueline de Bellefort couldn't have got hold of the pistol. But somebody did. And somebody overheard the scene. And somebody was B.F. enough to write a big J on the wall."

There was a tap on the door and Miss Bowers entered.

The hospital nurse sat down in her usual composed efficient manner. In answer to Poirot she gave her name, address, and qualifications, adding:

"I've been looking after Miss Van Schuyler for over two years now."

"Is Miss Van Schuyler's health very bad?"

"Why, no, I wouldn't say that," said Miss Bowers. "She's not very young and she's nervous about herself and she likes to have a nurse around handy. There's nothing serious the matter with her. She just likes plenty of attention and she's willing to pay for it."

Poirot nodded comprehendingly. Then he said:

"I understand that Miss Robson fetched you last night?"

"Why, yes, that's so."

"Will you tell me exactly what happened?"

"Well, Miss Robson just gave me a brief outline of what had occurred and I came along with her. I found Miss de Bellefort in a very excited hysterical condition."

"Did she utter any threats against Mrs. Doyle?"

"No, nothing of that kind. She was in a condition of morbid self-reproach. She'd taken a good deal of alcohol, I should say, and she was suffering from reaction. I didn't think she ought to be left. I gave her a shot of morphia and sat up with her."

"Now, Miss Bowers, I want you to answer this. Did Miss de Bellefort leave her cabin at all?"

"No, she did not."

"And you yourself?"

"I stayed with her until early this morning."

"You are quite sure of that."

"Absolutely sure."

"Thank you, Miss Bowers."

The nurse went out. The two men looked at each other.

Jacqueline de Bellefort was definitely cleared of the crime. Who then had shot Linnet Doyle?

CHAPTER 13

Race said:

"Some one pinched the pistol. *It wasn't Jacqueline de Bellefort.* Some one knew enough to feel certain that his crime would be attributed to her. But that some one did *not* know that a hospital nurse was going to give her morphia and sit up with her all night. Add one thing more. Some one had already attempted to kill Linnet Doyle by rolling a boulder over the cliff—that some one was *not* Jacqueline de Bellefort. *Who was it!*"

Poirot said:

"It will be simpler to say who it could not have been. Neither Mr. Doyle, Mrs. Allerton, Mr. Tim Allerton, Miss Van Schuyler nor Miss Bowers could have had anything to do with it. They were all within my sight."

"H'm," said Race, "that leaves rather a large field. What about motive?"

"That is where I hope Mr. Doyle may be able to help us. There have been several incidents—"

The door opened and Jacqueline de Bellefort entered.

She was very pale and she stumbled a little as she walked.

"I didn't do it," she said. Her voice was that of a frightened child. "I didn't do it. Oh, please believe me. Every one will think I did it—but I didn't—I didn't. It's—it's awful. I wish it hadn't happened. I might have killed Simon last night—I was mad, I think. But I didn't do the other . . ."

She sat down and burst into tears.

Poirot patted her on the shoulder.

"There, there. We know that you did not kill Mrs. Doyle. It is proved—yes, proved, *mon enfant*. It was not you."

Jackie sat up suddenly, her wet handkerchief clasped in her hand.

"But who did?"

"That," said Poirot, "is just the question we are asking ourselves. You cannot help us there, my child?"

Jacqueline shook her head.

"I don't know . . . I can't imagine . . . no, I haven't the faintest idea."

She frowned deeply.

"No," she said at last. "I can't think of any one who wanted her dead"—her voice faltered a little—"except me."

Race said:

"Excuse me a minute—just thought of something."

He hurried out of the room.

Jacqueline de Bellefort sat with her head downcast nervously twisting her fingers.

She broke out suddenly:

"Death's horrible—horrible. I—I hate the thought of it."

Poirot said:

"Yes. It is not pleasant to think, is it, that now, at this very moment, some one is rejoicing at the successful carrying out of his or her plan."

"Don't—don't!" cried Jackie. "It sounds horrible, the way you put it."

Poirot shrugged his shoulders.

"It is true."

Jackie said in a low voice:

"I—I wanted her dead—and she is dead. . . . And what is worse—she died—just like I said."

"Yes, Mademoiselle. She was shot through the head."

She cried out:

"Then I was right, that night—at the Cataract Hotel. There *was* some one listening!"

"Ah!" Poirot nodded his head. "I wondered if you would remember that. Yes, it is altogether too much of a coincidence—that Madame Doyle should be killed in just the way you described."

Jackie shuddered.

"That man that night—who can he have been?"

Poirot was silent for a minute or two, then he said in quite a different tone of voice:

"You are sure it was a man, Mademoiselle?"

Jackie looked at him in surprise.

"Yes, of course. At least—"

"Well, Mademoiselle?"

She frowned, half closing her eyes in an effort to remember. She said slowly:

"I *thought* it was a man. . ."

"But now you are not so sure?"

Jackie said slowly:

"No, I can't be certain. I just assumed it was a man—but it was really just a—a figure—a shadow. . . ."

She paused and then, as Poirot did not speak, she asked:

"You think it must have been a woman? But surely none of the women on this boat can have wanted to kill Linnet?"

Poirot merely moved his head from side to side.

The door opened and Bessner appeared.

"Will you come and speak with Mr. Doyle, please, M. Poirot. He would like to see you."

Jackie sprang up. She caught Bessner by the arm.

"How is he? Is he—all right?"

"Naturally he is not all right," said Dr. Bessner reproachfully. "The bone is fractured, you understand."

"But he's not going to die?" cried Jackie.

"Ach, who said anything about dying? We will get him to civilisation and there we will have an X-ray and proper treatment."

"Oh." The girl's hands came together in a convulsive pressure. She sank down again on a chair.

Poirot stepped out on to the deck with the doctor and at that moment Race joined them. They went up to the promenade deck and along to Bessner's cabin.

Simon Doyle was lying propped with cushions and pillows an improvised cage over his leg. His face was ghastly in colour, the ravages of pain with shock on top of it. But the predominant expression on his face was bewilderment—the sick bewilderment of a child.

He muttered:

"Please come in. The doctor's told me—told me—about Linnet. . . . I can't believe it. I simply can't believe it's true."

"I know. It's a bad knock," said Race.

Simon stammered:

"You know—Jackie didn't do it. I'm certain Jackie didn't do it! It looks black against her, I dare say, but *she didn't do it*. She—she was a bit tight last night and all worked up and that's why she went for me. But she wouldn't—she wouldn't do *murder* . . . not cold-blooded murder. . . ."

Poirot said gently:

"Do not distress yourself, Mr. Doyle. Whoever shot your wife, it was not Miss de Bellefort."

Simon looked at him doubtfully.

"Is that on the level?"

"But since it was not Miss de Bellefort," continued Poirot, "can you give us any idea of who it might have been?"

Simon shook his head. The look of bewilderment increased.

"It's crazy—impossible. Apart from Jackie nobody could have wanted to do her in."

"Reflect, Mr. Doyle. Has she no enemies? Is there no one who has a grudge against her?"

Again Simon shook his head with the same hopeless gesture.

"It sounds absolutely fantastic. There's Windlesham, of course. She more or less chucked him to marry me—but I can't see a polite stick like Windlesham committing murder and anyway he's miles away. Same thing with old Sir George Wode, he'd got a down on Linnet over the house—disliked the way she was pulling it about—but he's miles away in London and anyway to think of murder in such a connection would be fantastic."

"Listen, Mr. Doyle," Poirot spoke very earnestly. "On the first day we came on board the *Karnak* I was impressed by a little conversation which I had with Madame your wife. She was very upset—very distraught. She said—mark this well—that *everybody* hated her. She said she felt afraid—unsafe—as though *every one* round her were an enemy."

"She was pretty upset at finding Jackie aboard. So was I," said Simon.

"That is true—but it does not quite explain those words. When she said she was surrounded by enemies, she was almost certainly exaggerating—but all the same she did mean *more than one person*."

"You may be right there," admitted Simon. "I think I can explain that. It was a name in the passenger list that upset her."

"A name in the passenger list? What name?"

"Well, you see, she didn't actually tell me. As a matter of fact I wasn't even listening very carefully. I was going over the Jacqueline business in my mind. As far as I remember Linnet said something about doing people down in business and that it made her uncomfortable to meet any one who had a grudge against her family. You see, although I don't really know the family history very well, I gather that Linnet's mother was a millionaire's daughter. Her father was only just ordinary plain wealthy but after his marriage he naturally began playing the markets or whatever you call it. And as a result of that, of course, several people got it in the neck. You know, affluence one day, the gutter the next. Well, I gather there was some one on board whose father had got up against Linnet's father and taken a pretty hard knock. I remember Linnet saying: 'It's pretty awful when people hate you without even knowing you.'"

"Yes," said Poirot thoughtfully. "That would explain what she said to me.

For the first time she was feeling the burden of her inheritance and not its advantages. You are quite sure, Mr. Doyle, that she did not mention this man's name?"

Simon shook his head ruefully.

"I didn't really pay much attention. Just said: 'Oh, nobody minds what happened to their fathers nowadays. Life goes too fast for that.' Something of that kind."

Bessner said dryly:

"Ach, but I can have a guess. There is certainly a young man with a grievance on board."

"You mean Ferguson?" said Poirot.

"Yes. He spoke against Mrs. Doyle once or twice. I myself have heard him."

"What can we do to find out?" asked Simon.

Poirot replied:

"Colonel Race and I must interview all the passengers. Until we have got their stories it would be unwise to form theories. Then there is the maid. We ought to interview her first of all. It would, perhaps, be as well if we did that here. Mr. Doyle's presence might be helpful."

"Yes, that's a good idea," said Simon.

"Had she been with Mrs. Doyle long?"

"Just a couple of months, that's all."

"Only a couple of months," exclaimed Poirot.

"Why, you don't think—"

"Had Madame any valuable jewellery?"

"There were her pearls," said Simon. "She once told me they were worth forty or fifty thousand."

He shivered.

"My God, do you think those damned pearls—"

"Robbery is a possible motive," said Poirot. "All the same it seems hardly credible. . . . Well, we shall see. Let us have the maid here."

Louise Bourget was that same vivacious Latin brunette whom Poirot had seen one day and noticed.

She was anything but vivacious now. She had been crying and looked frightened. Yet there was a kind of sharp cunning apparent in her face which did not prepossess the two men favourably towards her.

"You are Louise Bourget?"

"Yes, Monsieur."

"When did you last see Madame Doyle alive?"

"Last night, Monsieur. I waited in her cabin to undress her."

"What time was that?"

"It was some time after eleven, Monsieur. I cannot say exactly when. I undress Madame and put her to bed and then I leave."

"How long did all that take?"

"Ten minutes, Monsieur. Madame was tired. She told me to put the lights out when I went."

"And when you had left her, what did you do?"

"I went to my own cabin, Monsieur, on the deck below."

"And you heard or saw nothing more than can help us?"

"How could I, Monsieur?"

"That, Mademoiselle, is for you to say, not for us," Hercule Poirot retorted.

She stole a sideways glance at him.

"But, Monsieur, I was nowhere near. . . . What could I have seen or heard? I was on the deck below. My cabin it was on the other side of the boat even. It is impossible that I should have heard anything. Naturally, if I had been unable to sleep, if I had mounted the stairs, *then* perhaps I might have seen this assassin, this monster enter or leave Madame's cabin, but as it is—"

She threw out her hands appealingly to Simon.

"Monsieur, I implore you—you see how it is? What can I say?"

"My good girl," said Simon harshly. "Don't be a fool. Nobody thinks you saw or heard anything. You'll be quite all right. I'll look after you. Nobody's accusing you of anything."

Louise murmured:

"Monsieur is very good," and dropped her eyelids modestly.

"We take it, then, that you saw and heard nothing?" said Race impatiently.

"That is what I said, Monsieur."

"And you know of no one who had a grudge against your mistress?"

To the surprise of her listeners Louise nodded her head vigorously.

"Oh, yes. That I do know. To that question I can answer 'Yes' most emphatically."

Poirot said:

"You mean Mademoiselle de Bellefort?"

"She, certainly. But it is not of her I speak. There was some one else on this boat who disliked Madame, who was very angry because of the way Madame had injured him."

"Good Lord," said Simon. "What's all this?"

Louise went on, still emphatically nodding her head with the utmost vigour.

"Yes, yes, yes, it is as I say! It concerns the former maid of Madame—my predecessor. There was a man, one of the engineers on this boat who wanted her to marry him. And my predecessor, Marie her name was, she would have done so. But Madame Doyle, she made inquiries and she discovered that this Fleetwood already he had a wife—a wife of colour, you understand, a wife of this country. She had gone back to her own people but he was still married to her, you understand. And so Madame she told all this to Marie and Marie she was very unhappy and she would not see Fleetwood any more. And this Fleetwood, he was infuriated, and when he found out that this Madame Doyle had formerly been Miss Linnet Ridgeway he tells me that he would like to kill her! Her interference ruined his life, he said."

Louise paused triumphantly.

"This is interesting," said Race.

Poirot turned to Simon.

"Had you any idea of this?"

"None whatever," said Simon with patent sincerity. "I doubt if Linnet even knew the man was on the boat. She had probably forgotten all about the incident."

He turned sharply to the maid.

"Did you say anything to Mrs. Doyle about this?"

"No, Monsieur, of course not."

Poirot said:

"Do you know anything about your mistress's pearls?"

"Her pearls?" Louise's eyes opened very wide. "She was wearing them last night."

"You saw them when she came to bed?"

"Yes, Monsieur."

"Where did she put them?"

"On the table by the side as always."

"That is where you last saw them?"

"Yes, sir."

"Did you see them there this morning?"

A startled look came into the girl's face.

"Mon Dieu, I did not even look. I come up to the bed, I see—I see Madame, and then I cry out and rush out of the door and faint."

Hercule Poirot nodded his head.

"You did not look. But I, I have the eyes which notice, and there were *no pearls on the table beside the bed this morning*."

CHAPTER 14

Hercule Poirot's observation had not been at fault. There were no pearls on the table by Linnet Doyle's bed.

Louise Bourget was bidden to make a search among Linnet's belongings.

According to her all was in order. Only the pearls had disappeared.

As they emerged from the cabin a steward was waiting to tell them that breakfast had been served in the smoking-room.

As they passed along the deck, Poirot paused to look over the rail.

"Aha! I see you have had an idea, my friend."

"Yes. It suddenly came to men when Fanthorp mentioned thinking he had heard a splash, that I too had been awakened some time last night by a splash. It's perfectly possible that, after the murder, the murderer threw the pistol overboard."

Poirot said slowly:

"You think that is possible, my friend?"

Race shrugged his shoulders.

"It's a suggestion. After all, the pistol wasn't anywhere in the cabin. First thing I looked for."

"All the same," said Poirot, "it is incredible that it should have been thrown overboard."

Race said:

"Where is it then?"

Poirot said thoughtfully:

"If it is not in Mrs. Doyle's cabin, there is, logically, only one other place where it could be."

"Where's that?"

"In Mademoiselle de Bellefort's cabin."

"Yes. I see—"

He stopped suddenly.

"She's out of her cabin. Shall we go and have a look now?"

Poirot shook his head.

"No, my friend, that would be precipitate. *It may not yet have been put there*."

"What about an immediate search of the whole boat?"

"That way we should show our hand. We must work with great care. It is very delicate, our position at the moment. Let us discuss the situation as we eat."

Race agreed. They went into the smoking-room.

"Well?" said Race as he poured himself out a cup of coffee. "We've got two definite leads. There's the disappearance of the pearls. And there's the man Fleetwood. As regards the pearls, robbery seems indicated, but—I don't know whether you'll agree with me—"

Poirot said quickly:

"It was an odd moment to choose?"

"Exactly. To steal the pearls on a voyage such as this invites *a close search of everybody on board*. How, then, could the thief hope to get away with his booty?"

"He might have gone ashore and dumped it?"

"The company always has a watchman on the bank."

"Then that is not feasible. Was the murder committed to divert attention from the robbery? No, that does not make sense—it is profoundly unsatisfactory. But supposing that Mrs. Doyle woke up and caught the thief in the act?"

"And therefore the thief shot her? But she was shot whilst she slept."

"So that too does not make sense. . . . You know, I have a little idea about those pearls—and yet—no—it is impossible. Because if my idea was right the pearls would not have disappeared. Tell me, what did you think of the maid?"

"I wondered," said Race slowly, "if she knew more than she said."

"Ah, you too had that impression?"

"Definitely not a nice girl," said Race.

Hercule Poirot nodded.

"Yes, I would not trust her, that one."

"You think she had something to do with the murder?"

"No, I would not say that."

"With the theft of the pearls, then?"

"That is more probable. She had only been with Mrs. Doyle a very short time. She may be a member of a gang that specialises in jewel robberies. In such a case there is often a maid with excellent references. Unfortunately we are not in a position to seek information on these points. And yet that explanation does not quite satisfy me. . . . Those pearls—ah *sacré*, my little idea *ought* to be right. And yet nobody would be so imbecile—" he broke off.

"What about the man Fleetwood?"

"We must question him. It may be that we have there the solution. If Louise Bourget's story is true, he had a definite motive for revenge. He could have overheard the scene between Jacqueline and Mr. Doyle, and when they have left the saloon he could have darted in and secured the gun. Yes, it is all quite possible. And that letter J scrawled in blood. That, too, would accord with a simple rather crude nature."

"In fact, he's just the person we are looking for?"

"Yes—only—"

Poirot rubbed his nose. He said with a slight grimace:

"See you, I recognise my own weaknesses. It has been said of me that I like to make a case difficult. This solution that you put to me—it is too simple—too easy. I cannot feel that it really happened. And yet, that may be sheer prejudice on my part."

"Well, we'd better have the fellow here."

Race rang the bell and gave the order. Then he said:

"Any other—possibilities?"

"Plenty, my friend. There is, for example, the American trustee."

"Pennington?"

"Yes, Pennington. There was a curious little scene in here the other day."

He narrated the happenings to Race.

"You see—it is significant. Madame, she wanted to read all the papers before signing. So he makes the excuse of another day. And then, the husband, he makes a very significant remark."

"What was that?"

"He says: '*I never read anything. I sign where I am told to sign.*' You perceive the significance of that? *Pennington did.* I saw it in his eye. He looked at Doyle as though an entirely new idea had come into his head. Just imagine, my friend, that you have been left trustee to the daughter of an intensely wealthy man. You use, perhaps, that money to speculate with. I know it is so in all detective novels—but you read of it too in the newspapers. It happens, my friend, *it happens*."

"I don't dispute it," said Race.

"There is, perhaps, still time to make good by speculating wildly. Your ward is not yet of age. And then—she marries! The control passes from your hands into hers at a moment's notice! A disaster! But there is still a chance. She is on a honeymoon. She will perhaps be careless about business. A casual paper slipped in among others, signed without reading. But Linnet Doyle was not like that. Honeymoon or no honeymoon, she was a business woman. And then her husband makes a remark and a new idea comes to that desperate man who is seeking a way out from ruin. If Linnet Doyle were to die, her fortune would pass to her husband—and he would be easy to deal with, he would be a child in the hands of an astute man like Andrew Pennington. *Mon cher* Colonel, I tell you I *saw* the thought pass through Andrew Pennington's head. 'If only it were Doyle I had got to deal with. . . .' That is what he was thinking."

"Quite possible, I dare say," said Race dryly. "But you've no evidence."

"Alas, no."

"Then there's young Ferguson," said Race. "He talks bitterly enough. Not that I go by talk. Still, he *might* be the fellow whose father was ruined by old Ridgeway. It's a little far-fetched but it's *possible*. People do brood over bygone wrongs sometimes."

He paused a minute and then said:

"And there's my fellow."

"Yes, there is 'your fellow' as you call him."

"He's a killer," said Race. "We know that. On the other hand I can't see any way in which he could have come up against Linnet Doyle. Their orbits don't touch."

Poirot said slowly:

"Unless, accidentally, she had become possessed of evidence showing his identity."

"That's possible, but it seems highly unlikely." There was a knock at the door. "Ah, there's our would-be bigamist."

Fleetwood was a big truculent looking man. He looked suspiciously from one to the other of them as he entered the room. Poirot recognised him as the man he had seen talking to Louise Bourget.

Fleetwood said suspiciously:

"You wanted to see me?"

"We did," said Race. "You probably know that a murder was committed on this boat last night?"

Fleetwood nodded.

"And I believe it is true that you had reason to feel anger against the woman who was killed."

A look of alarm sprang up in Fleetwood's eyes.

"Who told you that?"

"You considered that Mrs. Doyle had interfered between you and a young woman."

"I know who told you that—that lying French hussy. She's a liar through and through, that girl."

"But this particular story happens to be true."

"It's a dirty lie!"

"You say that although you don't know what it is yet."

The shot told. The man flushed and gulped.

"It is true, is it not, that you were going to marry the girl Marie, and that she broke it off when she discovered that you were a married man already."

"What business was it of hers?"

"You mean, what business was it of Mrs. Doyle's? Well, you know, bigamy is bigamy."

"It wasn't like that. I married one of the locals out here. It didn't answer. She went back to her people. I've not seen her for half a dozen years."

"Still you were married to her."

The man was silent. Race went on.

"Mrs. Doyle, or Miss Ridgeway as she then was, found out all this?"

"Yes, she did, curse her. Nosing about where no one ever asked her to. I'd have treated Marie right. I'd have done anything for her. And she'd never have known about the other, if it hadn't been for that meddlesome young lady, and I felt bitter about it when I saw her on this boat, all dressed up in pearls and diamonds and lording it all over the place with never a thought that she'd broken up a man's life for him! I felt bitter all right. But if you think I'm a dirty murderer—if you think I went and shot her with a gun, well, that's a damned lie! I never touched her. And that's God's truth."

He stopped. The sweat was rolling down his face.

"Where were you last night between the hours of twelve and two?"

"In my bunk asleep—and my mate will tell you so."

"We shall see," said Race. He dismissed him with a curt nod. "That'll do."

"*Eh bien?*" said Poirot as the door closed behind Fleetwood.

Race shrugged his shoulders.

"He tells quite a straight story. He's nervous, of course, but not unduly so. We'll have to investigate his *alibi*—though I don't suppose it will be decisive. His mate was probably asleep and this fellow could have slipped in and out if he wanted to. It depends whether any one else saw him."

"Yes, one must inquire as to that."

"The next thing, I think," said Race, "is whether any one heard anything which might give us a clue to the time of the crime. Bessner places it as having occurred between twelve and two. It seems reasonable to hope that some one among the passengers may have heard the shot—even if they did not recognise it for what it was. I didn't hear anything of the kind myself. What about you?"

Poirot shook his head.

"Me, I slept absolutely like the log. I heard nothing—but nothing at all. I might have been drugged I slept so soundly."

"A pity," said Race. "Well, let's hope we have a bit of luck with the people who have cabins on the starboard side. Fanthorp we've done. The Allertons come next. I'll send the steward to fetch them."

Mrs. Allerton came in briskly. She was wearing a soft grey striped silk dress. Her face looked distressed.

"It's too horrible," she said as she accepted the chair that Poirot placed for her. "I can hardly believe it. That lovely creature with everything to live for—dead. I almost feel I can't believe it."

"I know how you feel, Madame," said Poirot sympathetically.

"I'm glad *you* are on board," said Mrs. Allerton simply. "You'll be able to find out who did it. I'm so glad it isn't that poor tragic girl."

"You mean Mademoiselle de Bellefort. Who told you she did not do it?"

"Cornelia Robson," said Mrs. Allerton with a faint smile. "You know, she's simply thrilled by it all. It's probably the only exciting thing that has ever happened to her and probably the only exciting thing that ever will happen to her. But she's so nice that she's terribly ashamed of enjoying it. She thinks it's awful of her."

Mrs. Allerton gave a look at Poirot and then added.

"But I mustn't chatter. You want to ask me questions."

"If you please. You went to bed at what time, Madame?"

"Just after half-past ten."

"And you went to sleep at once?"

"Yes. I was sleepy."

"And did you hear anything—anything at all—during the night?"

Mrs. Allerton wrinkled her brows.

"Yes, I think I heard a splash and some one running—or was it the other way about? I'm rather hazy. I just had a vague idea that some one had fallen overboard at sea—a dream, you know, and then I woke up and listened but it was all quite quiet."

"Do you know what time that was?"

"No, I'm afraid I don't. But I don't think it was very long after I went to sleep. I mean it was within the first hour or so."

"Alas, Madame, that is not very definite."

"No, I know it isn't. But it's no good my trying to guess, is it, when I haven't really the vaguest idea?"

"And that is all you can tell us, Madame?"

"I'm afraid so."

"Had you ever actually met Mrs. Doyle before?"

"No, Tim had met her. And I'd heard a good deal about her—through a cousin of ours, Joanna Southwood, but I'd never spoken to her till we met at Assuan."

"I have one other question, Madame, if you will pardon me for asking."

Mrs. Allerton murmured with a faint smile:

"I should love to be asked an indiscreet question."

"It is this. *Did you, or your family, ever suffer any financial loss through the operations of Mrs. Doyle's father, Melhuish Ridgeway!*"

Mrs. Allerton looked thoroughly astonished.

"Oh, no! The family finances have never suffered except by dwindling. . . . You know, everything paying less interest than it used to. There's never been anything melodramatic about our poverty. My husband left very little money but what he left I still have, though it doesn't yield as much as it used to yield."

"I thank you, Madame. Perhaps you will ask your son to come to us."

Tim said lightly when his mother came to him:

"Ordeal over? My turn now! What sort of things did they ask you?"

"Only whether I heard anything last night," said Mrs. Allerton. "And unluckily I didn't hear anything at all. I can't think why not. After all, Linnet's cabin is only one away from mine. I should think I'd have been bound to hear the shot. Go along, Tim, they're waiting for you."

To Tim Allerton Poirot repeated his previous question.

Tim answered:

"I went to bed early, half-past ten or so, I read for a bit. Put out my light just after eleven."

"Did you hear anything after that?"

"Heard a man's voice saying good-night, I think, not far away."

"That was I saying good-night to Mrs. Doyle," said Race.

"Yes. After that I went to sleep. Then, later, I heard a kind of hullabaloo going on, somebody calling Fanthorp, I remember."

"Miss Robson when she ran out from the observation saloon."

"Yes, I suppose that was it. And then a lot of different voices. And then somebody running along the deck. And then a splash. And then I heard old Bessner booming out something about, 'Careful now,' and 'Not too quick.'"

"You heard a splash?"

"Well, something of that kind."

"You are sure it was not a *shot* you heard?"

"Yes, I suppose it might have been. . . . I did hear a cork pop. Perhaps that was the shot. I may have imagined the splash from connecting the idea of the cork with liquid pouring into a glass . . . I know my foggy idea was that there was some kind of party on. And I wished they'd all go to bed and shut up."

"Anything more after that?"

Tim thought.

"Only Fanthorp barging round in his cabin next door. I thought he'd never get to bed."

"And after that?"

Tim shrugged his shoulders.

"After that—oblivion."

"You heard nothing more?"

"Nothing whatever."

"Thank you, Mr. Allerton."

Tim got up and left the cabin.

CHAPTER 15

Race pored thoughtfully over a plan of the promenade deck of the *Karnak*.

"Fanthorp, young Allerton, Mrs. Allerton. Then an empty cabin—Simon Doyle's. Now who's on the other side of Mrs. Doyle's? The old American dame. If any one heard anything she should have done. If she's up we'd better have her along."

Miss Van Schuyler entered the room. She looked even older and yellower than usual this morning. Her small dark eyes had an air of venomous displeasure in them.

Race rose and bowed.

"We're very sorry to trouble you, Miss Van Schuyler. It's very good of you. Please sit down."

Miss Van Schuyler said sharply:

"I dislike being mixed up in this. I resent it very much. I do not wish to be associated in any way with this—er—very unpleasant affair."

"Quite—quite. I was just saying to M. Poirot that the sooner we took your statement the better, as then you need have no further trouble."

Miss Van Schuyler looked at Poirot with something approaching favour.

"I'm glad you both realise my feelings. I am not accustomed to anything of this kind."

Poirot said soothingly.

"Precisely, Mademoiselle. That is why we wish to free you from the unpleasantness as quickly as possible. Now you went to bed last night—at what time?"

"Ten o'clock is my usual time. Last night I was rather later as Cornelia Robson, very inconsiderately, kept me waiting."

"*Très bien, Mademoiselle*. Now what did you hear after you had retired?"

Miss Van Schuyler said:

"I sleep very lightly."

"*A merveille!* That is very fortunate for us."

"I was awoken by that rather flashy young woman—Mrs. Doyle's maid who said 'Bonne nuit, Madame,' in what I cannot but think an unnecessarily loud voice."

"And after that?"

"I went to sleep again. I woke up thinking some one was in my cabin but I realised that it was some one in the cabin next door."

"In Mrs. Doyle's cabin?"

"Yes. Then I heard some one outside on the deck and then a splash."

"You have no idea what time this was?"

"I can tell you the time exactly. It was ten minutes past one."

"You are sure of that?"

"Yes. I looked at my little clock that stands by my bed."

"You did not hear a shot?"

"No, nothing of the kind."

"But it might possibly have been a shot that awakened you?"

Miss Van Schuyler considered the question, her toad-like head on one side.

"It might," she admitted rather grudgingly.

"And you have no idea what caused the splash you heard?"

"Not at all—I know perfectly."

Colonel Race sat up alertly.

"You know?"

"Certainly. I did not like this sound of prowling around. I got up and went to the door of my cabin. Miss Otterbourne was leaning over the side. She had just dropped something into the water."

"Miss Otterbourne?"

Race sounded really surprised.

"Yes."

"You are quite sure it was Miss Otterbourne?"

"I saw her face distinctly."

"She did not see you?"

"I do not think so."

Poirot leant forward.

"And what did her face look like, Mademoiselle?"

"She was in a condition of considerable emotion."

Race and Poirot exchanged a quick glance.

"And then?" Race prompted.

"Miss Otterbourne went away round the stern of the boat and I returned to bed."

There was a knock at the door and the manager entered.

He carried in his hand a dripping bundle.

"We've got it, colonel."

Race took the package. He unwrapped fold after fold of sodden velvet. Out of it fell a coarse handkerchief faintly stained with pink, wrapped round a small pearl-handled pistol.

Race gave Poirot a glance of slightly malicious triumph.

"You see," he said. "My idea was right. It *was* thrown overboard."

He held the pistol out on the palm of his hand.

"What do you say, M. Poirot? Is this the pistol you saw at the Cataract Hotel that night?"

Poirot examined it carefully, then he said quietly.

"Yes—that is it. There is the ornamental work on it—and the initials J.B. It is an *article de luxe*—a very feminine production—but it is none the less a lethal weapon."

".22," murmured Race. He took out the clip. "Two bullets fired. Yes, there doesn't seem much doubt about it."

Miss Van Schuyler coughed significantly.

"And what about my stole?" she demanded.

"Your stole, Mademoiselle?"

"Yes, that is my velvet stole you have here."

Race picked up the dripping folds of material.

"This is yours, Miss Van Schuyler?"

"Certainly it's mine!" the old lady snapped. "I missed it last night. I was asking every one if they'd seen it."

Poirot questioned Race with a glance—and the latter gave a slight nod of assent.

"Where did you see it last, Miss Van Schuyler?"

"I had it in the saloon yesterday evening. When I came to go to bed I could not find it anywhere."

Race said quietly:

"You realise what it's been used for?"

He spread it out, indicating with a finger the scorching and several small holes.

"The murderer wrapped it round the pistol to deaden the noise of the shot."

"Impertinence!" snapped Miss Van Schuyler.

The colour rose in her wizened cheeks.

Race said:

"I shall be glad, Miss Van Schuyler, if you will tell me the extent of your previous acquaintance with Mrs. Doyle."

"There was no previous acquaintance."

"But you knew of her?"

"I knew who she was, of course."

"But your families were not acquainted?"

"As a family we have always prided ourselves on being exclusive, Colonel Race. My dear mother would never have dreamed of calling upon any of the Hartz family who, outside their wealth, were nobodies."

"That is all you have to say, Miss Van Schuyler?"

"I have nothing to add to what I have told you. Linnet Ridgeway was brought up in England and I never saw her till I came aboard this boat."

She rose.

Poirot opened the door for her and she marched out.

The eyes of the two men met.

"That's her story," said Race, "and she's going to stick to it! It may be true. I don't know. But—Rosalie Otterbourne? I hadn't expected that."

Poirot shook his head in a perplexed manner. Then he brought down his hand on the table with a sudden bang.

"But it does not make sense," he cried. *"Nom d'un nom d'un nom!* It does not make sense."

Race looked at him.

"What do you mean exactly?"

"I mean that up to a point it is all the clear sailing. Some one wished to kill Linnet Doyle. Some one overheard the scene in the saloon last night. Some one sneaked in there and retrieved the pistol—Jacqueline de Bellefort's pistol, remember. Somebody shot Linnet Doyle with that pistol and wrote the letter J on the wall. . . . All so clear, is it not? All pointing to Jacqueline de Bellefort as the murderess. And then what does the murderer do? Leave the pistol—the damning pistol—Jacqueline de Bellefort's pistol for every one to find? No, he—or she—throws the pistol, *that particular damning bit of evidence,* overboard. Why, my friend, why?"

Race shook his head.

"It's odd."

"It is more than odd—it is *impossible!*"

"Not impossible since it happened!"

"I do not mean that. I mean that *the sequence of events is impossible*. Something is wrong."

CHAPTER 16

Colonel Race glanced curiously at his colleague. He respected—he had reason to respect—the brain of Hercule Poirot. Yet for the moment he did not follow the other's process of thought. He asked no question, however. He seldom did ask questions. He proceeded straightforwardly with the matter in hand.

"What's the next thing to be done? Question the Otterbourne girl?"

"Yes, that may advance us a little."

Rosalie Otterbourne entered ungraciously. She did not look nervous or frightened in any way—merely unwilling and sulky.

"Well?" she said. "What is it?"

Race was the spokesman.

"We're investigating Mrs. Doyle's death," he explained.

Rosalie nodded.

"Will you tell me what you did last night?"

Rosalie reflected a minute.

"Mother and I went to bed early—before eleven. We didn't hear anything in particular, except a bit of fuss outside Dr. Bessner's cabin. I heard the old man's German voice booming away. Of course, I didn't know what it was all about till this morning."

"You didn't hear a shot?"

"No."

"Did you leave your cabin at all last night?"

"No."

"You are quite sure of that?"

Rosalie stared at him.

"What do you mean? Of course I'm sure of it."

"You did not, for instance, go round to the starboard side of the boat and throw something overboard?"

The colour rose in her face.

"Is there any rule against throwing things overboard?"

"No, of course not. Then you did?"

"No, I didn't. I never left my cabin, I tell you."

"Then if any one says that they saw you—"

She interrupted him.

"Who says they saw me?"

"Miss Van Schuyler."

"Miss Van Schuyler?" She sounded genuinely astonished.

"Yes. Miss Van Schuyler says she looked out of her cabin and saw you throw something over the side."

Rosalie said clearly:

"That's a damned lie."

Then, as though struck by a sudden thought, she asked:

"What time was this?"

It was Poirot who answered.

"It was ten minutes past one, Mademoiselle."

She nodded her head thoughtfully.

"Did she see anything else?"

Poirot looked at her curiously. He stroked his chin.

"See—no. But she heard something."

"What did she hear?"

"Some one moving about in Mrs. Doyle's cabin."

"I see," muttered Rosalie.

She was pale now—deadly pale.

"And you persist in saying that you threw nothing overboard, Mademoiselle?"

"Why on earth should I run about throwing things overboard in the middle of the night?"

"There might be a reason—an innocent reason."

"Innocent?" said the girl sharply.

"That is what I said. You see, Mademoiselle, something *was* thrown overboard last night—something that was not innocent."

Race silently held out the bundle of stained velvet—opening it to display its contents.

Rosalie Otterbourne shrank back.

"Was that—what—she was killed with?"

"Yes, Mademoiselle."

"And you think that I—I did it? What utter nonsense! Why on earth should I want to kill Linnet Doyle? I don't even know her!"

She laughed and stood up scornfully.

"The whole thing is too ridiculous."

"Remember, Miss Otterbourne," said Race, "that Miss Van Schuyler is prepared to swear she saw your face quite clearly in the moonlight."

Rosalie laughed again.

"That old cat. She's probably half-blind anyway. It wasn't me she saw."

She paused.

"Can I go now?"

Race nodded and Rosalie Otterbourne left the room.

The eyes of the two men met. Race lighted a cigarette.

"Well, that's that. Flat contradiction. Which of 'em do we believe?"

Poirot shook his head.

"I have a little idea that neither of them was being quite frank."

"That's the worst of our job," said Race despondently. "So many people keep back the truth for positively futile reasons. What's our next move? Get on with the questioning of the passengers?"

"I think so. It is always well to proceed with order and method."

Race nodded.

Mrs. Otterbourne, dressed in floating batik material, succeeded her daughter. She corroborated Rosalie's statement that they had both gone to bed before eleven o'clock. She herself had heard nothing of interest during the night. She could not say whether Rosalie had left their cabin or not. On the subject of the crime she was inclined to hold forth.

"The *crime passionel!*" she exclaimed. "The primitive instinct—to kill! So closely allied to the sex instinct. That girl, Jacqueline, half Latin, hot-blooded—obeying the deepest instincts of her being, stealing forth, revolver in hand—"

"But Jacqueline de Bellefort did not shoot Mrs. Doyle. That we know for certain. It is proved," explained Poirot.

"Her husband, then," said Mrs. Otterbourne rallying from the blow. "The blood lust and the sex instinct—a sexual crime. There are many well-known instances."

"Mr. Doyle was shot through the leg and he was quite unable to move—the bone was fractured," explained Colonel Race. "He spent the night with Dr. Bessner."

Mrs. Otterbourne was even more disappointed. She searched her mind hopefully.

"Of course," she said. "How foolish of me. *Miss Bowers!*"

"Miss Bowers?"

"Yes. Naturally. It's so *clear* psychologically. Repression! The repressed virgin! Maddened by the sight of these two—a young husband and wife passionately in love with each other—of course it was her! She's just the type—sexually unattractive—innately respectable. In my book, *The Barren Vine*—"

Colonel Race interposed tactfully:

"Your suggestions have been most helpful, Mrs. Otterbourne. We must get on with our job now. Thank you so much."

He escorted her gallantly to the door and came back wiping his brow.

"What a poisonous woman! Whew! Why didn't somebody murder *her!*"

"It may yet happen," Poirot consoled him.

"There might be some sense in that. Whom have we got left? Pennington—we'll keep him for the end I think—Richetti—Ferguson."

Signor Richetti was very voluble—very agitated.

"But what a horror—what an infamy—a woman so young and so beautiful—indeed an inhuman crime—!"

Signor Richetti's hands flew expressively up in the air.

His answers were prompt. He had gone to bed early—very early. In fact immediately after dinner. He had read for a while a very interesting pamphlet lately published—Prähistorische Forschung in Kleinasien—throwing an entirely new light on the painted pottery of the Anatolian foothills.

He had put out his light some time before eleven. No, he had not heard any shot. Not any sound like the pop of a cork. The only thing he had heard—but that was later—in the middle of the night—was a splash—a big splash—just near his porthole.

"Your cabin is on the lower deck—on the starboard side, is it not?"

"Yes, yes, that is so. And I hear the big splash." His arms flew up once more to describe the bigness of the splash.

"Can you tell me at all what time that was?"

Signor Richetti reflected.

"It was one, two, three hours after I go to sleep. Perhaps two hours."

"About ten minutes past one, for instance?"

"It might very well be, yes. Ah! but what a terrible crime—how inhuman. . . . So charming a woman . . ."

Exit Signor Richetti—still gesticulating freely.

Race looked at Poirot. Poirot raised his eyebrows expressively. Then shrugged his shoulders. They passed on to Mr. Ferguson.

Ferguson was difficult. He sprawled insolently in a chair.

"Grand to-do about this business!" he sneered. "What's it really matter? Lot of superfluous women in the world!"

Race said coldly:

"Can we have an account of your movements last night, Mr. Ferguson?"

"Don't see why you should. But I don't mind. I mooched around a good bit. Went ashore with Miss Robson. When she went back to the boat I mooched around by myself for a while. Came back and turned in round about midnight."

"Your cabin is on the lower deck—starboard side?"

"Yes. I'm not up among the nobs."

"Did you hear a shot? It might only have sounded like the popping of a cork."

Ferguson considered.

"Yes, I think I did hear something like a cork. . . . Can't remember when—before I went to sleep. But there were still a lot of people about then—commotion, running about on the deck above."

"That was probably the shot fired by Miss de Bellefort. You didn't hear another?"

Ferguson shook his head.

"Nor a splash?"

"A splash? Yes, I believe I did hear a splash. But there was so much row going on I can't be sure about it."

"Did you leave your cabin during the night?"

Ferguson grinned.

"No, I didn't. And I didn't participate in the good work, worse luck."

"Come, come, Mr. Ferguson, don't behave childishly."

The young man reacted angrily.

"Why shouldn't I say what I think? I believe in violence."

"But you don't practise what you preach?" murmured Poirot. "I wonder."

He leaned forward.

"It was the man, Fleetwood, was it not, who told you that Linnet Doyle was one of the richest women in England?"

"What's Fleetwood got to do with this?"

"Fleetwood, my friend, had an excellent motive for killing Linnet Doyle. He had a special grudge against her."

Mr. Ferguson came up out of his seat like a Jack-in-the-Box.

"So that's your dirty game, is it?" he demanded wrathfully. "Put it on to a poor devil like Fleetwood who can't defend himself—who's got no money to hire lawyers. But I tell you this—if you try and saddle Fleetwood with this business you'll have me to deal with."

"And who exactly are you?" asked Poirot sweetly.

Mr. Ferguson got rather red.

"I can stick by my friends anyway," he said gruffly.

"Well, Mr. Ferguson, I think that's all we need for the present," said Race.

As the door closed behind Ferguson he remarked unexpectedly:

"Rather a likeable young cub, really."

"You don't think he is the man you are after?" asked Poirot.

"I hardly think so. I suppose he *is* on board. The information was very precise. Oh, well, one job at a time. Let's have a go at Pennington."

CHAPTER 17

Andrew Pennington displayed all the conventional reactions of grief and shock. He was, as usual, carefully dressed. He had changed into a black tie. His long clean-shaven face bore a bewildered expression.

"Gentlemen," he said sadly. "This business has got me right down! Little Linnet—why, I remember her as the cutest little thing you can imagine. How proud of her Melhuish Ridgeway used to be too! Well, there's no point in going into that. Just tell me what I can do—that's all I ask."

Race said:

"To begin with, Mr. Pennington, did you hear anything last night?"

"No, sir, I can't say I did. I have the cabin right next to Dr. Bessner's, No. 38-39, and I heard a certain commotion going on in there round about midnight or so. Of course I didn't know what it was at the time."

"You heard nothing else? No shots?"

Andrew Pennington shook his head.

"Nothing whatever of the kind."

"And you went to bed?"

"Must have been some time after eleven."

He leaned forward.

"I don't suppose it's news to you to know that there's plenty of rumours going about the boat. That half-French girl—Jacqueline de Bellefort. There was something fishy there, you know. Linnet didn't tell me anything but naturally I wasn't born blind and deaf. There'd been some affair between her and Simon some time, hadn't there? *Cherchez la femme*—that's a pretty good sound rule—and I should say you wouldn't have to *cherchez* far."

Poirot said:

"You mean that in your belief Jacqueline de Bellefort shot Mrs. Doyle?"

"That's what it looks like to me. Of course I don't *know* anything . . ."

"Unfortunately we do know something!"

"Eh?" Mr. Pennington looked startled.

"We know that is quite impossible for Miss de Bellefort to have shot Mrs. Doyle."

He explained carefully the circumstances. Pennington seemed reluctant to accept them.

"I agree it looks all right on the fact of it—but this hospital nurse woman—I'll bet she didn't stay awake all night. She dozed off and the girl slipped out and in again."

"Hardly likely, M. Pennington. She had administered a strong opiate, remember. And anyway a nurse is in the habit of sleeping lightly and waking when her patient wakes."

"It all sounds rather fishy to me," said Pennington.

Race said in a gently authoritative manner:

"I think you must take it from me, Mr. Pennington, that we have examined all the possibilities very carefully. The result is quite definite—Jacqueline de Bellefort did not shoot Mrs. Doyle. So we are forced to look elsewhere. That is where we hope you may be able to help us."

"I?"

Pennington gave a nervous start.

"Yes. You were an intimate friend of the dead woman's. You know the circumstances of her life, in all probability, much better than her husband does, since he only made her acquaintance a few months ago. You would know, for instance, of any one who had a grudge against her—you would know, perhaps, whether there was any one who had a motive for desiring her death."

Andrew Pennington passed his tongue over rather dry looking lips.

"I assure you, I have no idea. . . . You see Linnet was brought up in England. I know very little of her surroundings and associations."

"And yet," mused Poirot, "there was some one on board who was interested in Mrs. Doyle's removal. She had a near escape before, you remember, at this very place, when that boulder crashed down—ah! but you were not there, perhaps?"

"No. I was inside the temple at the time. I heard about it afterwards, of course. A very near escape. But possibly an accident, don't you think?"

Poirot shrugged his shoulders.

"One thought so at the time. Now—one wonders."

"Yes—yes, of course." Pennington wiped his face with a fine silk handkerchief.

Colonel Race went on:

"Mrs. Doyle happened to mention some one being on board who bore a grudge—not against her personally—but against her family. Do you know who that could be?"

Pennington looked genuinely astonished.

"No, I've no idea."

"She didn't mention the matter to you?"

"No."

"You were an intimate friend of her father's—you cannot remember any business operation of his that might have resulted in ruin for some business opponent?"

Pennington shook his head helplessly.

"No outstanding case. Such operations were frequent, of course, but I can't recall any one who uttered threats—nothing of that kind."

"In short, Mr. Pennington, you cannot help us?"

"It seems so. I deplore my inadequacy, gentlemen."

Race interchanged a glance with Poirot, then he said:

"I'm sorry too. We'd had hopes."

He got up as a sign the interview was at an end.

Andrew Pennignton said:

"As Doyle's laid up, I expect he'd like me to see to things. Pardon me, Colonel, but what exactly are the arrangements?"

"When we leave here we shall make a non-stop run to Shellal, arriving there to-morrow morning."

"And the body?"

"Will be removed to one of the cold storage chambers."

Andrew Pennington bowed his head. Then he left the room.

Poirot and Race again interchanged a glance.

"Mr. Pennington," said Race, lighting a cigarette, "was not at all comfortable."

Poirot nodded.

"And," he said, "Mr. Pennington was sufficiently perturbed to tell a rather stupid lie. He was *not* in the temple of Abu Simbel when that boulder fell. I—*moi qui vous parle*—can swear to that. I had just come from there."

"A very stupid lie," said Race, "and a very revealing one."

Again Poirot nodded.

"But for the moment," he said, and smiled, "we handle him with the gloves of kid, is it not so?"

"That was the idea," said Race.

"My friend, you and I understand each other to a marvel."

There was a faint grinding noise, a stir beneath their feet. The *Karnak* had started on her homeward journey to Shellal.

"The pearls," said Race, "that is the next thing to be cleared up."

"You have a plan?"

"Yes." He glanced at his watch. "It will be lunch time in half an hour. At the end of the meal I propose to make an announcement—just state the fact that the pearls have been stolen, and that I must request every one to stay in the dining-saloon while a search is conducted."

Poirot nodded approvingly.

"It is well imagined. *Whoever took the pearls still has them*. By giving no warning beforehand, there will be no chance of their being thrown overboard in a panic."

Race drew some sheets of paper towards him. He murmured apologetically:

"I like to make a brief précis of the facts as I go along. It keeps one's mind free of confusion."

"You do well. Method and order, they are everything," replied Poirot.

Race wrote for some minutes in his small neat script. Finally he pushed the result of his labours towards Poirot.

"Anything you don't agree with there?"

Poirot took up the sheets. They were headed:

MURDER OF MRS. LINNET DOYLE

Mrs. Doyle was last seen alive by her maid Louise Bourget. Time: 11.30 (approx).

From 11.30—12.20 following have alibis—Cornelia Robson, James Fanthorp, Simon Doyle, Jacqueline de Bellefort—*nobody else*—but crime almost certainly committed *after* that time, since it is practically certain that pistol used was Jacqueline de Bellefort's which was then in her handbag. That her pistol was used is not *absolutely* certain until after post mortem and expert evidence re bullet—but it may be taken as overwhelmingy probable.

Probable course of events: X (murderer) was witness of scene between Jacqueline and Simon Doyle in observation saloon and noted where pistol went under settee. After the saloon was vacant, X procured pistol—his or her idea being that Jacqueline de Bellefort would be thought guilty of crime. On this theory certain people are automatically cleared of suspicion.

Cornelia Robson since she had no opportunity to take pistol before James Fanthorp returned to search for it.

Miss Bowers—same.

Dr. Bessner—same.

N.B. Fanthorp is not definitely excluded from suspicion since he could actually have pocketed pistol while declaring himself unable to find it.

Any other person could have taken the pistol during that ten minutes' interval.

Possible motives for the murder:

Andrew Pennington. This is on the assumption that he has been guilty of fraudulent practices. There is a certain amount of evidence in favour of that assumption, but not enough to justify making out a case against him. If it was he who rolled down the boulder he is a man who can seize a chance when it presents itself. The crime, clearly, was not premeditated except in a *general* way. Last night's shooting scene was an ideal opportunity.

Objections to the theory of Pennington's guilt. *Why did he throw the pistol overboard since it constituted a valuable clue against J.B.*

Fleetwood. Motive, revenge. Fleetwood considered himself injured by Linnet Doyle. Might have overheard scene and noted position of pistol. He may have taken pistol because it was a handy weapon rather than with the idea of throwing guilt on Jacqueline. This would fit in with throwing it overboard. But *if that were the case, why did he write J. in blood on the wall!*

N.B. Cheap handkerchief found with pistol more likely to have belonged to a man like Fleetwood than to one of the well-to-do passengers.

Rosalie Otterbourne. Are we to accept Miss Van Schuyler's evidence or Rosalie's denial? Something *was* thrown overboard at that time and that something was presumably the pistol wrapped up in the velvet stole.

Points to be noted. Had Rosalie any motive? She may have disliked Linnet Doyle and even been envious of her—but as a motive for murder that seems grossly inadequate. The evidence against her can only be convincing if we discover an adequate *motive*. As far as we know there is no previous knowledge or link between Rosalie Otterbourne and Linnet Doyle.

Miss Van Schuyler. The velvet stole in which pistol was wrapped belongs to Miss Van Schuyler. According to her own statement she last saw it in the observation saloon. She drew attention to its loss during the evening and a search was made for it without success.

How did the stole come into the possession of X? Did X purloin it some time early in the evening? But if so, why? Nobody could tell *in advance* that there was going to be a scene between Jacqueline and Simon. Did X find the stole in the saloon when he went to get the pistol from under the settee? But if so, why was it not found when the search for it was made? *Did it ever leave Miss Van Schuyler's possession?*

That is to say:

Did Miss Van Schuyler murder Linnet Doyle? Is her accusation of Rosalie Otterbourne a deliberate lie? If she did murder her, what was her *motive?*

Other possibilities.

Robbery as a motive. Possible—since the pearls have disappeared and Linnet Doyle was certainly wearing them last night.

Some one with a grudge against the Ridgeway family. Possible—again no evidence.

We know that there is a dangerous man on board—a killer. Here we have a killer and a death. May not the two be connected? But we should have to show that Linnet Doyle possessed dangerous knowledge concerning this man.

Conclusions. We can group the persons on board into two classes—those who had a possible motive or against whom there is no definite evidence, and those who, as far as we know, are free of suspicion.

Group I.
Andrew Pennington
Fleetwood.
Rosalie Otterbourne.
Miss Van Schuyler.
Louise Bourget (Robbery?)
Ferguson (Political?)

Group II.
Mrs. Allerton.
Tim Allerton.
Cornelia Robson.
Miss Bowers.
Dr. Bessner.
Signor Richetti.
Mrs. Otterbourne.
James Fanthorp.

Poirot pushed the paper back.

"It is very just, very exact, what you have written there."

"You agree with it?"

"Yes."

"And now what is your contribution?"

Poirot drew himself up in an important manner.

"Me, I pose to myself one question!

"Why was the pistol thrown overboard?"

"That's all?"

"At the moment, yes. Until I can arrive at a satisfactory answer to that question, there is no sense anywhere. That is—that must be—the starting point.

You will notice, my friend, that in your summary of where we stand, you have not attempted to answer that point."

Race shrugged his shoulders.

"Panic."

Poirot shook his head perplexedly.

He picked up the sodden velvet wrap from the table and smoothed it out, wet and limp, on the table. His finger traced the scorched marks and the burnt holes.

"Tell me, my friend," he said suddenly. "You are more conversant with firearms than I am. Would such a thing as this, wrapped round a pistol, make much difference in muffling the sound?"

"No, it wouldn't. Not like a silencer, for instance."

Poirot nodded. He went on.

"A man—certainly a man who had had much handling of firearms—would know that. But a woman—a woman would *not* know."

Race looked at him curiously.

"Probably not."

"No. She would have read the detective stories where they are not always very exact as to details."

Race flicked the little pearl-handled pistol with his finger.

"This little fellow wouldn't make much noise anyway," he said. "Just a pop, that's all. With any other noise around, ten to one you wouldn't notice it."

"Yes, I have reflected as to that."

He picked up the handkerchief and examined it.

"A man's handkerchief—but not a gentleman's handkerchief. *Ce cher* Woolworth, I imagine. Threepence at most."

"The sort of handkerchief a man like Fleetwood would own."

"Yes. Andrew Pennington, I notice, carries a very fine silk handkerchief."

"Ferguson?" suggested Race.

"Possibly. As a gesture. But then it ought to be a bandana."

"Used it instead of a glove, I suppose, to hold the pistol and obviate fingerprints," Race added with slight facetiousness: "The Clue of the Blushing Handkerchief."

"Ah, yes. Quite a *jeune fille* colour, is it not?" He laid it down and returned to the stole, once more examining the powder marks.

"All the same," he murmured, "it is odd. . . ."

"What's that?"

Poirot said gently:

"*Cette pauvre Madame Doyle*. Lying there so peacefully. . . . With the little hole in her head. You remember how she looked?"

Race looked at him curiously.

"You know," he said, "I've got an idea you're trying to tell me something—but I haven't the faintest idea what it is."

CHAPTER 18

There was a tap on the door.

"Come in," Race called.

A steward entered.

"Excuse me, sir," he said to Poirot. "But Mr. Doyle is asking for you."

"I will come."

Poirot rose. He went out of the room and up the companion way to the promenade deck and along it to Dr. Bessner's cabin.

Simon, his face flushed and feverish, was propped up with pillows.

He looked embarrassed.

"Awfully good of you to come along, M. Poirot. Look here, there's something I want to ask you."

"Yes?"

Simon got still redder in the face.

"It's—it's about Jackie. I want to see her. Do you think—would you mind—would she mind, d'you think—if you asked her to come along here. You know I've been lying here thinking. . . . That wretched kid—she is only a kid after all—and I treated her damn badly—and—"

He stammered to silence.

Poirot looked at him with interest.

"You desire to see Mademoiselle Jacqueline? I will fetch her."

"Thanks. Awfully good of you."

Poirot went on his quest. He found Jacqueline de Bellefort sitting huddled up in a corner of the observation saloon. There was an open book on her lap but she was not reading.

Poirot said gently.

"Will you come with me, Mademoiselle? M. Doyle wants to see you."

She started up. Her face flushed—then paled. She looked bewildered.

"Simon? He wants to see me—to see *me?*"

He found her incredulity moving.

"Will you come, Mademoiselle?"

"I—yes, of course I will."

She went with him in a docile fashion like a child—but like a puzzled child.

Poirot passed into the cabin.

"Here is Mademoiselle."

She stepped in after him, wavered, stood still . . . standing there mute and dumb, her eyes fixed on Simon's face.

"Hallo, Jackie. . . ."

He, too, was embarrassed. He went on:

"Awfully good of you to come. I wanted to say—I mean—what I mean is—"

She interrupted him then. Her words came out in a rush—breathless desperate. . . .

"Simon—I didn't kill Linnet. You know I didn't do that. . . . I—I—was mad last night. Oh, can you ever forgive me—?"

Words came more easily to him now.

"Of course. That's all right! Absolutely all right! That's what I wanted to say. Thought you might be worrying a bit, you know. . . ."

"Worrying? A bit? Oh! Simon!"

"That's what I wanted to see you about. It's quite all right, see, old girl? You just got a bit rattled last night—a shade tight. All perfectly natural."

"Oh, Simon! I might have killed you. . . ."

"Not you. Not with a rotten little peashooter like that. . . ."

"And your leg! Perhaps you'll never walk again. . . ."

"Now, look here, Jackie, don't be maudlin. As soon as we get to Assuan they're going to put the X-rays to work, and dig out that tinpot bullet and everything will be as right as rain."

Jacqueline gulped twice, then she rushed forward and knelt down by Simon's bed, burying her face and sobbing. Simon patted her awkwardly on the head. His eyes met Poirot's and with a reluctant sigh the latter left the cabin.

He heard broken murmurs as he went. . . .

"How could I be such a devil. . . . Oh, Simon! . . . I'm so dreadfully sorry. . . ."

Outside Corneila Robson was leaning over the rail.

She turned her head.

"Oh, it's you, M. Poirot. It seems so awful somehow that it should be such a lovely day."

Poirot looked up at the sky.

"When the sun shines you cannot see the moon," he said. "But when the sun is gone—ah, when the sun is gone."

Cornelia's mouth fell open.

"I beg your pardon?"

"I was saying, Mademoiselle, that when the sun has gone down, we shall see the moon. That is so, is it not?"

"Why—why, yes—certainly."

She looked at him doubtfully.

Poirot laughed gently.

"I utter the imbecilities," he said. "Take no notice."

He strolled gently towards the stern of the boat. As he passed the next cabin he paused for a minute.

He caught fragments of speech from within.

"Utterly ungrateful—after all I've done for you—no consideration for your wretched mother . . . no idea of what I suffer. . . ."

Poirot's lips stiffened as he pressed them together. He raised a hand and knocked.

There was a startled silence and Mrs. Otterbourne's voice called out:

"Who's that?"

"Is Mademoiselle Rosalie there?"

Rosalie appeared in the doorway. Poirot was shocked at her appearance. There were dark circles under her eyes and drawn lines round her mouth.

"What's the matter?" she said ungraciously. "What do you want?"

"The pleasure of a few minutes' conversation with you, Mademoiselle. Will you come?"

Her mouth went sulky at once. She shot him a suspicious look.

"Why should I?"

"I entreat you, Mademoiselle."

"Oh, I suppose—"

She stepped out on the deck, closing the door behind her.

"Well?"

Poirot took her gently by the arm and drew her along the deck, still in the direction of the stern. They passed the bathrooms and round the corner. They had the stern part of the deck to themselves. The Nile flowed away behind them.

Poirot rested his elbows on the rail. Rosalie stood up straight and stiff.

"Well?" she said again, and her voice held the same ungracious tone.

Poirot spoke slowly, choosing his words.

"I could ask you certain questions, Mademoiselle, but I do not think for one moment that you would consent to answer them."

"Seems rather a waste to bring me along here then."

Poirot drew a finger slowly along the wooden rail.

"You are accustomed, Mademoiselle, to carrying your own burdens. . . . But you can do that too long. The strain becomes too great. For you, Mademoiselle, the strain is becoming too great."

"I don't know what you are talking about," said Rosalie.

"I am talking about facts, Mademoiselle—plain ugly facts. Let us call the spade the spade and say it in one little short sentence. Your mother drinks, Mademoiselle."

Rosalie did not answer. Her mouth opened, then she closed it again. For once she seemed at a loss.

"There is no need for you to talk, Mademoiselle. I will do all the talking. I was interested at Assuan in the relations existing between you. I saw at once that, in spite of your carefully studied unfilial remarks, you were in reality passionately protecting her from something. I very soon knew what that something was. I knew it long before I encountered your mother one morning in an unmistakable state of intoxication. Moreover, her case, I could see, was one of secret bouts of drinking—by far the most difficult kind of case with which to deal. You were coping with it manfully. Nevertheless, she had all the secret drunkard's cunning. She managed to get hold of a secret supply of spirits and to keep it successfully hidden from you. I should not be surprised if you discovered its hiding-place only yesterday. Accordingly, last night, as soon as your mother was really soundly asleep, you stole out with the contents of the *cache,* went round to the other side of the boat (since your own side was up against the bank) and cast it overboard into the Nile."

He paused.

"I am right, am I not?"

"Yes—you're quite right." Rosalie spoke with sudden passion. "I was a fool not to say so, I suppose! But I didn't want every one to know. It would go all over the boat. And it seemed so—so silly—I mean—that I—"

Poirot finished the sentence for her.

"So silly that you should be suspected of committing a murder?"

Rosalie nodded.

Then she burst out again.

"I've tried so hard to—keep every one from knowing. . . . It isn't really her fault. She got discouraged. Her books didn't sell any more. People are tired of all that cheap sex stuff. . . . It hurt her—it hurt her dreadfully. And so she began to—to drink. For a long time I didn't know why she was so queer. Then, when I found out, I tried to—to stop it. She'd be all right for a bit—and then suddenly, she'd start and there would be dreadful quarrels and rows with people. It was awful."

She shuddered. "I had always to be on the watch—to get her away. . . .

"And then—she began to dislike me for it. She—she's turned right against me. I think she almost hates me sometimes. . . ."

"*Pauvre petite,*" said Poirot.

She turned on him vehemently.

"Don't be sorry for me. Don't be kind. It's easier if you're not." She sighed—a long heartrending sigh. "I'm so tired . . . I'm so deadly, deadly tired."

"I know," said Poirot.

"People think I'm awful. Stuck up and cross and bad-tempered. I can't help it. I've forgotten how to be—to be nice."

"That is what I said to you—you have carried your burden by yourself too long."

Rosalie said slowly:

"It is a relief—to talk about it. You—you've always been kind to me, M. Poirot. I'm afraid I've been rude to you often."

"*La politesse,* it is not necessary between friends."

The suspicion came back to her face suddenly.

"Are you—are you going to tell every one? I suppose you must because of those damned bottles I threw overboard."

"No, no, it is not necessary. Just tell me what I want to know. At what time was this? Ten minutes past one?"

"About that, I should think. I don't remember exactly."

"Now tell me, Mademoiselle. Miss Van Schuyler saw *you,* did you see *her?*"

Rosalie shook her head.

"No, I didn't."

"She says that she looked out of the door of her cabin."

"I don't think I should have seen her. I just looked along the deck and then out to the river."

Poirot nodded.

"And did you see any one at all when you looked down the deck?"

There was a pause—quite a long pause. Rosalie was frowning. She seemed to be thinking earnestly.

At last she shook her head quite decisively.

"No," she said. "I saw nobody."

Hercule Poirot slowly nodded his head. But his eyes were grave.

CHAPTER 19

People crept into the dining-salon by ones and twos in a very subdued manner. There seemed a general feeling that to sit down eagerly to food displayed an unfortunate heartlessness. It was with an almost apologetic air that one passenger after another came and sat down at their table.

Tim Allerton arrived some few minutes after his mother had taken her seat. He was looking in a thoroughly bad temper.

"I wish we'd never come on this blasted trip," he growled.

Mrs. Allerton shook her head sadly.

"Oh, my dear, so do I. That beautiful girl! It all seems such a *waste*. To think that any one could shoot her in cold blood. It seems awful to me that any one could do such a thing. And that other poor child."

"Jacqueline?"

"Yes, my heart aches for her. She looks so dreadfully unhappy."

"Teach her not to go round loosing off toy firearms," said Tim unfeelingly as he helped himself to butter.

"I expect she was badly brought up."

"Oh, for God's sake, Mother, don't go all maternal about it."

"You're in a shocking bad temper, Tim."

"Yes, I am. Who wouldn't be?"

"I don't see what there is to be cross about. It's just frightfully sad."

Tim said crossly:

"You're taking the romantic point of view! What you don't seem to realise is that it's no joke being mixed up in a murder case."

Mrs. Allerton looked a little startled.

"But surely—"

"That's just it. There's no 'But surely' about it. Every one on this damned boat is under suspicion—you and I as well as the rest of them."

Mrs. Allerton demurred.

"Technically we are, I suppose—but actually it's ridiculous!"

"There's nothing ridiculous where murder's concerned! You may sit there, darling, just exuding virtue and conscious rectitude, but a lot of unpleasant policemen at Shellal or Assuan won't take you at your face value."

"Perhaps the truth will be known before then."

"Why should it be?"

"M. Poirot may find out."

"That old mountebank? He won't find out anything. He's all talk and moustaches."

"Well, Tim," said Mrs. Allerton, "I dare say everything you say is true, but even if it is, we've got to go through with it, so we might as well make up our minds to it and go through with it as cheerfully as we can."

But her son showed no abatement of gloom.

"There's this blasted business of the pearls being missing, too."

"Linnet's pearls?"

"Yes. It seems somebody must have pinched 'em."

"I suppose that was the motive for the crime," said Mrs. Allerton.

"Why should it be? You're mixing up two perfectly different things."

"Who told you that they were missing?"

"Ferguson. He got it from his tough friend in the engine-room who got it from the maid."

"They were lovely pearls," said Mrs. Allerton.

Poirot sat down at the table, bowing to Mrs. Allerton.

"I am a little late," he said.

"I expect you have been busy," said Mrs. Allerton.

"Yes, I have been much occupied."

He ordered a fresh bottle of wine from the waiter.

"We're very catholic in our tastes," said Mrs. Allerton. "You drink wine always, Tim drinks whisky and soda, and I try all the different brands of mineral water in turn."

"Tiens!" said Poirot. He stared at her for a moment. He murmured to himself. "It is an idea, that. . . ."

Then, with an impatient shrug of his shoulders, he dismissed the sudden preoccupation that had distracted him and began to chat lightly of other matters.

"Is Mr. Doyle badly hurt?" asked Mrs. Allerton.

"Yes, it is a fairly serious injury. Dr. Bessner is anxious to reach Assuan so that his leg can be X-rayed and the bullet removed. But he hopes that there will be no permanent lameness."

"Poor Simon," said Mrs. Allerton. "Only yesterday he looked such a happy boy, with everything in the world he wanted. And now his beautiful wife killed and he himself laid up and helpless. I do hope, though—"

"What do you hope, Madame?" asked Poirot as Mrs. Allerton paused.

"I hope he's not too angry with that poor child."

"With Mademoiselle Jacqueline? Quite the contrary. He was full of anxiety on her behalf."

He turned to Tim.

"You know, it is a pretty little problem of psychology that. All the time that Mademoiselle Jacqueline was following them from place to place he was absolutely furious—but now when she has actually shot him, and wounded him dangerously—perhaps made him lame for life—all his anger seems to have evaporated. Can you understand that?"

"Yes," said Tim thoughtfully, "I think I can. The first thing made him feel a fool—"

Poirot nodded.

"You are right. It offended his male dignity."

"But now—if you look at it a certain way, it's *she* who's made a fool of herself. Every one's down on her and so—"

"He can be generously forgiving," finished Mrs. Allerton. "What children men are!"

"A profoundly untrue statement that women always make," murmured Tim.

Poirot smiled. Then he said to Tim:

"Tell me, Madame Doyle's cousin, Miss Joanna Southwood, did she resemble Madame Doyle?"

"You've got it a little wrong, M. Poirot. She was our cousin and Linnet's friend."

"Ah, pardon—I was confused. She is a young lady much in the news that. I have been interested in her for some time."

"Why?" asked Tim sharply.

Poirot half rose to bow to Jacqueline de Bellefort who had just come in and passed their table on the way to her own. Her cheeks were flushed and her eyes bright, and her breath came a little unevenly. As he resumed his seat Poirot seemed to have forgotten Tim's question. He murmured vaguely:

"I wonder if all young ladies with valuable jewels are as careless as Madame Doyle was?"

"It is true, then, that they were stolen?" asked Mrs. Allerton.

"Who told you so, Madame?"

"Ferguson said so," said Tim.

Poirot nodded gravely.

"It is quite true."

"I suppose," said Mrs. Allerton nervously, "that this will mean a lot of unpleasantness for all of us. Tim says it will."

Her son scowled. But Poirot had turned to him.

"Ah! you have had previous experience, perhaps? You have been in a house where there was a robbery?"

"Never," said Tim.

"Oh, yes, darling, you were at the Portarlingtons that time—when that awful woman's diamonds were stolen."

"You always get things hopelessly wrong, Mother. I was there when it was discovered that the diamonds she was wearing round her fat neck were only paste! The actual substitution was probably done months earlier—as a matter of fact a lot of people said she'd had it done herself!"

"Joanna said so, I expect."

"Joanna wasn't there."

"But she knew them quite well. And it's very like her to make that kind of suggestion."

"You're always down on Joanna, Mother."

Poirot hastily changed the subject. He had it in mind to make a really big purchase at one of the Assuan shops. Some very attractive purple and gold material at one of the Indian merchants. There would, of course, be the duty to pay, but—

"They tell me that they can—how do you say—expedite it for me? And that the charges will not be too high. How think you, will it arrive all right?"

Mrs. Allerton said that many people, so she had heard, had had things sent straight to England from the shops in question and that everything had arrived safely.

"*Bien*. Then I will do that. But the trouble one has, when one is abroad, if a parcel comes out from England! Have you had experience of that? Have you had any parcels arrive since you have been on your travels?"

"I don't think we have, have we, Tim? You get books sometimes but of course there is never any trouble about them."

"Ah, no, books are different."

Dessert had been served. Now, without any previous warning, Colonel Race stood up and made his speech.

He touched on the circumstances of the crime and announced the theft of the pearls. A search of the boat was about to be instituted, and he would be obliged if all the passengers would remain in the saloon until this was completed. Then, after all, if the passengers agreed, as he was sure they would, they themselves would be kind enough to submit to a search.

Poirot slipped nimbly along to his side. There was a little buzz and hum all round them. Voices doubtful, indignant, excited. . . .

Poirot reached Race's side and murmured something in his ear just as the latter was about to leave the dining-saloon.

Race listened, nodded assent, and beckoned a steward.

He said a few brief words to him, then, together with Poirot he passed out on to the deck, closing the door behind him.

They stood for a minute or two by the rail. Race lit a cigarette.

"Not a bad idea of yours," he said. "We'll soon see if there's anything in it. I'll give 'em three minutes."

The door of the dining-saloon opened and the same steward to whom they had spoken came out. He saluted Race and said:

"Quite right, sir. There's a lady who says it's urgent she should speak to you at once without any delay."

"Ah!" Race's face showed his satisfaction. "Who is it?"

"Miss Bowers, sir, the hospital nurse lady."

A slight shade of surprise showed on Race's face. He said:

"Bring her to the smoking-room. Don't let any one else leave."

"No, sir—the other steward will attend to that."

He went back into the dining-room. Poirot and Race went to the smoking-room.

"Bowers, eh?" murmured Race.

They had hardly got inside the smoking-room before the steward reappeared with Miss Bowers. He ushered her in and left, shutting the door behind him.

"Well, Miss Bowers?" Colonel Race looked at her inquiringly. "What's all this?"

Miss Bowers looked her usual composed unhurried self. She displayed no particular emotion.

"You'll excuse me, Colonel Race," she said. "But under the circumstances I thought the best thing to do would be to speak to you at once"—she opened her neat black handbag. "—and to return you these."

She took out a string of pearls and laid them on the table.

CHAPTER 20

If Miss Bowers had been the kind of woman who enjoyed creating a sensation, she would have been richly repaid by the result of her action.

A look of utter astonishment passed over Colonel Race's face as he picked up the pearls from the table.

"This is most extraordinary," he said. "Will you kindly explain, Miss Bowers?"

"Of course. That's what I've come to do." Miss Bowers settled herself comfortably in a chair. "Naturally it was a little difficult for me to decide what it was best for me to do. The family would naturally be averse to scandal of any kind, and they trust my discretion, but the circumstances are so very unusual that it really leaves me no choice. Of course, when you didn't find anything in the cabins your next move would be a search of the passengers, and if the pearls were then found in my possession it would be rather an awkward situation and the truth would come out just the same."

"And just what is the truth? Did you take these pearls from Mrs. Doyle's cabin?"

"Oh, no, Colonel Race, of course not. Miss Van Schuyler did."

"Miss Van Schuyler?"

"Yes. She can't help it, you know, but she does—er—take things. Especially jewellery. That's really why I'm always with her—it's not her health at all—it's this little idiosyncrasy. I keep on the alert and fortunately there's never been any trouble since I've been with her. It just means being watchful, you know. And she always hides the things she takes in the same place—rolled up in a pair of stockings—so that makes it very simple. I look each morning. Of course, I'm a light sleeper, and I always sleep next door to her and with the communicating door open if it's in a hotel so that I usually hear. Then I go after her and persuade her to go back to bed. Of course it's been rather more difficult on a boat. But she doesn't usually do it at night. It's more just picking up things that she sees left about. Of course, pearls have a great attraction for her always."

Miss Bowers ceased speaking.

Race asked:

"How did you discover they had been taken?"

"They were in her stockings this morning. I knew whose they were, of course. I've often noticed them. I went along to put them back, hoping that Mrs. Doyle wasn't up yet and hadn't discovered her loss. But there was a steward standing there and he told me about the murder and that no one could go in. So then, you see, I was in a regular quandary. But I still hoped to slip them back in the cabin later before their absence had been noticed. I can assure you I've passed a very unpleasant morning wondering what was the best thing to do. You see the Van Schuyler family is so *very* particular and exclusive. It would never do if this got into the newspapers. But that won't be necessary, will it?"

Miss Bowers really looked worried.

"That depends on circumstances," said Colonel Race cautiously. "But we shall do our best for you, of course. What does Miss Van Schuyler say to this?"

"Oh, she'll deny it, of course. She always does. Says some wicked person has put it there. She never admits taking anything. That's why if you catch her in time she goes back to bed like a lamb. Says she just went out to look at the moon. Something like that."

"Does Miss Robson know about this—er—failing?"

"No, she doesn't. Her mother knows, but she's a very simple kind of girl and her mother thought it best she should know nothing about it. I was quite equal to dealing with Miss Van Schuyler," added the competent Miss Bowers.

"We have to thank you, Mademoiselle, for coming to us so promptly," said Poirot.

Miss Bowers stood up.

"I'm sure I hope I've acted for the best."

"Be assured that you have."

"You see what with there being a murder as well—"

Colonel Race interrupted her. His voice was grave.

"Miss Bowers. I am going to ask you a question and I want to impress upon you that it has got to be answered truthfully. Miss Van Schuyler is unhinged mentally to the extent of being a kleptomaniac. Has she also a tendency to homicidal mania?"

Miss Bower's answer came immediately.

"Oh, dear me, no! Nothing of the kind. You can take my word for it absolutely. The old lady wouldn't hurt a fly."

The reply came with such positive assurance that there seemed nothing more to be said. Nevertheless Poirot did interpolate one mild inquiry.

"Does Miss Van Schuyler suffer at all from deafness?"

"As a matter of fact she does, M. Poirot. Not so that you'd notice it anyway, not if you were speaking to her, I mean. But quite often she doesn't hear you come into a room. Things like that."

"Do you think she would have heard any one moving about in Mrs. Doyle's cabin which is next door to her own?"

"Oh, I shouldn't think so—not for a minute. You see, the bunk is the other side of the cabin, not even against the partition wall. No, I don't think she would have heard anything."

"Thank you, Miss Bowers."

Race said:

"Perhaps you will now go back to the dining-saloon and wait with the others?"

He opened the door for her and watched her go down the staircase and enter the saloon. Then he shut the door and came back to the table. Poirot had picked up the pearls.

"Well," said Race grimly. "That reaction came pretty quickly. That's a very cool-headed and astute young woman—perfectly capable of holding out on us still further if she thinks it suits her book. What about Miss Van Schuyler now? I don't think we can eliminate her from the possible suspects. You know, she *might* have committed murder to get hold of those jewels. We can't take the nurse's word for it. She's all out to do the best for the family."

Poirot nodded in agreement. He was very busy with the pearls running them through his fingers, holding them up to his eyes.

He said:

"We may take it, I think, that part of the old lady's story to us was true. She *did* look out of her cabin and she *did* see Rosalie Otterbourne. But I don't think she *heard* anything or any one in Linnet Doyle's cabin. I think she was just peering out from *her* cabin preparatory to slipping along and purloining the pearls."

"The Otterbourne girl was there, then?"

"Yes. Throwing her mother's secret *cache* of drink overboard."

Colonel Race shook his head sympathetically.

"So that's it! Tough on a young 'un."

"Yes, her life has not been very gay, *cette pauvre petite Rosalie*."

"Well, I'm glad that's been cleared up. *She* didn't see or hear anything?"

"I asked her that. She responded—after a lapse of quite twenty seconds—that she saw nobody."

"Oh?" Race looked alert.

"Yes, it is suggestive, that."

Race said slowly:

"If Linnet Doyle was shot round about ten minutes past one or indeed any time after the boat had quieted down—it has seemed amazing to me that no one heard the shot. I grant you that a little pistol like that wouldn't make much noise, but all the same the boat would be deadly quiet and any noise, even a gentle pop, should have been heard. But I begin to understand better now. The cabin on the forward side of hers was unoccupied—since her husband was in Dr. Bessner's cabin. The one aft was occupied by the Van Schuyler woman who was deaf. That leaves only—"

He paused and looked expectantly at Poirot who nodded.

"The cabin next to hers on the other side of the boat. In other words—Pennington. We always seem to come back to Pennington."

"We will come back to him presently with the kid gloves removed! Ah, yes, I am promising myself that pleasure."

"In the meantime we'd better get on with our search of the boat. The pearls still make a convenient excuse even though they have been returned—but Miss Bowers is not likely to advertise that fact."

"Ah, these pearls." Poirot held them up against the light once more. He stuck out his tongue and licked them—he even gingerly tried one of them between his teeth. Then, with a sigh, he threw them down on the table.

"Here are more complications, my friend," he said. "I am not an expert on precious stones, but I have had a good deal to do with them in my time and I am fairly certain of what I say. *These pearls are only a clever imitation*."

CHAPTER 21

Colonel Race swore lustily.

"This damned case gets more and more involved." He picked up the pearls. "I suppose you've not made a mistake? They look all right to me."

"They are a very good imitation—yes."

"Now where does that lead us? I suppose Linnet Doyle didn't deliberately have an imitation made and bring it aboard with her for safety. Many women do."

"I think, if that were so, her husband would know about it."

"She may not have told him."

Poirot shook his head in a dissatisfied manner.

"No, I do not think that is so. I was admiring Mrs. Doyle's pearls the first evening on the boat—their wonderful sheen and lustre. I am sure that she was wearing the genuine ones then."

"That brings us up against two possibilities. First, that Miss Van Schuyler only stole the imitation string after the real ones had been stolen by some one else. Second, that the whole kleptomaniac story is a fabrication. Either Miss Bowers is a thief and quickly invented the story and allayed suspicion by handing over the false pearls, or else that whole party is in it together. That is to say, they are a gang of clever jewel thieves masquerading as an exclusive American family."

"Yes," Poirot murmured. "It is difficult to say. But I will point out to you one thing—to make a perfect and exact copy of the pearls, clasp and all, good enough to stand a chance of deceiving Mrs. Doyle is a highly skilled technical performance. It could not be done in a hurry. Whoever copied those pearls must have had a good opportunity of studying the original."

Race rose to his feet.

"Useless to speculate about it any further now. Let's get on with the job. We've got to find the real pearls. And at the same time we'll keep our eyes open."

They disposed first of the cabins occupied on the lower deck.

That of Signor Richetti contained various archæological works in different languages, a varied assortment of clothing, hair lotions of a highly-scented kind and two personal letters—one from an archæological expedition in Syria, and one from, apparently, a sister in Rome. His handkerchiefs were all of coloured silk.

They passed on to Ferguson's cabin.

There was a sprinkling of communistic literature, a good many snapshots, Samuel Butler's *Erewhon* and a cheap edition of *Pepys' Diary*. His personal possessions were not many—most of what outer clothing there was, was torn and dirty, the underclothing, on the other hand, was of really good quality. The handkerchiefs were expensive linen ones.

"Some interesting discrepancies," murmured Poirot.

Race nodded.

"Rather odd that there are absolutely no personal papers, letters, etc."

"Yes, that gives one to think. An odd young man, M. Ferguson."

He looked thoughtfully at a signet ring he held in his hand, before replacing it in the drawer where he had found it.

They went along to the cabin occupied by Louise Bourget. The maid had her meals after the other passengers, but Race had sent word that she was to be taken to join the others. A cabin steward met them.

"I'm sorry, sir," he apologised. "But I've not been able to find the young woman anywhere. I can't think where she can have got to."

Race glanced inside the cabin. It was empty.

They went up to the promenade deck and started on the starboard side. The first cabin was that occupied by James Fanthorp. Here, all was in meticulous order. Mr. Fanthorp travelled light, but all that he had was of good quality.

"No letters," said Poirot thoughtfully. "He is careful, our Mr. Fanthorp, to destroy his correspondence."

They passed on to Tim Allerton's cabin next door.

There were evidences here of an Anglo-Catholic turn of mind—an exquisite little triptych, and a big rosary, of intricately-carved wood. Besides personal clothing, there was a half-completed manuscript, a good deal annotated and scribbled over, and a good collection of books, most of them recently published. There were also a quantity of letters thrown carelessly into a drawer. Poirot, never in the least scrupulous about reading other people's correspondence, glanced through them. He noted that amongst them there were no letters from Joanna Southwood. He picked up a tube of secotine, fingered it absently for a minute or two, then said:

"Let us pass on."

"No Woolworth handkerchiefs," said Race, rapidly replacing the contents of a drawer.

Mrs. Allerton's cabin was the next. It was exquisitely neat and a faint, old-fashioned smell of lavender hung about it.

The two men's search was soon over. Race remarked as they left it:

"Nice woman, that."

The next cabin was that which had been used as a dressing-room by Simon Doyle. His immediate necessities—pyjamas, toilet things, etc., had been moved to Bessner's cabin, but the remainder of his possessions were still there, two good-sized leather suitcases and a kitbag. There were also some clothes in the wardrobe.

"We will look carefully here, my friend," said Poirot. "For it is very possible that the thief hid the pearls here."

"You think it is likely?"

"But, yes, indeed. Consider! The thief whoever he or she may be must know that sooner or later a search will be made and therefore a hiding-place in his or her own cabin would be injudicious in the extreme. The public rooms present other difficulties. But here is a cabin belonging to a man *who cannot possibly visit it himself*. So that if the pearls are found here it tells us nothing at all."

But the most meticulous search failed to reveal any trace of the missing necklace.

Poirot murmured "Zut!" to himself and they emerged once more on the deck.

Linnet Doyle's cabin had been locked after the body was removed but Race had the key with him. He unlocked the door and the two men stepped inside.

Except for the removal of the girl's body, the cabin was exactly as it had been that morning.

"Poirot," said Race. "If there's anything to be found here, for God's sake go ahead and find it. You can if any one can—I know that."

"This time you do not mean the pearls, *mon ami?*"

"No. The murder's the main thing. There may be something I overlooked this morning."

Quietly, deftly, Poirot went about his search. He went down on his knees and scrutinised the floor inch by inch. He examined the bed. He went rapidly through the wardrobe and chest of drawers. He went through the wardrobe trunk and the two costly suitcases. He looked through the expensive gold-fitted dressing-case. Finally he turned his attention to the washstand. There were various creams, powders, face lotions. But the only thing that seemed to interest Poirot were two little bottles labelled Nailex. He picked them up at last and brought them to the dressing-table. One, which bore the inscription Nailex Rose, was empty but for a drop or two of dark-red fluid at the bottom. The other, the same size, but labelled Nailex Cardinal, was nearly full. Poirot uncorked first the empty then the full one and sniffed them both delicately.

An odour of peardrops billowed into the room. With a slight grimace he recorked them.

"Get anything?" asked Race.

Poirot replied by a French proverb.

"*On ne prend pas les mouches avec la vinaigre*."

Then he said with a sigh:

"My friend, we have not been fortunate. The murderer has not been obliging. He has not dropped for us the cuff-link, the cigarette end, the cigar ash—or in the case of a woman, the handkerchief, the lip-stick, or the hair-slide."

"Only the bottle of nail polish?"

Poirot shrugged his shoulders.

"I must ask the maid. There is something—yes—a little curious there."

"I wonder where the devil the girl's got to?" said Race.

They left the cabin locking the door behind them and passed on to that of Miss Van Schuyler.

Here, again, were all the appurtenances of wealth, expensive toilet fittings, good luggage, a certain number of private letters and papers all perfectly in order.

The next cabin was the double one occupied by Poirot and beyond it that of Race.

"Hardly likely to hide 'em in either of these," said the colonel

Poirot demurred.

"It might be. Once, on the Orient Express, I investigated a murder. There was a little matter of a scarlet kimono. It had disappeared—and yet it must be on the train. I found it—where do you think?—*in my own locked suitcase!* Ah! it was an impertinence, that."

"Well, let's see if anybody has been impertinent with you or me this time."

But the thief of the pearls had not been impertinent with Hercule Poirot or with Colonel Race.

Rounding the stern they made a very careful search of Miss Bowers's cabin but could find nothing of a suspicious nature. Her handkerchiefs were of plain linen with an initial.

The Otterbournes' cabin came next. Here again, Poirot made a very meticulous search—but with no result.

The next cabin was Bessner's. Simon Doyle lay with an untasted tray of food beside him.

"Off my feed," he said apologetically.

He was looking feverish and very much worse than earlier in the day. Poirot appreciated Bessner's anxiety to get him as swiftly as possible to hospital and skilled appliances.

The little Belgian explained what the two of them were doing and Simon nodded approval. On learning that the pearls had been restored by Miss Bowers but proved to be merely imitation, he expressed the most complete astonishment.

"You are quite sure, Mr. Doyle, that your wife did not have an imitation string which she brought aboard with her instead of the real ones?"

Simon shook his head decisively.

"Oh, no. I'm quite sure of that. Linnet loved those pearls and she wore 'em everywhere. They were insured against every possible risk, so I think that made her a bit careless."

"Then we must continue our search."

He started opening drawers. Race attacked a suitcase.

Simon stared.

"Look here, you surely don't suspect old Bessner pinched them?"

Poirot shrugged his shoulders.

"It might be so. After all, what do we know of Dr. Bessner? Only what he himself gives out."

"But he couldn't have hidden them in here without my seeing him."

"He could not have hidden anything *to-day* without your having seen him. But we do not know when the substitution took place. He may have effected the exchange some days ago."

"I never thought of that."

But the search was unavailing.

The next cabin was Pennington's. The two men spent some time in their search. In particular Poirot and Race examined carefully a case full of legal and business documents, most of them requiring Linnet's signature.

He shook his head gloomily.

"These seem all square and above board. You agree?"

"Absolutely. Still, the man isn't a born fool. If there *had* been a compromising document there—a power of attorney or something of that kind, he'd be pretty sure to have destroyed it first thing."

"That is so, yes."

Poirot lifted a heavy Colt revolver out of the top drawer of the chest of drawers, looked at it and put it back.

"So it seems there are still some people who travel with revolvers," he murmured.

"Yes, a little suggestive, perhaps. Still, Linnet Doyle wasn't shot with a thing that size." He paused and then said, "You know, I've thought of a possible answer to your point about the pistol being thrown overboard. Supposing that the actual murderer *did* leave it in Linnet Doyle's cabin, and that some one else—some second person took it away and threw it into the river?"

"Yes, that is possible. I have thought of it. But it opens up a whole string of questions. Who was that second person? What interest had they in endeavouring to shield Jacqueline de Bellefort by taking away the pistol? What was that second person doing there? The only other person we know of who went into the cabin was Miss Van Schuyler. Was it conceivably Miss Van Shuyler who removed it? Why should *she* wish to shield Jacqueline de Bellefort? And yet—what other reason can there be for the removal of the pistol?"

Race suggested:

"She may have recognised the stole as hers, got the wind up, and thrown the whole bag of tricks over on that account."

"The stole, perhaps, but would she have got rid of the pistol, too? Still, I agree, that is a possible solution. But it is clumsy—*bon Dieu,* it is clumsy. And you still have not appreciated one point about the stole—"

As they emerged from Pennington's cabin Poirot suggested that Race should search the remaining cabins, those occupied by Jacqueline, Cornelia and two empty ones at the end, while he himself had a few words with Simon Doyle.

Accordingly he retraced his steps along the deck and re-entered Bessner's cabin.

Simon said:

"Look here, I've been thinking. I'm perfectly sure that these pearls were all right yesterday."

"Why is that, Mr. Doyle?"

"Because—Linnet"—he winced as he uttered his wife's name—"was passing them through her hands just before dinner and talking about them. She knew something about pearls. I feel certain she'd have known if they were a fake."

"They were a very good imitation, though. Tell me, was Mrs. Doyle in the habit of letting those pearls out of her hands? Did she ever lend them to a friend, for instance?"

Simon flushed with slight embarrassment.

"You see, M. Poirot, it's difficult for me to say . . . I—I—well, you see, I hadn't known Linnet very long."

"Ah, no, it was a quick romance—yours."

Simon went on:

"And so—really—I shouldn't know a thing like that. But Linnet was awfully generous with her things. I should think she might have done."

"She never, for instance—" Poirot's voice was very smooth, "—she never, for instance, lent them to Mademoiselle de Bellefort?"

"What d'you mean?" Simon flushed brick red—tried to sit up, and wincing, fell back. "What are you getting at? That Jackie stole the pearls? She didn't. I'll swear she didn't. Jackie's as straight as a die. The mere idea of her being a thief is ridiculous—absolutely ridiculous."

Poirot looked at him with gently twinkling eyes.

"Oh, la la la!" he said unexpectedly. "That suggestion of mine it has indeed stirred up the nest of hornets."

Simon repeated doggedly, unmoved by Poirot's lighter note.

"Jackie's straight!"

Poirot remembered a girl's voice by the Nile in Assuan saying:

"I love Simon—and he loves me . . ."

He had wondered which of the three statements he had heard that night was the true one. It seemed to him that it had turned out to be Jacqueline who had come closest to the truth.

The door opened and Race came in.

"Nothing," he said brusquely. "Well, we didn't expect it. I see the stewards coming along with their report as to the searching of the passengers."

A steward and stewardess appeared in the doorway. The former spoke first.

"Nothing, sir."

"Any of the gentlemen make any fuss?"

"Only the Italian gentleman, sir. He carried on a good deal. Said it was a dishonour—something of that kind. He'd got a gun on him, too."

"What kind of a gun?"

"Mauser automatic .25, sir."

"Italians are pretty hot tempered," said Simon. "Richetti got in no end of a stew at Wâdi Halfa just because of a mistake over a telegram. He was darned rude to Linnet over it."

Race turned to the stewardess. She was a big handome-looking woman.

"Nothing on any of the ladies, sir. They made a good deal of fuss—except for Mrs. Allerton who was as nice as nice could be. Not a sign of the pearls. By the way the young lady, Miss Rosalie Otterbourne, had a little pistol in her handbag."

"What kind?"

"It was a very small one, sir, with a pearl handle. A kind of toy."

Race stared.

"Devil take this case," he muttered. "I thought we'd got *her* cleared of suspicion and now—does every girl on this blinking boat carry around pearl-handled toy pistols?"

He shot a question at the stewardess.

"Did she show any feeling over your finding it?"

The woman shook her head.

"I don't think she noticed. I had my back turned whilst I was going through the handbags."

"Still—she must have known you'd come across it. Oh, well, it beats me. What about the maid?"

"We've looked all over the boat, sir. We can't find her anywhere."

"What's this?" asked Simon.

"Mrs. Doyle's maid—Louise Bourget. She's disappeared."

"*Disappeared?*"

Race said thoughtfully:

"She might have stolen the pearls. She is the one person who had ample opportunity to get a replica made."

"And then, when she found a search was being instituted, she threw herself overboard?" suggested Simon.

"Nonsense," said Race irritably. "A woman can't throw herself overboard in broad daylight from a boat like this without somebody realising the fact. She's bound to be somewhere on board."

He addressed the stewardess once more.

"When was she last seen?"

"About half an hour before the bell went for lunch, sir."

"We'll have a look at her cabin, anyway," said Race. "That may tell us something."

He led the way to the deck below. Poirot followed him. They unlocked the door of the cabin and passed inside.

Louise Bourget, whose trade it was to keep other people's belongings in order, had taken a holiday where her own were concerned. Odds and ends littered the top of the chest of drawers, a suitcase gaped open with clothes hanging out of the side of it and preventing it shutting, underclothing hung limply over the sides of the chairs.

As Poirot with swift neat fingers opened the drawers of the dressing-chest Race examined the suitcase.

Louise's shoes were lined along by the bed. One of them, a black patent leather, seemed to be resting at an extraordinary angle almost unsupported. The appearancc of it was so odd that it attracted Race's attention.

He closed the suitcase and bent over the line of shoes.

Then he uttered a sharp exclamation.

Poirot whirled round.

"Qu'est ce qui'il y a?"

Race said grimly:

"She hasn't disappeared. *She's here—under the bed . . .*"

CHAPTER 22

The body of a dead woman who in life had been Louise Bourget lay on the floor of her cabin. The two men bent over it.

Race straightened himself first.

"Been dead close on an hour, I should say. We'll get Bessner on to it. Stabbed to the heart. Death pretty well instantaneous, I should imagine. She doesn't look pretty, does she?"

"No."

Poirot shook his head with a slight shudder.

The dark feline face was convulsed as though with surprise and fury—the lips drawn back from the teeth.

Poirot bent again gently and picked up the right hand. Something just showed within the fingers. He detached it and held it out to Race—a little sliver of flimsy paper coloured a pale mauvish pink.

"You see what it is?"

"Money," said Race.

"The corner of a thousand franc note, I fancy."

"Well, it's clear what happened," said Race. "She knew something—and she was blackmailing the murderer with her knowledge. We thought she wasn't being quite straight this morning."

Poirot cried out:

"We have been idiots—fools! We should have known—then. What did she say? '*What could I have seen or heard. I was on the deck below. Naturally, if I had been unable to sleep, if I had mounted the stairs, then perhaps I might have seen this assassin, this monster, enter or leave Madame's cabin, but as it is—*' Of course, that is what did happen! She *did* come up. She did see some one going into Linnet Doyle's cabin—or coming out of it. And because of her greed, her insensate greed, she lies here—"

"And we are no nearer to knowing who killed her," finished Race disgustedly.

Poirot shook his head.

"No, no. We know much more now. We know—we know almost everything. Only what we know seems incredible. . . . Yet it must be so. Only I do not see. . . . Pah! what a fool I was this morning. We felt—both of us felt that she was keeping something back and yet we never realised the logical reason—blackmail."

"She must have demanded hush money straight away," said Race. "Demanded it with threats. The murderer was forced to accede to that request and paid her in French notes. Anything there?"

Poirot shook his head thoughtfully.

"I hardly think so. Many people take a reserve of money with them when travelling—sometimes five-pound notes, sometimes dollars, but very often French notes as well. Possibly the murderer paid her all he had in a mixture of currencies. Let us continue our reconstruction."

"The murderer comes to her cabin, gives her the money and then—"

"And then," said Poirot, "she counts it. Oh, yes, I know that class. She would count the money and while she counted it she was completely off her guard. The murderer struck. Having done so successfully, he gathered up the money and fled—not noticing that the corner of one of the notes was torn."

"We may get him that way," said Race doubtfully.

"I doubt it," said Poirot. "He will examine those notes, and will probably notice the tear. Of course, it he were of a parsimonious disposition he would not be able to bring himself to destroy a mille note—but I fear—I very much fear—that his temperament is just the opposite."

"How do you make that out?"

"Both this crime and the murder of Mrs. Doyle demanded certain qualities—courage, audacity, bold execution, lightning action—those qualities do not accord with a saving, prudent disposition."

Race shook his head sadly.

"I'd better get Bessner down," he said.

The stout doctor's examination did not take long. Accompanied by a good many Achs and Sos, he went to work.

"She has been dead not more than an hour," he announced. "Death, it was very quick—at once."

"And what weapon do you think was used?"

"Ach, it is interesting, that. It was something very sharp, very thin, very delicate. I could show you the kind of thing."

Back again in his cabin he opened a case and extracted a long delicate surgical knife.

"It was something like that, my friend—it was not a common table knife."

"I suppose," said Race smoothly, "that none of your own knives are—er—missing, doctor?"

Bessner stared at him, then his face grew red with indignation.

"What is that you say? Do you think I—I, Carl Bessner—who so well known is all over Austria—I with my clinics—my highly-born patients—I have killed a miserable little *femme de chambre!* Ah, but it is ridiculous—absurd, what you say! None of my knives are missing—not one, I tell you. They are all here, correct, in their places. You can see for yourself. And this insult to my profession I will not forget."

Dr. Bessner closed his case with a snap, flung it down and stamped out on to the deck.

"Whew!" said Simon. "You've put the old boy's back up."

Poirot shrugged his shoulders.

"It is regrettable."

"You're on the wrong tack. Old Bessner's one of the best even though he is a kind of Boche."

Dr. Bessner reappeared suddenly.

"Will you be so kind as to leave me now my cabin? I have to do the dressing of my patient's leg."

Miss Bowers had entered with him and stood, brisk and professional, waiting for the others to go.

Race and Poirot crept out meekly. Race muttered something and went off. Poirot turned to his left.

He heard scraps of girlish conversation, a little laugh. Jacqueline and Rosalie were together in the latter's cabin.

The door was open and the two girls were standing near it. As his shadow fell on them they looked up. He saw Rosalie Otterbourne smile at him for the first time—a shy welcoming smile—a little uncertain in its lines as of one who does a new and unfamiliar thing.

"You talk the scandal, Mademoiselles?" he accused them.

"No, indeed," said Rosalie. "As a matter of fact we were just comparing lipsticks."

Poirot smiled.

"Les chiffons d'aujourd'hui," he murmured.

But there was something a little mechanical about his smile and Jacqueline de Bellefort, quicker and more observant than Rosalie, saw it. She dropped the lipstick she was holding and came out upon the deck.

"Has something—what has happened now?"

"It is as you guess, Mademoiselle, something has happened."

"What?" Rosalie came out too.

"Another death," said Poirot.

Rosalie caught her breath sharply. Poirot was watching her narrowly. He saw alarm and something more—consternation—show for a minute or two in her eyes.

"Mrs. Doyle's maid has been killed," he said bluntly.

"Killed?" cried Jacqueline. *"Killed,* do you say?"

"Yes, that is what I said." Though his answer was nominally to her it was Rosalie whom he watched. It was to Rosalie to whom he spoke as he went on. "You see, this maid she saw something she was not intended to see. And so—she was silenced in case she should not hold her tongue."

"What was it she saw?"

Again it was Jacqueline who asked, and again Poirot's answer was to Rosalie. It was an odd little three-cornered scene.

"There is, I think, very little doubt what it was she saw," said Poirot. "She saw some one enter and leave Linnet Doyle's cabin on that fatal night."

His ears were quick. He heard the sharp intake of breath and saw the eyelids flicker. Rosalie Otterbourne had reacted just as he had intended she should.

"Did she say who it was she saw?" Rosalie asked.

Gently—regretfully—Poirot shook his head.

Footsteps pattered up the deck. It was Cornelia Robson, her eyes wide and startled.

"Oh, Jacqueline," she cried. "Something awful has happened. Another dreadful thing."

Jacqueline turned to her. The two moved a few steps forward. Almost unconsciously Poirot and Rosalie Otterbourne moved in the other direction.

Rosalie said sharply:

"Why do you look at me? What have you got in your mind?"

"That is two questions you ask me. I will ask you only one in return. *Why do you not tell me all the truth, Mademoiselle?*"

"I don't know what you mean. I told you—everything—this morning."

"No, there were things you did not tell me. You did not tell me that you carry about in your handbag a small calibre pistol with a pearl handle. You did not tell me all that you saw last night."

She flushed. Then she said sharply:

"It's quite untrue. I haven't got a revolver."

"I did not say a revolver. I said a small pistol that you carry about in your handbag."

She wheeled round, darted into her cabin and out again and thrust her grey leather handbag into his hands.

"You're talking nonsense. Look for yourself if you like."

Poirot opened the bag. There was no pistol inside.

He handed the bag back to her, meeting her scornful triumphant glance.

"No," he said pleasantly. "It is not there."

"You see. You're not always right, M. Poirot. And you're wrong about that other ridiculous thing you said."

"No, I do not think so."

"You're infuriating." She stamped an angry foot. "You get an idea into your head and you go on and on and on about it."

"Because I want you to tell me the truth."

"What is the truth? You seem to know it better than I do."

Poirot said:

"You want me to tell you what it was you saw? If I am right, will you admit that I am right? I will tell you my little idea. I think that when you came round the stern of the boat you stopped involuntarily because you saw a man come out of a cabin about half-way down the deck—Linnet Doyle's cabin as you realised next day—you saw him come out, close the door behind him and walk away from you down the deck and—perhaps—enter *one of the two end cabins*. Now then, am I right, Mademoiselle?"

She did not answer.

Poirot said:

"Perhaps you think it wiser not to speak. Perhaps you are afraid that if you do—you too will be killed."

For a moment he thought she had risen to the easy bait—that the accusation against her courage would succeed where more subtle arguments would have failed.

Her lips opened—trembled—then:

"I saw no one," said Rosalie Otterbourne.

CHAPTER 23

Miss Bowers came out of Dr. Bessner's cabin, smoothing her cuffs over her wrists.

Jacqueline left Cornelia abruptly and accosted the hospital nurse.

"How is he?" she demanded.

Poirot came up in time to hear the answer.

Miss Bowers was looking rather worried.

"Things aren't going too badly," she said.

Jacqueline cried:

"You mean, he's worse?"

"Well, I must say I shall be relieved when we get in and can get a proper X-ray done and the whole thing cleaned up under an anæsthetic. When do you think we shall get to Shellal, M. Poirot?"

"To-morrow morning."

Miss Bowers pursed her lips and shook her head.

"It's very unfortunate. We are doing all we can, but there's always such a danger of septicæmeia."

Jacqueline caught Miss Bowers's arm and shook it.

"Is he going to die? Is he going to die?"

"Dear me, no, Miss de Bellefort. That is, I hope not, I'm sure. The wound in itself isn't dangerous. But there's no doubt it ought to be X-rayed as soon as possible. And then, of course, poor Mr. Doyle ought to have been kept absolutely quiet to-day. He's had far too much worry and excitement. No wonder his temperature is rising. What with the shock of his wife's death, and one thing and another—"

Jacqueline relinquished her grasp of the nurse's arm and turned away. She stood leaning over the side, her back to the other two.

"What I say is, we've got to hope for the best always," said Miss Bowers. "Of course Mr. Doyle has a very strong constitution—one can see that—probably never had a day's illness in his life—so that's in his favour. But there's no denying that this rise in temperature is a nasty sign and—"

She shook her head, adjusted her cuffs once more, and moved briskly away.

Jacqueline turned and walked gropingly, blinded by tears towards her cabin. A hand below her elbow steadied and guided her. She looked up through the tears to find Poirot by her side. She leaned on him a little and he guided her through the cabin door.

She sank down on the bed and the tears came more freely punctuated by great shuddering sobs.

"He'll die. He'll die. I know he'll die. . . . And I shall have killed him. Yes, I shall have killed him. . . ."

Poirot shrugged his shoulders. He shook his head a little, sadly.

"Mademoiselle, what is done, is done. One cannot take back the accomplished action. It is too late to regret."

She cried out more vehemently:

"I shall have killed him! And I love him so. . . . I love him so."

Poirot sighed.

"Too much . . ."

It had been his thought long ago in the restaurant of M. Blondin. It was his thought again now.

He said, hesitating a little.

"Do not, at all events, go by what Miss Bowers says. Hospital nurses, me, I find them always gloomy! The night nurse, always, she is astonished to find her patient alive in the evening—the day nurse, always, she is surprised to find him alive in the morning! They know too much, you see, of the possibilities that may arise. When one is motoring one might easily say to oneself—if a car came out from that cross-road—or if that lorry backed suddenly—or if the wheel came off the car that is approaching me—or if a dog jumped off the hedge on to my driving arm, *eh bien*—I should probably be killed! But one assumes—and usually rightly—that none of these things *will* happen and that one will get to one's journey's end. But if, of course, one has been in an accident, or seen one or more accidents, then one is inclined to take the opposite point of view."

Jacqueline said, half-smiling through her tears:

"Are you trying to console me, M. Poirot?"

"The *bon Dieu* knows what I am trying to do! You should not have come on this journey."

"No—I wish I hadn't. It's been—so awful. But—it will be soon over now."

"*Mais oui—mais oui*."

"And Simon will go to the hospital and they'll give the proper treatment and everything will be all right."

"You speak like the child! *And they lived happily ever afterwards*. That is it, is it not?"

She flushed suddenly scarlet.

"M. Poirot. I never meant—never—"

"It is too soon to think of such a thing! That is the proper hypocritical thing to say, is it not? But you are partly a Latin, Mademoiselle Jacqueline. You should be able to admit facts even if they do not sound very decorous. *Le roi est mort—vive le roi!* The sun has gone and the moon rises. That is so, is it not?"

"You don't understand. He's just sorry for me—awfully sorry for me because he knows how terrible it is for me to know I've hurt him so badly."

"Ah, well," said Poirot. "The pure pity, it is a very lofty sentiment."

He looked at her half-mockingly, half with some other emotion. He murmured softly under his breath words in French:

La vie est vaine
Un peu d'amour
Un peu de haine
Et puis bonjour.

La vie est brève
On peu d'espoir
Un peu de rêve
Et puis bonsoir

He went out again on to the deck. Colonel Race was striding along the deck and hailed him at once.

"Poirot. Good man. I want you. I've got an idea."

Thrusting his arm through Poirot's he walked him up the deck.

"Just a chance remark of Doyle's. I hardly noticed it at the time. Something about a *telegram*."

"*Tiens—c'est vrai*."

"Nothing in it, perhaps, but one can't leave any avenue unexplored. Damn it all, man, two murders and we're still in the dark."

Poirot shook his head.

"No, not in the dark. In the light."

Race looked at him curiously.

"You have an idea?"

"It is more than an idea now. *I am sure*."

"Since—when?"

"Since the death of the maid—Louise Bourget."

"Damned if I see it!"

"My friend, it is so clear—so clear. Only—there are difficulties! Embarrassments—impediments! See you, around a person like Linnet Doyle there is so much—so many conflicting hates and jealousies and envies and meannesses. It is like a cloud of flies—buzzing—buzzing . . ."

"But you think you know?" The other looked at him curiously. "You wouldn't say so unless you were sure. Can't say I've any real light, myself. I've suspicions, of course . . ."

Poirot stopped. He laid an impressive hand on Race's arm.

"You are a great man, mon Colonel. . . . You do not say, *'Tell me.' 'What is it that you think?'* You know that if I could speak now, I would. But there is much to be cleared away first. But think, think for a moment along the lines that I shall indicate. There are certain points. . . . There is the statement of Mademoiselle de Bellefort that some one overheard our conversation that night in the garden at Assuan. There is the statement of Mr. Tim Allerton as to what he heard and did on the night of the crime. There are Louise Bourget's significant answers to our questions this morning. There is the fact that Mrs. Allerton drinks water, that her son drinks whisky and soda and that I drink wine. Add to that the fact of two bottles of nail polish and the proverb I quoted. And finally we come to the crux of the whole business, the fact that the pistol was wrapped up in a cheap handkerchief and a velvet stole and thrown overboard . . ."

Race was silent a minute or two then he shook his head.

"No," he said, "I don't see it. Mind, I've got a faint idea what you're driving at. But as far as I can see it doesn't work."

"But yes—but yes—you are seeing only half the truth. And remember this—we must start again from the beginning since our first conception was entirely wrong."

Race made a slight grimace.

"I'm used to that. It often seems to me that's all detective work is—wiping out your false starts and beginning again."

"Yes, it is very true, that. And it is just what some people will not do. They conceive a certain theory and everything has to fit into that theory. If one little fact will not fit, they throw it aside. But it is always the facts *that will not fit in* that are significant. All along I have realised *the significance of that pistol being removed from the scene of the crime*. I knew that it meant something—but what that something was I only realised one little half-hour ago."

"And I still don't see it!"

"But you will! Only reflect along the lines I indicated. And now let us clear up this matter of a telegram. That is, if the Herr Doktor will admit us."

Dr. Bessner was still in a very bad humour. In answer to their knock he disclosed a scowling face.

"What is it? Once more you wish to see my patient? But I tell you it is not wise. He has fever. He has had more than enough excitement to-day."

"Just one question," said Race. "Nothing more, I assure you."

With an unwilling grunt the doctor moved aside and the two men entered the cabin.

Dr. Bessner, growling to himself, pushed past them.

"I return in three minutes," he said. "And then—positively—you go!"

They heard him stumping down the deck.

Simon Doyle looked from one to the other of them inquiringly.

"Yes," he said. "What is it?"

"A very little thing," said Race. "Just now, when the stewards were reporting to me, they mentioned that Signor Richetti had been particularly troublesome. You said that that didn't surprise you as you knew he had a bad temper, and that he had been rude to your wife over some matter of a telegram. Now can you tell me about that incident?"

"Easily. It was at Wâdi Halfa. We'd just come back from the Second Cataract. Linnet thought she saw a telegram for her sticking up on the board. She'd forgotten, you see, that she wasn't called Ridgeway any longer and Richetti and Ridgeway do look rather alike when written in an atrocious handwriting. So she tore it open, couldn't make head or tail of it, and was puzzling over it when this fellow Richetti came along, fairly tore it out of her hand, and gibbered with rage. She went after him to apologise and he was frightfully rude to her about it."

Race drew a deep breath.

"And do you know at all, Mr. Doyle, what was in that telegram?"

"Yes, Linnet read part of it out aloud. It said—"

He paused. There was a commotion outside. A high-pitched voice was rapidly approaching.

"Where are M. Poirot and Colonel Race? I must see them *immediately!* It is most important. I have vital information. I— Are they with Mr. Doyle?"

Bessner had not closed the door. Only the curtain hung across the open doorway. Mrs. Otterbourne swept it to one side and entered like a tornado. Her face was suffused with colour, her gait slightly unsteady—her command of words not quite under her control.

"Mr. Doyle," she said dramatically, "I know who killed your wife!"

"What?"

Simon stared at her. So did the other two.

Mrs. Otterbourne swept all three of them with a triumphant glance. She was happy—superbly happy.

"Yes," she said. "My theories are completely vindicated—the deep primeval, primordial urges—it may appear impossible—fantastic—but it is the truth!"

Race said sharply:

"Do I understand that you have evidence in your possession to show who killed Mrs. Doyle?"

Mrs. Otterbourne sat down in a chair and leaned forward nodding her head vigorously.

"Certainly I have. You will agree, will you not, that *whoever killed Louise Bourget also killed Linnet Doyle*—that the two crimes were committed by one and the same hand?"

"Yes, yes," said Simon impatiently. "Of course. That stands to reason. Go on."

"Then my assertion holds. I know who killed Louise Bourget—therefore I know who killed Linnet Doyle."

"You mean, you have a theory as to who killed Louise Bourget," suggested Race sceptically.

Mrs. Otterbourne turned on him like a tiger.

"No, I have exact knowledge. I *saw* the person with my own eyes."

Simon, fevered, shouted out:

"For God's sake, start at the beginning. You know the person who killed Louise Bourget, you say."

Mrs. Otterbourne nodded.

"I will tell you exactly what occurred."

Yes, she was very happy—no doubt of it! This was her moment—her triumph! What of it if her books were failing to sell—if the stupid public that once had bought them and devoured them voraciously now turned to newer favourites. Salome Otterbourne would once again be notorious. Her name would be in all the papers. She would be principal witness for the prosecution at the trial.

She took a deep breath and opened her mouth.

"It was when I went down to lunch. I hardly felt like eating—all the horror of the recent tragedy—well, I needn't go into that.

"Half-way down I remembered that I had—er—left something in my cabin. I told Rosalie to go on without me. She did."

Mrs. Otterbourne paused a minute.

The curtain across the door moved slightly as though lifted by the wind, but none of the three men noticed it.

"I—er—" Mrs. Otterbourne paused. Thin ice to skate over here, but it must be done somehow. "I—er—had an arrangement with one of the—er—*personnel* of the ship. He was to—er—get me something I needed, but I did not wish my daughter to know of it—she is inclined to be tiresome in certain ways—"

Not too good, this, but she could think of something that sounded better before it came to telling the story in court.

Race's eyebrows lifted as his eyes asked a question of Poirot.

Poirot gave an infinitesimal nod. His lips formed the word, "Drink."

The curtain across the door moved again. Between it and the door itself something showed with a faint steel blue gleam.

Mrs. Otterbourne continued.

"The arrangement was that I should go round to the stern on the deck below this, and there I should find the man waiting for me. As I went along the deck a cabin door opened and somebody looked out. It was this girl—Louise Bourget or whatever her name is. She seemed to be expecting some one. When she saw it was me, she looked disappointed and went abruptly inside again. I didn't think anything of it, of course. I went along just as I had said I would and got the—the stuff from the man. I paid him and—er—just had a word with him. Then I started back. Just as I came round the corner I saw some one knock on the maid's door and go into the cabin."

Race said:

"And that person was—"

Bang!

The noise of the explosion filled the cabin. There was an acrid sour smell of smoke. Mrs. Otterbourne turned slowly sideways as though in supreme inquiry, then her body slumped forward and she fell to the ground with a crash. From just behind her ear the blood flowed from a round neat hole.

There was a moment's stupefied silence.

Then both the able-bodied men jumped to their feet. The woman's body hindered their movements a little. Race bent over her while Poirot made a catlike jump for the door and the deck.

The deck was empty. On the ground just in front of the sill lay a big Colt revolver.

Poirot glanced in both directions—the deck was empty. He then sprinted towards the stern. As he rounded the corner he ran into Tim Allerton who was coming full tilt from the opposite direction.

"What the devil was that?" cried Tim breathlessly.

Poirot said sharply:

"Did you meet any one on your way here?"

"Meet any one? No."

"Then come with me." He took the young man by the arm and retraced his steps. A little crowd had assembled by now. Rosalie, Jacqueline and Cornelia had rushed out of their cabins. More people were coming along the deck from the saloon—Ferguson, Jim Fanthorp and Mrs. Allerton.

Race stood by the revolver. Poirot turned his head and said sharply to Tim Allerton.

"Got any gloves in your pocket?"

Tim fumbled.

"Yes, I have."

Poirot seized them from him, put them on, and bent to examine the revolver. Race did the same. The others watched breathlessly.

Race said:

"He didn't go the other way. Fanthorp and Ferguson were sitting on this deck lounge, they'd have seen him."

Poirot responded:

"And Mr. Allerton would have met him if he'd gone aft."

Race said—pointing to the revolver:

"Rather fancy we've seen this not so very long ago. Must make sure, though."

He knocked on the door of Pennington's cabin. There was no answer. The cabin was empty. Race strode to the right-hand drawer of the chest and jerked it open. The revolver was gone.

"Settles that," said Race. "Now then, where's Pennington himself?"

They went out again on deck. Mrs. Allerton had joined the group. Poirot moved swiftly over to her.

"Madame, take Miss Otterbourne with you and look after her. Her mother has been"—he consulted Race with an eye and Race nodded—"killed."

Dr. Bessner came bustling along.

"*Gott im Himmel!* What is there now?"

They made way for him, Race indicated the cabin. Bessner went inside.

"*Find Pennington,*" said Race. "Any fingerprints on that revolver?"

"None." said Poirot.

They found Pennington on the deck below. He was sitting in the little drawing-room writing letters. He lifted a handsome clean-shaven face.

"Anything new?" he asked.

"Didn't you hear a shot?"

"Why—now you mention it I believe I did hear a kind of a bang. But I never dreamed—who's been shot?"

"Mrs. Otterbourne."

"*Mrs. Otterbourne?*" Pennington sounded quite astounded. "Well, you do surprise me. Mrs. Otterbourne." He shook his head. "I can't see that at all." He lowered his voice. "Strikes me, gentlemen, we've got a homicidal maniac aboard. We ought to organise a defence system."

"Mr. Pennington," said Race. "How long have you been in this room?"

"Why, let me see," Mr. Pennington gently rubbed his chin. "I should say a matter of twenty minutes or so."

"And you haven't left it?"

"Why, no—certainly not."

He looked inquiringly at the two men.

"You see, Mr. Pennington," said Race. "Mrs. Otterbourne was shot with your revolver."

CHAPTER 24

Mr. Pennington was shocked. Mr. Pennington could hardly believe it.

"Why, gentlemen," he said, "this is a very serious matter. Very serious indeed."

"Extremely serious for you, Mr. Pennington."

"For me?" Pennington's eyebrows rose in startled surprise. "But, my dear sir, I was sitting quietly writing in here when that shot was fired."

"You have, perhaps, a witness to prove that?"

Pennington shook his head.

"Why, no—I wouldn't say that. But it's clearly impossible that I should have gone to the deck above, shot this poor woman (and why should I shoot her anyway?) and come down again with no one seeing me. There are always plenty of people on the deck lounge this time of day."

"How do you account for your pistol being used?"

"Well—I'm afraid I may be to blame there. Quite soon after getting aboard there was a conversation in the saloon one evening, I remember, about firearms, and I mentioned then that I always carried a revolver with me when I travel."

"Who was there?"

"Well, I can't remember exactly. Most people, I think. Quite a crowd, anyway."

He shook his head gently.

"Why, yes," he said. "I am certainly to blame there." He went on:

"First Linnet, then Linnet's maid and now Mrs. Otterbourne. There seems no reason in it all!"

"There *was* reason," said Race.

"There was?"

"Yes. Mrs. Otterbourne was on the point of telling us that she had seen a certain person go into Louise's cabin. Before she could name that person she was shot dead."

Andrew Pennington passed a fine silk handkerchief over his brow.

"All this is terrible," he murmured.

Poirot said:

"M. Pennington, I would like to discuss certain aspects of the case with you. Will you come to my cabin in half an hour's time?"

"I should be delighted."

Pennington did not sound delighted. He did not look delighted either. Race and Poirot exchanged glances and then abruptly left the room.

"Cunning old devil," said Race. "But he's afraid. Eh?"

Poirot nodded:

"Yes, he is not happy, our Mr. Pennington."

As they reached the promenade deck again, Mrs. Allerton came out of her cabin, and seeing Poirot beckoned him imperiously.

"Madame?"

"That poor child! Tell me, M. Poirot, is there a double cabin somewhere that I could share with her? She oughtn't to go back to the one she shared with her mother, and mine is only a single one."

"That can be arranged, Madame. It is very good of you."

"It's mere decency. Besides, I'm very fond of the girl. I've always liked her."

"Is she very—upset?"

"Terribly. She seems to have been absolutely devoted to that odious woman. That is what is so pathetic about it all. Tim says he believes she drank. Is that true?"

Poirot nodded.

"Oh, well, poor woman—one mustn't judge her, I suppose, but the girl must have had a terrible life."

"She did, Madame. She is very proud and she was very loyal."

"Yes, I like that—loyalty, I mean. It's out of fashion nowadays. She's an odd character, that girl—proud, reserved, stubborn, and terribly warm-hearted underneath, I fancy."

"I see that I have given her into good hands, Madame."

"Yes, don't worry. I'll look after her. She's inclined to cling to me in the most pathetic fashion."

Mrs. Allerton went back into the cabin. Poirot returned to the scene of the tragedy.

Cornelia was still standing on the deck, her eyes wide.

She said, "I don't understand, M. Poirot. How did the person who shot her get away without our seeing him?"

"Yes, how?" echoed Jacqueline.

"Ah," said Poirot. "It was not quite such a disappearing trick as you think, Mademoiselle. There were three distinct ways the murderer might have gone."

Jacqueline looked puzzled. She said, *"Three?"*

"He might have gone to the right, or he might have gone to the left, but I don't see any other way," puzzled Cornelia.

Jacqueline too frowned. Then her brow cleared.

She said:

"Of course. He could move in two directions on one plane—but *he could go at right angles to that plane too*. That is, he couldn't go *up* very well—but he could go *down*."

Poirot smiled.

"You have brains, Mademoiselle."

Cornelia said:

"I know I'm just a plain mutt, but I still don't see."

Jacqueline said:

"M. Poirot means, darling, that he could swing himself over the rail and down on to the deck below."

"My!" gasped Cornelia. "I never thought of that. He'd have to be mighty quick about it, though. I suppose he could just do it?"

"He could do it easily enough," said Tim Allerton. "Remember there's always a minute of shock after a thing like this—one hears a shot and one's too paralysed to move for a second or two."

"That was your experience, Mr. Allerton?"

"Yes, it was. I just stood like a dummy for quite five seconds. Then I fairly sprinted round the deck."

Race came out of Bessner's cabin, and said authoritatively:

"Would you mind all clearing off. We want to bring out the body."

Every one moved away obediently. Poirot went with them. Cornelia said to him with sad earnestness.

"I'll never forget this trip as long as I live. . . . Three deaths. . . . It's just like living in a nightmare."

Ferguson overheard her. He said aggressively:

"That's because you're overcivilised. You should look on death as the Oriental does. It's a mere incident—hardly noticeable."

Cornelia said:

"That's all very well—they're not educated, poor creatures."

"No, and a good thing too. Education has devitalised the white races. Look at America—goes in for an orgy of culture. Simply disgusting."

"I think you're talking nonsense," said Cornelia, flushing. "I attend lectures every winter on Greek Art and the Renaissance—and I went to some on Famous Women of History."

Mr. Ferguson groaned in agony.

"Greek Art! Renaissance! Famous Women of History! It makes me quite sick to hear you. It's the *future* that matters, woman, not the past. Three women are dead on this boat—well, what of it? They're no loss! Linnet Doyle and her money! The French maid—a domestic parasite—Mrs. Otterbourne—a useless fool of a woman. Do you think any one really cares whether they're dead or not? *I* don't. I think it's a damned good thing!"

"Then you're wrong!" Cornelia blazed out at him. "And it makes me sick to hear you talk and talk—as though nobody mattered but *you*. I didn't like Mrs. Otterbourne much, but her daughter was ever so fond of her and she's all broken up over her mother's death. I don't know much about the French maid, but I expect somebody was fond of her somewhere, and as for Linnet Doyle—well, apart from everything else, she was just lovely! She was so beautiful when she came into a room that it made a lump come in your throat. I'm homely myself, and that makes me appreciate beauty a lot more. She was as beautiful—just as a woman—as anything in Greek Art. And when anything beautiful's dead, it's a loss to the world. So there!"

Mr. Ferguson stepped back a pace. He caught hold of his hair with both hands and tugged at it vehemently.

"I give it up," he said. "You're unbelievable. Just haven't got a bit of natural female spite in you anywhere." He turned to Poirot. "Do you know, sir, that Cornelia's father was practically ruined by Linnet Ridgeway's old man? But does the girl gnash her teeth when she sees the heiress sailing about in pearls and Paris models? No, she just bleats out, 'Isn't she beautiful?' like a blessed baa lamb. I don't believe she even felt sore at her."

Cornelia flushed.

"I did—just for a minute. Poppa kind of died of discouragement, you know, because he hadn't made good."

"Felt sore for a minute! I ask you."

Cornelia flashed round on him.

"Well, didn't you say just now it was the future that mattered, not the past? All that was in the past, wasn't it? It's over."

"Got me there," said Ferguson. "Cornelia Robson, you're the only nice woman I've ever come across. Will you marry me?"

"Don't be absurd."

"It's a genuine proposal—even if it is made in the presence of Old Man Sleuth. Anyway, you're a witness, M. Poirot. I've deliberately offered marriage to this female—against all my principles because I don't believe in legal contracts between the sexes, but I don't think she'd stand for anything else, so marriage it shall be. Come on, Cornelia, say yes."

"I think you're utterly ridiculous," said Cornelia, flushing.

"Why won't you marry me?"

"You're not serious," said Cornelia.

"Do you mean not serious in proposing or do you mean not serious in character?"

"Both, but I really meant character. You laugh at all sorts of serious things. Education and Culture—and—and Death. You wouldn't be *reliable*."

She broke off, flushed again, and hurried along into her cabin.

Ferguson stared after her.

"Damn the girl! I believe she really means it. She wants a man to be *reliable*. Reliable—ye gods!" He paused and then said curiously, "What's the matter with you, M. Poirot? You seem very deep in thought."

Poirot roused himself with a start.

"I reflect, that is all. I reflect."

"Meditation on Death. Death, the Recurring Decimal, by Hercule Poirot. One of his well-known monographs."

"Mr. Ferguson," said Poirot. "You are a very impertinent young man."

"You must excuse me. I like attacking established institutions."

"And I—am an established institution?"

"Precisely. What do you think of that girl?"

"Of Miss Robson?"

"Yes."

"I think that she has a great deal of character."

"You're right. She's got spirit. She looks meek, but she isn't. She's got guts. She's—oh, damn it, I want that girl. It mightn't be a bad move if I tackled the old lady. If I could once get her thoroughly against me, it might cut some ice with Cornelia."

He wheeled and went into the observation saloon.

Miss Van Schuyler was seated in her usual corner. She looked even more arrogant than usual. She was knitting.

Ferguson strode up to her. Hercule Poirot, entering unobtrusively, took a seat a discreet distance away and appeared to be absorbed in a magazine.

"Good-afternoon, Miss Van Schuyler."

Miss Van Schuyler raised her eyes for a bare second, dropped them again and murmured frigidly:

"Er—good-afternoon."

"Look here, Miss Van Schuyler, I want to talk to you about something pretty important. It's just this. I want to marry your niece."

Miss Van Schuyler's ball of wool dropped on to the ground and ran wildly across the saloon.

She said in a venomous tone:

"You must be out of your senses, young man."

"Not at all. I'm determined to marry her. I've asked her to marry me!"

Miss Van Schuyler surveyed him coldly, with the kind of speculative interest she might have accorded to an odd sort of beetle.

"Indeed? And I presume she sent you about your business."

"She refused me."

"Naturally."

"Not 'naturally' at all. I'm going to go on asking her till she agrees."

"I can assure you, sir, I shall take steps to see that my young cousin is not subjected to any such persecution," said Miss Van Schuyler in a biting tone."

"What have you got against me?"

Miss Van Schuyler merely raised her eyebrows and gave a vehement tug to her wool, preparatory to regaining it and closing the interview.

"Come now," persisted Mr. Ferguson. "What have you got against me?"

"I should think that was quite obvious, Mr.—er—I don't know your name."

"Ferguson."

"Mr. Ferguson." Miss Van Schuyler uttered the name with definite distaste. "Any such idea is quite out of the question."

"You mean," said Ferguson, "that I'm not good enough for her?"

"I should think that would have been obvious to you."

"In what way am I not good enough?"

Miss Van Schuyler again did not answer.

"I've got two legs, two arms, good health and quite reasonable brains. What's wrong with that?"

"There is such a thing as social position, Mr. Ferguson."

"Social position is bunk!"

The door swung open and Cornelia came in. She stopped dead on seeing her redoubtable Cousin Marie in conversation with her would-be suitor.

The outrageous Mr. Ferguson turned his head, grinned broadly and called out:

"Come along, Cornelia. I'm asking for your hand in marriage in the best conventional manner."

"Cornelia," said Miss Van Schuyler, and her voice was truly awful in quality. "*Have you encouraged this young man?*"

"I—no, of course not—at least—not exactly—I mean—"

"What do you mean?"

"She hasn't encouraged me," said Mr. Ferguson helpfully. "I've done it all. She hasn't actually pushed me in the face because she's got too kind a heart. Cornelia, your aunt says I'm not good enough for you. That, of course, is true, but not in the way she means it. My moral nature certainly doesn't equal yours, but her point is that I'm hopelessly below you socially."

"That, I think, is equally obvious to Cornelia," said Miss Van Schuyler.

"Is it?" Mr. Ferguson looked at her searchingly. "Is that why you won't marry me?"

"No, it isn't." Cornelia flushed. "If—if I liked you, I'd marry you no matter who you were."

"But you don't like me?"

"I—I think you're just outrageous. The way you say things. . . The *things* you say . . . I—I've never met any one the least like you. I—"

Tears threatened to overcome her. She rushed from the room.

"On the whole," said Mr. Ferguson, "that's not too bad for a start." He leaned back in his chair, gazed at the ceiling, whistled, crossed his disreputable knees and remarked, "I'll be calling you Auntie yet."

Miss Van Schuyler trembled with rage.

"Leave this room at once, sir, or I'll ring for the steward."

"I've paid for my ticket," said Mr. Ferguson. "They can't possibly turn me out of the public lounge. But I'll humour you." He sang softly, "Yo ho ho, and a bottle of rum." Rising, he sauntered nonchalantly to the door and passed out.

Choking with anger Miss Van Schuyler struggled to her feet. Poirot, discreetly emerging from retirement behind his magazine, sprang up and retrieved the ball of wool.

"Thank you, M. Poirot. If you would send Miss Bowers to me—I feel quite upset—that insolent young man."

"Rather eccentric, I'm afraid," said Poirot. "Most of that family are. Spoilt, of course. Always inclined to tilt at windmills." He added carelessly: "You recognised him, I suppose?"

"Recognised him?"

"Calls himself Ferguson and won't use his title because of his advanced ideas."

"His *title?*" Miss Van Schuyler's tone was sharp.

"Yes, that's young Lord Dawlish. Rolling in money, of course. But he became a communist when he was at Oxford."

Miss Van Schuyler, her face a battleground of contradictory emotions, said: "How long have you known this, M. Poirot?"

Poirot shrugged his shoulders.

"There was a picture in one of these papers—I noticed the resemblance. Then I found a signet ring with a coat of arms on it. Oh, there's no doubt about it, I assure you."

He quite enjoyed reading the conflicting expressions that succeeded each other on Miss Van Schuyler's face. Finally, with a gracious inclincation of the head, she said:

"I am very much obliged to you, M. Poirot."

Poirot looked after her as she went out of the saloon and smiled.

Then he sat down and his face grew grave once more. He was following out a train of thought in his mind. From time to time he nodded his head.

"*Mais oui,*" he said at last. "It all fits in."

CHAPTER 25

Race found him still sitting there.

"Well, Poirot, what about it? Pennington's due in ten minutes. I'm leaving this in your hands."

Poirot rose quickly to his feet.

"First, get hold of young Fanthorp."

"Fanthorp?" Race looked surprised.

"Yes. Bring him to my cabin."

Race nodded and went off. Poirot went along to his cabin. Race arrived with young Fanthorp a minute or two afterwards.

Poirot indicated chairs and offered cigarettes.

"Now, M. Fanthorp," he said. "To our business! I perceive that you wear the same tie that my friend Hastings wears."

Jim Fanthorp looked down at his neckwear with some bewilderment.

"It's an O.E. tie," he said.

"Exactly. You must understand that though I am a foreigner, I know something of the English point of view. I know, for instance, that there are 'things which are done' and things which are 'not done.'"

Jim Fanthorp grinned.

"We don't say that sort of thing much nowadays, sir."

"Perhaps not, but the custom, it still remains. The Old School Tie is the Old School Tie and there are certain things (I know this from experience) that the Old School Tie does not do! One of those things, M. Fanthorp, is to butt into a private conversation unasked when one does not know the people who are conducting it."

Fanthorp stared.

Poirot went on:

"But the other day, M. Fanthorp, *that is exactly what you did do*. Certain persons were quietly transacting some private business in the observation saloon. You strolled near them, obviously in order to overhear what it was that was in progress, and presently you actually turned round and congratulated a lady—Mrs. Simon Doyle—on the soundness of her business methods."

Jim Fanthorp's face got very red. Poirot swept on, not waiting for a comment.

"Now that, M. Fanthorp, was not at all the behaviour of one who wears a tie similar to that worn by my friend Hastings! Hastings is all delicacy, would die of shame before he did such a thing! Therefore, taking that action of yours in conjunction with the fact that you are a very young man to be able to afford an expensive holiday, that you are a member of a country solicitor's firm and therefore probably not extravagantly well off, and that you show no sign of recent illness such as might necessitate a prolonged visit abroad, I ask myself—and am now asking you—*what is the reason for your presence on this boat?*"

Jim Fanthorp jerked his head back.

"I decline to give you any information whatever, M. Poirot. I really think you must be mad."

"I am not mad. I am very very sane. Where is your firm? In Northampton—that is not very far from Wode Hall. What conversation did you try to overhear? One concerning legal documents. What was the object of your remark—a remark which you uttered with obvious embarrassment and *malaise?* Your object was *to prevent Mrs. Doyle from signing any documents unread*."

He paused.

"On this boat we have had a murder, and following that murder two other murders in rapid succession. If I further give you the information that the weapon which killed Mrs. Otterbourne was *a revolver owned by Mr. Andrew Pennington*, then perhaps you will realise that it is actually your duty to tell us all you can."

Jim Fanthorp was silent for some minutes. At last he said:

"You have rather an odd way of going about things, M. Poirot, but I appreciate the points you have made. The trouble is that I have no exact information to lay before you."

"You mean that it is a case, merely, of suspicion."

"Yes."

"And therefore you think it injudicious to speak? That may be true, legally speaking. But this is not a court of law. Colonel Race and myself are endeavouring to track down a murderer. Anything that can help us to do so may be valuable."

Again Jim Fanthorp reflected. Then he said:

"Very well. What is it you want you know?"

"Why did you come on this trip?"

"My uncle, Mr. Carmichael, Mrs. Doyle's English solicitor, sent me. He handled a good many of her affairs. In this way, he was often in correspondence with Mr. Andrew Pennington who was Mrs. Doyle's American trustee. Several small incidents (I cannot enumerate them all) made my uncle suspicious that all was not quite as it should be."

"In plain language," said Race, "your uncle suspected that Pennington was a crook?"

Jim Fanthorp nodded, a faint smile on his face.

"You put it rather more bluntly than I should, but the main idea is correct.

Various excuses made by Pennington, certain plausible explanations of the disposal of funds, aroused my uncle's distrust.

"While these suspicions of his were still nebulous Miss Ridgeway married unexpectedly and went off on her honeymoon to Egypt. Her marriage relieved my uncle's mind, as he knew that on her return to England the estate would have to be formally settled and handed over.

"However, in a letter she wrote him from Cairo, she mentioned casually that she had unexpectedly run across Andrew Pennington. My uncle's suspicions became acute. He felt sure that Pennington, perhaps by now in a desperate position, was going to try and obtain signatures from her which would cover his own defalcations. Since my uncle had no definite evidence to lay before her, he was in a most difficult position. The only thing he could think of was to send me out there, travelling by air, with instructions to discover what was in the wind. I was to keep my eyes open and act summarily if necessary—a most unpleasant mission, I can assure you. As a matter of fact, on the occasion you mention I had to behave more or less as a cad! It was awkward, but on the whole I was satisfied with the result."

"You mean you put Mrs. Doyle on her guard?" asked Race.

"Not so much that. But I think I put the wind up Pennington. I felt convinced he wouldn't try any more funny business for some time and by then I hoped to have got intimate enough with Mr. and Mrs. Doyle to convey some kind of a warning. As a matter of fact I hoped to do so through Doyle. Mrs. Doyle was so attached to Mr. Pennington that it would have been a bit awkward to suggest things to her about him. It would have been easier for me to approach the husband."

Race nodded.

Poirot asked:

"Will you give me a candid opinion on one point, M. Fanthorp? If you were engaged in putting a swindle over, would you choose Mrs. Doyle or Mr. Doyle as a victim?"

Fanthorp smiled faintly.

"Mr. Doyle, every time. Linnet Doyle was very shrewd in business matters. Her husband, I should fancy, is one of those trustful fellows who know nothing of business and are always ready to 'sign on the dotted line' as he himself put it."

"I agree," said Poirot. He looked at Race. "*And there's your motive.*"

Jim Fanthorp said:

"But this is all pure conjecture. It isn't *evidence*."

Poirot said easily:

"Ah bah! we will get evidence!"

"How?"

"Possibly from Mr. Pennington himself."

Fanthorp looked doubtful.

"I wonder. I very much wonder."

Race glanced at his watch.

"He's about due now."

Jim Fanthorp was quick to take the hint. He left them.

Two minutes later Andrew Pennington made his appearance.

His manner was all smiling urbanity. Only the taut line of his jaw and the wariness of his eyes betrayed the fact that a thoroughly experienced fighter was on his guard.

"Well, gentlemen," he said, "here I am."

He sat down and looked at them inquiringly.

"We asked you to come here, Mr. Pennington," began Poirot, "because it is fairly obvious that you have a very special and immediate interest in the case."

Pennington raised his eyebrows slightly.

"Is that so?"

Poirot said gently:

"Surely. You have known Linnet Ridgeway, I understand, since she was quite a child."

"Oh! that—" his face altered—became less alert. "I beg pardon, I didn't quite get you. Yes, as I told you this morning, I've known Linnet since she was a cute little thing in pinafores."

"You were on terms of close intimacy with her father?"

"That's so. Melhuish Ridgeway and I were close—very close."

"You were so intimately associated that on his death he appointed you business guardian to his daughter and trustee to the vast fortune she inherited."

"Why, roughly—that is so." The wariness was back again. The note was more cautious. "I was not the only trustee, naturally—others were associated with me."

"Who have since died?"

"Two of them are dead. The other, Mr. Sterndale Rockford, is alive."

"Your partner?"

"Yes."

"Miss Ridgeway, I understand, was not yet of age when she married?"

"She would have been twenty-one next July."

"And in the normal course of events she would have come into control of her fortune then?"

"Yes."

"But her marriage precipitated matters?"

Pennington's jaw hardened—he shot out his chin at them aggressively.

"You'll pardon me, gentlemen, but what exact business is all this of yours?"

"If you dislike answering the question—"

"There's no dislike about it. I don't mind what you ask me. But I don't see the relevance of all this."

"Oh, but surely, Mr. Pennington . . ." Poirot leaned forward, his eyes green and catlike—"there is the question of motive—in considering that, financial considerations must always be taken into account."

Pennington said sullenly:

"By Ridgeway's will, Linnet got control of her dough when she was twenty-one or when she married."

"No conditions of any kind?"

"No conditions."

"And it is a matter, I am credibly assured, of millions."

"Millions it is."

Poirot said softly:

"Your responsibility, Mr. Pennington, and that of your partner, has been a very grave one."

Pennington said curtly:

"We're used to responsibility. Doesn't worry us any."

"I wonder."

Something in his tone flicked the other man on the raw. He said angrily:

"What the devil do you mean?"

Poirot replied with an air of engaging frankness:

"I was wondering, Mr. Pennington, whether Linnet Ridgeway's sudden marriage caused any—consternation in your office?"

"Consternation?"

"That was the word I used."

"What the hell are you driving at?"

"Something quite simple. Are Linnet Doyle's affairs in the perfect order they should be?"

Pennington rose to his feet.

"That's enough. I'm through." He made for the door.

"But you will answer my question first?"

Pennington snapped:

"They're in perfect order."

"You were not so alarmed when the news of Linnet Ridgeway's marriage reached you that you rushed over to Europe by the first boat and staged an apparently fortuitous meeting in Egypt?"

Pennington came back towards them. He had himself under control once more.

"What you are saying is absolute balderdash! I didn't even know that Linnet was married till I met her in Cairo. I was utterly astonished. Her letter must have missed me by a day in New York. It was forwarded and I got it about a week later."

"You came over by the *Carmanic*, I think you said."

"That's right."

"And the letter reached New York after the *Carmanic* sailed?"

"How many times have I got to repeat it?"

"It is strange," said Poirot.

"What's strange?"

"That on your luggage there are no labels of the *Carmanic*. The only recent labels of transatlantic sailing are the *Normandie*. The *Normandie*, I remember, sailed two days after the *Carmanic*."

For a moment the other was at a loss. His eyes wavered.

Colonel Race weighed in with telling effect.

"Come, now, Mr. Pennington," he said. "We've several reasons for believing that you came over on the *Normandie* and not by the *Carmanic*, as you said. In that case, *you received Mrs. Doyle's letter before you left New York*. It's no good denying it, for it's the easiest thing in the world to check up the steamship companies."

Andrew Pennington felt absent-mindedly for a chair and sat down. His face was impassive—a poker face. Behind that mask his agile brain looked ahead to the next move.

"I'll have to hand it you, gentlemen. You've been too smart for me. But I had my reasons for acting as I did."

"No doubt."

Race's tone was curt.

"If I give them to you, it must be understood I do so in confidence."

"I think you can trust us to behave fittingly. Naturally I cannot give assurances blindly."

"Well—" Pennington sighed. "I'll come clean. There was some monkey business going on in England. It worried me. I couldn't do much about it by letter. The only thing was to come over and see for myself?"

"What do you mean by monkey business?"

"I'd good reason to believe that Linnet was being swindled."

"By whom?"

"Her British lawyer. Now that's not the kind of accusation you can fling around anyhow. I made up my mind to come over right away and see into matters myself."

"That does great credit to your vigilance, I am sure. But why the little deception about not having received the letter."

"Well, I ask you—" Pennington spread out his hands. "You can't butt in on a honeymoon couple without more or less coming down to brass tacks and giving your reasons. I thought it best to make the meeting accidental. Besides, I didn't know anything about the husband. He might have been mixed up in the racket for all I knew."

"In fact all your actions were actuated by pure disinterestedness," said Colonel Race dryly.

"You've said it, Colonel."

There was a pause.

Race glanced at Poirot. The little man leant forward.

"M. Pennington, we do not believe a word of your story."

"The hell you don't! And what the hell do you believe?"

"We believe that Linnet Ridgeway's unexpected marriage put you in a financial quandary—that you came over post haste to try and find some way out of the mess you were in—that is to say, some way of gaining time. That, with that end in view, you endeavoured to obtain Mrs. Doyle's signature to certain documents—and failed. That on the journey up the Nile, when walking along the cliff top at Abu Simbel, you dislodged a boulder which fell and only very narrowly missed its object—"

"You're crazy."

"We believe that the same kind of circumstances occurred on the return journey—that is to say, an opportunity presented itself of putting Mrs. Doyle out of the way *at the moment when her death would be almost certainly ascribed to the action of another person*—we not only believe, but *know*, that it was your revolver which killed a woman who was about to reveal to us the name of the person whom she had reason to believe killed both Linnet Doyle and the maid Louise—"

"Hell!" The forcible ejaculation broke forth and interrupted Poirot's stream of eloquence. "What are you getting at? Are you crazy? What motive had I to kill Linnet? I wouldn't get her money—that goes to her husband. Why don't you pick on him. *He's* the one to benefit—not me."

Race said coldly:

"Doyle never left the lounge on the night of the tragedy till he was shot at and wounded in the leg. The impossibility of his walking a step after that is attested to by a doctor and a nurse—both independent and reliable witnesses. Simon Doyle could not have killed his wife. He could not have killed Louise Bourget. He most definitely did not kill Mrs. Otterbourne! You know that as well as we do."

"I know he didn't kill her." Pennington sounded a little calmer. "All I say is, why pick on me when I don't benefit by her death?"

"But, my dear sir," Poirot's voice came soft as a purring cat, "that is rather a matter of opinion. Mrs. Doyle was a keen woman of business, fully conversant of her own affairs and very quick to spot any irregularity. As soon as she took up the control of her property which she would have done on her return to England her suspicions were bound to be aroused. But now that she is dead and that her husband, as you have just pointed out, inherits, *the whole thing is different*. Simon Doyle knows nothing whatever of his wife's affairs except that she was a rich woman. He is of a simple trusting disposition. You will find it easy to place complicated statements before him, to involve the real issue in a net of figures, and to delay settlement with pleas of legal formalities and the recent depression. *I think that it makes a very considerable difference to you whether you deal with the husband or the wife*."

Pennington shrugged his shoulders.

"Your ideas are—fantastic."

"Time will show."

"What did you say?"

"I said, 'Time will show!' This is a mtter of three deaths—three murders. The law will demand the most searching investigation into the condition of Mrs. Doyle's estate."

He saw the sudden sag in the other's shoulders and knew that he had won. Jim Fanthorp's suspicions were well founded.

Poirot went on:

"You've played—and lost. Useless to go on bluffing."

Pennington muttered:

"You don't understand—it's all square enough really. It's been this damned slump—Wall Street's been crazy. But I'd staged a comeback. With luck everything will be O.K. by the middle of June."

With shaking hands he took a cigarette, tried to light it—failed.

"I suppose," mused Poirot, "that the boulder was a sudden temptation. You thought nobody saw you."

"That was an accident—I swear it was an accident." The man leaned forward, his face working, his eyes terrified. "I stumbled and fell against it. I swear it was an accident. . . ."

The two men said nothing.

Pennington suddenly pulled himself together. He was still a wreck of a man but his fighting spirit had returned in a certain measure. He moved towards the door.

"You can't pin that on me, gentlemen. It was an accident. And it wasn't I who shot her! D'you hear? You can't pin that on me either—and you never will."

He went out.

CHAPTER 26

As the door closed behind him, Race gave a deep sigh.

"We got more than I thought we should. Admission of fraud. Admission of attempted murder. Further than that it's impossible to go. A man will confess, more or less, to attempted murder, but you won't get him to confess to the real thing."

"Sometimes it can be done," said Poirot. His eyes were dreamy—catlike.

Race looked at him curiously.

"Got a plan?"

Poirot nodded.

Then he said, ticking off the items on his fingers.

"The garden at Assuan. Mr. Allerton's statement. The two bottles of nail polish. My bottle of wine. The velvet stole. The stained handkerchief. The pistol that was left on the scene of the crime. The death of Louise. The death of Mrs. Otterbourne. . . . Yes, it's all there. *Pennington didn't do it, Race!*"

"What?" Race was startled.

"*Pennington didn't do it*. He had the motive, yes. He had the *will* to do it, yes. He got as far as *attempting* to do it. *Mais c'est tout*. Something was wanted for this crime *that Pennington hasn't got!* This is a crime that needed audacity, swift and faultless execution, courage, indifference to danger, and a resourceful, calculating brain. *Pennington hasn't got those attributes*. He couldn't do a crime unless he knew it to be safe. This crime wasn't safe! It hung on a razor edge. It needed boldness. Pennington isn't bold. He's only astute."

Race looked at him with the respect one able man gives to another.

"You've got it all well taped," he said.

"I think so—yes. There are one or two things—that telegram, for instance, that Linnet Doyle read. I should like to get that cleared up."

"By Jove, we forgot to ask Doyle. He was telling us when poor old Ma Otterbourne came along. We'll ask him again."

"Presently. First, I have some one else to whom I wish to speak."

"Who's that?"

"Tim Allerton."

Race raised his eyebrows.

"Allerton? Well, we'll get him here."

He pressed a bell and sent the steward with a message.

Tim Allerton entered with a questioning look.

"Steward said you wanted to see me?"

"That is right, Mr. Allerton. Sit down."

Tim sat. His face was attentive but very slightly bored.

"Anything I can do?"

His tone was polite but not enthusiastic.

Poirot said:

"In a sense, perhaps. What I really require is for you to listen."

Tim's eyebrows rose in polite surprise.

"Certainly. I'm the world's best listener. Can be relied on to say, 'OO-er!' at the right moments."

"That is very satisfactory. 'OO-er!' will be very expressive. *Eh bien,* let us commence. When I met you and your mother at Assuan, M. Allerton, I was attracted to your company very strongly. To begin with, I thought your mother was one of the most charming people I had ever met—"

The weary face flickered for a moment—a shade of expression came into it.

"She is—unique," he said.

"But the second thing that interested me was your mention of a certain lady."

"Really?"

"Yes—a Miss Joanna Southwood. You see, I had recently been hearing that name."

He paused and went on.

"For the last three years there have been certain jewel robberies that have been worrying Scotland Yard a good deal. They are what may be described as Society robberies. The method is usually the same—the substitution of an imitation piece of jewellery for an original. My friend, Chief Inspector Japp, came to the conclusion that the robberies were not the work of one person, but of two people working in with each other very cleverly. He was convinced, from the considerable inside knowledge displayed, that the robberies were the work of people in a good social position. And finally his attention became riveted on Miss Joanna Southwood. Every one of the victims had been either a friend or acquaintance of hers, and in each case she had either handled or been lent the piece of jewellery in question. Also, her style of living was far in excess of her income. On the other hand it was quite clear that the actual robbery—that is to say, the substitution—had *not* been accomplished by her. In some cases she had even been out of England during the period when the jewellery must have been replaced. So gradually a little picture grew up in Chief Inspector Japp's mind. Miss Southwood was at one time associated with a Guild of Modern Jewellery. He suspected that she handled the jewels in question, made accurate drawings of them, got them copied by some humble but dishonest working jeweller and that the third part of the operation was the successful substitution by another person—somebody who could have been proved never to have handled the jewels and never to have had anything to do with copies or imitations of precious stones. Of the identity of this other person Japp was ignorant.

"Certain things that fell from you in conversation interested me. A ring that had disappeared when you were in Majorca—the fact that you had been in a house-party where one of these fake substitutions had occurred, your close association with Miss Southwood. There was also the fact that you obviously resented my presence and tried to get your mother to be less friendly towards me. That might, of course, have been just personal dislike—but I thought not. You were too anxious to try and hide your distaste under a genial manner.

"*Eh bien*—after the murder of Linnet Doyle it is discovered that her pearls are missing. You comprehend, at once I think of you! But I am not quite satisfied. For if you are working, as I suspect, with Miss Southwood (who was an intimate friend of Mrs. Doyle's) then substitution would be the method employed—not barefaced theft. But then, the pearls quite unexpectedly are returned and what do I discover. That they are not genuine but *imitation*.

"I know then who the real thief is. It was the imitation string which was stolen and returned—an imitation which you had previously substituted for the real necklace."

He looked at the young man in front of him. Tim was white under his tan. He was not so good a fighter as Pennington—his stamina was bad. He said with an effort to sustain his mocking manner:

"Indeed? And if so, what did I do with them?"

"That I know also."

The young man's face changed—broke up.

Poirot went on slowly.

"There is only one place where they can be. I have reflected, and my reason tells me that that is so. Those pearls, Mr. Allerton, are concealed in a rosary that hangs in your cabin. The beads of it are very elaborately carved. I think you had it made specially. Those beads unscrew though you would never think so to look at them. Inside each is a pearl, stuck with seccotine. Most police searchers respect religious symbols unless there is something obviously queer about them—you counted on that. I endeavoured to find out how Miss Southwood sent the imitation necklace out to you. She must have done so, since you came here from Majorca on hearing that Mrs. Doyle would be here for her honeymoon. My theory is that it was sent in a book—a square hole being cut out of the pages in the middle. A book goes with the ends open and is practically never opened in the post."

There was a pause—a long pause, then Tim said quietly.

"You win! It's been a good game. But it's over at last. There's nothing for it now, I suppose, but to take my medicine."

Poirot nodded gently.

"Do you realise that you were seen last night?"

"Seen?" Tim started.

"Yes, on the night that Linnet Doyle died, some one saw you leave her cabin just after one in the morning."

Tim said:

"Look here—you aren't thinking . . . it wasn't I who killed her! I'll swear that! I've been in the most awful stew. To have chosen that night of all others. . . . God, it's been awful."

Poirot said:

"Yes, you must have had uneasy moments. But now that the truth has come out, you may be able to help us. Was Mrs. Doyle alive or dead when you stole the pearls?"

Tim said hoarsely:

"I don't know. Honest to God, M. Poirot, I don't know! I'd found out where she put them at night—on the little table by the bed. I crept in, felt very softly on the table and grabbed 'em, put down the others and crept out again. I assumed, of course, that she was asleep."

"Did you hear her breathing? Surely you would have listened for that?"

Tim thought earnestly:

"It was very still—very still indeed. No, I can't remember actually hearing her breathe. . . ."

"Was there any smell of smoke lingering in the air as there would have been if a firearm had been discharged recently?"

"I don't think so. I don't remember it."

Poirot sighed.

"Then we are no further."

Tim asked curiously.

"Who was it saw me?"

"Rosalie Otterbourne. She came round from the other side of the boat and saw you leave Linnet Doyle's cabin and go to your own."

"So it was she who told you."

Poirot said gently:

"Excuse me—she did not tell me."

"But then—how do you know?"

"Because I am Hercule Poirot! *I do not need to be told*. When I taxed her with it, do you know what she said? She said, '*I saw nobody*.' And she lied."

"But why?"

Poirot said in a detached voice:

"Perhaps because she thought the man she saw was the murderer. It looked like that, you know."

"That seems to me all the more reason for telling you."

Poirot shrugged his shoulders.

"She did not think so, it seems."

Tim said, a queer note in his voice:

"She's an extraordinary sort of a girl. She must have been through a pretty rough time with that mother of hers."

"Yes, life has not been easy for her."

"Poor kid," Tim muttered.

Then he looked towards Race.

"Well, sir, where do we go from here? I admit taking the pearls from Linnet's cabin and you'll find them just where you say they are. I'm guilty all right. But as far as Miss Southwood is concerned I'm not admitting anything. You've no evidence whatever against her. How I got hold of the fake necklace is my own business."

Poirot murmured:

"A very correct attitude."

Tim said with a flash of humour:

"Always the gentleman!"

He added: "Perhaps you can imagine how annoying it was to me to find my mother cottoning on to you! I'm not a sufficiently hardened criminal to enjoy sitting cheek by jowl with a successful detective just before bringing off a rather risky coup! Some people might get a kick out of it. I didn't. Frankly, it gave me cold feet."

"But it did not deter you from making your attempt?"

Tim shrugged his shoulders.

"I couldn't funk it to that extent. The exchange had to be made sometime and I'd got a unique opportunity on this boat—a cabin only two doors off and Linnet herself so preoccupied with her own troubles that she wasn't likely to detect the change."

"I wonder if that was so—"

Tim looked up sharply.

"What do you mean?"

Poirot pressed the bell.

"I am going to ask Miss Otterbourne if she will come here for a minute."

Tim frowned but said nothing. A steward came, received the order and went away with the message.

Rosalie came after a few minutes. Her eyes, reddened with recent weeping, widened a little at seeing Tim, but her old attitude of suspicion and defiance seemed entirely absent. She sat down and with a new docility looked from Race to Poirot.

"We're very sorry to bother you, Miss Otterbourne," said Race gently. He was slightly annoyed with Poirot.

The girl said in a low voice:

"It doesn't matter."

Poirot said:

"It is necessary to clear up one or two points. When I asked you whether you saw any one on the starboard deck at 1.10 this morning, your answer was that you saw nobody. Fortunately I have been able to arrive at the truth without your help. Mr. Allerton has admitted that he was in Linnet Doyle's cabin last night."

She flashed a swift glance at Tim. Tim, his face grim and set, gave a curt nod.

"The time is correct, Mr. Allerton?"

Allerton replied:

"Quite correct."

Rosalie was staring at him. Her lips trembled—fell apart. . . .

"But you didn't—you didn't—"

He said quickly:

"No, I didn't kill her. I'm a thief, not a murderer. It's all going to come out so you might as well know. I was after her pearls."

Poirot said:

"Mr. Allerton's story is that he went to her cabin last night and exchanged a string of fake pearls for the real ones."

"Did you?" said Rosalie.

Her eyes, grave, sad, childlike, questioned his.

"Yes," said Tim.

There was a pause. Colonel Race shifted restlessly.

Poirot said in a curious voice:

"That, as I say, is Mr. Allerton's story, partially confirmed by your evidence. That is to say, there is evidence that he did visit Linnet Doyle's cabin last night, *but there is no evidence to show why he did so*."

Tim stared at him.

"But you know!"

"What do I know?"

"Well—you know I've got the pearls."

"*Mais oui—mais oui*—I know you have the pearls—*but I do not know when you got them*. It may have been *before* last night. . . . You said just now that Linnet Doyle would not have noticed the substitution. I am not so sure of that. Supposing she *did* notice it. . . . Supposing, even, she knew who did it. . . . Supposing that last night she threatened to expose the whole business and that you knew she meant to do so. . . . And supposing that you overheard the scene in the saloon between Jacqueline de Bellefort and Simon Doyle and as soon as the saloon was empty you slipped in and secured the pistol, and then an hour later, when the boat had quieted down, you crept along to Linnet Doyle's cabin and made quite sure that no exposure would come. . . ."

"My God," said Tim. Out of his ashen face, two tortured agonised eyes gazed dumbly at Hercule Poirot.

The latter went on:

"But somebody else saw you—the girl Louise. The next day she came to you and blackmailed you. You must pay her handsomely or she would tell what she knew. You realised that to submit to blackmail would be the beginning of the end. You pretended to agree, made an appointment to come to her cabin just before lunch with the money. Then, when she was counting the notes, you stabbed her.

"But again luck was against you. Somebody saw you go to her cabin—" he half turned to Rosalie. "Your mother. Once again you had to act—dangerously—foolhardily—but it was the only chance. You had heard Pennington talk about his revolver. You rushed into his cabin, got hold of it, listened outside Dr. Bessner's cabin door and shot Mrs. Otterbourne before she could reveal your name—"

"N-o!" cried Rosalie. "He didn't! He didn't!"

"After that, you did *the only thing you could do*—rushed round the stern, and when I rushed after you, you had turned and pretended to be coming in the *opposite* direction. You had handled the revolver in gloves—those gloves *were in your pocket when I asked* for them. . . ."

Tim said.

"Before God, I swear it isn't true—not a word of it."

But his voice, ill assured and trembling, failed to convince.

It was then that Rosalie Otterbourne surprised them.

"Of course it isn't true! And M. Poirot knows it isn't! He's saying it for some reason of his own."

Poirot looked at her. A faint smile came to his lips. He spread his hands in token of surrender.

"Mademoiselle is too clever. . . . But you agree—it was a good case?"

"What the devil—"

Tim began with rising anger, but Poirot held up a hand.

"There is a very good case against you, Mr. Allerton. I wanted you to realise that. Now I will tell you something more pleasant. *I have not yet examined that rosary in your cabin.* It may be that, when I do, *I shall find nothing there.* And then, since Mademoiselle Otterbourne sticks to it that she saw no one on the deck last night—*eh bien,* there is no case against you at all. The pearls were taken by a kleptomaniac who has since returned them. They are in a little box on the table by the door if you would care to examine them with Mademoiselle."

Tim got up. He stood for a moment unable to speak. When he did, his words seemed inadequate but it is possible that they satisfied his listeners.

"Thanks!" he said. "You won't have to give me another chance."

He held the door open for the girl, she passed out, and picking up the little cardboard box, he followed her.

Side by side they went. Tim opened the box, took out the sham string of pearls and hurled it far from him into the Nile.

"There!" he said. "That's gone. When I return the box to Poirot the real string will be in it. What a damned fool I've been."

Rosalie said in a low voice:

"Why did you come to do it in the first place?"

"How did I come to start, do you mean? Oh, I don't know. Boredom—laziness—the fun of the thing. Such a much more attractive way of earning a living than just pegging away at a job. Sounds pretty sordid to you, I expect—but you know there was an attraction about it—mainly the risk, I suppose."

"I think I understand."

"Yes, but you wouldn't ever do it."

Rosalie considered for a moment or two, her grave young head bent.

"No," she said simply. "I wouldn't."

He said:

"Oh, my dear—you're so lovely . . . so utterly lovely. Why wouldn't you say you'd seen me last night?"

Rosalie said: "I thought—they might suspect you."

"Did you suspect me?"

"No. I couldn't believe that you'd kill any one."

"No. I'm not the strong stuff murderers are made of. I'm only a miserable sneak thief."

She put out a timid hand and touched his arm.

"Don't say that. . . ."

He caught her hand in his.

"Rosalie, would you—you know what I mean? Or would you always despise me and throw it in my teeth?"

She smiled faintly.

"There are things you could throw in my teeth, too. . . ."

"Rosalie—darling. . . ."

But she held back a minute longer.

"This—Joanna—?"

Tim gave a sudden shout.

"Joanna—? You're as bad as Mother. I don't care a damn about Joanna—she's got a face like a horse and a predatory eye. A most unattractive female."

Presently Rosalie said:

"Your mother need never know about you."

Tim said thoughtfully.

"I'm not sure. I think I shall tell her. Mother's got plenty of stuffing, you know. She can stand up to things. Yes, I think I shall shatter her maternal illusions about me. She'll be so relieved to know that my relations with Joanna were purely of a business nature that she'll forgive me everything else."

They had come to Mrs. Allerton's cabin and Tim knocked firmly on the door. It opened and Mrs. Allerton stood on the threshold.

"Rosalie and I—" said Tim.

He paused.

"Oh, my dears," said Mrs. Allerton. She folded Rosalie in her arms. "My dear, dear child . . . I always hoped—but Tim was so tiresome—and pretended he didn't like you. But of course I saw through *that!*"

Rosalie said in a broken voice:

"You've been so sweet to me—always. I used to wish—to wish—"

She broke off and sobbed happily on Mrs. Allerton's shoulder.

CHAPTER 27

As the door closed behind Tim and Rosalie, Poirot looked somewhat apologetically at Colonel Race. The colonel was looking rather grim.

"You will consent to my little arrangement, yes?" Poirot pleaded. "It is irregular—I know it is irregular, yes—but I have a high regard for human happiness."

"You've none for mine," said Race.

"That *jeune fille,* I have a tenderness towards her—and she loves that young man. It will be an excellent match—she has the stiffening he needs—the mother likes her—everything is thoroughly suitable."

"In fact the marriage has been arranged by heaven and Hercule Poirot. All I have to do is to compound a felony."

"But, *mon ami,* I told you, it was all conjecture on my part."

Race grinned suddenly.

"It's all right by me," he said. "I'm not a damned policeman, thank God! I dare say the young fool will go straight enough now. The girl's straight all right. No, what I'm complaining of is your treatment of *me!* I'm a patient man—but there are limits to my patience! *Do* you know who committed the three murders on this boat or *don't* you?"

"I do."

"Then why all this beating about the bush?"

"You think that I am just amusing myself with side issues? And it annoys you? But is is not that. Once I went professionally to an archæological expedition—and I learnt something there. In the course of an excavation, when something comes up out of the ground, everything is cleared away very carefully all around it. You take away the loose earth, and you scrape here and there with a knife until finally your object is there, all alone, ready to be drawn and photographed with no extraneous matter confusing it. That is what I have been seeking to do—clear away the extraneous matter so that we can see the truth—the naked shining truth."

"Good," said Race. "Let's have this naked shining truth. It wasn't Pennington.

It wasn't young Allerton. I presume it wasn't Fleetwood. Let's hear who it was for a change."

"My friend, I am just about to tell you."

There was a knock on the door. Race uttered a muffled curse.

It was Dr. Bessner and Cornelia. The latter was looking upset.

"Oh, Colonel Race," she exclaimed. "Miss Bowers has just told me about Cousin Marie. It's been the most dreadful shock. She said she couldn't bear the responsibility all by herself any longer, and that I'd better know as I was one of the family. I just couldn't believe it at first, but Dr. Bessner here has been just wonderful."

"No, no," protested the doctor modestly.

"He's been so kind, explaining it all, and how people really can't help it. He's had kleptomaniacs in his clinic. And he's explained to me how it's very often due to a deep seated neurosis."

Cornelia repeated the words with awe.

"It's planted very deeply in the subconscious—sometimes it's just some little thing that happened when you were a child. And he's cured people by getting them to think back and remember what that little thing was."

Cornelia paused, drew a deep breath, and started off again.

"But it's worrying me dreadfully in case it all gets out. It would be too terrible in New York. Why, all the tabloids would have it. Cousin Marie and mother and everybody—they'd never hold up their heads again."

Race sighed.

"That's all right," he said. "This is Hush Hush House."

"I beg your pardon, Colonel Race."

"What I was endeavouring to say was that anything short of murder is being hushed up."

"Oh!" Cornelia clasped her hands. "I'm *so* relieved. I've just been worrying and worrying."

"You have the heart too tender," said Dr. Bessner and patted her benevolently on the shoulder. He said to the others, "She has a very sensitive and beautiful nature."

"Oh, I haven't really. You're too kind."

Poirot murmured:

"Have you seen any more of Mr. Ferguson?"

Cornelia blushed.

"No—but Cousin Marie's been talking about him."

"It seems the young man is highly born," said Dr. Bessner. "I must confess he does not look it. His clothes are terrible. Not for a moment does he appear a well-bred man."

"And what do you think, Mademoiselle?"

"I think he must be just plain crazy," said Cornelia.

Poirot turned to the doctor.

"How is your patient?"

"Ach, he is going on splendidly. I have just reassured the little Fräulein de Bellefort. Would you believe it, I found her in despair. Just because the fellow had a bit of a temperature this afternoon! But what could be more natural? It is amazing that he is not in a high fever now. But now, he is like some of our peasants, he has a magnificent constitution—the constitution of an ox. I have seen them with deep wounds that they hardly notice. It is the same with Mr. Doyle. His pulse is steady, his temperature only slightly above normal. I was able to pooh-pooh the little lady's fears. All the same, it is ridiculous, *nicht wahr?* One minute you shoot a man, the next you are in hysterics in case he may not be doing well."

Cornelia said:

"She loves him terribly, you see."

"Ach! but it is not sensible, that. If *you* loved a man, would you try and shoot him? No, you are sensible."

"I don't like things that go off with bangs anyway," said Cornelia.

"Naturally you do not. You are very feminine."

Race interrupted this scene of heavy approval.

"Since Doyle is all right, there's no reason I shouldn't come along and resume our talk of this afternoon. He was just telling me about a telegram."

Dr. Bessner's bulk moved up and down appreciatively.

"Ho, ho, ho, it was very funny that! Doyle, he tells me about it. It was a telegram all about vegetables—potatoes—artichokes—leeks—Ach! pardon?"

With a stifled exclamation, Race had sat up in his chair.

"My God," he said. "So that's it. Richetti!"

He looked round on three uncomprehending faces.

"A new code—it was used in the South African rebellion. Potatoes mean machine guns, artichokes are high explosives—and so on. Richetti is no more an archæologist than I am! He's a very dangerous agitator, a man who's killed more than once. And I'll swear that he's killed once again. Mrs. Doyle opened that telegram by mistake, you see. *If she were ever to repeat what was in it before me,* he knew his goose would be cooked!"

He turned to Poirot.

"Am I right?" he said. "Is Richetti the man?"

"He is your man," said Poirot. "I always thought there was something wrong about him! He was almost too word-perfect in his rôle—he was all archæologist, not enough human being."

He paused and then said:

"But it was not Richetti who killed Linnet Doyle. For some time now I have known what I may express as the 'first half' of the murder. Now I know the 'second half' also. The picture is complete. But you understand that although I know what must have happened. I *have no proof that it happened*. Intellectually the case is satisfying. Actually it is profoundly unsatisfactory. There is only one hope—a confession from the murderer."

Dr. Bessner raised his shoulders sceptically.

"Ach! but that—it would be a miracle."

"I think not. Not under the circumstances."

Cornelia cried out:

"But who is it? Aren't you going to tell us?"

Poirot's eyes ranged quietly over the three of them. Race smiling sardonically, Bessner, still looking sceptical, Cornelia, her mouth hanging a little open, gazing at him with eager eyes.

"*Mais oui,*" he said. "I like an audience, I must confess. I am vain, you see. I am puffed up with conceit. I like to say, 'See how clever is Hercule Poirot!'"

Race shifted a little in his chair.

"Well," he said gently, "just how clever *is* Hercule Poirot?"

Shaking his head sadly from side to side Poirot said:

"To begin with I was stupid—incredibly stupid. To me the stumbling-block was the pistol—Jacqueline de Bellefort's pistol. Why had that pistol not been left on the scene of the crime? The idea of the murderer was quite plainly to incriminate her. Why then did the murderer take it away? I was so stupid that I thought of all sorts of fantastic reasons. The real one was very simple. The murderer took it away because he *had* to take it away—because *he had no choice in the matter*."

CHAPTER 28

"You and I, my friend," Poirot leaned towards Race, "started our investigation with a preconceived idea. That idea was that the crime was committed on the spur of the moment without any preliminary planning. Somebody wished to remove Linnet Doyle and had seized their opportunity to do so at a moment when the crime would almost certainly be attributed to Jacqueline de Bellefort. It therefore followed that the person in question had overheard the scene between Jacqueline and Simon Doyle and had obtained possession of the pistol after the others had left the saloon.

"But, my friends, *if that preconceived idea was wrong*, the whole aspect of the case altered. And it *was* wrong! This was no spontaneous crime committed on the spur of the moment. It was, on the contrary, very carefully planned and accurately timed, with all the details meticulously worked out beforehand, even to the drugging of Hercule Poirot's bottle of wine on the night in question!

"But, yes, that is so! I was put to sleep so that there should be no possibility of my participating in the events of the night. It did just occur to me as a possibility. I drink wine, my two companions at table drink whisky and mineral water respectively. Nothing easier than to slip a dose of harmless narcotic into my bottle of wine—the bottles stand on the tables all day. But I dismissed the thought—it had been a hot day—I had been unusually tired—it was not really extraordinary that I should for once have slept heavily instead of lightly as I usually do.

"You see, I was still in the grip of the preconceived idea. If I had been drugged that would have implied premeditation, it would mean that before 7.30, when dinner is served, *the crime had already been decided upon*. . . . And that (always from the point of view of the preconceived idea) was absurd.

"The first blow to the preconceived idea was when the pistol was recovered from the Nile. To begin with, if we were right in our assumptions, the pistol *ought never to have been thrown overboard at all*. . . . And there was more to follow."

Poirot turned to Dr. Bessner.

"You, Dr. Bessner, examined Linnet Doyle's body. You will remember that the wound showed signs of scorching—that is to say that the pistol had been placed close against the head before being fired."

Bessner nodded.

"So. That is exact."

"But when the pistol was found it was wrapped in a velvet stole and that velvet showed definite signs that a pistol had been fired through its folds—presumably under the impression that that would deaden the sound of the shot. *But if the pistol had been fired through the velvet, there would have been no signs of burning on the victim's skin*. Therefore the shot fired through the stole *could not have been the shot that killed Linnet Doyle*. Could it have been the other shot—the one fired by Jacqueline de Bellefort at Simon Doyle? Again no, for there had been two witnesses of that shooting and we knew all about it. It appeared, therefore, as though a *third* shot had been fired—one we knew nothing about. But only two shots had been fired from the pistol, and there was no hint or suggestion of another shot.

"Here we were face to face with a very curious unexplained circumstance. The next interesting point was the fact that in Linnet Doyle's cabin I found two bottles of coloured nail polish. Now ladies very often vary the colour of their nails, but so far Linnet Doyle's nails had always been the shade called Cardinal—a deep dark red. The other bottle was labelled Rose, which is a shade of pale pink, but the few drops remaining in the bottle were not pale pink but a bright red. I was sufficiently curious to take out the stopper and sniff. Instead of the usual strong odour of pear drops, the bottle smelt of vinegar! That is to say, it suggested that the drop or two of fluid in it was *red ink*. Now there is no reason why Mrs. Doyle should not have had a bottle of red ink, but it would have been more natural if she had had red ink in a red ink bottle and not in a nail polish bottle. It suggested a link with the faintly stained handkerchief which had been wrapped round the pistol. Red ink washes out quickly but always leaves a pale pink stain.

"I should perhaps have arrived at the truth with these slender indications, but an event occurred which rendered all doubts superfluous. Louise Bourget was killed in circumstances which pointed unmistakably to the fact that she had been blackmailing the murderer. Not only was a fragment of a *mille* franc note still clasped in her hand, but I remembered some very significant words she had used this morning.

"Listen carefully, for here is the crux of the whole matter. When I asked her if she had seen anything the previous night she gave this curious answer. *'Naturally, if I had been unable to sleep, if I had mounted the stairs, then perhaps I might have seen this assassin, this monster enter or leave Madame's cabin. . . .'* Now what exactly did that tell us?"

Bessner, his nose wrinkling with intellectual interest, replied promptly:

"It told you that she *had* mounted the stair."

"No, no—you fail to see the point. Why should she have said that—to *us?*"

"To convey a hint."

"But why *hint* to us? If she knows who the murderer is, there are two courses open to her—to tell us the truth, or to hold her tongue and demand money for her silence from the person concerned! But she does neither. She neither says promptly: 'I saw nobody. I was asleep.' Nor does she say: 'Yes, I saw some one, and it was so and so.' Why use that significant indeterminate rigmarole of words? *Parbleu*, there can be only one reason! She is *hinting to the murderer*—therefore the murderer *must have been present at the time*. But besides myself and Colonel Race only two people were present—Simon Doyle and Dr. Bessner."

The doctor sprang up with a roar.

"Ach! what is that you say? You accuse me? Again? But it is ridiculous—beneath contempt."

Poirot said sharply:

"Be quiet. I am telling you what I thought at the time. Let us remain impersonal."

"He doesn't mean he thinks it's you now," said Cornelia soothingly.

Poirot went on quickly.

"So it lay there—between Simon Doyle and Dr. Bessner. But what reason has Bessner to kill Linnet Doyle? None, *so far as I know*. Simon Doyle, then? But that was impossible! There were plenty of witnesses who could swear that Doyle never left the saloon that evening until the quarrel broke out. After that he was wounded and it would then have been physically impossible for him to have done so. Had I good evidence on both those points? Yes, I had the evidence of Miss Robson, of Jim Fanthorp and of Jacqueline de Bellefort as to the first, and I had the skilled testimony of Dr. Bessner and of Miss Bowers as to the other. No doubt was possible.

"So Dr. Bessner *must* be the guilty one. In favour of this theory there was the fact that the maid had been stabbed *with a surgical knife*. On the other hand Bessner had deliberately called attention to this fact.

"And then, my friends, a second perfectly indisputable fact became apparent to me. Louise Bourget's hint could not have been intended for Dr. Bessner, *because she could perfectly well have spoken to him in private at any time she liked*. There was one person, *and one person only* who corresponded to her necessity—*Simon Doyle!* Simon Doyle was wounded, was constantly attended by a doctor, was in that doctor's cabin. It was to him, therefore, that she risked saying those ambiguous words in case she might not get another chance. And I remember how she had gone on, turning to him: 'Monsieur, I implore you—you see how it is? What can I say?' And his answer, *'My good girl, don't be a fool. Nobody thinks you saw or heard anything. You'll be quite all right. I'll look after you. Nobody's accusing you of anything.'* That was the assurance she wanted, and she got it!"

Bessner uttered a colossal snort.

"Ach! it is foolish, that! Do you think a man with a fractured bone and a splint on his leg could go walking about the boat and stabbing people! I tell you, it was *impossible* for Simon Doyle to leave his cabin."

Poirot said gently:

"I know. That is quite true. The thing was impossible. It was impossible—but it was also true! There could be *only one logical meaning* behind Louise Bourget's words.

"So I returned to the beginning and reviewed the crime in the light of this new knowledge. Was it possible that in the period preceding the quarrels Simon Doyle had left the saloon and the others had forgotten or not noticed it? I could not see that that was possible. Could the skilled testimony of Dr. Bessner and Miss Bowers be disregarded? Again I felt sure it could not. But, I rememered, *there was a gap between the two*. Simon Doyle had been alone in the saloon for a period of five minutes, and the skilled testimony of Dr. Bessner only applied to the time *after that period*. For that period we had only the evidence of *visual appearance*, and though apparently that was perfectly sound, it was no longer *certain*. What had actually been *seen*—leaving assumption out of the question?

"Miss Robson had seen Miss de Bellefort fire her pistol, had seen Simon Doyle collapse on to a chair, had seen him clasp a handkerchief to his leg and seen that handkerchief gradually soak through red. What had Mr. Fanthorp heard and seen? He heard a shot, he found Doyle with a red-stained handkerchief clasped to his leg. What had happened then? Doyle had been very insistent that Miss de Bellefort should be got away, that she should not be left alone. After that, he suggested that Fanthorp should get hold of the doctor.

"Accordingly Miss Robson and Mr. Fanthorp go out with Miss de Bellefort and for the next five minutes they are busy *on the port side of the deck*. Miss Bowers's, Dr. Bessner's and Miss de Bellefort's cabins are all on the port side. Two minutes are all that Simon Doyle needs. He picked up the pistol from under the sofa, slips out of his shoes, runs like a hare silently along the starboard deck, enters his wife's cabin, creeps up to her as she lies asleep, shoots her through the head, puts the bottle that has contained the red ink on her washstand (it mustn't be found on him), runs back, gets hold of Miss Van Schuyler's velvet stole which he has quietly stuffed down the side of a chair in readiness, muffles it round the pistol and fires a bullet into his leg. His chair into which he falls (in genuine agony this time) is by a window. He lifts the window and throws the pistol (wrapped up with the tell-tale handkerchief in the velvet stole) into the Nile."

"Impossible!" said Race.

"No, my friend, not *impossible*. Remember the evidence of Tim Allerton. He heard a pop—*followed* by a splash. And he heard something else—the footsteps of a man running—a man running past his door. *But nobody should have been running along the starboard side of the deck*. What he heard was the stockinged feet of Simon Doyle running past his cabin."

Race said:

"I still say it's impossible. No man could work out the whole caboodle like that in a flash—especially a chap like Doyle who is slow in his mental processes."

"But very quick and deft in his physical actions!"

"That, yes. But he wouldn't be capable of thinking the whole thing out."

"But he did not think it out himself, my friend. That is where we were all wrong. It looked like a crime committed on the spur of the moment. As I say it was a very cleverly planned and well thought out piece of work. It could not be *chance* that Simon Doyle had a bottle of red ink in his pocket. No, it must be *design*. It was not *chance* that he had a plain unmarked handkerchief with him. It was not *chance* that Jacqueline de Bellefort's foot kicked the pistol under the settee where it would be out of sight and unremembered until later."

"Jacqueline?"

"Certainly. The two halves of the murderer. What gave *Simon* his alibi? The shot fired by *Jacqueline*. What gave Jacqueline *her* alibi—the insistence of *Simon* which resulted in a hospital nurse remaining with her all night. There, between the two of them, you get all the qualities you require—the cool resourceful planning brain, Jacqueline de Bellefort's brain, and the man of action to carry it out with incredible swiftness and timing.

"Look at it the right way, and it answers every question. Simon Doyle and Jacqueline had been lovers. Realise that they are still lovers and it is all clear. Simon does away with his rich wife, inherits her money, *and in due course will marry his old love*. It was all very ingenious. The persecution of Mrs. Doyle by Jacqueline, all part of the plan. Simon's pretended rage. And yet—there were lapses. He held forth to me once about possessive women—held forth with real bitterness. It ought to have been clear to me *that it was his wife he was thinking about*—not Jacqueline. Then his manner to his wife in public. An ordinary inarticulate Englishman, such as Simon Doyle, is very embarrassed of showing any affection. Simon was not a really good actor. He overdid the devoted manner. That conversation I had with Mademoiselle Jacqueline, too, when she pretended that somebody had overheard. *I* saw no one. And there *was* no one! But it was to be a useful red herring later. Then one night on this boat I thought I heard Simon and Linnet outside my cabin. He was saying, 'We've got to go through with it now.' It was Doyle all right, but it was to Jacqueline he was speaking.

"The final drama was perfectly planned and timed. There was a sleeping draught for me in case I might put an inconvenient finger in the pie—there was the selection of Miss Robson as a witness—the working up of the scene, Miss de Bellefort's exaggerated remorse and hysterics. She made a good deal of noise in case the shot should be heard. *En verité*, it was an extraordinarily clever idea.

Jacqueline says she has shot Doyle, Miss Robson says so, Fanthorp says so—and when Simon's leg is examined he *has* been shot. It looks unanswerable! For both of them there is a perfect alibi—at the cost, it is true, of a certain amount of pain and risk to Simon Doyle, but it is necessary that his wound should definitely disable him.

"And then the plan goes wrong. Louise Bourget has been wakeful. She has come up the stairway and she has seen Simon Doyle run along to his wife's cabin and come back. Easy enough to piece together what has happened the following day. And so she makes her greedy bid for hush money and in so doing signs her death warrant."

"But Mr. Doyle couldn't have killed *her?*" Cornelia objected.

"No, the other partner did that murder. As soon as he could Simon Doyle asks to see Jacqueline. He even asks me to leave them alone together. He tells her then of the new danger. They must act at once. He knows where Bessner's scalpels are kept. After the crime the scalpel is wiped and returned and then, very late and rather out of breath, Jacqueline de Bellefort hurries into lunch.

"And still all is not well. *For Mrs. Otterbourne has seen Jacqueline go into Louise Bourget's cabin.* And she comes hot-foot to tell Simon about it. Jacqueline is the murderess. Do you remember how Simon shouted at the poor woman. Nerves, we thought. But the door was open and he was trying to convey the danger to his accomplice. She heard and she acted—acted like lightning. She remembered Pennington had talked about a revolver. She got hold of it, crept up outside the door, listened and at the critical moment fired. She boasted once that she was a good shot and her boast was not an idle one.

"I remarked after that third crime that there were three ways the murderer could have gone. I meant that he could have gone aft (in which case Tim Allerton was the criminal) he could have gone over the side (very improbable) or he could have gone into a cabin. Jacqueline's cabin was just two away from Dr. Bessner's. She had only to throw down the revolver, bolt into the cabin, ruffle her hair and fling herself down on the bunk. It was risky, but it was the only possible chance."

There was a silence, then Race asked:

"What happened to the first bullet fired at Doyle by the girl?"

"I think it went into the table. There is a recently made hole there. I think Doyle had time to dig it out with a penknife and fling it through the window. He had, of course, a spare cartridge so that it would appear that only two shots had been fired."

Cornelia sighed. "They thought of everything," she said. "It's—horrible!"

Poirot was silent. But it was not a modest silence. His eyes seemed to be saying: "You are wrong. They didn't allow for Hercule Poirot."

Aloud he said: "And now, doctor, we will go and have a word with your patient. . . ."

CHAPTER 29

It was very much later that evening that Hercule Poirot came and knocked on the door of a cabin.

A voice said, "Come in," and he entered.

Jacqueline de Bellefort was sitting in a chair. In another chair, close against the wall, sat the big stewardess.

Jacqueline's eyes surveyed Poirot thoughtfully. She made a gesture towards the stewardess.

"Can she go?"

Poirot nodded to the woman and she went out. Poirot drew up her chair and sat down near Jacqueline. Neither of them spoke. Poirot's face was unhappy.

In the end it was the girl who spoke first.

"Well," she said. "It is all over! You were too clever for us, M. Poirot."

Poirot sighed. He spread out his hands. He seemed strangely dumb.

"All the same," said Jacqueline reflectively. "I can't really see that you had much proof. You were quite right, of course, but if we'd bluffed you out—"

"In no other way, Mademoiselle, could the thing have happened."

"That's proof enough for a logical mind—but I don't believe it would have convinced a jury. Oh, well—it can't be helped. You sprang it all on Simon—and he went down like a ninepin. He lost his head utterly, poor lamb, and admitted everything."

She shook her head. "He's a bad loser."

"But you, Mademoiselle, are a good loser."

She laughed suddenly—a queer, gay, defiant little laugh.

"Oh, yes, I'm a good loser all right." She looked at him.

She said suddenly and impulsively:

"Don't mind so much, M. Poirot! About me, I mean. You do mind, don't you?"

"Yes, Mademoiselle."

"But it wouldn't have occurred to you to let me off?"

Hercule Poirot said quietly:

"No."

She nodded her head in quiet agreement.

"No, it's no use being sentimental. I might do it again. . . . I'm not a safe person any longer. I can feel that myself. . . ." She went on broodingly. "It's so dreadfully easy—killing people. . . . And you begin to feel that it doesn't matter. . . . That it's only *you* that matters! It's dangerous—that."

She paused, then said with a little smile.

"You did your best for me, you know. That night at Assuan—you told me not to open my heart to evil. . . . Did you realise then what was in my mind?"

He shook his head.

"I only knew that what I said was true."

"It was true. . . . I could have stopped, then, you know. I nearly did. . . . I could have told Simon that I wouldn't go on with it. . . . But then perhaps—"

She broke off. She said:

"Would you like to hear about it? From the beginning?"

"If you care to tell me, Mademoiselle."

"I think I want to tell you. It was all very simple, really. You see, Simon and I loved each other. . . ."

It was a matter-of-fact statement, yet underneath the lightness of her tone there were echoes. . . .

Poirot said simply:

"And for you love would have been enough—but not for him."

"You might put it that way, perhaps. But you don't quite understand Simon. You see, he's always wanted money so dreadfully. He likes all the things you get with money—horses and yachts and sport—nice things, all of them. Things a man ought to be keen about. And he'd never been able to have any of them. . . . He's awfully simple, Simon is. He wants things just like a child wants them—you know—terribly.

"All the same he never tried to marry anybody rich and horrid. He wasn't that sort. And then we met—and—and that sort of settled things. Only we didn't see when we'd be able to marry. He'd had rather a decent job, but he'd lost it. In a way it was his own fault. He tried to do something smart over money and got found out at once. I don't believe he really meant to be dishonest. He just thought it was the sort of thing people did in the city."

A flicker passed over her listener's face, but he guarded his tongue.

"There we were, up against it, and then I thought of Linnet and her new country house, and I rushed off to her. You know, M. Poirot, I loved Linnet, really I did. She was my best friend and I never dreamed that anything would ever come between us. I just thought how lucky it was she was rich. It might make all the difference to me and Simon if she'd give him a job. And she was awfully sweet about it and told me to bring Simon down to see her. It was about then you saw us that night at *Chez Ma Tante*. We were making whoopee although we couldn't really afford it."

She paused, sighed, then went on.

"What I'm going to say now is quite true, M. Poirot. Even though Linnet is dead it doesn't alter the truth. That's why I'm not really sorry about her even now. She went all out to get Simon away from me. That's the absolute truth! I don't think she even hesitated for more than about a minute. I was her friend, but she didn't care. She just went bald-headed for Simon. . . .

"And Simon didn't care a damn about her! I talked a lot to you about glamour, but of course that wasn't true. He didn't want Linnet. He thought her good-looking but terribly bossy, and he hated bossy women! The whole thing embarrassed him frightfully. But he did like the thought of her money.

"Of course I saw that. . . . And at last I suggested to him that it might be a good thing if he—got rid of me and married Linnet. But he scouted the idea. He said, money or no money, it would be hell to be married to her. He said his idea of having money was to have it himself—not to have a rich wife holding the purse strings. 'I'd be a kind of damned Prince Consort,' he said to me. He said, too, that he didn't want any one but me. . . .

"I think I know when the idea came into his head. He said one day: 'If I'd any luck I'd marry her and she'd die in about a year and leave me all the boodle.' And then a queer startled look came into his eyes. That was when he first thought of it. . . .

"He talked about it a good deal one way and another—about how convenient it would be if Linnet died. I said it was an awful idea and then he shut up about it. Then, one day, I found him reading up all about arsenic. I taxed him with it then, and he laughed and said, 'Nothing venture, nothing have! It's about the only time in my life I shall be near to touching a fat lot of money.'

"After a bit I saw that he'd made up his mind. And I was terrified—simply terrified. Because, you see, *I realised that he'd never pull it off*. He's so childishly simple. He'd have no kind of subtlety about it—and he's got no imagination. He would probably have just bunged arsenic into her and assumed the doctor would say she's died of gastritis. He always thought things would go right.

"So I had to come into it, too, to look after him. . . ."

She said it very simply but in complete good faith. Poirot had no doubt whatever that her motive had been exactly what she said it was. She herself had not coveted Linnet Ridgeway's money. But she had loved Simon Doyle, had loved him beyond reason and beyond rectitude and beyond pity.

"I thought and I thought—trying to work out a plan. It seemed to me that the basis of the idea ought to be a kind of two-handed *alibi*. You know—if Simon and I could somehow or other give evidence against each other—but actually that evidence would clear us of everything. It would be easy enough for me to pretend to hate Simon. It was quite a likely thing to happen under the circumstances. Then, if Linnet was killed, I should probably be suspected, so it would be better if I was suspected right away. We worked out details little by little. I wanted it to be so that if anything went wrong, they'd get me and not Simon. But Simon was worried about me.

"The only thing I was glad about was that I hadn't got to do it. I simply couldn't have! Not go along in cold blood and kill her when she was asleep! You see, I hadn't forgiven her—I think I could have killed her face to face—but not the other way. . . .

"We worked everything out carefully. Even then, Simon went and wrote a J in blood which was a silly melodramatic thing to do. It's just the sort of thing he *would* think of! But it went off all right."

Poirot nodded.

"Yes. It was not your fault that Louise Bourget could not sleep that night. . . . And afterwards, Mademoiselle?"

She met his eyes squarely.

"Yes," she said. "It's rather horrible, isn't it? I can't believe that I—did that! I know now what you meant by opening your heart to evil. . . . You know pretty well how it happened. Louise made it clear to Simon that she knew. Simon got you to bring me to him. He told me what I'd got to do. I wasn't even horrified. I was so afraid—so deadly afraid. . . . That's what murder does to you. . . . Simon and I were safe—quite safe—except for this miserable blackmailing French girl. I took her all the money we could get hold of. I pretended to grovel. And then when she was counting the money—I—did it! It was quite easy. That's what's so horribly frightening about it. . . . It's so terribly easy. . . .

"And even then we weren't safe. Mrs. Otterbourne had seen me. She came triumphantly along the deck looking for you and Colonel Race. I'd no time to think. I just acted like a flash. It was almost exciting. I knew it was touch or go that time. That seemed to make it better. . . ."

She stopped again.

"Do you remember when you came into my cabin afterwards? You said you were not sure why you had come. I was so miserable—so terrified. I thought Simon was going to die. . . ."

"And I—was hoping it," said Poirot.

Jacqueline nodded.

"Yes, it would have been better for him that way."

"That was not my thought."

Jacqueline looked at the sternness of his face.

She said gently:

"Don't mind so much for me, M. Poirot. After all, I've lived hard always, you know. If we'd won out, I'd have been very happy and enjoyed things and probably should never have regretted anything. As it is—well, one goes through with it."

She added:

"I suppose the stewardess is in attendance to see I don't hang myself or swallow a miraculous capsule of prussic acid like people do in books. You needn't be afraid! I shan't do that. It will be easier for Simon if I'm standing by."

Poirot got up. Jacqueline rose also. She said with a sudden smile:

"Do you remember when I said I must follow my star? You said it might be a false star. And I said, 'That very bad star, that star fall down.'"

He went on to the deck with her laughter ringing in his years.

CHAPTER 30

It was early dawn when they came into Shellal. The rocks came down grimly to the water's edge.

Poirot murmured:

"*Quel pays sauvage. . . .*"

Race stood beside him.

"Well," he said, "we've done our job. I've arranged for Richetti to be taken ashore first. Glad we've got him. He's been a slippery customer, I can tell you. Given us the slip dozens of times."

He went on:

"We must get hold of a stretcher for Doyle. Remarkable how he went to pieces."

"Not really," said Poirot. "That boyish type of criminal is usually intensely vain. Once prick the bubble of their self-esteem and it is finished! They go to pieces like children."

"Deserves to be hanged," said Race. "He's a cold-blooded scoundrel. I'm sorry for the girl—but there's nothing to be done about it."

Poirot shook his head.

"People say love justifies everything, but that is not true. . . . Women who care for men like Jacqueline cares for Simon Doyle are very dangerous. It is what I said when I saw her first. She cares too much, that little one! It is true."

Cornelia Robson came up beside him.

"Oh," she said. "We're nearly in."

She paused a minute or two then said:

"I've been with her."

"With Miss de Bellefort?"

"Yes. I felt it was kind of awful for her boxed up with that stewardess. Cousin Marie's very angry though, I'm afraid."

Miss Van Schuyler was progressing slowly down the deck towards them. Her eyes were venomous.

"Cornelia," she snapped. "You've behaved outrageously. I shall send you straight home."

Cornelia took a deep breath.

"I'm sorry, Cousin Marie, but I'm not going home. I'm going to get married."

"So you've seen sense at last," snapped the old lady.

Ferguson came striding round the corner of the deck.

He said: "Cornelia, what's this I hear? It's not true!"

"It's quite true," said Cornelia. "I'm going to marry Dr. Bessner. He asked me last night."

"And why are you going to marry him?" said Ferguson furiously. "Simply because he's rich?"

"No, I'm not," said Cornelia indignantly. "I like him. He's kind, and he knows a lot. And I've always been interested in sick folks and clinics, and I shall have just a wonderful life with him."

"Do you mean to say," said Mr. Ferguson incredulously, "that you'd rather marry that disgusting old man than me?"

"Yes, I would. You're not reliable! You wouldn't be at all a comfortable sort of person to live with. And he's *not* old. He's not fifty yet."

"He's got a stomach," said Mr. Ferguson venomously.

"Well, I've got round shoulders," said Cornelia. "What one looks like doesn't matter. He says I really could help him in his work, and he's going to teach me all about neuroseses."

She moved away. Ferguson said to Poirot.

"Do you think she really means that?"

"Certainly."

"She prefers that pompous old bore to me?"

"Undoubtedly."

"The girl's mad," said Ferguson.

Poirot's eyes twinkled.

"She is a woman of original mind," he said. "It is probably the first time you have met one."

The boat drew in to the landing stage. A cordon had been drawn round the passengers. They had been asked to wait before disembarking.

Richetti, dark faced and sullen, was marched ashore by two engineers.

Then, after a certain amount of delay, a stretcher was brought. Simon Doyle was carried along the deck to the gangway.

He looked a different man—cringing, frightened, all his boyish insouciance vanished.

Jacqueline de Bellefort followed. A stewardess walked beside her.

She was pale but otherwise looked much as usual.

She came up to the stretcher.

"Hallo, Simon," she said.

He looked up at her quickly. The old boyish look came back to his face for a moment.

"I messed it up," he said. "Lost my head and admitted everything! Sorry, Jackie. I've let you down."

She smiled at him then.

"It's all right, Simon," she said. "A fool's game and we've lost. That's all."

She stood aside. The bearer picked up the handles of the stretcher.

Jacqueline bent down and tied the lace of her shoe. Then her hand went to her stocking top and she straightened up with something in her hand.

There was a sharp explosive "pop."

Simon Doyle gave one convulsed shudder and then lay still.

Jacqueline de Bellefort nodded. She stood for a minute, pistol in hand. She gave a fleeting smile at Poirot.

Then, as Race jumped forward, she turned the little glittering toy against her heart and pressed the trigger.

She sank down in a soft huddled heap.

Race shouted:

"Where the devil did she get that pistol?"

Poirot felt a hand on his arm. Mrs. Allerton said softly:

"You—knew?"

He nodded.

"She had a pair of those pistols. I realised that when I heard that one had been found in Rosalie Otterbourne's handbag the day of the search. Jacqueline sat at the same table as they did. When she realised that there was going to be a search she slipped it into the other girl's handbag. Later she went to Rosalie's cabin and got it back after having distracted her attention with a comparison of lipsticks. As both she and her cabin had been searched yesterday it wasn't thought necessary to do it again."

Mrs. Allerton said:

"You wanted her to take that way out?"

"Yes. But she would not take it alone. That is why Simon Doyle has died an easier death than he deserved."

Mrs. Allerton shivered.

"Love can be a very frightening thing."

"That is why most great love stories are tragedies."

Mrs. Allerton's eyes rested upon Tim and Rosalie standing side by side in the sunlight and she said suddenly and passionately:

"But thank God, there is happiness in the world."

"As you say, Madame, thank God for it."

Presently the passengers went ashore.

Later the bodies of Louise Bourget and of Mrs. Otterbourne were carried off the *Karnak*.

Lastly the body of Linnet Doyle was brought ashore, and all over the world the wires began to hum, telling the public that Linnet Doyle, who had been Linnet Ridgeway, the famous, the beautiful, the wealthy Linnet Doyle was dead. . . .

Sir George Wode read about it in his London club, and Sterndale Rockford in New York, and Joanna Southwood in Switzerland, and it was discussed in the bar of the Three Crowns in Malton-under-Wode.

And Mr. Burnaby's lean friend said:

"Well, it didn't seem fair, her having everything."

And Mr. Burnaby said acutely:

"Well, it doesn't seem to have done her much good, poor lass."

But after a while they stopped talking about her and discussed instead who was going to win the Grand National. For, as Mr. Ferguson was saying at that minute in Luxor, it is not the past that matters but the future.